THE MIND OF JENNIFER RUSSELL

SYDNEY JAMES CARD

First published in Great Britain as a softback original in 2019

Copyright © Sydney Card

The moral right of this author has been asserted.

Typeset in Minion Pro

Editing, design, typesetting and publishing by UK Book Publishing

www.ukbookpublishing.com

ISBN: 978-1-913179-21-2

THE MIND OF
JENNIFER RUSSELL

PART ONE:

THE GIRL WITH SILVERY HAIR

CHAPTER I:

THE STRANGER

EXMOOR, DEVON

JULY 2127

The summer sun was high up in the cloudless sky; it was a hot and humid afternoon. They sat sweltering on a grassy hill, three boys and three girls. They were the elite in a class of their own. Their attention was occupied by the work being done on a construction site on the other side of the track in front of the hill. They had no idea of the final product of all the hard work being done on the building site. All the adults they encountered were deaf to their queries. Beyond the construction site was the Research Complex where men and women wearing white lab coats could be seen wandering about the grounds of the compound.

Steven Calvert, as he was fourteen, was the elected leader. He sat on the slope of the hill, gazing at the huge concrete pylons being erected on each end of the construction site. He was impressed even though he had no idea what they were for. On the opposite side of the hill a girl of twelve was standing gazing down at the copse at the bottom of the hill. She found the heat overpowering and oppressive. She wore a white blouse and a white skirt that clung to the sweat of her body. Juliet Prentice turned on her heel and strode across the summit to her friends and stepped over prone bodies that lay about on the grass. She stopped when she reached her best friend Janice Clarke, who was looking down at Steven with love and admiration in her eyes. They were seldom out of each other's sight. Janice turned her head and stared up at Juliet and smiled fondly at her friend, she reached out her right hand and ran it caressingly over Juliet's left thigh.

Juliet called to Steven and he got up when he heard his name being called and joined Juliet where she was standing. Janice stood up and though she was only three months older than Juliet, she made the black-haired girl look small. Being short for her age did not worry Juliet, as she was tough and stood up to anyone who decided to give her grief. Janice was timid and shy. She gained strength from being close to Juliet. Janice wore a cream coloured dress that clung to her shapely body. She ran a hand through her curly blonde hair.

'What's up?' Steven asked Juliet.

Juliet took hold of Steven's hand and led him across the summit to the other side; Janice followed behind them, wondering what Juliet had found. Juliet pointed down towards the copse below them. A tall girl was gazing up at them from the bottom of the hill.

'She has just emerged from the trees. I have never seen her before, I wonder what she wants,' Juliet said.

'We can soon find out,' Steven said.

Steven shouted down at the tall stranger and told her to come up.

Juliet waved a warning hand at him. He gazed at the worried expression on her pretty face.

'Is it wise to have her here among us?'

Steven smiled at Juliet.

'With six of us up here, she can hardly be a threat to us,' Steven observed.

The three of them watched the tall girl clamber up the side of the hill. She wore a yellow dress and sandals on her feet. She came up and stood in front of Steven, who had to look up to see her face. The stranger was the tallest girl they had ever seen, she must have been nearly seven foot in height. Steven was just over six foot. She had long ginger hair that grew down to her slim waist. Her bright emerald green eyes regarded him with interest. The two boys and the other girl that were lying on the grass got up and joined them and they had surrounded the tall girl, who showed no fear of them.

'I've come to join you,' the girl said in a strong commanding voice.

'We don't allow strangers amongst us,' Juliet told her.

The tall girl ignored Juliet and kept her eyes on the boy in front of her.

'They treat me without respect. I've tried to reason with them without success. So, I've come to try my luck with you.'

'We don't want you either,' Juliet said, coldly.

The girl who had just joined them pushed in front of Juliet.

'Let's vote on it,' the girl said.

Hazel Johnson was eleven, the youngest of the group; her shoulder length auburn hair was a mass of curls. Her chubby smiling face was full of freckles.

'What's your name?' Hazel asked the stranger.

The tall girl gazed down at the cheerful, smiling young girl, the stern expression on the thin face evaporated and she smiled at the small girl. Hazel beamed back at her. For the first time in her life the tall girl had found someone who was emanating warm feelings towards her.

'Samantha Edwards, I'm fifteen.'

Simon James asked for a show of hands in favour of letting Samantha join them. He put his hand up as did John Stephenson who stood beside him – Steven and Hazel put their hands up too. Janice voted with her best friend Juliet against the tall stranger.

'Well, Samantha, it looks as if you are in,' Steven said.

Samantha showed her gratitude by thanking them. She had to find someone she could trust.

'Fear made me seek you out.'

'You look the type of girl who is afraid of nothing,' Hazel said.

Samantha gazed down at the younger girl.

'I wish I could say the same.'

Juliet made a face at the tall girl and walked away. Janice joined her as she started down the hill. Samantha went down the other side of the hill and Steven followed her; he was intrigued by the tall mysterious girl and he wanted to know more about her. Samantha hated the hot weather – it made her dress stick to her sweaty body. It gave her headaches. At the bottom of the hill they made their way round the nearby copse, and they came to an overgrown orchard that belonged to a large house.

'Have you ever experienced déjà-vu?'

Steven shook his head.

'No, I can't say I have,' he replied. Samantha pushed open the front door; the rusty hinges protested noisily. Steven could see the house had not been used for a long time. There was dust and cobwebs everywhere.

'I found this house yesterday, I've explored it and found it familiar, I am sure I've been in this house before at some time, but I only arrived here last week.'

'Very interesting,' Steven said.

'I told my guardians I had been here, and they weren't very nice about it, I thought they were going to hit me.'

Samantha climbed the stairs and Steven followed her; the stairs creaked with age as they arrived at the landing. They went up another flight of stairs that led to the attic. Samantha walked to the window and looked out at the panoramic view of the moorland. Steven stood beside her. Steven could see the hill on the other side of the overgrown copse. His five friends had gone home.

Samantha started talking about herself with no prompting from Steven. She had recovered from a long illness at the age of twelve, they had told her. Samantha had no memories for her life before the age of twelve. The next three years she had been plagued with bad dreams and blackouts. Samantha would miss a whole day and have no idea what had happened to her. Her guardians showed no concern that she could not account for her whereabouts on each occasion, and it seemed to Samantha, they did not care about her.

'Do you know anything about your true parents?'

'I was told they died while I was ill,' Samantha replied.

Samantha turned from the window and left the attic. Steven followed her out of the house. They made their way back to the hill. Samantha strode towards the Research Complex and Steven decided to follow her. They walked round the side of the compound and came up to the special school Steven and his friends attended in the afternoons. Samantha told him she attended the school early in the mornings. They were obviously trying to keep her away from Steven and his friends. That was why Samantha had decided to join them. Samantha gripped the metal railings and stared at the empty courtyard at the side of the school building.

'I wish I could break out of the prison I find myself in,' Samantha said, softly.

The metal railings bit into her soft cheeks as she pressed her face harder against them. The sun was hot on her back. The sweat from her body soaked her dress and underwear. Steven gazed at her in amazement and he called her name and she seemed to be unaware of him standing close to her.

'Are you all right?' Steven asked in a voice full of concern.

Steven tapped her on the shoulder, and she moved away from the railings – they had made angry marks down her pale cheeks. Samantha ran her hand over her face. She walked to the far side of the school and went down an alley between the school and the infirmary building. Steven walked beside her.

'Will you accompany me to my home? I have something I want to show you,' she said.

Steven nodded and he saw her face break into a smile for the first time. They turned left at the rear of the alley and a short walk took them to a cottage standing alone. Samantha took out the key from her dress pocket and opened the door. Steven entered the cottage behind her.

'My guardians are working at the Research Complex at the moment, so we won't be disturbed.'

Steven followed Samantha up the stairs to her bedroom and sat in a chair beside the bed. Samantha removed her dress and tossed it onto the bed; she seemed unconcerned that he was seeing her just in bra and panties. She left the bedroom, and Steven gazed round the room; the cream coloured walls were bare. There was nothing to show him what the tall girl was interested in. After a while Samantha returned with a large towel wrapped round her body, she felt clean and refreshed after her shower. Steven turned around as she walked to the wardrobe and pulled the towel off her slim figure; she put on a clean pair of panties and bra, she picked out a pink dress and put it on. Steven heard her approach him and he turned and faced her.

'I feel a lot better now,' she said. Steven gave her a smile as she sat on the bed.

'You look a lot better; you are very pretty; you have a nice figure,' Steven said.

Samantha blushed. She needed a friend badly and the boy's words had told Samantha she had found one. She held a metal box and she opened it, she took out some photographs and she handed them to Steven.

'Do any of you know why we are here and what is expected of us?' Samantha asked in a serious voice.

The top photograph was the inside of the military encampment beside the hill. Steven and his friends had been chased away by the soldiers if they got too close to it. His father was in the photograph walking with an army officer Samantha referred to as the General. Three more photographs showed the inside of the Research Complex; Samantha pointed out her guardians in one they were walking across the compound with the General.

'Your guardians won't be pleased if they find these,' Steven said.

'It won't be any worse than what they do to me now,' she assured him.

Steven handed the photographs back to Samantha and he got up off the chair and sat beside her on the bed.

'Can you meet me by the hill tonight at eleven?'

Samantha wanted to know why.

Steven kissed her on the cheek.

'I'll tell you then, will you come?'

Samantha nodded her head and agreed to make the appointment; she was mystified, and she wanted to know what the boy had in mind for her.

Steven stood up and said it was time for him to go, so they left the cottage together and Steven stretched up onto his toes and kissed Samantha on the lips.

'Until tonight,' he said. Steven turned and made his way home. Samantha placed her fingers onto her lips. She hoped Steven would kiss her again. She entered the cottage and went up to her room and got a shock. A tall, stout woman stood by her bed holding the metal box. Her female guardian had entered the cottage by the back door, while she was saying goodbye to Steven.

'You are for it now, my girl, if you can't curb your rebellious ways, I will beat them out of you,' the woman said coldly.

Before Samantha could turn and run the woman grabbed her right arm and pulled her face down on the bed. She put the metal box down and pulled up the hem of Samantha' s dress and slapped her bottom and the backs of her thighs. Samantha cried out in pain and humiliation. When the woman's violent rage abated, she picked up the box and strode out of the room. Samantha got off the bed and tried to keep her mind off the excruciating pain in her bottom and thighs. She went to the door and listened; she heard the front door slam. Samantha opened the bedroom door and crept down the stairs. She had to get away. She left the house and ran as fast as her ailing legs could carry her. Samantha made her way to the old house on the other side of the overgrown copse. She went up to the attic and sat on the dusty floor and waited for night to fall.

CHAPTER II:

A NIGHT IN THE COPSE

Steven Calvert gazed at the luminous dial of his digital watch. It was eleven fifteen. Juliet and Janice stood beside him. John Stephenson was standing a few feet away by the edge of the overgrown copse, which looked more foreboding in the dark. Though it was night the temperature was warm.

'Perhaps she's not coming,' Juliet said.

'Samantha might be having trouble getting away from her guardians, she told me they treat her roughly,' Steven said.

'You spent a long time with her,' Janice said.

'Nothing happened – I just wanted to know more about her.'

A tall figure detached itself from the overgrown copse making John jump; he called to the others and they joined him.

'I thought you weren't coming,' Steven said.

Samantha stood close to him and told him they were waiting for her when she entered her bedroom.

'The woman threw me on the bed and beat me. When she left the house I ran away.'

'Perhaps you should have kept running,' Juliet offered.

Samantha scowled at Juliet's smiling face.

'I've already tried that; I wouldn't get far.'

Samantha told Steven she had thoroughly reconnoitred the surrounding area and found an invisible barrier surrounding them.

'They have a strange defensive shield around this whole area; there is no escape for either of us. We have to stick together; I need your help.'

Juliet stared at her sceptically. She put a finger to her head and grinned.

'The girl's crazy,' Juliet said.

Samantha stood over her menacingly, and Juliet wondered if the tall girl was going to hit her.

"Who are you calling crazy?'

Juliet stood her ground and stared defiantly up at Samantha.

'You,' Juliet said.

Samantha placed her right fist under Juliet's nose; her dark brown eyes did not stray from Samantha's angry face. Juliet clenched her fists waiting for Samantha to hit out at her. It was a comical scene: a girl just over five foot, squaring up to someone nearly two foot taller. Samantha towered over her and Juliet showed no fear, she enjoyed battles with girls taller than herself, she was of the opinion the taller they were the harder they fell.

'We haven't come here for a punch up,' Steven said, taking Samantha's fist away from Juliet's nose.

Janice Clarke moved close to Samantha.

'You have to take a test if you want to join us.'

Janice explained to the tall girl, she had to spend the night in the overgrown copse. One of them would stay with her to make sure she did not cheat. Samantha had been in the copse at night before, so it held no fears for her. To her surprise and distaste Juliet offered to stay with her. Juliet wanted to have some fun with this tall, overbearing girl. Samantha was obviously not happy about it, which would make the coming night more enjoyable for Juliet.

'We'll see you at dawn,' Steven said.

Steven, John and Janice made their way home.

'If they don't tear each other to pieces beforehand,' Janice commented.

Samantha walked to the copse. At the edge she stopped and turned to Juliet who had not moved.

'Well, aren't you coming?'

Juliet followed the tall girl into the overgrown copse, they went into the heart of the thick foreboding copse and Samantha settled down on the ground.

'Watch out for large, hairy creepy-crawlies, I'm sure they will have fun crawling up that dress of yours,' Juliet said, with a satisfied smile.

Juliet was wearing a black T-shirt and black slacks, she sat down beside Samantha.

'I'm not dressed for the occasion. I had to leave home in a hurry.'

'Have you really left home?'

'Yes, I'm not going back there again,' Samantha said.

'What are you going to do if they catch you? They'll probably give you a harder beating,' Juliet observed.

Samantha had no idea what she was going to do, apart from making sure they did not catch her. They would send out a search party for her; Samantha could not defy capture indefinitely. But she knew the terrain and she would make it difficult for them to find her.

Juliet's digital watch chimed midnight. They listened to the normal night sounds that surrounded them. Then suddenly groans and other noises broke the silence of the night. Samantha looked towards Juliet, who was sitting beside her.

'Your friends seemed to be enjoying themselves, is this part of the test too?'

Juliet feigned innocence as to who was making the noises, but she was disappointed that the tall girl was unperturbed by the racket that was going on around them.

'I'd wish they would hurry up and go home, I want my beauty sleep,' Samantha said.

Samantha closed her eyes and waited for silence to come back to the overgrown copse. At last Juliet's friends gave up their game and went home. Samantha opened her eyes and stood up and then disappeared into the undergrowth. Juliet sat and waited for the tall girl to return. After a while there was still no sign of Samantha coming back, so Juliet decided to go and look for her. Juliet made her way through the tangled undergrowth of the copse in the direction taken by Samantha. Juliet came out of the overgrown copse and spied Samantha's bright pink dress by the high fence surrounding the military encampment. The tall girl was on all fours.

'What do you think you are doing?' Juliet asked Samantha.

Samantha grabbed Juliet's hand and pulled her down to the ground and told the girl to be quiet. Juliet settled down beside Samantha who pointed to two men standing inside the boundary fence a couple of yards away. One was a high-ranking army officer. The other was a civilian, who Juliet recognised straight away. The man was Steven's father, she told Samantha.

General Heywood looked towards the overgrown copse, unaware of the two girls hiding in the bushes outside the boundary fence. Samantha was very much on his mind – from the age of six Samantha's her life had been balanced on a knife's edge. She had spent most of her time in hospital and in surgery. The biggest problem Samantha had was inside her head; they had one of the top neurosurgeons in the world working on her. The conditioning she had been receiving to keep her mental state steady was breaking down and her constant disappearing acts were not helping matters. In spite of her troubles Samantha was a very intelligent person and she had no trouble with the tests they gave her, and she was not afraid of hard work.

'How long will it take us to catch her this time?' David Calvert inquired.

'She won't stray far away, she'll go to ground and make it more difficult to find her,' the General replied.

'The heavy-handed tactics dealt to her this time would not have helped,' David observed.

'When we finally get hold of Samantha, we'll have to find someone else to take her in.'

The two men walked along the boundary fence; Samantha kept track of them as she moved along on her hands and knees amongst the bushes on the other side of the fence.

'How are Steven and the others getting on?' David asked.

'All except Janice is doing very well – she is cheating.'

General Heywood stared up at the starry night sky, as if expecting to find answers to his problems up there. David suddenly gazed beyond the boundary fence and he thought he saw a flash of pink amongst the bushes.

'Janice, that's a surprise, I didn't think she would have the nerve.'

'That's precisely what she wants us to think, Janice is a very devious young girl,' General Heywood explained.

Janice Clarke was quiet and shy; she thought the tests were a waste of time. Janice knew how intelligent she was, she did not need a machine to tell her. Janice had devised a formula to fool the teaching machines so they would not make a true assessment of her intelligence quotient. She had done a good job, too well – for their liking. Heywood was of the opinion she was only cheating herself. They could use desperate measures to get Janice to do the tests properly, but Heywood would rather have the girl's cooperation.

'I was hoping Steven might have a word with her, they seem to be thick as thieves.'

'I'll have a word with Steven, I'm sure he will want to help.'

'I hope so; we could feed her to the machines and have numbers pouring out of her ears,' Heywood said.

The two girls in the bushes were listening with deep interest. Juliet had to warn Janice as soon as possible. Juliet did not mind the tests and enjoyed letting them know how clever she was. Juliet could not understand why Janice would want to cheat.

'I'll have to have a word with Janice when I see her,' Juliet said.

The two men walked away, and Samantha got up and ran towards the copse; Juliet chased after her. When they entered the copse, they settled down on the ground. Juliet gazed at Samantha' s pale face and saw for the first time the girl's bright green eyes were luminous in the darkness. She guessed Samantha's night vision was far superior to her own.

'Did you know your eyes shine in the dark?' Juliet inquired.

Samantha nodded. 'That's one of the reasons they hate me, but I'm not as nasty as you seem to think I am.'

Juliet curled up and let sleep overtake her. Samantha could not sleep, she was too keyed up. She sat and waited for dawn to come. Steven came at first light and Samantha met him at the edge of the overgrown copse.

'I'm afraid Juliet has fallen asleep on the job,' she told him.

CHAPTER III:

THE GIRL WHO WOULD NOT TRY

Janice Clarke sat at her desk and gazed down at the test paper before her. Janice had solved the problem as soon as she had scanned the test paper, but Janice did not want them to know she had solved it so quickly, so she turned her head and gazed out of the window. She thought about what Juliet had told her about what she had heard during the night. Janice wondered what they were going to do to her to make her do the test the way they wanted her to. Janice was waiting for them to take her away and do their worst.

The instructor came over and tapped her on the shoulder, making her jump as her attention was far away from the classroom. She gazed up at the instructor's stern expression. He told her to leave the room and make her way up to the next floor. She did as she was told, and she arrived in a large white-walled room filled with teaching machines. A tall man in his late thirties approached her and gave her a warm smile.

Professor Albert Harris guided her to one of the teaching machines and Janice sat in front of it. The Professor touched a button and the screen lit up.

'We had a problem with your last session here, so we have to go through it again,' Professor Harris explained.

The threat in his voice was not lost on Janice.

'If you think it will help,' Janice said, not bothering to hide her boredom.

Professor Harris placed a headset on her, and she went through the test program calmly; she completed two thirds of it without trouble, then she deliberately pressed the wrong key and a sharp pain ran through her head. Janice pressed the right key, and nothing happened. The next problem she pressed the right key, but after that she decided to hit the wrong key and received another shock in her head for her troubles. Janice went through the rest of the test without making any more mistakes. She took off the headset and gazed up at the Professor.

'Do it right and you get a banana, do it wrong and you get the shock treatment.'
Janice had not liked the experience.

'You are a very bright child; you are only cheating yourself by not doing the tests properly.'

Janice went back to the classroom in deep thought – they had found a way to punish her for cheating. Juliet smiled and winked at her as Janice sat at her desk beside Juliet. Steven got up from his desk behind her and sat on her desk. He had been asked by his father to have a word with Janice.

'I suggest you do the tests properly from now on,' he told her.

'And if I don't?'

'Well if you want to be a dummy, carry on as you are,' Steven replied.

Janice stood up and raced from the classroom and left the school building. She ran all the way home and when she got to her room, Janice lay on the bed. A black kitten jumped on the bed and curled up on her stomach. Janice ran a hand soothingly over the top of the cat's head, which purred loudly with pleasure. After a while there came a knock on the front door. The kitten leapt off her and Janice stood up and went downstairs and opened the door. Steven was stood outside. She moved to let him in, and they stood in the hallway.

Steven accused her of letting the side down and he was very disappointed in her. He warned her they may send her away if she did not cooperate. Janice bit her lip to stop herself from crying.

'Tomorrow I expect a change in you,' Steven said.

Steven kissed her on the lips and left the house, leaving Janice to her thoughts. She entered the lounge; her father was sitting on the couch and she sat next to him. They had a visitor: Dr Bishop, the school's psychoanalyst, was sitting on an armchair opposite them.

'I have come to talk to you – I want to ease any worries you might have. I want to put your mind at rest,' Dr Bishop said.

'I've got no worries – I just don't want to be here,' Janice said.

'We are only trying to get the best out of your unique talents.'

Janice stared hard at Dr Bishop.

'To what ends, that's what's bothering me.'

'How much does the girl Samantha contribute to your unease?' Dr Bishop asked her.

Janice fidgeted with the hem of her skirt.

'Juliet thinks she's crazy.'

'Where is Samantha now?' her father asked.

Janice turned her head and gazed at her father.

'I don't know, I haven't seen her since last night. Steven told me she ran away when he went to see how she was in the morning,' Janice told him.

Janice had told the two men about the ordeal of staying all night in the overgrown copse – they were surprised they had got Samantha to do it. General Heywood had been disappointed in the news that he had missed the chance of catching her.

Janice turned her attention on Dr Bishop.

'If I don't do the tests properly, will I get my bottom smacked like Samantha? They really laid into her.'

'No, the person who struck Samantha has been chastised and Samantha will be getting someone new to look after her,' Dr Bishop assured Janice.

Dr Bishop stood up and Julian Clarke saw him out and then came back and sat on the couch beside his daughter.

Janice had a gold locket around her neck and Julian opened it and placed it in front of her eyes. Janice stared at the tiny photograph of her mother inside it; she had died when Janice was six.

'If you won't do it for yourself – then why don't you do it for your mother? She wanted the best for you, you are a very intelligent girl, you've come this far, why not go all the way.'

He gave her a hug and kissed her on the cheek.

'Janice, you know I love you and I am here for you; I won't let anyone hurt you, sweetheart, you are too precious to me,' her father said.

Janice laid her head on his shoulder.

'I will try, Daddy, honestly I will,' Janice said.

CHAPTER IV:

THE RUNAWAY

Samantha spent her days avoiding the search parties that were sent out for her, by the soldiers from the military encampment. When they approached the old house from the front, she left by the back door, then she returned to the house when it had been thoroughly searched and the soldiers had left. She moved silently and swiftly as she moved from place to place to avoid the searchers. Her keen senses could see, hear and smell them before they got near to her. Samantha moved like a phantom; they could not perceive her presence, though she was almost close enough to touch. She would lie quiet and still in the bushes until they had passed by. General Heywood was amazed at how well Samantha had dropped out of sight – it was obvious the girl was always one step ahead of them. He was aware Samantha was determined to stay free for as long as she could, and she was expertly doing just that. Something else had to be done to get the girl back in the fold.

Samantha sat on the dusty floor of the old attic – she back lay against the wall and her long legs stretched out before her. The pink dress she wore was dirty and torn in several places. Her face, arms and legs were equally dirty, and her long ginger hair was a mess and no longer glossy. Samantha did not care about her appearance as she could not do anything about it for the moment. She ignored the hunger rumblings in her stomach. She closed her eyes and let her mind drift away.

'Is this a private party, or can anyone join in?' a female voice said.

A hand tapped Samantha on the shoulder and her eyes flashed open and she saw it was the blonde girl sitting beside her. She stared at Janice with wild green eyes.

'I'm sorry I startled you,' Janice apologised.

Janice gazed at the tall girl – she was horrified at her appearance, and Janice had never seen anyone so dirty and run down.

'You look terrible, have you eaten lately?'

Samantha gave a weak smile and shook her head. Janice took a chocolate bar out of her yellow dress pocket and gave it to her.

'Why don't you give yourself up, I'm sure they won't hurt you. My father told me the woman who hit you has been punished, you won't be going back to her,' Janice said.

Samantha gazed at the blonde girl as she took the paper off the chocolate bar.

'If they want me, they'll have to come and get me,' Samantha said, defiantly.

Samantha quickly devoured the chocolate bar.

'They do, but you are never at home,' Janice said.

'I'm not going to make it easy for them,' Samantha assured her.

'We are both rebels in our way,' Janice said.

Janice told her about how she cheated the test results by tampering with the teaching machines. Now they had discovered it and she had to do the tests properly.

Samantha kissed her on the cheek.

'I'm impressed, I wish I had thought of that,' Samantha said in admiration.

There came a sound from the lower part of the house. Janice put a hand on Samantha's shoulder to stop her from leaping to her feet.

'It's all right, that will be Steven, he is coming to talk to you,' Janice said.

Samantha got up and walked across the floor, Janice followed her down the attic steps and crossed the landing then went down the stairs to meet Steven at the bottom of them.

'Hullo Steven, you are my second visitor.'

Steven was as shocked as Janice at Samantha's untidy appearance.

'They have asked me to get in contact with you, to persuade you to come out from hiding – Janice and I have been very worried about you. You look as if you could use a good bath and a hot meal,' Steven said.

Samantha sat on the stairs and stared up at Steven.

'You can come to my home, nobody will hurt you there,' Steven promised.

Janice sat beside Samantha and put her arm round the girl's thin waist.

'You can trust us, Samantha.'

Janice found herself under the hard stare of two bright green eyes. She wondered if Samantha was trying to see inside her head.

'We want to be your friend, if you'll let us,' Steven said.

Samantha turned her head and stared up at Steven and studied his face; he seemed sincere in what he said. Samantha was well aware she had to trust someone, and she liked Janice and Steven.

'All right, I'll trust you, I'll come to your home at ten tonight, but I shall be looking out for a trap,' Samantha said at last.

Janice kissed Samantha on the grubby cheek.

'You won't be sorry for your decision,' Janice assured her.

Samantha and Janice stood up and Steven went to the tall girl and kissed her on the lips. He gave her instructions on how to get to his house. Then he left the house with Janice. Samantha returned to the attic with her fingers touching her lips and thought about the kiss she had received from the boy.

Steven Calvert gazed at the clock on the mantel as it chimed ten o'clock. He turned away and gazed at General Heywood, who stood by the lounge door. Steven wondered if he would keep his word about not harming Samantha when she arrived at the house. His father and stepmother sat on the couch. Steven crossed to the window and pushed the curtain aside and looked out – there were two soldiers standing by the front gate. He wondered if Samantha could slip past them without their knowledge.

Hilary Calvert got up and left the room. She approached the kitchen and she heard the sound of the back door opening; she strode to the kitchen door and opened it. General Heywood came up behind her. Hilary opened the door and switched on the light. Standing by the back door was a tall girl in a torn and dirty pink dress – she stared wide-eyed at Hilary and the General.

They were both shocked at the sight of the fifteen-year-old girl covered from head to toe in dirt and grime – the girl looked as if she had risen from the grave. Her long ginger hair was untidy and tangled. Hilary moved slowly towards Samantha who stared at her in suspicion.

General Heywood stayed by the door and let Hilary try to gain the girl's confidence. Hilary moved slowly and deliberately towards Samantha, who stood like a frightened and timid animal – that with the slightest wrong move would be away with a burst of speed. Samantha moved back away from the advancing woman. Seeing this, Hilary stopped moving and smiled at the girl.

'Nobody in this house is going to harm you, Samantha. Nobody is going to hurt you, while I'm here,' Hilary said in a soft soothing voice.

Hilary held out her right hand to the girl, as she stood against the back door as if trying to push herself into it. Samantha stared at the hand outstretched towards her.

'Come on, darling, I am not going to hurt you. You can have a refreshing bath and a good meal, after which you will feel like a new girl,' Hilary said.

Hilary took a slow step forward as Samantha still stared at her offered hand. As Hilary got close to her, Samantha's head came swiftly up and Hilary was caught by the hard stare of two wide green eyes. They bore into her – Hilary felt as if she was being evaluated for her honesty and trustworthiness.

'You can trust me, Samantha, I mean you no harm, and I wouldn't hurt one of Steven's friends.'

Samantha made up her mind and decided to trust Steven's stepmother. She laid her right hand timidly into Hilary's outstretched hand. Hilary held Samantha's hand firmly but gently and guided her out of the kitchen and up the stairs to the bathroom, General Heywood returned to the lounge and informed David and Steven that Samantha had arrived. Hilary ran the bath while Samantha removed the dirty and torn dress, she took off her underwear. Hilary helped the girl into the bath. She sat in the warm scented water and stared at the tiled wall. Samantha allowed the woman to wash the grime off her body. Hilary sometimes gazed at the young tormented face – she wondered what was going on in the girl's mind, as the bright green eyes stared into space.

Hilary shampooed the girl's ginger hair – then she got a comb and carefully removed the tangles and soon got it to its natural glossy state.

'How does a pretty thing like you get in such a state?'

Samantha came to life and started to scrub her grimy knees. Hilary let the girl finish washing her body, when she had done Samantha let Hilary help her out of the bath and dry her wet body.

'Do you like me?'

Hilary was glad to hear the girl's voice at last, but the sudden enquiry surprised her.

'Why shouldn't I, you haven't got two heads, have you?'

A smile softened the hard-facial features.

'I wonder sometimes, because I'm unusually tall and not very good looking, people seem to have the idea I'm a monster.'

Hilary was dismayed to hear that; she was going to have a hard word with the General. She wrapped the large bath towel round Samantha and guided the girl to the spare bedroom and sat the girl on the bed.

'I don't know who told you that, but you are a very pretty girl and don't let anyone tell you otherwise.'

Samantha gazed at the woman – Hilary gazed at the watery green eyes.

'If you want to have a good cry, go ahead. There's no shame in it. I'm here for you,' Hilary said, sincerely.

Hilary put her arms around Samantha and hugged her, the girl's tears came in a flood. She felt the convulsions run through the girl's body as Samantha released her pent-up emotions. Hilary held the slim body tightly and ran a hand through the long ginger hair. Finally, the tears stopped, and Hilary released the girl and Samantha dried her tear stained face on the bath towel.

'Feeling better?' Hilary asked.

Samantha nodded and gave the woman a smile. Samantha decided she liked Steven's stepmother.

'You are a good person,' Samantha told her.

Hilary kissed the girl on the cheek. She stood up and left the room for a moment then returned with a red dress. She was a tall slim woman and gave it to Samantha who put it on.

'It's a bit short as you are taller than me; it's lucky you have nice legs.'

Samantha gazed down and ran a critical eye over her bare legs.

'Do you think so?'

Hilary nodded and kissed the girl on the cheek.

'Let's go down to the kitchen and get some hot food into you,' Hilary said.

Hilary cooked Samantha a meal and sat at the breakfast table with her and watched Samantha happily fill her empty stomach. When she finished the meal, Samantha looked up at the woman and gave her a satisfied smile.

'You are a wonderful cook; Steven is very lucky.'

General Heywood walked into the kitchen and sat beside Samantha and watched her sip at a mug of coffee. He waited until she was ready. At last Samantha placed the empty mug down on the table. She felt Hilary standing by her chair; the woman started to massage the girl's thin shoulders. Samantha told General Heywood she was not going back to the home she had run away from. She wanted a house of her own, Samantha assured him – she was quite capable of looking after herself.

Samantha had resigned herself to carry on with what they had planned for her. She promised not to run away again, as long as she got some concessions which she outlined to General Heywood. He accepted them as he wanted to keep her happy so she could continue the work she had started. Hilary and the General looked at Samantha in admiration – she knew what she wanted and presented herself well. Samantha looked up on occasions at Hilary, who stood by her chair with a comforting hand on her right shoulder; she gave the girl a smile of encouragement. Samantha felt the woman was on her side.

General Heywood told Samantha he would be expecting some hard work from her.

General Heywood and Samantha stood up – she gave a deep sigh and then held out her hands to him.

'Well, I'm ready to have the chains put on,' she said, dryly.

'We prefer the invisible chains,' he assured her.

Hilary placed her hands on the girl's shoulders.

'I'll keep Samantha here for a couple of days, so I can keep an eye on her, while she recovers from her ordeal,' Hilary said.

General Heywood nodded his head and gave his consent and left the house; he was glad the crisis was over. Samantha was very important to him and he would have to try and keep her happy, so she would stay on the path he had planned out for her.

Hilary could see the girl was tired and worn out, so she guided Samantha to the spare room and Samantha fell asleep the instant her head hit the pillow.

Samantha awoke next morning and sat up in bed, she stretched out and gave a deep sigh. The sun shone brightly through the window. She got out of bed and crossed over to the window and opened it. A slight breeze blew in and caressed her naked body. She took several deep breaths. Hilary had been right: after being well fed and groomed, Samantha did feel like a new girl. She felt the sun's warmth on her naked skin. She felt a lot better; she felt her strength returning.

A few moments later the door opened, and Hilary entered the room carrying a tray. Samantha returned to the bed, as the tray was placed on the bedside table, and she gazed at the food on it.

'Breakfast in bed, you are so nice to me.'

Samantha got into bed and sat up – Hilary handed her the tray and Samantha tucked into her breakfast. Hilary sat on the edge of the bed.

'How is my patient this morning?'

Samantha gave Hilary a satisfied smile.

'It was nice sleeping in a bed again, you are being so kind to me, and I really appreciate it.'

Hilary sat beside Samantha and gave her a kiss on the cheek.

'Nobody should end up in the state you were in last night. Kindness and respect are what you can expect in this house,' Hilary said.

Samantha emptied the plate then picked up the mug of tea and sipped it. Hilary went to the wardrobe and opened the door.

'We got some clothes for you, Samantha – while you slept. There's plenty here for you to wear, so you don't have to walk about the house naked,' Hilary said.

When Samantha had drank her tea, she placed the empty mug on the bedside table, she got up and walked to the wardrobe. Hilary handed her a pale blue bra and matching panties. Samantha put them on and stood in front of the full-length mirror on the inside of the wardrobe door. She stared at her reflection, the hollow cheeks and sunken eyes reminded Samantha of the girl in her dreams. Hilary placed her hands on the girl's shoulders and slowly massaged them.

'We'll soon have you back to normal,' Hilary said.

'I don't think I know what normal is, you are the only person I've met so far that has taken my feelings into consideration, and you seem to see me in a very different light to the others that rule my life.'

Hilary moved in front of Samantha and ran a hand caressingly over her cheek – the green eyes studied her face.

'Well that's going to change, I've had a strong word with the General and things are going to change for you, Samantha; you will be joining Steven and the others at school. If you have any more problems come and see me, you know where I'll be, and I shall be there for you, so never forget that.'

Samantha liked Hilary very much – at last she had met someone who thought she was human. Hilary gave her a pink blouse and maroon skirt and Samantha put them on.

'Now there's a pretty schoolgirl,' Hilary commented.

'You are doing wonders to my confidence – I can't find the words to thank you.'

Hilary gave the girl a hug.

'It's a pleasure, Steven likes you, he will help build up your confidence even more.'

They left the bedroom. Samantha felt a lot better now someone was fighting in her corner, and she was ready to face whatever they threw at her. Samantha knew what she had to do – there were going to be people who were going to give her grief like Juliet. Samantha was well aware she was going to have trouble with that girl.

CHAPTER V:

ACCIDENTS WILL HAPPEN

Karen Thompson was sat back in her seat with her eyes closed. She wondered about the little horrors they had given her to instruct. They had not been clear about her new post – she was surprised to learn it was at a research facility. Her job was teaching children and she would not be changing her methods for the special bright children she was about to teach. Karen was going to work them hard.

A new note in the motors of the helicopter told Karen she was at her destination. She opened her eyes and gazed out of the window. The helicopter landed in the courtyard of the special school she would be teaching in. She saw there was a reception party waiting for her. The rotors stopped turning and she stepped out of the helicopter. Karen was glad to have her feet on solid ground again. General Heywood approached her and held out his hand.

'I'm glad to see you, Miss Thompson, how was your flight?'

Karen shook the General's hand and asked him to lead her to the little monsters she was to teach. She told him the journey had been too noisy for her liking. General Heywood assured her the classroom would be quieter.

Six faces were pressed against the classroom window looking at the helicopter – they gazed down at their new instructor. When the people down below walked out of sight, they returned to their seats. Five minutes later the door opened and they expected their new teacher to walk in, but to their surprise and Juliet's disappointment, Samantha strode into the room. Steven gave her a friendly smile as she came to the line of desks; he had not told the others the tall girl would be joining them. A tall sandy haired boy walked in next. Samantha found an empty desk on Steven's right, Janice was sat on his left, the desk behind Samantha was owned by Juliet and she glared at Samantha.

'I would have thought they would have done away with you.'

Samantha grinned at the black-haired girl.

'They're obviously of the mind, I'm too good to lose,' Samantha said.

The boy who had followed Samantha into the classroom sat next to Juliet. Samantha turned to the boy.

'You'll have to watch that one, she has a bad attitude problem,' Samantha told him, pointing to Juliet.

Henry Jones smiled up at her, he was sure he was going to enjoy his time here.

Hazel who sat on the other side of Juliet laughed out loud – Juliet scowled at the younger girl. Janice turned around to her friend.

'You asked for that, Juliet.'

Hazel patted Samantha on the back. 'It's good to see you again, Samantha.'

Samantha turned and thanked her. 'I don't think Juliet shares your feelings.'

'Forget her – Juliet has a chip on her shoulder – the size of an oak tree.'

The door opened again, and eight pair of eyes watched Karen walk into the room. She walked up to her desk and stood and faced the eight children. She soon found the one she was looking for; the General had told Karen about the tall ginger haired girl. She had no time for rebels in her class; she had a formula for rebellious pupils. Samantha gazed at the woman and could see her eyes were turned her way, Samantha had no doubt the General would have told the new instructor to be especially hard on her and Samantha was going to expect the worse from the new instructor.

Karen called out the names alphabetically and she got them to stand so she could get a good look at them. Janice Clarke was first, and Steven Calvert came next. Samantha was third. Karen stared hard at the tall girl; she made an impressive sight; Karen knew she was going to have to stamp her authority on the girl from the very first. She called out Paul James, who was sitting next to Hazel. Samantha decided to sit, but the teacher told her to keep standing.

'The first lesson, don't move until I say so,' Karen said sharply, keeping her eyes on Samantha.

Karen read out the names of the other pupils she had not yet called out. Samantha had to stand all through the first lesson, then after an hour she was told to sit down, and she gave a deep sigh of relief. At the end of the day they filed out of the classroom. Juliet came up to Samantha.

'The new teacher has certainly got it in for you,' Juliet said.

'They are certainly getting their revenge on you – for giving them the slip for so long,' Steven said.

'It gives Juliet some enjoyment,' Samantha said.

Samantha walked away from the smiling girl and left the school building; she found Hilary Calvert waiting for her at the gate. Steven kissed Janice and she went off with Juliet, who shouted goodbye to Samantha, using the name Sammy, which she knew Samantha detested. Samantha ignored the tiresome girl. Hilary told Samantha she had a surprise for her. Samantha was glad to hear it, she wanted something pleasurable after the day she had had. She followed Hilary along the path away from the school, and Steven walked beside her. They walked past the turning that led to the homes of Steven and his friends. After a short walk Hilary stopped outside a vacant house, she gave Samantha a set of keys and told her the house was her new home. Samantha walked up to the front door and put the key in the lock and opened the door and stepped into the hallway. Hilary stood beside her and kissed her on the lips.

'I've been here all day getting it ready for you, if there's anything else you need, just let me know,' Hilary said.

They went on a tour of the house, starting with the lower floor. There was a comfortable fully furnished lounge, the kitchen was well stocked, and the back room had been made into a gymnasium as to Samantha's instructions.

'I'll come over on occasions and have a workout on this equipment,' Hilary said.

'Come around anytime – you've been so good to me, I really appreciate it,' Samantha said.

'Nobody should be allowed to get in the state you were in, when you came to my house; anytime you need me, just call,' Hilary said.

They went up the stairs and visited the bathroom, the main bedroom and the spare bedroom. Samantha was glad they had given her a house far from the others, especially Juliet. They went down to the kitchen and Hilary prepared them a meal. After they had eaten and washed up, Steven hugged Samantha and kissed her on the lips. He left with Hilary, so Samantha could settle

Samantha undressed and had a shower, after which she dried herself and lay on the bed in the main bedroom. At last she was alone and free to do what she wished, with nobody around to watch her.

The room was dark, and a voice was heard crying out of the darkness.

LET ME OUT!

Samantha awoke next morning with a splitting headache, the dream still floating around in her aching mind. She got off the bed and staggered to the window and looked out. The sky was blue and cloudless; the sun shone brightly, it told her it was going to be another scorching day. She just made it to the bathroom in time before she was violently sick in the toilet. She went in the shower and let the running warm water wash the cold sweat from her body.

Samantha got dressed and left the house, she felt drowsy and sick, and she decided to visit the infirmary. It was hot and a slight breeze blew against her. Samantha stared ahead of her, as she walked along the track towards the boundary fence of the Research Complex.

Juliet Prentice was sitting on the low wall at the front of her house, she saw Samantha walk past and she called out to the tall girl in the name she did not like. Samantha showed no sign she was aware of Juliet. She watched Samantha approach the main gate of the Research Complex. A jeep suddenly came out of the main gate. Unaware of it, the girl stepped in front of it, as Juliet stood up and shouted a warning. The driver swerved to miss her, but he hit Samantha a glancing blow and she fell to the ground senseless. Juliet ran up to her and knelt down and saw Samantha was unconscious. The jeep had stopped nearby, and an army officer got out and picked up Samantha's prone body and laid her gently on the back seat of the jeep. He got in next to the driver and Juliet watched the jeep speed in the direction of the infirmary.

Hazel Johnson was mysteriously drawn to the construction site in front of the Research Complex. The sun beat down on her, the hot air shimmered about her body, and her red dress clung to her sweaty skin. She stood by one of the huge concrete pylons that held a great dish of a radio telescope. She stared up at it. Hazel suddenly felt dizzy; she moved away from the pylon and noticed a dumper truck backing towards her. Hazel tried to move out of the way, but she found her reactions were sluggish. The dumper truck hit her and knocked Hazel against the concrete pylon and she feel senseless to the ground.

Hazel lay in bed in a light blue walled room; there were other beds in the room, but they were all empty. Machines were attached to her body as they monitored her life signs. She lay in a room that was part of Laboratory 3 on the compound of the Research Complex. A door slid open and a tall slim figure strode into the room. Her pale blue eyes glazed round the room and spied the occupied bed. She approached it and gazed down at the pretty face on the pillow. She shook her head and the long silvery hair cascaded around her thin shoulders. She wished the unconscious girl would wake so she could talk to her. It was the first time she had seen someone close to her own age – she was alone and a virtual prisoner.

She stood motionless by the bed staring down at the occupant. The door slid open again and footsteps approached the bed.

'You are back with the living once again, I see,' the newcomer said in a cold, hard voice.

The silver blonde girl turned and faced the newcomer. She was a brown-haired girl in a white lab coat; she was very disappointed the tall girl had not been killed in the accident with the computer.

Hazel woke and gazed at the vision standing by the bed. The tall thin figure wore a long flowing white nightgown. The face was thin and ghostly white – the wide deep-set ice blue eyes glazed back at her. The thin lips formed a smile, there was no warmth in it. Hazel closed her eyes. There was an aura emanating from the tall slim girl; Hazel felt her head ache and she slipped back into unconsciousness.

'It seems she can't stand your presence either.'

The girl in the white lab coat grinned at the girl in the white nightgown, who walked away from the bed and walked out of the room with the other girl's laughter ringing in her ears.

CHAPTER VI:

ESCAPADE IN THE NIGHT

Two days later Samantha came out of the dark pit of unconsciousness. She stared up at the white ceiling and realised she was not at home. She sat up and found she was wired to some machines by the bed. Hazel was sitting on a chair by the bed.

'I'm glad you are awake at last. I've been worried about you.'

Hazel's face lit up as Samantha gazed at her through blurred vision.

'You are probably the only one who was,' Samantha said.

Hazel assured Samantha they had all been worried about her, Juliet as well as she had seen the accident and was hoping she had a speedy recovery. Hazel told Samantha about her own accident at the construction site and that she had been taken to a hospital ward inside the Research Complex.

'When I woke there was a tall thin girl standing by the bed, she had long silvery hair and she was very pale,' Hazel said.

Hazel stared at the expression of horror on Samantha's face.

'You look as if you've seen a ghost; that girl certainly looked like one,' Hazel said.

Samantha disconnected herself from the machines by the bed and pulled the sheet down and swung her long legs over the side of the bed. She wondered if the girl Hazel saw was the same one in her dreams.

'I have nightmares about the girl you saw.'

'That's strange,' Hazel said.

Hilary entered the infirmary and saw Samantha sitting on the side of the bed; she gave a deep sigh of relief. She approached the bed and told Hazel to go home.

'That wasn't a good idea, throwing yourself in front of Major Collins' jeep.'

'I didn't exactly throw myself. I was coming here, because I woke with a splitting headache and I felt sick. The hot sun was making me feel worse; I had no idea what I was doing. I just felt something hit me and I blacked out,' Samantha explained.

Hilary ran a soothing hand over Samantha's forehead.

'Do you have these headaches often?' Hilary asked.

'Quite often and I have blackouts as well, it's not that I always run away, I have these headaches and my mind goes blank, I end up a long way from home and I don't know how I got there or why. They refuse to tell me what's wrong with me, but I'm sure they know,' Samantha explained.

Hilary sat beside Samantha and put a comforting arm round the girl's waist; she kissed the girl on the cheek.

'I'll start asking questions for you, I'll see what I can find out. I care for you, Samantha, and I don't want to see you in so much pain.'

A tall man in his early fifties approached the bed; he wore a grey suit. He stood over Samantha and gave her a warm smile.

'How is my young patient?'

'You tell me, you're the doctor,' Samantha said.

Dr Forbes asked Samantha about the accident and she could only tell him what she had told Hilary. He put the girl through several tests and Samantha cooperated and did as she was told, without making a fuss. Hilary helped the doctor and Samantha was glad the woman was here. When they had finished with her, Samantha gazed up at Dr Forbes and waited for his verdict.

'Have I passed the medical?'

'Yes, I shall keep you here for one more day under observation. You didn't break any bones, just bruised where the car hit you,' Dr Forbes told her.

Two hours later Steven and Janice came to see her. They both kissed Samantha on the lips.

'We're glad you weren't damaged too severely,' Steven said.

'With Hazel being knocked down also – we are walking around looking nervously about us,' Janice said.

'Accidents will happen,' Samantha observed.

When Samantha left the infirmary in the evening of the next day, she went straight to the hill overlooking the construction site. She was glad to see Steven and his friends were not there, as she wanted to be alone. She watched the sun sink slowly behind the distant hills on the other side of the Research Complex. She had taken off her pink dress and she sat in her bra and panties; a cool breeze blew against her skin. After a while she heard a sound behind her. Samantha turned her head and to her annoyance, Juliet was stood behind her, wearing a white blouse and blue shorts.

'If you've come here to tell me I'm crazy for sitting here alone, don't bother,' Samantha said.

Juliet sat beside her.

'I wasn't, I saw you get hit by the jeep, I wanted to see if you were all right.'

'As you can see, I'm still in one piece.'

Samantha stood up and put on her pink dress, Juliet also stood up.

'You look great in shorts, Juliet; I could not wear them.'

'Have you anything planned for tonight?' Juliet asked.

Samantha pointed towards the Research Complex.

'I'm going to wait for darkness and sneak over there and try to find out what they are hiding.'

Juliet was shocked, she could imagine the many painful punishments Samantha would receive if she was caught on the other side of the boundary fence. What lay there was none of their business.

'That's crazy–' Juliet cut off the last word by biting her lower lip.

Juliet had not come to annoy Samantha, she wanted to end the animosity that was growing between them and she had received an ultimatum from Janice – her best friend would not speak to her until she had made peace with Samantha.

'You love playing it close to the wind, don't you?'

Samantha smiled and gazed at the deep brown eyes that studied her facial expression for an insight as to what might be on her mind. Samantha found the girl very tiresome, but she had to admit, Juliet was very bright for a girl of twelve.

'Mysteries are there to be solved; they're not boosting our intelligence for nothing.'

'I expect when we get older, they will tell us what they require us for,' Juliet said.

'I aim to find out before then,' Samantha said.

She walked slowly down the hill and Juliet followed close behind her.

'Why don't you come with me? I could use your talents,' Samantha said.

'Are you serious?' Juliet asked in a shocked voice.

At the bottom of the hill Samantha turned and faced Juliet.

'Are you scared?' Samantha goaded.

'Yes, and I'm not afraid to admit it.'

'I'll protect you,' Samantha assured her.

They walked together along the track that took them round the research facility and up to the school and they turned right towards the group of eight houses. Against her better judgement Juliet decided to accompany Samantha on her risky quest.

Outside her house Juliet agreed to meet Samantha by the school gates at midnight.

'I'll see you later, Sam, and don't forget to wear something appropriate, we don't want you to stick out like a sore thumb,' Juliet said, without turning around. Samantha ran off towards her own home.

When Samantha got home she heard someone working in the kitchen. She entered the kitchen and found Janice cooking supper.

'Hilary gave me a spare key, so I could cook a meal for you.'

Samantha told her about the meeting with Juliet and how they were going to the Research Complex to find out what was going on over there.

'That sounds risky,' Janice observed.

Samantha smiled at her. 'It is – but I must learn more about myself.'

'I hope Juliet was better behaved towards you. I had a serious talk with her.'

'That was good of you and nice to have you here waiting for me.'

'Juliet's mother mysteriously disappeared, and Juliet thinks she has abandoned her,' Janice explained.

Samantha nodded. 'I can see why a girl like Juliet had problems with girls as tall as me. What you say would be a catalyst for her being more aggressive.'

After they had eaten supper they went to the lounge and sat on the couch. 'The General won't like what you have planned.'

Samantha grinned at her. 'That's why I'm not going to tell him.'

Janice kissed her on the cheek. 'I'll be here when you get back and you can tell me all about it.'

'I'll look forward to that,' Samantha said.

Juliet crept out of her house at midnight. She went swiftly towards the hill and reached it first as there was no sign of Samantha. In a couple of the buildings on the compound lights were on, showing someone was up and about.

Juliet hoped Samantha would abandon her mission, but knowing the girl, Juliet thought Samantha would still go through with it.

Juliet crossed over to the other side of the track towards the construction site, which was now fenced off and was now part of the compound so inquisitive people like Hazel could not get in and come to harm. She started to walk round the high perimeter fence of the Research Complex, keeping a sharp eye out for any kind of movement, and she half expected to be grabbed by something nasty. She detected no movement inside the complex. Juliet gazed nervously around her as if something or somebody was lurking in the darkness. She wondered if Samantha was lurking nearby waiting to leap out at her and give her a fright. Juliet made it to the rear of the complex. A hundred yards away from the rear boundary fence was the large ancient wood; it curved round the Research Complex. She had never been here before, the trees were dark and foreboding and Juliet did not want to go near them, it was obviously home to wild creatures that may not welcome her in their habitat. A place Samantha would be at home in, Juliet was sure of that. Juliet wondered where the girl had got to. She slowly walked back the way she had come. Juliet had reached halfway when she was suddenly grabbed from behind. Juliet opened her mouth to scream and a hand was clamped over it. A voice whispered in her ear; Juliet tore herself out of the grip of her assailant. She spun round and faced a tall dark figure standing over her. Juliet swore.

'Tut, tut, such language is not ladylike,' Samantha scalded her.

'You are late; do you have to creep up on people like that?'

'I couldn't help it, I've been following you since you left the hill, you are so easy to sneak up on,' Samantha said.

'It must be great to have perfect night vision,' Juliet said.

'I know the fact my eyes shine in the dark – freaks you out – but you need not fear it,' assured Samantha.

'It's just disconcerting, that's all. We are all trying to get used to it.'

Samantha was wearing a black sweater and black skirt and black tights; her long ginger hair was tied up under a black woollen cap. Juliet gazed at the only bright part of Samantha, her green eyes – Juliet and the others still could not get used to the way the tall girl's eyes shone in the dark, two small green spots of light shining out of the dark shadows of her thin face. She had better night vision than them. Juliet decided her mind was not playing tricks on her, when her sixth sense seemed to be aware of someone close watching her. Juliet saw Samantha in a new light.

'Now you are here, how are we going to get in?'

'We are going in by the main gate.'

'Of course, it's so obvious, why didn't I think of that,' Juliet said, sarcastically.

Samantha strode off and Juliet followed her, mumbling to herself. They went around to the other side of the Research Complex where the main gate was situated. When they arrived there Samantha went to the control box by the side of the main gate. She took out a small metal box from her skirt pocket. Juliet stood close to her.

'It's not as strange as you might think; you'll notice there is no guard in the security office,' Samantha said.

Samantha opened the control box and placed her gadget inside it. She kept her eyes on the Liquid Crystal Display on her electronic device, and she told Juliet to stand by the keypad on the gate control box. After a while she called some numbers to Juliet who tapped them out on the keypad. As Juliet tapped in the last number spoken to her the gates slid open. Samantha took her device out of the control box and placed it in her skirt pocket; she closed up the panel in the gate control. Samantha dashed through the gateway and ducked under the window of the security office. Juliet quickly joined her.

When Samantha got to the end of the small building, she looked around the corner and saw the security guard enter the building. Samantha gazed through the window above her head and made sure the guard was facing the other way; she dashed across the compound with Juliet in hot pursuit. In the centre of the compound was a large blockhouse. Samantha stopped when she reached it, to let the slower Juliet catch up.

'There are not many people about, so far so good,' Juliet said.

'I've been watching this place for ages, I have checked on movements going on here, they shouldn't catch us if we're careful,' Samantha said in a voice full of confidence.

'You're a cool one and no mistake,' Juliet said in admiration of the tall girl.

Along the west side of the compound were two large single storey buildings which contained the research laboratories. Samantha ran off and headed for the rear building, which contained Lab 3, the one Hazel was taken to after her accident. Samantha tried the door and found it unlocked, Juliet kept an eye out for any movement in the darkness, and then followed Samantha into the building, closing the door behind her.

'I hope nobody is at home,' Juliet said.

They walked along a corridor dimly lit. The first door they came to Samantha tried and found it unlocked. She pushed it open and the room beyond lit up and she surveyed the room: it was full of filing cabinets and desk top computers. She closed the door and walked on until she got to the end where she turned right. Juliet followed close behind – she was waiting for Samantha to bump into someone; she hoped the tall girl had a good excuse for being here if they were caught. Samantha was not worried about being caught as they could not treat her any worse than they had already; Samantha was out for answers to questions that filled her curious mind.

They came to a door on each side of the corridor. Samantha chose the left one and it slid open when she touched the control pad. They entered a large room which lit up when they were past the doorway; it was the main laboratory. Juliet was drawn to the computers like a magnet, and she sat in one of the chairs at the control desk. Samantha gazed round the room at the benches filled with scientific equipment. She went over to Juliet who was running her fingers over the computer control surfaces. Her eyes were fixed on the screen. Juliet was engrossed in what she was doing, she was in her element. Juliet discovered they were in the genetics laboratory – the information she was getting told her that and it was a subject more suited to her friend Janice, whereas computers were Juliet's love.

Samantha stood over her.

'There's plenty of info on us, but nothing concerning you,' Juliet told her.

'Such is life,' was all Samantha had to say.

Juliet had no trouble getting the general data, though sometimes she got an access denied, which she expected. She was not after any state secrets, though she would break into them if she worked at it, but they did not have the time and the sooner they were gone the better Juliet would like it. Juliet had formulated a way of getting into access denied data in the school's computer system. She knew the authorities would love to catch her at it, but Juliet was expert in being one step ahead of them.

'You should have brought Janice, she would love all this,' Juliet said.

'Can you memorize some of the interesting data?' Samantha asked.

Juliet nodded her head.

'Good, I'm just going to see what else I can find out,' Samantha said.

Samantha left the laboratory and walked up the corridor to the end and turned right; she came up to some double doors with some round windows in them. She looked through one and surveyed the hospital ward on the other side of the doors. There were rows of beds on both sides of the room and a brown-haired female in a white lab coat was walking down the aisle. Samantha recognised her at once. Livonia Wagstaffe was the same age as Samantha, she was nasty and malicious and completely without scruples. She had a hatred for Samantha that was intense to the extreme. They had both attended the school at the same time and clashed violently on many occasions. When they met next Samantha was sure it would be explosive, she was certain.

Lavonia Wagstaffe moved to the only bed that was occupied. She gazed down at the thin white face on the pillow. The girl should wake soon, and history would be in the making. Lavonia held the limp left wrist and felt the pulse – it was strong and steady. She gazed at the peaceful face, and the eyes suddenly flashed open and stared up at Lavonia standing by the bed.

'Good, you are awake at last,' Lavonia said.

'Where am I?'

'You are in hospital, you have just recovered from a very bad illness,' Lavonia told her.

The girl ran a hand over her forehead; she tried to remember, but nothing came to her hazy mind, her head throbbed.

'I don't remember, I have a headache,' the girl said.

Lavonia gave the girl two white pills to swallow and poured out a glass of water to wash them down with.

'Don't worry, it'll come back to you in time, just relax.'

Samantha watched with interest through the window in the door; the girl in the bed had long silvery blonde hair. Someone tapped her on the shoulder, making her jump; she turned and faced the grinning Juliet.

'Sorry, did I give you a fright?'

Juliet was glad to have got Samantha back for jumping out at her in the dark and grabbing her.

'The computer froze me out, I think I touched a nerve, so I think they will be coming to search for us,' Juliet warned.

Juliet gazed through the round window in the door and saw Lavonia standing by the occupied bed. She turned to her companion.

'Sammy, I would never have believed it, there's someone in there that is uglier than you,' Juliet taunted.

Samantha stared down at the grinning face. Juliet enjoyed goading Samantha too much to quit straight away. Samantha could see she got a strange pleasure out of it.

'You really are very tiresome at times,' Samantha said.

Juliet giggled and turned her head and gazed through the window in the door. She asked Samantha who the girl in the ward room was.

'That is Lavonia; if you think I'm nasty, wait until you meet her – she makes me seem just a pussy cat,' Samantha said.

'I've considered you many things, Sammy, but pussy cat is not one of them,' Juliet said.

Samantha turned away and went back the way they had come, with Juliet following behind her.

In the ward room the door on the opposite side of the room slid open and Hilary Calvert stepped in, joined Lavonia at the bedside and smiled warmly at the patient.

'Hullo Jennifer, how are you feeling?'

'I'm feeling much better, I feel my strength returning,' the girl said.

'Good, we'll soon have you up on your feet,' Hilary said.

A smile lit up the thin pale face. She could not wait to be up and about, she had things to do.

Samantha and Juliet were in the laboratory as they had heard someone entering the building by the main door and they could not get out that way. Samantha opened the window and helped Juliet clamber out into the night. Samantha quickly vacated the building after her. They found themselves by the boundary fence. They went to the other side of the building and Samantha scanned the compound for movement; she checked nobody was standing by the entrance to the building they had just left. Then she shot across the compound at high speed. Juliet was amazed at the turn of speed the tall girl could produce – there was a lot of power in her long legs. Juliet was impressed. Juliet darted after her and caught up with Samantha at the large concrete blockhouse at the centre of the compound.

'Are we going out the way we came in?' Juliet inquired.

'Why not? It's only natural to use the front door, when entering and leaving a place.'

'Of course, how silly of me to ask,' Juliet mumbled.

Samantha darted off in the direction of the security hut. Juliet ran as fast as she could to keep up with the tall athletic girl. Samantha crouched under the window of the security hut as Juliet joined her.

'The guard is at home,' Samantha told her.

'So, when the guard turns his back, we fly out the open gate,' Juliet said.

'You are a little heavy for flying, Juliet, just run as fast as you can,' Samantha advised.

Juliet nudged her and growled.

'I might be a big girl, but I can run, you don't have to worry about me.'

Samantha moved round to the other side of the security hut, just as a military jeep was coming through the open main gate. When it had gone past them,

Samantha told Juliet to make a run for the main gate. Juliet did not have to be told twice. As Juliet reached the gate, Samantha made sure the guard had his attention on the military jeep; then she ran towards the open gate. Juliet did not wait for Samantha as she ran off to her home. When she got to her gate she stopped and turned and saw Samantha just behind her.

'That was quite an adventure, we'll have to do it again sometime,' Samantha said.

'I was wrong, Samantha, you're not crazy, you are quite mad,' Juliet said without a hint of malice.

Samantha was happy Juliet had not used that awful name for her.

'Goodnight Juliet.' Samantha turned away and made for her own home.

Samantha went to the kitchen and made two coffees and took them to the lounge; she found Janice asleep on the sofa. She put the coffees on the low table and sat beside Janice and slowly woke her up; her eyes flashed open and smiled to see Samantha; safe and sound.

'They did not catch you?'

'No, we were too clever for them,' Samantha said.

Samantha handed her a coffee and told her how they had got on inside the compound. Janice was interested and amazed at what they had done.

'The General is going to be mad – when he learns of all these times – you keep doing all these things against his authority.'

'He hasn't told me I can't have fun every now and again.'

Janice giggled and drank her coffee.

CHAPTER VII:

JENNIFER RUSSELL

Hazel Johnson was sitting on her garden wall, her boyfriend Paul James sat beside her; they watched an army jeep park outside the empty house next door. Two girls got out of the back, the first was nearly as tall as Samantha with long silvery blonde hair, Hazel was sure it was the girl she had seen in the Research Complex when she had awakened from her accident. The other girl was several years younger; she walked close to her tall companion, who made her way to the empty house. The young girl clung to her.

'I can walk on my own, I'm not helpless.'

'I lost you, Jenny, I'm going to take care of you, I don't want to lose you again,' the little girl said.

Hazel and Paul watched them enter the house. Once the door was shut, Hazel and Paul got off the wall and made their way to the school building.

When Juliet left her home, she found Samantha waiting at her gate – it was a surprise as the tall girl had tried to avoid her at all times. It had been two days since their nightly sojourn in the Research Complex and they had neither spoken about it nor come within speaking distance of each other. Juliet had a sudden fear Samantha had thought up another weird idea.

'Morning Juliet, I hope you don't mind if I accompany you to school.'

'All right, but I think I'm going to regret it,' Juliet said.

Samantha grinned at her worried expression.

'You are too suspicious for your own good,' Samantha assured her.

They walked to the school building in silence. When they entered the classroom, they found the girl they had seen in the Genetics Laboratory sitting at a desk in front of Steven Calvert. As Samantha approached the desk to get to her own, the brown-haired girl glared up at her.

'I can't say it's nice to see your ugly mug again, Sammy.'

Samantha walked away and sat at her desk next to Steven; Juliet moved to Lavonia and returned the glare.

'You obviously haven't looked in the mirror, lately,' Juliet said.

Samantha giggled; she was glad Juliet was on form. Lavonia gave Juliet a stare of pure hatred. Juliet showed Lavonia she was not afraid of her and gave Lavonia a stare of dislike with the same intensity.

An hour later the tall silvery blonde girl Hazel had seen in Lab 3, walked into the room. Juliet turned and gazed at Samantha; her face was more pale than usual. The girl crossed to Karen Thompson's desk and introduced herself. Karen told her to sit next to Lavonia. Samantha just stared at her in silent shock; here she was again, and Samantha was not dreaming this time.

Jennifer Russell was glad to be back in school after her mystery illness that almost brought her life to an end. Now she was fully recovered, and her strength was back to normal. Her brain was ready to devour everything the instructor could teach her, so she could get on with everything they had planned out for her. They were not going to be disappointed in her work. Jennifer Russell was going to excel and thrust all the other students aside.

Jennifer gazed at the girl sitting next to her, who was staring at her in fascination. Jennifer gave Lavonia a thin smile; Jennifer was aware she could use a girl like Lavonia. Jennifer would use her to weed out the weak links in this class. She looked round the room and noticed the ginger haired girl staring at her, she would be her greatest threat, Jennifer was sure. Get them before they get you, that was Jennifer's motto. That was what she had to do, and Lavonia was going to help her.

The next day Juliet Prentice woke late and rushed to the school building without her breakfast. She entered the classroom and went to her desk. On the way she had to pass Lavonia, who stuck out her foot and the unwary Juliet tripped over it.

'Did you enjoy your trip?' Lavonia asked Juliet, as she picked herself up.

Jennifer Russell grabbed her by the arm, the ice blue eyes staring hard at Juliet.

'You really must look where you are going, they will think you are heading for a reversal and you know what will happen to you then.'

Juliet clenched her fists and tried to cool her boiling temper. Karen Thompson came into the room and told Juliet to sit down. Juliet went to her desk.

Late one evening Janice called on her friend. Juliet, like Samantha, had been rushing out of the school and avoiding contact with anybody. She found Juliet lying on her bed reading a book. Janice sat on the bed and Juliet put down her book and gave Janice a weak smile.

'You are spending a lot of time alone, have we upset you somehow?'

Juliet swung her legs over the side of the bed and sat next to Janice.

'Lavonia and her freaky friend are keeping up their hate Juliet campaign. I don't want you to get the same treatment, because of me.'

Janice put her arms round her friend and hugged her.

'We have been friends since we were five, a fine friend I would be, if I deserted you in your hour of need,' Janice said.

Juliet explained how her references books and pens were disappearing from her desk. Silly tricks were being played on her by the two malicious older girls. Juliet assured Janice they were out to get her.

'They are not going to succeed, Steven and I won't let them bring you down,' Janice promised.

Juliet clung to her friend and Janice kissed her on the cheek.

'Never turn your back on the people that care for you. We are all here for you,' Janice said.

Outside Steven's house he kissed Janice several times; then they parted, and Janice went to her house.

The next morning when Juliet entered the classroom, she was ordered to report to Dr Bishop's office – he was the school psychoanalyst. Juliet made her way to the next floor expecting the worst. She entered the office and sat on the other side of Anthony Bishop's desk. He gazed at the pretty freckled round face and the worried expression. Juliet fidgeted with the hem of her black skirt.

'Do you have any problems?' he asked.

Juliet told him what had been happening to her; she knew it was Jennifer and Lavonia going through her desk, but she could not prove it.

'Jennifer keeps telling me, I'm going through a reversal,' Juliet said.

Dr Bishop gave her a warm smile and Juliet sat more at ease.

'I must have a word with that young lady. I've had reports she's been trying to do the same to Samantha,' he said.

'Samantha told us she had bad dreams most nights and Jennifer was in most of them. It must be quite a shock to have your worst nightmare walk into your reality,' Juliet said.

Juliet was given several vigorous intelligence tests; Juliet was doing what she liked the most and her two enemies were a world away. When it was over, she sat and waited for the result of her endeavours. Bishop told Juliet, she done the tests extremely well and she should be more confident in her abilities and ignore the likes of Lavonia and Jennifer Russell, who put unwanted pressures on her mind.

At break time Samantha was passing the classroom and she looked through the window and saw Lavonia going through Juliet's desk. She made her way to Karen Thompson's office and told her about Lavonia's activities. Karen went straight to the classroom and found Lavonia still rummaging through Juliet's desk. She approached the girl silently and grabbed her left ear painfully; Lavonia jumped with fright and squealed with pain. Karen stared coldly at the sixteen-year-old girl.

'The next time I find your hands in someone else's desk, I'll have you scrubbing the walls and floors throughout the building; I'll curb your spiteful ways,' Karen told her icily.

Karen guided the girl out of the room by her ear, and in the corridor Lavonia was sent on her way with a hard kick against her backside. Lavonia took her hurt pride and went in search of Jennifer Russell, who laughed when she heard what had happened to Lavonia, which made her angry.

When Jennifer and Lavonia returned to the classroom, they found themselves under the cold stare of Karen's dark eyes.

She had never liked Jennifer from the first – Karen thought the tall girl was mean and calculating and her character was predominating, she was intelligent but arrogant to the extreme.

Jennifer had tried it on once with Karen, who made it known to Jennifer in no uncertain terms she was playing with fire. Karen taught Jennifer who was boss, and the tall silver blonde girl received a slapped face for her troubles. Karen got the full blaze of hatred from the ice blue eyes. Karen silently challenged the tall girl to hit her back, it was a fight for dominance and Karen won as Jennifer turned away and went back to her seat.

Juliet came back to the classroom with a blank expression on her face. She returned to her desk. Hazel sitting next to her gave her a soft slap on the back. At the end of the day Janice and Samantha caught hold of Juliet at the school gate. Janice inquired how she had got on with Dr Bishop.

'All right,' Juliet said.

Janice gripped Juliet by the shoulders at the sound of her unconcerned voice and shook her in frustration.

'Oh Juliet, even if you don't care how you got on, I do.'

Juliet smiled broadly.

'I took a lot of hard tests and passed them all; the terrible twins have not got rid of me yet.'

Juliet turned to Samantha.

'The instructor told me, you told her about Lavonia going through my desk – I owe you one,' she said.

'Oh Juliet, you really are a silly girl, you just don't know who your friends are.' Samantha turned to Janice.

'Does she?'

Janice and Samantha smiled broadly at each other and then Samantha walked away. Janice hugged Juliet and they went on to their homes.

CHAPTER VIII:

THE OBSERVATORY

MAY 2128

Samantha woke up and slid out of bed and went to the bathroom and had a shower, she dried herself and returned to the bedroom. She stood naked in front of the full length mirror on the door of her wardrobe and wished herself a happy birthday – she was now sixteen, and she gazed at her slim body, no change there.

Samantha got dressed and she went down the stairs and had breakfast and then she left the house. She walked up the track leading from her house to the group of houses further up. When she got there, Samantha turned left and made for the main gate of the Research Complex. At the gate she was met by Professor Atwood, a tall stout man in his late forties. He was warm and pleasant, she liked him at once. He gave her a pass with her name and photograph on it. They passed through the gateway and Samantha showed her pass to the security guard, who stared at her in suspicion. Samantha wondered if he had been on the gate on the night she and Juliet paid a visit to the Research Complex.

Professor Atwood guided Samantha to the radio telescope; they stood under the great dish.

'What do you think of it?'

Samantha gazed up at the radio telescope dish.

'Very impressive,' she observed.

Professor Atwood laughed and took her arm and guided her into the observatory building; they entered the control room. A tall young man emerged from a group of technicians and approached them; he stared at the tall ginger haired girl – he did not trust girls taller than himself. The professor introduced him to Samantha. She had a feeling he did not like her.

'Another young genius, just like her friend Jennifer,' the man said.

Michael Palmer found himself under the glare of her bright green eyes.

'Jennifer is no friend of mine,' Samantha assured him.

'We've got something in common then,' Michael said dryly.

Samantha moved away from the two men and stood by the observation window, she gazed out at the radio telescope; the dish was moving slightly aligning to a certain point in space. The speaker on the wall above her head gave out a hissing sound that buzzed round her ears. A certain note in it kept time with a throb inside her head. A hand settled on her right shoulder making her jump; a tall well-built girl stood beside her, she wore steel rimmed glasses and she gave Samantha a friendly smile and introduced herself.

'I'm Michelle – you will be working with me.'

Michelle Gowning was twenty four and she was a couple of inches above six foot. She gazed up at the new member of the team, fascinated by Samantha – she was the tallest person Michelle had ever met, an impressive sight with her bright green eyes and long glossy ginger hair. Michelle put her arm round Samantha's waist and guided her to a nearby desk, Michelle sat down in front of a desk top monitor, and she motioned Samantha to sit in a vacant seat beside her. All day Samantha worked with her new instructor. The radio telescope had not picked up anything unusual in space. Samantha asked Michelle if she knew what they were looking for. The older girl was evasive and told Samantha they would know when they found it. It was obvious to Samantha that once again she was expected to work and not ask questions.

At the end of the day Michelle invited Samantha to her accommodation hut for dinner. Samantha eagerly accepted as she liked the older girl. Professor Atwood congratulated her on the hard work she had put in and hoped she would become a regular member of the team. She accepted his praise gracefully and thanked him for his support in treating her as an intelligent adult.

'That's quite all right; I've heard all sorts of tales about you. But I make up my own mind about a person. You can be quite at ease with me, I don't believe half the things they say about you, Samantha,' Professor Atwood said with a grin.

'I might be a rebel, but I have my good points,' Samantha said.

'I'll vouch for that,' Michelle said.

Samantha followed Michelle out of the building. She was happy she had gained another friend; they made their way down the compound until they got to the centre, where Samantha stopped and gazed at a large concrete blockhouse. Samantha looked through one of the small windows; she could only see dark shadows.

'I wonder what they keep in there.'

Michelle put a finger to her lips.

'Top secret, if I tell you, I'll have to shoot you,' she said, humorously.

Michelle moved towards the accommodation huts at the rear of the compound, and Samantha followed her. Michelle had the end hut close to the helipad. Samantha studied the large squat helicopter that occupied the space.

'Doesn't that wake you when it takes off?'

'No, they don't take off at night,' Michelle informed her.

Samantha wondered if the General would let her learn to fly it.

So you can fly away and escape, no chance.

Michelle took the electronic key out of the pocket of her white lab coat and slid it in the lock on the door of her living quarters; she walked in and Samantha followed and closed the door behind her. Michelle removed her white coat and hung it up; she wore a short green dress underneath. The low-cut bodice of the dress showed a generous amount of cleavage. The hem was way up her buxom thighs. Samantha was impressed, she could never wear a dress like that, and she did not have the figure for it.

'How tall are you, if you don't mind me asking?' Michelle inquired.

Samantha followed the older girl into the kitchen area.

'Six foot ten, I don't know why I've grown so tall, perhaps it's because I always eat my greens,' Samantha replied, giggling.

Samantha sat on a chair and gazed at Michelle.

'You must have given them a headache heightening the doorways.'

Samantha helped her new friend to prepare the evening meal. Michelle was pleased to see Samantha was as enthusiastic about cooking as she was. After an enjoyable meal; they settled down on a comfortable couch in another room. Michelle had a bottle of wine and two glasses. She filled them and gave one to Samantha.

'Thank you, this is the first time I've had alcohol, I hope it does not make me drunk.'

The hem of her brown skirt had ridden up her slim thighs; Michelle laid a warm hand on her right thigh and squeezed it gently.

'It's your sixteenth birthday; you are entitled to get drunk. I am completely honourable, I shall not take advantage of you,' Michelle assured her.

Samantha sipped the red wine and gazed at Michelle and decided she would not mind if the older girl took advantage of her. Samantha warmed to her new working partner, she hoped they would be good friends. Michelle told her how happy she was when she got the job at the observatory, she had worked hard, and Michelle had been rewarded for her endeavours. Samantha wished they would reward her for the hard work she did, but they just gave her work, work and more work. Michelle filled her glass when it was empty, the hand stayed on her right thigh and Samantha felt no danger, so she did not knock it off. It started to run up and down her thigh caressing her skin. As they talked, they lost all knowledge of the time and it was dark before they knew it.

Samantha put her glass down and stood up, she felt dizzy and the room seemed to be going around, she had drunk too much wine. Michelle stood up and helped to steady her and Samantha leaned against the older girl.

'You are in no state to walk home; you'd better stay the night. The bedroom is through there,' Michelle said pointing to a nearby doorway.

Samantha stumbled to the bedroom and Michelle put the empty bottle and glasses away. Samantha removed her blouse and skirt and placed them on a chair by the bed. She kept her bra and panties on and removed her socks and shoes. She slid between the sheets and closed her eyes. When Michelle entered the bedroom, her guest was fast asleep.

CHAPTER IX:

THE DREAM

O ut in the blackness of space the searching scout ship had left the immense shape of the mother ship as it moved against the backdrop of the innumerable points of light that made up the galaxy. The scout ship entered the next planetary system they came to; they had been searching for a millennium for a stolen shuttlecraft, and they entered system after system searching for their prey without success.

The stolen shuttlecraft had a tracer on it and if it was near, the scanners on the searching scout ship would pick it up. As they moved through the system a blip came up on the scanners and the scout ship unloaded its cargo and the recovery of the stolen craft and the criminals that commanded it had started.

Samantha woke with a start and found herself on the floor, she got up and went to the kitchen and made herself some strong coffee as she was still tipsy from the wine she had drunk. A moment later Michelle walked into the room. Samantha told her about her dream.

'You'll have to tell the Professor about it, he'll be very interested in your dream,' Michelle said.

Michelle made herself some coffee and they returned to the bedroom and sat on the bed and sipped their hot drink. Michelle ran her free hand over Samantha's cheek, and she gave Michelle a weak smile.

'Are you all right?' Michelle asked.

Samantha nodded her head and drank the black coffee.

Janice was standing by the marshland; darkness was spreading over the cloudy sky. She started to move forward, and her feet slowly sank into the boggy ground, but she kept going until the marsh water was up to her waist. A loud whine sounded over her head and then something hit the marsh close to her. The marsh started to glow green around her and she felt something enter her mind. Her voice screamed out.

The welcoming sight of her bedroom greeted Janice, as she opened her eyes and sat up in bed. Her body was covered in a cold sweat. Janice tried to get out of bed but to her horror she could not feel her legs. Screams were forced out of her.

Julian Clarke was woken by his daughter's screams. He rushed into her bedroom and turned on the light. As he reached the bed Janice threw her arms round him.

'I can't feel my legs,' Janice wailed.

Julian pulled the sheet back and showed Janice she was still in one piece.

'It was just a bad dream, sweetheart,' Julian said, comforting his frightened daughter.

Janice brought her legs up and fondled her toes with nervous fingers. She could happily feel the lower half of her body again.

CHAPTER X:

SOMETHING OUT THERE

S amantha woke just after dawn and found herself alone in bed; she got up and got dressed, cooking smells drawing her to the kitchen, where Michelle was preparing breakfast for the both of them.

'Good morning, glad to see you up at last, you are just in time for breakfast,' Michelle said.

'You are spoiling me, and we've only just met,' Samantha said.

Samantha sat down and Michelle placed a filled plate in front of her and she dug into the fried breakfast. Michelle sat at the table opposite her.

'Did you have any more interesting dreams?'

Samantha shook her head.

'None I can tell you about,' assured Samantha.

'Spoilsport,' Michelle said in disappointment.

After they had eaten, they left the building and made their way towards the observatory. When they arrived, they caught Steven Calvert leaving the building.

'Was there any success last night?' Michelle asked him.

'Nothing unusual, I hope you have better luck.'

Steven went up to Samantha and planted a vigorous kiss on her mouth.

'That is a birthday kiss for yesterday, as I missed you,' he said.

Samantha and Michelle entered the building and got down to work.

At the end of the day Michelle left the building, but Samantha elected to stay and wait for her replacement, which was Jennifer Russell. Steven Calvert came in and was surprised to see her still hard at work.

'You're late going home.'

'Jennifer hasn't turned up and I suppose I'll have to do her shift. Nothing exciting has happened yet,' Samantha explained.

Steven bent over her and kissed her on the lips.

'We'll have to do something about that.'

Samantha pushed him away.

'I don't know what you mean,' she said in complete innocence.

Steven laughed and kissed her again and then went to the computer room. Samantha got on with her work and tried to shake off the tiredness from her mind and body.

In the morning Professor Atwood and Michelle came into the control room together and found Samantha still at her post.

'Have you been at it all night?' Michelle asked.

Samantha gazed at her with tired eyes.

'Jennifer Russell did not turn up, so I had to do her shift.'

Samantha stood up and stretched her aching body; Michelle sat in the seat Samantha had vacated. Samantha went to the observation window and stared out at the morning sunshine. She was exhausted and her head ached. The speaker on the wall close to her head was emitting a low incessant hiss, a pulse she had noticed before came through and activated a throb inside her head. A sudden piercing whine came out of the speaker, it hurt her ears and it cut through her brain like a knife. Samantha fell to the floor on her hands and knees. The throb in her head felt as if it was about to split her skull. She closed her eyes and tears forced their way through her closed eyelids.

Michelle got out of her seat and rushed up to the speaker and turned it off. Professor Atwood helped Samantha to her feet. A thunderous noise outside did not help Samantha's aching head and did nothing to ease her shattered nerves. Michelle gazed out of the window and watched a huge black shape fly pass the building.

'It looks as if Jo's back,' she said.

Michelle watched the huge helicopter head for the rear of the compound. Then she turned away from the window and helped the Professor guide the ailing Samantha towards his office.

'That's one way to blow your mind,' Samantha said in a trembling voice.

In the office Samantha sank into a chair and Michelle stood close to her, while Professor Atwood went to the drinks machine and got her a black coffee. He handed it to her, and she sipped it slowly. Her head still hurt, and she felt utterly drained.

Colonel Hopkins, head of security of the Research Complex, stood still and waited for the noise of the helicopter to cease; the immense span of the rotors gradually slowed and stopped. When all was quiet, he gave a sigh of relief as his ears welcomed the silence. The cockpit hatch opened, and the pilot left the aircraft and approached the Colonel. Joanna Lumsden saluted respectfully and asked if General Heywood was ready to receive her.

'He's in the operations room, in the main building, ready and waiting for you.'

Joanna followed Colonel Hopkins across the compound. She was at the pinnacle of her young life and at twenty-eight she was heading for her greatest adventure. Joanna was overjoyed to be part of the project and now things were starting to happen, and something was out there, Joanna was where she wanted to be.

They made their way across the compound to the other side to where the administrative building stood, which was where the offices and operations room was housed. Joanna held a briefcase tightly under her right arm. They entered the building and went up to the second floor. They entered the operations room; there were two people with the General, a man and a woman. Joanna had not met either. She handed General Heywood the briefcase and followed the General into his office and shut the door behind her.

'There's something out there all right,' Joanna said.

'How far out?' the General asked.

Before Joanna answered the tall slim woman she had seen in the operations office had moved silently into the room and stood behind Joanna before she realised the woman was there.

'It is between the orbits of Pluto and Neptune, it's huge and seems to be in no hurry to get here,' Joanna said.

The General stared at the tall blonde standing behind Joanna.

'It looks as if your friends have arrived.'

'Now they are here, what are you going to do about it,' the woman said in a soft silky voice.

Joanna moved away from the woman and looked her up and down. Her slim figure was clothed in a long cream coloured dress, the hem lay around her ankles, the face was oval and deep set blue eyes stared back at her; the high forehead was crowned by curly blonde hair.

'The project is well in advance and we are ready for any contingency. They won't be here for a while yet, we have plenty of time to get ready for them,' the General said.

General Heywood dismissed Joanna and she left the office closing the door behind her. As she crossed the operations room, the tall dark man left in the room approached her and slid his arm round her waist and Joanna shuddered. To say she did not like the man was an understatement, Joanna had only been in his presence twice and both times he gave her the creeps. The General would not tell her what part in the project the man was involved in. She found him overbearing and oppressive. He was a big man dressed in a dark suit; she wanted to get away from him. Joanna wriggled out of his grasp and stared at his dull grey eyes; she was sure there was an evil mind behind them. He smiled at her and saw the disgust in her face. Joanna almost ran away from him as she left the room in a hurry, with his evil laugh ringing in her ears.

When Joanna left the building, she ran into the two passengers on the flight over, she knew one of the girls and they had not talked much during the journey as Melanie McAllister made it obvious Joanna was not her favourite person. Melanie was two inches short of six foot and had long brown hair and sparkling brown eyes. The short green dress she wore emphasised her well-built figure.

'Are you going back?' Melanie said in a cold voice.

Joanna gave the girl a warm smile and Melanie did not wave her hard expression at all. Her mother had died when she was thirteen and Melanie had blamed her father for her demise; now she was fifteen their father-daughter relationship had disintegrated to a hatred Melanie fuelled with every chance she got. She had been very close to her mother and loved her very much; now she was gone, Melanie had only her hate for her father to keep her going. When her father received his post at the Research Complex, Melanie stayed with friends of her mother. Now to her horror her father had had her brought here so he could keep an eye on her.

'Are you in a hurry to get rid of me?'

Joanna was fond of Melanie's father and he was helping her to rise in her career, Melanie had turned her hate onto her, Joanna, and the older girl was very disappointed as she liked Melanie very much. Joanna tried to get on with her, but Melanie was having none of it.

'The further you are away from Father the better I like it,' Melanie said.

'I like you, Melanie, there's no way I want to hurt you,' Joanna implored.

'I wouldn't find you so disagreeable, if you kept away from Father,' Melanie said.

Joanna sighed deeply; she was beating her head against a wall in trying to show Melanie she was not a threat to her or her father.

'That's hard, as work brings us together.'

Melanie turned on her heal and went to her companion and they made their way to the entrance of the main building, Joanna shook her head and made her way to the observatory building.

'It doesn't look as if you want to join the military, Mel.'

She turned to Wendy Goodman. 'You are right there, Wendy. I am going to be their worst nightmare.'

'Just as long as I don't upset you – like they obviously have.'

They walked into the building. 'You don't have to worry – I like you, Wendy.'

'I like you too, Mel.'

General Heywood and the tall blonde woman left the building as Melanie was about to enter; she stood to attention and clicked her heels and Melanie gave a military salute.

The General decided to ignore the disrespect in her attitude, as he knew she did not want to be here. He introduced her to his companion who would be taking charge of Melanie and keep her hard at work. Melanie gazed at the tall blonde woman, who stared back at her with an air of authority, challenging Melanie to use the same tone on her, but Melanie did not rise to the challenge as she had no quarrel with the woman.

'I hope I will respond adequately to your instruction, Doctor.'

Dr Hamilton smiled putting Melanie at ease; she liked the strong will the girl showed.

'I'm sure you will.'

When they had left, someone knocked on the door. A few moments later a tall, well-built girl walked in.

'I'm Wendy Goodman. I was told to report to you.'

'Good I'll get someone to show you your new home,' the General said.

General Heywood was gazing towards the other side of the compound and when he saw Samantha exit the observatory building and head towards the rear of the compound, he wondered where she was going. Samantha was on her way to the living quarters as Michelle had given her electronic key to Samantha, as she was in no fit state to take the long walk home. As she passed the building of Lab 3, she met Hilary Calvert coming out.

'You look rough, Sam, what's up?'

Samantha told Hilary what had happened at the observatory; Hilary was concerned the girl had been working all day and all night.

'Michelle has given me the key to her hut so I can rest there; I haven't the strength to walk home.'

Hilary placed a hand on Samantha's sweating forehead; it felt cool on her skin, her head was still pounding.

'They're certainly getting their pound of flesh out of you, I don't want you ending up like the first time I met you,' Hilary said.

'I don't mind the hard work, I'm not going to run away from my responsibilities, and I am going to keep my promise to the General.'

'That doesn't mean you have to overdo it, go straight to bed, I'll look on you later,' Hilary said.

'You are so nice to me, I really appreciate what you do for me,' Samantha said, sincerely.

Hilary kissed the girl on the cheek and watched her make for the living quarters. She waited until the girl had reached Michelle's hut and entered it and she made her way across the compound, when she got to the middle, she met General Heywood and she stopped him.

'Overworking your star pupil again, I see,' Hilary said.

Hilary explained what she meant and told him what Samantha had just gone through, she told him something must be done about that girl Jennifer Russell. The relationship between the two girls was very volatile.

'A little rivalry never hurt anyone,' the General commented.

'That does not mean Samantha has to do Jennifer's work, as well as her own.'

General Heywood assured Hilary he would look into it.

'Samantha is a nice girl, it's about time you got to know her – why don't you talk to her, let her know you care.'

'I do care,' Heywood assured her.

'You've got a strange way of showing it; she has done what you have asked of her and more. I think it's about time you filtered some of the truth out to her, it can't be nice for a person to have no past life,' Hilary said.

Samantha removed her clothes and had a cool shower to relieve her sweaty skin; she then went to the medicine cabinet to take something for her headache. She went to the bedroom and got in bed and closed her eyes and sleep soon overtook her.

Samantha was brought out of the depths of sleep by a sound of incessant banging; she sat up in bed and tried to decide if the banging was inside her head or outside the building. The dream was still in her mind, an opaque glass prison and something moving inside it is banging against the glass walls. The shrill cry of:

Let me out Let me out.

Samantha got out of bed and got dressed, she left the bedroom and opened the door, and General Heywood stood outside.

'Can't a girl get her beauty sleep in peace?'

'You look terrible,' he said.

Samantha smiled and moved aside so he could enter the living quarters. Samantha settled on the couch and General Heywood sat in a chair opposite her, after handing her a briefcase.

'What's this?' Samantha asked.

Samantha opened the briefcase and pulled out a thick file. She opened it up and found a large photograph on top; she picked it up and gazed at it. Her first thought was it was a still from some deep space movie, but the General's serious expression and the secret file told her otherwise. It was very impressive as star ships went; it had been photographed by a probe that orbited Neptune.

'I don't suppose it's one of ours.'

Samantha suddenly remembered the pulse that was coming out of the hiss from the speaker in the observatory. It had tuned into a part of her brain that recognised it for what it was. Samantha had found out she was different to everyone else, but how different was ever nagging her mind.

'Whoever they are, they are sending out a signal to us,' Samantha said.

General Heywood sat up and stared hard at the weary face before him and wondered what was going on inside her head.

'When it first came through, I thought it was one of my usual headaches, as it was pulsating at the same pitch as the throbbing in my head, until they boosted the signal and nearly blew my brains out. When I've rested from the experience, I'll get back to the observatory and try to work out what sort of message they are sending us.'

Samantha placed the briefcase on the couch beside her. General Heywood watched her stand up and approach his chair and then stand over him and it made him realise how tall she was.

'I don't suppose you'd like to tell me, who this Jennifer Russell really is?'

'Just a girl who was struck down by a mystery illness, she was brought here so we could find out what was killing her.'

'Yes, that's the official story, I came here one night last year and got that much from the Lab 3 computers,' Samantha confessed.

'Yes, we know, I'd like to know how you conned Juliet into joining you on the venture.'

Samantha grinned and wondered if they had purposely left the gates open so they could leave the compound.

'I wanted to prove to her I was not crazy.'

'And did you?'

'Juliet is just suspicious of people taller than herself; she no longer matters. I have to prove to myself I'm not crazy.'

Samantha turned and went back to the couch and settled on it, folding her long legs on it. Samantha told him that when Jennifer Russell entered the classroom it was not the first time she had seen the girl. She had been a ghostly figure in her dreams. She would be laid out on a bed in an oxygen tent. General Heywood kept his face expressionless. Samantha was not dreaming, she was remembering something that actually happened to her. Except the dream she had of a being locked in a glass cage, he could not think where Samantha dreamed that one up from.

'I find nothing crazy about you Samantha, trust me,' he said.

General Heywood watched the brightness of her green eyes change to a dull green.

'How can I trust you, when you and the people around you don't trust me,' Samantha said.

General Heywood stood up and walked to the couch.

'I trust you, Samantha, you've given me no reason not to,' he said.

'I promised to do the work you give me; I keep my promises. The people you had me live with first, were treating me as if I was something to be feared, that was why they were not very nice to me.'

General Heywood placed a hand on her shoulder.

'I'm truly sorry about that, I know you want to know more about your past life. I hope you can be patient for a little while longer, Samantha, and then I will tell you all that you need to know.'

'Well I'm not going anywhere, I've really got no choice but to do as you say, I just want to be trusted a bit more,' Samantha said.

'You have a choice, Samantha, you have just made it,' he said.

General Heywood moved away and went to the door; Samantha got up to see him out.

'I hope it was the right choice,' she said.

Samantha opened the door for him, and he stepped out of the building then turned and faced her.

'Of course it was, I trust you to take the right choice every time and don't tell anyone, but I do care about you, I'm not about to throw you off the deep end without your safety in mind,' he assured her.

Samantha watched him walk towards the large helicopter parked at the helipad, with the briefcase under his arm. Joanna was sat in the pilot seat gazing down at her instruments, and when the General entered the helicopter, she started the motors. Samantha watched the large helicopter rise up into the sky and fly off to the west. Samantha shut the door and went back to bed.

Wendy was having coffee in the kitchen when Melanie entered the house. She sat at the table and Wendy made her a mug of coffee.

'I'm glad it's you, Mel, I'm sharing the house with. Pick the bedroom you want. I have no preference.'

'Thanks – I'll have the back bedroom,' Melanie said.

After they had drunk their coffees, they took their cases upstairs and unpacked.

'Not a bad pad,' Wendy said.

Melanie agreed with her. 'It certainly is.'

They went to the lounge and sat on the sofa.

'I haven't had a stable home for some time – as I move around a lot,' Wendy said.

'Can't your parents find a place to plant their roots?'

'My father disappeared mysteriously, and I have no idea who my mother was,' Wendy explained.

'That's rough. My mother died two years ago, and I have no faith in my father.'

'I'm sorry for your loss, Mel.'

'Thanks – I hope you father turns up safe and well.'

'Amen to that,' Wendy said.

When Melanie had finished her coffee; she stood up. 'I'm going to have a shower.'

CHAPTER XI:

SARAH MULLEN

General Heywood arrived in London and went to the private apartments where he was to have the meeting with the Premier. He was a tall slim man in his early forties, with short iron grey hair. He had been in office for six years and his friendship with the General had been as long. General Heywood opened the briefcase and handed Graham Mullen the file. He sat in a comfortable armchair and gazed round the room and his eyes settled on a girl curled up on a leather couch. She had short sandy coloured hair and her small round face was lightly freckled. Her grey eyes met his stare and a smile played on her full red lips.

Sarah Mullen's eyes flitted from the General to her father, who was engrossed in the file of the proceedings of the project so far and the huge alien starship in the outer boundary of the solar system. Sarah wished she could mind read as her father would probably not show her the file he was reading. When Graham had finished reading the file, he turned to the General and hoped he was ready for the first contact.

'Is there still a problem with the girl Samantha?'

'We've had no trouble over the last year, she is being very cooperative,' the General assured him.

Sarah decided to interrupt so as to let them know she was still in the room.

'Beaten into submission, was she?'

General turned to the girl and shook his head.

'Not at all, Samantha is well aware of what is good for her,' the General said.

Sarah turned to her father.

'Just like me, Daddy,' she said with a grin.

Graham Mullen ignored his daughter and told the General Sarah would be his new charge. Sarah got off the couch and stood up and curtsied; she gave the General her best mischievous smile. Graham told him there were no university or college that would take her. The General guessed it was more than that, but it was not for him to question what the Premier wanted to do with his daughter.

'I associate with the wrong type of people and Daddy is trying to get rid of me. Out of sight, out of mind, that's me.'

She fixed her grey eyes on the General; behind her light-hearted facade was a keen and alert, intelligent mind. She was a girl who knew what she wanted, and the General was sure Sarah was quite capable of getting it.

'How very undisciplined of you,' General Heywood said.

'Isn't it just, I unfortunately step on toes, but if they stick out their feet, it's not my fault.'

Graham Mullen took his daughter by the arm and showed her the door. He told her to get packed and closed the door behind her.

'I hope you don't mind taking Sarah with you, I'm sure you can give her some work that will keep her out of trouble. Sarah is very intelligent in spite of her mischievous character,' the Premier said.

General Heywood understood completely.

'With the political atmosphere as it is at the moment, it's best to have her out of the way,' he observed.

'That's right, her ideas are unconventional to say the least,' Graham Mullen said.

A little while later Sarah joined them, carrying a large suitcase. She had changed into a large grey sweatshirt with the words, Listen, Learn and Understand. She wore a matching pleated grey skirt that came down to her knees.

'I hope we will have a good working relationship, General, you'll find my bark is worse than my bite,' Sarah assured him.

'I can't wait.'

Henry Jones was in the kitchen preparing lunch. The door buzzer went, and Henry went to answer the door. Melanie McAllister stood on the doorstep. She wore a short brown dress and long white socks. The night before Melanie had gone for a walk and met Henry – something clicked, and he had invited her to lunch on the next day.

'It's nice to see you again,' Henry said.

Melanie smiled and followed Henry to the kitchen and sat at the table; he made her a mug of coffee.

'Have they told you anything about what you may be working on?'

Henry shook his head and dished out the meal.

Samantha woke with a start from dreams of tall, dark, menacing aliens out to get her; luckily, she had awoken before they laid hands on her. Samantha stared up at the smiling face of Michelle Gowning – she was just back from her shift at the observatory, and she offered a mug of tea to Samantha, as she sat up.

'That must have been quite a dream you were having, don't tell me, you woke before the ending.'

Samantha took the offered mug and sipped the strong tea.

'Thankfully I did just that and I'm not disappointed,' Samantha assured her.

'You can tell me after dinner, when you're dressed it will be ready,' Michelle said.

Samantha watched Michelle walk out of the bedroom, while she drank the strong tea; it was helping her frayed nerves. She placed the empty mug on the bedside table and got out of bed and showered then got dressed, Samantha entered the kitchen as Michelle was dishing out the dinner. Michelle looked the girl up and down, starting with her long, glossy ginger hair and bright green piercing eyes in a strong, thin face, which was not unattractive, Michelle found the girl striking, she wore a pale yellow blouse and short brown skirt, Michelle gazed at her long shapely legs and gave Samantha a smile of approval. Samantha was used to being stared at as if she was under a microscope; she hoped Michelle liked what she saw. After an enjoyable meal Samantha went into the next room and settled onto the comfortable couch while Michelle made coffee for them both. Samantha thought over her chat with the General and wondered what her next actions should be. She was going to give them the loyal work they wanted from her, but she was not going to let them have it all their own way.

'Penny for them,' Michelle said.

Samantha had not heard the older girl approach, who held out a mug of coffee to her and Samantha took it. Michelle settled down beside her and kissed her on the cheek and the green eyes were on her in an instant studying her face.

'What was that for?'

Michelle sipped her coffee then gave Samantha a warm smile.

'You looked so rough this morning, I'm glad you look a lot better.'

'I feel a lot better; I thought my skull was going to split,' Samantha said.

Michelle told her Jennifer had been given a roasting for not turning up and she was there now working with Steven.

'She's not a happy bunny,' Michelle said.

Samantha gave her a wicked smile and Michelle kissed her.

'What a shame.'

Michelle laughed as she thought Jennifer Russell was a pain also. Samantha was drinking her coffee and Michelle moved closer to her and kissed her on the cheek.

'I like you, Samantha, I like you a lot,' Michelle confessed sincerely.

Samantha was happy to hear that; she liked the older girl and she enjoyed being kissed by her and working with her. Michelle tapped her mug against the one Samantha held, they kissed and smiled at each other.

'Here's to friendship and long may it reign,' Michelle said.

'I'll drink to that,' Samantha concurred.

Samantha drained her coffee mug and placed it on the floor and lay back on the couch. Michelle put her empty mug on the floor and sat up on the couch and gazed at her guest; then kissed her.

'What do you think of the discovery out in space?' Michelle asked.

Samantha had been thinking about it from the first time the General told her of the starship in the outer regions of the solar system.

'They are searching for something,' Samantha said.

Michelle ran her hand over the top of Samantha's left thigh.

'You sound so certain,' Michelle observed.

'They were sending a signal and the radio telescope was picking it up, but I did not recognise it for what it was, though part of my brain was trying to tell me,' Samantha explained.

'Getting no reply, they boosted the signal and that's what nearly blew my brains out.'

'I'm glad you survived it; have you worked out what they were saying?' Michelle asked.

Samantha had been wrapping her brains round it ever since she left the observatory and had come to only one conclusion.

'I don't think it's a message as such, I think they are sending out a signal pulse and they are expecting a similar signal back,' Samantha said.

'Well I hope they don't get a reply and go away,' Michelle said.

Samantha gazed at her and smiled, she had a feeling it was not going to go away, and the occupants were after something and they would find it here on Earth. Samantha was going to keep that thought to her.

'If they detect us, which they will if they come closer, they might want to come here and say hello,' Samantha said.

'Let's hope they're friendly,' Michelle said.

Michelle sat back close to Samantha, who gazed at the hand that lay still on the middle of her left thigh.

Michelle ran a caressing hand over Samantha's cheek. Her world was changing; people were being nice to her and treating her with respect.

'We make a fine team, you and me. Don't let Jennifer and Lavonia get inside your head. You have gained a lot of good friends, think of them when that pair irritate you,' Michelle reminded her.

Michelle kissed her again then stood up. She was tired and ready for bed. Samantha ran her eyes over the well-built curvaceous figure encased in a tight blue dress.

'You are very beautiful, Michelle; I don't know what you see in a tall skinny girl like me.'

Michelle smiled and reached out her hand and Samantha took it and the girl pulled her off the couch.

'You are not skinny, and you have great legs,' Michelle argued.

Samantha kissed her and thanked Michelle for the compliment. She went towards the exit door and told Michelle she was going out for a walk. Michelle went to the bedroom and Samantha walked out into the cool night. A breeze caressed her face and bare legs. She gazed up at the night sky and thought of the alien spaceship that was heading towards them. It was another conundrum for her to solve, in her bid to learn why she was here and what was expected of her.

Samantha, old girl – You think too much.

CHAPTER XII:

COLLISION COURSE

A hand settled on her shoulder and Samantha woke with a start, she found herself on the couch and Michelle standing over her and offering her a mug of strong tea.

'You could have used the bed, I wouldn't have charged you anything,' Michelle said.

Samantha took the mug of tea and sipped it.

'I'm sorry, I went for a walk after you retired to bed, then I came back here and I must have dropped off here,' Samantha said.

'Are you ready for work?'

'Yes, but if you don't mind, I'll wait until Jennifer has left the building, I don't want to put myself off my breakfast,' Samantha said.

Michelle giggled and strode off to the kitchen.

Michelle sat staring at the radar screen as a large blip ran slowly across the screen. The object was just passing the orbit of Mars. Samantha came up behind Michelle and asked her what was happening. Michelle pointed at the radar screen.

'A sizeable space vehicle is heading this way, the Mars base had been tracking it, and now we have it on our screens.'

They both stared at the screen; Samantha laid her hands-on Michelle's shoulders. Suddenly several smaller blips separated themselves from the larger one.

'Just like my dream,' Samantha said.

Janice Clarke, who had been working in the computer room, came in and joined them. She stood beside Samantha and gazed at the screen, then muttered something under her breath. Michelle told her to be quiet as the muttering girl was disturbing her concentration. Janice ignored the older girl and continued to talk to herself. Samantha told Janice to go and leave them in peace. Janice stuck her fist under Samantha's nose and accused her of bringing doom down upon them; she turned away and ran out of the room.

'Why does everybody blame me? Not every bad thing that happens is my fault,' Samantha complained.

Michelle looked up at her and gave Samantha a warm smile.

'I don't blame you.'

Samantha was glad of that; she wanted at least one person on her side.

'I'd better go after Janice, I know where she'll be,' Samantha said.

'I wonder what has got into her.'

'I wonder.'

Samantha left the building and walked out of the main gate of the Research Complex. She found Janice sitting cross legged on the summit of the hill, Samantha settled down beside her.

'Do you want to talk about it?' Samantha asked softly.

Janice stayed silent keeping her thoughts to herself; Samantha placed a hand on her shoulder. Janice turned her head and stared at the older girl.

'Like your friend Juliet, you are still suspicious of me, but something is bothering you and has been before I came on the scene. Believe it or not I do like you, Janice, and I want to help.'

Janice gazed at the thin face and bright green eyes; she could see Samantha was sincere in what she said.

'No matter what Juliet thinks, I'm no monster and I don't want to be put in the same category as Jennifer Russell and Lavonia.'

Janice gave up on her solemn expression and smiled broadly, showing Samantha what a very beautiful girl she was.

'I never thought you were a monster, even from the first time we met you. I don't think you are anything like the terrible twins, neither do the rest of us,' Janice assured the tall ginger haired girl.

Janice kissed her on the lips.

Janice turned her head and stared out ahead of her.

'I'm disturbed at what is coming. I'm sorry, I blamed you, Samantha, and of course I don't think it's your fault. There is a terrible atmosphere hanging over us.'

Janice told Samantha about the dream she had had the other night, it told her something nasty was going to happen to her. When Jennifer Russell and Lavonia joined them at the school, something malignant had come into their lives.

'Have they started on you, Janice? I won't have the terrible twins bothering you – as you are special to all of us.'

Janice shook her head and Samantha asked her to promise to say something if she has trouble with the two older girls.

'We may be genetically improved, and they may find a genius superhuman amongst us, but they can never breed the primeval fear out of us. You shouldn't give in to your fears, as you have five loyal friends standing at your side to give you strength. We haven't got all the answers to why we are here, but we will get there in the end, if we listen, learn and understand,' Samantha said.

'Don't you mean six? You are wrong if you think I don't count you as a friend, we need you and Juliet will see that too.'

Janice stood up and held out her hand to Samantha and she took it and Janice pulled her up on her feet.

'I'm sorry we have isolated you from us recently, our attitude towards you will change from now on.'

'I hope so, an ugly girl like me needs all the friends she can get.'

Janice giggled and kissed her; they started down the hill; she assured Samantha there were at least two girls around uglier than her. She did not have to tell Samantha who they were.

'You know, Samantha, you should not take Juliet's jibes to heart, there's nothing ugly about you – any sensible person can look at you and see a pretty girl. You are very striking – your glossy ginger hair is gorgeous, as are your green eyes,' Janice said.

'Thanks Janice, that's very nice of you to say so, I'm tall and strong, but I have no wish to harm you or your companions,' Samantha said.

Janice stood on tiptoe and kissed Samantha on the lips and winked at her.

'You're all right, Samantha.'

Samantha smiled with pleasure.

'My friends can call me Sam.'

'OK, Sam it is and don't worry about Juliet, I'll deal with her,' Janice promised.

Janice turned away and made for home, Samantha made for the main gate of the Research Complex. Samantha was happy Janice was accepting her, in time Samantha was sure they were going to need each other. Deep in thought she was unaware that Jennifer Russell was bearing down on her from another direction on a collision course as she slowly lost control of the bicycle she was riding. She called out a warning, but Samantha did not hear her as her mind was on other things. Jennifer Russell collided with her and they both hit the ground painfully. The bicycle ended up in the ditch on one side of the track. Samantha sat up and surveyed the damage done to her by the runaway bicycle. Her right knee was grazed and bleeding, an impression of the tyre tread ran up the whiteness of her thigh. Samantha got up and brushed herself down.

'I'm terribly sorry, I lost control of my bicycle, I am having trouble riding it,' Jennifer Russell said.

'So, I've noticed.'

Samantha took out a handkerchief from her skirt pocket and tied it round her damaged knee.

'Is there anything I can do for you?' the silver haired girl asked.

'No thanks, you've done enough already. Why are you in such a hurry?'

Jennifer Russell grinned broadly lighting up her pale thin face.

'I'm organizing a Ceremony and I don't want to be late.'

'What kind of Ceremony?'

Her curiosity aroused.

'It's an idea of mine. Hazel and Paul have paired off so I've thought up a Ceremony so they can make their vows to each other. We are going to hold it on the hill later,' Jennifer Russell said, excitedly.

'Perhaps we should hold one for you and the computer, you'd make a lovely pair,' Samantha said with a smile.

Jennifer Russell glared at her rival in distaste.

'And by the way, where were you the other night? I had to work your shift.'

Samantha did not bother to hide the anger in her voice – she stared at the ice-blue eyes glaring at her; they suddenly changed to a deep blue.

'I had a headache, why should I work so hard, when I have you to do it for me,' she said, icily.

Samantha stood up to her and matched her icy glare.

'Not anymore, I've heard you have to do your own work from now on, you lazy bitch.'

Jennifer Russell turned angrily on her heels and picked up her bicycle and got on it and tried riding it across the track. Samantha giggled as she watched Jennifer fall off the bicycle several times. When the irritating girl was out of sight, Samantha returned to the observatory and carried on with her work in a quiet and subdued manner. Michelle did not press her as she could see the girl had something on her mind. If Samantha wanted to tell her about it, Michelle would let her friend tell her in her own time. She concentrated on her own work. Samantha left the observatory early so as not to run into Jennifer Russell and her obnoxious sidekick. But outside the building she bumped into the General and a young female stranger.

'This is Sarah Mullen, I hope you don't mind, she'll be staying with you.'

Sarah provided Samantha with a beaming smile on cue. Samantha gazed at the older girl in distaste, but Sarah assured Samantha she would be no trouble and she would obey her every wish.

'I'm perfectly house trained,' Sarah said.

Samantha took out her house key and tossed it to Sarah, who caught it easily.

'Let yourself in and make yourself at home, I hope you can cook, I don't know when I'll be back.'

Samantha walked away and headed for the rear of the compound; Sarah turned to the General.

'How much do you want me to tell her? I'm sure she would be very interested in what I could tell her,' Sarah said; the beaming smile had gone.

'I want you to tell her nothing, we have a nice cold and damp glasshouse ready for you, if you say anything you shouldn't,' the General said, coldly.

Sarah smiled at the threat; he would do it she was sure, in spite of her father.

'I don't think Daddy will like that.'

'Your father gave me leave to treat you as I see fit, I'm in charge here and you will do as I command.'

Sarah stood up straight and saluted.

'Yes, sir, it will be as you say, mustn't upset the routine even though you are messing about with her brain,' Sarah said, her voice thick with distaste.

General Heywood stood over Sarah Mullen, she stood firm, he was in command, but she was not going to wilt under pressure.

'There's something about Samantha, you don't know, we will feed her information when the need arises; you are here to observe, not to interfere.'

'Samantha's a human being, isn't she?' Sarah argued.

The General stared at her. 'Is she?'

General Heywood guided her to a jeep, and they got in the back; the army corporal driver steered the jeep out of the compound and drove to the house Samantha occupied. Sarah sat in silence, thinking about the General's last words. The General deposited the girl outside the house and the jeep turned and went back to the Research Complex.

Hilary Calvert slipped out of the entrance of the Lab 3 building. She suddenly heard cries of anger and pain, from a female voice, and it was coming from the side of the building. She walked round the building and came upon Samantha venting her frustration and rage on the building wall. The clash with Jennifer Russell had flared her nerves and emotions. Hilary shouted out her name and Samantha took no notice and continued to scream out at the wall, beating it with her fists. Hilary grabbed Samantha by the left forearm and turned the girl to face her. Her face was red with her exertions, her deep-set eyes were alight with a green fire, and her heart beat at a fast rate inside her chest; her blood raced round her body as she trembled all over.

'Calm down, Sam, calm down, it's Hilary.'

Samantha closed her eyes and relaxed her speeding metabolism; her heart gradually slowed the fast thumping in her chest. She opened her eyes and tears ran down her flushed cheeks. Hilary still had hold of her forearms; she had stripped some skin from her wrists and fists.

'The buildings are firmly built here; you'll find it hard to knock them down with your fists,' Hilary said.

'It was either that or strangle the life out of that girl Jennifer, she really does my head in,' Samantha said.

Samantha told the woman of her run in with Jennifer while Hilary guided her into the Laboratory building; they walked down the long corridor and entered the hospital ward. At the other end of the long bed-filled room, a door slid open to allow them entrance to the next room. Hilary told Samantha to sit on the operating table in the centre of the room. Hilary went through another door and returned a moment later with a tall dark-haired man in a white coat.

'Well Samantha, what have you been up to this time?'

Samantha stared blankly at him, as he injected serum into her upper arm with a hypodermic needle. Samantha stared past him and gazed at the far window that showed some of the room beyond. It seemed familiar.

'You must take care of yourself, Samantha, you are a very important person,' the doctor said.

Samantha stared at his face for the first time.

'I'm glad someone thinks so,' she said.

Hilary dressed the wounds to her wrists and the knee damaged by the collision with Jennifer and her bicycle. When she had finished Samantha slid off the table and walked slowly to the window and stared into the room beyond it. Hilary came and stood beside her.

'I've been in that room and that girl Jennifer was there also. I thought it was a dream, but it wasn't. What were they doing to me in there?'

'Perhaps they brought you here, after your mystery blackouts,' Hilary said.

Hilary turned to her companion and Dr Richard Blake nodded his head.

'I don't think they are a mystery to some people round here,' Samantha said.

Dr Blake found her sharp green eyes on him; he admired Samantha, and she did not miss a thing.

'Everything that is done here is for your own wellbeing, Samantha,' Dr Blake said.

Samantha left the room followed by Hilary; they remained silent until they had left the building.

'The next time you come across Jennifer, come and see me, before you decide to injure yourself.'

'I will, but I feel much better now I've let off a bit of steam,' Samantha said.

Hilary watched the tall girl head towards the living quarters; she knew the girl had been staying with Michelle.

Michelle Gowning was cooking dinner when a knock came on her door, she opened it and her face lit up when she saw Samantha standing outside. She thought her friend had gone back to her own home, but she was glad the girl was here now. Michelle stood aside and Samantha moved past her and the door was shut behind her.

'You've been in the wars,' Michelle said, as she saw the bandages on Samantha's wrists.

Samantha told her about her collision with Jennifer, which made her take it out on the outside wall of Lab 3.

'I wondered why you were so quiet when you returned from tracking down Janice,' Michelle said.

'I was cooling down my blazing temper; I didn't want to take it out on you or the electronic machinery.'

Michelle ran her hand over Samantha's left cheek, then kissed her on the lips.

'You wouldn't have done that, I have no fear of you ever wanting to hurt me,' Michelle assured her.

'I wish others felt the same.'

Michelle kissed her on the lips and Samantha felt more of the tensions in her body slip away.

'They don't know you like I do. I have made it a point to get to know you.'

They went into the kitchen and had a meal together, and then they returned to the next room and settled on the comfortable couch.

'The General has lumbered me with a lodger; I gave her my key and told her to make herself at home.'

'You are welcome to stay here another night, we can carry on getting to know each other better,' Michelle said.

'There isn't much more I can tell you about me,' Samantha said.

'I bet there are some secrets about yourself you haven't told me yet,' Michelle said.

'When I discover them, I'll let you know,' Samantha declared.

Michelle laughed and got up and went to make coffee for them both.

CHAPTER XIII:

MENACE

Jennifer Russell stared transfixed at the radar screen; the seven blips were getting closer to Earth, whatever they were it was not going to be for their benefit she was sure. Jennifer Russell stood up and crossed over to the drinks machine and got herself a strong coffee. She turned away from the machine and Lavonia materialized beside her, much to her distaste. Jennifer had enjoyed using the spiteful girl to annoy the other students at the school, but now the girl was just an irritation.

'What do you think those blips represent?' Lavonia asked, as if she thought Jennifer would know.

'When they land in our backyard, you can go and look, and then you can tell me,' Jennifer said, scornfully.

Lavonia grabbed Jennifer by the arm to stop her from walking away from her.

'Do you think they are heading for this place?'

'A high-security Research Establishment? If they don't land here, I shall be very surprised.'

Jennifer Russell tore herself from Lavonia and sat at the radar screen and sipped her coffee.

'I have plotted their trajectory and calculated their likely landfall. They will hit the ground somewhere near the marshland,' Jennifer said.

Lavonia thought for a moment then her face lit up.

'So, they could in fact fall in Samantha's backyard,' she observed with glee.

Jennifer stared at the girl for a moment; she was not as dumb as she looked. She put her arm round Lavonia's waist.

'Now there's a highly entertaining probability. Right in Samantha's lap, the best place for them,' Jennifer said, happily.

The technicians in the room stared in amazement at the two girls as they burst out laughing.

Samantha drank her coffee and retired to bed; Michelle stayed up a while longer. When she finally went to bed, she found Samantha fast asleep. Michelle undressed and got in beside Samantha gently so as not to wake the sleeping girl.

Samantha woke first and got dressed and left the living quarters. She made her way out of the complex and ran leisurely towards her house. She got in by using her spare key; she found her lodger in the kitchen, eating breakfast. Samantha made herself some coffee and sat on the table and stared at Sarah Mullen, who felt herself under scrutiny from the bright green eyes – she felt like a specimen under examination. Sarah suddenly felt vulnerable under the penetrating stare. After a while Samantha looked down at her drink and Sarah was released, she felt as if a great weight was lifted off her.

'What has the General told you about me?' Samantha suddenly asked.

'Nothing, if I want to get to know you, I will have to do it myself.'

Samantha finished her coffee and went up to her bedroom to change her clothes. She undressed and showered and put on a red dress and went back downstairs; she went into the lounge and found Sarah sitting on the couch. Samantha sat in an armchair opposite her lodger. Sarah could see the tall girl did not trust her as she was a stranger; Samantha was entitled to be unsure of a newcomer to her home.

'What's it like, on the outside?' Samantha asked.

Sarah stared at her.

'The special school and the Research Complex are my world, surrounded by thick woodland, hills and desolate moorland. You are an outsider,' Samantha explained.

'You yearn to escape,' Sarah said.

Sarah felt the power of Samantha's stare again, her green eyes flashed; Sarah had a strange feeling of an invisible force knocking her back.

'I've tried to escape without success. I suppose the General sent you here to keep an eye on me.'

'I'm no spy, my father sent me here because I'm an embarrassment to him,' Sarah explained.

'He has a lot of power over you,' Samantha observed.

Sarah giggled.

'He has a power over everybody,' Sarah declared.

Then Sarah explained who her father was, and Samantha reacted by laughing.

'So, you've been sent to spy on the General.'

Sarah shook her head.

'Not at all, the General and my father are good friends, he knows everything about the General, there's no need for espionage.'

Samantha stood up and crossed the room and sat beside Sarah on the couch.

'How much do you know of what goes on here?'

Sarah turned her face away from Samantha. She had been aware that question would come up sooner or later. Samantha was very astute, and she would have to watch herself, she was sure the tall intelligent girl could spot a lie when she heard one. Sarah could not say much, or she would be condemning herself to the cold damp glass house the General had waiting for her, if she gave Samantha information she was not supposed to have.

'I don't know much; my father does not confide in me on matters of state.'

'Do you hate your father?' Sarah turned and faced Samantha.

'On the contrary, I love my father, it's his job I want,' Sarah declared.

Samantha smiled.

'And you'll get it.'

'Of course, there's a revolution coming, it won't last long, and it won't be violent, but it will end when I get the top job,' Sarah prophesied.

'There's something heading for Earth, that may put pay to your schemes and ascertains,' Samantha warned.

Samantha stood up and walked out of the room, Sarah stared at her retreating back. She did not like the sound of what Samantha had just told her. Sarah felt her father had dropped her right in it.

Karen Thompson got an unpleasant surprise as she sat at her desk and waited for her students to enter the room, Sarah Mullen walked in and approached her desk – they already knew each other as Sarah had been her student previously.

'Sarah, I can't say it's a pleasure to see you again, your father obviously has decided to put you out of society. I'm glad the Premier has realised at last what a danger you represent.'

'We have the right to follow our own convictions, perhaps I am a rebel, but I mean no harm to anyone. I can reach my goals without coercion and violence,' Sarah explained

Karen stared at the girl with an expression of menace.

'We'll see. While you are here, Sarah, you will follow my orders and convictions, if not I'll do violence to your backside. I hope I make myself clear.'

Sarah nodded her head.

'Clear as crystal, Miss.'

Sarah turned away and strolled over to the group of desks. She found a vacant one next to Juliet, who gave her a welcoming smile.

In the afternoon Jennifer and Lavonia entered the classroom. They noted Samantha was not in yet. Lavonia sat at her own desk and Jennifer sat on Samantha's desk. She had seen Karen was not in the room, which gave Jennifer another chance to have a stab at her rival. Steven and John, who sat on either side of it, knew there was going to be trouble. Jennifer ignored Steven when he told her to go back to her own desk. All eyes turned to the door when it opened, and Samantha walked into the room. The silence that greeted her rang alarm bells in her head; there was trouble in the air. When she saw Jennifer sitting on her desk, she gave a deep sigh.

'The prodigal returns,' Lavonia said.

Samantha reached her desk and stood still as she waited for Jennifer to get off her desk so she could sit at it.

All eyes were on the two oldest girls as they sized up to each other. They felt the tension in the room rise as both girls had an aura about them.

'Hullo Sammy, long time, no sees,' Jennifer said, insolently.

Juliet sitting behind them realised Jennifer was using the name she used to irritate Samantha.

'Get off my desk and don't call me by that stupid name,' Samantha said, icily.

Lavonia was standing by her own desk which was in front of the two antagonists.

'I think Sammy is a nice name,' Lavonia said.

Samantha ignored the troublemaker and kept her eye on Jennifer Russell.

'Can you move, please, Jennifer, I want to sit down.'

'Why, are you thinking of staying?'

Jennifer Russell glared at her rival and silently challenged Samantha to move her off the desk physically. Samantha was tired and bored with the antics of Jennifer, always spoiling for a fight; she would not stop goading Samantha until there was one. Samantha felt a shiver run through her body; her head started to throb.

'Come on, Sammy, why you don't remove me from your desk, let's see what you're made of,' Jennifer taunted.

The tension in the room was electric; every other person in the room was waiting for the fight to begin, as the two girls squared up to each other like two strong titans. Lavonia waited eagerly for the explosive outcome of this confrontation, as Jennifer had told her she was going to give Samantha hell. Samantha felt the throb in her head beat faster as the hot anger brewed up inside her. Her skin felt prickly and sweaty; her vision became blurred. The ice-blue eyes of her rival glared at her in defiance. She could see the anger inside Samantha, by her flushed cheeks. Jennifer slid off the desk and stood in front of Samantha.

'It's time, Sammy darling, to show you who's boss round here. And it's definitely not you.'

Samantha clenched her fists; she was trying to fight the impulse to hit out at Jennifer, her nails dug into her palms. Something snapped inside her, and Samantha hit out with her right fist and it slammed into Jennifer's nose and blood sprayed over her pale face, her head was knocked back and Jennifer fell backwards into the seat behind her. Blood flowed from both nostrils and tears filled her eyes. Samantha stood over her, shaking uncontrollably.

Lavonia moved towards Samantha ready to get revenge for what she had done to Jennifer. Janice got in first and pushed Lavonia back towards her own desk. Janice then turned on Jennifer Russell, her face even paler than before and blood ran over her lips and chin.

'You did that on purpose, I hope you're satisfied,' Janice said, angrily.

Steven Calvert got out of his seat and went to Samantha, who stood still and looked as if she had no idea what was happening. He took hold of her and guided her to Jennifer's desk and pushed her into the vacant seat. Lavonia had the next desk and she was not happy.

'I don't want her sitting near me,' she complained.

'Tough.'

Juliet had joined her friend in front of Jennifer and told her what a creep she was. Lavonia was quick as usual to defend her friend and she hated Juliet nearly as much as Samantha. Lavonia stood over the short dark-haired girl.

'You'll stick your nose in once too often, Shorty.'

Juliet glared at her and showed Lavonia she had no fear of her.

'You can try and do something about it, if you like,' Juliet offered.

Lavonia squared up to the short thirteen-year-old girl; she could look after herself and never worried about the size or age of her opponent. She could hit hard and fast, she was ready for a scrap if Lavonia wanted one. Seeing Juliet was ready for action, Lavonia turned away and went back to her seat.

'You're all mouth, Lavonia,' Juliet shouted back at her.

Juliet grabbed Jennifer by the arm and pulled her roughly out of the chair.

'Come on, wretch, let's get your ugly mug cleaned up,' Juliet said with a smile.

Juliet pulled the tall girl roughly across the room. Jennifer made no attempt to pull away from Juliet, as she seemed in a state of shock, and her plan had backfired very painfully.

'Never a dull moment – is it always like this?' Sarah inquired.

Janice turned and faced the new girl.

'Oh yes, this is just an ordinary day,' she remarked dryly.

Sarah Mullen burst out laughing; it helped to dampen the tension in the room, and everyone joined in with her, with the exception of Lavonia.

CHAPTER XIV:

AFTERMATH

Karen Thompson entered the room and Steven told her what had happened. She saw Samantha sitting in the front, staring into space. She told Steven to take her to Dr Bishop's office. Samantha let the boy guide her out of the room. She mutely followed him up to the next floor.

Juliet was in the girl's washroom cleaning the blood from Jennifer's face. The tall girl made no complaint at the rough treatment, as Juliet was not very kind to her, and she was having fun. She had wanted to hit the tall girl herself; Samantha had really given her a good one – Jennifer Russell would have a misshapen nose for the rest of her miserable life, Juliet thought with glee.

'I can't say it's an improvement, but it will be a reminder of a bad mistake you made, and you won't forget it in a hurry,' Juliet said.

'I – I don't understand, it wasn't me,' Jennifer moaned.

Juliet shook her head, the girl was still in shock after almost having her head knocked off, but Juliet still thought the girl was nuts.

Samantha was slumped in a chair beside Dr Bishop's desk; he gave her a small glass of brandy to steady her shattered nerves. Her head still throbbed continuously; even more Samantha wanted to know what was happening inside her head and why Jennifer had the power to make her feel so nauseous. Samantha was now aware of where she was and knew she was in trouble; again.

Dr Anthony Bishop looked down at Samantha; she made a sorry picture. What he knew of the girl, she had her troubles, but he knew it was unlike her to hit anyone. She seemed to be in command of her negative emotions. Bishop was aware of the bitter rivalry between the two older girls; he was disappointed it had ended in a fight. That was something they did not want, and Bishop was sure there was something wrong here. Steven had given him a thorough account of what had happened, and he had put the blame entirely at Jennifer's door.

'Samantha!' he called sharply.

Samantha looked up from the empty glass and stared up at him. The light in her watery green eyes was subdued.

'Why did you hit Jennifer, it was very unlike you?'

'She made me do it, I was not myself,' Samantha replied.

Samantha put the empty brandy glass on the desk and placed her hands together in her lap.

'I had a headache and Jennifer would not let me sit at my desk. She was spoiling for a fight, everything was a blur and the next thing I know, Jennifer was sat in a chair with blood all over her face.'

'How often do you get these headaches?' he asked in deep concern.

Samantha gazed at the psychoanalyst; tears filled her green eyes.

'Too often. I want someone to tell me what's wrong with me.' Samantha put a finger to her forehead. 'Something is not right inside my head.'

Samantha let her head fall. Tears dropped onto her hands that lay on the top of her thighs. She was crying freely as her pent-up emotions were released. Her head started to throb again, she shivered as she felt sick inside. Samantha wriggled uncomfortably in her seat; she wanted to leave the room and be alone. Bishop stared at Samantha as the agitation of her body became clear to him. The door opened and Jennifer Russell entered the room. The closer she got to Samantha, the more agitated she got, the blood drained from her face, her fists clenched, Samantha fought hard to subdue the anger that was burning inside her. Samantha got shakily to her feet and stumbled away from the desk and approached the car window. Jennifer Russell sat in the chair Samantha had vacated.

'How are you feeling now?' Bishop asked her.

Jennifer fingered her misshapen nose.

'Apart from a sore nose, I feel fine,' she replied calmly.

'Have you any idea why Samantha hit you?'

Jennifer glanced across towards the window, Samantha had her back to them, and Jennifer gave a wry smile.

'Perhaps she does not like me.'

'You must have given Samantha a reason to hit you, it is very unlike her,' Bishop told her.

Jennifer was calm and assured; she kept her ice-blue eyes fixed on his face.

'They have put it in her mind, she is better than everybody else; I am a danger to that idea.'

'The story I get is you are to blame for Samantha hitting you, Jennifer, you set up the whole thing; unfortunately for you, your plan went slightly wrong. Your negative ability to antagonise people is not a way to show people you are better than them.'

He stopped talking and noticed her eyes had gone a shade darker.

'You have never tried to get on with Samantha or any of the others since you arrived here,' he continued.

'We are not compatible, I'm too much of a threat to Samantha,' Jennifer said, icily.

Samantha, standing by the window, placed her palms against the window; her body was sweating, and her head continued to hurt more. Her heart beat faster, the blood raced through her veins, her metabolism was running riot; in her mind she was screaming for release from whatever was tearing her mind and body apart.

'You've got that right, Jennifer, you are a threat, but not just to Samantha, you've already tried to undermine Juliet, but she was more intelligent than you give her credit for.'

Jennifer Russell shot to her feet, the calm facade gone, her eyes were a deep blue, and a fire he could almost feel.

'Do you find me a threat?' Bishop threw at her.

Samantha felt a sharp bolt of pain run through her aching brain; she wanted to die.

Jennifer Russell wanted to run out of the room in fear this man was getting to her. Dr Bishop stood up and walked round his desk and approached Jennifer and grabbed her wrists; he felt her strength as she tried to pull away from him.

Her eyes flashed at him.

'Let go, you are hurting me,' Jennifer ordered.

Her face was contorted with rage, he could almost feel the hate for him through the hold he had on her wrists, and her body trembled as she fought to get away from him. She was very strong and he had to apply a lot of strength to keep hold of her. Bishop released her and Jennifer turned and rushed out of the room. By the window Samantha fell senseless to the floor.

Angie Russell left her house and went in search of her big sister as she had not returned from school. The nine-year-old girl walked along the track between the two rows of houses. She made her way to the hill, as all the older children seemed to congregate there. When she finally reached it, there was no sign of her big sister or anyone else. Angie hoped Jennifer had not been struck down by illness again. Jennifer was her whole life, she was more than a big sister, and she was Angie's best friend. She moved towards the overgrown copse; a sound came above her head. A strange whining sound in the sky made her look up. A stiff breeze blew around her and ruffled her short blonde hair. Something shot over her head and crashed into the nearby bushes at the edge of the overgrown copse. The sphere had broken apart and between the two halves was a glowing green orb; the many facets sparkled with several different shades of green. Angie took off her blazer and put it over the green orb and wrapped the blazer around it; she picked it up and ran home with her prize.

Sarah Mullen sat on Juliet Prentice's bed drinking a glass of beer; Juliet was standing by the window sipping a glass of orange juice.

'What do you think of Samantha?' Juliet inquired.

From the window of the learning room they had seen Samantha ushered out of the school building on a stretcher, they had left the teaching machines together and gazed down at the courtyard below. Lavonia in her usual ungracious manner had hoped Samantha had finally dropped dead. Sarah had gone to the drinks machine and took out a cup of ice-cold orange juice and went to Lavonia and threw it in her face.

'Oh sorry, I slipped.'

Lavonia had run out of the room with a chorus of cheering behind her retreating back.

Sarah Mullen stared at Juliet as the girl stood with her back to her.

'You have to work hard to gain her trust, she is a strange girl, who is not surprising, knowing what they are doing to her brain,' Sarah said.

Juliet turned away from the window and went to the bed and sat beside her guest.

'What do you mean?'

Sarah placed the empty glass on the floor and gazed at her new friend. She wondered how much she dared tell Juliet, she wanted to avoid being locked away. She had been told not to tell Samantha, but there was nothing stopping her telling Juliet.

'They are giving her mind conditioning treatments. I did not get all of it, but they are somehow messing about with her brain,' Sarah said in deadly seriousness.

Juliet was shocked, she thought back to the first time she had met Samantha – she had called the girl crazy. Now she wished she had not. Samantha had appeared frightened and Juliet could now see why, Juliet would be frightened too if they were digging inside her head.

'I wonder if they are doing the same to all of us here,' Juliet said.

'I don't think so, only Samantha was mentioned in that context. Perhaps she is more unstable than the rest of you,' Sarah said.

'You would be unstable too, if someone was messing about with your mind.'

John Stephenson and Steven Calvert went out looking for the runaway, they went to the home of Jennifer Russell, but she was not there, and her young sister had not seen her.

'She could have gone to ground anywhere,' John said.

Steven had an idea.

'There's an old house on the other side of the overgrown copse; Samantha hid there when she ran away – we could start there.'

They raced to the overgrown copse and then slowed and went around it. They moved past the old orchard, and they were soon standing facing the old house.

'How quaint, is it haunted?'

'Only by Jennifer, if she's in there,' Steven replied.

Steven went to the door and pushed it open, the hinges creaking loudly.

'Spooky,' John muttered.

Steven walked into the hallway and made for the staircase; John followed behind him. Steven slowly made his way up the stairs; he was half expecting Jennifer to leap out at him at the top of the stairs. He hoped the girl was in a better mood than the one she'd been in when she ran out of the school building.

Jennifer Russell stood in the master bedroom gazing out of the cracked window. The burning rage in her head had gone, she felt calm and steady, she felt good inside. She had seen the two boys approach the house; she knew they were looking for her. When Jennifer heard them coming up the stairs, she turned away from the window and went to the open door. She must go and greet them; she was going to let them know she had changed. As soon as she had reached the house, Jennifer had felt the tension slip from her body, the anger faded from her mind. When she got up to the main bedroom, she felt good.

As Steven reached the top of the stairs Jennifer came out of the room to his right and a moment later, they stood facing each other.

'Hullo Steven, are you looking for me?'

'You must come back with us,' Steven told her.

Jennifer Russell gave him her best smile, Steven noticed her eyes were pale blue, so he knew she was not agitated about them being here.

'Of course, it's so nice of you to worry about me.'

Steven and John exchanged glances and John shook his head and then stared down the stairs followed by Steven and Jennifer bringing up the rear. They left the house.

Juliet and Sarah were eating in the kitchen.

'I like the way you threw that cold orange juice in Lavonia's face,' Juliet said.

'That girl is a real creep,' Sarah said.

Juliet liked the older girl; she was a lot of fun.

'I hope you can see me as a friend, Juliet.'

'We need as many friends we can get around here.'

Sarah laughed. 'With girls like Jennifer and Lavonia around – I can see why.'

'They don't frighten you?' Juliet inquired.

Sarah shook her head. 'If they start on me – I shall eat them for breakfast.'

Juliet giggled. 'That's definitely something that would spoil anyone's appetite.'

'There's no need to be frightened of them – they are cowards on their own.'

'They don't use their fists; they know that wouldn't work. They try to get inside your head,' Juliet said.

Sarah put her arm round Juliet's waist. 'I've got a few tricks of my own to fight that sort of mischief.'

Henry and Melanie washed up and then retired to the lounge and sat on the couch.

'We had one of your school friends in the medical lab, this afternoon,' Melanie said.

'That would be Samantha. The terrible twins were at their very worst.'

'She was unconscious when I left. I suppose the General is keeping the two wicked girls here because he sees them as a challenge,' Melanie said.

'Would you be mad at me, if I kissed you?' Henry asked.

Melanie smiled and shook her head. Henry kissed her lightly on the lips. Melanie thought that would be another thing the General would be angry at her for.

'When they decide what I will be working on, I hope it's near you, so I can protect you.'

Melanie giggled and kissed him. 'Do you think I need protecting?'

'You told me you were an angry girl – I want to be there, so you don't get into trouble,' Henry said.

Melanie kissed him. 'I want to work close to you also, Henry, you are different to all the other boys I have associated with.'

Janice met Hilary at the main gate and asked if she could visit Samantha; as they were all worried about her.

'You have a good bond with Samantha. That is something she needs at the moment,' Hilary said.

They walked across the compound. 'I have spent a few nights at her house – she has only good dreams or none at all. Sam asked me how I stopped her from having bad dreams. I could not give her an answer. If I knew what gave Samantha a peaceful night, I would bottle it and made sure she had a dose every night.'

'Dr Blake gave her every test and examinations he could think of and we scanned her brain, but we could not find an answer to her ailments,' Hilary explained.

Janice thought for a moment. 'What if the problem is external of Samantha's brain, not internal?'

Hilary stopped and stared at the thirteen-year-old girl. Janice was showing why she was selected for the Research Complex.

'It would need a strong mind.'

'Or a warped one like Jennifer and her freaky friend.'

'We'll have to keep them separated if Jennifer is the cause,' Hilary said.

Samantha came to in a white walled room; her eyes glazed up at a white ceiling. Her head ached slightly, her senses told her brain her metabolism had slowed, and her heart was beating normally in her chest. She gazed down and saw she was wired to machines by the bed; something was clamped to her forehead. Her sharp hearing heard someone humming and she turned her head. A computer system lined the wall; a female in a white lab coat was bent over a machine running her fingers over the lighted sensor pads. The bottom of the coat had ridden over her ample bottom showing she wore a dark brown skirt underneath; the hem had ridden up also giving Samantha a good view of the backs of her buxom thighs.

'Nice legs,' Samantha said, hoping to get the girl's attention.

Naomi Evans stopped humming and stood up straight; she turned and walked to the bed. She took hold of Samantha's thin right wrist and felt her pulse.

'There's nothing wrong with your eyesight anyway.'

Naomi checked the machinery by the bed and told Samantha she was in perfect health.

'As far as the machines are concerned, I'd like a second opinion,' Samantha said.

Naomi brought forward the machine she had been working on when Samantha had spoken, she placed it by the bed then she pulled the sheet back over Samantha's body; she was just wearing bra and panties. Naomi left the sheet at Samantha's long slender feet.

'Nice legs,' Naomi said.

A ghost of a smile flitted over her thin face. Samantha was disappointed at her figure, but this girl was the third person to give her a compliment on her legs – perhaps her body was not a complete disaster area after all.

'I'm Samantha, what's your name?'

'Naomi, just lie back and be still. We'll soon see if you are falling apart at the seams.'

Samantha turned her head and gazed at the monitor on the machine by the bed, Naomi held a probe that was attached to the machine. She placed the probe over Samantha's small left breast. The screen lit up and Samantha saw her heart beating away merrily.

'Nothing wrong there, as you can see, you've got a strong heart and it's working perfectly.'

'It's not my heart I'm worried about,' Samantha told her.

Naomi moved the probe down and Samantha kept her eyes on the screen seeing her insides revealed to her eyes fascinated her. Naomi was keeping an eye on the screen and when the probe reached the reproductive organs, Naomi held the probe still.

'That's strange.'

Samantha was suddenly alarmed. 'What?'

'Your ovaries are unusually small.'

Samantha watched the probe circle her belly; Naomi kept her eye on the screen.

'I hope you aren't expecting to have too many children.'

'At this time of my life having babies is light years from my mind. Perhaps me reproducing is not on their agenda.'

'Just as well, you are only going to give birth once and then your reproductive organs will shut down,' Naomi explained.

'As I'm not contemplating having sex in the near future, I'll worry about that piece of news, when the time comes,' Samantha said.

'Which won't be for some time yet, you can have as much sex as you like, you won't conceive, you are quite unique.'

Naomi grinned at her patient. Samantha took the probe away from Naomi and placed it against her forehead. Samantha wanted to see what was going on inside her head. Samantha stared at the monitor screen. The image of her brain was clear and surprising.

'Does the scan pick up any abnormalities?'

Naomi gazed at a screen on the body of the medical machine, as clear and precise. Samantha ran the probe over her head; Naomi watched the brain scan and started to shake her head.

'According to this your brain is quite healthy.'

Samantha stared wide eyed at the images of her brain coming up on the probe monitor. Her brain was made up of three separate parts, the forebrain the largest mass in her head, which showed the reason for her domed forehead, which she kept well hidden under her bushy ginger hair. Behind the forebrain were two smaller brain masses; all were connected by a mass of organic filaments. She was different in more ways than one.

'This gets better every minute,' Naomi observed.

A door slid open and Dr Blake entered the room. Naomi pulled the sheet up and covered Samantha's slim body.

'Your patient, Doctor, is healthy and strong, a fine specimen,' Naomi said.

Samantha stared hard at her, and then she turned to the doctor, who stood by the bed studying the machines wired to her body.

'I'm a specimen now, am I?'

'We are not sure what ails you, any more than you do, at this time. Why don't you tell me in your own words, about your confrontation with Jennifer,' Blake said.

Samantha explained to him what had happened in the classroom; Jennifer was spoiling for a fight. She suddenly felt ill and her headache, she did not remember hitting Jennifer; everything was a blur until she was sitting in Dr Bishop's office.

'Jennifer came into the room and I got up and went to the window and she sat down. The longer she was in the room the worse I felt. My head hurt and I thought my skull was about to burst. My body was on fire and I was trembling all over. I must have passed out and I woke up here.'

'There's nothing physically wrong with you now,' Dr Blake told her.

Her face flushed with anger.

'So, I'm crazy as Juliet keeps telling me and I'm imagining it all,' she said coldly.

'Calm down, Sam,' Naomi cautioned.

'Of course not, I've had Dr Bishop's report on his interview with you. He finds nothing wrong with your mental state and neither do I. Just relax while I make a few tests on you.'

Naomi injected a drug into Samantha's upper left arm; Samantha closed her eyes, she felt drowsy and soon drifted off to sleep.

Dr Blake left the room followed by Naomi, and then entered the Lab 3 hospital ward. Jennifer Russell was sitting on one of the beds and Hilary Calvert was standing over her. Ever since she had been brought here Jennifer had been questioned by Hilary and the doctor; they had given her all kinds of tests on her body. She wished they would let her go home to her younger sister. Dr Blake seemed to know what was going on in her mind.

'I don't think there's any need to keep you here any longer, Jennifer, you can go. But no more tricks. If you don't like Samantha, keep out of her way and keep out of trouble,' he said.

Jennifer Russell stood up and gave him a smile.

'I will, I'm sorry about my behaviour at the school, it won't happen again,' Jennifer said.

Hilary guided her out of the ward and out of the building.

Naomi was holding a medical instrument in her hand, she was running it over Jennifer as she spoke to the doctor, and she looked up at Dr Blake.

'She is a clone,' Naomi declared.

Dr Blake grinned at her and nodded; he turned and went to the room where Samantha was sleeping.

'What about Samantha? – she is not entirely human,' Naomi said.

'Samantha is half human – I can't tell you more than that – I have a mission for you,' he said.

Naomi smiled, things were speeding up – it was about time they gave her something better to do, she had not joined the research team just to be a nurse.

Hilary met Janice Clarke outside the gate to the research complex – she told Janice, Samantha was feeling a lot better and she was sleeping comfortably.

'Samantha has made a bond with you, Janice,' Hilary said.

'I have spent a few nights with Samantha – she has told me when I was there, she had only good dreams or none at all. Samantha asked me how I did it – but I had no answer for her. If I knew how I influenced her dreams – I would bottle it and make sure she got a regular dose,' Janice said.

'We did every test on Samantha and we are no nearer discovering why she has headaches and bad dreams,' Hilary said.

Janice was depressed to hear that – she liked Samantha and knew the girl was not being treated right – Janice thought for a moment – she wished she was older and more intelligent so she could provide an answer to Samantha's problem – apart from the big problem – the girl Jennifer Russell. She stared at Hilary – suddenly Janice got an idea.

'What if the problem is external – not internal to Samantha's brain?'

Hilary stared at the thirteen-year-old girl – she was showing why she was here at the research complex.

'It would need a strong mind,' Hilary said.

Janice had a serious expression. 'Or a warped mind like Jennifer Russell,' she said.

Hilary knew what Janice meant – the girl certainly liked to rub Samantha up the wrong way.

'We'll have to make sure they are kept apart at all times,' Hilary said.

CHAPTER XV:

THE CEREMONY

Janice Clarke and Steven Calvert stood hand in hand on the summit of the hill. In the distance the setting sun was disappearing behind some high hills. Jennifer stood facing them. When she had left the compound she had gone in search of Steven and Janice; she was very apologetic and begged their forgiveness and Jennifer assured them she was going to change. They were still suspicious of Jennifer, though they agreed to set up her plan of holding this ceremony for them. They stood in a circle of six boys and six girls sitting cross legged on the grass. Hazel and Paul were there – they had just gone through their own ceremony and they stared up at Janice and Steven, giving them smiles of encouragement.

'Do you, Steven, agree to uphold the rules of the Ceremony?' Jennifer asked in a sharp clear voice.

'I do,' Steven answered.

Jennifer repeated the same query to Janice, and she gave the same response. Jennifer turned back to Steven.

'Do you, Steven, agree to remain faithful to Janice and let nobody come between you?' Jennifer asked.

'I do,' he replied.

Jennifer turned to Janice.

'Do you Janice, agree to remain faithful to Steven and let nobody split you up?'

'I do,' Janice assented.

Samantha came out of a drugged sleep and found herself lying in her own bed. She slid out of bed and looked round her bedroom; she found nothing out of place, and nothing added. Her head was clear and no longer throbbed. She removed the nightdress and gazed down at her naked body. She was glad to see her skin as pale and unblemished. The dream, if it had been a dream, was still clear in her mind; she wondered what sorts of experiments were done on her mind and body while she was in the drugged sleep. She went to the wardrobe and took out her underwear and put it on, and then she put on her pink dress. Samantha went to the door and opened it, she heard sounds downstairs, she thought there was a burglar, and then she decided it was probably Hilary come to see if she was all right.

Samantha moved slowly down the stairs at the bottom; she detected the sounds were coming from the kitchen. She walked quietly along the hallway; she opened the kitchen door. The girl stood with her back to Samantha, she wore a short brown dress, and she had medium length bushy dark brown hair.

'I'm glad I didn't dream you up.'

Naomi Evans spun round and gave Samantha a wide grin.

'Ah, my patient's awake at last.'

Samantha settled down in a chair by the breakfast table; she watched Naomi move round the kitchen as she made coffee and a small snack for her patient. Sudden sounds outside made her look towards the back door. The whining sound was gradually getting closer and louder. Something shot over the house and headed for the marshes beyond.

'What was that?' Naomi asked sharply.

Naomi stared at Samantha, her face was calm and without expression.

'They're here,' Samantha said in a toneless voice.

Naomi kept staring at Samantha trying to think what she meant by those words. Dr Blake had told her about Samantha, the real story and Naomi got a clue to why she had been sent here to this research facility. Another whining object flew over the house.

Jennifer Russell stood at the base of the hill close to the overgrown copse. The Ceremony was breaking up because of the whining object shooting across the night sky. The breeze caressed her bare midriff as she gazed up at the sky. She listened to the missiles whining over her head. She thought of Samantha and wondered if she was outside her house when they hit her property. The thought made her smile. Jennifer suddenly felt a sharp pain in the exposed part of her back. Her skin went goosepimply, and she suddenly felt dizzy. She blacked out and collapsed to the ground and lay unconscious by the side of the overgrown copse.

Steven Calvert got parted from Janice and found himself alone on the hill, he went down the side of the hill, he heard the whining sounds in the sky, and something hit the hill close to him.

A strange odour assailed his nostrils and a green mist slowly enveloped him. Coldness touched his body, and something entered his head, and all went black.

Samantha sipped a mug of coffee and Naomi sat on the table close to her. The hem of the short brown dress had ridden up her tanned buxom thighs. She gazed at Samantha.

'I made myself at home, I hope you don't mind.'

Samantha shook her head; she was glad of her company.

'Why are you here?'

'I just wanted to make sure you came out of the drugged sleep all right,' Naomi said.

'Why drug me in the first place?'

Naomi gave her a warm smile; she wanted Samantha to know she was not her enemy.

'It was just to give you a deep sleep, so your shattered nerves can settle down.'

Naomi found herself under deep scrutiny by the bright green eyes. Samantha wanted to trust Naomi, she liked her.

'Jennifer Russell is a clone,' Naomi informed her, calmly.

Naomi stared at Samantha studying her reaction to the news.

'What?'

Samantha was not sure how to take this piece of information. Naomi kept quiet and let Samantha chew over that titbit.

'I don't believe it,' Samantha said at last.

Naomi put her hand on Samantha's shoulder.

'I found out when she was brought to the medical lab, don't tell anyone I told you, Samantha, I am on your side.'

Samantha would like to believe Naomi wanted to be true to her. Jennifer Russell being a clone made this bad day worse than her other bad days and it made her wonder who else was a clone.

'Is anyone else a clone? I hope your answer will be in the negative.'

'Yes, she is the only one; Dr Blake would not tell me why we have a clone here.'

'That's a relief.'

Naomi slid off the table and stood behind Samantha and started to massage her shoulders.

'Getting back to your problems, we can find nothing wrong inside your head; perhaps the problem is not internal to your mind and body, but there must be an external influence working on you.'

Samantha gazed up at the ceiling and let her thoughts run riot. Was Naomi trying to tell her something, without committing herself? Naomi was obviously trying to gain her trust.

Lavonia in her rush to get away from the strange whining missiles that were falling from the night sky, found herself near the marsh. The ground was soft and boggy. She wrinkled her nose at the dank rotting odour that pervaded the marshland. The sky was full of noise and bright lights, then something crashed into the bushes near Lavonia and made her jump. She saw a green glow shining up from the bushes as she approached them. Lavonia detected another odour as she stared at the misty greenness. Lavonia was transfixed as she stared at the green glowing mist; she shuddered as an immense coldness crept up her body. She stared into the depths of the green glow, then something entered her skull and she fell to the ground senseless.

Janice appeared close to the marshes some way off from Lavonia. She was close to the marsh water; a few feet away across the water something glowed turning the water green. Janice stared at it in fascination; she moved forward and stepped into the cold water of the marsh. Janice moved further into the water, something compelled her to reach the glowing waters ahead of her. The water level crept up her shapely thighs; she kept going until the water reached her waist. The stagnant odour did not deter her from reaching the glowing water close by. Janice was soon standing in the centre of the green glowing patch of water; her body trembled from the cold water. A ball of green light rose up from the water and travelled up her body until it got to her head. She was bathed in the green light. Something entered her head, a cold energy filtered into her brain.

'Jennifer Russell certainly exerts some sort of power over you,' Naomi said.

Samantha turned her head and faced Naomi.

'She makes my skin crawl when I'm close to her, I find the experience very nauseating,' Samantha said.

Samantha slid off the stool and walked to the back door and opened it and stepped out into the night; a stiff breeze ruffled her long hair, a loud whine shot over her head. Naomi came out and stood beside her.

'They have come at the right time,' Naomi said

'I hope the others stayed at home,' Samantha said.

'They were up on the hill just before the sun went down, some sort of Ceremony or other,' Naomi said.

Samantha remembered Jennifer Russell telling her about it, it was strange after what had happened in the schoolroom, and they trusted Jennifer enough to go through with her Ceremony. Samantha hoped they would not live to regret it.

'I'd better go there and make sure they have left the hill in time,' Samantha said.

'The military camp would be alerted, and the soldiers will be out in force,' Naomi said.

Samantha turned and faced Naomi who was illuminated by the light from the kitchen.

'Are you afraid?'

Naomi surprised Samantha by laughing sharply. Naomi liked the tall girl; she was a sharp one.

'No, do you feel up to running about in the dark?'

'I feel just fine. You take the marsh area and I'll make for the hill,' Samantha said.

Samantha went back into the house and returned with two torches, she gave one to Naomi and then ran in the direction of the hill. Naomi switched on the torch and made a slower journey down the garden towards the distant marshland. Samantha ran into John, Juliet and Wendy Goodman. John Stephenson told her all hell had broken loose and the night sky was filled with strange noises and flashes of light; something had happened to Jennifer Russell and she was last seen falling down the side of the hill towards the overgrown copse. Samantha left them and when she got to the hill it was alive with armed troops who told her to go back to her home. Samantha did not stay to argue, she left them and headed for the overgrown copse, she wanted to find the body of Jennifer Russell to confirm whether the nauseous girl was alive or dead. She made for the spot where her body was supposed to have ended up. Samantha flicked the torch on and surveyed the base of the hill but found no body.

Juliet arrived at her home and found Sarah waiting at her door.

'I lost sight of you, Juliet, so I came back here to wait for you.'

They entered the house and went into the kitchen and Juliet made some coffee.

'I was joined by John and Wendy, we met Samantha and she told us to rush off home,' Juliet said.

'It was quite a night. I wonder if they were meteors, or something darker,' Sarah said.

'Definitely something dark,' assured Juliet.

They went to the lounge and sat on the couch and sipped their coffees.

'I'm glad you've stayed here – you give me a lot of self-confidence.'

'I'm sure you would have found it sooner or later. The trip you did last year, making an unauthorized visit to the Research Complex, took guts. Samantha would not have taken you, if she did not think you were a girl she could trust. She finds you irritating, but she obviously thinks you are a girl who can make the right decisions,' Sarah said.

'I feel guilty about the way I've treated her, after what you told me about having your brain messed with.'

'You'll have to sit and talk with the girl. I like Samantha; she had steel to her character. Steven and Janice like her a lot.'

'She might not want to talk to me,' Juliet confessed.

'You'll find a way; I have confidence in you.'

'Will you stay the night with me?' Juliet asked.

Wendy Goodman arrived at an empty house and she had a shower and went to bed. She had thoughts of what might be happening outside, none of them nice.

Henry Jones and Melanie McAllister were sitting on the couch drinking coffee.

'That was a strange night,' she said.

'It certainly was. I wonder what those flying objects were.'

Melanie kissed him on the cheek. 'Unidentified Flying Objects,' she corrected.

Henry laughed and kissed her on the lips. 'I hope your house mate got back all right.'

'I hope she stayed at home,' Melanie said.

'I hope your father won't mind you being here with me.'

'It's nothing to do with him who I associate with.'

Melanie had not told Henry who her father was.

Samantha decided to enter the overgrown copse, she tried to keep her mind off what might and might not be lurking in the dark foreboding copse, waiting to grab her at any moment. Samantha moved cautiously through the overgrown vegetation, then she stepped on something and she pointed the torch down to her feet. The body of Jennifer Russell lay still on her back, she had the torch light on the head, not much remained of the face, it was melted and corroded, it was just a mush of tissue, the hands and legs were the same – whatever had attacked Jennifer Russell had made a good job of destroying her body. Samantha had been sure the girl would have come to a no-good end and now she had.

Samantha heard a sound behind her and before she could move an arm came around her body and clamped on her body like a vice, a hand was clamped over her mouth. She was pulled deeper into the overgrown copse, she tried to struggle but her assailant was strong and held her tighter.

'Don't struggle please, I could easily break your neck,' a sharp female voice said.

As to emphasize her words the hand that gripped Samantha's jaw moved her head round slowly, Samantha felt the pressure rise in the back of her neck.

'I don't want to hurt you, but I can if I must. I will release you if you promise not to shout out, nod your head,' the voice whispered in her ear.

Samantha nodded her head and the hand was removed from her mouth and chin. She heard her assailant move back away from her. Samantha turned slowly and turned the torch light on the tall figure standing in front of her. Samantha stood still frozen to the spot – she could only stare in disbelief with her mouth wide open.

PART TWO:

THE MIND OF JENNIFER

CHAPTER XVI:

MIRROR, MIRROR

MAY 2124

For twelve years the girl lay under an oxygen tent, on this day the twelfth year of her birth, the first signs of movement came to her prone slender body. The senses and nerves hurriedly sent messages to the waking brain. The eyes fluttered open and finding the first sensation of bright light too many the eyes closed. After a while the eyes reopened to get used to the light, they gazed up at the obscuring cloud that surrounded them. The tall slim body wriggled under the software cocoon it lay in. The sharp hearing detected sounds beyond the opaque cloudiness that domed over the girl.

Suddenly the curtain of mist was drawn back, and a brighter light assailed her eyes and they quickly closed again.

She blinked her eyes several times to get her eyes used to the brighter light. She noticed a large round face peering at her, a hand reached out and stroked the place above her eyes, it was warm and gentle, the girl liked it; after a while the hand was removed.

Valerie Peterson was glad the girl had come out of the coma at last. She was aware of the ice blue eyes studying her face. There was some colour appearing on the thin pale face. The long blonde hair cascaded about her head. Valerie gave the girl a warm smile to put her at ease. The girl made her thin lips imitate the smile on the face beaming down on her. After a while Valerie left the room to report the girl was awake and alert.

The girl sat up and pulled the covering off her body, so she could see what she was made of. She could only use one hand because her other wrist was strapped to the bed and a thin tube rose from the bandage on her thin wrist. Her eyes followed the tube up to a drip-feed above her bed. She then gazed at the long nightgown that covered her body down to her long slender feet. Her brain sent a message to her senses and her toes started to wriggle, she smiled in triumph. Her eyes went to the bodice of the nightgown: it was pushed out firmly and she could see down it.

The door opened and the girl turned her head and watched the woman return to her bedside. Valerie spoke softly and clearly to her patient; she was aware the girl could not understand her. Valerie removed the bandage and tube from the thin wrist and moved the drip-feed away from the bed. The ice blue eyes watched her every movement. The girl had decided the woman was not going to hurt her, so there was no danger. She was comforted by the soft voice; the girl was sure the woman was trying to put her mind at ease.

The girl made a sudden movement and avoided Valerie and dived off the bed; she caught sight of her reflection in a mirror on the bedside table. The girl grabbed it and skated across the parquet floor. Her long legs unused to her body weight collapsed under her and she fell and slid across the polished floor on her bottom until she came to a stop and sat cross legged in the middle of the room. The girl gazed at the mirror and stared at the face in it, wide ice blue eyes stared back at her. She gazed at the long thin face and long blonde hair that hung over her thin shoulders. The girl was pleased with what she saw, a smile appeared on the thin pick lips, the ice blue eyes became brighter, the face in the mirror matched her own, her mind was now awake and alert.

A door at the other end of the room slid open and a tall dark-haired man in a white lab coat walked in and made his way to the girl sat on the floor. The girl looked up from the mirror when he stood over her; he spoke softly to her. The girl kept her eyes on him in case he was after her prize; she held it tight against the bodice of her nightdress. Dr Richard Blake could read what was going through the mind of the girl. Valerie came up to them.

'She thinks I am after her mirror; we'll have to get her off the floor before she freezes her bottom on the cold floor,' he said.

The girl watched the woman kneel in front of her. Valerie held out her hand to the girl in the hope of enticing the girl up onto her feet. The girl had a name and Valerie said it breaking it up into three syllables.

'Jen –in- fer,' the girl muttered.

After a while the girl pursed her lips and started to try and repeat what the woman had said to her.

Valerie gave the girl a smile of encouragement.

'Jen – ni – fer,' the girl muttered to herself.

The girl offered her right hand to the woman, the left hand held the mirror tight to her chest. She allowed the woman to lift her up onto her feet.

Valerie supported the girl as they approached the bed. The girl jumped onto the bed, still clinging tightly onto the mirror. She lay on the bed and Valerie pulled the sheet over her. Dr Blake stood by the bed. The girl looked up at him with interest, she did not protest when the doctor put her through a medical examination.

Richard Blake was aware he was under the sharp scrutiny of the deep-set ice blue eyes. At the end of the examination the girl was chuckling to herself as if she had enjoyed the experience.

'How is she?' Valerie asked.

'Jennifer is simply glowing with health; she's obviously unharmed by her twelve-year sleep.'

Jennifer watched them leave the room, and then she held the mirror up to her face.

'Jen-ni-fer,' she muttered proudly.

CHAPTER XVII:

A GIRL NAMED JENNIFER

Valerie Peterson was placed in charge of the girl Jennifer. She fed her and taught her to speak and read. Jennifer enjoyed the lessons and she was very attentive to what Valerie told her. Jennifer was a very good pupil and she wanted to know everything, her sharp mind devoured all that Valerie told her. Jennifer was occasionally visited by the doctor and she obediently let him examine her and glowed with pleasure when he told her she was strong and healthy.

One morning when Valerie entered the room with a breakfast tray, she saw Jennifer standing by the wall behind her desk on the opposite side of the room to her bed. Valerie placed the tray on the desk and the girl came to her.

'I want a mirror as tall as me on this wall, do you think they'll let me have one?' the girl inquired in a soft silky voice.

'Of course they will, I will see to it. Now eat your breakfast like a good girl,' Valerie said.

Jennifer sat at the desk and tucked into her breakfast.

'You are such a good cook, I like you,' Jennifer told her.

'I like you too, Jennifer.'

The girl gave her a beaming smile.

After breakfast Valerie continued schooling the young girl, she went through the lessons with enthusiasm,

Jennifer was enjoying the learning process and she proudly accepted all the praise Valerie bestowed on her. Two days later to the extreme delight of Jennifer a full-length mirror was placed on the wall behind her desk. When she was left alone Jennifer threw off her clothes and stood naked in front of the mirror; she studied her body from all angles. Jennifer looked for the best elegant pose she could throw herself into, she was very pleased with her tall slender body, with very defined curves and straight lines. Valerie came into the room and slapped her bare bottom.

'Stop preening yourself and get to bed.'

Jennifer went to the bed and put on her nightgown and got under the sheets, Valerie kissed her on the cheek and tucked her in. Valerie walked to the door and turned around after she had plunged the room into darkness, she saw two tiny points of light that told her the girl was watching her. It was a weird experience seeing the pale blue light of the girl's eyes shining in the dark, she was not quite like other little girls, and Valerie wondered what other strange attributes the girl had.

When the door slid shut behind Valerie the girl jumped out of bed and made for the door. When she got there, she looked up at the red light above it, where she knew a camera was concealed in the wall. Did they watch her day and night, she wondered.

I am a specimen for their scientific experiments. A Curio.

In the operations room a blonde curly haired woman was looking at the monitor that showed Jennifer sitting on the floor staring back at her. The woman wondered what the girl was thinking.

Are you aware of me here watching you? Jenny?

Valerie Peterson walked into the huge room and sat beside the woman and gazed up at the screen – though the room was in darkness the camera showed clearly the girl sitting on the floor gazing up at the hidden camera.

'The little terror, I'll have to teach her once she is in bed, she is to stay there,' Valerie said.

'Don't be too hard on her, Jenny only wants to know who's watching her.'

The woman stood up and turned away from the row of monitors and crossed the room. Valerie got up and followed her.

'When are you going to call on her?' Valerie asked.

'When the time is right. I must learn more about her before stepping into that room.'

'You have nothing to worry about, Jennifer is a very intelligent girl, her thirst for knowledge is insatiable,' Valerie told her.

When the girl reached the age of thirteen, two men entered her room. She sat at her desk and Valerie sat on the opposite side of the desk. Jennifer watched the two men approach her – one was tall and dressed in a military uniform, he was broad and strongly built, and Jennifer was impressed as she studied his face. Jennifer decided he was a man of importance.

'Are you in charge here?' she asked.

General Heywood raised his eyebrows and gazed at his companion, who wore a white lab coat. Professor Albert Harris grinned at him.

'Something like that,' Heywood told the girl.

The Professor asked the girl if she had everything she wanted, and she was getting attention to all her needs.

'Yes, thank you,' Jennifer said in a soft voice.

After answering several questions, she watched the two men walk back to the door, she hoped they were pleased with her. Valerie continued the lessons and Jennifer was ready as usual.

The next night Jennifer had a bad dream, and, in the morning, Valerie found the girl irritable and unmanageable. The lessons were cancelled, and Jennifer was left to her own devices. The next morning Valerie found the girl sitting naked in the middle of the room. She called her name and got no answer; Jennifer was staring into space. Valerie draped the sheet off the bed around the girl's shoulders to protect her naked body from draughts. In the afternoon the girl came to life and jumped to her feet; the sheet dropped from her naked body. She paced the room like a caged tiger. When her legs got tired of walking aimlessly around the room, she sat at her work desk in an effort to ease her troubled mind by feeding her brain data from her desk computer.

In the evening Valerie came into the room carrying the girl's lunch on a tray, she placed it on the work desk and turned to the bed, where the girl was sitting with her head in her hands. When Valerie approached the bed, the girl jumped up and ran to Valerie and threw her arms round the woman.

'What's the matter, Jenny? You can tell me.'

'I had a bad dream, it was awful,' the girl sobbed.

Valerie took the girl to the work desk and sat her down in from of her lunch.

'Try to forget about it, nothing is going to hurt you, while I'm here to protect you,' Valerie said.

Jennifer started to eat her lunch and Valerie ran a soothing hand over the girl's forehead.

'Do you still like me?' Jennifer asked.

Valerie kissed her on the cheek.

'Of course I do, you are a very nice girl, Jenny.'

In the night Jennifer had another bad dream. The same tall ginger-haired girl that was in her first bad dream was there and she had had an axe and she had attacked Jennifer and split her skull like a melon. Then the ginger-haired girl got down on knees and started to rip the brain out of the shattered skull and devour it. Jennifer woke in the morning irritable and thoroughly miserable. She picked at her breakfast and refused to do any lessons, so Valerie left her alone. Jennifer sat in front of the door and stared up at the hidden camera. She knew someone was watching her, so she decided to stare back at them.

In the operations room General Heywood was sitting beside the curly haired woman.

'It looks as if she is aware – we are watching her,' he said.

'She knows someone is watching her, the camera is there for us to keep an eye on her,' the woman said.

CHAPTER XVIII:

THE BRAINCHILD

MAY 2126

When Jennifer turned fourteen, she was taken out of the room. Jennifer hoped they would allow her outside to feel the sun on her body and the wind ruffling her long blonde hair. She followed Valerie along the long corridor outside the room. At the end of it they got into a lift and as the door slid shut Jennifer gazed round the small compartment and wondered what was going to happen next. As the lift started going up, she looked nervously around her as she had the feeling, she was leaving her stomach behind. Noticing the discomfort on her face Valerie put her arm round her waist and gave the girl a warm smile. When the lift reached the top of the shaft it stopped, and the door slid open. Valerie guided Jennifer into a large room full of electronic machinery and people. Jennifer stared about her in astonished wonder. She walked along the computer banks; they were hugely better than her small desk top computer. She could be happy in this room, Jennifer told herself. The technicians working in the room gave her a fleeting glance as she moved among them. Jennifer had never been amongst so many people before, Jennifer hoped she would make a good impression; she wanted them to like her.

A man detached himself from a crowd of technicians and approached Jennifer. He had short black hair and wore glasses. She recognised him as he had visited Jennifer in her room.

'Hello Jennifer, this is where you will receive your real training,' Professor Harris said.

Jennifer gave him a beaming smile.

'Oh goody, it's about time I got something to get my teeth into. I must work my brain to its fullest capacity,' Jennifer said.

'And how much is that?'

Jennifer gazed at the man who had joined them; he did not wear a white lab coat like the Professor, and he was a lot younger. Jennifer gazed at his face; his blue eyes were looking her up and down. Jennifer hoped he liked what he saw. She wore a crisp white blouse and black skirt and her long blonde hair was neatly brushed.

'Is this the brainchild you've had hidden away?'

The Professor nodded and introduced Jennifer to Michael Palmer. She gave him one of her sweetest smiles, that made her look more the schoolgirl she was, but the ice blue eyes told him something else. He would have to keep a close eye on her, he thought to himself.

'Well, Missy, let's see what you're made of.'

Michael grabbed her arm and led her out of the main computer room. They entered a smaller room filled with teaching machines. He sat Jennifer in front of the nearest.

'OK, Missy, let's get started.'

'The name's Jennifer,' she corrected him.

Michael turned the machine on.

'OK, Missy.'

Michael smiled when he heard her gasp of exasperation.

Jennifer was aware he did not like her and was unimpressed with her talents. But actions spoke louder than words, she would show him, Jennifer thought to herself. Jennifer sat at the learning machine and gazed at the first problem, while Michael stood over her and watched the long thin fingers flit over the keyboard tapping out the answer. When Jennifer had gone through all the problems in the first machine she moved off to the next; she was enjoying herself. Michael had to reluctantly admit the girl knew her stuff. All through the day she took everything Michael could throw at her. Jennifer happily came through it with flying colours.

At the end of the day Valerie came into the room to collect her charge. Jennifer was full of herself and could not refrain from telling Valerie how well she had done. Michael had told Jennifer she had done all right and she accepted the small praise graciously. It had been better than nothing. Valerie took Jennifer out of the learning hall and they walked down a long corridor and passed a number of doors until they got to the one Valerie stopped at and it slid open to admit them. They walked through the open doorway.

'This is your new living quarters.'

Jennifer gazed round the furnished room; there was everything she wanted, including her own computer work desk. There was a full-length mirror on the wall beside the wardrobe that was filled with clothes for her to wear. Jennifer did a victory dance in the middle of the room, and when she had finished, she ran to Valerie and hugged her tight.

'You think I'm an awful bighead, don't you?'

'Yes, I do and if I didn't love you so much, I'd want to give your bottom a good spanking, so you wouldn't be able to sit down for a week,' Valerie said.

'You old fraud, you know you wouldn't spank me, I would like it too much,' Jennifer retorted.

'Not so much of the old, you little scamp.'

Jennifer got on the bed and smoothed the skirt over her thighs and lay back.

'I do appreciate all you have done for me, I will never do anything that would bring you harm, Val.'

Valerie Peterson stood over the bed, the pale blue eyes glazed up at her.

'I am here to protect you, Jenny, I shall be next door. If you have any more bad dreams, I shall be there to comfort you,' Valerie said.

Michael Palmer was about to leave the learning hall when a tall woman came in. She wore a cream coloured blazer and skirt, she had thick curly blonde hair.

'Hello Doctor,' he greeted.

'How did she perform?' she asked.

'She's the nearest I've seen to a human computer, but don't tell her I said that.'

The woman gave him a wide grin, her deep blue eyes shone.

'I won't. I'm glad everything is going to plan.'

The two of them left the room together.

In the night Jennifer had another nightmare.

Jennifer was in a dusty attic of an old house; she lay on the rubble strewn floor. A dark loathsome shadow monster stood over her. Jennifer was paralysed with fear. The thing fell on her and began to pull her body apart and devour her. Standing behind the beast was a tall thin girl with long flowing ginger hair that hung down to her waist. She wore a long white dress that clung to her slim body. She stood and watched while Jennifer was eaten alive until there was nothing left.

Jennifer woke in a cold sweat; she got out of bed and paced the floor. She suddenly remembered what Valerie had told her and left the room; the corridor was in darkness. She went to the door next to her own and knocked. A while later the door slid open; and Jennifer entered the room; and the lights came on.

Valerie sat on the bed dressed in a blue nightgown, she watched Jennifer run to her and sit on the bed beside her.

'What is it, Jenny darling?'

Jennifer told Valerie about the nightmare; tears ran down her cheeks. Valerie put a comforting arm round her waist.

'It was horrible,' Jennifer cried.

'Try to forget it, you are safe now, I'm here and I won't let anything hurt you,' Valerie said softly.

Every time she entered the learning hall, Jennifer found work was the best way to forget her fears and bad dreams. Michael Palmer put her to work. There was also another girl in the room, who was about a year older than Jennifer, and she was slightly shorter and had long brown hair. Lavonia Wagstaffe held out her hand to Jennifer, who ignored it – there was something in the face and brown eyes Jennifer did not like. She got on with her work. Lavonia stood by the machines and watched her progress. Because the girl was in her domain Jennifer thought the older girl was bound to be clever, but Jennifer discovered the girl was just above average intelligence. Jennifer wondered if Lavonia was put under her wing to learn from a more intelligent person to boost her knowledge.

Lavonia decided she did not like Jennifer, she was overbearing, and she strode about the room with an air of complete authority as if she was in control of everything about her. Michael Palmer was amused by her arrogance and did not let it disturb him, like it did Lavonia and the other technicians. Every time Jennifer got out of hand, he called her 'Missy' which to his utmost pleasure, Jennifer disliked immensely.

JULY 2126

In the locker and laundry room just off the learning hall, Lavonia Wagstaffe was pacing the floor in a fit of anger, her face was flushed red, and she was ready to do a murder.

'That girl will have to go, we have to kill her,' Lavonia stormed.

A woman of thirty-six with short fair hair smiled at the girl when she turned to her.

'I agree,' the woman said.

The woman gazed down at the man sitting on a bench close to her. He nodded his head.

'It will be dangerous, that girl is still a mystery and we don't know what hidden talents Jennifer has,' he said.

'We have to kill her before she starts to display them,' Lavonia said.

The woman went to the girl and put her arm round her waist and kissed Lavonia on the cheek.

'You are a girl after my own heart.'

The man sat and stared at them with dark eyes that shared the darkness of his mind.

'She should be, she's your daughter, after all,' he said.

Lavonia went over to him and stood in front of him and waited for orders.

'You'll have to kill her, you know, you will have the best opportunity as you work with her. Can you kill, Lavonia?'

Lavonia thought about the question and then thought of Jennifer and how irritating the girl was, Lavonia would have no qualms about putting an end to the girl.

'I can kill Jennifer, it will be an extreme pleasure to do away with her,' Lavonia said.

'Good girl, you are nearly as nasty as me,' the man said.

JULY 2126

Jennifer was working alone in the main computer room in the late evening when Lavonia suddenly materialized beside her.

'Can I help you in any way?'

Jennifer was about to throw her out, when she changed her mind. She tried to think up some menial task for the irritating girl. When she had given Lavonia some instruction, Jennifer moved off to continue her work at the computer control desk. Lavonia got down to her plan of getting rid of Jennifer once and for all; she was going to make Jennifer pay for her arrogance. Lavonia went to the work bench along the wall opposite the computer system. She picked up the tool box and carried it over to the computer a little way from where Jennifer was working at the control desk. She opened the inspection hatch and carrying the tool box she crawled into the dark cavern inside the machine. Lavonia moved slowly along the channel, shining the beam of the small torch she carried in front of her. When she found the place she was looking for she got down to work.

When Lavonia had finished, she crawled out of the crawl space and closed the inspection hatch. She returned the tool box to the work bench. Jennifer suddenly appeared besides her gazing at her in deep suspicion, Lavonia feigned innocence. Jennifer went back to the control desk to complete her work there. Lavonia raced out of the room to make good her escape – she did not want to be found anywhere near when Jennifer met her end.

There was a flash of light and a loud crackling sound as Jennifer was hit by a power surge, she gave a piercing scream as the electronic power ran through her body. She fell to the floor, her face was deathly white.

Pain, Excruciating pain.

Every nerve was on fire as the power surge ran through her body. The mind wanted to be free of the pain and torment. The mind fell into the dark pit of unconsciousness, where there were no memories, no feelings and no life. The body was an empty shell.

Michael Palmer stood by the control desk scratching his head and gazing at the control panel. He tried to keep his eyes and mind off the twenty-three-year-old girl on her hands and knees under the control desk. She had just arrived, and he found her excellent at her work, but her pretty face and figure a distraction. Colonel Hopkins, the head of security, was standing behind him, waiting patiently for Michael to tell him how the girl was injured. The lifeless body was taken away to the medical centre in the Lab 3 building. The girl on the floor stood up and brushed her hands over the front of her dark brown skirt. Her medium length dark brown hair was bushy and ruffled. Her dark brown eyes were fixed on Michael.

'What did you find, Naomi?'

'Someone has cross wired the power grids, so the control desk became live,' Naomi said.

Michael turned to the Colonel.

'It looks like someone wants our brainchild dead,' he said.

Naomi Evans had rewired the power grids to their original positions, she had found some fascinating work that had been done to the computer control desk, and two speaker units were fitted into it and a sensor panel.

'I'd like to meet the person who has been working on this computer,' she said to Michael.

'If she recovers, I shall introduce you, but I don't think much for her chances,' he said.

'That would be a shame if your colleague does die, I'm sure she was trying to interact with the computer and give it a voice,' Naomi said.

Michael knew what Naomi was getting at and he wondered if she was working on a computer that she could hold a conversation with.

'I haven't personally, but I have some friends who are looking into it, if your colleague does recover, I shall introduce her to my friends,' Naomi said.

Naomi turned away from him and made for the exit door; he watched her retreating back.

INTERIM

The body lay lifeless in a bed in a small white-walled room. Machines around the bed recorded almost non-existent life signs. For a year the body lay thus.

The mind had fallen deeper into the abyss and it suddenly sensed intelligence nearby. In an effort to free itself from the pain of the body, the mind had seemed to have found refuge in another brain. It had crossed a bridge, but to where? And could it find a way back?

CHAPTER XIX:

OVER THE BRIDGE

AUGUST 2127

Valerie Peterson walked into the small room and stood by the bed. She looked down at the placid white face. The girl had once before come out of a deep coma, and Valerie was sure Jennifer would do it again. As long as that tiny spark of life burned inside the body there was hope for the girl. Valerie ran a hand through the long hair that had turned silvery by the accident with the computer; they had not told her that someone had tried to murder the girl. She caressed the high forehead and wondered what dreams the girl was having; Valerie hoped they were not like the nightmares the girl used to have. It seemed the beast in the dream had finally got to Jennifer.

Under the closed eyelids rapid eye-movement started, the electroencephalograph started to monitor a waking brain. Valerie picked up the limp right wrist and felt for the pulse. It was getting stronger.

'Come on, Jenny, you can make it,' Valerie muttered softly.

Valerie left the room to report the girl was showing signs of life. The girl suddenly sat up and held her head in her hands. She had crossed over the bridge and she was back in her own body. Jennifer detached herself from the machines that were monitoring her life signs or the lack of them. She pulled the sheet off her body and swung her long legs over the side of the bed. She was wearing a long white nightgown, she pulled it up over her slender thighs and ran her hands over them massaging her leg muscles, when she had finished, and she stood up and got her legs used to carrying her weight again. She wondered how long she had been in the white room, she was glad to be alive – when the power surge ran through her body she had thought she was a goner.

She made a few tentative steps forward. She slowly headed for the door. She found it hard going as her legs had forgotten how to walk. Eventually she got to the door and ran her hand over it and the door slid open and she stepped out into a long corridor; she turned right and moved forward until she got to the end. She stood and stared at the metal door barring her way forward. She ran her long delicate fingers over the keypad on the door control panel. She searched for the combination that would open the door. Her long fingers flitted over the keypad; her brain was getting into gear as she worked faster. Speed was the essence. At last; the door slid open.

'Eureka!'

She entered a large room with a lift terminal. She remembered being in a similar room with Valerie, the woman took her up to a new environment. She had been underground and now she was back there. She wondered why they wanted to keep her away from everybody else, why they dug a hole in the ground to hide her from the world. She stood in front of the lift door and hit the controls and the double doors slid open and she entered the lift and the doors closed behind her. The lift went up and her stomach went down; she wished it would not do that. She waited patiently until the lift finished the journey upwards, then it stopped, and the doors slid open and she vacated the lift. She strode into a large room filled with the hum of sophisticated machinery. She walked round the room gazing in wonder at the computers and other strange machinery that she had no knowledge of.

Fascinating.

She eventually came to three large capsules standing in the middle of the room. She approached them. One of them was open and she looked inside – it was empty. The size and shape of the inside told the girl she could get her tall frame in easily. She went to the middle one and stared through the transparent part of the lid. There was a thin pale face inside, the eyes were closed, it was female and even worse the face was her own; she stepped back in shock.

She went to the next capsule knowing already what she would find there. She stared dumbfounded at the second effigy of herself. She gazed back at the empty capsule that told her there might be a third effigy of her wandering about somewhere.

Perhaps this is a dream and I'm still in a coma, hooked to the machines.

She turned away from the capsules. When she found Valerie, she had a few questions for the woman, who she saw as her friend.

This is no dream, pinch yourself and see.

She pinched her right forearm.

Ouch.

If you think this is bad. Just wait and see what else they have in store for you.

She found the door out of the room and stepped into a passage and turned right, she came to some double doors and pushed them open and walked into a long room with light blue painted walls; it was full of hospital beds. One of them was occupied. She walked over to it, and a red-haired young girl was lying in it. She heard someone approach her.

'You are back with the living again, I see,' a cold female voice said.

She spun round and once again stared at the evil face of Lavonia. The memory of the power surge in the computer she was working on came flooding back to her mind. The girl before her was in the room just before it happened. She remembered her name, Lavonia that was it. She turned back to the girl in the bed. The eyes opened and stared up at her, and then the eyes closed.

'It seems she can't stand your presence either,' Lavonia said.

Lavonia grinned at the girl; she was very disappointed the girl had not died; she would have to try again at a later date.

Lavonia laughed at her retreating back.

We are going to have a reckoning – you and. I'm going to see you die, Lavonia. You are going to die slowly and painfully.

She went through another doorway and she found herself outside. It was a new experience for her; she had never been fully exposed to the elements. The wind tugged at her white nightdress – it ruffled her silver blonde hair. The bright sunshine bathed her in light and warmth. She felt suddenly dizzy – her sight blurred. She collapsed to the ground and everything went black.

CHAPTER XX:

THE AMBIGUOUS JENNIFER RUSSELL

CONSCIOUSNESS THREE QUESTIONS WHO AM I? WHAT AM I? WHERE AM I?

Eyes fluttered open and bright light stung the optic nerves; the eyes closed. The eyes reopened and stared up at the pale blue ceiling. The girl in the bed sat up and held her head in her hands. She tried to get her foggy mind to do some thinking. She pulled the sheets down the bed and swung her long legs over the side of the bed. She looked down at herself. She gazed at the bodice of her nightgown.

Now I know what I am. Now – Who am I?

She moved to the end of the bed and picked up the chart hanging on the end of the bed. There was a name on it.

JENNIFER RUSSELL: FIFTEEN.

She placed the chart on the bed and spied a mirror on the bedside table. She moved towards it and picked up the mirror and gazed at her reflection; she stared at the light blue eyes and long silver blonde hair; the face was very pale.

The girl in the mirror – looks as if she has seen a ghost.

She put the mirror down and tried to sort out her confused thoughts.

Is that it? I have come back from the dead.

She heard footsteps approaching her, she turned and watched a woman in a white coat walk to the bed, and she gave the girl a warm smile.

'You're awake at last, Jennifer.'

'I seem to have no memories of who I am and what has happened to me,' the girl said.

The woman doctor told the girl she had been in a coma for a year after a mysterious illness had struck her down. The girl had no memory of that so she could not dispute the story.

'How are you feeling?'

'Rough is an apt word to how I'm feeling,' the girl replied.

'Well let's see if we can do something about that. My name is Hilary by the way.'

Hilary Calvert gave the girl a complete medical examination. After which she gave Jennifer Russell a clean bill of health.

'What happens now?' the girl asked.

'We have someone who is waiting to see you again,' Hilary said.

Hilary left the ward room and the girl went to the window above the front of the bed and gazed out at the clear blue sky; the sun shone brightly. Hilary came back with a little girl in tow. The girl turned away from the window. The little girl ran to her and hugged her tight.

'You are not going to be taken away from me again, I am going to take care of you, Jenny,' the little girl sobbed.

I don't know this small girl.

The next day clothes were brought to the girl to wear. She decided to take the name Jennifer Russell as her own; though she was sure she was not sister of the little girl Angie Russell. She got dressed and Hilary guided her out of the ward and out of the building, she stepped out into the bright sunshine. The little girl was there waiting for her, sitting in the back of an army jeep; she sat next to her and Angie kissed her on the cheek. A soldier sat at the wheel of the jeep and he drove through the compound to the main gate and headed towards the group of small cottages.

When Jennifer went to the school building, she met a girl about the same age as herself by the gates. The girl went by the name of Lavonia. She warned Jennifer to look out for a tall ginger haired girl – she was not a nice person, Lavonia told Jennifer and the girl would take an instant dislike to Jennifer. Lavonia made an alliance with Jennifer to make sure they got no trouble from the ginger haired girl.

CHAPTER XXI:

A MULTITUDE OF JENNIFERS

The eyes flashed open and her senses told her body, she was lying in a warm cocoon. Above her head was a square window where the light filtered in. A rush of data ran through her brain, the memories came flooding back. She remembered the computer hurting her and next she was outside, and she had felt ill and blacked out.

My name is Jennifer – just Jennifer.

She remembered the large room with the three life support capsules, there was one empty and she was now lying inside it. She raised her hands and ran her fingers over the lid in search of a catch so she could open the lid and escape. She could not find anything, and she hit the lid with her fists in frustration, she screamed out for release.

There was a sudden hiss and the lid swung away to one side. She clambered slowly out of the capsule and stood by it and looked round the room, she was alone amongst the machinery. She looked down at herself and found the long white nightgown had gone and she wore a white blouse and black skirt. She looked down at her feet, she had on long white socks and blue trainers. She was glad she was suitably dressed for going outside as she was going to try her hardest to get out of this place she was trapped in. She checked the other two capsules and they were still occupied by her effigies, she hoped she did not bump into the third on her way out. She left the room by the same door she had gone through the last time she was in the room. Out in the familiar passage she decided to take the left turn. She came to a dead end, a wall with a window in it, she found how to open it and she clambered out of it; the ground luckily was not far from the window and she was soon standing outside the building.

It was dark and her eyes automatically switched to night vision and she could see clearly all that was around her. She took several deep breaths; she was not feeling dizzy like the first time she had managed to get outside. It brought a thought to her mind she did not like. Was she the same Jennifer or just another effigy? She suddenly felt like a rat in a maze going through several tests, if she went through the tests successfully, what sort of reward would she receive?

They have to be sure you are strong and intelligent enough, to survive any vigorous and dangerous test they can throw at you.

If she did not survive, they had another replacement ready to take over from her.

Expendable – that's the word.

'Being almost roasted alive by a power surge was a test, was it?' she asked, as she stared up at the night sky.

She looked about for the best direction to take. She was close to a boundary fence, she had to find the gate and avoid being seen. She kept close to the wall of the building and moved forward until she came to the end of it and she found another single storey building close by. She moved on to the back of the next building and ducked under windows until she got to the other end. A few yards in front of her was a huge concrete pylon which held the immense dish of a radio telescope. Next to it was the observatory building. There was a track running across the front of it; she decided to follow it and see where it would lead her. She came across several people she did not know, and they ignored her. The track went to a T-junction, the left track would take her back into the heart of the compound. She took the right path, which passed by the security hut. The track then curved to the right close to a second radio telescope. Turning, she spied the main gate which was shut. When she got to the main gate she gazed at the control box. She ran her long fingers over the keypad; she worked fast and in deep concentration, until the gate slid open.

Eureka!

A voice shouted behind her and she saw the security guard coming towards her. She did not wait to see what he wanted – she ran out of the compound.

Step One: Find freedom. Accomplished.

Step Two: Find the Ginger-haired girl.

She turned right. Something whined over her head; she looked up at the night sky. She walked along the path and she came to a high hill which was on the right side of the path. There were some young people on the summit; she walked round it, keeping an eye on the boys and girls above her. As she approached the overgrown copse she gazed up at the hill and saw a tall girl standing with her back to her. She noticed the long silvery hair being ruffled by the wind. Something whistled past her head. A little while later the girl standing on the hill toppled over backwards and started to roll down the hill. She stepped back and the body landed at her feet. She knelt down and placed a hand on the chest and detected no heartbeat, she took hold of the limp wrist and felt for a pulse and found none, and her effigy was quite dead.

Better her than me.

She dragged the body into the overgrown copse; she heard more whining noises in the sky. Something was coming, but what? She thought it would be best if she kept hidden in the safety of the overgrown copse, while there was so much activity around the hill. She sat on the ground and waited for the commotion outside the copse to die down.

Sometime later she heard someone enter the overgrown copse; and a torch beam stabbed the darkness. She stood up and moved away from the body. She saw a tall girl come into view – she carried a torch and she had long ginger hair. The girl inhaled deeply: her quarry was in reach. The girl of her dreams came to the body, while the girl studied the body the girl moved round to get behind her. She brought her right arm round the girl's body and clamped her left hand over the jaw.

'Don't struggle please, I could easily break your neck,' she told her captive.

She gave the girl a demonstration of her strength. She gripped the girl's chin and turned her head round.

'I don't want to hurt you, but I can if I must. I will release you if you promise not to shout out, nod your head,' she whispered in her ear.

After a moment the ginger haired girl nodded her head, Jennifer released her and stood back and watched the tall girl turn and shine a torch in her face, Jennifer blinked and studied the girl in front of her. She found the expression of shock interesting; it was the same shock she felt seeing the vision of her dreams standing in front of her. After a while Jennifer smiled and held out her hand.

'Hello, I'm Jennifer.'

PART THREE:

VICTIMS

CHAPTER XXII:

SAMANTHA AND JENNIFER

OCTOBER 2128

Samantha could only stand and gape at the girl in disbelief. Was this another clone?

'I don't understand,' Samantha said at last.

The silver blonde girl moved close to her.

'I don't want your understanding, I just need you to tell me what is going on around here,' Jennifer demanded.

Samantha switched off the torch and gazed at the luminous blue eyes in front of her. They had something in common at least.

'Don't ask me, they tell me nothing,' Samantha assured her.

Jennifer grabbed her arm.

'Why don't you take me to your home and tell me your story and I'll tell you mine,' Jennifer advised.

Samantha gazed down at the body of the clone, it was bloated, and the face was a melted mess.

'If you are thinking I killed her, I can assure you, I didn't.'

'I don't know of any weapon that can do that to a body,' Samantha said.

'Yes, it's a mess all right, I'm just glad it was her and not me,' Jennifer said.

Samantha grinned at her.

'It was you, that's a clone.' The ice blue eyes lit up.

'Of course, I should have realised.'

They walked out of the overgrown copse.

'Whoever killed it might still be about,' Samantha said.

'Now there's a sobering thought,' Jennifer observed.

Samantha made her way home and Jennifer followed her; the dark night sky was quiet as last. When they got to the house, they entered by the back door. Jennifer sat at the table and Samantha went around the house and found out Naomi had not come back. Back in the kitchen she made coffee for them both; she could not wait to learn about this Jennifer.

'Can you cook?' Jennifer inquired.

Samantha nodded and gave her guest a mug of coffee.

'Good, I can't remember the last time I had a meal. I will tell you my story while you knock up something for me, if you will be so kind.'

'I'd be glad to.'

Samantha set about fixing a meal for her guest, while Jennifer told her story in a calm level voice. She kept her eyes on Samantha as she moved round the kitchen. Jennifer made a concentrated study of the ginger-haired girl to see if she was a threat to her like her image in the dreams. Jennifer needed to know. At the moment Samantha was pleasant enough, after the initial shock of seeing her for the first time and the death of her effigy.

Samantha was aware of the eyes following her around the room, she felt like a specimen on a slide under a microscope. She glanced at Jennifer on several occasions while she worked, the face was a mask of concentration, not on the story being told, but on her – Samantha was being assessed and evaluated.

When Jennifer had finished talking, she sat at the table and dug ravenously into what Samantha had prepared for her. Samantha sat opposite her.

'I'm glad I wasn't having all the fun,' Samantha said.

Samantha gave Jennifer details of her own history, which as far as her memory was concerned, started like Jennifer at the age of twelve. Jennifer listened while she ate, she found the story intriguing. She told Samantha to tell all no matter how trivial it might seem. Samantha told her about the dreams which had either Jennifer or her effigy, Jennifer Russell, Samantha did not know which. When Samantha had finished Jennifer realised, they had the same enemy, a girl named Lavonia. She sat back in silence and her mind sifted through the data Samantha had given her. After a while she stood up and moved to the other side of the table and stood close to Samantha, who stared up at the ice blue eyes.

'You say the effigy made you sick to the stomach, when she stood close to you. What do you feel, now I'm standing close to you?' Jennifer asked.

Samantha had never thought of it until this girl mentioned it. No, she did not have the same feelings, for which Samantha was glad. She looked the girl up and down; there were several differences now she was studying the girl more closely. This Jennifer was taller and not so thin, the face was prettier too. It had a mischievous smile as opposed to the sly grin of the effigy.

'If you aren't a threat to me, then I am no threat to you. I had to contact you to find out,' Jennifer said.

'We are both in need of answers, we would be in a better position if we worked together to get them,' Samantha advised.

Samantha stifled a yawn with the back of her hand; Jennifer placed a hand on her shoulder.

'You are tired, you must get some sleep. I have had enough sleep to last me a while, I shall stay up and protect you and the house while you sleep,' Jennifer said.

Samantha stood up and left the room and went up to her bedroom. Samantha could not afford to put her complete trust in Jennifer, so she locked her door just in case. Jennifer went into the lounge and sat on the couch. She did not put on the light in case a killer was prowling outside. She thought about the girl sleeping upstairs and decided she liked Samantha and hoped they would eventually trust each other. At the moment they had just met and obviously would not be sure of each other and what they could be capable of.

Suddenly her senses were alerted to sounds outside the window, someone was outside. Jennifer was up in an instant. She left the room and heard someone at the front door. Jennifer stood close to the wall as the door started to open and a dark figure entered the house. As the door was closed Jennifer switched on the light. The burglar wore a dark brown coat with a hood; the person wearing it turned and faced Jennifer, who smiled at the familiar face.

'Hello Valerie, what can I do for you?' Jennifer asked.

Valerie Peterson hugged and kissed the girl and then stood back.

'I'm glad to see you are still in one piece.'

'Which is more than can be said for my effigy,' Jennifer said.

The smile faded from Valerie's face. 'You know what happened to the clone?'

Jennifer's mind raced, clone, of course. Jennifer told her friend about finding the body and meeting up with the girl in her dreams.

'Why was I cloned?'

'We didn't know if you were coming out of the coma you were born in. You are vital to the work being done here, if we couldn't have you, we would have to settle for the next best thing, so three clones were made from your cells,' Valerie explained.

Jennifer sat on the stairs and looked up at Valerie.

'The person who killed the clone will be coming after me next?'

Valerie nodded her head. Someone had tried once to kill Jennifer so it was reasonable to assume they would try again. Valerie had dressed Jennifer in the clothes while she had been unconscious after her first entry to the outside and the elements. After the dreams Jennifer had had of a ginger-haired girl, she had made enquiries and came up with Samantha. She knew Jennifer would want to meet her, so Valerie had worked to get Jennifer her wish and made it easy for her to get outside.

'You think I'll be safer outside with more places to hide, than the environment I escaped from?'

'It would be reasonable to think so, if you can befriend this girl, Samantha, it would be a help. Because she is a danger in your dreams, does not mean she is a threat to you in real life. You must evaluate the dream for what it is, just a dream,' Valerie said.

'I already have, and I must confess I like the girl, though naturally we are still suspicious of each other,' Jennifer said.

Valerie ran a hand soothingly over Jennifer's cheek.

'Take care, Jenny,' Valerie said.

'I will and you do the same,' Jennifer said.

Valerie Peterson left the house and Jennifer shut the door and returned to the lounge. She went to Samantha's work desk and activated her desk top computer and hacked into the computer system in the Lab 3 building. She was after data on their cloning program.

Samantha woke in the first light of dawn; she slid out of bed and unlocked her door and went to the bathroom for a shower. Later she entered the lounge with a mug of tea for her guest; she found Jennifer curled up on the sofa. She sat on the edge of the sofa and Jennifer's eyes flashed open. Samantha offered her the mug of tea and she took it and sipped it.

'I had a visitor while you were asleep, she told me they had found the body of Jennifer Russell, no wonder you didn't get on with her, the clone was an inferior model, I'm afraid,' Jennifer said.

'Let's hope they don't use the other two clones in the life support capsules, you told me about,' Samantha said.

'So, do I – it would mean I'd be incapacitated, or worse, dead,' Jennifer said.

'I'd gladly watch your back for you,' Samantha said, sincerely.

Jennifer put the empty mug on the floor and moved closer to Samantha and kissed her on the cheek.

'That's very nice of you; I think we are going to be good friends.'

Samantha smiled at her and tried to determine what kind of a girl Jennifer was. One thing was obvious, she was only going to display as much of her intelligence that she wanted Samantha to know about. Samantha was not going to be fooled by the mischievous smile Jennifer flashed often.

'Only time will tell. Have you decided what you are going to do next?' Samantha inquired.

Jennifer stood up.

'I want to have a look round the Russell cottage; you can show me where it is.'

'Do you want to go now?'

Jennifer nodded and Samantha stood up and they left the house.

'No time like the present,' Jennifer said.

They walked leisurely along the track running from the house towards the main housing estate. Jennifer wondered why Samantha was isolated from everyone else, she was sure Samantha was not unhappy about the situation, as she had said, it had been hard to make friends.

Dark clouds in the sky started to shed rain on them. Jennifer gazed up at the sky and let the rain run over her face.

'Are you enjoying the rain?'

'It's a new experience.'

They got to the end of the track and turned right into the main estate, there were four houses on each side of the track, and the ninth was on the end of the estate facing them, where Jennifer and Angie lived. Samantha went to the front door and found it open; she entered the house followed by Jennifer. They looked round the rooms on the ground floor; finding nothing of interest they went up the stairs. The first bedroom they came to belonged to the little girl Angie. The curtains covered the windows and it was a real grey day, the room was dark, Jennifer scanned the room with her night vision, Samantha went to the next bedroom. Something caught her eye and Jennifer moved cautiously across the room. She spied a tiny spark of green light coming from behind the wardrobe. Jennifer pulled it away from the wall. Behind the wardrobe on the floor was a satchel and a green glow was emanating from it. She called for Samantha.

Samantha was soon standing close to Jennifer, as she picked up the satchel by the strap and took it to the bed.

'What have we here, I wonder,' Jennifer said.

'Be careful,' Samantha warned.

Jennifer slowly opened the satchel and gazed down at the green glowing globe at the bottom of the satchel. She felt the cold energy touch her right hand, as she moved down into the satchel, the coldness touched her fingers, and it brought goose pimples all over her body. Jennifer felt her energy ebbing away. Jennifer withdrew her hand, she felt dizzy and fell against Samantha who stood beside her. Samantha put an arm round her waist and supported her.

'How do you feel?' Samantha asked, her voice full of concern.

'I suddenly felt weak, as if something was sucking the energy from my body,' Jennifer said.

'Some objects we have been tracking in space, fell to Earth last night – that object in the satchel could be part of one of the objects,' Samantha said.

'See if you can find a suitcase,' Jennifer said.

Samantha went into the other bedroom and found a suitcase and brought it back to Jennifer, who was sitting on the bed. She laid the suitcase on the bed and Jennifer gingerly placed the satchel inside it and then closed down the top.

'You look rough,' Samantha said.

Jennifer looked up at Samantha as she stood over her; she held the suitcase.

'I haven't fully recovered from that power surge that nearly killed me. My body is still in a weakened state,' Jennifer explained.

Samantha held out her free hand and Jennifer took it and let Samantha pull her up from the bed.

'Then the sooner we get back to my house, the sooner I can pack you off to bed,' Samantha said.

Jennifer gave her a weary smile; the belief she had nothing to fear from Samantha was getting stronger.

'I like you, Samantha, you have no reason to trust me, but you care that I'm not feeling well.'

'We can't work together if there is mistrust between us, I shall trust you, Jennifer, and you have not given me reason not to. And you can be sure I have no thoughts of bringing harm to you in any way.'

Jennifer kissed her on the cheek.

'We are going to make a good team, you and I,' Jennifer said.

Jennifer walked out of the room. Samantha watched her retreating back, and she ran her free hand over the cheek Jennifer had kissed. Samantha had to admit she was warming to Jennifer. They left the house and Samantha led Jennifer between the two houses belonging to Janice and Juliet, so she could get home quicker by the short cut. When they got there, Samantha ordered Jennifer to bed and the girl did not argue. She went to the spare room and collapsed onto the bed and dozed off.

Jennifer woke at midday, a blanket had been draped over her body, and she pulled it away and stretched herself and then got off the bed. She went to the bathroom and undressed. She got under the shower and gave a deep sigh as the warm water flowed over her nude body.

Ecstasy.

Jennifer stood still and let the water run over her, she was going to enjoy the pleasure of the shower to the full. Her mind was sharp and alert; she had some work to do on her body to get herself to a hundred per cent fitness. After a while she turned off the shower and dried herself and got dressed. She went down the stairs and Samantha was just entering the house by the front door.

'I'm glad you are awake at last, I have something to tell you,' Samantha said.

They went into the lounge and sat on the couch. Samantha had discovered Angie was very ill and near death. Steven had been found unconscious on the hill and Janice had been pulled out of the marsh by Naomi. All three were in the infirmary. The General had caught up with her and told her about Jennifer and he had asked Samantha if she had seen her. Samantha lied and said she had not, though Samantha was sure he did not believe her. Jennifer thanked her for not giving her away.

'If the General wants to get you, he will have to catch you himself,' Samantha said.

Samantha got up and left the room, Jennifer sat back on the couch. Samantha returned with two mugs of coffee and she gave Jennifer one and sat next to her.

'What are you going to do now?' Samantha asked.

'I want to look in on the little girl Angie, perhaps we can help her.'

'What can we do, we aren't medical students?' Samantha said.

'I think that thing we found in the satchel is the cause of her illness, you told me your speciality is physics, so you should be able to find out something about it.'

Samantha shook her head; she did not have the same faith in her abilities that Jennifer seemed to have.

'Sometimes I wish I'd never been born,' Samantha decided.

Jennifer grinned at her and their eyes met.

'I get the same feeling,' Jennifer agreed.

Jennifer put her arm round Samantha's waist and kissed her cheek.

'About me, or yourself?' Samantha wondered.

Jennifer giggled, this girl was sharp, and she was going to enjoy working with Samantha.

'That's something your simulacrum could never achieve.'

'What's that?'

'A smile and a laugh – the clone was cold as ice,' Samantha explained.

'It was an inferior model; I hope they do better with the next one.'

'I hope there isn't a next one, you are a much better person,' Samantha said.

Jennifer moved closer to Samantha and was glad she did not pull away.

'I hope you did not mind, but that was a nice thing you said about me,' Jennifer said softly.

Jennifer gazed at Samantha's face and the warm smile on it. Then she stood up and held out her hand and Samantha took it and Jennifer pulled her up onto her feet.

'Does this make you feel uncomfortable?' Jennifer asked.

Samantha shook her head. 'No, I feel pleasure from your touch; you have a better figure than me.'

Jennifer smiled and kissed her on the cheek.

CHAPTER XXIII:

THE INFIRMARY

They made their way to the infirmary, Samantha leading the way. She decided to take the long way round as there were too many soldiers patrolling around the direct route. It was still raining and Samantha gave Jennifer a coat to wear, it had a hood and she had it pulled over her head, to hide her silver blonde hair rather than just to keep her head dry. They crossed the moorland at the back of the house towards the estate, they passed along the alley between the houses of Juliet and Janice then crossed the track and passed up the alley between John and Steven's houses. The ground beyond that was part woodland and they walked along the tree line until they got to the rear of the infirmary and entered the building by the back door. Jennifer kept the hood of the coat up over her head to hide her silver blonde hair. They entered the ward room and went to the closest bed where Steven Calvert lay unconscious. Jennifer wandered to the next bed which contained a curly haired girl – she was very beautiful, Jennifer noted. A girl sat at the bedside, she gazed at Jennifer with dark suspicious eyes.

'What do you want?' the girl asked.

Samantha joined them and told Juliet about Jennifer and explained to her that the Jennifer Russell she knew was a clone.

'Are you serious?' Juliet asked, dumbfounded.

'Absolutely, believe me, Juliet, I'm not going to invent a story like that,' Samantha said.

Juliet shook her head, she had to believe Samantha's tale as it was not stranger to what had happened to Steven and Janice.

'OK, Samantha, I believe you.'

Juliet went to Jennifer and pulled the hood over her head and gazed at the ice blue eyes.

'Not much improvement – this Jennifer is just as ugly,' Juliet observed, amusingly.

'You'll have to excuse Juliet, she has a bad sense of humour,' Samantha said.

'Damn right, Sammy.'

Samantha shook her head and looked towards Jennifer.

'See what I mean?' Samantha asked Juliet how Janice was. 'We are still waiting for her to come round.'

Jennifer moved to the next bed which contained a girl of nine. She went to the head of the bed, she lifted up the thin wrist and felt for a pulse, it was very weak, which showed her life was hanging by a thread. The little girl's eyes flickered open and stared at her.

'Jenny.' The voice was weak and trembling.

'What was it?'

Jennifer sat on the edge of the bed and held the little girl's right hand.

'A green globe, so cold, it hurts,' Angie murmured in a weakened voice.

Jennifer ran a hand over the girl's forehead.

'You'll make me well again, won't you, Jenny? I love you and I know I can count on you.'

Jennifer felt her eyes water – it told Jennifer that she cared about this little girl. Angie slipped into unconsciousness,

'I don't think I can, Angie.'

Tears slid down her pale cheeks, this was a new feeling and it had brought tears to her eyes. A man in a white coat came up to her.

'We've done all we can, it's up to Angie now,' Dr Forbes said.

Samantha approached them and Jennifer stood up and wiped her eyes with the back of her hand. Samantha asked if she could see the report on Angie's illness. Dr Forbes took them to his office, and he went to the filing cabinet and took out Angie's file and handed it to Samantha. She looked through it, while Jennifer stayed by the door; she had pulled the hood over her head again. The door opened and hit her in the back; Jennifer turned and sighed deeply, as she stared at the General.

'Oho,' Jennifer mumbled.

General Heywood stood close to Jennifer like an avenging angel.

'The game is up,' Samantha said.

Jennifer stared at General Heywood.

'You've come to take me away?'

'We are worried about you, Jennifer; you are not strong enough to be running around.'

Jennifer's face went red with anger.

'I'm tired of being locked up in a white room and treated like an exhibit in a freak show.'

Samantha raised her eyebrows at the show of anger; it was similar to the anger of the clone. Samantha also felt an ache in her head, the first time she had felt that while she had been with this Jennifer.

'Your clone Jennifer Russell has been destroyed – who's going to mourn poor Angie?' Jennifer said.

General Heywood found himself in the full glare of Jennifer's ice-blue eyes.

'I want to be here for Angie, she is alone, like me. I have nowhere to run, Samantha can vouch for that.'

Jennifer switched her gaze to Samantha, who nodded in agreement. There was nowhere to go, they were stuck here.

'Is it too much to ask, for Angie to have something familiar in front of her. Would you deny Angie a friend in her hour of need?' Jennifer said.

'Jennifer can stay with me, she'll be there if you want her,' Samantha said.

'It all comes down to your trust in us, or the lack of it.'

'Well said, Jenny,' Samantha echoed.

General Heywood consented to let Jennifer have her way; she was a strong-willed person, just like Samantha. He had not wanted the two girls coming together yet, but now it was too late. He had to hope they would not have a volatile relationship – at the moment they seemed to be getting on.

'I want you to realise this, someone has tried to kill you once, they will obviously try again,' he warned.

'I haven't forgotten, they'll find it hard a second time, they'll find me a dangerous adversary,' Jennifer said, with ice in her voice.

General Heywood studied her face, the eyes had bluer in them, there was no doubt Jennifer meant what she said. They still did not know what her full capabilities were, she was a genius with computers, but what other secrets she had in her head could only be guessed at. Perhaps they would learn more about Jennifer if they let her out on a short leash. He hoped Jennifer would not prove to be a problem Samantha could not solve. He turned away and strode out of the office.

'Is anyone going to tell me what is going on?' Dr Forbes said, as he stared straight at Jennifer.

Samantha left the office and let Jennifer explain to the doctor who she was. Samantha walked past Juliet sitting at Janice's bedside and went to Steven's bed. The boy was awake, and he gazed up at her and gave her a pained smile.

'How are you feeling?'

Apart from a splitting headache and his body aching all over and being asked a lot of awkward questions he had no answers for, he felt fine. Steven told her he could not remember what had happened to him. Jennifer joined them and Steven gave her a surprised look.

'The General told me you were dead.'

Jennifer gave him a wry smile.

'The reports of my death were highly exaggerated,' Jennifer said.

Juliet came up behind Jennifer.

'That's a shame.'

Jennifer laughed and Juliet gazed at her in surprise.

'That's strange: your clone was not renowned for its sense of humour,' Juliet said.

'Oh, I am, I'm famous for my sense of humour, just ask Samantha.'

Steven wanted to know what they were talking about and Samantha told him that the girl who was found dead was a clone, made from Jennifer's cells. Juliet went back to her friend's bed and saw with delight that Janice had her eyes open.

'What happened to you, Jan?'

Janice felt weak and she had a headache, she could not remember what had happened to her in the night. She saw Jennifer and asked Juliet what she was doing here. She was not worried about what had happened to them.

'That is Jennifer, it seems she was cloned and that gave us Jennifer Russell, the one we know and love; I don't think,' Juliet informed her.

Janice tried to sit up and Juliet helped her and pulled the pillows up against her back.

'I hope she has a better disposition than the clone,' Janice said.

'She told us she had a sense of humour,' Juliet said.

'That'd be a first,' Janice said.

Juliet laughed and Samantha came up to her to see what laughter was for. Seeing Janice sitting up, Samantha asked her how she was feeling.

'Rough,' Janice said.

Samantha found out Janice was in the same boat as Steven, as she had no idea what had happened to her. Janice asked about her new friend and Samantha told her Jennifer's tale. When she finished Janice stared hard at her.

'You believe her?' Janice asked.

Samantha nodded her head.

'I don't think she has a reason to lie to me, she is desperate for answers just like me.'

Samantha turned to see where Jennifer was and saw her talking to Steven; she turned back to Janice.

'I'm going to watch her carefully before I fully trust her, but at the moment I don't think she's a danger to us.'

Janice reached out and took Samantha's hand.

'Just be careful, Sam,' she warned.

'I will, Jan, don't fear.'

CHAPTER XXIV:

EUREKA

Jennifer woke next morning with the sun shining on her face; she stretched out her body, then sat up and gazed out of the window. She had enjoyed her first day of freedom and was looking forward to the second. A few white clouds crossed the blue sky. Jennifer got out of bed and left the bedroom and entered the bathroom. A few minutes later she made her way down the stairs, then went into the back room that was kitted out as a gymnasium. Jennifer had decided to give her body a workout. She gave her body a hard time with the exercise apparatus. After half an hour Jennifer was panting hard and sweating profusely. Her heart beat rapidly inside her chest. She wore a black bra and matching panties.

'You put up a good show, Jenny.'

Jennifer looked towards the door and stared at Samantha, who stood watching her. Jennifer wondered how long she had been there.

'My body needs knocking into shape, I shan't survive if I don't keep myself strong and fit,' Jennifer explained.

Jennifer walked up to Samantha.

'Is it that bad?' Samantha asked.

'The power surge that hit me turned my hair silvery, what it did to my body, I can only guess.'

You are paying the price for not being vigilant.

Jennifer walked past her and went up to the bathroom and took off her bra and panties. She got under the shower; the hot water ran over her sweaty body. She closed her eyes and let her mind drift away.

I'll be more careful this time.

Too late – You are dying.

Jennifer opened her eyes and saw Samantha standing by the door watching her.

No, I am indestructible.

Jennifer got out of the shower; Samantha gazed at her naked body; as she handed her a large towel and Jennifer started drying her wet body.

We'll see.

Jennifer put on her underwear and went to the spare room, Samantha followed behind her. Valerie Peterson had sent over some clothes for Jennifer to wear. She went to the wardrobe and gazed at the selection of clothes inside it. She took out a black dress and put it on; she twirled round in front of Samantha.

'How do I look?' Jennifer asked.

Samantha ran her eyes over Jennifer from head to foot. The girl had a fuller figure than her and Samantha was slightly envious.

'Very sexy,' Samantha said, truthfully.

Jennifer moved close to Samantha and kissed her on the cheek.

'You are a real darling – do you know that?'

They went down the stairs and went into the kitchen to start preparing breakfast. Jennifer suddenly felt faint and Samantha noticed her face was paler.

'Are you all right, you look terrible?'

'I think I overdid it with the exercising. My body wasn't ready for such punishment. My conscience is annoyed at my lack of sense,' Jennifer said.

Jennifer sat in a chair and Samantha stood over her.

'I wouldn't worry about that, my conscience gave up on me a long time ago,' Samantha said with a smile.

An hour later they were standing by the main gate of the Research Complex. The security guard stared at Jennifer in suspicion, as he checked her pass.

'Why couldn't you have used this the last time you went through the gate,' he said.

'I was in a hurry,' Jennifer said.

The guard gave Jennifer back her pass and she put it in the pocket of her black dress. She followed Samantha across the compound to the long single storey building that housed the labs 1 and 2. They went straight through the main doors and turned left; they entered a small room filled with safe deposit boxes. Samantha went to the one with her own personal number on it. She opened the safe and took out a large lead-lined box. She shut the safe door and carried the lead box out of the room; Jennifer followed behind her. They entered another room and they crossed it to another door, and it slid open. They entered a room full of lockers; Samantha went to the locker that was her own and opened it and took out a white lab coat and put it on. She took out another and gave it to Jennifer who also put it on. Samantha gave her an anti-radiation badge to clip onto her lapel, Samantha clipped one on her lapel and she shut the locker. They left the locker room and turned left and went through another door. They entered the first laboratory room, and Jennifer went to the computer room. Samantha went to a work bench and placed the lead box on it. She put on a pair of protective gloves and then opened the lead-lined box. The green faceted globe sat on the bottom of the box. A cold green light touched her face. She stared transfixed at the glowing globe which shimmered with different shades of green.

Visions suddenly filled her mind; particles of her past dreams came to her. Samantha kept her eyes locked on the green globe. Her mind was being filled with things she had not experienced before, alien things and worlds of difference.

Jennifer sat at the computer control desk. She went through the data Samantha had collected on the strange green globe, she had worked hard, and Jennifer was very pleased with her work rate. She was impressed; Samantha had a good brain. As she stared at the data her eyes started to blur and she suddenly felt she was looking through a green mist. Jennifer blinked her eyes; something strange was happening to her and her mind was wandering; she had experienced something similar, if she could only remember. The computer was no longer in front of her; Jennifer was somehow looking through the eyes of another person.

Eureka!

CHAPTER XXV:

MIND TRANSFERENCE

Jennifer tried to stand, and the swivel chair slid away from her. Jennifer fell to the floor; she felt sick. Jennifer crawled along the floor towards the exit door. When she got there she struggled to her feet, then she moved through the doorway and she saw Samantha standing by the work bench as she stared in a trance down at the green globe in the lead box. It was drawing her mind into it; Jennifer knew she had to get to Samantha quickly before she lost her mind to it. When she eventually reached the work bench, Jennifer closed the lid on the lead box. She then grabbed Samantha roughly and spun her round; the bright green eyes were staring through her.

'It's you,' Jennifer shouted.

Jennifer slapped Samantha hard on the right cheek; Samantha blinked her eyes and then stared at Jennifer's face. She moved closer to Samantha and kissed her lightly on the lips. For a few seconds they stared at each other. Samantha's mind began to clear of the alien images brought to it by the glowing green globe. She was back to reality. She smiled at Jennifer.

'Thanks, you saved my mind.'

Jennifer felt relieved, she did not like slapping Samantha, she did not want to hurt the girl, but it was the only action she could think of at the time, to bring Samantha out of the trance.

'I'm sorry I struck you, I hope I did not hurt you too much,' Jennifer apologized.

Samantha shook her head.

'It's lucky you did, I was seeing things not of this Earth, the visions were completely alien, and I thought my dreams were bad enough.'

Jennifer ran her hand over the cheek she had slapped and caressed it gently.

'I had a dream, it contained a girl who looked like you, she bashed my head in and ate my brains,' Jennifer said.

Samantha brought her right arm up and held the hand that caressed her cheek.

'I don't eat brains, they're bad for the digestion,' Samantha said.

Jennifer burst out laughing and Samantha joined her; she could not remember the last time she had had a good laugh. Jennifer kissed her.

'I want to be your friend, Samantha,' Jennifer said.

Jennifer moved away from her and Samantha turned and picked up the lead-lined box.

'You are, Jenny, I like you very much.'

Jennifer's face beamed; she was happy to know Samantha was enjoying her company. They went to the safe deposit room and Samantha locked away the lead box. Then they went to the locker room, Samantha took off her white lab coat and hung it up in her locker, she then sat on a bench and watched as Jennifer removed her white coat and hand it up inside the locker. Samantha tried to get her thoughts into perspective about this new Jennifer. She got no bad vibes when she was close to her like she had done with Jennifer Russell. Samantha was sure there was no danger represented by Jennifer and the girl truly wanted to be her friend. Jennifer was taking charge in their relationship and Samantha did not mind that. She had a conceited air about her but that was to be expected as Samantha was well aware of the girl's intelligence. Jennifer was aware of her importance. Samantha liked the mischievous smile that Jennifer gave on occasions, when she decided to keep the essence of herself locked in her brain. Samantha knew the girl was keeping things from her. Jennifer was going to keep an air of mysteriousness about her.

Jennifer shut the locker door and turned and noticed Samantha watching her intently. She gave the girl a smile; she moved to the bench and placed her hand on Samantha's knees.

'A penny for your thoughts,' Jennifer said.

'I was thinking about you.'

Jennifer gave her a wide grin.

'Nothing bad, I hope.'

Samantha shook her head.

'Of course not, what possible bad thoughts could I have about you?'

Samantha stood up as Jennifer beamed at her, the ice blue eyes went a darker hue and a wicked smile crossed her thin lips. She threw her arms round Samantha and hugged her.

'I can see we are going to get on like a house on fire,' Jennifer said.

CHAPTER XXVI:

THE THING IN THE ...
BLOCKHOUSE

They left the building and Samantha suddenly decided to have a look at the large concrete blockhouse in the middle of the compound. Jennifer followed her. When they got there Jennifer gazed wonderingly at it.

'I wonder what they've got hidden in there,' Jennifer said.

'So, do I – do you have any suggestions of how we can get in there?'

Jennifer's face shined and the wicked smile was back.

'Just leave it to the expert. If I open it; you'll have to give me a kiss,' Jennifer said.

Jennifer went to the door on the front of the blockhouse and ran her expert eye over the electronic lock. Samantha stood beside her.

Jennifer's nimble fingers ran over the keypad. Samantha was amazed at the speed she went at her work. Her face was a mask of concentration; her brain was fixed in a computation mode. After a while there was a sound of a click and a hiss of sound and the door slid open. Jennifer gazed triumphantly at Samantha.

'Nothing to it,' Jennifer said.

'You're a genius.'

'I know,' Jennifer declared.

Jennifer reset the electronic lock and the door slid shut.

'We'll come back when it's dark and see what they have in there,' Jennifer said.

Samantha started walking quickly towards the main gate – Jennifer had to run to catch up with her.

Jennifer walked past her and Samantha laughed and quickly caught up with her. At the main gate Samantha met Sarah Mullen; Jennifer passed by and left the compound.

'Hullo Sarah, long time no see,' Samantha said.

'General Heywood has been keeping me busy as his private secretary,' Sarah said.

'That'll keep you out of mischief, that should please your father,' Samantha said.

'Which is more than I can say for your friend – they are not very happy she has teamed up with you. I hope she has a better temperament, than her double,' Sarah said.

'Jennifer is a much better person,' Samantha assured her.

'Look after yourself,' Sarah said.

Samantha walked through the gateway and went in search of Jennifer. She found her standing by her front door, Jennifer asked about her friend and Samantha explained who Sarah was as she opened her door and they entered the house. They went into the lounge.

'Someone is not very pleased we are together,' Samantha told Jennifer.

'I wouldn't worry about it, that's their problem,' Jennifer said.

Jennifer sat on the couch and pulled the hem of her black dress up her thighs. She gazed at the ice blue eyes staring up at her. Samantha wished she could see inside her head. Jennifer grabbed her hand and pulled Samantha down onto her lap. Jennifer pulled the hem of the maroon skirt Samantha wore; further up her slim thighs and ran her hands over the cool pale skin.

'I hope you don't mind me taking liberties with your shapely thighs.'

'Your legs are better than mine,' Samantha said.

Jennifer bent her fingers and ran her long nails across the skin on the inside of Samantha's right thigh.

'You don't cut your nails very often,' Samantha said.

Jennifer giggled and kissed her on the cheek.

'Are you being naughty; Jenny?'

'You are a lovely girl, Sam.'

Jennifer got up and stood in front of Samantha and kissed her on the cheek.

'If we are going out tonight, you'd better get some rest,' Samantha said.

Jennifer got off the couch and left the room and went up to her bedroom. She lay on the bed, she closed her eyes and thought of Samantha. Jennifer was very glad her dreams were wrong; she liked the girl very much and they were getting very close.

Jennifer dozed off a very happy girl. Samantha sat in the kitchen drinking a mug of strong sweet tea. She was thinking of Jennifer; the girl was testing her emotions. The clone did it in the nastiest way possible, but Jennifer was the complete opposite; Samantha hoped there was nothing nasty hidden behind her nice characteristics.

At midnight Samantha entered Jennifer's room with a mug of coffee. She switched on the light and saw Jennifer lying on the bed. Samantha sat on the edge of the bed and ran a hand over Jennifer's cheek, her eyes were closed, and the pale face was in a serene sleep. After a while the eyes flashed open and stared at her.

'I'm sorry, did I startle you?'

Jennifer sat up and took the mug of coffee from her and sipped it.

'No, you didn't,' Jennifer said.

Jennifer placed her free hand on Samantha's left thigh and felt the warm texture of her skin.

'I heard you enter the room.' The hand moved further up Samantha's thigh.

'Do you feel ready to go out?' Samantha asked.

Jennifer nodded and drank her coffee and placed the empty mug on the bedside table; she sat on the edge of the bed beside Samantha and kissed her lightly on the lips. Samantha felt her hand caress the inside of her right thigh.

'I hope you don't mind me taking liberties with your shapely legs?'

Samantha shook her head; Jennifer's touch was electric. Samantha pulled the hem of her dark blue skirt up to the tops of her slim thighs. Jennifer saw she wore a pair of white panties. Jennifer rubbed her hand over the front of the panties.

'I take no offence with your touch, I like it,' Samantha said.

Jennifer gazed at the long shapely legs as she ran her hand over them.

'I'm glad you like it, I'm very fond of you and I'm going to be very good to you.'

Jennifer kissed her on the cheek.

'You are a good girl, Sam.'

Samantha felt the wandering hand move up and down the inside of her right thigh; it felt hot on her cool skin; the other hand lay on the front of her panties.

Jennifer bent her fingers and ran her long sharp fingernails along the soft skin it brought shivers down her thigh. Jennifer did the same to Samantha's left thigh.

'Do you like that?'

'You know I do, Jenny.'

Jennifer grinned and kissed her again and rubbed her body against her.

'When you were gazing in that green globe in that fixed trance, you were transferring the images into my mind, then I realised I was looking through your eyes. You are important to me, Sam, you really are,' Jennifer explained.

'You are a strange girl, Jenny. You are important to me also.'

Jennifer was pleased to hear that and gave Samantha a big hug and kissed her several times; then stood up.

'You're telepathic, I don't think your thoughts are any more fantastic than my own,' Samantha said.

Samantha stood up and Jennifer moved close to her, their bodies touched. Samantha enjoyed being close to the girl, it made her feel good and nothing throbbed inside her head. She was sure it was something to do with Jennifer.

'I'm not telepathic, the way you mean it. I detect your feelings and emotions and read you from them.'

Samantha was drawn to Jennifer's hypnotic eyes; they were no longer ice blue, but a darker blue. As well as being mysterious, Jennifer was a very hypnotic person, she wanted to pull away, but the smile on the thin lips put her at ease.

'I can probe your mind, but not without your permission.'

Samantha was interested in that – perhaps Jennifer could detect her hidden memories.

'I give it, I want you to probe my mind,' Samantha said, eagerly.

Jennifer gave her a warm smile; inside her head her mind could not believe its luck.

'I will, Sam, I promise.'

'You are so good to me, Jenny.'

'That's what I'm here for. Are you ready for our voyage of discovery?'

Samantha nodded her head.

'Ready as I'll ever be.' They left the bedroom and went downstairs and left the house.

'When we get back, I'll probe your mind for you.'

'I shall look forward to that,' Samantha assured her.

They made their way to the research compound, they found the main gate open, they searched for the guard and saw him by the radio telescope pylon, and he had his back to them, so they rushed through the gate and hid behind the security hut. Jennifer gave out an excited giggle. Samantha could see she was enjoying this. They made their way swiftly towards the blockhouse. Keeping their eyes open for trouble with their perfect night vision. A light drizzle was drifting across the compound. They got to the blockhouse metal door; she waited for Jennifer to do her stuff.

Jennifer activated the lock and the door slid open; Samantha slid inside the blockhouse. Jennifer followed her and shut the door behind her.

Samantha took a small torch out of her coat pocket and switched it on. They both stared in amazement at what stood before their eyes.

'Now there's a surprise,' Samantha said.

The spacecraft took up most of the room in the blockhouse. They stood at the front end of it. Jennifer moved and gazed at the squat oval body – this was worth the chances they were taking. They went to the rear of the spacecraft; there was a wing that curved downwards and ended in the power plant, it was the same on the other side. They searched the craft for a way in.

CHAPTER XXVII:

HOSTILE ACTION

They found a hatch and Jennifer activated the control box and the hatch slid open.

'Eureka.'

Samantha slid into the open hatchway and Jennifer followed her, the lights lit up when they entered the inner compartment.

'You stay here and keep guard, I'll have a look round,' Samantha said.

Jennifer went through the hatch and stood outside the spacecraft. She suddenly heard a slight sound close to her. Jennifer became aware of danger as a dark shape descended on her, something hard hit the back of her head and she saw stars, the pain made her eyes water and then everything went black and she collapsed to the ground.

Samantha stood in the main compartment; it was flooded with light. She studied the computer system that ran along one wall. It was completely alien to her. In the centre of the room was a conference table with six chairs around it. She sat in one and found it completely surrounded her slim form; the owners of the spacecraft had similar bodies to her own. She got up and moved to the rear of the compartment. On her left she found a recess and she stepped into it. She gazed at the control panel at the rear of the recess.

After a while she stepped out, her mind was a buzz of excitement, she had to make sure she did not touch anything. Samantha made her way to the front compartment. She stood in front of the bulkhead; she stared at the control panel by the closed hatch that barred her way into the next compartment. She wished Jennifer was here as she would have the hatch open in no time. Samantha ran her fingers lightly over the multi-coloured keypad.

BLUE.

Samantha spun round and found she was alone. The voice seemed to be all around her. Samantha turned back to the hatch and pressed the blue button on the keypad. There came a loud hiss and the hatch door slid upwards. She moved slowly and cautiously through the open hatchway. The air was stale on the other side and she wrinkled her nose in distaste. She found herself on the flight deck. There were two large seats in front of her, Samantha stepped between them and gasped when she saw one was occupied.

Beware.

Suddenly her senses were keyed up for danger. She heard someone enter through the open hatch. She thought it might be Jennifer and she was about to turn around, when a sharp hostile voice spoke out.

'Don't move; I'm armed.'

The voice was female with a slight foreign accent.

'Your friend is at this moment incapacitated, I will finish her off, when I've dealt with you.'

Samantha stared in front of her searching for a way out of her predicament. She moved forward slightly.

'Keep still.'

'Surely you don't expect me to give up my life without a fight. Where's the logic in that?'

The evil laughter echoed round the flight deck.

'The logic is, I have a weapon and there's nothing to stop your demise.'

'The gods decree otherwise,' Samantha said.

Samantha dived to the floor as she heard the discharge of an energy weapon. The floor fell away in front of the seats; she felt an excruciating burning pain in her back. Her body fell into the shallow pit in front of the seats, Samantha blacked out.

Jennifer came to with a burning pain in her head; she blinked her watery eyes. She got up on her hands and knees, she felt nauseous and her stomach wanted to eject its contents. Jennifer took deep breaths and felt the back of her head; the hair was wet and matted.

Vigilance – You just won't learn.

Jennifer got shakily to her feet.

'You are a fool, Jennifer. Letting someone creep up on you, a fine predator you'd make,' she scolded.

Jennifer held onto the side of the hatch to steady herself. She heard someone moving inside the spacecraft close to the hatchway. Jennifer dived to the rear of the spacecraft and watched a tall figure exit the open hatch and make for the door of the blockhouse. Jennifer suddenly thought of Samantha, perhaps she lay dying in the spacecraft. She had to go to her. Jennifer entered the spacecraft and made her way through it until she reached the control room. She was drawn to the alien computer system like a magnet. She stared at the strange characters and symbols. Her eyes lit up in spite of the pain in her head. This is what she was born to do, she could not get enough, her curiosity was aroused. Jennifer was in her element and all else was forgotten. Her thin face was a mask of concentration. Jennifer had no doubts she would eventually decipher the strange language of the alien computers. She just had to find a focal point she could recognise. Her long nimble fingers worked fast to feed her hungry mind.

Jennifer moved away from the computer system to give her mind a breather. She strode to the bulkhead that led to the next compartment. She stood by the hatch and gazed at the colour keypad. She pressed the blue button and the hatch slid upwards. Jennifer moved slowly into the flight deck.

Jenny.

Her body stiffened, she wished the voices in her head would disappear and leave her alone.

Jenny – Help me.

'Samantha!'

Jennifer sneezed as the stale air irritated her nostrils. She moved between the seats and screamed when she saw one of the seats was occupied. It was a tall mummified body with long grubby red hair on the domed skull. It was not a pretty sight. Jennifer gazed down at the floor and noticed the crumpled form of Samantha in the shallow pit.

'Sam!'

Jennifer knelt down beside the stricken girl. The back of her coat was burnt away. Samantha's back was red raw. Samantha gave a stifled cry. Jennifer gently pulled her friend out of the pit. Samantha's face was filled with pain; the green eyes were dull and filled with tears.

'Sam, I'm here.' Jennifer ran a caressing hand over Samantha's forehead.

'It was a woman,' Samantha said with a struggle.

Jennifer helped Samantha to her feet, keeping a supporting arm round her.

'Did you recognise her?'

Samantha shook her head.

'I didn't see her face.'

Samantha clung to Jennifer, as they moved out of the flight deck. They made their way slowly through the spacecraft until they reached the exit hatch. When they left the blockhouse, Jennifer inhaled the night air deeply; it was raining steadily.

'That's nice, the weather is trying to put out the fire in my back,' Samantha said.

They made their way to the Lab 3 building so Samantha could get medical help for her injured back. They met Hilary Calvert in the ward room and she took charge of Samantha and helped her to one of the beds. Jennifer left the building. Jennifer went to the Lab 1 building; she saw Michelle working at one of the work benches, and she strode over to her.

'What have we here?' Jennifer asked. Michelle looked up from her work and stared at Jennifer.

'Where did you spring from?'

'It's a long story,' Jennifer said.

Michelle picked up half a spherical container and handed it to Jennifer, who studied it with fascinated interest.

'Have you got the other half?'

Michelle handed her the other half sphere and Jennifer fitted the two halves together. She had a large matt black sphere with four long spikes on it.

'Have you any ideas?' Colonel Hopkins asked, as he came up behind her.

'It's a container of some sort,' Jennifer observed.

Michelle told her they had found seven opened spheres all empty; ten had come down so there were another three; somewhere.

'Have Steven and Janice remembered anything more about their experiences that night?'

Colonel Hopkins shook his head, whatever had happened to them, it was still a mystery.

'What do you think the containers might have contained?' Michelle asked.

Jennifer smiled at her. 'I have an idea – but it is too fantastic to mention.'

Michelle smiled at her. 'I like fantastic ideas.'

'I'd like to confirm it first.'

In the Lab 3 building Samantha lay on a hospital bed on her front while Hilary tended to her injured back.

'What happened to you, Sam? This is a very bad injury.'

Samantha told Hilary she had been shot in the back with some sort of energy weapon. Hilary picked up a jar labelled S/156 that lay on top of the bedside cupboard and unscrewed the lid.

'Did you see who did it?'

'No, I only know it was a woman with a foreign accent,' Samantha said.

Samantha gritted her teeth as Hilary smeared the contents of the jar over her burnt back. She tried to be as gentle as she could. Jennifer entered the ward room and stood by the bed and held Samantha's hand and squeezed it gently.

'Thanks for coming to my aid, Jenny.'

'Don't mention it, Sam, I'm sorry I did not protect you well enough.'

Dr Richard Blake walked in and was glad to see Jennifer was there.

'Come on, you,' he said, as he grabbed Jennifer by the arm.

'Why do you scientists have so much difficulty in using my name, I'm not you or Missy, my name is Jennifer, Jen-ni -fer,' she complained.

'My, you have developed a temper,' Richard Blake said.

In the next room he told Jennifer to lie on the operating table. She lay down and stared up at the ceiling. He placed the medical hood over her body and set the probe going. He stared at the monitor on the hood and gazed at the pictures of what was going on inside Jennifer's body. She waited patiently while the examination went on. When Dr Blake pulled the hood from her body and turned off the probe, Jennifer gazed up at him in expectation of bad news.

'Well, Doctor, how long have I got? I can take it on the chin.'

He picked up her right hand and studied it, he squeezed it gently.

'I didn't know you cared,' Jennifer beamed.

Dr Blake ignored her witticism and asked her if she had any pain in her hand.

'It feels cold and slightly numb,' Jennifer said.

'You have the same disruption of cells in your hand that Angie Russell has in her whole body.'

Now we know.

'Is there anything else?'

Jennifer sat up and swung her long legs over the side of the table. She listened soberly to what the doctor told her. Her body and metabolism were still in a weakened state after the effects of the power surge. She needed rest and plenty of it, the work she was giving her body was holding up her recuperative powers. She had to stop her mind ruling her body.

'I want to keep you here under surveillance.'

'I can't, I have things to do,' Jennifer argued.

'I can easily keep you here if I wanted.'

Jennifer slid off the table and stood up to her full height in front of the doctor.

'I hope you won't stop me; I want to be there for Angie, I am something familiar she can hold onto,' Jennifer said.

Dr Blake studied her determined expression; she was silently challenging him to keep her in the room against her will. Jennifer was quite aware she did not have the strength to put up a fight. She did not let the fatigue her body was feeling show on her face.

'OK, I hear you are staying with Samantha, I'll contact Dr Forbes in the infirmary, if you promise to cooperate with him. You can continue to stay where you are; I expect Samantha will benefit from your company, now that she has been hurt.'

'Thank you, Doctor, I'll promise I'll be a good girl,' Jennifer said.

CHAPTER XXVIII:

EXPEDITION TO THE MARSH

Jennifer entered the infirmary and found Hazel sitting at Angie's bedside; she remembered the time she had seen Hazel lying in one of the beds in Lab 3. Hazel got up to go.

'Don't go, Hazel, please, Angie needs all her friends round her at this time,' Jennifer said.

Hazel sat back in the chair; Jennifer took a seat on the other side of the bed. Angie was asleep. Jennifer took the girl's small hand in her own.

'I'm sorry, Jenny,' Hazel said.

'I know, we all are,' Jennifer said.

Samantha lay on her left side and stared at the rain outside the window. The last hour she had been interrogated about her nightly adventure with Jennifer. General Heywood made it clear he was angry with the pair of them, as his aggressive questioning showed. He blamed Samantha for everything, as if she had gone out to get herself killed on purpose. Samantha told him, she was exercising her right to gather information on her own, as he did not give her the data she needed. Her back still burned with pain, but it did not stop her giving as well as she got. Though he was angry with her, he still had respect for the way she stood up to him.

Samantha got out of the bed and grimaced at the pain in her back. She was bored and wanted to leave the ward and get back home. She stood by the window and looked out at the rain-soaked compound.

General Heywood walked into his office in the main administrative building. He sat at his desk and after a while the door opened and Melanie McAllister strolled into the room and stood to attention in front of his desk; she clicked her heels and saluted. She met his angry gaze with a smile.

'God calls and I come running,' Melanie said.

General Heywood glared at her; he was disappointed with himself for letting the girl's manner get under his skin. He asked Melanie if she had been up to no good, during the night before. Melanie assured him she had been tucked up in bed, dreaming of freedom. When he told her about the attack on Samantha, her flippant manner dissolved.

'She was attacked by a female,' he told her.

'Well it wasn't me; I have no reason to hurt her and I haven't even been in the same room with the girl.'

'We know.'

A large delicate hand was placed on her shoulder; Melanie looked up at Dr Hamilton as she stood beside her.

Though Melanie was six foot in height, the tall blonde-haired woman made her feel short.

'You have nothing to worry about, child, we don't blame you for what happened to Samantha,' the woman assured her.

General Heywood stared up at the woman; her deep set dark blue eyes returned his gaze. Her height and intelligence did not intimidate him like it did when they first met. Their working relationship was now on equal terms.

'Samantha wants more information,' he said.

'Logical,' said the girl sitting at the other desk.

Dr Hamilton turned to the desk on the other side of the room; Sarah sat at it and watched the woman with interest. Dr Sally Hamilton turned back to the General.

'She is here to look, listen and learn, it is not yet time to give her more information, she has to continue her education.'

'This unknown attacker is making things difficult – until this person is caught, Samantha and Jennifer are in danger,' the General said.

'We must be vigilant, Colonel Hopkins must step up the security here and catch this person,' Sally Hamilton said.

Sarah decided to break into the conversation.

'Give them enough rope and they may hang themselves.'

Dr Hamilton turned and studied the round freckled face; the grey eyes stared back at her. A sardonic smile played on the full red lips; the tall woman took a silent appraisal of Sarah. The jovial exterior of her character was a front, the grey eyes showed the intelligence that lay behind them. Dr Hamilton smiled at her.

'You may be right, Sarah, perhaps you can keep your eyes open, I'm sure you are a girl who surveys all she sees.'

The tall woman turned and walked out of the room; Melanie followed behind her. The General and Sarah exchanged glances.

'She'll have her eyes on you now, Sarah.'

'Dr Hamilton is a powerful woman,' Sarah observed.

'Do I detect a note of fear?'

Sarah shook her head and grinned.

'Respect; not fear,' she said.

Samantha was sat up in bed, when a nurse entered the room.

'I'm Melanie McAllister.'

'Henry's girlfriend,' Samantha said.

Melanie smiled and sat on the edge of the bed. 'Don't tell the General, he wouldn't understand.'

'Your secret is safe with me. He doesn't tell me anything so I'm not going to tell him other people's secrets,' Samantha assured her.

'I came here because I heard about the attack on you. Before people think it was me, I had to see you, so I could tell you I have no wish to harm you in any way.'

Samantha smiled. 'We know it wasn't you, it was a woman with a foreign accent.'

'This is the first time we have spoken to each other – I wanted you to know what sort of girl I was. Henry likes you and worries when you get harmed,' Melanie said.

When Melanie got home, she found Wendy Goodman in the kitchen fixing lunch; she asked Melanie how Samantha was.

'I went to see her; Samantha was sitting up in bed.'

'That's good. It seems someone doesn't like her,' Wendy said.

'The security doesn't seem so good round here,' Melanie said.

Janice popped to see how Samantha was faring; she sat on the edge of the bed. Janice could see Samantha was glad to see her.

'Hilary told me what had happened to you.'

'You must watch out, Jan – someone is after me and I don't want them to hurt you because of me.'

Janice gave her friend a determined expression. 'I'm not going to turn my back on you – neither is Steven. We aren't going to let you face danger alone,' Janice assured her.

The next morning Melanie came to see her again.

'How's your back?'

'It seems to be getting better, Hilary tells me, and my body heals itself quickly.'

'My house mate, Wendy, sends her best wishes for a speedy recovery,' Melanie said.

'Thank her for me. How is Henry?'

Melanie sat on the edge of the bed. 'The General has him working with security. Wendy and I were talking about security last night, certainly when it applies to you.'

Melanie stood up and left the room and a few minutes later Steven entered the room and sat on the edge of the bed and kissed Samantha on the lips. He told her the girl Lavonia had disappeared.

'Something good has come at last. I hope she stays disappeared.'

Steven laughed and asked her if she had any idea who had attacked her. Samantha shook her head.

'Have you any idea what had happened to you and Janice that night?'

Steven shook his head. 'We both can't recall anything of that night.'

A week later, Samantha left the hospital ward, in the Lab 3 building and returned to her house. Her body was quickly mending the damaged flesh and skin of her back. Dr Blake was surprised at her fast recovery powers. Her back still ached but she found it was something she could put up with. She found Jennifer in the house.

'That was a close call, I'm so glad you survived it,' Jennifer said, sincerely.

'So am I, but I was not overjoyed by the pain. Now there is a killer after us both,' Samantha said.

'So, we must be even more vigilant.'

Samantha went into the lounge and collapsed onto the couch, Jennifer went to make coffee for them both. She entered the lounge and handed Samantha a mug of coffee then sat on the couch beside her. She kissed Samantha on the lips.

'The General and the Colonel have no ideas on who the attacker is yet,' Samantha said.

'I've been in contact with Valerie, she has been working on unmasking the culprit, but she has had not success yet. Lavonia was the girl who caused the power surge in the computer that injured me, but she did not attack you, because the girl is missing,' Jennifer said.

'And I hope she stays missing,' Samantha said.

Jennifer nodded in agreement. They sat in silence for a while going through their own thoughts.

Samantha placed the empty cup on the floor and stood up; she went to the window, and Jennifer turned and gazed at her back. The wind was blowing wildly; the sky was thick with grey cloud. A cold shiver ran through Samantha's body and it made her back ache painfully. There was a predator outside and it wanted to make a meal of her and Jennifer. Jennifer sitting on the couch noticed the unsteadiness in the stature of Samantha's body. She got up and went to the window; Samantha felt her presence beside her and stayed staring out of the window.

Jennifer knew all about the interrogation by the General after their misfortunate experience, she had told Samantha to forget about it, he was only doing his job; she must not let it intimidate her. Jennifer stood behind her and put her arms round Samantha.

'I don't think it's your fault, Sam. It is their fault for not giving you enough information.'

Samantha stood still while Jennifer gently squeezed her breasts; her nipples went hard as nuts. After a while she moved away and Samantha turned away from the window and walked out of the room. Jennifer followed behind her, to see what she was going to do next. Samantha went into the kitchen and opened the back door and stepped out; Jennifer stayed inside the doorway. Samantha stood still as the wind blew her long ginger hair into her face and tugged at her blouse and skirt.

'If you are going out, you should put a coat on,' Jennifer advised.

A loud whining sound crossed the sky above their heads.

'What was that?' Jennifer wanted to know.

'Whatever it is, it's heading for the marsh,' Samantha said.

Samantha turned and looked Jennifer up and down, she was wearing, what Samantha called 'That dress'. It was black and clinging, it showed the contours of Jennifer's shapely figure, and the bodice was low and showed a generous amount of cleavage; the hem ended just below the tops of her milky white thighs. Apart from being a highly intelligent person, Jennifer was also an exhibitionist. At the moment Jennifer's habit was turned on her, a person of her own sex. Samantha had not pushed away Jennifer's advances, as she was one of the few who liked her. She needed the girl as a companion, and they were good at working as a team. Great minds thought alike, and Samantha and Jennifer did just that.

'Can you tell what I'm thinking?' Samantha asked all of a sudden.

Jennifer's face changed expression several times before she spoke.

'I can tell you are thinking of me, but that is obvious by the way you are looking at me.'

Samantha smiled.

'Would you react the same way towards me, if I wasn't a girl?'

Jennifer turned away and moved further into the kitchen; Samantha went in and shut the door.

'You are the only person I've reacted that way to, it is just a coincidence that you are female; I told you, it is my way to feel what kind of person you are. I like you very much, you have not pushed me away and you said you liked the idea of continuing the experience I gave you.'

Samantha placed a hand on shoulder; Jennifer regarded her with wide open ice blue eyes.

'I wouldn't push you away, I might offend you. I need your friendship, Jenny, you have become important to me,' Samantha said.

'You are no less important to me – I will only touch you in the way you want me to and whenever you want me to. I do not want to offend you either.'

'Put your coat on, we are going for a stroll,' Samantha said.

They went up the stairs to put on a warm coat to protect them from the cold wind and rain. Back in the kitchen Samantha stood close to Jennifer.

She kissed her softly on the lips. Then Samantha headed for the back door and opened it and they went out. Jennifer shut the door behind her, the wind howled around them and they were rained upon from a great height. They made their way to the marsh; they held hands. Their boots squelched in the wet muddy ground.

When they got to the marsh they moved slowly and cautiously. Jennifer groped about amongst the bushes, hoping she would not lay her hands on something slimy that moved. After a while her long searching fingers touched something. She picked the object up and went to Samantha and showed her a silver bracelet with the name Lavonia inscribed on it.

'That might be a clue to what happened to her,' Samantha said.

Samantha put the bracelet in her coat pocket. She removed her socks and shoes.

'What are you up to now?' Jennifer asked.

Samantha waded into the marshy water; she moved slowly forward; Jennifer watched her. Samantha suddenly touched something with her foot; she stood still, and the only sound was the wind and rain. Samantha bent down and slid her hands into the cold dark water of the marsh; they touched the object at her feet. It was a sphere with long sharp spikes protruding from it, which would have gone through her foot if she had stepped on one of them. Samantha made her way back to hard ground where Jennifer waited for her. Samantha decided it was time to get out of the wind and rain. Jennifer agreed and they started towards the house. She entered the house by the back door, Jennifer was in the kitchen and she handed her a mug of coffee. She gazed at Samantha with an expression of deep concern.

Samantha sat up on a stool and sipped the hot strong coffee – Jennifer stood close to her and kissed her on the lips.

'There is a complete sphere in the marsh, in the morning you'll have to contact Major Harrington and he can retrieve it,' Samantha said.

Jennifer nodded.

'Then you can investigate it and see what it contains,' Samantha said.

'You can count on me,' Jennifer assured her.

Samantha put the empty cup down and slid off the stool.

'I know I can.'

Samantha made her way upstairs and went into her bedroom and undressed and then went to the bathroom and got under the shower. Jennifer appeared and she gazed at her back. Samantha turned and saw her watching with wide searching eyes.

'Why don't you come in with me, you can assist me, by doing my back, I need a pair of soft soothing hands,' Samantha said.

'I'll be right with you – I don't like showering alone either.'

Jennifer quickly peeled off her clothing and stepped naked in the shower; it was the first time Samantha had seen her entirely nude. Jennifer was seven foot in height, two inches shorter than Samantha, though her body was fuller than her – Samantha was envious of her.

'You are a very lucky girl, Jenny, you have a figure I would kill for,' Samantha said.

'As long as it's not me you'd kill, I don't mind,' Jennifer said.

Samantha felt Jennifer's slender hands run softly up and down back. Jennifer was amazed at the quick regeneration of Samantha's skin and flesh; she was almost good as new.

'Does it hurt much?'

Samantha shook her head. 'It just aches continuously to remind me to watch my back.'

'You are not the only one that needs reminding, the back of my head is still sore, it was a wonder I did not get my skull split open.'

Samantha smeared shower gel over the front of her body; she felt the soft gentle hands run down her back; soft lips kissed her left shoulder. Jennifer spread her hands over Samantha's shapely bottom. Samantha sighed as the long slender fingers massaged her firm flesh. After a while Jennifer bent her fingers and ran her sharp nails gently over Samantha's buttocks and down the backs of her thighs, it sent shivers up and down her body.

"I can see why you never cut your fingernails. I love the feeling it gives me; it gives me goose bumps,'

Jennifer giggled; she gave tender loving care to her fingernails as she did to the rest of her curvy body. Jennifer received much pleasure from running her long sharp fingernails over her own body, so she was sure Samantha liked it.

'Tell me if you are enjoying it.'

Jennifer pressed her firm breasts against Samantha's back, she closed her eyes and placed her hands over Samantha's small breasts. She gasped as Jennifer continued to excite her senses.

'I like it, Jenny, but I don't know if I should be; I like the feeling of your tits pressing against my back,' Samantha said.

Jennifer gently nibbled her left ear lobe and squeezed her small breasts firmly.

'I sense that, Samantha, but you are not pulling away from me.'

'I'm enjoying your caressing and fondling of my body; to pull away. Are you trying to probe my mind, you said you would?'

'I feel your emotions rising as I caress you, let your mind go blank,' Jennifer said.

'I'll try, but you are driving my senses wild.'

Samantha closed her eyes and tried to get all thoughts out of her mind, she sighed deeply, while Jennifer's hands continued their journey of discovery over all parts of her body.

'You have a very complex mind, Sam. There are a lot of dark places I can't comprehend,' Jennifer said.

They got out of the shower and dried each other; Samantha kept her thoughts to herself. They stood and kissed each other for a few moments.

Samantha woke late morning and got out of bed and got dressed and went down to the kitchen to make tea. When she had drunk hers, Samantha took a mug upstairs for Jennifer. She entered the spare bedroom and sat on the bed and shook the sleeping girl gently to wake her. Samantha gave her the mug of hot strong tea. Jennifer kissed her on the lips.

'Thanks, Sweetie.'

'We must shower together again; that was tremendous; you know how to give someone an orgasm,' Samantha said.

'I hope we'll shower together all the time,' Jennifer said.

'What do you think those spheres contained?' Samantha inquired.

Jennifer sipped her tea and gazed at Samantha.

'The first thing that came into my mind is they may have contained some kind of alien conscience.'

'That's my theory too,' Samantha said.

Jennifer put the empty mug on the bedside table and moved forward and kissed Samantha.

'Great minds think alike.' They kissed again.

Downstairs the doorbell rang, Samantha got off the bed.

'I wonder who that is, we haven't forgotten to do something this morning?' Samantha wondered.

'No, we are not wanted until this afternoon,' Jennifer said.

Samantha went downstairs to answer the door; she found Juliet standing on her doorstep. Samantha sighed deeply. Juliet knew what the tall girl was thinking. What does that nuisance girl want?

'It's good to see you, Juliet!'

Samantha ushered the girl into the kitchen and gave her a mug of tea. Juliet removed her coat and draped it over the back of a chair. Juliet was wearing a short purple dress with a low-cut top frilled with white lace; that showed a generous amount of cleavage.

'Nice dress; shows off your body magnificently.'

Juliet nodded and smiled.

'What can I do for you?' Samantha asked.

'I want you to tell me what's going on here,' Juliet said, as she sat down.

Juliet sipped her tea as she stared hard at Samantha's expression of amusement.

'You think I know more than you?'

Juliet was sure she did, Samantha was the oldest of them, after all.

'You are their favourite.'

Samantha could not stop herself from laughing. If only she knew?

'I'm sorry for laughing, but if they have a favourite, it certainly isn't me.'

'You set yourself apart from the rest of us and that Jennifer.'

'And whose fault is that?'

Juliet did not need reminding, when they first met Samantha, she was the one who mistrusted and disliked the tall girl. Juliet had been suspicious of her and did not want to give Samantha the chance to prove herself. Now she felt very guilty about that, after what Sarah had told her, Juliet wanted to let Samantha know, she had been wrong about her.

'Yes, I only know too well, that's why I'm here. I have a lot to apologize for,' Juliet said, sincerely.

Samantha softened her expression. This was a new Juliet.

'I am here to learn just like you are, I am just a slave, an intelligent one, but a slave nonetheless,' Samantha explained.

She heard sounds from upstairs, Jennifer was moving about. Juliet stared up at the ceiling; Samantha could see the Juliet did not want to meet up with the girl.

'Why don't we continue this at your house, this evening,' Samantha advised.

Juliet stood up and put on her coat and Samantha saw her to the door.

'I don't want to fight with you, Sam, I want to make my peace with you,' Juliet said.

Juliet left the house and Samantha went slowly up the stairs. She had been touched by what Juliet had said. She entered the spare room and found Jennifer sitting on the side of the bed.

'That was Juliet, she wanted information from me, because she thought I was the favourite one,' Samantha informed her.

Jennifer stood up and put her arms round Samantha and kissed her.

'Of course, you're not, I am.' Samantha laughed as Jennifer stood behind her.

'You are a girl of two halves, you are the positive and the clone was the negative. You possess the good emotions the clone never had,' Samantha said.

Samantha felt Jennifer pull down the zip of her dress.

'Are you telling me, you like me, Sam?'

Samantha nodded her head as the dress was slid down her slim body.

'Absolutely, I've been waiting for a girl like you to walk into my life, for a long time.'

Jennifer hugged her and kissed her lightly on the lips; their bodies rubbed together.

'As our relationship builds up, you will discover more about me,' Jennifer said.

'I hope so; you are a real girl of mystery.'

'I'm not going to tell you all my secrets in one go,' Jennifer assured her.

Jennifer grabbed her hand and guided her to the bed, and they sat down on it.

'I look forward to hearing a few secrets at least,' Samantha said.

Jennifer winked at her; then kissed her.

'I thought there'd be a catch,' Samantha said, as she left the room.

Samantha left the house and made for the school house; she had a date with her psychoanalyst. She entered the school and went to Dr Bishop's office and sat down at his desk.

'How's your back?' he asked.

'Sore but it's healing nicely.'

'Have you any other problems?'

Samantha shook her head.

'How are you getting on with the girl Jennifer?'

'Very well, she is a lot better than her clone.'

Dr Bishop was keeping a special eye on Samantha after the fight in the classroom; he wanted to make sure the girl did not have any more headaches or blackouts. Samantha answered his questions calmly and truthfully. At the end of the session, she walked out of the office and sighed deeply. She went back to the house. Jennifer was in the kitchen preparing lunch, and she had on a short black dress.

'Samantha told her about her session with Dr Bishop.

'You got a good report from him, that's all that matters, Darling.'

Samantha was glad she was pleased for her.

'The reason I feel so good in mind and body, is obviously something to do with you, Jenny.'

They had lunch together and then they went their separate ways. Jennifer had work in the observatory to do and Samantha had to visit Juliet. When Samantha knocked on the door, Juliet opened it immediately; she still wore the purple dress she had had on earlier. She had a purple ribbon in her black hair.

'You look very pretty, Juliet.'

'Thank you.'

Juliet led her visitor to the lounge, and they sat on a black leather sofa.

'You saw Dr Bishop this afternoon – how did it go?' Juliet asked.

'Fine, thanks.'

Juliet gave her a warm smile.

'I'm glad to hear it.'

Juliet stayed quiet for a while collecting her thoughts, Samantha waited patiently for her to talk.

'With her spineless friend Lavonia, they cruelly bated you. It made me feel guilty, as I was the same when we first met. I shouted insults to you every chance I got. I know I've wronged you in the past and I want to apologize for it, until I do, I'm no different to Jennifer and Lavonia. Because I don't see you much these days the guilt is eating me up inside.'

Juliet stopped talking; Samantha placed a hand on her shoulder.

'You are nothing like the terrible twins, when we sneaked into the Lab 1 building – I was very impressed on your hacking into the computer system there.'

Juliet gazed at her face.

'Were you?'

'Absolutely, you are a very clever girl, don't let anyone tell you different,' Samantha replied.

Juliet felt much better after hearing that, it helped to bring their relationship a little closer to being good friends.

'I'd given up hope that we might develop a bond together, like you and Janice. So, I kept away.'

'Hazel blamed me for you keeping away from us, which she let me know in no uncertain terms, every time we were together.'

Samantha smiled; she got on well with the youngest member of the team.

Juliet got up and went to the kitchen to make them both some tea. Samantha got up and went to the hi-fi and put on a CD.

She sat back down on the sofa. Soft music filled the room. Juliet came back with two mugs of strong tea; she handed one to Samantha.

'You have good taste in music, Juliet, we have something in common.'

'I want us to have a lot more in common, after that,' Juliet said, sincerely.

Samantha sipped her tea.

'I'll drink to that,' she said.

They sat in silence listening to the music and drinking their tea, after a while Juliet placed her empty mug on the floor.

'I think Lavonia and Jennifer were put amongst us to weed out the weak, those that don't come up to scratch,' Juliet said.

'Lavonia always preyed on the weak, cowardly bullies always do,' Samantha said, icily.

'Jennifer is a predator and when her job is done...' Juliet stopped and stared hard at the bright green eyes gazing at her.

'They bring in a more furious animal to rid us of the predator,' Juliet continued.

Juliet noticed the brightness fade from the emerald green eyes. Samantha knew what was coming next.

'You!'

Samantha finished her tea and left the house, Juliet's words echoed through her aching brain. She made her way to the research facility.

You must get Jennifer – before she gets you.

Samantha moved through the main gate unchallenged and walked swiftly across the compound towards the Lab 3 building. She found Dr Blake in his office; he was surprised to see her.

'What can I do for you, Samantha?'

She placed her long slender hands on the desk. 'Have you discovered what killed the clone, yet?'

Dr Blake sat up straight and told her he would have to get the authority to tell her. Samantha was a girl on a mission, and she had no time to lose. She picked up the telephone and dialled General Heywood's number.

General Heywood was talking to a tall blonde woman wearing a white lab coat. When the telephone buzzed it made him jump. He picked up the receiver and heard the calm voice of Samantha on the other end. He stared up at the woman.

'Samantha wants to know what killed the clone. Do we tell her?'

The woman smiled and nodded her head. Samantha was following the course she had predicted.

'I will have to go soon, Samantha will be seeing you next,' the woman said.

'How do you know that?'

The woman grinned at him.

'I know my own creation,' she said.

Samantha put the receiver down and stared hard at the doctor.

'You now have the authority to tell me. So, what killed it?'

Dr Blake noted her referring to the clone as it.

'A new strain of virus, we have never seen before, it was injected into her back.'

Samantha stared at him; he could see the deep concentration on her expression.

'Not of this Earth, I suppose,' Samantha said, after a few moments.

'You know something I don't?'

Samantha turned and headed for the door.

'Not yet,' she replied.

Samantha ran across the compound and made for the administrative building. As she got to the main door a tall figure slipped round the other side of the building; in a strange quirk of fate, mother and daughter missed each other by inches. Samantha ran up the stairs and entered General Heywood's office; he greeted her with a smile.

'What's up, Sam?'

Samantha stood over him like an avenging angel.

'On the coast you have a facility called the Fortress?'

The General stared at her in surprise.

'I take it you got that information when you and Juliet sneaked in here last year.'

'Yes, Juliet's a genius when it comes to hacking into computers,' Samantha said.

'I'll have to have another word with that young lady,' he said.

'I was wondering if they had developed any energy weapons there,' Samantha said.

General Heywood shook his head.

'Not when I was last there.'

'Contact them now and find out,' Samantha demanded.

She strode towards the door.

'I'm not waiting to get shot at again.'

Samantha left the office and closed the door.

Samantha returned to Juliet's house. They had a meal together and she told Juliet the General thought she was a naughty girl for helping her look into the information on Research Complex computers.

Juliet smiled at her. 'Spank me.'

Samantha laughed.

'They are not going to give me information freely – I have to search for it in any way I can. You are better at computers than me – that's why I wanted you with me. '

'I misinterpreted the situation, I'm sorry – you are just as blind as the rest of us,' Juliet apologised.

Samantha showed Juliet the bracelet Jennifer had found at the marshland.

'Lavonia vanished in the marsh – even bad things happen to the bad. I want you to tell Janice about the virus, that's her field of research,' Samantha said.

'I will,' Juliet promised.

They sat in the lounge and drank coffee.

'Janice told me you thought you had been abandoned by your mother. She doesn't think that's the case and neither do I. Something bad may have happened to stop her contacting you. Wendy has a father who is missing; she does not think he had abandoned her. I have no idea who my parents are, neither does Hazel. Like you we have scientists who are our guardians. I will try and find something about your mother; I shall keep digging until I turn up something. I like this new Juliet – don't lose her.'

Juliet gazed at Samantha. 'You'll do that for me?'

'Of course, I will. You came with me when I wanted to enter the Research Complex. And we are friends, aren't we?'

Juliet nodded and Samantha smiled happily.

In the morning Samantha went to the kitchen and had some coffee.

Jennifer soon joined her. She wore a thick black woollen jumper and black pleated skirt; her long silvery hair was tied up into a ponytail. They kissed passionately.

'You look nice this morning, Jenny.'

Jennifer beamed at her; it was important what Samantha thought of her.

'Thank you, Darling,' Jennifer said and kissed Samantha on the lips.

Jennifer ate her breakfast, Samantha did not tell Jennifer about her visit to Juliet, but she told her about what she learned at the research facility.

'I wondered where you had got to, I stayed up as long as I could,' Jennifer said.

They left the house together.

CHAPTER XXIX:

THE ALIEN MIND

Jennifer made for the military camp at the side of the hill. Jennifer showed her pass at the gate and made her way to Major Harrington's office. She told him about the sphere they saw fall into the marsh.

'If that's the reason Samantha was out that night, why didn't she tell us, instead of giving us so much lip?'

Jennifer shook her head and told the Major that was something he had to sort out with Samantha herself.

A little while later Jennifer sitting in the front of an army truck that headed for the marsh. Major Harrington was driving. When they reached the marsh, the truck slowed and Jennifer jumped out and the Major swerved the truck so it would miss her; Jennifer was sprayed with wet smelly mud.

'Thank you, for the mud bath.'

Major Harrington grinned at her angry expression and the soldiers nearby showed they were enjoying her predicament.

Jennifer moved off in a huff and went to the edge of the marsh; she pointed to the spot where the object hit the marsh.

'Who's going in for a dip?'

'If you think something is there, you'll have to find it yourself,' the Major told her.

Jennifer pulled up the hem of her skirt and tucked it into her panties. She removed her socks and shoes. Jennifer strode into the marsh and made for the spot where Samantha had found the sphere, she took the utmost care where she put her feet as she did not want the spikes on the sphere going through her foot. The water was ice cold and smelly. Her right foot touched something, and she stood still. Jennifer bent down and put her hands under the water of the marsh; she gripped the sphere and lifted it out of the murky water.

'Here it is.'

Jennifer waded out of the water with her prize; she placed it in the back of the truck. She pulled her skirt out of her panties and let the hem fall to below her knees.

She put on her socks and shoes and got in the back of the truck. She was aware the soldiers in the back with her were keeping their distance from her.

'I hope you are going to have a bath when you get back,' the Major said.

'Are you insinuating that I smell?' Jennifer complained.

'Let's just say we'll make sure we're not downwind of you,' Major Harrington said.

They drove to Samantha's house and Jennifer had a quick shower and got back in the military truck and it set off in the direction of the Research Complex. It drove through the main gate. The truck parked outside the building that housed the Labs 1 and 2, Jennifer picked up the sphere and leapt out of the back of the truck and raced through the main doors. She turned right and entered Lab 2. She made her way to the main computer room; she placed the black sphere on the computer control desk. Michael Palmer came up to her and greeted Jennifer in his usual way.

'Hello Missy, it's nice to see you again.'

Jennifer ignored him and ran her hands over the rough surface of the sphere. Michelle appeared at her side, and Colonel Hopkins was standing nearby. They watched Jennifer with fascinated interest. Michelle eagerly helped her; she could see Jennifer knew what she was doing. Her long slender fingers flitted over the control panel, touching the coloured touch pads. The black sphere sat on a turntable and it spun slowly, a beam was emitted by the computer and it probed the sphere.

Jennifer ran her fingers over the sphere in search of an opening. Suddenly there was a soft hiss and the two hemispheres came apart.

'Eureka!'

A green mist covered her hands; it brought cold shivers through her body. A strange voice spoke in her mind.

Who are you?

She stared into the depths of the green glowing mass that throbbed inside the split sphere.

How can I tell you that, when I do not know myself?

Jennifer felt something inside her head, her brain was being probed.

You are the Pariah.

'Are you all right, Jenny?' Michelle said.

Giving birth to you, they have given birth to chaos. You are a danger to the Universe.

Jennifer gripped the two hemispheres and clamped them together. She ran her fingers over the control desk and the sphere was immediately surrounded by a force field.

'What is it?' Michael asked.

Jennifer shook her head; Michelle had a hand on her shoulder.

'It's a mind, a very powerful one, we seem to have an invasion on our hands,' Jennifer said, turning to Colonel Hopkins.

The head of security walked out of the room; Jennifer turned back to the black sphere confined in the force field. The alien mind seemed to know who or what she was.

'How are you feeling, Jenny? You did not look at all well just now,' Michelle asked in a voice full of concern.

'I am now, that was a very weird experience, having another mind running about inside my head.'

CHAPTER XXX:

THE HAUNTED DREAMER

S amantha was in the locker room in Lab 1. She placed the satchel she carried onto a low bench; inside it was the lead box that contained the alien power cell. She took off the white lab coat and placed it in the locker. Someone entered the room and she spun round. Steven Calvert strode up to her and kissed her on the lips.

'You are a hard girl to keep up with,' he complained.

'I've been busy, and Janice should be the girl you give a kiss to – I don't want her running after me, accusing me of trying to steal her boyfriend.'

Steven was sure the tall girl was avoiding them for other reasons. After Juliet had told him she had eventually caught up with the girl, Steven decided to seek her out.

'You don't have to worry about Janice, I kiss her in an entirely different way, I'm just trying to show you, we are your friends and you don't have to avoid us all the time,' Steven said.

Samantha secured her locker and picked up the satchel, Steven followed her to the door.

'Have they discovered the identity of the person who tried to murder you?' Steven asked.

Samantha shook her head.

'I've been with your father nearly all day, going through the profiles of every female working here, all those with a foreign accent, of which there are a few, but we had to rule them all out, as some had alibis, and some weren't tall enough. I didn't see the person's face, so we'll have to wait until they try again.'

Steven did not like the sound of that, he liked Samantha and told her he hoped she would get plenty of protection.

'I'm in the General's bad books again after last night; I wouldn't be surprised if he used me as bait to catch the culprit.'

They left the building, Steven had to go to the observatory building, and he kissed her on the cheek and told her he would see her the next day. Samantha left the compound and made her way to her house.

Jennifer had gone to the special school for an interview with Dr Bishop. She sat at his desk and waited for him to question her. He studied her face and her ice-blue eyes that stared at him with interest. Like Samantha told him – there were a lot of similarities between them but Jennifer was not as slim as the clone and there was no hostility in this girl's expression.

'Do you know why I asked to see you?'

Jennifer smiled. 'You want to know if I'm like the clone and want to harm Samantha in some way.'

The girl was honest – that was something in her favour.

The smile stayed on her face. 'Outwardly I'm similar – but inside I'm a very different person. Samantha does not feel nauseous when we are close together. I don't give her headaches.'

'I'm going to add you to my records of the other young people at this school,' he said.

'I understand. The others tell me how at ease they are having these sessions with you – who are different to some of the people who work round her,' Jennifer said.

Dr Bishop smiled – he was well aware of the problems General Heywood had with Samantha.

'I'm here to make sure they are not too rough on her.'

Jennifer smiled and was glad he was looking out for Samantha. She answered all the questions he threw at her without any problem. After the session was over, Jennifer stood up and thanked him for understanding her. Dr Bishop watched the tall girl walk out of his office.

Her walk was a lot different to the clone – he wanted to find out more about this Jennifer. Her expressions throughout the interview seemed to show she was enjoying the experience.

It was getting dark when Jennifer entered the house, she had just left the infirmary, she had been sitting at Angie's bedside, and her life was slipping away fast. Jennifer and Samantha had gone as far as they could, Angie had been exposed to the alien power cell for too long and they could not reverse the effects of it. Jennifer had gone to Dr Blake so he could examine the hand that had been close to the glowing green globe and to her relief her hand was no longer showing the effects of the power cell. He gave her some other good news: her body was getting stronger and her metabolism had thrown off the effects of the power surge.

She found Samantha dozing on the couch, she left her to it and Jennifer went to the backroom that had been made into a gymnasium; she threw off her black jumper and skirt. Jennifer gave her body a hard workout on the exercise equipment. She was doing better than the first time she used Samantha's equipment.

At the end of her workout Jennifer stood in the middle of the room, inhaling and exhaling deeply. She felt exhilarated; she was now strong in mind and body.

Samantha stood by the door and gazed at Jennifer as she stood in her bra and panties. Her skin glistened with sweat.

'Having fun?' Samantha inquired.

Jennifer turned and faced her; she wondered how long she had been standing there. She approached Samantha and stood in front of her; Jennifer put her arms round Samantha and kissed her several times.

'My strength is back to normal, my health is a hundred per cent,' Jennifer said.

Jennifer told her the result of her examination she had had in the afternoon.

'I'm glad,' Samantha said.

They went into the kitchen and Samantha made coffee for them both. Jennifer told her about the sphere and the mind it contained. Samantha was enthralled; one of these minds could be in Steven and Janice. She voiced her thoughts to Jennifer, who nodded in agreement.

'When it was probing my brain, I had the feeling I was in the presence of a great evil,' Jennifer said.

'It seems it felt the same about you,' Samantha said.

Jennifer sat on a stool and sipped her coffee. Samantha stood beside her and placed a hand on her shoulder.

'Don't worry, Jenny, I don't think you're a pariah,' Samantha said, trying to keep a straight face.

'I feel better already.' Jennifer kissed her and Samantha smiled happily.

'I saw Steven today and I felt nothing evil about him, in fact he was quite charming,' Samantha said.

'It would stay hidden until the time was right to take over Steven and Janice's mind, when that spaceship gets here, I suppose,' Jennifer said.

Samantha finished her coffee and left the room and went upstairs to her bedroom, she removed her dress and hung it up in her wardrobe, and she heard Jennifer go into the next room. She took off underwear and put on her nightdress and turned off the light; she got into bed.

A girl stood trapped in a glass cage, which was misty and obscured the girl's features. Her hands beat against the glass.

Let me out Let me out.

Samantha woke as if someone had shouted in her ear; she sat up and suddenly noticed a tall dark shadow by the bed, two pin-points of blue light gazing down at her. Samantha switched on the bedside lamp and Jennifer blinked as the light struck her face.

'I wish you'd make some noise when you come in, Jennifer, you nearly gave me a heart attack.'

A loud crack of thunder shook the night; Jennifer noticed Samantha had spoken her name in full, which meant she was angry with her. Jennifer did not want that.

'I'm sorry, Samantha; I did not mean to scare you. I was passing your door, when I heard you calling out.'

Samantha told her about the dream. Thunder crashed and lightning lit up the night sky, rain beat against the windows. Samantha lay back down and saw Jennifer had not moved from the bedside.

'Was there anything else you wanted, Jenny?'

'I just want to make sure you are all right, I was worried about you,' Jennifer said.

'I'm fine and just don't stand there, you're making the place look untidy.'

Jennifer sat in a chair by the bed, Samantha shook her head.

'Are you going to sit there all night?'

Jennifer winked at her.

'Do I disturb you?'

'Just sitting there – like that - Yes,' Samantha said.

Jennifer stood up and started to walk to the door. Samantha called her back. Jennifer stood by the bed and Samantha took hold of her hand.

'If you want to share my bed, why don't you just ask?'

'I'm afraid you'll say no,' Jennifer said, softly.

Samantha let go of her hand and pulled the sheet back and moved across the bed to make room.

'But I will probably say yes.'

Jennifer swiftly got on the bed beside Samantha, who pulled the sheet back over them.

They listened to the storm raging outside. Samantha kissed Jennifer.

'If the storm frightens you, Jenny, I shall protect you.'

'Storms don't frighten me, I'm indestructible,' Jennifer said.

Jennifer kissed her on cheek.

Jennifer moved away from her and lay on her back. Samantha turned on her side, with her back to Jennifer. They let sleep take over their tired bodies.

The tall slim shape was obscured by the opaque glass prison, the shouts became more urgent.

Let me out Let me out.

Samantha tossed and turned in her sleep, her movements woke Jennifer and she switched on the bedside lamp. She gazed at Samantha's sweaty face.

Samantha stood in front of a full-length mirror; the reflection in it was not her. It was Jennifer, she was laughing at her. Samantha put her hands to her ears in an effort to drown out the laughter, she screamed out to Jennifer to stop, but she kept on laughing in her evil tone.

Jennifer ran a hand over Samantha's face; she seemed to be fighting for breath as the nightmare took hold of her. The torment in her expression increased, Jennifer called her name.

The face in the mirror began to welt, the tall figure in the mirror held a long thin blade in one hand, it suddenly shot out of the mirror and buried the blade in Samantha's chest.

Samantha screamed out making Jennifer jump; she sat up and Jennifer put a comforting arm round her. Samantha held her head in her hands.

'That must have been a hell of a dream,' Jennifer said.

Samantha took deep breaths; Jennifer could see she was physically shaken by the nightmare. Jennifer pulled her close and laid Samantha's head on her ample breasts.

'How long have you been having these nightmares?' Jennifer asked.

'All my life, they're a punishment for my sins.'

Samantha told her about the dream. Jennifer was apprehensive in the fact she was in the nightmare.

'Do you think that was me in your dream?'

Samantha lifted her head and smiled at Jennifer.

'Of course not, I feel no fear from you, Jenny. It's like the dreams you have of a person looking like me; which is not me. I won't let my dreams spoil our friendship. I love you too much,' Samantha said.

'I love you too, Sam. If I knew I was doing something to give you these dreams – I would stop it. It is a mystery to me – as it is to you, Sam,' Jennifer said, sincerely.

Jennifer kept a tight hold of her and kissed her on the lips.

'I love your kisses, Jenny,' Samantha said.

'I hate seeing you in pain, Sam. The mind that is working on you is very much alive – we must find it and destroy it,' Jennifer said, defiantly.

They lay down on the bed, their arms round each other; they kissed each other passionately.

The storm still raged outside, and it matched the storm inside Jennifer's head.

CHAPTER XXXI:

THE DEATH OF ANGIE RUSSELL

Samantha woke in the middle of the morning, the storm had blown itself out and the sun was shining brightly, she was alone in bed. She got dressed and had breakfast. She left the house and made her way to the infirmary.

In the infirmary Steven stood by the bed that contained the dying Angie Russell, Janice sat by the bedside playing her guitar and singing in a soft voice.

'Angie, can you hear me?' Steven asked.

Angie moved her head and groaned.

'Where did you hide it?' Angie groaned and Steven placed a hand on her forehead.

'The thing you found has made you ill, we must find it before another person touches it and ends up like you,' Steven said.

Angie tried to speak but she could not find the strength, she just wanted to sleep. She slipped into unconsciousness. Steven moved away from the bed and glanced at Janice then left the infirmary. Melanie McAllister came to the bedside and nodded to Janice, she picked up the small thin wrist and felt for a pulse and found none, and she stared at Janice and shook her head. Janice kept playing her guitar and singing softly; tears ran down her cheeks. Jennifer came in the room and strode to the bedside and Melanie placed a hand on her shoulder.

'Angie's suffering has ended at last,' Melanie said, softly.

'Thanks for all that you've done for her, Mel.'

Jennifer walked out of the infirmary and almost collided with Samantha who was approaching fast. Jennifer shook her head and Samantha knew Angie had died. She gave Jennifer a hug.

'I'm so sorry, Jenny.' Jennifer moved away and gazed down at the ground.

'I didn't even know the girl, Sam.'

'But you cared for her, Jenny.'

But it wasn't enough.

Jennifer walked away from the building with a heavy heart. Samantha followed behind her, sifting through her own private thoughts.

****

Dr Hamilton gazed down at the small body on the operating table in the autopsy room in the Lab 3 building. She knew what had killed the little girl; the medical probe had picked up the radiation contaminating the small body. Whatever the object she had touched must be found before somebody else discovered it. She turned to Valerie Peterson, who stood gazing at the probe monitor.

'Have you been keeping yourself informed about Jennifer and Samantha's activities?' Valerie asked.

Dr Hamilton stared at her companion; Valerie had formed a special bond with Jennifer – they had a mutual trust for each other. She had a high respect for Valerie, as she had done an expert job in training Jennifer. Dr Hamilton had been worried when Jennifer eventually met Samantha. It had been too early for the two girls to meet, as Dr Hamilton had wished it had been sometime longer before they eventually met. As they had not killed each other yet, the signs were favourable for the two girls to hopefully get on with each other. She was sure about Samantha, but Jennifer was another matter, Dr Hamilton was still not sure what was going on in the girl's head. She would have like to question Samantha about her relationship with Jennifer, but that was out of the question. As far as she was concerned Dr Hamilton did not exist and it had to stay that way.

'Yes, General Heywood keeps me informed, they are working well together.'

'Your doubts about Jenny are unfounded,' Valerie said.

'We shall see.'

As if on cue General Heywood walked into the autopsy room, Valerie walked past him and left the room. Dr Hamilton asked him if the object that had killed Angie had been found yet. They had searched the house of the little girl and found traces of radiation behind the wardrobe in her bedroom. There were reports that Jennifer and Samantha had visited the house. Dr Blake had told him about Jennifer's hand.

'I'll give you some anti-radiation pills, you can give Jennifer.'

'They had been doing a lot of work in the physics department of Lab 1, so it's possible they may have it,' the General said.

Dr Hamilton wanted to know what the two girls were up to; they were becoming thick as thieves.

'Have we any idea who attacked them?' she inquired.

General Heywood shook his head and then left the room; he found Valerie outside waiting for him.

'She still has doubts about Jenny.'

The General gazed at her.

'Jennifer is a very strong-willed girl, I haven't found anything bad in her yet and neither has Samantha,' he told her.

'I've worked with Jenny longer than anyone, I trust her.'

They walked down the long corridor.

'I don't know Samantha, I don't want her to hurt Jenny,' Valerie said in a voice full of concern for her former charge.

CHAPTER XXXII:

ENEMY ACTION

Samantha and Jennifer walked slowly along the track towards their home; they had kept silent ever since they left the infirmary.

'Our suffering has only just begun,' Jennifer said, at last.

Samantha stared at her.

'I don't know what you mean.' Samantha smiled as the ice blue eyes seemed to bore into her skull.

'Things have fallen on us from the night sky and there is a large alien spaceship heading towards us,' Jennifer said.

Samantha stared at her sternly; the girl was definitely agitated about something.

'You are not mad at me, Jenny?'

Jennifer stopped walking and laid a hand on her cheek.

'Of course not; I could never be mad at you, Sam,' assured Jennifer.

'I'm glad; I'd die if you were mad at me,' Samantha said.

Samantha put her arms round Jennifer and kissed her. Then she stared at the strain on her pale face.

'Angie's death has hit you hard.'

Jennifer nodded her head.

'And I touched the thing.' Jennifer held up her right hand and Samantha grabbed it.

'How does it feel, Jenny?'

Her hand tingled still and was slightly numb, Jennifer was glad it had not spread up her arm.

'IT'S NOT TOO BAD, IT HAS NOT GOT WORSE.'

They continued walking towards Samantha's house, unknown to them they were being watched. Samantha still held Jennifer's hand.

'You can let go, if you want to,' Jennifer said, amusingly.

Samantha let go of it, as she had not realised she still had hold of Jennifer's hand.

'Sorry.'

The tall dark figure shadowing them, kept concealed amongst the trees on the right side of the track. They had to get rid of the two girls as soon as possible - they were becoming a threat.

They stood by the front door. Jennifer ran her hand over Samantha's cheek, and then she ran her fingers over her thin lips. Samantha opened her mouth and Jennifer slid her index and middle fingers into it. Samantha closed her sharp teeth gently onto them.

'I hope you aren't hungry, Sam.'

Samantha opened her mouth and Jennifer withdrew her fingers.

'If you stick your fingers in people's mouths, you expect to get them bitten,' Samantha said.

Samantha opened the front door and let Jennifer go in first. She turned and looked towards the trees lining the other side of the track. A telescopic gun sight was fixed on the centre of her forehead. The finger tightened on the trigger. Jennifer grabbed her hand and pulled her violently into the house; the finger slackened the pressure on the trigger.

'Hey, you nearly pulled my arm off,' Samantha complained.

Jennifer was staring hard at her, the eyes started to get bluer colour in them – it showed Samantha she was up to something. The face was a mask of concentration. It seemed as if Jennifer wanted to have another go at getting inside her head. On the few occasions Jennifer had tried to sense what Samantha was thinking – she had got nowhere – unconsciously Samantha had been putting up barriers to stop her. The last time – the night she had spent in Samantha's bed – Jennifer had made her strongest effort yet. Boosting Samantha's sexual emotions – her mind was getting stronger and Jennifer found more of her mental powers coming into fruition.

'If you tell me what you're looking for, I might be able to help you,' Samantha said.

The sapphire blue eyes stared hard at her – it was hypnotic – she could not pull away from Jennifer.

'I was trying to probe your mind and access your memories.'

Samantha moved closer to her until their bodies touched.

'Is that what you were doing last night?' Samantha asked.

Jennifer put her hands on each side of her face and gazed into Samantha's bright green eyes. After a few moments Samantha felt a throb inside her head. Jennifer noticed the change of hue in the green eyes and she moved away from Samantha.

'Were you getting a headache?'

Samantha nodded her head. 'I had a slight throb in the head,' Samantha replied.

Jennifer kissed her passionately; Samantha sighed with pleasure.

'That was my fault, I'm afraid, part of your mind is fighting me, when I probe deeper into your memories.'

Samantha ran a hand over Jennifer's face; then kissed her. Jennifer purred with delight.

'I'm not consciously fighting your attempts to read my mind, if you can help me to sort my head out, I shall be forever grateful.'

Jennifer smiled; Samantha had complete trust in her. Samantha belonged to her. Jennifer's mind buzzed with excitement. The deep depression that had plagued her mind all morning was fading away. Samantha had a calming effect on her. She pushed Samantha firmly against the wall and kissed her full on the mouth. Samantha's head began to throb again, she closed her eyes and Jennifer kept kissing her. Samantha put her arms round Jennifer and gave herself up to Jennifer's passion. Her head began to throb slightly, but did not get any worse so she let it be, as she did not want Jennifer to stop kissing her.

After a while Jennifer moved away from her.

'I'm sorry, Sam; I got quite carried away there.'

'You can get carried away like that, whenever you like, you have a strong mind and a very passionate personality,' Samantha said.

They walked down the hallway hand in hand.

'I can use your negative emotions to probe your mind, but that would be more painful to you. I won't do that because I care for you too much,' Jennifer said.

A man approached the open front door, as Samantha had all her attention on Jennifer; she had forgotten to shut it. He stepped over the threshold, he saw the two girls by the stairs. He stood still and held the blade firmly in his hand.

'Do you want me to keep trying?' Jennifer asked.

Jennifer laid her back against the banister and ran a hand over Samantha's cheek.

'Yes,' Samantha replied without hesitation.

'Good girl.'

Jennifer slowly unbuttoned the pink blouse Samantha was wearing and removed it. She stared at the sapphire blue eyes. Jennifer removed the maroon skirt Samantha was wearing.

'I noticed you weren't wearing a bra and you've got no panties on either.'

Jennifer kissed her on the lips then moved down to Samantha's slender neck. She kissed Samantha's bare breasts.

Watching the two girls the assassin was sure he could get close to them before they noticed him. As they seemed to be more interested in the game they were playing.

'Are you getting anywhere?' Samantha asked.

Jennifer grinned and kissed her; Samantha felt a hand slip between her slim thighs.

The man in the gymnasium was close to the door that stood ajar. He could hear the two girls as they stood close to the door.

Jennifer moved away from Samantha at last.

'Was that nice for you, Sam?'

Samantha smiled at her.

'Very nice, you're a very sexy girl, Jenny.'

Jennifer beamed at her and ran her hand over Samantha's cheek.

'I've still got a few more surprises up my sleeve for your body,' Jennifer said.

'I can't wait,' Jennifer said.

Jennifer went into the kitchen to get a glass of water – she needed cooling down, and she was too hot to handle in more ways than one. Samantha made her way down the hallway; she stopped at the lounge door. She noticed the front door was open.

Careless.

She had been attacked once; someone out there wanted her out of the way. Jennifer had made her forget security. Samantha cursed herself for letting her emotions cloud her sense of survival. She would have to be more alert when she was dealing with Jennifer. She did not fully trust the girl yet; Jennifer had a powerful personality, something she had to beware of.

Samantha closed the front door and walked towards the lounge door; she pushed it with the tip of her right foot. As the door opened wider, she stared into the room. Nothing moved and no unusual sound was detected by her sensitive hearing.

Surprise is everything.

The assassin was not behind the lounge door as Samantha thought. He was in the room opposite. He watched her cross the threshold of the lounge, and then he moved silently across the hallway towards her. The long thin blade held firmly in his right hand.

First attack is to maim.

He lunged forward thrusting the blade into the back of the tall girl before him.

The sharp pain in her back told Samantha someone was behind her. Samantha moved away and swung her right fist in an arc at whoever was behind her.

His eyes never left the target before him and he ducked his head under the flying bony fist and kicked out hard with his right leg and the steel toecap of his shoe struck her bottom and knocked her forward, Samantha lost her footing and went down flat on her face.

Second attack is to finish off the victim.

The assassin slammed his right foot down on her back, knocking the wind out of her. With his other foot he aimed a kick at her head.

Come on, Sammy. Where is your killer instinct?

His foot failed to hit the target as Samantha grabbed it with her hand and at the same moment lifted her body off the floor with her other arm; losing his balance the assassin fell sideways onto the sofa. Samantha leapt to her feet. She watched the killer get onto his feet; she bent down quickly and lifted up the heavy coffee table. The man was fast but Samantha was quicker; as he leapt forward aiming the his thin blade at the girl, he came in collision with the flying coffee table. Samantha heard a cracking sound, could not be sure if it was the table or the killer's skull. He fell in a heap on the floor. Samantha gazed down at the still form; there was a lot of blood on the face. He looked dead. This was her first kill. Samantha felt no remorse; it was him or her.

Jennifer stood in the kitchen sipping iced water from a glass, when she heard the crash in the lounge. She dropped the glass and ran out of the kitchen, her first mistake. She ran into the man coming out of the gymnasium, he swung the heavy wooden club he was holding and aimed for her head. Jennifer cried out and put her arms up to protect her precious head. The club hit her right wrist she heard the bones breaking and the pain shot up her arm. She was grabbed from behind and a sharp point of a blade was pressed against her slender neck.

Samantha came out of the lounge, she had heard Jennifer cry out. She gazed down the hallway and immediately saw Jennifer's predicament. She would not be able to get to Jennifer before the blade slit her throat – Samantha was fast on her feet, but not that fast. Her eyes fell on the small high table she had at the side of the hall – a large crystal ball sat on a matt black plinth.

Could she throw it and hit the assassin before he plunged the blade into Jennifer's neck?

Velocity.

It depends on how hard you can throw it.

With one quick movement Samantha picked up the crystal ball and threw it with all her might.

Jennifer felt the blade cut into her neck and something flashed by an inch from her head. Suddenly she was free. She turned and gazed down at her attacker – the top of his skull had been cracked like an eggshell by the heavy crystal ball. She looked up and stared towards Samantha, who was walking slowly towards her.

'Bullseye,' Samantha exclaimed.

Samantha stared down at the body and the crushed skull, and then she looked up at Jennifer.

'Are you hurt?'

Jennifer lifted her right arm. Samantha gazed at the thin wrist; the pale skin was now flushed and discoloured.

'My wrist is broken.'

Jennifer placed her left hand on Samantha' s back and guided her into the kitchen; she felt the wetness and gazed at her hand and saw in horror, her hand was covered in blood. She stood behind Samantha and saw the back of the blouse had blood on it.

'You're bleeding.'

Samantha knew she had been knifed in the back; she removed the blouse.

'You've been stabbed in the back.'

Jennifer sat her down on a stool and she looked for the med-kit. When she found it, Jennifer washed the blood from Samantha's back and dressed the wound.

'Thanks, Jenny, we should get your wrist to hospital.'

Samantha went up to her bedroom and put on a clean blouse and came back down and found Jennifer in the lounge. She gazed down at the body on the floor.

'Two attempts at the same time, they must be getting desperate.'

'It doesn't say much for the security round here,' Samantha observed.

After she spoke the last word the window shattered, and something hit the floor by the sofa. Jennifer shoved Samantha towards the open door. She shouted to Samantha to get out of the house quick. Samantha ran to the front door, hoping Jennifer was right behind her. Jennifer started to chase after her, but her leading foot hit something and she fell headlong on the floor. Then there was a loud explosion. A blast of hot air rushed over her; the room disintegrated around her.

Samantha had the door open as the lounge wall was blown outwards and she was hit by an invisible force that thrust her out of the house. She heard a scream inside her head.

Jenny.

With his telescopic sight on the front door of the house, he was disappointed to see Samantha exit the house. He wondered if he should bring her down with one shot or play the prey for a bit, get some target practice in. His finger tightened on the trigger as he kept the tall ginger-haired girl in his sights.

As Samantha made her way onto the track, something slammed into her side almost knocking her over, she felt a burning pain, and she looked down and saw the left side of her blouse was blossoming red. Someone was shooting at her. Samantha started to run away from her attacker, but she hadn't got far when a second bullet hit her in the back; the impact sent her sprawling headlong onto the dusty track. She lay still hoping the hit man would think she was dead. The killer wanted to make sure – Samantha felt another bullet slam into her body.

Steven and Janice were just entering the main gate of the research facility when they heard the distant explosion. Steven gazed down the track and saw the smoke rising up into the sky in the direction of Samantha's home. He told Janice to get the emergency services out to Samantha's home. He ran off down the track until he came to Samantha's prone body on the track; he turned her over onto her back. The eyes fluttered open and all life seemed to have left the pale green eyes. Her expression told him the pain she was feeling.

'Hang on, Sam, Janice is getting help.'

'J-Jenny is still in the house.' The voice was weak and just audible, and then she passed out.

Janice ran across the research compound and met Melanie and got her to contact Hilary and inform her there had been an explosion at Samantha's house. Then she went to the building that held the fire truck and informed the crew they were wanted. Hilary immediately got her paramedics suitably equipped and the military ambulance raced out of the compound and went into the direction of the marsh.

Steven Calvert was kneeling beside the still body of his friend. He held her long delicate right hand, and he knew a spark of life was still inside her. Over the time they had known each other he had grown a deep affection for the tall girl. He ran a hand over her cheek.

'Stay with us, Sam, we don't want to lose you, now we have grown to love you,' he said, softly.

Steven stood up as the ambulance drew up to him, Hilary leapt out with her med kit, and Steven told her Samantha had been shot three times, twice in the back, and once in the side. The other paramedics brought out a stretcher and loaded the injured girl onto it. Steven informed Hilary that Jennifer was still in the house.

The fire truck drove past the ambulance and parked by the front of the house and began to put the fire out, and then they made sure the house was safe for the security team to enter. Colonel Hopkins arrived on the scene; Michelle Gowning drove the jeep up to the house.

'Someone just doesn't like Sam,' she said, as she got out of the car.

Before the Colonel could comment Steven came up to him and informed him about Jennifer.

'It doesn't look good,' was all Michelle could say.

Colonel Hopkins and Michelle entered the house by the back door and went through the kitchen; they found the corpse by the door of the gymnasium. They gazed at the crushed head, then Michelle spied the large crystal ball by the door, she picked it up and saw the blood and hair on it.

'This is what killed him,' she said.

'You'd better put it down where you found it, the forensic team won't like you touching the evidence,' Hopkins said.

Michelle placed the crystal ball down on the floor where she had found it. Then she followed the Colonel slowly up the hallway towards the devastation that was the lounge. Captain Rogers stood by the door of the opposite room as he supervised his men who were slowly clearing out the debris from the lounge. He saluted the Colonel as he approached.

'Any sign of the girl yet, Captain?'

Captain Rogers shook his head and motioned to the damage in the lounge. 'The ceiling has come down. If she wasn't killed by the explosion, she would have been crushed by part of the ceiling falling on her.'

John Walsh and his forensic team took photographs of the corpse in the hallway and the crystal ball. Paramedics then loaded the dead man onto a stretcher and took him out to the waiting truck. Steven Hilbert and his father were walking slowly down the track from where Steven had found Samantha towards the house; a forensic man was with them carrying a camera. Steven stepped amongst the trees opposite the house and studied the ground around them. After a while Steven knelt down and noticed a shoe print in the earth. He called his father.

'I didn't find any spent cartridges, so the shooter probably took them with him,' Steven said.

Steven gazed down at the ground at the footprint; the man from the forensic team was photographing it.

'It looks like a man's shoe, by the deep impression of the footprint I would say it was male. There are not too many females here that handle firearms.'

David Calvert was impressed with his son.

Eventually the corpse in the lounge was uncovered and it had caught the full force of the explosion. The sofa had been blown against the wall. One of the soldiers was about to move it and he noticed a hand lying against the wall protruding from behind the sofa. He called to Captain Rogers and he helped the soldier move the sofa slowly away from the wall. Colonel Hopkins came up to them and gazed down at Jennifer, as she lay on her side – the sofa had protected her body from the explosion. Michelle knelt down and lifted the thin wrist and felt for a pulse, then looked up at the Colonel.

'Lucky girl, she's still alive.'

Colonel Hopkins went out and called the paramedics in to take the unconscious girl out of the wrecked lounge. Jennifer was placed into the ambulance and driven to the hospital in the research facility.

Juliet Prentice and Hazel Johnson were leaving the observatory as they had finished their shift there. They met Janice outside and she told them about Samantha. Juliet raced off towards the medical lab. She came across Melanie McAllister and questioned her about Samantha. She told Juliet that Samantha was still in surgery, which meant the girl was hanging onto life. Juliet found a seat and sat down and waited for news of Samantha. Half an hour later Hilary Calvert came up to her. Juliet leapt to her feet.

'Is Sam going to be all right?'

Hilary placed a hand on Juliet's shoulder and nodded. Samantha was still unconscious, but she was stable, and Hilary was sure Samantha would pull through. Hilary told the young girl to home; there was nothing she could do.

JANUARY 2129

Juliet Prentice was at her station beside the hospital bed her friend lay in. Hilary knew nothing short of an explosion would remove the girl from Samantha's bedside, so Hilary let her stay. On the other side of the bed machines were monitoring Samantha's body as it got on with the work of repairing itself. Though Samantha was still unconscious her body was getting stronger. They all hoped she would soon come out of the coma. Juliet kept her eyes on Samantha's face as she waited for a sign to show the older girl was waking up. When the eyes flittered open, Juliet got to her feet, Samantha blinked as the bright light irritated her eyes.

'At last, Sam, why take so long to wake from a snooze?'

Samantha had been so sure she would wake up dead after being shot three times, but now had to hear one of Juliet's bad jokes; Samantha knew she was very much alive. She tried to sit up and felt queasy; Juliet put a hand on her chest and pushed her back down on the bed; then kissed her on the lips.

'What are you playing at, Sam, keep still,' scolded Juliet.

'Yes, Doctor.'

Juliet walked out of the ward room door and caught sight of Hilary. Juliet informed her Samantha was back with the living. Hilary raced into the ward room and found Samantha sitting up in bed; she gave the girl a smile and detached Samantha from the machinery at the side of her bed. Hilary took her temperature and felt her wrist for her pulse.

'How are you feeling, Sam?'

'I'm happy to be alive. How about Jennifer, did she survive?'

Hilary nodded her head; Juliet answered her query.

'We don't know how, the bedroom above the lounge fell on her, Jennifer's got more lives than a cat.'

Samantha sighed deeply; she was very glad Jennifer was still alive. Hilary told her Jennifer was still in a coma.

'The General will want to see you, when you're ready,' Hilary said.

Samantha made a sour face; she would get the blame for everything.

'I can't wait.'

Hilary got Melanie to fix up a light meal for Samantha. Later in the day she was visited by her friends who cheered her up. In the late evening Naomi Evans visited her dressed in a nurse's uniform.

'Hi Sam, nice to see you looking well,' Naomi said.

Naomi sat in a chair beside the bed; Samantha had not seen the older girl since the time she had turned up in her home, the night the spheres fell from the sky. Naomi started to question Samantha about her lapses into lengthy comas after the assorted injures that her body had endured. Hilary had told her the date and Samantha was shocked herself to know she had been out for three months.

Samantha could not think of a reason for it, Dr Blake had told her it was her body's way of getting time to heal itself.

'You seemed to be checking my medical records thoroughly.'

Samantha stared hard at Naomi, who could almost feel the bright green eyes boring into her skull.

'I'm a good judge of how intelligent a person is...' Samantha started.

Naomi kept silent waiting for Samantha to continue.

'I bet that nurse's uniform hides a multitude of sins.'

Naomi was already aware that Samantha was a girl you could not pull the wool over her eyes so easily. The green eyes were putting her under a microscope.

'You are the last person I want to deceive,' Naomi said, truthfully.

Naomi stood up.

'I'll let you get some rest; I'll see you tomorrow, Sam.'

Samantha watched her walk down the ward room. There was more to Naomi that meets the eye. Samantha was going to enjoy working the girl out. She liked a challenge.

In the morning General Heywood and Colonel Hopkins came to see her. The General asked how she was, and Samantha knew by the tone in his voice that he was very concerned about her. Samantha gave them a report on what had happened to Jennifer and herself as far as she could remember it. Samantha owned up to killing the two men and she did not have any choice, but to do what she had done, it was them or her. When she had finished her narrative, she sighed and closed her eyes.

'It's all right Samantha, you won't be charged with anything,' the General told her.

Samantha opened her eyes and stared at him sharply.

'Have you found the person that was shooting at me?'

Colonel Hopkins shook his head; the perpetrator had covered their tracks well. They had found a footprint – but it did not lead to their capture.

'Someone knows more about me, than I do myself, they see a reason why I should die,' Samantha said, bluntly.

The General tried to avoid her piercing green eyes. That told Samantha a lot about him.

And, so do you, General.

In the afternoon Karen Thompson came to see Samantha, carrying her schoolbooks with her. She told Samantha, just because she was in a hospital bed, it was no reason not to continue her schoolwork.

'Thanks, Miss Thompson, that's just what I need.'

Karen gazed at her sternly.

'I hope you're being sarcastic,' Karen said in a warning tone.

Samantha shook her head.

'Of course not, Miss.'

Karen Thompson smiled to herself as Samantha got down to doing her schoolwork. She was glad the tall girl knew who the boss was. Karen took no nonsense from any student who thought they were bigger and more intelligent than the rest. Samantha knew Karen was not a woman to trifle with and Samantha knew she still had a lot to learn, before she did what the General expected of her.

Three hours later Hilary came in to do some tests on Samantha, and Karen left the ward.

'It's nice to see you trying to make up the months of schooling you've missed,' Hilary said.

'I didn't have much choice.'

In the middle of the night Samantha woke and slid out of bed. She had had a dream and Jennifer was in it; she had to find out where she was being kept. Jennifer had told her there was a way to get down to the underground facility from Lab 3. Samantha had to find it and see what was happening to Jennifer with her own eyes. She walked out of the ward and walked past the operating rooms and walked along a short corridor which led her to a large room. She surveyed it and discovered a security camera above some lift doors – there was no way she could do anything unobserved, which did not worry her, as she had to be watched in case the shooter came for her again. Samantha wanted to get down to the lower level before she was apprehended. She strode quickly to the lift and gazed at the control panel. Luckily Jennifer had given her the code numbers. She ran her long slender fingers over the keypad and the doors slid open. Samantha got in the lift and pressed the button that took the lift downwards. The doors slid shut and the lift made its descent.

The lift stopped and the doors slid open, she exited the lift and found herself in a large medical room, with three life capsules as described to her by Jennifer. She gazed down at the occupants and gave out a loud gasp of astonishment.

Three capsules, three Jennifers. Samantha gazed at them and tried to distinguish which was the real Jennifer and which were the clones. Samantha heard footsteps approaching and she looked up. A pretty woman of average height wearing a white lab coat gazed at her suspiciously. Jennifer had told her about Valarie Peterson, who used to look after her.

'Valerie!'

'You must be Samantha, Jenny told me about you.'

Samantha told Valerie she had come down to see how Jennifer was. They would not tell her anything.

'Jenny told me how much you care for her and I don't care for her less,' Samantha said.

Valerie opened the lid of one of the end capsules and motioned Samantha to come close to her.

'Jenny used to have bad dreams concerning you and when she left here, I thought you might hurt her.'

Samantha shook her head.

'When we met and got to know each other, Jenny saw I was no danger to her.'

Samantha gazed down at the pale serene face; Jennifer was in a place where there was no pain.

'Her life signs have stabilized, she will pull through, once her body has repaired itself,' Valerie said

'I'm so glad and relieved; it was a miracle Jenny survived the explosion.'

Valerie put a hand on her shoulder.

'Jenny is a very strong girl, she always tells me, and she is indestructible.'

Samantha laughed softly.

'She told me that too; now I believe her.'

Dr Sally Hamilton walked out of her office and turned the corner to approach the life support capsules; she stopped dead when she saw who Valerie was talking to. It was the first time she had had a good look at her daughter, since leaving her with foster parents at the age of twelve. Sally fought the urge to race over to Samantha and gives her a motherly hug. She had to be dispassionate about Samantha; she did not have the luxury of having a normal mother-daughter relationship. Samantha had a destiny to follow and Dr Hamilton had to let her go. Even now that she knew someone wanted Samantha dead, the dangers for her daughter had only just begun. There was something more sinister waiting for her. Studying Samantha as she talked to Valerie, she could see Samantha was developing into a strong athletic person, she was a lot taller than her and she could see Samantha was taller than Jennifer.

'You'd better go back up where you came from, before they come and get you,' Valerie said.

Samantha took out an envelope from her nightgown pocket and gave it to Valerie.

'Can you give that to Jenny for me; don't let anybody else read it, please.'

Valerie slid the letter in her lab coat pocket.

'Trust me, Samantha, I shall give it to Jenny as soon as she comes to,' Valerie promised.

Samantha walked away and returned to the lift doors and got in the lift. When she was gone, Dr Hamilton walked over to Valerie.

'What did Samantha want?'

Valerie told her. 'You'll have to tell me about Samantha, she seems a very nice girl,' Valerie said.

Sally Hamilton walked away. Jennifer was Valerie's concern, and Samantha had to look after herself.

When the lift doors opened she saw Naomi waiting for her.

'Did you enjoy your little trip?'

Samantha walked out of the lift and made her way back to the ward. Naomi followed behind her, as she could not walk as fast as Samantha and she did not feel like running to keep up with the tall athletic girl. Samantha got back in bed and stared up at Naomi, as she stood over the bed.

'The General sent you to slap my wrist, did he?'

Naomi grinned.

'I think he wants to slap more than your wrist.'

'I've been a very naughty girl, well I never saw myself as an angel,' Samantha said, coldly.

In the morning after Hilary had done some tests to see if she was healthy enough to leave the ward and get on with her studies, Samantha was released from the hospital ward. She walked out of the main gate of the facility and made her way to the school building. Karen Thompson gave her a warm welcome when she entered the classroom, Samantha sat next to Steven Calvert, who kissed her on the cheek. At the end of the school day, Samantha and Steven left the school together.

'You'll be staying with us, Sam, so we can keep an eye on you.'

Samantha pulled a face and shook her head. 'It's not your eye I'm worried about, it's the wandering hands.'

Steven laughed. He liked Samantha a lot and was always trying to steal a kiss from her.

'At home I shall be on my best behaviour,' Steven promised.

'Good, you seem to forget Janice is your girlfriend,' Samantha reminded him.

Samantha slowly got back to the continuation of her life, work, work and more work. In the mornings she attended school to get on with her vigorous learning schedules. In the afternoons she worked in the physics laboratory with Michelle Gowning, who was the only one of the military scientists that she could call a friend. Samantha spent several nights with her and enjoyed making love to the full-bodied girl. Security never let her out of their sight. Some of the evenings she visited the observatory and used the huge telescope to gaze at the stars and planets. Close to the orbit of the planet Jupiter was the great alien spaceship, sitting there waiting, waiting for what?

The right time.

The right time for what? Samantha wondered.

That's what Samantha wanted to know.

Steven Calvert left the research complex and Samantha called on Janice.

'I'll be going away soon; so, I want to spend as much time making love to you, as I can,' Samantha said.

'You'd better stay here until that time comes, Sam.'

'I'd hope you'd say that, Janice,' Samantha said.

The doorbell rang and Juliet answered the door; she smiled happily when she saw Samantha standing on the doorstep. Juliet let her in and shut the door.

'Janice told me you were leaving soon,' Juliet said.

'I shall miss you both,' Samantha said.

'Have you found a girl for yourself?'

Juliet shook her head. 'Not since Sarah went away.'

'What about Wendy Goodman; she is going with anyone and her house mate is going with Henry Jones. Wendy is very much like you in a lot of ways and I think she's just waiting for you to make the first move,' Samantha said.

Juliet thought for a moment; she liked Wendy; though they had only spoken a few times; while at school; they had never worked together at the research facility.

'Do you think I'm her sort of girl?'

'Of course, you are,' Samantha assured her.

Juliet giggled and stood on tip toe and kissed Samantha on the lips.

The next day Juliet went in search of Wendy; she found the girl by the marsh.

'Are you having fun, Wendy?' Juliet asked.

'Yes, I love swimming in the marsh,' Wendy said.

'On a hot day in the summer it gets a bit smelly,' Juliet said.

'I wait until the rains fill it up after the summer,' Wendy said.

They started walking towards the houses.

'Are you still living alone, Wendy?'

'More or less; Mel spends most of her time with Henry – don't tell the General; it's a secret.'

'Would you like to come and stay with me?'

Wendy stopped and gazed at Juliet. 'I did not know if you liked me.'

'The times I see you, you seem to be a pleasant girl; I want to get to know you more,' Juliet said.

Wendy put her arm round Juliet's waist and kissed her on the cheek. They made their way to Juliet's house. They had dinner together and then they relaxed on the sofa.

Janice entered the school and the two new boys came and walked on either side of her. Malcolm Williams and David Murray had arrived two days earlier.

PART FOUR:

THE FORTRESS

CHAPTER XXXIII:

THE MACHINE

MAY 2130

Eighteen-year-old Samantha Hamilton stared up at the high walls of the high-tech facility called the Fortress. She was glad to finally learn her real surname and the General promised her he would tell her about her parents. She hoped they would tell her what they wanted of her.

Sarah Mullen drove the car up to the main gate; General Heywood sat beside her. Samantha sat back in the back seat. The gates opened and Sarah drove into this new place Samantha was being deposited in. Here she was to find out the purpose of her learning and training, to at last find out what they wanted her to do. She hoped to get an insight into why someone wanted to murder her. Samantha still had to look over her shoulder to make sure nobody was about to creep up on her and do her some harm.

Samantha had spent the last year in the Capital, she had lived with Sarah in her flat. Samantha was very happy, and she had had several meetings with her father, who had been very impressed with her. She had met several of the people in his Government. Samantha looked, listened and learnt while she was in conversation with them. They wanted to know about her, and Samantha was going to acquire all the knowledge she could about the Government that wanted to use her in whatever plan they had in mind. Samantha wanted to use the system for her own ends. Some days she was free to do whatever she wanted, Sarah was her guide round the Capital, and she introduced Samantha to her friends in her organisation, as Sarah called it. Sarah told her a change was coming and she was going to be the catalyst. Samantha believed her, she was a very intelligent girl, an ideal person to have as a friend, if you were devising a campaign of their own, like Samantha was.

Sarah parked the car by the office building; the General got out of the car and entered the office building. Samantha got out of the car and approached Sarah, who stood by the car.

'Thank you, Sarah, for everything, I appreciate all that you have done for me.'

Sarah grinned and put her arms round Samantha and hugged her hard, then stood on tiptoe and kissed Samantha on the lips.

'It's been a pleasure and don't forget: if you get into any trouble, call me.'

Samantha winked at her. 'If you find a place for me in your organisation – let me know.'

'I will,' Sarah promised.

Sarah got back in the car.

'I will,' Samantha said.

Samantha watched the car drive out of the gates, then went into the office building. General Heywood was waiting patiently for her. He was talking to another high-ranking officer. Colonel Jackson was chief of security at the Fortress, he gazed at Samantha; General Heywood had briefed him about her abilities. She stared back at him as he ran a speculative eye over her. She was sure the General had warned him about her. Colonel Jackson found Samantha an interesting subject, as he gazed at the thin freckled face with the deep set bright green eyes; her ginger hair had been cut short.

General Heywood told Samantha to follow him and he made for a door behind the desks. It slid open and they entered the operations room. Samantha looked round the room with her inquisitive eye. White coated technicians walked about the large room and some tended computers that lined one side of the room. It was a hive of activity; there were several army officers there too. The General gave her a tour of the operations room; the technicians greeted her warmly as they had been advised of her coming. She came across a familiar face; her dark hair had been shortened.

'Well, Naomi, this is a pleasant surprise.'

Naomi Evans looked away from her computer monitor and gazed up at Samantha.

'Hello Sam, I like the dress.'

Samantha was wearing a figure-hugging cream coloured dress; the hem came down to her knees. She left Naomi to her work. General Heywood guided her out of the room and out of the building; he gave her a tour of the rest of the Fortress.

'You didn't tell me Naomi was here.'

'It was a surprise to me also, she works for Dr Blake and she had clearance to work here, so I won't throw her out.'

Samantha was pleased about that, she liked Naomi and she wanted to know why Naomi was following her about.

In the centre of the compound was a large single-storey building which served as barracks for the troops stationed in the military facility. In front of it just past the main gate was a firing range. Samantha hoped the General would allow her to use it; after the attacks on her person he had issued her with a hand gun, which lay in her dress pocket. On the west side of the compound was the accommodation huts, General Heywood opened the door of the first one and told Samantha it would be her living quarters. She entered the dwelling; it was partitioned into four rooms, equipped with everything she would need for an easy living. Samantha was pleased with her new temporary home.

'I'm glad you're happy with your living quarters, it may help you to be contented in your work.'

Samantha made a face.

'Work. I thought there would be a catch,' she said.

General Heywood smiled at her and they left the building. The laboratory buildings ran along the rear boundary fence. They approached the first one and alongside it she saw a familiar sight. The large glistening shape of the alien scout ship sat on the grass at the side of the building.

'How did that get here?'

The General told her it had been airlifted here, as they had nobody who could fly it. He cheered Samantha up by telling her it was up to her to get it up and running. He guided her into the laboratory. She walked round the room, where she was going to work. She had her own compact computer system. There was a long work bench in the middle of the room. Along the wall opposite the computer was a strange looking machine, Samantha walked along its length and stared at it; the machine was long and filled with coloured tubes and wires. It was the weirdest thing she had ever laid eyes on.

'What does it do?' she asked.

'That is what you have to find out.'

Samantha shook her head.

'How did I know you were going to say that?'

He grinned at her and Samantha had a nasty thought.

'What if it blows me up into a lot of small pieces?'

'I've got complete faith in your abilities. I hope you don't damage yourself; I have got used to having you around.'

Samantha stared at him. Their working relationship had got better over the last year and they had softened their attitude towards each other. The General would not tell Samantha, but he liked her. He was going make sure she was not injured by the machine. He would make sure she followed safety procedures. Samantha sat on a low bench in front of the machine.

'Why don't you start from the beginning,' she said.

Stanley Hamilton, Samantha's father, a physicist of renowned repute, was working to perfect a new fuel for the spacecraft XS 150, which was kept at the Fortress when it was not in space. One day while driving along the road towards the Fortress he came across a girl of about fifteen years of age, walking along the side of the road. He stopped the car in front of her and opened the passenger door.

The girl got in beside him. Stanley Hamilton asked her several questions, but the girl remained silent. She was a tall girl, well over six feet in height, she wore a rough brown habit, and she pulled the cowl off her head and turned her pale thin face to him. She had short curly hair above a high domed forehead and deep set dark blue eyes that studied him with concentrated interest. Seeing he was not a threat to her, the girl gave him a beaming smile with her thin lips.

Stanley drove into the Fortress taking the girl with him. She was taken to the medical research laboratory and Dr Richard Blake gave the girl a full medical examination. The girl remained silent throughout the tests and never complained at the treatment she received. She was housed in one of the living quarters and Stanley taught her how to use the appliances. The girl attached herself to Stanley and every morning he went to his lab, she was waiting outside for him. He named her Sally and she started to speak to him in an undefined language. He took her to Dr Erika Strasberg's department and Erika and her colleagues set about teaching the girl the English language and trying to learn her language.

Sally became his loyal assistant and companion, when she was able to speak his language. Two years later he married her and a year later she gave birth to Samantha. When her daughter was six, Sally embarked on a project of her own. She was very secretive, and she kept her work to herself and her daughter. She kept the lab locked up and little Samantha was the only person to accompany Sally in the lab.

Then tragedy struck. Stanley Hamilton crashed his car, killing himself and leaving Sally in a critical condition. Little Samantha managed to drag her mother from the wreckage. They broke into the laboratory and found the machine. They were unable to access the computer system and get into Sally's private database.

The spacecraft standing outside the building was found in the wood a mile away from the Fortress, it had crashed into the trees. The hatch was open, and they got into the flight deck and they found a tall red headed female sitting in one of the seats; she was dead.

When General Heywood had finished his narrative, Samantha stood up and paced the room.

There it is, Sam – Not only are you different and mistrusted, you are also half alien – Isn't that the killing joke?

Samantha stopped pacing and turned to the General.

'I have no memories of my life under the age of twelve.'

'After the accident you became seriously ill, you were in and out of hospital until Dr Blake finally found what was ailing you. After your erratic body condition was stabilized, it was found your alien brain was not working in conjunction with each other. Dr Blake has operated on your brain as far as he can go. It is now up to you. He thinks when you finally stabilize your two different brains start working together you will get your memories back.'

Samantha sat down on the bench beside the General.

'That's a lot to take in at once, it's a pity Juliet isn't here, she would just love to hear that, not only am I crazy, but I'm an alien also,' Samantha said.

The General put a hand on her shoulder.

'You're not crazy and to me, you're as human as anyone I know.'

Samantha's eyes brightened and she gave him a smile.

'Thank you for that.'

She stood up and went to the machine.

'With no papers or instruction manual, what am I supposed to do with it?' Samantha asked, puzzled.

'Your mother may have passed something on to you, locked in your memory when you were six.'

'As far as my memory is concerned that six-year-old girl is no more, she worked with Mother, I don't have that luxury,' Samantha said.

General Heywood stood up.

'You won't be working alone, I've got the right person to give you a hand,' he said.

CHAPTER XXXIV:

WHERE THERE'S A WILL. . .

Samantha lay on her bed and gazed up at the ceiling in the hope of inspiration. She let her mind drift away. She was born of two worlds, the significance of her brain configuration was driven home to her. Samantha had a lot of hard thinking to do, she was a different person now and she had to come to terms with her differences. She was heading for enlightenment or total destruction.

A knock on her front door brought her out of her reverie, she got off the bed and went to the wardrobe, as she could not answer the door naked. She put on her underwear, and then she put on the military uniform the General had given her. When she went to answer the summons, she wondered about the assistant the General had for her – he had not told her who it was. Samantha opened the door and a wide smile spread over her thin lips. She stepped back and allowed her visitor to enter her quarters.

Naomi Evans rushed in and slammed the door shut. She threw her arms round Samantha and hugged her.

'You are a military girl now.'

'You seem to be following me about,' Samantha said.

'Dr Blake assigned me here – to watch over you.'

'You are certainly a sight for sore eyes – I thought I would be working with strangers.'

Naomi smiled. 'It'll be great working with you, Sam.'

'You haven't heard what we are working on yet,' Samantha warned her.

'Well, Boss, how about filling me in on the task we are about to undertake,' Naomi said.

They left the living quarters and made their way to the laboratory building. They entered the building and Samantha showed Naomi the strange alien machine.

'It's lovely, what does it do?'

'That's what I asked the General. It's our task to find out,' Samantha said.

'Nothing tricky, then,' Naomi observed, dryly.

Samantha took Naomi by the arm and took her to the compact computer system.

'I want you to work on the computer, you are a better specialist in that field than me,' Samantha said.

Naomi sat in front of the computer and activated the control desk.

'Access denied, there's always a catch,' Naomi said.

'We can't have everything,' Samantha observed.

Samantha stood behind Naomi while she worked on the computer, searching for the code to break the lockout. Samantha started to massage Naomi's shoulders, she sighed with pleasure.

'That's lovely, darling.'

Samantha told her the story the General had told her concerning her parents. Naomi listened with interest.

'You remember the probe picture of my brain configuration, now we know the reason for it, half human and half alien; I hope our friendship has not been damaged by this information.'

Naomi stood up and faced her.

'I would not abandon our friendship for anything – you look human enough to me,' Naomi said

Naomi kissed her on the cheek.

'I trust you, Naomi, above all else.'

Naomi went back to the computer and Samantha walked across the room and stood over the machine and stared at the control panel. It seemed simple enough, it was colour coded like the controls in the alien scout ship. If she pressed the wrong button, that would be the end of her. She opened the inspection cover to see what powered it. In amongst the wiring and power coils was a strange green faceted globe. It was similar to the one in her suitcase still in the lead box. She closed up the cover. She gazed at the control box; there were three coloured touch pads on the control panel, red, blue and green. Samantha supposed the red one was stop; green might be started, and blue was anybody's guess.

Samantha held her breath and pressed the green button; the machine started to hum, and a green haze surrounded the machine. She suddenly felt nauseous and she stepped away from the machine. Samantha shook her head as it started to throb. She pressed the red touchpad and the machine went dead. Naomi was at her side and put an arm round her waist.

'Are you all right? You've gone quite pale,' Naomi said in a voice full of concern.

Naomi guided her to the low bench and sat her down on it, Naomi went to the drinks dispenser and brought back a cup of strong coffee and handed it to Samantha, who sipped it gratefully. The throb in her head started to abate. Naomi sat beside her and put a comforting arm round her shoulders.

'Did you have any luck with the computer?'

Naomi shook her head.

'We'll have to get more information about your mother, we have to get to know the person, we'll have to go to the admin building and look through the records,' Naomi said.

Samantha put the empty cup down and stood up and made for the exit, Naomi followed her out of the lab building. They went to the administrative building and entered the records office and Naomi sat at one of the desk top computers and accessed the database for the records of Dr Sally Hamilton. Samantha stood beside her and gazed at the monitor.

Dr Sally Hamilton was a psychologist who had working theses on the minds of twins and their relationship with each other. Sally had written a book with another woman, Melissa Harris, on the subject. Samantha stared hard at the young woman – the face was familiar – then it came to her. Melissa Harris was Juliet's mother. There was no information on what might have happened to her. They were also studying ESP in young people – particularly twins. It brought warning bells to her mind as she read – Dr Sally Hamilton was working with another girl to produce a human clone. There was no data on which the girl was.

'Curiouser and curiouser,' Samantha mumbled.

'Do you see something?' Naomi asked.

Samantha stared at her. 'A load more questions and no answers.'

'Isn't that the way of it all?'

Samantha nodded in agreement.

'I wonder what she did in her spare time,' Samantha said.

'Bringing you up I expect,' Naomi said.

Before they left the building, Samantha reported to the General. He had told her to keep him informed of her progress. He gave her a bundle of clothes and told her it was the uniform she had to wear while she was on the base. Naomi walked with Samantha to her living quarters and Samantha took the gun out of her dress pocket and laid it on the table.

'You are armed and dangerous, Sam.'

Samantha removed the dress and sorted through the clothes she had been given.

'I'm going to make sure I don't get shot at again, without firing back.'

Samantha put on a white blouse and an olive drab skirt that went down to just above her knees, there was a jacket made of the same olive drab material. She smiled at Naomi.

'What do you think?'

'You look gorgeous as ever,' Naomi observed.

Samantha giggled.

'Thank you for that exaggeration.'

Naomi kissed her on the lips and left the hut. Samantha undressed and went to bed; it had been a long tiring day.

Samantha woke next morning, the bright sun shining on her face. She got out of bed and got dressed and left the accommodation hut. She walked towards the laboratories. As she reached the end of the row of huts, a voice called out to her. There was a large open space in the corner of the compound just past the accommodation huts, a large silvery spaceship sat in the middle of it; a familiar face stared at her from an open hatch. Samantha walked towards Joanna Lumsden as she slid out of the hatch.

'Do you like my new toy?'

Samantha gazed at the silvery spacecraft XS 150. Joanna stood by the hatch under the blunt nose of the craft. She told Samantha to follow her into the hatch, which they entered by a metal ladder, which took them up to the flight deck. Samantha sat in the seat of the navigation/observation position under the starboard transparent bubble. Joanna sat under the port bubble as she was the pilot.

'I'll ask the General if you can come on a flight with me,' Joanna said.

'Great, I'd love that. I will be your friend for life.'

After a short while they left the spacecraft and Samantha found a friend waiting for her. Steven Calvert hugged her hard and kissed her full on the mouth.

'A simple hello would have done,' Samantha said when he eventually released her.

Steven looked her up and down; she had filled out slightly since he last saw her.

'I like the uniform, it suits you.'

'How long have you been here?'

Steven put his arm round her waist, and they made a move towards the laboratory buildings.

'I just arrived this morning; they told me you were here.'

They entered the building and Samantha showed him the mysterious machine built by her equally mysterious mother. She activated it and a low hum vibrated round the room.

'Have you had breakfast yet?'

Steven shook his head and Samantha turned off the machine. They left the laboratory and walked across the compound towards the canteen. They found Naomi and Joanna sitting together so they joined them. Samantha had a light breakfast while Steven had something more substantial.

'What is your mission here?' Naomi asked, as she gazed at Steven's face.

Steven stared back at her and made a mental note to ask Samantha if she trusted this woman.

'I'm here to keep an eye on Sam, she's a valuable commodity.'

Samantha coughed on her breakfast.

'That's something new, who gave you that idea?' Samantha inquired.

Steven grinned at her and put his arm round her slim waist.

'You are very valuable to us,' Steven told her.

When they had all finished breakfast, Samantha and Naomi went back to the laboratory. Samantha sat at the computer system and stared hard at it, as if it would give up the data if she glared at it continuously. Naomi stood behind her chair.

'Why don't you swear at it?' offered Naomi, who started to massage her thin shoulders.

After a while Samantha stood up and went to the machine and activated it. Naomi stood beside her.

'Do you think it's possible to link the machine with the computer?' Samantha asked.

Naomi thought for a moment.

'I should think so.' Samantha grinned at her.

'Let's get to work then.'

Naomi left the laboratory and went to the stores to get the equipment she needed. Samantha turned off the machine and waited for Naomi to get back. Then they got down to work on combining the computer and the machine. Samantha hoped it would give her an idea of what the machine was for and what it was capable of. Watching Naomi work she could see the older girl was an expert in electronics; she was learning more about Naomi. When the work was completed Naomi sat at the computer console; Samantha stood behind her.

'You did a good job, Naomi. I appreciate what you've done.'

'I'm here for you, Sam and I'm going to help you in every way I can,' Naomi said, honestly.

Samantha went back to the machine and activated it and pressed the green button and a shaft of green light emanated from the front of the machine ended up at the far wall above a low bench. Samantha gazed at the circle of green light on the wall. Samantha approached the bench. As she reached the circle of light, Steven walked into the laboratory.

'What are you doing?' Steven asked, as he approached Samantha.

Samantha turned and gave him a smile.

'We need a guinea pig; I can't ask anyone else to do it.'

Steven did not like the idea, but there was logic in what she had said. He went back to the machine and stood by the control panel. Naomi gazed at the computer monitor; the data coming from the machine was fascinating. Some of it was understandable, but a lot of it was alien to her. Naomi was sure Samantha would understand it all.

Samantha sat on the bench; her head was in the circle of light, she felt a slight discomfort, and she closed her eyes and let her mind go blank. She regulated her breathing and relaxed her body and let the tension fade away. A vision came into her mind.

The car ran off the road out of control, the little girl clung to the back seat. The windscreen shattered as the car hit a tree. The door beside the ginger-haired little girl opened and she was plucked out of the car by a strong force. She struck the ground hard and painfully. The car ended upside down.

The little girl sat up and stared in horror at the crashed car and her parents still in it. Panic seized her young mind. She got up and went towards the car, the passenger door was open, and her mother sat still in the seat. The little girl struggled to get her mother out of the car. The girl strained as she used all the strength in her small body, as she pulled her mother from the wrecked car. She felt the heat from the flames in the car. The little girl knew she had to get her mother away from the burning car. She dragged her mother slowly across the rough ground further away from the car. Then it exploded and she fell across her mother to shield her from the blast.

An army General came on to the scene. The little girl sat cross legged on the ground, her mother's head in her lap. She stared up at the man with watery green eyes.

'Can you help? Mummy's dying,' the little girl sobbed.

A hand settled on her shoulder and Samantha opened her eyes. Her emotions echoed the emotions of the vision; she had felt what the little girl had felt about her dying mother. Steven had turned off the machine and he stood over her.

'Are you all right?'

Samantha stared blankly at him for a moment, and then nodded her head.

'That was a hell of an experience,' Samantha said.

Steven and Naomi sat on either side of her.

'I called your name several times, but you did not answer me, you seemed to be in a deep trance,' Steven explained.

Samantha stood up on shaky legs; she leant against Steven who had got up at the same time. When she had steadied herself, Samantha went to the computer and sat down; she stared at the data on the monitor screen. Naomi stood behind her and massaged her shoulders, while Samantha studied the data the computer had collected on the trial run with the strange machine.

After some time, she looked away from the computer screen. She told them about the vision she had had while sitting in the energy beam. It had felt so real as if she had been in the little girl's mind. It was a shock to the system when Samantha realised that she had been the little girl in the vision. The machine had dragged up a hidden memory from her brain. A dark realisation came into her mind, her face went pale and Steven ran a soothing hand over her cheek.

'What is it, Sam?' Steven asked. Samantha stared up at his face.

'There was a car crash, they were being shot at, and it was murder.'

Samantha stood up and Steven took hold of her left hand.

'They murdered my parents, now they are after me,' she said in a shaky voice.

Steven and Samantha left the laboratory and made for the office building. General Heywood looked up as she flew into his office like a tornado; she stood at his desk; her bright green eyes glared at him.

'They were murdered.'

Samantha told him of the vision she had had with the help of the machine.

'Whoever killed my parents, are now after me.'

'Your protection is our number one priority. That's why Steven is here,' General Heywood assured her.

Samantha turned and left the office with Steven. The General watched her go. He did not like misleading her about her mother, but that was how Dr Sally Hamilton wanted it.

Samantha returned to her living quarters and lay on her bed and stared up at the ceiling. A few minutes later there was a knock on the door, she got of the bed and went to see who wanted her. Steven grinned at Samantha after she had opened the door; she stood aside so he could enter. He was carrying a large brown paper bag.

'I've got some food for you, in case you're hungry.'

Steven laid the bag on the table.

'That's very thoughtful of you, Steven.'

As they ate Samantha was quiet and withdrawn. Steven waited patiently for her to become more talkative. When they had eaten, they went into the next room and sat on a couch.

'Are you all right, Sam?'

Samantha nodded and managed to give him a weak smile.

'That vision has given me a lot to think about.'

Steven put an arm round her waist.

'You know I'm here for you, Sam.'

Samantha saw the expression of concern on his face, Samantha was very glad he was here in the Fortress. They were very close, and she trusted him implicitly.

'Thanks, that means a lot to me, Steven.'

Steven saw the strain on her face. Samantha was mentally tired as well as physically.

'You should go and get some rest,' Steven advised.

Samantha smiled and he kissed her on the cheek.

'Can you stay the night; I don't feel like sleeping alone.'

'Are you sure?'

Samantha stood up and gazed down at him, a mischievous smile played on her thin lips.

'It wouldn't be the first time we have shared a bed.'

While Samantha had stayed with Steven at his home, he had enticed her to his bed when his parents were out working. It had been her first time and he had not rushed into it; he had made love to her slowly and gently. Samantha cared for him deeply and they made love a couple of times more before she left.

'I'm glad it's not going to be the last,' he said.

Steven followed her to the bedroom.

'You're going to behave yourself,' she ordered.

'Of course, Sam, I'm going to be the perfect gentleman.'

Samantha laughed.

'That'll be the day,' she said.

Steven sat on the bed and watched her undress. When she was down to her bra and panties, she slid under the sheet. She closed her eyes and was soon asleep. Steven undressed and got in beside her.

The door opened and a tall dark shape entered the room, it slid silently to the bed, amber eyes gazed at the head on the pillow. The girl was pretty and vulnerable. A thin white hand took hold of the sheet and pulled it down the bed, the girl wore black matching bra and panties. The other hand held a long thin blade and the figure thrust it deep into the girl's chest.

Samantha woke and cried out. Steven woke and put an arm round her.

'Sam!'

Samantha took several deep breaths then gazed at Steven. She told him of her dream, it had been so real. Steven lay on top of her and slowly entered her; he kissed her small breasts.

'Why can't you have some pleasant dreams for a change?'

'Because I'm cursed,' Samantha said. Steven held her close and kissed her.

'We'll have to do something about that, Sam.'

Samantha lay back down on the bed, Steven settled down beside her.

'If you can stop me having any more dreams like that, would be nice.'

Steven placed a hand on her flat stomach and kissed her several times.

'I'll see what I can do,' he said.

Samantha turned onto her side and drifted off to sleep. She woke again with the room full of daylight. She sat up as the door opened and Steven walked in carrying two mugs of tea. He handed her one and he sat on the edge of the bed.

'Morning, Sam.'

'I don't know how you did it, Steven, but I did not have another dream,' Samantha said.

Steven kissed her.

'I'm glad I could help.'

Samantha drank her tea then got dressed. She entered the laboratory alone and activated the machine and sat on the bench and moved her head, so it was within the circle of light. The coldness of the energy beam made her shiver. Samantha closed her eyes and let her mind go blank. She felt a pulse beat deep inside her head.

The small ginger-haired girl entered the laboratory in search of her mother. She heard a strange humming noise; she saw a green glow inside the room, and she was drawn towards a strange machine along the side of one wall of the laboratory. The girl stood beside it and ran a small hand over the machine. She fingered the control panel, and then went around to the front of the machine; she was bathed in a cold blue light. Something was tugging at her small body, and then there were two little girls in the room, both facing each other across the expanse of the room.

A woman ran into the laboratory and put a hand over her mouth, when she saw her daughter. She rushed to the machine and deactivated it. The little girl standing in front of it disappeared. The little girl standing by the bench gazed at her mother, as she wondered how she got there.

The woman rushed over and picked up her daughter.

'I'm sorry, Mummy, I did not mean to be naughty, and I could not find you. I'm sorry, truly I am,' the little girl sobbed.

'That's all right, sweetheart, I'm not going to scold you.'

The woman carried her daughter out of the laboratory.

'Did you ever want another little girl like me?'

'Why do you ask?' the woman inquired.

The woman gazed at the little girl's sparkling green eyes.

'I just wondered; I often think what it would be like to have a little sister. Like just now, but not exactly like me. That was me, wasn't it, Mummy, the other one?'

Naomi entered the laboratory and gazed in horror at Samantha as she sat in a trance on the bench. She ran to the machine and deactivated it. She went to the bench and sat beside Samantha, who stared blankly across the room.

'Sam, speak to me.'

Samantha's face was frozen, devoid of expression. Naomi slapped her face firmly, the face muscles flinched. Her mind was still locked in on the vision, despite the machine being turned off.

The little girl stood in front of the machine and gazed at her mother, who stood beside the control panel. She gave her daughter a reassuring smile. The little girl enjoyed helping her mother in her experiments. The machine started to hum, and the girl waited expectantly as the energy field wrapped itself round her body. The woman stared at her daughter inside the pulsating blue light. The little girl started to dissipate, when the little girl had disappeared as the energy field dispersed.

'Mummy.'

The woman gazed towards the bench on the other side of the room, the little girl stood beside it smiling at her mother. The woman ran towards her and picked up the child. The little girl gave her mother a wet kiss on the cheek.

'How are you feeling?'

'I'm fine, Mummy. I love helping you.'

The woman deactivated the machine and carried her daughter out of the laboratory.

The vision disappeared from inside her head and she heard someone calling her name. Her mind and body were ecstatic, she wanted more. But another vision did not come and the throb in her head faded away. Samantha opened her eyes, Naomi was a blur as she ran a hand over Samantha's cheek, and her sight began to clear.

'Sam, darling, are you back with us?'

Samantha nodded as Naomi gripped her shoulders. Samantha began to breathe deeply as her body shivered.

'That machine does weird things to your mind and body. It's addictive, I wanted more,' Samantha explained.

Samantha told Naomi about her vision, while Naomi held her close to her. When she had finished her narrative, Naomi kissed Samantha full on the mouth, Samantha put her arms round her and held Naomi tight against her body.

'You should leave that machine alone, the energy field had you locked too tight in that vision, you may not come out of it next time,' Naomi warned.

Samantha kissed her.

'I have to keep going, that's why I'm here. That little girl was me, that machine is dragging up lost memories.'

'There are some things that should remain lost.'

Naomi stood up and stared down at her friend.

'It seems to me your mother was using you as a guinea pig for her experiments,' Naomi said.

Samantha stood up and both girls stared at each other.

'Mother's prerogative, I expect she had her reasons.'

They left the laboratory and went to the canteen to get some lunch; they found Steven there and they sat with him. Samantha told him of her new vision.

'I suppose you are going to ignore my warnings and carry on trying to scramble your brain?' Naomi inquired, after Samantha had finished her narrative.

'I'm going to carry on, but I'm not going to ignore your warnings.'

They went to Naomi's quarters and she cooked a meal for them both; they had a bottle of wine to wash it down with; when they had eaten, they sat on a couch and Naomi filled the glasses up with wine.

'Are you trying to get me drunk?' Samantha asked.

Naomi smiled and kissed her on the lips. 'How else can I seduce you?'

'You don't have to get me drunk for that,' Samantha assured her.

CHAPTER XXXV:

... THERE'S A WAY

Samantha sat cross-legged on the grass at the side of the laboratory building. The alien spacecraft stood behind her. The blue sky was cloudless; the heat of the sun beat down on her. Samantha was taking her time to get back to work, as she was still suffering from the last vision from the machine. Naomi was engaged elsewhere; she was sure the older girl was avoiding her.

'How's it going?'

Samantha looked up at the speaker; Colonel Jackson gave her a pleasant smile. 'It isn't.'

Samantha held out her right hand and the army officer took it and pulled her up onto her feet. She asked him if she could have permission to leave the facility for a short time, Samantha wanted to visit the place where her parents were killed in the car crash.

'General Heywood told me you might; I'll take you as I'm responsible for your safety.'

Samantha went to find Steven, and then they went to the main gate where the Colonel was waiting for them in a jeep. Samantha and Steven got in the back and the corporal drove the jeep out of the Fortress.

'What are you hoping to find?' the Colonel asked.

'Everything and nothing,' Samantha replied.

The Fortress was surrounded on three sides by ancient woodland; beyond the trees at the rear of the facility were the unstable cliffs of the coastline. They reached a sharp bend in the road. The corporal drove the jeep off the road and Samantha jumped out of it before it stopped.

'Is this it?' she inquired.

Colonel Jackson came up to her and pointed towards the point in the road.

'The car missed the bend and hit the trees and turned over.'

Samantha studied the tree line; there twelve years ago, she had been involved in a tragedy.

'What are you looking for?'

Samantha smiled at him. 'I'll let you know – when I find it.'

She knelt down and ran her hands through the leaf mould. Steven stood over her.

'Found anything?'

Samantha shook her head and continued to search the ground for any sign of something left behind after the fateful crash. After a while her long sensitive fingers touched something that was not organic. Samantha gripped it and stood up and held out her hand to Steven, he gazed at the silvery cube in her palm.

'It's a computer data cube, I've never seen its like before,' Samantha said.

'Neither have I.'

Samantha slipped the disc into her olive drab skirt pocket. She walked away from the trees and started to walk aimlessly down the road. Steven followed at a distance; he knew she wanted to be alone. In the jeep Colonel Jackson kept a sharp eye on them. Samantha kept walking along the road; she gazed at the open moorland. Steven a little way behind heard the jeep moving slowly behind him. Samantha saw a car parked at the side of the road in front of her. When she drew level with it the door opened and a tall girl stepped out, she wore a white T-shirt and light grey shorts and an evil smile on her chubby face.

'Sammy, this is a pleasant surprise.'

Samantha glared at Lavonia Wagstaffe as she stood menacingly in front of her.

'Just when it was hoped we were rid of you at last,' Samantha said.

It was an unexpected bonus to Lavonia; her arch enemy was out in the open and could be disposed of at last.

'You won't get rid of me that easily, Sammy.'

Samantha ignored the fact Lavonia was using the name Samantha hated to rile her. Samantha stared at the eyes; there was a green tint in the whites of her eyes. The girl was infected with whatever was in the spheres that had fallen to Earth. The obnoxious girl was now twice as evil. Barnaby Morgue got out of the driving seat and looked at the two girls sizing up to each other. When his companion gave the signal, he would kill the ginger-haired girl. He put a hand inside his jacket pocket and brought out his handgun. Samantha had an eye on them both. Her senses were alert as she was in a vulnerable position. The man was her biggest danger. She knew Steven was behind her and knew he would be ready for anything.

'There is nowhere to run to, Sammy.'

Samantha slid a hand inside the pocket of her skirt; she felt the coolness of the metal against her long delicate fingers.

'I wouldn't run away from a creep like you.'

Lavonia turned and moved towards the car and Samantha pulled the handgun out of her skirt pocket – if Lavonia wanted to be shot in the back, it was all right with Samantha.

'There's no place on this Earth for you, Sammy, in the coming order of things,' Lavonia said, as she moved away from Samantha.

Samantha kept a sharp eye on the man as he trained a telescopic rifle at her. In a burst of speed Samantha shot Lavonia in the left thigh and the infected girl screamed in pain. Samantha sped off the road as a shot was fired at her and a high velocity bullet flashed past her head. Barnaby was surprised by the speed of the tall girl. He saw there was a lot of power in those long athletic legs. He fired another shot at the fleeing girl. Lavonia struggled to get in the car as she cursed Samantha for being a slippery customer. Samantha had given her a painful lesson: do not turn your back on an enemy.

Bullets whistled past Samantha as she ran a zig zag course to some nearby trees. Samantha suddenly felt a burning pain in her left shoulder; she dived to the ground. Steven fired at the car when he got in range. Barnaby got in the car and gave Lavonia the rifle and started the car and accelerated away at high speed. Steven made his way across the moorland to where Samantha was picking herself up and surveying the damage to her shoulder.

'That'll teach you to go off on your own,' scolded Steven.

Samantha gave him a pained smile.

'I wasn't expecting something nasty to crawl out from under a stone and attack me.'

They made their way to the jeep; Colonel Jackson drove them back to the Fortress and Steven took Samantha to the hospital building to get medical attention.

'Lavonia had a strange green tint to the whites of her eyes. I don't think she's human anymore,' Samantha said.

'She never was,' Steven assured her.

Samantha went to the medical centre and got her shoulder fixed up. General Heywood was not very happy about Samantha being shot at again. Samantha lay on her back on the bed; she did not want to work on the machine, while her shoulder hurt. She held the computer disc in her left hand and gazed at it. She wondered if it belonged to her mother. Did it fall out of her pocket when her daughter dragged her out of the burning car?

More questions than answers.

What are you doing to me, Mother?

Lavonia coming back on the scene was a bad omen. Lavonia was out for her blood and would not rest until she had utterly destroyed Samantha. She did not fear Lavonia; she would take any challenge the obnoxious girl threw at her. Lavonia was infected with something alien that made her doubly dangerous.

There came a knock on the door; she swung her long legs over the side of the bed and placed the computer disc on the bedside table. She left the sleeping compartment and opened the main door and stared at the smiling face of Steven Calvert.

'Can I come in, or do you want to get dressed first?'

Samantha looked down and noticed she only wore bra and panties.

'It's nothing you haven't seen before.'

Steven walked in and she shut the door behind him.

'The General's not very happy with you, getting yourself shot again.'

'Tell me something I don't know.'

Steven sat on the couch and stared up at her, running his eyes over her tall athletic figure.

'Nobody could have anticipated Lavonia turning up like that. They are going to find a way to get at me, wherever I am,' she explained.

Steven grabbed her left hand and pulled her down onto the couch beside him.

'In that case I'll have to stick a little bit closer to you.'

He put his hand on her chin and kissed her softly on the lips, he stared at her bright green eyes, as ever he thought she was trying to read his mind.

'I don't want anyone to get into danger because of me,' she said, sincerely.

Steven ran a soothing hand over her right cheek; he kissed her again.

'When you first came to us, you did not want to be alone. It's too late to back out now. You've got friends who want to stick by you, whatever the danger.'

Samantha blinked her watery eyes. She suddenly realised how much he really cared about her.

'You are one of the few people I would trust my life to, Steven.'

Samantha studied his handsome face, the calm blue eyes staring back at her. The sincerity in his expression, she did not need to question, she had known him too long. She ran her left hand over his face; he gazed at the long slender fingers as they caressed his skin. He took her hand away from his face and studied it. The long and shapely hand and long delicate, fragile looking fingers, he knew there was a lot of strength in the soft hand.

'I shall never betray that trust, Sam, you are very important to me,' he said.

Steven kissed the palm of her hand. Samantha enjoyed his touch.

'You are no less important to me, Steven.'

Their bodies touched as she kissed him, he released her hand. Steven put his arms round her taking care not to touch her injured shoulder.

'Do you want me to stay tonight?' Steven asked.

Samantha nodded and turned around and laid her back against him.

'You are very beautiful, Sam.'

'I suggest you get your eyes tested.'

Steven placed his hands gently on the clasp of her bra.

'There's nothing wrong with my eyesight,' assured Steven.

Samantha placed her hands-on hips and pressed them tighter to her small hard breasts.

'Are you trying to have your wicked way with me?'

Steven nuzzled the side of her neck and brought tremors to her skin.

'Of course not; I won't do anything you don't want me to.'

'Liar,' she said.

Steven kept kissing her neck as she sighed deeply, Samantha could feel her body responding to his attentions.

'Do you want me to stop?'

Samantha shook her head; she liked the way he kissed and caressed her.

'There is something you should know, Steven.'

Samantha told him what General Heywood had told her about her mother, that she belonged to another civilization out in deep space. While she spoke, he removed her bra.

'That doesn't make any difference to me or your other friends; we shall never think less of you.'

Samantha closed her eyes as she lay against him; Steven gently ran his hands over her bare breasts.

'I know we have done it before, but we're older. I don't know how my alien half will react, you will have to be prepared for the unexpected,' Samantha explained.

Steven laughed and kissed her on the cheek.

'I'm always prepared for the unexpected where you're concerned, Sam. We have nothing to worry about.'

Samantha stood up and took his hand and pulled him up and they went hand in hand to the bedroom. Samantha removed her panties and got between the sheets and watched Steven undress and get into bed beside her.

'I'm not worried, you'll be the one who's going to get injured if anything goes wrong,' Samantha said.

Steven slid slowly on top of her and kissed her.

'Then I'll be extra careful, Sam.'

Samantha clung to him. Steven kissed her face and neck. Steven felt the heat of her body rise.

'You really are hot stuff, Sam.'

'That's why you can't get enough of me,' Samantha said.

Steven could not argue with that; he continued to kiss and caress her naked body.

As the dawn; light filtered through the window of the bedroom. Samantha opened her eyes and stretched out her body, which had returned to normal temperature. She sat up and the door opened, and Steven entered carrying mugs of strong sweet tea; he handed one to Samantha and sat on the bed and kissed her.

'How are you feeling this morning, Sam?'

Samantha took a sip of her tea.

'I'm positively glowing inside.'

Steven kissed her full on the mouth.

'That's sounds bad.'

Samantha giggled and drank her tea. Steven put his mug on the bedside table and left the bedroom and returned a few moments later with her breakfast on a tray.

'You're spoiling me.'

'How's the shoulder?'

'It's a little stiff and sore,' Samantha replied.

Samantha finished her breakfast.

'I'll get dressed and we can run that computer disc I found through the computer in the laboratory,' Samantha said.

'Not so fast, you'll spend the day here resting that shoulder.'

Samantha lay back down on the bed and stared up at him, with her sparkling green eyes.

'Will you spend the day with me, Steven?'

Steven stood up.

'I suppose I'll have to, I'm in charge of your protection,' he said.

Samantha giggled.

'The only thing I need protecting from is you.'

Steven smiled and shook his head.

'I don't know what you mean.'

Samantha gave him a seductive smile.

'Come here, I'll show you what I mean.'

Steven got down on the bed and Samantha put her arms round him and rubbed her naked body against him.

'I told you. You can't get enough of me,' Samantha reminded him.

The next day as the dawn light approached, Steven and Samantha got up and went to the shower and ran cold water over their over-heated bodies to cool them off. She dried her body and they got dressed. Steven and Samantha left the living quarters. She ran around the inside of the boundary wall several times. The soldiers on the compound cheered her on. After she had finished her run, she entered the laboratory. She went to the machine and activated it and pressed the blue button. It was time for phase two. She stood in front of the machine and she was bathed in a blue energy field. It made her flesh tingle, her body started to tremble, and a throb started to beat inside her head. The perception of the laboratory was changing.

On the other side of the room by the bench, a blue haze materialised out of thin air. It rose to a height of seven feet, and then a shape started to appear inside the blue haze, it started to solidify. When it was finally formed into a tall slim girl, the blue mist dissipated, and Samantha gazed around her.

'That was one hell of an experience,' Samantha muttered.

Samantha walked across the room towards the computer system. She took the computer disc that she had found, out of her skirt pocket. She found a slot by the computer terminal and slid the disc into it. The computer hummed into life. A hologram was emitted from it. The image was of a tall figure, female and almost human, yet completely alien. The large domed skull was topped with blonde curly hair, the deep-set blue eyes stared at Samantha, as she stood close by, the face was thin and pale with an angular jaw, and the mouth was open and showed long pointed teeth. A vibrating female voice echoed round the room from the computer speakers.

Daughter.

'Mother,' Samantha said.

I have put a heavy burden on you.

The fight for our survival falls on your shoulders. You are being thrown to the wolves – You are being conditioned for this moment. They have been chasing us through the Universe for centuries. There are only a few of us left. The final battle will be fought here on this World. You will be our enemies' nemesis.

You were born for this fight – you are the product of two worlds. The machine you helped me to experiment with, was just a prototype, for something more potent.

The final design is in your brain and another. This is what you have to do. Think, Listen and Learn.

I have complete faith in you, Sam.

At this very moment they are drawing near to us. They will search you out – you are on your own. Trust no one. People close to you may be infected. You must be vigilant. Your life will depend on it.

Your grandmother was a great fighter and she fought for the freedom of our people. You have her DNA in your body, and it will help you free the Universe of a monster.

Perhaps when this is all over and you are triumphant – you will be able to forgive me for dropping you in at the deep end.

It is the only way – there is no soft option. You are strong and capable and there is another – she has what you need. You both need to work together. It is your destiny. You must keep growing and learning.

Don't think too harsh of me – Samantha. The time we had together was the best six years of my life. I love you, dear daughter.

The hologram dispersed – Samantha continued to stare at the spot on the floor where the image of her mother had stood.

'What do you think of that?' Naomi inquired.

The visions Samantha had got from the machine gave her insight into how much her mother loved her. The hologram image had given her a clear picture of what her mother looked like. Samantha ran her hands over her own face and over the top of her head. Who were these people that were after her mother and now had turned their attention on to her? Samantha did not like the idea of mistrusting the people she cared for, the friends she had made. Suddenly Lavonia came into her mind, the time she had met the girl on the road outside the Fortress. Samantha remembered the green tint in the whites of her eyes. There was a way she could identify the infected. Samantha was going to make sure she was not truly alone.

'I wonder who the female is I have to work with and what has she got that I need?' Samantha said.

Samantha being deep in thought did not hear Steven creep up on her. He grabbed her round the waist and nuzzled her neck. Samantha reacted swiftly and violently. Samantha twisted round and threw Steven against the computer console, giving him an idea of her immense strength. For a moment the dark green eyes glared at him. Then they went bright green, her expression softened.

'Never creep up on me like that again.'

Samantha moved close to him and ran a hand over his cheek, then kissed him on the lips.

'Are you hurt?'

Steven shook his head, but his body still trembled from the shock of her speed and strength that she showed when throwing him off her.

'Only my pride,' he said. Samantha put her arms round him and kissed him several times; she rubbed her body against him.

'I suppose your alien half doesn't like being caught by surprise,' Steven said. Samantha smiled at him.

'My human half is not keen on it either.'

They stood by the computer desk for a few moments, kissing each other.

'We are both here for you – Sam – you are not alone in this,' Naomi said.

CHAPTER XXXVI:

THE ALIEN SCOUTSHIP

S amantha stood in front of the machine and Steven stood at the control panel. Steven activated the machine and pressed the blue button. Samantha shivered as she was enveloped in the blue energy beam. Samantha closed her eyes and her brain started to throb. General Heywood and Colonel Jackson stood in the middle of the room watching Samantha as she stood in the column of blue energy. The tall slim girl started to fade inside the energy field; when Samantha had disappeared the energy field dissipated. Samantha materialized close to the bench and she called out to them, Steven deactivated the machine. General Heywood strode over to her.

'That was fantastic, how are you feeling?'

Samantha smiled at him to let him know she felt fine.

'It's a weird experience,' she said.

Samantha went to the computer and the General followed her. She ran the computer disc she had found, and he gazed at the hologram image of her mother. When the hologram message had finished, Samantha stared hard at him and inquired if the General knew anything about what the hologram revealed about her mother.

'Axerus, that's your mother's name, told us she had come from the planet Imera, which had been overrun by a parasitic alien life form led by Zindra and Boraus.'

'The black spheres that fell to Earth,' Samantha interrupted.

'Imera and her daughter fled the planet and they have been pursued through the Universe until Imera crash landed not far from here.'

'Have you caught up with Lavonia yet?' Samantha asked.

General Heywood shook his head, the car she had been in had been found abandoned a few miles away.

'She must be found at all costs; she is one of them now.'

The General assured Samantha a wide search for her was in operation.

'I don't like the idea of being thrown to the wolves,' Samantha said, icily.

'You shouldn't take that literally, you are going to get all the protection we can give you,' the General assured her.

'It's not protection I want, it's information.'

Samantha sat on the seat in front of the computer desk.

'I'm being pushed down a path full of pitfalls and dark shadows.'

Samantha got up and left the laboratory, Steven Calvert followed her out and they went to the canteen for lunch. Then they returned to Samantha's living quarters. Steven sat on the couch and grabbed her hand and pulled her down onto his lap.

'You really are something, Sam, do you know that?'

'It's nice to be appreciated by someone,' Samantha said, sternly.

Steven kissed her and Samantha relaxed and let the tension slip from her body.

'Let me show you how much I appreciate you.'

Samantha grinned and poked him in the ribs.

'You are just after my body,' accused Samantha.

Steven nuzzled her neck and ran his hand up and down her left thigh.

'And a lovely body it is too.'

Samantha put her arms round his neck and gazed into his blue eyes. Steven stared back at her, both trying to read each other's thoughts.

'You know, Sam. I shall travel that path with you.'

Samantha removed her blouse and tossed it onto the floor. She wriggled her bottom as she sat in his lap.

'You are a very striking girl, Sam.'

Samantha kept staring at his face; their relationship had been growing closer from the first time they met. Now they had turned into lovers, Samantha knew he would follow her to hell, if she asked him.

'You fancied me from the first time we met,' Samantha said.

'Guilty as charged,' he admitted.

Samantha felt his fingers behind her back unfastening her bra.

'Do you know exactly what we are being asked to do?'

There was a change in her voice and expression. As if she was implying there was something General Heywood was not telling them.

'I know as much as you. My job is to back you up and give you protection.'

Samantha stood up and walked towards the bedroom; he followed her. She removed her skirt and panties and got under the sheets and watched Steven undress and he got in beside her.

'It's nice having you here and protecting me while I sleep.'

'That's what I'm here for,' Steven assured her.

Samantha woke at the first light of dawn; she nudged the sleeping Steven in the back.

'Wakey. Wakey,' she said.

Steven sat up and glared at her. Samantha kissed him and got out of bed. She had a cold shower to cool off her overheated body.

Samantha had her usual run around the complex boundary, then she went to the alien spacecraft that stood beside the laboratory wall. The hatch was open, so she entered the spacecraft. She made it to the central compartment. A tall dark-haired man was working at the alien machinery alongside one wall. She moved quietly towards him and tapped him on the shoulder. Simon Beresford jumped in surprise and spun round, he scolded Samantha for giving a fright. She apologised sincerely, she had a habit of moving quietly round a room, she had annoyed a lot of people doing it, but it was just her way and a lot of the time it was instinctive.

'How are you progressing?' she asked

'Slowly,' he replied.

Samantha stood beside him and stared at the alien computer system. The data in the laboratory computer had given her an understanding of the alien symbols; she explained them to Simon as they worked together. After a while she left him and made her way to the rear of the spacecraft, where the power plants were. She opened the hatch that led to the rear compartment and went through it. She walked between the two propulsion units and found the control panel. She ran her long fingers over it and the power plants roared into life. She made her way back to Simon and saw he had been joined by Joanna Lumsden.

'What are you up to, Sam?' she asked. 'I thought I'd warm the motors up.'

Samantha made her way up to the flight deck; Joanna followed her. Samantha slid into the left-hand seat; it fitted the contours of her slim body comfortably as if it had been made for her. Joanna sat in the seat beside her and found it was not made for her fuller figure.

'They'll have to redesign the seating if they want me to fly this,' Joanna complained.

Samantha giggled and ran her nimble fingers over the instrument panel in front of her. After a while the spacecraft lifted off the ground.

'We have lifted off,' Samantha said. Joanna nudged her.

'Magnificent, General Heywood was sure you'd get it off the ground, Sam.'

'What I lack in good looks, I make it up in brains,' Samantha said, light-heartedly.

Simon came onto the flight deck and Samantha asked him if all the hatches were closed.

'Yes, are we going for a trip round the Universe?'

As if in answer Samantha sent the spacecraft higher up into the sky. Simon gripped the back of Joanna's seat, as Samantha concentrated hard on the computer control board. She sent the spacecraft up to the stratosphere. Being this high in the World was new to Samantha; Joanna and Simon were used to it, as they flew the solar system in the XS 150.

'Where are you going, Sam?' Joanna inquired.

The spacecraft travelled up through the Ionosphere and Samantha settled it into an orbit round their mother planet. She stood up.

'Let me show you something,' she said.

They went back to the middle compartment. Samantha stood by the machinery at one side of the room, Joanna and Simon stood against the far wall. Samantha ran her fingers over the control panel. The floor started to move down to the rear of the compartment, Joanna and Simon pressed their backs against the wall, as they stared down at space and the Earth below their feet.

Simon looked shocked.

Samantha grinned at the shock on his face.

'It's all right, Simon, it's a projection.'

Samantha walked forward and stood in the middle of the room; she spread her arms out.

'To them down there, we are gods, Simon.'

Samantha gazed down at the image of the Earth far down below her feet.

'We are the owners of all that we survey,' Samantha quoted.

Joanna stared across at the tall slim figure of Samantha standing as if in mid-air and nothing visible to stop her from falling down into space. The bright green eyes stared back at her. Joanna knew all about her parentage, but it did not change her impression of the girl. Joanna liked her and enjoyed working with her. Samantha was in her element as she stood with nothing under her feet except space and the planet Earth.

'You've found your ideal vocation, at last, Sam,' Joanna observed.

Samantha laughed and gazed down at the image at her feet.

'Is this as high as I can get?' Samantha pondered.

Joanna and Simon returned to the flight deck. Samantha walked to the rear of the compartment and sat in one of the seats. The rhythm of the motors changed, and the spacecraft started to descend towards the Earth. Samantha watched the image as they entered the atmosphere. Joanna flew the spacecraft back to the Fortress and landed against the side wall of the laboratory building. She got out of her seat and Simon ran a hand up and down her right thigh, Joanna kissed him on the lips. They entered the middle compartment and the floor was back in place. Samantha opened the hatch and left the spacecraft. Samantha entered the laboratory and a smile of delight spread over her face, as she saw Naomi sat at the computer.

'Naomi, I'd thought you had gone for good, it's such a relief to see you again.'

Samantha moved towards the computer system and Naomi got up and moved away from her.

'How are you proceeding with your mother's invention?'

Samantha detected a strange note in Naomi's voice and her actions were somehow different too.

'Very well, I've found other properties it has,' Samantha said.

Naomi faced her and Samantha saw it. The green tint in the whites of her eyes – they had got hold of Naomi. Samantha kept her face expressionless, her mind working furiously to come up with an answer to Naomi's infection. She stared at the machine and it gave her an idea.

'Why don't you sit in front of it, Naomi, and we'll see what happens,' Samantha said.

'Not on your life.'

Samantha went to the machine and activated it. Naomi had turned her head and was staring towards the far wall above the bench. Samantha took her chance and brought the edge of her right hand down on the back of Naomi's neck; she fell to the floor. Samantha lifted up the unconscious girl and carried her to the bench. She sat Naomi up and went to get some rope to tie her hands behind her back and tie her ankles to the rung of the bench. Her head was inside the circle of the energy field from the machine. Samantha waited for Naomi to regain consciousness. When Naomi came to, she fixed Samantha a stare of pure hate.

'You will release me.'

Samantha shook her head and stood up and went to the machine and turned up the intensity of the energy field.

'What are you doing?'

Samantha walked over to the bench and stared at Naomi's dark eyes.

'I'm going to force you out of my friend's head.'

'You are no match for us.'

Samantha grinned at the conceit in the voice, which was part Naomi and part alien.

'We'll see about that,' Samantha said.

'It is useless to obstruct us.'

Samantha did not agree. 'You are the one trapped in the energy field.'

Samantha walked back to the machine and adjusted the energy field. The pain and distress Naomi was feeling was clearly visible on her face. Samantha was aware she could lose her friend as well as kill the alien mind in her head.

'How much pressure can you take?'

'You will kill your companion.'

Samantha stood stone faced; she was not going to deviate from the path she had taken.

'That's a sacrifice I'm willing to take.'

Samantha increased the crushing pressure of the force field, Naomi cried out in pain and her body trembled.

'Free me.'

'Free you, vacate that body.'

Samantha gazed at the pain on the pretty round face in the energy field.

'We will destroy you all.'

Not if I have anything to do with it.

'You win.' Samantha turned off the energy field.

For now.

A pulsating mass of energy rose from Naomi's head, Samantha activated the machine and an energy beam shot out and impaled the alien mind in its field.

'Do you think the others of your kind will do any better than you?' Samantha wanted to know.

Samantha heard the voice in her head.

'Our minds are connected, the others will know my fate and they will act accordingly.'

Samantha turned up the pressure of the energy field up to maximum. The alien mind was crushed to oblivion. She turned off the machine. She untied the unconscious girl and lifted her off the bench. Samantha carried her out of the laboratory building and made for the medical building. She left Naomi in their care and made for the General's office and told him everything that had happened with Naomi. After making her report Samantha went to the assault course and threw herself vigorously at the obstacles in an attempt to take her mind off what she had done to Naomi. After a couple of hours, she sank to the ground; her heart pounded inside her chest, her body was hot and sweaty.

'Do you feel better for that?'

Samantha looked up and saw Steven grinning down at her.

'I love a good work out before dinner,' she lied.

'So, I see.' Steven held out his hand and she took it and he pulled Samantha up onto her feet. She fell against him and Steven held onto her.

'Sometimes it's easier to sort out a problem by talking to a friend,' Steven advised.

Steven walked with Samantha to her quarters. Samantha went to have a shower and Steven brewed some hot strong tea for them both. He sat in a chair sipping his tea while he waited for her to return. Sometime later Samantha walked in wearing just bra and panties; he handed her a mug of tea and patted his thighs. She settled down on his lap without hesitation and sipped her tea.

'It's typical of you, Sam, to take it out on your body, when your mind is at fault.'

Steven put his arms round her and held her tight and kissed her on the cheek.

'I didn't realise you know me too well, Steven.'

'I couldn't protect you, if I didn't,' Steven said.

'I could have killed her.'

Steven nuzzled her neck.

'You had to do what you did; Naomi will be the first person to agree with it, she'll be glad you took the demon out of her head.'

Samantha turned her head and stared at his handsome face.

'It's scarier than just a demon. You should have been there,' Samantha said in a trembling voice.

Steven could see the experience had got through her hardened exterior.

'You're not alone, Sam.'

If only that were true, she thought. In the next phase of her plan, she had to be just that: alone. Samantha stood up and looked down at him. Steven stared hard at her face. Samantha was up to something; they had been friends long enough for him to read her facial expressions.

'Something tells me, you have a plan that doesn't feature me and the General.'

Samantha smiled and ran a hand over his face.

'You do know me, Steven. We've got too close,' Samantha observed.

'What are you going to do?'

Samantha walked into the sleeping compartment and sat on the bed; Steven sat beside her.

'I'm going for a little trip,' she said.

Samantha grinned at him; there was going to be nothing nice about her planned trip into space.

'I'm going to borrow the alien scout ship and visit the mother ship, making its leisurely course towards us,' Samantha said.

Steven stared at her in disbelief.

'Before we can take them on, we must learn all we can about our enemy,' Samantha said.

'That's logical, Sam,' Steven agreed.

'I'm going to try and get Naomi to come with me, I shall need her expert skills,' Samantha said.

Steven put his arm round her waist and hoped she wanted him with her too.

'And me?'

Her expression was deadly serious, she shook her head.

'You can come with us on the scout ship, but I can't risk you on the mother ship, Steven.'

'You forget I'm here to give you protection,' he reminded her.

'I'm not going to play all my important cards on one hand.'

Samantha moved closer to him and kissed him.

'You are too important to me to risk you in this trip. I have other plans for you, Steven.'

'The most important person you can't take a risk with, is yourself,' argued Steven.

Samantha was well-aware of that, but she was the one that had to leap headfirst into danger.

'That doesn't apply, I'm expendable. I take all the risks, which is why I'm here.'

'I'm sure the General doesn't see think you're expendable.'

Samantha grinned at Steven and then shook her head. He had no idea of the turmoil that was going on inside her head, he had to remain in the dark about the true nature of the destiny, and she had planned out for herself.

Samantha slid across the bed and got under the sheets, they stared at each other for a moment.

'Do you want to join me?' she asked. Steven stood up and smiled at her.

'You ask a lot of silly questions, Sam.'

Samantha poked her tongue out at him and watched him undress. They romped wildly on the bed; Samantha enjoyed having him thrust vigorously inside her. After two hours they were hot and sweaty; they had a shower; then went to bed and were soon asleep.

In the morning they made love and then got up and had breakfast. Samantha went to the medical centre to see Naomi; she sat at the bedside.

'How are you feeling?'

Naomi managed to conjure up a smile for her friend.

'Rough.'

Naomi had woken up with a splitting headache and an aching body. She was glad the voice in her head had gone.

'Wrenching that mind out of your head was very painful and stressful, I hope there was no brain damage,' Samantha said.

Naomi shook her head and assured Samantha her brain was none the worse after the experience.

'Don't worry too much, Naomi, you are safe now. Tell me what happened if you feel up to it,' Samantha said in a soft comforting voice.

Naomi let her mind go back; her recent memories were dark and confusing. The thing that had inhabited her head had made her do things against her will; it made plots against her friends. They had come for her at night as she lay in her bed waiting for sleep to come to her weary mind and body. Two dark shapes entered her room and violently dragged her out of bed. Something wet and clammy was pressed against her nose and mouth.

Naomi lost consciousness.

Naomi had come to and found herself strapped down on a bed. Her head ached. She was lying in a small white-walled room. There was a small table and a black sphere was sat upon it. A tall figure entered the room dressed in dark clothing, the face was masked, and Naomi could not see who it was. It stood by the table and picked up the black sphere. It was picked up and broken in two. Naomi stared at the pulsating green glow. Naomi watched in horror as the thing in the sphere floated towards her, Naomi wriggled but she was held down tight to the bed. It enveloped her head and it got into her brain.

'You are ours now, Naomi, you are to get rid of Samantha for us.'

Naomi stopped speaking and stared at Samantha.

'It controlled me, it wanted me to kill you, and there was nothing I could do.'

Samantha ran a hand over her cheek.

'You're free of it now and you are back with your friends.'

Samantha kissed her on the cheek.

'The next time you feel like going off on your own, let me know first.'

'I left some equipment at the Research Complex. I thought it might help in your experiments with the machine,' Naomi explained.

'Where's the equipment now?' Samantha asked.

'It's in my living quarters.'

'Do you feel strong enough to leave here?'

Naomi pulled the sheets down and swung her legs over the side of the bed. Samantha opened the door of a small cupboard by the bed and pulled out a folded dark brown dress. She tossed it to Naomi who stood up and put it on.

'I was getting bored lying here anyway,' Naomi said.

They walked out of the medical centre and made for the living quarters.

'They are telling you, that wherever you are, they can get to you,' Naomi said.

She was sat on the couch with her legs folded under her; Samantha stood by the coffee table and studied the medical equipment on it. She picked up one and activated it and held it over Naomi's head. The scanner would tell Samantha if there was any residue left in Naomi's head, when the alien mind had been forced out.

'Lucky for me they failed to make it fatal,' Samantha said.

'Not with the lack of trying,' Naomi pointed out.

After a while she deactivated the scanner and placed it on the table; she sat on the couch.

'Your mind's your own now,' Samantha said.

'I'm glad of that.'

Samantha placed a hand on Naomi's knee.

'I hope you can forgive me for the pain and stress I caused you, I hope it hasn't damaged our friendship,' Samantha said.

'You did what you had to do, to free me from that horror, I care for you too much to walk out on you,' Naomi said, sincerely.

Samantha slid her hand up Naomi's thigh and it pushed the hem of the dress up as it went. Naomi gazed at Samantha' s green eyes, they were bright and glittering. Naomi had been attracted to them the first time she laid eyes on Samantha. The long slim hand caressed the softness of the inside of her thigh.

'I missed you when you went away, I blamed myself for it. I need you, Naomi, I have some work that needs to be done and you are the only person I can trust to get it done,' Samantha said.

Naomi gripped the hand on her thigh and lifted it to her face; she slid the long slender fingers into her mouth and sucked them. Samantha moved closer to her.

'You can rely on me; I shall never betray your trust in me.'

Samantha put her hand on the back of Naomi' s head and planted a long firm kiss on her mouth, Naomi lay back on the couch and Samantha went with her and kissed Naomi more passionately. After a while Samantha sat up and feared she had gone too far.

'I'm sorry, Naomi, I got quite carried away,' Samantha apologised.

Naomi sat up and winked at her.

'That's quite all right, Sam. I've had an urge to kiss you also.'

They got off the couch and collected the electronic equipment that lay on the table and carried it across the compound towards where the scout ship was parked. Joanna and Simon were waiting for them. They knew what Samantha had in mind. As Joanna Lumsden was an officer in the military, she was duty bound to advise the General of what she was up to. As she was not going to accompany Samantha on boarding the alien mother ship, she did not mention it. Samantha was going to get all the flak from the General for the escapade, so she told Joanna her job and rank was safe. General Heywood was going to let Samantha carry out her own plans within reason.

Samantha and Naomi went to study the propulsion units. Naomi studied the control panel. Samantha had explained to her how it worked, as she wanted Naomi to learn all she could about the alien spacecraft and how it functioned. She activated the motors and gazed across at Samantha.

'In my wildest dreams I never thought one day I would be leaving Earth in an alien spacecraft,' Naomi said.

Samantha winked at her.

'This is only the tip of the iceberg, I've got a lot of more interesting jobs for you to do, Naomi,' Samantha assured her.

They walked towards the exit hatch.

'I can't wait, Sam.'

The scout ship escaped the Earth's atmosphere and headed towards the red planet. Steven Calvert sat across from Joanna and stared out of a side window. This was a new experience for him, and he was enjoying every minute of it. Samantha and Naomi entered the main compartment; they made for a large recess on the left of the hatch that led to the flight deck. Naomi stepped into the recess and gazed at the machinery it contained, and then she turned to Samantha.

'What do you think they used this for?' Naomi inquired.

Samantha got in beside her and Naomi put her arm round her waist.

'I would say it is a device to allow the occupants of this spacecraft to leave it without having to land,' Samantha guessed.

'A teleport,' Naomi said, excitedly.

Samantha kissed Naomi and patted her bottom.

'Clever girl, go to the top of the class.'

'Do you think we could work out how it works?' Naomi asked.

Naomi moved out of the recess so Samantha could have more room while she studied the instrumentation. She found the control box and ran an exploratory eye over it. Samantha was sure it would not be too difficult to sort out. She had studied the alien-database on the spacecraft's main computer. Naomi stepped back into the recess to see if she could help. Samantha found the activation switch and the machinery lit up and hummed.

'I suppose you are going to use this to board the mother ship?'

'That's the general idea,' Samantha said.

Samantha put her arms round the girl and stared down at her dark eyes.

'Are you sure you want to do this? I won't mind if you want to back out, Naomi.'

Naomi kissed her softly on the lips.

'You need me for what you plan to do; I have a deep affection for you, Sam. Where you go, I go.'

CHAPTER XXXVII:

THE ENEMY

Samantha made her way up to the flight deck; she outlined her plan to Joanna, while Simon and Steven listened with interest. When Samantha had finished, she waited for Joanna's opinion.

'It's your show, just make sure you bring yourself back from there,' Joanna said, after a few moments' thought.

Samantha returned to the main compartment, she found Naomi working in the teleport recess.

'How's it going?'

Naomi smiled and stepped out of the recess; they walked across to the main computer system.

'We can work it all right, but what it will do to our bodies is anyone's guess,' Naomi said.

'Nobody said it was going to be easy,' Samantha said.

Naomi shook her head and made a face at Samantha. Then she turned her attention to the data in the alien computer memory.

They wanted a blueprint of the mother ship they were approaching. They knew the parts of the spaceship they wanted to see, but they had to find a quick route to get there. Naomi knew what parts of the alien ship that would interest her, and she was determined to find them. The data on the mother ship came up on the computer screens. Samantha stood beside her.

'A cargo bay would be the best bet.'

Naomi agreed with her; they wanted to enter the spaceship far away from the places that contained the most crew members.

'We're here.'

The two girls turned to face Simon Beresford, who told them they were moving close to the alien mother ship that had an orbit round Neptune. They seemed to be in no hurry to get to Earth. Whatever their plans were they had no intention of rushing into anything blindly. Joanna had put the scout ship in an orbit round Neptune keeping the planet between them and the mother ship.

Samantha and Naomi went to the teleport recess and Naomi dialled in the co-ordinates that would put them inside the mother ship.

Samantha turned to Simon.

'When we've gone tell Jo to keep the scout ship out of teleport range – we don't want any uninvited guests turning up. There's a communicator on the bracelets, so I'll contact you when we are ready to come back,' Samantha said.

Simon watched Samantha and Naomi step into the teleport booth and a few moments later they slowly faded from view. Simon returned to the flight deck and gave Joanna the message Samantha had given him.

'I hope this is not the last time we see them,' Joanna said.

'Amen to that,' Simon said.

Amron Rufus sitting in the tactical station in the control room of the star ship had been watching the sensors as they picked up the scout ship and showed him it was one of their own. It had disappeared behind the planet they were orbiting then after a while it had moved away at a high velocity back the way it had come. Amron made his report to the Supreme Leader, who advised him to check if there had been any teleport traces inside the star ship. Amron checked the sensors and found a teleport trace in Cargo Bay 5. The Supreme Leader sent his second in command to investigate and detain their uninvited guest.

Inside Cargo Bay 5 Samantha and Naomi stared about them in wonder. Samantha moved forward between two rows of containers of various sizes and shape, covered with the alien script. Samantha turned her attention to the walls of the cargo bay and searched for a way out. When she discovered the exit doors not far from her position, Samantha made straight for them. As she got close to them, they started to slide open. Samantha darted away and stood against the wall. Naomi dived behind the containers. Samantha got ready for action as two tall dark shapes stepped into the cargo bay.

Roth stepped cautiously into the cargo bay; he sniffed the air and detected the scent of his prey nearby. Roth was just less than seven feet in height and his tall bulky frame was rippling with brute strength. His red scaly skin shone in the light, his head was round, and the face was elongated, his dark beady eyes surveyed the cargo bay for his prey. The Ixxion was born and bred to kill and Roth did his killing with the ease of an expert. He could smell his quarry; the prey was definitely female. He could not smell her fear; that was good, he was sure her eyes were watching him from wherever she had hidden herself.

Samantha inched herself towards the open doorway, as she kept a sharp eye on the alien just in front of her. She was aware of him sniffing the air trying to catch her scent; she hoped his sense of smell was not as good as her own. Samantha found his odour very unpleasant; it told her the alien was a very expert predator. As she reached the doorway Roth spun round as he detected the odour of his prey lay behind him. Samantha stepped away from the wall and readied herself for his eventual attack. His impulse to charge at the tall female in front of him was stopped short as he stared at the thin face and deep-set green eyes that suddenly lost their brightness and went to a dark deep green. The prey was ready for him.

'Imera'

The alien word meant nothing to Samantha, though something about her had made the alien hesitate. Though she was at least a foot taller than her adversary, he was armed to the teeth – he had a large belt round the waist which had several assortments of weapons fixed to it. The alien started to move towards her. Roth seeing his quarry was unarmed had decided to subdue her with his bare hands. The face and body of the prey was showing no fear as it prepared for battle. Samantha's expression was a mask of concentration – she was about to fight for her life.

Roth made a sudden charge at her and in an instant, she moved to the side and swung her right fist and hit him in the side of the head. Roth moved away stunned by the force that the bony fist had hit him, the female prey was strong and fast on her feet.

Roth faced his prey and Samantha stared at the murderous intent on the alien face, she stood her ground defiantly, then something hit her hard in the back. Samantha moved away as another huge bulky shape loomed over her. Another alien had entered the cargo bay; this one had a green sheen to his leathery skin.

Roth moved in while the prey had her attention on Ruin, he struck out with his right foot and struck the female prey in the back of her right knee and her leg gave way. Ruin struck her viciously across the face with his broad leathery hand; she went down. Roth placed his right foot on her stomach and pulled out a thick bladed machete. A sharp voice behind Roth made him stand up straight taking his foot off the prey lying on the floor. Ruin followed his companion's example and stood up respectfully before the newcomer. He was taller than Samantha and wore a silvery overall that clung to his slim frame. The long thin face had deep set grey eyes; the high domed forehead was topped with short cropped blonde hair.

'Manners, Roth, that's no way to treat a guest.'

Aplon Whan, the second in command, stared down at the captive, held the energy weapon firmly in his right hand and aimed it at her. A beam of energy hit her in the chest and her whole body was aflame with pain and then she passed out. Aplon looked up at Roth.

'Pick her up, let's get her to the examination room, this creature must get our full attention.'

Roth picked up the unconscious female and carried her out of the cargo bay, followed by the other Ixxion and Aplon Whan. Naomi emerged from a large container and made her way to the exit door. She took the automatic out of her skirt pocket and held it firmly in her right hand; the doors slid open and she stepped cautiously into a bright corridor. She looked to the right and saw the three aliens up ahead. She wondered what they had in mind for Samantha; Naomi knew it would not be for the good of her health. She held the handgun tight in her hand, her senses alert and ready for action – she was a girl out of place, but Naomi was well prepared to adapt to any situation she found herself in. Naomi was not going to let a few hostile aliens stop her reaching her goal.

CHAPTER XXXVIII:

EXAMINATIONS

Samantha woke and found herself strapped down to an operating table, her clothes had been removed, and a probe was running up and down her naked body. A screen on the left of the table was showing pictures of her anatomy. The tall alien in the silver overall uniform was standing on the right-hand side of the operating table.

Adon Ducros, the Supreme Leader, strode into the room and stood beside his second in command; he wore a gold overall uniform. He stared at the female on the table.

'The resemblance to Imera is striking, is it not?' Ducros said.

'It is a hybrid, the young immature female has the genes of Imera's people, but she is not pure Moran. Imera's offspring must have bred from a species in this solar system,' Aplon Whan explained.

Ducros stared down at the bright green eyes staring up at him.

'Do you usually strip your guests naked? It's not very dignified being treated like this.'

'We are able to understand its language, it seems,' Aplon said.

Roth the Ixxion stood at the foot of the table; he made his report about finding and subduing the female prey.

'You are impressed, Roth?' Aplon inquired.

Roth bowed his head.

'We must find out as much as we can about it,' Ducros said.

'What are you going to do with me?'

Adon Ducros stared down at the captive.

'We need information and you are going to provide it.'

Samantha glared at the alien leader.

'I'm not going to tell you anything you can use against my planet,' Samantha assured him.

'We aren't interested in your primitive planet, we just want the two fugitives and the stolen spacecraft,' Ducros informed her.

'They are both dead, they won't bother you again.'

'Good.' Ducros was glad of that.

Adon Ducros walked out of the examination compartment; Aplon Whan and Roth followed close behind. Ruin stayed behind to keep an eye on the female alien. Samantha kept an eye on him, as he looked at her as if trying to decide which part of her body to eat first. Her survival was up to Naomi, she hoped the older girl had not got lost.

The door slid open and Ruin turned towards it and Samantha saw the answer to her prayers moving through the open doorway. Naomi fired her automatic as the tall monstrosity rushed towards her. Ruin fell dead at her feet; she ejected the empty clip from her automatic and took out a full clip from her skirt pocket and slipped it into the butt of her automatic. She strode over to the metal table Samantha was secured to.

'You took your time,' she complained.

Naomi searched for a way to free Samantha.

'I was collecting information; I can't help it if you can't stay out of trouble.'

Naomi managed to release Samantha and she found her clothes lying on the floor in one corner of the room; luckily the teleport bracelet was also there, and she slipped it on her thin right wrist. When she was dressed, they left the examination room and Naomi guided her to the compartment opposite. Samantha found herself in a large computer room. Naomi went to the terminal she had been working at and she told Samantha to watch the computer screen as she ran her nimble fingers over the control desk. A face came up on it. Samantha stared at the high domed forehead and the deep-set eyes in a thin face with a ruddy complexion; she translated the alien script and found it was a female by the name Imera, the same word the alien had thrown at her – now she knew why.

'She must be your long-lost grandmother,' Naomi said.

'Now have you any doubts to my alien parentage?'

'Not now, but don't worry, I still like you.'

Naomi winked at her and removed the computer storage unit she had fixed to the alien computer terminal. It had been taking selected data from the computer files Naomi had found to be of the most interest to Samantha.

'You'll like Imera; she is a rebel, just like you, Sam.'

Samantha contacted the scout ship on the communicator on her teleport bracelet and told Joanna they were ready to come back. Simon stood by the teleport booth waiting for the machine to drag the two girls back to the spacecraft. Two shapes suddenly took shape in the booth and a few moments later Samantha and Naomi stepped out of the booth. Simon went to the intercom and informed Joanna they were back. She moved the scout ship away from the star ship at high velocity and headed it back to Earth. When the scout ship was hovering high over the Fortress, Samantha and Naomi were standing by the teleport booth.

'This is it, Naomi, you know what you have to do?'

Naomi nodded her head; Samantha had briefed her all through the journey back to Earth.

'Everything's all clear, you know you can trust me, but I don't think Sarah will be pleased with me being the usurper in her plans – we are not really the best of friends,' Naomi said.

'Leave Sarah to me, we are not taking over, just bringing her deadline a little closer. We shall need her organization,' Samantha said.

Naomi stepped into the teleport booth. Inside the backpack Naomi carried was the power cell in the lead lined box. Samantha reminded Naomi to be careful and not open the box and keep it well hidden.

'I shall be fine, just take care of yourself and don't take any unnecessary risks.'

Samantha activated the teleport and watched Naomi fade from sight. The scout ship settled down on the ground in the usual parking place by the lab buildings; the crew left it and walked towards the Administrative building.

'Where is Naomi?' Joanna asked.

'I don't know, I haven't seen her for some time,' Samantha said, innocently.

'Perhaps she wanted some time to herself,' Simon suggested.

General Heywood stared stone-faced at the three individuals that sat on the other side of his desk; Samantha had given him her report on their unofficial visit to the alien star ship. After listening to Joanna, and Simon had given their side of the story, he told them to leave. General Heywood stared at Samantha; the anger he felt showed on his stern expression. Samantha was sure she was in for another telling off. He did not like the way she went off on her own and shunning officialdom, but it was her way and he would have to put up with it, if he wanted her to work for him. The fact she had been nearly killed twice, Samantha knew she could trust no one.

'I don't know whether to congratulate you on a job well done, or throw you in the glasshouse for a week, for putting yourself and three other lives in unnecessary danger,' he said, coldly.

'Joanna and Simon were in no danger; they don't want to destroy their own spacecraft; it was necessary for me to get information from that star ship. The mission was a success so why not treat it as such,' Samantha argued.

'That's all very well, but how can I organize protection for you, if I don't know what you are going to do from one minute to the next.'

Samantha smiled as she became aware of how difficult she was making his job. If he knew what she had planned, he would go ballistic and have her locked away for good. There was a world outside the high walls of the Fortress, and she wanted to experience the feeling of being outside and free. Samantha had gone as far as she could with the machine in the laboratory and to perfect the invention of her mother, she had to go elsewhere and with the help of Naomi they got into database and found the very place that was suitable for continuing her work. The Research Laboratories at Exeter close to the river. Naomi was already on her way to the city. She had connections to the local government there as her father was a politician. Though Naomi had warned Samantha she had not seen her father for a few years, and he may have disowned her. Samantha told Naomi to flash her hazel eyes and beg his forgiveness and Samantha was sure Naomi would get her father to grant her anything she asked for.

'I've got some strange notion, you are planning to do a runner,' General Heywood said.

The guilty expression that flitted over her thin face told the General all he needed to know. Samantha realised she still was not old enough or bright enough to fool him.

'I see I've underestimated your intelligence, I'm sorry, my arrogance is only overshadowed by my foolishness.'

The General was amazed at the sincerity of her admission.

'Someone told me a long time ago, I should get to know you, so I did. I just want you to know, I'm not your enemy and I do care what happens to you,' he said.

Samantha stared at him intently and his expression showed no signs that his words were false; she had not realised she had given him the impression she thought the General was the enemy. Samantha just thought they had different ways of working; she did not have his military mind.

'I have never thought of you as an enemy. I have never broken my promise to give the work you want from me. I have to do this my way, no matter how dangerous it gets. There is only one place where I can continue the work you have set me.'

'Could you enlighten me on where this place is?'

Samantha told him and made him aware she wanted to make her own way to Exeter. She was tired of being hidden behind high walls and boundary fences, she wanted freedom.

'When were you planning to make your escape?'

'As soon as possible, I've sent Naomi ahead to make things easier for me.'

'You seem to put a lot of trust in that girl, I hope she does not fail you,' he cautioned.

'Naomi has earned my trust; she has a job to do and she will do it expertly. If you trust Dr Richard Blake, then you can trust Naomi, as I do,' Samantha said.

General Heywood stood up and told her to wait in the office for a few moments and he left. He went to the operations room and contacted the Research Facility and got hold of Dr Sally Hamilton. He had never told Samantha that her mother was still alive, though he had not exactly told the girl her mother was dead; he knew Samantha had just thought she had died with her father in the crash. For her own reasons, Dr Hamilton did not want Samantha to know she was still alive and kicking. General Heywood informed Dr Hamilton that her daughter wanted to go off on her own away from the protection they could give her and get to know the country she was living in. He told her Samantha had wiped her computer files and downloaded the data into her own computer, her brain. Dr Sally Hamilton was impressed her daughter was coming along nicely – if Samantha wanted to get away, then she should be allowed to do just that. They had plenty of resources to keep her under observation.

General Heywood returned to his office and Samantha looked up at him expectantly.

'OK, Samantha, we shall do it your way, we'll give you a communicator so in any sign of danger I want you to contact me.'

Samantha nodded her head.

'I have no wish to get myself killed, I assure you. Before I go, I want to know if you trust me. You have earned my trust and I want you to trust me in return.'

The General stared at her appealing bright green eyes. He put a comforting hand on her shoulder.

'I've always trusted you, Sam, but you are a very irritating person to work with.'

Samantha laughed.

'I know, I'm sorry about that, but you are a soldier, I'm not, we are bound to do things differently,' Samantha said.

Samantha left the building and made her way to the living quarters, she found Steven Calvert waiting outside her hut. She invited him in, and Samantha told him she was leaving the Fortress. Steven put his arms round her and Samantha allowed him to kiss her on the lips. Steven told her he would accompany her. Samantha shook her head.

'I go alone, I have Naomi waiting for me when I get to Exeter, you have your own work to do,' Samantha said.

Steven walked with her to the main gate and it opened, and Steven hugged and kissed her, then Samantha walked out of the Fortress to follow her destiny.

PART FIVE:

HIDE AND SEEK

CHAPTER XXXIX:

ASYLUM

NOVEMBER 2130

Barnaby Morgue kept his eyes on the road while his partner in crime Lavonia Wagstaffe gazed at the open moorland. After a while her eyes shifted to the road they were driving leisurely along. Up ahead she noticed a tall figure strolling along the side of the road. As the car drew closer Lavonia saw it was girl wearing a black sweater and slacks, she had short ginger hair. Lavonia pointed her out to Barnaby.

'Christmas has come early this year,' she said, excitedly.

Barnaby slowed the car and as they drew up to the girl, Barnaby swerved the car at the girl and hit her, knocking her to the ground. He stopped the car and Lavonia jumped out carrying a handgun. The girl struggled onto her hands and knees and Lavonia fired at her twice and she lay still on the ground.

Barnaby got out of the car and helped his partner drag the girl to the car and lay her unconscious on the back seat. They got back in the car and drove away.

THE STONEHOUSE CLINIC: NR. EXTON, EXMOOR.

Carrie Scott knocked on the door of Dr Stonehouse's office and opened the door. She closed the door behind her and walked to his desk. Dr Brian Stonehouse was in his early fifties, he was a plump man of average height, and the strong-featured face had an iron grey beard the same colour of his short hair. He gave Carrie a pleasant smile. She had met him at medical school at the age of nineteen. He found her a very capable student and ready to learn all he could teach her. Two years later he gave her a job at his clinic. She enjoyed the work and she learnt a lot from him in taking care of his patients. She was of average build and height and she had short brown hair – she wore a nurse's uniform.

Carrie informed the doctor there was no change in the new patient. He stood up and walked round the desk and they left the office. They walked up the corridor and got in the lift and went up to the top floor.

Samantha came to in the worst pain and discomfort she had ever experienced. She opened her eyes and groaned and tried to remember what had happened to her. She had been run down by a car and then shot. She tried to sit up but a sharp pain in the back made her lie down again. She was in a small yellow-walled room. She heard a door open and she watched the man and girl walk to the bedside.

'How are you feeling?' Dr Stonehouse inquired.

Samantha stared at the man; he wore a white lab coat and the girl was dressed in a green nurse uniform.

'You are the doctor, you tell me,' Samantha said.

Stonehouse gave her a reassuring smile and told her; they would soon have her back on her feet. He ordered Carrie to fix his patient a meal. He followed her out of the room. Samantha stared up at the ceiling and wondered what was going to happen to her now; the people who ran her down must have brought her here. She was in danger, Samantha had no doubt. A little while later Carrie returned to the room and gave Samantha the meal she had prepared for her.

'Is this the last meal for the condemned?'

Carrie shook her head and left the room. Dr Stonehouse would not say who the mystery patient was. Carrie hoped she was not dangerous, as the girl did not seem to be at all happy.

When Dr Stonehouse entered his office there were a man and a girl waiting for him. Dr Stonehouse recognised the man by his strong lean face; he wore a dark suit; the last time the doctor had seen him the man was dressed in a military uniform. He stood by his desk. The girl was sat in a chair by the door, she wore a black sweatshirt and black skirt, and he gazed at her thin face and pale blue eyes. Dr Stonehouse gave her a friendly smile, but the girl did not acknowledge it. She stared straight at the big man standing by his desk. Stonehouse moved up to his desk and the man struck him gently on the shoulder.

'Hello Brian, nice to see you again.'

'Are you here for the new patient?'

The man nodded his head.

'She is a very dangerous person; we want you to help us with her.'

'She has something I want,' the girl by the door said.

The girl stood up and walked out of the office.

'She had run away from the Research Facility where we used to work together; fortunately she was caught before she got to any large city,' the man told Stonehouse.

Dr Stonehouse stared in horror at his companion.

'She's not carrying some sort of disease, is she?'

The man shook his head.

'No nothing like that, we just want her where we can keep an eye on her.'

Samantha slid painfully out of bed; she had on a long white nightgown. The door opened and she suddenly felt nauseous and her head began to throb. The tall girl walked into the room with a familiar evil smile on her thin face.

'Hello Sammy, it's nice to see you again.'

'I can't say the same about you, the last time I saw you, you were a mess and quite dead,' Samantha said.

The tall silver blonde girl approached Samantha; when she was in reach, she lashed out swiftly with her right fist and struck Samantha on the chin with all her strength, Samantha was knocked backwards, and the back of her head struck the window ledge as she went down.

'I take it she was no friend of yours,' a female voice said at the door.

The tall girl turned and faced Carrie and ordered her to give her a hand to get Samantha back on the bed. They picked up the unconscious girl between them and unceremoniously threw her onto the bed. Carrie noticed the back of the girl's head was bleeding.

'The way her head hit the window ledge, I wouldn't be surprised if you haven't cracked her skull,' Carrie said.

'She's alive, that's all that matters,' the tall girl said without a care.

Carrie followed the tall girl out of the room and closed the door behind them.

'Come with me and help get some equipment out of my car.'

'Don't you ever say please?' Carrie inquired.

'No!'

They left the square three storey building; the sky was grey and overcast. The grounds of the clinic were set inside a small wood. They followed the path that led out of the wood and ended at the roadside where the tall girl had her car. The girl opened the boot and pulled out a large box and gave it to Carrie, who struggled to keep hold of it as the box was heavy. She turned and carried it back to the clinic. The tall girl took out another large box and, taking a tight hold of it, she followed Carrie into the clinic and up to the top floor to the room where Samantha was being kept. Carrie helped the domineering girl to unpack the boxes and set the electronic equipment they contained up by the head of the bed, wires were fixed to the unconscious girl's head. When they were done, Carrie was dismissed and she gladly made a hasty retreat.

Samantha returned to consciousness the following night with a searing pain in her head and she felt sick to the stomach. She got a sudden feeling there was something awful close by; it stretched out of the darkness and touched her mind. She blinked her watery eyes as the moonlight filtered in through the window above the bed and settled on a ghostly figure standing by the bed.

You have something I want.

Samantha stared at the thin white hand that reached out for her; she moved away from the expected touch.

You must die – so I can be free.

The voice inside her head started to plague her again.

You know I can cause you pain and discomfort. Give in to the inevitable. Close your eyes and give up your life to me.

The thin hand gripped her shoulder in a vice like grip, Samantha tried to move but she found herself securely strapped to the bed.

You are not needed anymore, you are redundant.

Steely fingers dug into her flesh.

You must die so I can reach my full potential.

An evil giggle filled the room and Samantha slipped into unconsciousness.

'Do the right thing, Sammy, just die.'

The lights came on the tall thin girl was laughing at the girl on the bed, her companion was watching the images from the brain scanning equipment.

'Good work, Jennifer, you have done well,' he complimented.

'I'm eager to please, her mind is so inferior to mine,' she said, arrogantly.

The second clone Jennifer Russell strode out of the room – he had told her that was the name she was to go by, she had no memory of it, and she accepted it. Jennifer Russell wanted to please her companion. He had a strong predatory mind like her own, he had told her the ginger haired girl was her deadly rival and Jennifer Russell had to beat her into oblivion, she had got into her mind and found Samantha had something she must possess and she would take it and then destroy Samantha.

After a few words with Dr Stonehouse the man left. Samantha would stay locked up in the room; he would contact the doctor if he had a change of orders.

Deep in the unconscious mind of Samantha a vision from her past filtered out of her memory.

The little girl of six years of age runs around the large bushes bordering the large back garden. Her mother was standing close by.

'Where can I hide, they're after me, help me, Mummy.'

'Why not hide amongst the bushes,' the woman said.

The woman entered-into the little girl's game.

'They can see into my mind, what shall I do?'

The woman smiled at her daughter.

'Well they won't find much there to help them – you do not know enough yet.'

The little girl stared up at her mother.

'When will I know enough?'

'When you are a big girl,' her mother replied.

'Then I won't be a big girl, if I keep my mind empty, then they won't hurt me,' the girl said.

The woman picked up her daughter and kissed her cheek.

'They will never hurt you, not while I'm here,' the woman assured her daughter. *Where are you now, Mother? When I need you the most?*

Dr Stonehouse and his companion walked down the corridor – away from the room where Samantha lay as if in death. The next door up opened and a girl in a black nightgown came out and stood by the door; she watched the two men approach her, the pretty round face was expressionless, the grey eyes stared intently at the two men. They watched them as they passed by.

After a moment he turned and saw the girl had shifted position and was still staring at them intently. Something told him the face was familiar, but he could not place where he had seen the girl before.

'How long has she been here?' he asked the doctor.

Dr Stonehouse turned and watched the girl slip back into her room and close the door.

'Phoebe? About a year, after they eventually caught her. It's a strange case and a very violent one,' Dr Stonehouse replied.

Phoebe sat on the bed and stared into space, and the vision of the night of horror that had turned her life upside down was replayed again in her mind. A dark force had come into the house and butchered her parents in the dark of night, everything was red and black. A tall dark figure without a face had caused mayhem, she had been fifteen and she had been severely beaten and he did other awful things to her, while her twelve-year old sister looked on in a petrified state. They had found her in the morning with the long sharp blade in her hand and she was accused of the slaughter of her parents. Her sister was too hysterical to comment on what had happened.

Carrie entered the room and walked to the bed and asked the girl if she needed anything. She remained still and quiet as she continued to stare at the far wall. Carrie shook her head and left the room, closing the door behind her. The girl had not spoken since her arrival and whatever was going on inside her head only she knew. Carrie was unable to get a word out of her.

As she stared at the wall the vision changed and the faceless figure that killed and tortured her now had a face. Her hands made fists and her long nails dug into her palms and broke the skin. Now her enemy had a face she could start her revenge on the demon that had ruined her life. When that was accomplished, she could go and find her sister and tell her the nightmare was finally over.

Jennifer Russell – clone 2 – sat in the passenger seat and stared at the torrential rain crashing against the windscreen as she waited for her travelling companion to return to the car. When he eventually came back to the car, he got in and started up the motor.

'Where are we off to now?' she inquired.

'I'm taking you to the big city, I have an idea Naomi will be making for Exeter,' he said.

Naomi Evans was up to something he had no doubt and he had to catch her before she became a danger.

'When you find her give her to me and I'll get the information out of her for you.'

'I'm sure you will, that's why I brought you with me,' he said.

CHAPTER XL:

INVEIGLE, OBFUSCATE

JANUARY 2131.

EXETER, DEVON.

Naomi Evans was relieved her father still lived at the same house that she had left to gain a higher education at college and find a profession for herself. Naomi pressed the doorbell and put her hands behind her back and crossed her fingers. The door opened and a tall heavily built man stared at her as if trying to recognise her.

'Hello Daddy, it's me again.'

George Evans stood aside so his daughter could enter the house and then he shut the door behind her.

'Hello Naomi, long time, no see.'

Naomi took off her coat and hung it up; she went into the lounge and settled down on the sofa, while her father went to the kitchen to make some tea. She gazed round the room and found nothing changed from the last time she was here. Naomi gave a sigh as the hardest part of her venture had been accomplished; her father had let her in, so he was not too mad at her for not calling on him sooner. George Evans came back and handed his daughter a mug of strong tea, then sat in an armchair opposite her.

'I'm sorry I've been so long coming to see you. I know you were slightly disappointed I was not the son you wanted, so I did not want to come back until I'd done something to make you proud of me,' Naomi confessed.

George shook his head and sighed.

'If I've given you that impression, I'm sorry. I've always been proud of you, Naomi,' he said, sincerely.

'Thank you, Daddy, that's nice to know. Do you trust me?'

George Evans put his cup down and got up and sat on the sofa beside his daughter.

'You are here for a reason, so, Naomi, let's have it.'

When Naomi had finished telling her story and outlining her future plans, George Evans sat back and inwardly digested what he had heard. To say his daughter was ambitious was an understatement. He did not know she was so devious; she was setting her sights high, but how high? Her determination to get him to endorse her campaign reminded him of her mother. It was through her that Naomi had decided to get a degree in the sciences, she had gone into medicine because Naomi wanted to learn how and why her mother was taken away from her so early in her life and she had been unable to realize her own ideas and goals. Naomi was going to succeed in the plan Samantha had formulated with her, it was for her mother, as she had always told Naomi never start anything she could not finish. She needed the help of her father to get started as she had to get into the City Government building so she could get into the database and formulate a new identity for herself. Naomi Evans had to disappear as she was a wanted person.

'You've changed, Naomi; I did not see you as the revolutionary type.'

Naomi smiled and shook her head and assured her father, she was not in the government toppling game, she acknowledged his superior experience in being a politician, and she was not in it for that sort of power. But a thought still nagged in his mind – was his daughter trying to deceive? George knew his daughter was very bright, but was not quite sure how high was her intelligence; it was obvious she had done exceedingly well in college to get a job at a high technical research facility.

Naomi could see the doubts in his change of expressions.

'Now you know why I asked you if you trusted me, I would never do anything to dishonour you, Daddy. You and Mother helped me get to where I am now, so I would never do anything to hurt you. I know it has been a long time since I have contacted you, but I still look up to you.'

George stared hard at her face and the emotion of her expression brought the truth to her words.

'The change that is being proposed is long in the future and it won't be because of me, I have plans of my own. I need to build up a new identity for myself and I need your help. Nobody will know of your involvement, I assure you. I am not going to endanger you, I love and respect you too much, Daddy.'

'There is a lot of your mother in you, Naomi, your strong will and determination of purpose, she would be very proud of you.'

George kissed his daughter on the cheek and Naomi beamed at him.

'It's for Mummy that I want to be somebody, and I want you to be very proud of me,' Naomi said, sincerely.

'If you succeed in your campaign, I shall be astonished.'

Naomi stood up and looked down at her father.

'Does that mean you will help me?'

George smiled and winked at her.

'I suppose it does.'

Naomi left the room and climbed the stairs and entered her old bedroom; nothing had changed, the room was the same as she had left it. She went to the bedside table and picked up a large framed photograph of her mother, and her eyes started to water. Naomi put it down and went over to the wardrobe and slid the door open. Naomi removed her dress and took out a denim shirt from the wardrobe and put it on and then put on a matching pair of blue jeans. She removed the wig from her head and gazed at her reflection in the wardrobe mirror, Naomi had had her hair cut short. She left the room and went back downstairs and met her father in the hallway. He gave her a thick sheepskin coat.

'It was your mother's, it should fit you, and it has started to snow.'

Naomi put on the coat and George opened the door.

'Are you ready?' he asked.

Naomi nodded her head; she was as ready as she would ever be. She followed her father out of the house and shut the door behind her. George opened the passenger door of his car and Naomi got in.

'People will think I've got a new girlfriend,' he said, light-heartedly.

'Good, it will make my disappearance easier for you – as far as they are concerned you have not seen me for years,' Naomi said.

George slammed the door shut and got in the driving seat and drove away from the house. Naomi gazed at the river Exe as the road ran alongside it. George drove out of Exeter and made for London. Naomi felt the excitement build up inside her; Naomi could not wait to get started on her new career.

JANUARY 2132

EXETER, DEVON.

Gerald Pollard sat at his desk on the thirtieth floor of the Government Administrative building. There were several rows of desks in the large room that made up the database. He was working on the middle row. While his eyes were firmly staring at the screen of his desktop computer, his ears detected footsteps approaching him. He stopped working and turned his head. When he saw who it was, he jumped to his feet. Sarah Mullen smiled as he stood to attention. It was the first time she had been able to meet with her friends and colleagues since her father had had her hidden away in the Research Complex. Gerald was the oldest and most important man in her group, and he was also part of the National Government as he was attached to the Home Office. Her father was not aware of their working relationship, as they rarely met in public and she always had an innocent reason for them to bump into each other. She had entered the office when there were not too many people around to see them meet and she would tell anyone who inquired about her that she was just searching for information, which was what Sarah was after and she wanted to tell Gerald all that she knew about the Research Complex and the alien star ship that was still at the outer regions of the solar system. Gerald sat down and listened to her narrative without interruption. When she had finished Sarah gave him a description of Samantha and inquired if any of the others in the group had contacted such a person. Gerald shook his head. Sarah knew the girl was heading for Exeter and told him to keep an eye out for her.

'There is another girl you should look out for, she is the same height as me, but with a fuller figure and long dark hair that's all over the place,' Sarah said.

Gerald knew who she meant – anyone not agreeing with her ideas, Sarah would tell him about.

'You mean Naomi?'

Sarah nodded her head – Sarah did not want Naomi involved in her plans as Naomi was the kind of girl that would muscle in and take over.

'You won't have to worry about her anymore, Naomi is dead, killed in a fatal car crash in London,' Gerald informed her.

Sarah put a hand to her mouth and sat in a chair at the next desk; he could see she was physically shocked over the news.

'Was it an accident?' Sarah asked after a while.

'The investigation team found nothing suspicious. It's a shame, her father's a nice man, and he's very distraught at losing his only daughter so soon after his wife's death.'

Sarah stood up.

'I'd better go and inform the General.'

Gerald watched her walk along the aisle between the work desks; he wondered if she believed Naomi was murdered – there had been no evidence pointing to that assumption.

Sarah Mullen got in the lift and went down the thirty floors to the bottom; she left the building by a rear exit and walked into Paul Street, and she crossed the road and walked into a beauty parlour. As the door closed a girl standing looking down at her desk looked up. Lisa Booth looked the customer up and down and shook her head.

'This could be a tough one, I don't think I can do anything to improve you, madam,' Lisa said.

'Your jokes haven't improved over the years, Lisa,' Sarah said.

Sarah went to the counter and lifted up the flap and moved to the other side of it. She took a painting off the wall and laid it on the counter; she turned back to the wall and where the painting had been was an electronic control panel. Sarah ran her fingers over it and a partition of the wall slid back. She stepped into the dark recess that lit up and revealed a stairway, Sarah walked up it and Lisa followed her and the panel slid back. At the top of the stairway Sarah stepped into an office room, almost completely filled with desks and filing cabinets; there was not much space to walk along the floor. Sarah shook her head and muttered under her breath.

'We really must get a bigger building,' Sarah observed.

Sarah perched herself on a desk and gazed at her friend, Lisa was just below average height, slim figure with a small round face that did not need any beauty treatment.

'Have we managed to secure that new office building in North Street?' Sarah inquired.

Lisa shook her head. They had found ideal premises for their group, they had the money ready – but someone had got in before them. Lisa had not been able to find the identity of the buyer, or what the building was going to be used for. Sarah was disappointed and wanted Lisa to continue to try and find out who now owned the building and what they were going to use it for.

'Where is Xanthe?' Lisa's expression turned grave.

'Don't you know what day it is today?'

Sarah thinking of the date suddenly became aware of the horror that had come into the life of one of her friends, which had also touched Lisa who had an experience of horror on the same night ten years before. Sarah was living in London at the time and she had not met Xanthe or Lisa at that time.

'She's at the abandoned housing estate where it all happened, I would have been with her, but Gerald contacted me to say you were on your way,' Lisa said.

Sarah slid off the desk and stood close to Lisa and ran a soothing hand over her cheek.

'Has the sister turned up?' Lisa shook her head.

'Not as far as I know. How Phoebe escaped being locked up, is beyond me. She has gone to ground, and I hope she stays there for Xanthe's sake,' Lisa said.

Lisa let her mind drift back ten years when at the age of eleven she had watched Phoebe Cross being dragged out of the house screaming, her hands and clothes covered with blood. She had turned her staring wide eyes on Lisa and she suddenly felt guilty as if the whole horrible business was her fault; Lisa did not know why she felt that way, she had her own terrors to worry about. Xanthe slid out of the house of horrors and went straight to Lisa and clung tight to her, as she whispered over and, over again in her ear: she didn't do it, she didn't do it.

'Do you think Phoebe killed her parents?' Sarah asked, breaking into Lisa's thoughts.

'The two girls were going to be separated, they wanted to give Xanthe up for adoption so she could have a better home – perhaps Phoebe resented that, they were inseparable. If Phoebe wasn't mad before the incident, she was quite insane when they dragged her out of the house. Xanthe remains silent about the horrors that went on in that house, she has got her life on track and I want it to stay that way,' Lisa said.

Xanthe Cross sat on her old bed staring across the bedroom; the windows had been boarded up like all the other windows in the old house she had been brought up in. She came here on every anniversary of her parents' death to face her ghosts and in the hope she would run into her sister. Xanthe was sure of her sister's innocence over the horrible death of her parents; nobody, not even her mother and father, really knew Phoebe, and she was not the evil person people made her out to be. Xanthe could never tell the real truth of what had happened that night; she had locked the horrors in the back of her memory in a door never to be opened, until Xanthe came face to face with her older sister. Phoebe was big and strong with a frightful temper, Xanthe was the very opposite, timid and frail with dark wide eyes, like depthless pools. Her parents thought Phoebe was having a domineering effect on Xanthe, so they wanted to send Xanthe off to be adopted so Phoebe would have no influence over her. But the relationship between the two sisters was quite the opposite, Phoebe loved her sister and was trying to protect her from something nasty and nobody understood it.

Xanthe stood up and walked across the room and walked out to the landing. The ghosts stood around her, Xanthe could not see them, but she knew they were there. Opposite her old bedroom was the door to the bedroom where her parents were slaughtered, and her sister was abused and tortured. She walked to the end of the landing and walked slowly down the stairs as they creaked loudly in the silent house. As she stepped down into the hallway the front door slowly creaked open. Xanthe moved quickly and stayed behind the opening door, she slipped the automatic out of the inside pocket of her coat. She had not used it yet but Xanthe knew there would be a first time. A tall dark figure stepped into the murky light of the hallway and Xanthe moved silently up behind it.

'Keep still and stay facing forward,' Xanthe said.

Xanthe stabbed the automatic in the back of the intruder and ran her left hand down the body as she searched for any weapons the intruder might be carrying; she gave a silent sigh when her probing hand found the stranger was a woman. Xanthe stepped away when she was satisfied the intruder was unarmed.

'I'm not a girl you should creep up on,' Xanthe warned.

'Can I turn around now – I assure you I am not your enemy.'

'Yes, why not?' she asked.

She turned and gazed at the weapon being pointed at her, and then she gazed up at the pale round face and the dark eyes.

'I thought people didn't walk about with guns in their pockets.'

Xanthe smiled and kept her eyes on the face, as the sharp hazel coloured eyes regarded her with interest.

'I'm a special case,' Xanthe said.

'You work for the Government?'

Xanthe shook her head. 'Not this Government,' Xanthe assured the stranger.

The stranger was several years older than her; she gave Xanthe a smile as she kept staring at the gun aimed at her.

'Why don't you put the weapon away, we can talk better without it.'

Xanthe shook her head, she was not that trusting.

'Why don't you tell me; who you are.'

'My name is Zenobia Madison, I've been living abroad for ten years, and I had a friend who used to live on this estate at that time.'

'Nobody lives here now, only the ghosts walk about this housing estate now,' Xanthe explained, moodily.

Zenobia grinned and hoped this girl was not one of the ghosts that haunted this place.

'What would a ghost want with a gun?'

Xanthe gazed at the automatic in her hand and then relaxed; she returned the gun to the inside of her coat.

'I'm real enough; I used to live in this house, the name's Xanthe.'

Zenobia held out her hand. Zenobia had hit the jackpot in one go, this was the girl she had hoped to contact.

'I'm glad to meet you.'

Xanthe took the offered hand and stared hard at the round face bordered by the fur outline of the hood of her coat. Was this a coincidental meeting or was Zenobia here for a reason? Xanthe turned and walked out of the old house and Zenobia followed behind her.

'Do you come here to converse with the spirits of the former occupants?' Zenobia asked.

Their boots crunched through the thin layer of snow covering the ground, the freezing wind blew in their faces.

'Something like that; my parents were murdered here in a horrifying circumstances. They weren't the only deaths round here, a lot of strange things happen at night that made everyone move out and the housing estate was left abandoned, I come here on this date every year, because something compels me to,' Xanthe explained.

Xanthe came to beg forgiveness of the spirits of her dead parents; she felt a guilt that would never go away – the silence after the event and hiding the details of the murder deep inside her subconscious. She had not seen the demon that had come into the house at night and torn her world apart; her older sister had been accused of the hideous murder.

'What made you enter that house in particular?' Xanthe wanted to know.

'No mystery there, I saw footprints in the snow leading to the house, so I knew someone was in there, because there were no footprints coming out. I wanted to find someone who could tell me what happened to a friend of mine, who used to live on this estate,' explained Zenobia.

The houses bordered a single straight road, they stood two houses away from the end of the road, and Zenobia stared down at the end house.

'Who was your friend?'

Zenobia stared at the house on the left of the end house, it was just a burnt-out shell.

'Amy Thornton.'

Xanthe turned and knew the house that Zenobia had her eyes on. Amy had been seen outside her house and was laughing hysterically as she watched it burn, her parents still inside the burning house.

'Amy told me before I went abroad that her parents had changed, and they were going to kill her. I thought perhaps she was having a bad day,' Zenobia said.

'Everybody living here has had the same bad day, but with different horrifying circumstances,' Xanthe said.

Zenobia turned and made for the other end of the housing estate where she had parked her car. She offered Xanthe a lift and she accepted. Zenobia removed her coat and tossed it on the back seat; underneath she wore a dark brown blazer and skirt. Xanthe sat in the passenger seat and closed the car door and unbuttoned her coat. The sleek comfortable limousine showed Zenobia was a girl with money. Xanthe gazed at her manicured fingers curled round the steering wheel – she had several glittering rings on several fingers of both hands; her wedding finger had no ring on it. So, she was rich and available. Zenobia swerved onto the main road; the River Exe ran parallel to the road on their right. On the other side of the river was the Exeter Experimental Laboratories. It was a large array of buildings surrounded by a high fence. It had taken up a larger area since Zenobia lived nearby ten years ago.

'They must be doing something special over there to take up so much room, there were only two buildings when I knew it,' Zenobia said.

Xanthe gazed across the river at the Experimental facility. She had been taken there after the murder of her parents, she had stayed behind the high fence until she was sixteen and Xanthe was let out to take up her life where she had left off. She had searched out her friend who had lived opposite, Lisa had an apartment in the city and she instantly took Xanthe in as Lisa had never been more pleased to see someone before, she had never stopped thinking of Xanthe and what might have happened to her after that horrific night. They were once again firm friends, they were going to protect each other with their lives.

'I spent four years in there, they were studying children for E S P at that time,' Xanthe said.

'Did they find any in you?' Zenobia asked.

Xanthe shook her head. They had given her every test imaginable. Several children from the housing estate were with her, if they discovered anything strange about them, Xanthe did not know or care.

'I'm just boring Miss Average,' Xanthe said.

'I don't believe that, not many people want to face their fears regularly the way you do.'

Xanthe shook her head and smiled.

'Don't read too much into that, I'm just a glutton for punishment.'

Zenobia drove leisurely along the road as a new fall of snow started to drift across the dull cloudy sky.

'Or you're feeling a deep guilt about something that is not your fault.'

Xanthe turned her head and gazed at Zenobia, her suspicions raised, she began to wonder if their meeting was not a coincidence.

'How very astute of you, just who are you?'

'I'm who I said I was, Zenobia Madison. I have told you no lies and I'm not trying to deceive you,' Zenobia said, sincerely.

Xanthe was not convinced that bumping into this woman was just an innocent act. Her silky-smooth voice could hide a multitude of sins. As they drove into North Street and parked in front of the new twenty-five storey building that Sarah Mullen wanted to acquire, Xanthe's interest in the woman mounted. Zenobia got out of the car and told Xanthe she would not be long and Xanthe watched the woman walk to the building entrance and disappear into it.

Zenobia entered the foyer and strode over to the desk, where a girl in her late twenties stood on the other side of the reception desk waiting for her employer to come up to her.

'Everything all right, Jacqui?'

Jacqui Taylor nodded her head and told Zenobia everything was going to plan and they were well ahead of the deadline. Zenobia had put Jacqui in charge of the preparations in getting her business up and running, she had known the girl before she had gone abroad and when she came back, Zenobia had looked her up and offered her the job and Jacqui had gratefully accepted, so Zenobia could get on with recruiting more staff.

'Did you find her?'

Zenobia nodded and told her Xanthe was sitting in her car at this very moment.

'I found her in a very strange place, the old abandoned housing estate by the river, where you lived as a child. I think she blames herself for the murder of her parents and she seeks the forgiveness from the ghosts she thinks still inhabit her old house,' Zenobia said.

'She sounds a girl in pain,' Jacqui said.

Zenobia nodded her head.

'In her own stumbling way, Xanthe is a survivor, just like you, Jacqui. Amy Thornton was not so lucky.'

After they had taken Amy away, after she had set fire to her home and not told her parents about it when they were still inside the house, Amy kept quiet and soon after the incident she had killed herself. When Jacqui had told her, Zenobia refused to believe Amy was an arsonist and murderer. Jacqui told her about Xanthe and her sister, Phoebe. Jacqui had been friends with Phoebe before the deaths of her parents; she had a terrible temper, but she was no killer. Zenobia found the whole business about the housing estate very strange and she was immediately suspicious there had been something going on there that had not come to light.

'I must get Xanthe to where she wants to go; I'll see you later, Jacqui.'

Jacqui watched her friend walk across the foyer towards the entrance doors.

'Good luck, Zen.'

Zenobia left the building and got back in her car and asked Xanthe where she wanted to be dropped off. She started the car and drove up to the end of the road.

'Are you in a steady employment at the moment, Xanthe?'

'I'm working part-time at the moment, I…'

Xanthe stopped talking as if she was about to say too much about her work.

'It's all right; I'm not trying to pry. If you want full employment, I have a position for you in my business.'

'What kind of employment?'

Zenobia turned into Paul Street and made for the beauty parlour owned by Lisa Booth.

'Why don't you come to my office tomorrow morning and we can talk about it then,' Zenobia said.

She drove up to the kerb and turned off the engine, Lisa and Sarah were standing outside the beauty parlour, Zenobia nodded to them as they gazed at the car. Xanthe got out and promised to call on Zenobia in the morning. She stepped onto the pavement and approached her two friends; they watched the car drive away.

'Who is your new friend, Xanthe?' Sarah asked.

Xanthe told her friends who she was and how they met. Sarah whistled.

'Have I ever told you, Xanthe, you are a gem,' Sarah said.

Xanthe smiled at the praise.

'She has offered me employment,' Xanthe said.

'That's lucky, now we can find out more about this woman who has gazumped us,' Lisa said.

Sarah put her arm round Xanthe's waist and told her to accept the job she had been offered. Xanthe moved away from her, she was not fooled.

'If you are asking me to spy on her, don't. I'm not a spy and I don't want to be.'

There was anger in her voice. Lisa stood close to her and put a comforting hand on her left shoulder.

'It's all right, Xanthe. Of course, Sarah does not want you to spy on her. It is entirely your choice if you take the job or not,' Lisa said.

'I'm just naturally curious about her, that's all,' Sarah said.

Sarah left the two girls and made her way back to the administrative building before the General sent out a search party for her. Lisa took Xanthe by the arm and took her home and they had lunch together.

Sarah Mullen went up to the top floor as soon as she entered the Government building and got Gerald Pollard to find out about Zenobia Madison. She left the database room and let Gerald get on with his work. She took the lift down to the next floor and when the doors opened, she saw George Evans walking towards the lift; she went to him and offered her condolences on the death of his daughter.

'Thank you, she told me once, Sarah, that you two did not get on, when you met at college.'

'We had a difference of opinion on some subjects, but I did not dislike her, and it saddens me Naomi's life was cut short so tragically.'

George nodded his head and gave her a warm smile. Suddenly Zenobia came into her mind and Sarah asked George Evans if he knew the woman.

'I knew her father, he was a very rich man, Zenobia inherited his fortune and she went abroad ten years ago. She's back now as Naomi met her before the accident.'

George Evans walked into the lift and Sarah moved down the corridor muttering under her breath, curiouser and curiouser.

Zenobia Madison stood in her twenty fifth floor office gazing out of the large window at the panoramic view of the city spread out before her. Zenobia was where she wanted to be, up high looking down at everyone else. Zenobia had inherited her father's talent to let money make money: while abroad she had increased her fortune tenfold. A large map of the world was stretched over the wall on her left, showing how far across many countries her small empire stretched. Now she had to build a powerhouse here in her country of birth, she wanted power and she would go to any lengths to get it. When she had met Naomi in the Capital, she had told Zenobia of Sarah Mullen and her campaign to be Premier like her father in a few years' time. Naomi told her Sarah had the organisation and resources; Zenobia had the vast wealth. Zenobia had liked Naomi a lot; she was not a girl that beat about the bush, she came straight out with what she had in mind, and Zenobia was pleased to meet someone as devious as herself. Naomi had given her licence to produce and market her medical equipment she had constructed, they had struck up an immediate partnership, Naomi was a scientist and Zenobia found she could use a person like Naomi; she was ingenious and wanted to improve her lot in life, though the tragic car crash had put a short end to that. Zenobia was going to continue the plan they had formulated.

Zenobia turned and walked out of the luxurious air-conditioned office and stepped into the outer offices and made for the lift doors, they opened, and she entered the lift and the doors slid shut behind her. She stared out of the transparent lift tube as the lift descended the side of the building. Zenobia watched the city get closer to her as she dropped to their level. The lift stopped at the bottom of the shaft and the doors opened and she walked into the foyer. Jacqui Taylor still sat at the reception desk even at this late hour. Evan after a ten year absence she was still a loyal friend to Zenobia and she rewarded Jacqui for that.

'Are you doing anything tonight, Jacqui?'

Jacqui Taylor stood up and shook her head. Zenobia pulled up the flap and waited for her friend to move to her side of the reception desk then dropped the flap down.

'Why don't we go out and get drunk?' Zenobia said.

'That's the best offer I've had all week,' Jacqui said.

Zenobia left the building and waited for Jacqui to lock up, they got in the car parked at the kerb and Zenobia drove into the heart of the city.

When Xanthe entered the foyer, she found Zenobia waiting for her. She thanked Xanthe for coming in and she guided the girl to the lift. They were soon travelling up the building and Xanthe gazed in wonder out of the transparent lift tube. She gazed at the panoramic view of the city and the covering of snow over everything made the scene more amazing. At the twenty-fifth floor the lift doors opened, and they vacated it and entered the outer office, where Xanthe would be put to work. She was going to be the personal secretary to Zenobia.

'Why me, we've only just met?' Xanthe was naturally wary.

'You are suspicious, that is quite normal,' Zenobia admitted.

Zenobia guided her into the main office, Xanthe gazed round the large office room in wonder, and she knew Sarah Mullen would love to have an office like this.

'I'm not trying to deceive you, Xanthe, I'm going to be up front with you, I shall put all my cards on the table,' Zenobia assured her.

Zenobia guided Xanthe to the wall covered by the World Map. She pointed out the markers that showed the extent of her business empire.

'Of course, I've found out all about you and I have found you are reliable, intelligent and ambitious. Just the type of person I'm looking for,' Zenobia said.

Zenobia sat the bewildered Xanthe down at the desk in front of a compact computer system. Xanthe stared at the screen as the financial details of Zenobia's company appeared, she stared in amazement at the spiralling profits – Zenobia had a hand in everything. Xanthe could not understand why she was being shown all this and she told Zenobia so, Xanthe was a friend of the Premier's daughter and

Sarah Mullen would love to get hold of some of this data Xanthe was being shown. Why was Zenobia so sure she would not speak of this to Zenobia's competitors?

'You are putting a hell of a lot of trust in a person who has ties with people who could use the information for their own ends,' Xanthe warned her.

'Would you tell anyone about my financial details?'

Xanthe did not hesitate to shake her head.

'I told Sarah I'm not a spy, when she told me to take the offer of employment with you.'

Zenobia smiled at her as if she was absolutely sure Xanthe would keep the confidentiality between the two of them.

'There you are, Xanthe, you have another redeeming quality.'

Zenobia started to ask Xanthe questions about what she had seen; she did not see the reason for it, but she gave the answers almost automatically. Zenobia was impressed.

'I thought you told me, they found nothing remarkable about you at the Experimental Laboratories?'

'They weren't looking for people with an exceptional memory, obviously.'

Zenobia grinned and shook her head.

'There's always a use for a photographic memory, whatever business you're in, but they know where to find you if the need arises.'

Xanthe stared up at Zenobia; she did not like the sound of her voice or the implications of what she had said

Sarah Mullen stormed into the beauty parlour after a very frustrating morning, Lisa watched her approach the reception desk, and she could see Sarah was not a happy bunny. Lisa took her into the back room and made some tea to help calm her down. Sarah sat on a stool and told Lisa about her search to find some incriminating evidence about Zenobia Madison had come to a dead end and she was squeaky clean. When Gerald Pollard came up with nothing, she went to see her father, who was having a meeting with General Heywood and Henry Jackson, the administrator for the county. They were discussing the problem of Samantha, who had not surfaced yet; they knew she would be coming to Exeter, because of the Research Laboratories by the river, where she would have to finish off her work.

Graham Mullen could not help his daughter as he had the highest regard for Zenobia and her late father and reminded his daughter that every rich person was not necessarily a criminal. Sarah argued the fact she was after Xanthe to work for her was a sign the woman was up to something. General Heywood, who was in the room and listening to the conversation, offered to use his security team to look into the affairs of Zenobia Madison. Graham told the General to be discreet, as Graham was sure his daughter was barking up the wrong tree. Sarah left the room in a huff after the General had told her not to disappear and be sure she was ready to leave Exeter when he was.

Lisa was sympathetic to her cause but told Sarah, Zenobia was a very intelligent woman and would leave nothing criminal about her for people to find.

'I know you care about Xanthe as much as I do, but she is a big girl now and can look after her. I'm sure Zenobia just wants Xanthe to work for her because she had a talent Zenobia wants in her business,' Lisa assured her.

'I hope you are right.'

Sarah was still not convinced, Zenobia was a threat, the woman was moving into her territory for one purpose only: to oust her out and gain the power Sarah wanted for herself.

Zenobia gave Xanthe a tour of the floors of the building that were in use, as some parts of the building were still empty as she had not found a use for them yet, but she was ever hopeful. When she had got Xanthe working for her, she would then work on Lisa Booth, then she would use them to reel in the big fish, Sarah Mullen, then the game could really begin. A bit of obfuscate planning and Zenobia could inveigle Sarah and her friends in doing just what she wanted them to do.

At noon she took Jacqui and Xanthe out to lunch and Xanthe gave her the news she was happily waiting for. Xanthe was very excited about the work Zenobia wanted her to do and as it was the proverbial offer that could not be refused, Xanthe had no intention of refusing the employment Zenobia was offering her.

After lunch Xanthe returned to the beauty parlour and found Sarah was there with Lisa. She announced to them her decision to work for Zenobia. Sarah marvelled at the enthusiasm Xanthe showed in telling them the work she had to do. She was very impressed with Zenobia's organisation that was worldwide. She told Lisa about the fully equipped medical facilities in the Zen Industries building, as Lisa Booth was a qualified doctor. Xanthe told Sarah about the advanced technology Zenobia had under her control. Sarah smiled as she realised Xanthe was a good propaganda machine for Zenobia. As the woman she would be, she hoped Sarah and Lisa would be enticed to see for themselves the Worldwide Organization she was head of. Zenobia could help Sarah realise her ambitions for a price.

CHAPTER XLI:

PHOEBE CROSS

MAY 2133

THE STONEHOUSE CLINIC

EXTON, DEVON

Phoebe Cross took the key out of her coat pocket and slipped it into the lock and the front door swung open. There was a slight sound behind and when she was about to turn round a strong force pushed her into the hallway and she was thrown against a wall; the shock of the pain in her face and body stunned her and she fell to the floor. The door was shut behind her and Phoebe was picked up and dragged up the stairs as a clock chimed midnight, as if counting the many minutes of her life that remained to her. As the huge dark shape got her onto the landing, through watery eyes she saw a bedroom door open and her twelve-year-old sister stared at them wide-eyed. Phoebe was thrown bodily against her young sister knocking her back in the room. Phoebe lay in pain on the threshold of the bedroom, she was kicked until her body was further in the room and the door was slammed and locked.

Phoebe was lifted up into a sitting position on the floor and her younger sister clung to her whimpering as they heard screams and noises coming from their parents' room, then there was silence for a moment, then footsteps came to their door; something was coming for them. Phoebe got to her feet as the door crashed open and a dark figure moved menacingly towards Phoebe. She was grabbed and thrown round the room like a rag doll, her little sister dived and hid under the bed. Phoebe was stunned and in pain as the strong force assaulted her in many other ways. Then she was dragged from the room and into the next room and with watery eyes she saw the carnage, blood was everywhere so were parts of her parents' bodies.

Phoebe Cross sat on the bed with her thighs up against her chest and her chin rested on her knees. She stared trance-like at the bare white wall opposite the bed, in her mind everything was dark and red, she replayed the horror over and over again even in her dreams. Phoebe did not know how long she been in the small white walled room, neither did she care; she could spend the rest of her life here, however long that may be. The demon that had torn her life apart was aware she was here, Phoebe was sure, she had seen him, and she had felt the same horrific fear when he had visited the asylum some time ago, as on the night of her parents' death and she had been dragged away as the guilty one. The end had been a blur and Phoebe did not know why she had been covered in her parents' blood or why the murder weapon was gripped tight in her right hand. Phoebe would try to find out when the demon came back for her.

The door opened and Carrie Scott walked into the room carrying Phoebe's lunch on a tray. She sighed and shook her head; the girl was in the same position as she had been at breakfast, Carrie had been trying to talk to her, but the girl ignored her. Carrie wondered what was going on in her mind, whatever it was the girl kept it to herself. Carrie placed the tray on the bedside table and nudged the girl on the shoulder and told her lunch was served. Phoebe did not move and continued to stare into space. Carrie turned and walked out of the room, shutting the door behind her.

Phoebe moved and swung her bare legs over the edge of the bed; she picked up the tray and began to eat her lunch.

Carrie Scott went into the next room and walked to the bed that was surrounded by machinery that monitored the life signs of the tall female patient lying like death. Carrie wondered why Dr Stonehouse did not have her sent to the hospital where she would be properly cared for. She must be missed by somebody; relatives would be out looking for her. The doctor told her the patient was better here until she woke up,

Carrie was not sure the patient ever would come out of the coma, she was being kept here for a reason and the doctor knew what it was, but he was not going to tell her. Carrie had been worried about the girl ever since she almost had her skull cracked by hitting her head against the window sill three years ago. Carrie checked the monitors and noticed no change; the girl was barely alive with little brain activity. She was having no active dreams if she was capable of dreaming as her brain was locked into the machine that was scanning it. Though Carrie did not know that but the machine and what it might be doing to the patient's brain made Carrie very suspicious of it, even though Dr Stonehouse tried to put her mind at ease, by telling her the tall girl was not being harmed by the machinery monitoring her, it did not help and Carrie remained suspicious. There was nothing she could think of doing but waiting for the girl to wake up, if she was capable of doing so.

Carrie left the room and went down to Dr Stonehouse's office to inform him there was no change in Samantha and Phoebe was as uncommunicative as ever. He received the report with a lack of interest Carrie found curious. Carrie left the office and was in a determined mood, she would concentrate on Phoebe and get her to speak, and she went to her own office and sat at her desk and patched her computer into the database to get details on Phoebe Cross.

Dr Stonehouse got on the telephone and contacted his associate and reported the condition of the two girls as he did now on a regular basis. Phoebe Cross was a danger to the both of them, because of the secrets locked deep in her memory. It was ideal she was being silent and unresponsive.

Carrie walked into the room and found the girl sitting on the bed in her usual position, her head resting on her knees and her dark eyes staring out into space. Phoebe heard the door open and footsteps approach the bed. She continued to stare at the far wall, as her never ending nightmare went on and on inside her head. Carrie pulled up a chair and sat at the bedside, Carrie hoped she would be in the way and Phoebe would have to acknowledge her existence especially if Phoebe tried to leave the bed on the side where Carrie sat waiting. Carrie studied the girl – if the data she had read was right, she was staring at a cold-blooded killer; she could not see it as Phoebe was placid enough, but Carrie had no idea what was going on inside her head. Of course, Phoebe did not have to be guilty of everything reported against her, the reputation she built up would follow Phoebe wherever she went, and every bad event would be laid at her door, whether she was guilty or not.

Whatever it took Carrie was determined to let Phoebe know she was a likely friend and somebody she could depend on. Carrie did not like Phoebe thinking she was alone and there was nobody around who cared about her plight, if only Carrie could get through to her.

'You have had quite a violent life so far, Phoebe,' Carrie said, softly.

The girl did not speak or move.

'That's it, Phoebe, you just sit there staring into space, I'll just stay here and be a constant irritation,' Carrie said.

Phoebe kept her stone face and inside her head the vision of violent death faded away, she turned her head at last and stared at the irritation sitting by the bed. Carrie had a smile of triumph on her pretty face.

'Now I have your attention, why don't you go the whole way and say something.'

Phoebe did not change her stony expression as the vision of her strangling the young nurse came into her mind.

'If you like, you can jump on me and beat me to a bloody pulp, if it would make you feel better, I won't mind, that's what friends are for,' Carrie said.

Her lips broke into a smile before Phoebe could stop herself, causing the nurse harm would only be a temporary solution to her problems, it would just provide them with an excuse to keep her locked up for longer.

'If you want to be a friend, you can show me a way to get out of this place,' Phoebe said.

Phoebe moved her legs and swung round and sat on the side of the bed; her dark eyes stared at Carrie waiting for her response.

'I'd have to know a lot more about you, before I decide what I shall do about you, Phoebe.'

Carrie stood up and walked out of the room. Phoebe sat on the bed and stared at the closed door, sometime later Carrie came back with a tray and two mugs of hot strong tea, she offered Phoebe one and she took it and sipped the tea and watched Carrie sit on the chair in front of her.

'I've researched into your life, Phoebe, I suppose most of it is a fabrication, you don't look like a homicidal maniac, but I don't know what's going on inside your head,' Carrie explained.

'If I told you I have not killed anybody, would you believe me?' Phoebe asked.

'If you assure me of your innocence of any crime that has been assigned to you, I would believe you.'

'I have killed no one, there is an evil one after me, that is why I'm being kept in this place, so he knows where I am, so he can come for me.'

Carrie gazed at the dark eyes that stared back at her. Carrie told of Phoebe of the man and girl who had come here a year ago, Phoebe nodded her head.

'He is the one, how much do you trust your employer?'

Carrie had to confess she was not so sure about Dr Stonehouse, he had changed from when she first met him and she owed him a lot, but something was going on.

'Do you know Dr Stonehouse?' Carrie asked.

Phoebe nodded her head. At the time when her parents were killed Dr Stonehouse lived on the same housing estate. Phoebe was not the only person living on the estate who had had something happen to them, lots of strange things happened growing in seriousness until all broke loose and Phoebe was dragged away as an insane killer. Phoebe had managed to keep her sanity by letting it all wash over her head. At the time she did not think that Dr Stonehouse had anything to do with the strange happenings, but now she was not so sure – after all he was keeping her here and Phoebe was sure the doctor had no intention of letting her go.

'You have to help me get out of here; if I am to die, I want to do it out there,' Phoebe said, pointing to the window.

'I don't want to be here, when Dr Stonehouse's companion comes back; if he wants me, he will have to come and find me. I don't want to die in this locked cage.'

Carrie stood up and paced the room while Phoebe stayed on the bed and waited for the nurse to decide whether to help her or not. Phoebe had to get away somehow before he came back for her. Phoebe was aware of what the nurse was thinking – even if Phoebe was in danger could she set free an alleged insane violent person and set in motion another killing spree like the one that killed the girl's parents. Carrie was sure Phoebe wanted some kind of revenge for what had happened to her. She had to be sure of her actions before she did anything to help Phoebe. Right now, Carrie wished she was telepathic. She went back to the bed and stood over the girl; the dark eyes stared up at Carrie as if she was about to pass sentence on her.

'If I am to help you get out of here, I have to be very sure of your motives,' Carrie said.

'I have only one agenda and that is, I must contact my sister before he catches up with me, I must discover what she retains of the incident, we are the two halves of the whole. Only when we come together again will the truth be known.'

Carrie opened the cupboard by the bed and pulled out the clothes Phoebe had arrived in and tossed them to her and told her to get dressed. Phoebe stood up and pulled off the nightgown and put on the short brown dress and slipped on a pair of black shoes.

'You are sure your sister is alive? He may have got to her first.'

Phoebe shook her head.

'I don't think so, I would have felt it,' Phoebe said.

Carrie walked to the door and looked out and found the passage was clear, she stepped out of the room and Phoebe followed her up the passage until they came to the next door and Phoebe stopped and opened the door.

'Who's in here?'

'The other girl I told you about,' Carrie replied.

Phoebe walked into the room and went to the bed and stared down in amazement at the tall girl lying on it.

'They breed them tall around here, that's the kind of friend I could use,' Phoebe said.

'She's not from round here, she's been in that state for three years, I can't see her waking up now,' Carrie explained.

Phoebe stared at the machine at the head of the bed; it reminded her of something, and the wires running from the machine were fixed to implants at the left side of the head. She turned to Carrie.

'She won't wake while that machine is fixed to her head,' Phoebe said.

Phoebe ran her fingers gently over the wires to see if she could free them from the girl's head. She must be a special person to be treated in this way. With the help of the machine the girl was living an imaginary life that seemed real to her, while in the real world she was lying like death on a hospital bed. When she explained the process to Carrie, she was horrified.

'I can't believe Dr Stonehouse would do such a thing to a person.'

'I expect it's his companion that is keeping her this way; if I can free the wires from the implants – we can free her from her imaginary lifestyle.'

'It won't kill her, will it?' Carrie inquired.

'She's as good as dead now, I'm sure they are not going to release her, we will be giving her a chance for life,' Phoebe argued.

Carrie nodded and watched Phoebe work on the implants and after a while Phoebe managed to free the wires from the implants, which would have to be removed by surgery. There was a drip feed attached to the right wrist. She pulled the thin tube from under the bandage, she then picked up the hand and held it, Phoebe felt a shock run up her arm and goose pimples covered her skin.

Samantha was caught in a maze that seemed to have no exit, whatever path she took ended up in a dead end, she was like a rat in a laboratory, and she had no idea of time as there was no day or night. She was in a prison where there was no escape and nobody to talk to. Alone; all alone. She turned another corner and there was a bright flash, and everything disappeared, and a bright whiteness stung her eyes.

Phoebe saw the eyelids open and the bright green eyes stared up at her.

'Where am I?'

The voice was faint, and Phoebe just about heard what the girl had said. Phoebe told her who they were and told her where she was. Phoebe explained about the machine that had been attached to implants fixed to her head and she had been living in a reality made up by the machine and whoever had programmed it. Samantha listened in silence and brought her left hand up and touched the left side of her head.

'How do you feel?' Carrie asked in deep concern.

'How do I look?'

'Bloody awful,' Phoebe told her.

Samantha managed a weak smile. 'That's how I feel.'

Samantha started to struggle up into a sitting position and Carrie moved quickly to help her up and the green eyes gave her a cold stare.

'I know you.'

'I work here, and I have no relationship with the terrible girl that hit you. I am concerned about your health.'

Samantha turned her gaze on Phoebe.

'What is the date?'

When Phoebe told her, Samantha could not believe it; she had lost three years of her life.

'I'm twenty-one today,' was all she could think of saying.

'Happy birthday,' Phoebe wished her.

Samantha managed a weak smile and stared at her right-hand which Phoebe still clutched in her own.

'You can let go of my hand now.'

Phoebe was unaware she still held it; she let go of it and apologised.

Carrie told them she was leaving the room for a while and told them she would not be long. She told Phoebe to stay put as she had not decided what to do about

Phoebe yet. Carrie left the room. Samantha pulled the sheet down and swung her long legs over the side of the bed. She told Phoebe to look in the cupboard at the bedside and see if her clothes were inside. Phoebe looked inside and pulled out a black sweater and black slacks, she gave them to Samantha, who removed the white nightgown she wore and tried to stand up. Phoebe came close to her and supported Samantha as she stood on her weak shaky legs.

'Core, I've seen better shaped beer bottles,' Phoebe commented on Samantha's slim figure.

'There's no need to be personal, I am just a naturally skinny girl,' Samantha said.

Samantha put on the sweater and slacks, and then she sat back on the bed. Phoebe handed her a pair of trainers that she had found in the cupboard. Samantha put them on her long slim feet. Carrie entered the room carrying a glass filled with a green liquid, she handed it to Samantha, who gave her a frosty look.

'It's all right, it's not poisonous.'

Samantha took the glass and drank the liquid and made a face after she had drained the glass. Carrie told Phoebe Dr Stonehouse had gone out and now was the best time to leave the building.

'Thanks, Carrie, you won't regret it,' Phoebe assured her.

Carrie and Phoebe moved to leave the room – Samantha got to her feet.

'Do you mind if I join you?'

Phoebe went to her and supported her as they walked to the door. Carrie took the lead as they went out into the passage; they went to the end and got into the lift. When it reached the bottom floor, Carrie left the lift to see if the coast was clear.

Carrie went to the main doors and opened them, then she waved to the two girls in the lift and Phoebe helped Samantha to the doors and out of the building. Samantha decided to have a slow walk round the grounds so she could get her legs in good working order. Carrie guided Phoebe along the driveway that led to the main road; on the other side of the road Carrie had her home a small cottage. She walked along her driveway up to the garage where she kept her car, she opened the door and they entered the garage and Phoebe closed the door. There was plenty of light coming through the window. Carrie took out a set of keys out of her skirt pocket and removed her car keys from the ring and handed them to Phoebe.

'The tank's full, when you've cleared your name, you can return the car,' Carrie said.

'Are you sure about this? It's very good of you.'

'Just promise me you'll keep in touch.'

Phoebe put her arms round Carrie and kissed her full on the mouth, she then moved away.

'I'm forever in your debt,' Phoebe said.

Samantha sat down on the cool grass and lay her back against a tree, the sky was covered in a thick grey cloud, and there was dampness in the air. She lay her head back against the bark of the tree and closed her eyes. Samantha tried to get her mind round the idea she had been asleep for three years. Samantha was glad her mind was now free from the never-ending nightmare it had been stuck in.

I don't see why I had to be stuck in there with you.

'I thought I'd be rid of you.'

No such luck. The only way we can be free of each other, is for you to die.

'My death is not an option.'

As far as I can see, your death might be the only option.

Not going to happen.

Samantha stood up and took a deep breath; she was not going to let the thing inside her head drive her out of her mind.

CHAPTER XLII:

CHARLOTTE WILSON

Carrie crossed the road and headed for the clinic. As she got to the other side a car drew up to her and a man got out and approached her. Carrie gazed at the tall handsome man, he was in his early twenties and had sandy coloured hair cut short. She turned her head and looked at the car. There was a man in the driving seat and a girl sat on the back seat; their eyes met. She was the prettiest girl Carrie had ever set eyes on, she had shoulder length blonde hair. Carrie was shown a photograph by the man standing beside her; it was the tall girl Samantha.

'She is here at the clinic, I will take you to her,' Carrie said.

The car drove up the driveway and made for the entrance to the clinic, Steven Calvert fell in beside the nurse and followed the car.

'I don't suppose you have a doctor with you?' Carrie inquired.

'Yes, we have, why?'

Carrie told him about the mind lock his friend had been in for the past three years, she mentioned the implants and that they would need a surgeon to remove them.

Steven motioned to the girl in the car to join them and told Carrie to give her the details of Samantha's condition. Janice Clarke leapt out of the car carrying her med kit and approached the nurse. Steven walked round the grounds of the clinic in search of Samantha, and he found her at the tree line at the back of the building sitting down with her back against a tree.

'Is this a private party or can anyone join in?'

Samantha stared up at him and after her memory had told her who she was looking at, Samantha managed a smile; she was glad to see a friend again. She held out her hand and he took it and pulled Samantha onto her feet.

'You look only half the girl you used to be, Sam.'

They made their way to the front of the clinic and walked into the entrance where Janice strode up to Samantha and ran a hand over her left cheek.

'Who's done this to you, Sam?'

'I had a run in with one of Jennifer's clones.'

Janice nodded her head as she knew all about the cloning of Jennifer.

'We wondered where the second one went; I don't suppose you saw who was with her?' Janice inquired.

Samantha shook her head. Janice asked the nurse and Carrie gave her a rough description of the tall thin man, as she had not had a clear look at his face as he always seemed to have it turned away from her. They entered the medical room and Janice got Samantha to lie on the operating table and Janice made an exploratory examination of the implants. Carrie stood by ready to help.

'Very advanced technology,' Janice muttered.

'Can you remove them?'

David Calvert walked into the room and informed Janice that Dr Bishop was on his way by helicopter, and David had contacted the Research Facility and told them they had found Samantha.

Steven Calvert walked out of the grounds of the clinic and turned right and strolled slowly up the road, which was bordered on both side by trees. He gazed up at the grey cloudy sky and spots of rain hit his face. He heard a sound and scanned the sky and noticed a helicopter approaching from the North-west. That would be Bishop and the mystery doctor Janice had told him about. Steven stood still and watched it get closer. Steven was glad they had responded quickly when his father had told them they had found Samantha. He cared a lot for the tall girl. The helicopter flew over his head and made for the clinic. He started walking forward and passed the village of Exon which lay on high ground to his left. Steven saw a car approaching and he stopped walking. It drew up to him and stopped and the passenger door opened, and a tall girl stepped out and stood over him.

'Hello Steven.'

Steven stared at Jennifer Russell and suddenly got a vision of him grabbing her thin neck and throttling the life out of her.

'You're too late if you are here to finish the job you started on Samantha.'

The tall girl shook her head and gave him a smile that was as cold as her voice.

'If we had wanted her dead, I would have killed her right of way. We just wanted her out of commission for a while.'

'We?'

The girl giggled and turned her back on him.

'That's for me to know and you to find out.'

Steven watched the clone get in the car and saw it drive away, then he made his way to the clinic.

Janice Clarke now 18 watched the tall elegant figure of Dr Sally Hamilton walk into the medical room. Janice had received all her medical training from her at the Research Facility. Janice was also studying genetics. Carrie Scott moved away from the operating table as the tall woman stood over the two girls. Carrie had anaesthetized the patient. Janice knew how Carrie was feeling, as Janice had wilted under the awesome power when she first met Dr Sally Hamilton. When Janice learned the woman was Samantha's mother, she was not surprised as Samantha had a very powerful character of her own. General Heywood had warned Janice not to tell Samantha her mother was alive if their paths crossed. Janice was not pleased as it meant she would be deceiving Samantha, a person she cared for a lot. Dr Sally Hamilton had assured Janice it would not benefit the mission if Samantha knew, so she ordered Janice to keep it a secret.

First glance at the implants told Dr Sally Hamilton all she needed to know: her enemies were nearby; they were lot closer than the mother ship in space. They were using the second clone to experiment on her daughter. The clone had been activated without her knowledge, which told her they had enemies working inside the Research facility who were still active after the other two attacks on Samantha. With the help of Janice, they removed the implants from Samantha's head. She barked the occasional order to Carrie, who obeyed the commands without hesitation, as Carrie had not wish to annoy the tall domineering woman. Janice gave her a warm smile to put her at ease.

'Do you think they caused any brain damage? Samantha is aware of who we are.'

Dr Hamilton shook her head; whoever had connected the implants to Samantha's head knew what they were doing, they did not want to damage her daughter too much as they wanted to use her for some plan of their own.

'She'll be fine after some rest and a good meal inside her.'

'When she is fit enough to travel, are we to take Samantha back with us?' Janice inquired.

Dr Hamilton shook her head, she wanted Samantha to carry on following her own course, her daughter had a job to do and Samantha was to be allowed to get on with it.

'No, we'll let her move around freely for the moment.'

'But she must be watched closely, we know someone is intent on causing Samantha harm,' Janice observed.

'Of course, that's where you and Steven come in. Perhaps you can convince Samantha to take you with her for security.'

'We'll try, she is a very strong-willed person and seems to want to go it alone,' Janice said.

While going through Dr Stonehouse's records Dr Bishop came upon a familiar name, it was an ex-patient of his. He stood up and walked out of the offices, he passed Dr Hamilton coming out of the medical room and asked her about Samantha and she assured him Samantha was on the road to recovery. She made her way out of the building and went to the waiting helicopter. Dr Bishop turned down a left passage and knocked on the first door he came to and a female voice called for him to enter. He opened the door and walked into the room. A girl was sitting on a couch playing a guitar; she stopped when he made his way towards her.

Charlotte Wilson stood the guitar on the floor at the side of the couch and listened to the footsteps moving casually towards her. She had been blinded by a car crash that had killed her parents when she was ten. After they tended to her treatable injuries Charlotte was taken from the hospital by a Professor Fairclough, who assured her with kindly words that she had nothing to worry about, he was going to see she would be well cared for now she was alone as Charlotte had no relatives in the country now her parents were dead. She was taken to the Research Laboratories in Exeter and she met Dr Anthony Bishop for the first time. He helped her through the trauma of being in a fatal car crash and her blindness. He helped her get over the anger and guilt she felt inside, as she blamed herself for her parents' death because she had survived, and they had not. With his soft comforting voice Dr Bishop got Charlotte to put her trust in him and released her pent-up emotions. Dr Bishop left the facility and Professor Fairclough took charge of her. Charlotte stayed there for six years, there were other children there and she soon made new friends – so she did not feel she was alone. Charlotte was given many strange tests to see if her other senses had been heightened after she lost her sight and if she had developed a sixth sense to compensate for her blindness. Charlotte did not want people to think she was a little weird after the accident so if she found there was anything different about herself, Charlotte was determined to keep it to herself.

At the age of sixteen Charlotte left the research establishment and Dr Bishop met her outside the gate and took her to a family had got to take her in. Unfortunately, it did not last long and after two months, Charlotte was on the move again.

Charlotte Wilson now seventeen found herself at Dr Stonehouse's clinic. When the door opened and someone entered her room, she immediately thought it was Stonehouse come to ask her more strange questions. But the footsteps were not as heavy as his and were not light, so it was not the nurse. She stood up and listened as her visitor approached her and stopped a foot away from her.

'Hullo Charlotte, what are you doing here?'

Charlotte gave a deep sigh of relief as she realised who her visitor was.

'Dr Bishop, I'm so glad you are here. You're going to be very mad at me.'

Dr Bishop laid a comforting hand on her shoulder.

'I've been very naughty, I can't seem to get people to like me, and I don't do it on purpose.'

They sat down on the couch.

'Of course not, it's hard to have a stable life when you're being sent from one place to another. We'll have to find a permanent home for you.'

Charlotte shook her head and the long blonde hair cascaded over her shoulders. She was sure Dr Bishop would never find a person that was tuned to her wavelength; the only person she had found that understood her was Dr Bishop. She did not like or trust Dr Stonehouse, he was only after what was inside her head, that was the reason he had brought her here.

'If you are here, does that mean Dr Stonehouse has gone away?'

'Yes, you won't have to worry about seeing him again,' Dr Bishop assured her.

Charlotte took off her dark glasses and turned her face to him and gave him a bright smile. She was a very beautiful girl and her bright blue eyes would never see it. He assured Charlotte he would do everything to get her settled down to a comfortable life.

'You've done too much for me already; I really appreciate the care you show for me. I don't want to be a burden to you,' Charlotte said, sincerely.

'You'll never be that, Charlotte; you are a very pretty and bright girl.'

Dr Bishop stood up and Charlotte replaced her dark glasses and stood up and followed the psychoanalyst to the door.

'While I'm here you can put me to work, I want to be useful around here,' she said.

'All right, Charlotte, you're hired,' he told her.

Charlotte giggled as they walked into the passage. She followed Bishop back to the offices, where he found the nurse and David Calvert waiting for him. Bishop got Charlotte to sit at the reception desk and he went to the main desk and the nurse gazed nervously at him; seeing her discomfort Bishop gave her a friendly smile. He informed the young nurse that her employer would no longer be in the clinic. He assured Carrie her job was safe as he needed the young nurse to help him go through the records of the people being treated in the clinic.

Janice Clarke walked into the canteen and got herself a coffee and spied Steven sitting at a table by the window, she crossed the room and Steven gazed up at Janice as she stared at the tall girl sitting opposite him.

'Where did you pick up that creature?' she inquired.

Janice sat next to Steven as he told her where he had met Jennifer Russell. He told Janice the clone was being very uncooperative about the identity of her companion.

'We'll take her back to Dr Hamilton, she will know how to get the information out of her,' Janice said.

Jennifer Russell grinned and stared across the table at Janice.

'How is Samantha?'

'She'll be fine now the implants have been removed,' Janice replied.

Charlotte left the offices and walked along the corridor until she came to the medical room door; there she stopped, and she opened the door and stepped into the room. She listened and as nobody challenged her, Charlotte decided she was alone in the room. She walked forward until she got to the centre of the room where Samantha lay asleep on the operating table. She held onto it to steady herself and her right hand came in contact with a face. Samantha's eyes flashed open and gazed at a girl in a dark blue dress. Dark glasses hid the girl's eyes. Samantha sat up. Charlotte stepped back from the operating table – she was not alone in the room after all, and she felt a strange sensation run through her body.

'I'm sorry to disturb you, I had a strange feeling come over me as I touched your face, I feel a presence around you,' Charlotte said.

Samantha giggled.

'I have that effect on everyone I meet - my name is Samantha.'

'I'm Charlotte; I feel you are a girl with a problem.'

Samantha swung her long legs over the side of the table. This girl was very perceptive.

'Isn't that why we are here?'

Charlotte shook her head and smiled.

'No, I haven't got a problem, I AM the problem, and they can't manage me.'

'You sound all right to me,' Samantha assured her.

Charlotte reached out with her hands and ran them gently over Samantha's face. She kept still while Charlotte surveyed her face with searching fingers.

'You have a very strong facial bone structure; I can see you are a girl who knows what she wants.'

Samantha laughed.

'I can't get it, that's the trouble,' Samantha explained.

Samantha slid off the operating table.

'What was that strange feeling you had?'

Charlotte took hold of Samantha's hand and squeezed it gently.

'I felt another presence around you, an aura of hate, not like the real you at all,' Charlotte said.

'You don't know me.'

'Inside you are a decent person, when you eventually find yourself, you will see I'm right, I like the feel of your face, it is beautiful.'

'Thank you, Charlotte I shall remember that.'

They walked towards the door; Samantha liked Charlotte even though she was a little strange. She had got too near the truth for her liking, but being forever in the dark Samantha felt for the girl. Samantha opened the door and they stepped out of the room. They walked along the corridor and parted company when Samantha went into the offices and Charlotte made for the rest room. She got herself a cup of tea and made for the other side of the rest room. As she came up to the table occupied by Steven and Janice, Jennifer Russell stood up and moved away from the table and Charlotte bumped into her.

'Sorry,' Charlotte said.

'That's all right, Jennifer never looks where she's going,' Janice said.

Charlotte Wilson shied away from the girl she had bumped into as Charlotte felt a nasty aura emanating from her, Charlotte recognised it straight away, and she had felt the same aura when she had touched Samantha's face. It was stronger in this girl, she was the owner of the evil presence surrounding Samantha, and Charlotte grabbed an arm.

'It's you,' Charlotte accused.

Jennifer Russell tore herself from Charlotte's grip.

'I don't know you.'

Charlotte found the cold female voice devoid of emotion.

'You are not complete, you have no conscience,' Charlotte told her.

Jennifer Russell rushed past Charlotte and left the room; Janice stood up and guided the blind girl to the seat the clone had vacated.

'Thank you. I seem to have upset your friend.'

'Believe me, she is no friend of mine,' Janice said.

'Then I hope you are a friend of Samantha, I have just met her, and she is in need of good friends.'

'Samantha has made quite an impression on you,' Steven said.

Charlotte sipped her tea, Janice asked her how she lost her sight and Charlotte told her of the car crash that robbed her of her parents and her sight. Her hearing had sharpened, and she had developed another sense she had not experienced before.

'That girl I bumped into has a very evil aura about her; it haunts the girl Samantha as well. I felt her try to get into my mind, but I was able to keep her out, she has one single aim in life, she thinks Samantha has something of hers and she will stop at nothing to get it. In the process she wants to destroy Samantha completely,' Charlotte explained.

Steven and Janice stared at each other – the clone made their skin crawl as well. They could see this blind girl was very perceptive as she had gained a lot of information about the clone in only a small amount of time they had been in contact with each other.

'What did you mean by saying she was not complete?' Janice asked.

'She is a copy of another person, a much more powerful being with a very strong mind, she is chaos, totally without conscience and she is not entirely human.'

Again Steven and Janice exchanged glances.

'You have hit the nail on the head, that girl is indeed a copy, she is a clone,' Janice told her.

Charlotte drank her tea, she knew about animal cloning, but she was unaware they had started cloning humans.

'I hope the person she was cloned from has a better attitude,' Charlotte said.

Steven and Janice looked at each other. The girl Jennifer had still not regained consciousness after the explosion at the house she was sharing with Samantha, she had seemed amicable enough when they had met her for the first time; now after what Charlotte had said about the clone, they would have to be aware of Jennifer when she finally recovered.

CHAPTER XLIII:

GONE TO BLAZES

EXETER CITY, JULY 2133

Lisa Booth drew her car up to the entrance of the beauty parlour at the crack of dawn. She got out of the car and opened the front doors of the shop. She stepped into the foyer and was suddenly alert. She stared across at the counter and beyond, the panel on the rear wall was open showing the stairs that led to the upper office. She went to the counter and listened and there was the sound of someone moving about upstairs. She took out her cell phone from her coat pocket and rang Xanthe's number. When her voice came on the phone, Lisa told her to come at once as there had been a break-in and someone was moving around in the offices.

Xanthe rushed into the inner office and informed Zenobia Madison she had to go and help her friend Lisa, as her beauty parlour had been burgled. Zenobia got up from her desk and offered to drive her there. They took the lift down to the underground car park under the building. Zenobia drove out of the car park and the car sped to the next street where the beauty parlour was situated. A shock waited for them when they got there. Smoke was rising up into the morning sky, the building was on fire. Zenobia stopped the car and told Xanthe to phone the fire services and she jumped out of the car and ran to the entrance of the beauty parlour; the doors were open and she entered the foyer, which was filled with smoke. Zenobia searched for Lisa and found her body lying by the counter; flames licked out from the opening in the wall on the other side of the counter. Zenobia lifted up Lisa and carried her as she rushed out of the building. Xanthe helped her lay Lisa on the back seat of the car, Zenobia felt for a pulse in the right wrist and found the girl was alive.

If you are mega-rich and have a very impressive lifestyle, you need an impressive home to live in and Zenobia had just that. She was a person who could say her home was a castle and mean it. The main building was square with a tower built in each corner of it. On the grounds at the rear of it were stables and several assorted outhouses. The whole complex was surrounded by a high grey stone wall. Zenobia drove up to the main gate, Xanthe sat beside her stared out of the windscreen in amazement.

'Wow!' was all she could think of to say.

'My father built the main castle building; when I came back home, I had the wall built around the place, for extra security,' Zenobia said.

Zenobia got out and went to the gate and opened it with her electronic key and the gate swung inwards, she walked through the gateway. Xanthe slid into the driving seat and drove the car through the gateway and parked the car at the left hand side of the main building. Zenobia had invited Xanthe over for dinner to get her mind off the attack on her friend and the destruction of her business. Lisa was still in hospital – she was conscious but still very ill. Both Zenobia and Xanthe were questioned by the police. Zenobia met Lisa's friend Gerald Pollard, and though he did not accuse her outright, Zenobia was sure he thought she was involved with the crime against Lisa, even though she had Xanthe as her alibi.

It was late evening and it was still warm. Xanthe wore a short brown dress, she stood and gazed at the huge castle. Zenobia came up to her.

'It's a big place just for one person,' Xanthe observed.

'I'm not the only person living here,' Zenobia said.

Zenobia had several people living in who helped with the upkeep of the castle and outhouses. Jacqui Taylor and her partner, who was the security man, and a personal friend of Zenobia. The three of them had grown up together. She guided Xanthe into the building and she gave Xanthe a guided tour of the castle building. Xanthe marvelled at the richness of the furnishings in every room, which was another example that showed how wealthy the woman was. She had worked for Zenobia for eighteen months and Xanthe had made more money than she had ever done before. They finished up in a huge banqueting hall; Jacqui Taylor was talking to a tall man in his late thirties, as they approached them. Xanthe found out from Jacqui the man was her partner and head of security. Zenobia left the room to change and Jacqui offered Xanthe a glass of white wine.

'Thanks, this is a magnificent place, I wish I could afford something like this,' Xanthe said.

Jacqui gave her a sly smile and winked.

'In these times anything is possible.'

Xanthe had a feeling Jacqui was trying to tell her something; she wondered if Zenobia had something else in store for her. While Xanthe waited for Zenobia to make her entrance she walked round the large banqueting hall, she gazed up at the paintings on the wall and the luxurious draperies, Xanthe thought she was in another world; she wanted to pinch herself to see she was not dreaming that she was not asleep at her work desk. Jacqui moved along beside her.

'Do you know anything about medieval history?'

Xanthe nodded her head; history was one of her main interests, and most of the castle inside was authentic, apart from the modern luxuries. Zenobia's father had done a good job in recreating a bygone age.

'Do you ever dress the part?' she asked Jacqui.

'I do sometimes when Zenobia is entertaining a lot of people.'

They went back to the large banqueting table and Jacqui refilled Xanthe's wine glass. Beautiful waitresses were laying the table for dinner. The large entrance doors opened, and Zenobia strode majestically across the tiled floor. Christopher Thornton whistled sharply. Zenobia was dressed in a long flowing cream coloured gown; the low-cut bodice hugged her small firm breasts. She wore a sparkling tiara in her hair. Xanthe had never seen the woman look so beautiful; she really was the queen of the castle. She moved to one end of the banqueting table and sat down. Xanthe sat down on her right and Jacqui sat on Zenobia's left and Christopher sat beside her.

After lunch Zenobia guided Xanthe out of the castle through the huge kitchen area and out the rear door. The light of day was rapidly disappearing, and it was going to be a warm night; a slight breeze blew against them.

'You look stunning in that gown, Zenobia, you certainly know how to make a grand entrance,' Xanthe said.

'Thank you, I hope you enjoyed the meal tonight.'

'I've had a wonderful time, this place is just unbelievable,' Xanthe said.

They walked across the cobbled yard.

'How would you like to live here?'

Xanthe stopped walking and stared at Zenobia as if she was not sure she had heard right.

'You deserve something better than that apartment you live in,' Zenobia said.

Zenobia pointed to three cottages against the boundary wall. Two were empty and Christopher Thornton lived in one. Zenobia offered Xanthe one of the empty cottages. They walked across the garden towards the cottages; Xanthe followed the woman into the first cottage. Zenobia stood in the hallway while Xanthe walked round the cottage checking all the rooms, then she returned to Zenobia.

'Well what do you think?' Zenobia inquired.

Xanthe was hooked, the cottage was a lot better than her apartment and she might be invited to more dinner dates in the castle banqueting room with Zenobia and her friends.

'It's an offer I can't refuse,' Xanthe declared.

Zenobia smiled happily; everything was going to plan.

She walked out of the cottage and Xanthe followed her. There came a gunshot and a bullet thudded into the door close to Xanthe and she dived back into the cottage. A tall dark figure ran towards Zenobia with a gun in the right hand,

Zenobia put her right hand in the pocket of her gown, the hand flashed out instantly holding an automatic and she shot the assailant dead in its tracks. There came the sound of gunfire in the direction of the stables at the rear of the complex. She ran over to the stables, Xanthe followed behind her. In front of the stable building they found Christopher standing over a body of a man in a dark uniform.

'Anyone you know?' Zenobia asked.

'He's part of the security team at the research laboratories,' Christopher told her.

Zenobia told him of the man she had shot.

'It looks like you upset somebody, Zenobia,' Xanthe said.

Zenobia turned and faced Xanthe; her expression was grave.

'Not me, the man I shot was firing at you.'

Xanthe stared at her in horror, Lisa had been attacked and now they had come for her. Xanthe had always wondered when her happiness was going to end.

'Do you think he was part of the attack on Lisa?' Xanthe asked.

Zenobia nodded her head.

'It's a good bet.' Zenobia turned to Christopher.

'You'd better call the police and tell them there are two dead bodies here for them to collect.'

Zenobia and Xanthe walked back to the castle and in the banqueting hall Zenobia gave Xanthe a glass of brandy to steady her nerves.

CHAPTER XLIV:

A COMPULSION TO REPRODUCE

AUGUST 2133

Samantha jogged up the road away from the clinic; she was much stronger, and the colour had come back to her cheeks. She was ready to continue her journey to the City of Exeter where she could continue her work. Steven and Janice were determined to go with her. But she did not want to travel in the car with them as they had the clone with them, and Samantha wanted to steer clear of her. Samantha had to get herself another car just for herself, and Steven could drive his car behind her at a safe distance so they would not be connected with her; there was something else on her mind, something her body was telling her. Samantha had a big decision to make. It was time to think about whether she wanted to bring another life into the world, at the moment there were not many candidates to mate with. Steven Calvert was the most obvious choice as he was part of the project, but there was the problem of Janice: Samantha did not want to hurt the girl by going after her partner. She would have to wait for something to present itself to help her come to a decision one way or another.

Janice walked out of the clinic; the tall figure of Jennifer Russell followed behind her. She opened the back door of the car and told the clone to get in; as she did Janice put her hand on the top of her head to make sure she did not hit her head as she got in, then Janice slammed the car door shut. She walked down the roadside and gazed up ahead. Janice wondered if Samantha would return with them. After a few moments the tall girl came into view jogging leisurely towards the clinic.

'You've returned then.' Samantha stood and smiled at Janice.

'I said I would.'

Samantha ran up to the clinic and entered it; she went to her room and removed her T-shirt and shorts. Samantha got under the shower and let cool water flow over her hot, sweaty body. A few minutes later someone knocked on her door; she left the shower and dried herself. Samantha went to the door and opened it and Steven walked in; seeing her naked he turned his back on her.

'I'll go while you get dressed,' Steven said.

'That's all right, it's not the first time you've seen me naked,' Samantha reminded him.

Samantha moved close to Steven and kissed him on the lips.

'I hope you're not going to race off and leave us, it'll feel as if you don't trust us,' Steven said.

Steven ran a hand over her cheek, Samantha surveyed his face.

'You know it's not that, of course I trust you and Janice, I don't want to put you in too much danger.

I don't want anyone to get harmed because of me.'

Steven put his arms round her.

'Janice and I care for you, Sam. Every time you go alone you end up in a deadly situation, we can't let that happen again,' Steven said.

Samantha pushed him towards the bed and pushed him onto it and she fell on top of him and kissed him hungrily.

'Sam, what are you doing?' Steven asked, as he tried to push her off him.

Samantha unbuttoned his shirt, Steven was surprised at the curiosity of her passion, and he hoped Janice did not walk in on them.

'You did enjoy making love to me those other times?' Samantha inquired.

Steven tried to turn over so he could turn the tables and get off her, but Samantha was very strong.

'I want us to make love, before we go, please Steven,' Samantha pleaded.

'What if Janice walks in?'

Samantha unzipped his trousers and started to pull them off him.

'She won't if we are quick.'

'All right, if that's what you want,' Steven said.

That was what Samantha wanted, her body was telling her brain it was time to conceive. Steven let her undress him, as she was well in charge. When she had undressed him, Samantha turned onto her back and pulled Steven on top of her. Steven was surprised how much he wanted her as they made love. Samantha was happy in the knowledge he was going to be the father of her offspring.

Twenty minutes later they lay still on the bed, Steven laid his head on her small conical breasts.

'You are a fiery lover, Sam.'

'You are not mad at me?'

Steven looked up at her and shook his head. Samantha grinned at him.

'Good, let's go one more time.'

Steven shook his head and moved on top of her.

'I love you, Steven.' This time they made love slow and easy.

Janice sat in the car and started the motor; she was beginning to wonder what had happed to Steven and Samantha.

Twenty minutes later Samantha walked into the offices, to say goodbye to Dr Bishop.

'I'll try but I can't promise anything,' she said.

Samantha walked out of the office and left the clinic and went to a car that was parked at the side of the building and got in it and drove off the grounds of the clinic and turned left, waving at Janice as she passed her car.

Steven opened the car door and got in beside Janice, who stared at him accusingly.

'You've been a long time, what kept you?'

'Nothing, let's go, we don't want her to get too far away,' Steven said.

CHAPTER XLV:

A PROMISE OF ANONYMITY

OCTOBER 2133

Lisa Booth sat at a table by the door of the public bar. She sipped her beer; Gerald Pollard sat beside her. He gazed at the door while Lisa studied the other people in the bar. Nothing bad had happened to her since the destruction of her beauty parlour, but she had not seen the person who had knocked her out and left her to burn with her business. To her surprise Zenobia Madison came to her and gave her the chance to set up her business again. She had plenty of empty space in her company building and offered her part of the rear of the building to use. Lisa took the woman up on her offer; Gerald was not very happy with her decision as he did not trust the woman. Zenobia also gave her all the equipment she needed. Zenobia did not charge her for it until she was up and running and making a profit. Lisa and Gerald thought it was too good to be true, but Zenobia had no wish to con Lisa any more than she wanted to deceive Xanthe. Lisa could be useful to her.

Gerald watched a tall slim girl stumble into the bar a little worse for wear. Her face was battered as if she had gone a few rounds with a heavy weight boxer. He nudged Lisa.

'There's a down and out, what can you do for her?' he said, pointing out the girl who had just walked through the doorway.

Lisa put her beer glass down and looked at the girl; the short-cropped ginger hair touched something in her memory, and she turned to her companion.

'Did Sarah ask you to look out for a girl with ginger hair?' Lisa inquired.

Gerald nodded and stood up and went to the girl and spoke to her.

'My friend would like to buy you a drink; you look as if you could use one.'

The girl stayed silent as he took her by the arm and led her to their table, she sat opposite Lisa, who gave her a friendly smile, and Gerald went to the bar and ordered some more drinks.

'You look as if you've had a rough time,' Lisa said.

'Yes, I've just arrived in the city and several people took an instant dislike to me,' the girl said in a shaky voice. Lisa could see the looked ill.

Gerald returned with the drinks and placed a glass of brandy in front of the girl.

'You look as if you could use that,' he said.

'Thanks.'

She picked up the glass and sipped the brandy, she welcomed the warm glow it brought to her insides. The beating she got was not the only thing her body was ailing from. She told them she had lost all her money and identity papers in the attack.

'If you've got nowhere to stay, I can put you up in my apartment,' Lisa offered.

'Are you this kind to all strangers?'

'Yes, our Lisa is the champion of the misfortunate souls of the city,' Gerald said.

Lisa nudged him painfully in the side with a well-aimed elbow. An hour later they left the public house. Gerald kissed Lisa on the lips and went on his way; the two girls crossed the road to the apartment building opposite where Lisa had her home. As they walked up the steps to the entrance, a tall dark figure stood in the dark shadows of a nearby building; dark brooding eyes studied the two girls, and the shorter of the two was the object of his interest. He knew her and he was back to renew their acquaintance, he was going to finish what he had started eleven years before.

When they entered the apartment Lisa took off her coat and hung it up; she relieved the stranger of her coat, underneath she wore a pink blouse and a short red skirt. Lisa told the girl to make herself at home while she went to the kitchen to make two strong coffees. The tall girl sank onto a couch and stretched out her long legs. She ached all over. Lisa came back in the room carrying two steaming mugs of coffee and handed one to her guest.

'I have only the one bed, I hope you don't mind sharing,' Lisa said, as she sat next to the girl.

'No, I don't snore.' She sipped the hot strong coffee, her mind as well as her body was in a mess. The brandy and now the coffee were beginning to bring her into some sort of normality. She remained silent and she was glad Lisa was not bombarding her with questions and was giving her time to volunteer information about herself in her own time. When they had drank the coffee, Lisa stood up.

'You look tired and worn out, let's get you to bed.'

Lisa grabbed the girl by the hand and pulled her up onto her feet. She groaned at the pain she was feeling; Lisa could see she was in a bad way.

'They gave you a good going over,' Lisa said.

In the bedroom she helped the injured girl out of her clothes and then left her to get into bed. The girl sat on the bed and ran her long delicate fingers over her ribcage; she discovered three cracked ribs, two on the right and one on the left side of her body. She slid between the sheets and groaned at the pain she was giving herself. She closed her eyes and waited for sleep.

Lisa woke next morning and got carefully out of bed so as not to wake the sleeping girl lying next to her. She showered and made her breakfast. She received a phone call from Gerald asking her to see him at the Administrative building as soon as she was dressed. Lisa wrote a note for her guest and then left the apartment. When she left the building a pair of eyes watched her stride along the street until she was out of sight.

Lisa arrived at the Administrative Building and made her way to the database room and found Gerald sitting at his desk. She sat on the desk and smoothed the hem of her dress down over her thighs. He showed her a data disc and then popped it into his desktop computer; she gazed at the information that came up on the screen. It showed her the face of the girl in her apartment. When she had read all the information on the data disc she gazed at Gerald.

'Do you think it's all true?' she asked.

'What does it matter, they can put as many lies on it as they want, just as long as they get the girl,' Gerald said.

Lisa took the data disc out of the computer and slid it into her dress pocket.

'I wonder how much they will give us, if we hand the girl in,' Gerald said.

A look of shock crossed her pretty face.

'You're joking!'

'Of course,' he said with a smile.

Gerald placed a hand on her left knee and Lisa picked up a ruler and struck the offending hand with it.

'That's for even harbouring such an idea,' she said, crossly.

Lisa spun round, turning her back on him and strode out of the room. He watched her go with the regret of making her cross – Gerald knew he would have to make up for it if he wanted to get back in her good books again.

Lisa went back to work and when she bumped into Zenobia during the day, she kept quiet about the girl in her apartment; she also kept it from her friend Xanthe, until Lisa knew exactly which way the wind was blowing. In the evening when she got back to her apartment she found her guest in the kitchen cooking a meal for them both.

'You should be in bed.'

The tall girl gave her a pained smile.

'I was bored just lying in bed; I wanted to fix lunch as a thank you for putting me up.'

Lisa told her it was a pleasure. Lisa helped her and when they had finished lunch, they sat on the couch drinking coffee. Lisa could see the girl was still in pain, though she tried to put a brave face on it. Lisa put her coffee cup down and unbuttoned the girl's blouse and opened it out, the girl held her breath as Lisa ran an exploratory hand over her ribs.

'You've got a nice soft touch.'

Lisa found the three cracked ribs and it told her how much pain the girl was feeling.

'I used to be a medical student once, amongst other things. I'm impressed – if I had so much damage to my body, I would be screaming the place down,' Lisa said.

Lisa moved away from the girl, who buttoned up her blouse.

'You'll have to rest up for a time, until your ribs heal.'

'Yes, doctor.'

Out in the night he was searching for his first victim in his new campaign of terror. He had to satisfy the craving that burned inside him. He prowled in the darkest shadows ever waiting to pounce on any unexpecting victim. He listened intently for any sound that told him someone was approaching his position.

Gerald Pollard came out of the nightclub in the early hours of the morning with a slightly tipsy girl clinging to him; he was going to see her safely to her door. He wished Lisa was with him, but he had not asked her to join him as she might still be angry with him. Gerald deposited the girl at her door and told her he would see her at work. She opened her door and she was just about to step into her house when a dark shape detached itself from the ornamental bushes that ran down either side of the path. She felt something hit her hard in the back thrusting her into the hallway, a hand was clamped over her mouth, she heard the door slam shut and she was thrust hard against the wall knocking the wind out of her. She fell to the floor stunned. He picked her up and found the bedroom and laid the girl on the bed. A thrill ran through him as he prepared to work on the body, it was good to be back at it again. He unzipped his backpack and pulled out his tools of trade; he tied the girl's ankles together.

Then he set about his work.

Lisa woke suddenly and screamed out and woke the girl lying beside her. Lisa was covered in a cold sweat; she held her head in her hands. The tall girl stared at her.

'I thought it was me who had the monopoly on nightmares.'

Lisa stared at her and smiled weakly.

'I haven't had this particular nightmare for a few years, I thought I was rid of it at last,' Lisa said.

'Something must have triggered it – has anything bad happened to you lately?'

Lisa told her about the beauty parlour being burned down and she almost went with it, but for someone dragging her out just in time.

'I know about bad dreams and I would not wish them on anyone, I sincerely hope I am not the cause of the reoccurrence of your nightmare,' the girl said.

'I'm sure you're not,' Lisa assured her.

Lisa got out of bed and left the room and a little while later she returned with two mugs of strong coffee; she handed one to her newfound friend. She sat on the side of the bed.

'I feel something dreadful is coming, perhaps the dream is an omen, some horror is out there in the dark waiting to get me,' Lisa said in a trembling voice full of fear.

A comforting hand was placed on Lisa's shoulder.

'You shouldn't let it get to you, I won't let anyone harm you while I'm here, and you have been good to me. Perhaps your brain is just throwing out old memories.'

'I hope you're right,' Lisa said.

'Of course, I am.'

Lisa turned and faced the girl and wished she had her confidence. She finished her coffee and got back into bed and turned off the bedside lamp.

'I've just realised, I don't even know your name,' Lisa said.

'It's Samantha, you can call me Sam.'

Lisa moved close to Samantha and kissed her.

'Sam, would you be offended if I asked you to put your arms round me,' Lisa said.

'Not at all,' Samantha assured her.

Lisa laid her head on Samantha's small breasts and strong arms held her close.

'I hope I'm not causing you pain,' Lisa said.

'Of course not, just relax,' Samantha said and kissed the girl.

Lisa closed her eyes and soon dozed off.

When Lisa came home next evening her guest was once again making lunch. They kissed passionately. She was told Gerald had phoned her and he had something important to tell her. When they had eaten Lisa showed her guest the data disc and put it in her computer and they both stared at the screen.

'Of course, I don't believe everything that's on it,' Lisa said.

'It doesn't have to be true, just as long they can convince people it's true.'

The tall girl moved away and sat on the couch; Lisa switched off the computer. The door buzzer went, and Lisa went to answer it, Gerald pushed passed her and Lisa shut the door.

'I've been at the police department all day,' he said.

Lisa stared at him in stunned silence. Gerald told her the girl he had been out with the night before had been found murdered in her home. He left out the grisly details of the murder, as it had not been a pretty sight. Gerald had told the police as much as he could – the girl was very much alive when he left her.

'I had that nightmare again, it's happening again, isn't it?' Lisa said.

Gerald shook his head and hugged her.

'Don't read too much into that, it was just a coincidence,' Gerald said.

'That's what I told her.'

Gerald started across at the girl sitting on the couch. He was glad she was sharing the apartment with Lisa. The tall girl made an imposing figure, he was sure a murderer would think twice before he tackled her. Gerald stayed for a while then left.

In the morning they left the apartment and Samantha had promised Gerald she would stick close to Lisa and she was determined to do just that. As they made their way to where Lisa had her business, she told Samantha about Zenobia Madison and Samantha was impressed and could not wait to meet the woman. They walked through the entrance of the twenty-five-floor building, Jacqui sitting at the reception desk gave her a wave and Lisa acknowledged it. They went to the far end of the foyer and Lisa took her electronic key from her dress pocket and opened the door to her new beauty parlour. Jacqui picked up the phone and contacted Zenobia.

Lisa gave the tall girl a guided tour of her business.

'If there's a part of your body you are not satisfied with, let me know, I'll do a professional job at a discount.'

'There's only one part of my body I'm depressed about and there's nothing anyone can do about that,' Samantha said.

Lisa diplomatically did not ask the girl what it was, though Lisa had a good idea. The back door opened, and Zenobia strode into the room and held out her hand to the tall girl.

'Hullo, your name wouldn't be Samantha by any chance?' Zenobia inquired.

Samantha nodded her head.

'And you must be the impressive Miss Madison.'

Zenobia laughed and gave the tall girl a friendly slap on the shoulder.

'I've been called a lot of things, but not that. Would you mind coming up to the main offices with me, I'd like to have a talk with you.'

'Lead the way.'

As they left Lisa wondered what Zenobia wanted with the tall girl and she had been surprised to see the woman knew the girl's name.

As the lift moved up the transparent tube, Samantha gazed out at the panoramic view of the city.

'How did you know my name?'

'We had a mutual friend,' Zenobia said.

Samantha turned and faced the woman.

'And who might that be?'

Zenobia told Samantha about meeting Naomi Evans just before the car crash and the business partnership they had made up together.

'She told me about you, I want to help you if I can,' Zenobia said.

'Do you think the crash was a set up to allow Naomi to make a disappearance?'

'It's possible, I don't know anything about the crash and Naomi never told me she was going to do that,' Zenobia said.

'I'll have to carry on without her for the time being, I hope she is still alive, she is the one person I trust without question and she is a loyal friend, Samantha said.

Samantha stayed silent until they were in Zenobia's main office. She asked Zenobia what she wanted to talk about.

'I want to do what I can for you.'

Samantha sat down and Xanthe came into room carrying two cups of coffee and she offered Samantha one and she took it. She put the other on the desk and walked out.

'I was hoping to get myself a new ID while I'm here and I have had my money stolen, so I shall need some more.'

Zenobia unlocked a drawer in her desk and pulled out a metal box, she opened it and pulled out a thick wad of bank notes and placed them on the desk in front of Samantha, she picked them up and whistled.

'You are very generous.'

'I can't help Naomi, but I can assist her friend. I'll organize a new ID for you,' Zenobia said

Samantha studied the woman's face as she tried to decide if Zenobia was trustworthy. She was a very wealthy and powerful woman. Naomi seemed to have put her trust in the woman, but she might have died in a car crash soon after – was Zenobia involved in that? She had to trust the woman for now; she was all Samantha had for the moment.

'OK, any help you can offer me will be gratefully appreciated.'

She watched Zenobia's face light up that made Samantha sure the woman had her own hidden agenda.

'I don't suppose you could give me an idea of your purpose for being here?'

Samantha shook her head.

'My real work is tied up with national secrecy, I couldn't tell you even if I wanted to.'

Samantha finished her coffee and placed the empty cup on the desk and then she stood up. Zenobia rose and held out her hand and Samantha gripped it in her own. Zenobia studied the long thin fingers.

'If you think of any way I can help you, don't hesitate to contact me.'

Samantha left the main office in the outer office Samantha gazed at the girl at the reception desk, the one that had brought in the coffee, her face was somehow familiar.

'Can I help you?' Xanthe inquired.

'You wouldn't have a sister, would you?'

The pleasant smile slid from Xanthe's face and she stood up.

'Yes, her name is Phoebe.'

It all came back to her; Samantha told Xanthe she had seen Phoebe in May.

'How was she?'

The tension built up inside Xanthe, tears started to trickle down her cheeks – this was the first time her sister had been sighted since they took her away. The thought that her sister was alive somewhere kept her going, now she had proof they had not killed Phoebe gave her extra strength.

'She was staying in a mental clinic on Exmoor; the nurse there gave Phoebe her car, that's all I know.'

Xanthe took Samantha's hands in her own.

'You don't know what this means to me, I can't thank you enough, for telling me.'

'That's all right, I'm just sorry I can't give you more information about her,' Samantha said.

'The fact Phoebe is still alive, and kicking is all I need at the moment,' Xanthe said.

Xanthe released Samantha's hands and she went into the lift, Xanthe sat at her desk and let the tears flow. It was still on, Phoebe was still alive and, on her way here. Retribution was going to be dealt out to the guilty ones and Phoebe would be free to walk at her side again.

'What is it, Xanthe?'

Xanthe looked up – she had not heard Zenobia come up to her desk.

'Your visitor has seen Phoebe; she's still alive and free.'

Zenobia had her own interests in the Phoebe Cross case; learning the girl was free gave Zenobia an idea at the reason behind the raid on her home, someone had tried to eliminate Xanthe before she came in contact with her sister.

'We'll have to keep a tighter security around you, Xanthe.'

Xanthe took out a handkerchief from her dress pocket and wiped her wet eyes and cheeks.

'I have always known, the closer Phoebe came to me, the more danger I was going to be in. I don't care, because it means the closer Phoebe is the stronger I will get,' Xanthe explained.

Zenobia stared at her wide dark eyes, she knew Xanthe felt she was weak without her older sister around to protect her, but Zenobia had got to know a lot about Xanthe since they started their working relationship and now they were firm friends, Xanthe had a hidden strength and it did not need her older sister to bring it out. They had not kept her locked up in the research laboratories for nothing. They had let her out at the age of sixteen, but someone was keeping a sharp eye on her.

'You are a lot stronger than you know,' Zenobia said.

Zenobia moved round to the side of the desk and bent over and kissed Xanthe lightly on the lips.

Samantha lay on the operating table; she gazed up at Lisa, who wore a white coat.

'Are you ready?' Lisa asked.

'Ready as I'll ever be.'

Zenobia was going to give Samantha a new ID and Lisa was going to give her a new face to go with it. Samantha decided to put herself in Lisa's hands, Lisa had shown Samantha several certificates to show she was in good hands as Lisa was an expert in her field.

'Let's do it,' Lisa said.

When she had finished Xanthe walked into the room. She looked down at Samantha, who lying quiet and still. Lisa put her arm round Xanthe's waist.

'Sam told me, she had seen Phoebe,' Lisa said.

'I've been waiting over ten years for news of Phoebe,' Xanthe said.

'You know I'm always here for you,' Lisa said.

'As I am here for you,' Xanthe said.

Samantha woke up and sat up, she swung her long legs over the side of the operating table, and Lisa came to her and placed a brunette wig on her head and brushed it out. Xanthe came over and studied Lisa's work.

'You've done magnificently as usual,' she told Lisa.

Lisa handed Samantha a mirror, she gazed at the face reflected in it. The hard-angular lines of her face had been softened and rounded.

'Lisa, you are a genius.'

Lisa beamed with pleasure, another satisfied customer. 'I can increase your bust size if you want me to,' Lisa said.

Samantha looked down at the blue bra she wore.

'I would love a larger bust size, but I don't want anything implanted inside me, I hoped they would increase in size naturally. I'll have to make do with what I've got,' Samantha said.

He sat on a seat against the wall as he looked down the corridor, towards the door of the apartment he was most interested in. The girl who lived there was a good friend of his; it would be nice to run his hands through her short blonde hair and caress her beautifully curved body. But the tall girl staying with her was a problem; he would have to wait until she was out of the way before he could reacquaint himself with Lisa. The two girls came into view. He stared at the tall girl; she was wearing a wig and her face had changed, but he knew it was the same girl by the way she walked and moved. He was going to go for her, as she would be a challenge. She did not hold herself like an ordinary female; this girl was a female predator. This was what he had been waiting for, a fight with one who was his equal and a female at that. A deep feeling of pleasure ran through his body. He closed his eyes and imagined the tall girl lying naked on a bed and he was running his expert hands over her slim athletic body. A thrill ran through him. He opened his eyes and the corridor was empty.

He stood up and made his way to his apartment to make plans.

Samantha woke with the early morning sunshine on her face, she sat up and saw she was alone in bed; Lisa had already gone to work. She got up and had a shower then got dressed. She had a quick breakfast then left the apartment.

He made his way to Lisa's apartment and he saw someone standing by the door, they had on a coat with a hood so he could not see who it was; he hoped it was Lisa – the height was right. The apartment door was opened, and he moved quickly as the person stepped into the apartment, he thrust them forward and kicked the door shut behind him.

When Samantha returned to the apartment, she found the door open. She cautiously crossed the threshold and called out Lisa's name. She got no answer. Samantha checked every room and she ended up at the bedroom door which was slightly ajar. She pushed the door open wider and then stepped into the room and saw the room was full of blood; the victim lay on her back. At first she thought it was Lisa, but as she knelt down beside the body, Samantha saw it was a stranger to her. Samantha stood up and heard someone enter the apartment. She walked to the door as Lisa reached it, she screamed when she saw the body on the floor of her bedroom.

'It wasn't me,' Samantha said.

Samantha held onto Lisa to keep her from falling. Lisa clung tightly to Samantha as she trembled.

'You'd better call your friend Gerald, he can inform the police for you,' Samantha advised.

After a while Lisa detached herself from Samantha and went to the phone and dialled Gerald's number. Samantha walked out of the apartment. She went to the seats by the wall at the end of the corridor. When she had returned to the apartment with Lisa the night before, she had noticed a dark figure sitting on one of the seats. He had been watching them she was sure. She spoke in a low voice.

'You were here, weren't you?'

The killer must have mistaken the dead girl for Lisa. He would have to come back and rectify his mistake, and then he would try for her. Samantha smiled down at the empty chairs. He can try his luck, but Samantha was no ordinary female, she would be his equal in strength, Samantha knew how to deal with murderous predators. She sat on the chair and looked towards the apartment door. Gerald Pollard turned up with the police and they entered the apartment. She hoped Lisa would not mention her name to the police as Samantha did not want to get involved, she had to keep her anonymity.

CHAPTER XLVI:

EVELYN STEVENS

Samantha went to the lift and rode up to the next floor. She got out and moved slowly down the corridor, gazing at the closed doors as she passed them. She wondered if the killer was lurking behind one of them. Samantha hoped he lived in the building as it would make it easier for her to seek him out. As she got to the end of the corridor the last door opened and a young girl wearing a black dress came out and stared at her. Samantha stopped walking.

'Another girl has been killed, hasn't she?'

Samantha stared at the girl.

'What would a girl of twelve know about such things?'

'I'm fourteen, actually,' the girl corrected.

Samantha studied the round impish face; it was slightly freckled, and her grey eyes shone with intelligence.

'I have an insight into such matters,' the girl said.

Samantha gave her a wry smile.

'I don't suppose you could point me in the direction of the killer's apartment?'

The girl shrugged off the hint of sarcasm in the tall girl's voice and nodded her head eagerly. She walked past her and made her way up the corridor until she got half way.

Samantha shook her head and made her way up to the young girl. When she got there the young girl pointed to a door and gave Samantha a triumphant grin.

'He's in there.'

Samantha stared at the girl sceptically, she was sure the young girl was having her on. She had a serious expression on her round pretty face.

'Why haven't you told the police?'

The young girl shook her head.

'It wouldn't have changed anything, and I don't want to be one of his victims.'

'What's your name?'

'Evelyn Stevens.'

Evelyn grabbed Samantha's right hand and gazed at it, she had not seen a hand like it, and she studied the palm.

'You've got beautiful hands, I like the long delicate fingers,' Evelyn said.

'Thank you, I'm Samantha.'

Evelyn ran a finger across the palm of Samantha's hand.

'Your future and his are fatefully linked,' Evelyn said, dramatically.

'You read palms?'

Evelyn released the hand and stretched out her right hand and ran it over Samantha's right cheek. The grey eyes fixed her with a hard stare.

'He haunts the night and preys on those foolish enough to step into his domain. He is after the girl you stay with, Lisa.'

Evelyn gave her a grave expression.

'I hope it wasn't her, the latest victim.'

Samantha shook her head and assured Evelyn; Lisa was safe and unharmed.

'You are a predator; I can tell by your luminescent eyes and strong hands. He won't tolerate another predator in his killing ground, especially a female predator; he will come for you at some time or another.'

Samantha sighed, another person who thought she was monster. She did not like what she had heard. Evelyn was sure of what she was saying, and her voice and manner was serious.

'It would be nice, just for once, for people to take me for what I am, just a girl with no homicidal tendencies,' Samantha complained.

'I know I have nothing to fear from you, I'm sure you're really a nice person at heart,' Evelyn said.

Samantha went to the apartment door and placed her hands flat against it. She closed her eyes and hoped her senses would pick up the evil lurking on the other side of the door. Evelyn watched her with excited interest.

'Do you think it is a coincidence you are both here at this moment in time?'

Samantha could detect nothing, the man was not at home. She took her hands away from the door and stepped back; she brought her right leg up and slammed the sole of her foot against the door. The lock splintered and the door swung inward. Samantha walked into the apartment followed by Evelyn.

'Is it wise to do this? He might come back any minute,' Evelyn warned.

'Don't worry, he will be outnumbered two to one,' Samantha said.

They went through all the rooms until they got to the bedroom. Samantha walked into the room and Evelyn stayed by the door. The bed was unmade, and the sheets were pulled down to the end of the bed. She checked the wardrobe and the chest of drawers, but she found nothing of interest. Samantha stared at the wall the bed lay against. There was a large rectangle chart on the wall with several small photographs on it. Two had been defaced by a red marker pen. One of which was the girl that had been killed in Lisa's apartment. Samantha pulled the chart off the wall and folded it up and stuffed it down the front of her skirt. She ushered Evelyn out of the apartment and pulled the door to.

'I'd stay in your apartment until he is caught,' Samantha said.

'Why?'

'One of those photographs on the chart was of you – what does your insight tell you about that?'

Evelyn gulped and stared white faced at the tall girl.

'Have you always lived in this apartment building?' Samantha inquired.

Evelyn shook her head. Up to the age of four she lived in a housing estate by the river; strange things were happening there, so her mother moved away. Evelyn told her Lisa was living there at the time, as was her friend Prue.

'Prue?'

'Prue Cross,' Evelyn said.

'I thought her name was Xanthe,' Samantha said.

Evelyn shrugged her shoulders.

'Perhaps she changed her name for some reason,' Evelyn proposed.

Evelyn went to her apartment and Samantha left the apartment building deep in thought. She went to see Zenobia to see if she had managed to fix up a new ID for her. She complimented Samantha on her new looks. Zenobia hand her some papers and an ID card.

'Thank you, this is much appreciated,' Samantha said.

'Is there anything else, I can do for you?' Zenobia said.

Xanthe walked in with two cups of coffee, Samantha took one and gave her a warm smile.

'Have you ever used the name Prue?'

Xanthe nodded her head and asked her if Lisa had told her.

'No, I met a fourteen old girl by the name of Evelyn.'

Xanthe remembered the name, a small four-year-old girl used to hang around Lisa when they both lived in the housing estate.

'They're not so far apart now, Evelyn lives on the floor above Lisa,' Samantha said.

Xanthe was about to leave the main office but Samantha asked her to stay and she stood up and turned to Zenobia.

'Could I have the use of your databank?' she asked.

Zenobia nodded and stood up, they crossed the office and went to a side door and it slid open and Zenobia walked through followed by Samantha and Xanthe.

CHAPTER XLVII:

SERIAL KILLERS AND GOVERNMENT AGENTS

The large room Samantha found herself in had several rows of desks with their own computer terminals. Her face broke into a smile; Jennifer would have a field day in this room, she thought to herself. Zenobia guided her to one of the desks and Samantha sat down and activated the computer. Lisa had given her the name of the girl killed in her apartment. She fed the name in the computer so she could activate the dead girl's data file. Samantha watched the data come up on the screen, Samantha sucked in her breath when a certain piece of information about the girl was revealed. Samantha checked the details of the murdered girl that worked with Gerald Pollard, Lisa had told her about that as it might have been the same killer who had murdered both girls. Samantha wondered how much Lisa really knew about the two girls – they both worked for the Government, but what department?

When she started to delve deeper into the activities of the two girls, she came up against ACCESS DENIED. Naomi had taught her several ways of getting past that obstruction. Samantha worked furiously at the computer; her long slim fingers darted over the keyboard. At last she broke into the guarded files; she gave a cry of triumph. The girls were Government Agents working for the same agency. It looked as if they were plants and was investigating Lisa and Gerald. Samantha stood up and turned off the computer.

'Did you get what you wanted?' Zenobia asked.

'Yes, thank you, I must see Lisa,' Samantha said.

'She is staying at Gerald's home at the moment, she phoned me to say she was too sick to come in,' Xanthe said.

Xanthe gave her Gerald's address and Samantha left the building and made way to Gerald's house. Lisa let her in, and she told Lisa about her friend who was killed in her apartment.

'Have you got any idea why the Government wants to spy on you?'

Lisa shook her head; she was not doing anything illegal.

'What about the work you do for Sarah Mullen?'

Lisa stared at her open mouthed.

'Sarah will be pleased when she finds out her father is checking up on her companions,' Samantha observed.

'She'll be even less pleased when she learns someone set fire to our secret offices,' Lisa said.

'Do you think there's a connection?'

Lisa nodded her head.

'And there was the attack on Xanthe at Zenobia's residence,' Lisa said.

Samantha took out the chart from down her skirt and opened it out and laid it on the table; Lisa gazed at the small photographs. Samantha told her where she had got it.

'What is it?'

'I've got a horrible feeling it's the murderer's hit list,' Samantha said.

'I don't like the sound of that; he's got a photo of me and Xanthe on it.'

Samantha told her about Evelyn who was also on the chart.

'I remember her, I was not aware she lived in the same apartment building, what's the connection?'

'The only connection I can see is you three used to live on the same housing estate a few years back,' Samantha said.

'I see Zenobia is here also.'

'She is a very powerful woman, I expect there are a lot of people who would like to see her bumped off,' Samantha observed.

Lisa went to the kitchen to make coffee and Samantha relaxed on the couch. After a while Lisa came back and handed her a mug of coffee and she sat next to her.

'What are you going to do?'

'We have to get him, before he gets us,' Samantha said.

Lisa stared at Samantha. Lisa suddenly wished Sarah had told her more about this strange girl, but she could not help liking the tall girl.

'How do you propose to do that?'

Samantha sipped her coffee; Lisa was not going to be happy about what she had in mind.

'We need a decoy to lure him out to a place and time of our own choosing,' Samantha said.

'Who have you in mind, me, Xanthe or this girl Evelyn?'

'Not Evelyn, she is too young,' Samantha said.

They sat in silence for a while and drank their coffee. Lisa wondered if this killer was the one that haunted her dreams. She had been 11 when he came to live next door to her on the housing estate by the river. He had had a lurid fascination for her. He was tall and dark with piercing yellowy eyes. Bad things started to happen on the estate and little Lisa was sure this man was to blame; he kept himself to himself and nobody knew his name. When Lisa left her house, he would be there standing by his open door, he would give her a cheery smile and she would run off and play with her friends.

Evelyn Stevens strode aimlessly along the side of the river. She had her hands deep in her skirt pockets. The light of day was rapidly diminishing. She came to the estate of derelict houses where she used to live at the age of four. It was the first time back for her, she did not come back regularly like Xanthe. Evelyn walked through the estate until she got to the house she used to live in. The house on the left of it was the one Lisa used to live in and the next house as usual had the front door open, but a tall dark man with yellowy eyes was not standing by it. Something made her body shiver and it was not the cold night air. Several people of all ages had been murdered on the estate. Just like the new murders, systematically carved up with a long thin blade, by the same evil mind, which was looking towards her from the shadows of one of the nearby houses.

Evelyn walked out of the housing estate and made her way further up the river, until she came to a roadway that crossed the river and she walked at the side of it and made her way to the other side. She came to a high fence that surrounded the Exeter Experimental Laboratories. Evelyn had been on the other side of the fence once when she was twelve. She was taking part in some strange experiments to assess the limits of her intelligence and if she had any E. S. P. They found out Evelyn had a very high IQ, but there were aspects of her brain she had no intention of telling anyone, she was keeping that to herself.

Evelyn suddenly became aware of a presence behind her and she was about to turn when she was grabbed and something wet and clammy was held over her nose and mouth, her lungs began to burn, and she lost consciousness.

NOVEMBER 2133

Steven Calvert drove his car down to the underground car park of the Zen Industries Building; he found an empty space and drove into it. He got out of the car and looked around and all was still and quiet. He moved away from the car and he heard a slight noise and Samantha came out of the shadows and pinned him against a pillar and kissed him hard on the mouth; he struggled to push her away, but once again he realised how strong the girl was. She rubbed her body against him.

'Samantha, you pick the strangest places,' Steven said, crossly.

Samantha stood away and grinned at the anger on his face.

'Don't you fancy me anymore?'

This was the first time he had been close to Samantha, since the time in that room in the clinic. She had shocked him, there had been no love in the sex act, it seemed to Steven, Samantha was just acting out a primeval urge, a need to reproduce. When it was done, she had dressed and left the room without a word.

'The last time we were together, you were hardly acting normally,' he said.

'Are you mad at me? I had to mate with someone; time was running short, I'm sorry if I've offended you. I still want us to be friends.'

Steven ran a hand over her cheek, he was finding things about her every time they met.

'So do I, just try to curb your lustful instincts.'

Samantha giggled and kissed him more softly. He moved away from her and went back to the car and she got in the seat beside him.

'I need your help to catch a serial killer.'

Steven could only sit and stare at her for a moment; she had said it as if catching dangerous killers was their normal employment. He had heard about the two girls that were killed.

'Why not leave it to the police? It's their job not ours.'

'I've got a nasty feeling about this particular killer,' Samantha said.

Steven did not like it; he did not want Samantha ending up the same way as the two dead girls.

'Even more reason to leave it to the experts,' Steven advised.

Samantha moved close to him and kissed Steven on the cheek.

'My dear Steven, we *are* the experts.'

Lisa Booth stood in front of her old home in the derelict housing estate that she had left at the age of 13. The door of the next house was wide open, enticing the unwary to enter, Lisa wondered if he was lurking in the old house once more, waiting to torment her again. He had got inside her head and he made her do things she bitterly regretted, she wanted to forget but the dreams would not let her.

After the day Xanthe's parents were killed and her sister was taken away as their murderer, Xanthe was sent away and Lisa lost her best friend. The demon that had lived next to her had disappeared as suddenly as he had appeared. Lisa's life had fallen apart, and she broke into pieces and it was not until she was once again reunited with her best friend five years later that Xanthe picked up the pieces and put them together again, they became inseparable. As long as they were together, Lisa knew she would never fall apart again.

Samantha came up to her and put an arm round her waist.

'Are you all right?'

Lisa nodded nervously; being near the old house was bringing back old memories, all bad.

'I'll be glad when it's all over.'

Samantha put her arms round her and hugged her.

'Steven and Xanthe are nearby, I just need one go at him, I'll make sure he does not touch you,' Samantha said, calmly.

Lisa walked to the door of her old home and pushed it open, she took a deep breath and stepped into the hallway, Samantha stayed by the door as Lisa moved slowly into the house.

In the house next door Evelyn Stevens lay on a bed covered with a thick layer of dust and dirt. Her wrists were tied together behind her back, her ankles were tied together. She slowly regained consciousness. She sat up and blinked, her head ached. She looked round the old bedroom; she wondered what house she was in. And worse, who had brought her here?

The air was musty and stale. Evelyn was aware she was being held in one of the houses on the derelict housing estate.

She had been caught as the night took over the land, now she was in daylight. The door creaked open and a tall man dressed in black walked into the room. Evelyn stared at him as he approached the bed.

'What are you going to do to me?'

He stood by the bed and kept quiet. Evelyn stared at the thin face, it was pale and pasty, and she decided he had disguised his true facial features. She did not want to think about what he might have in store for her. She did not want to be his next victim.

'It won't be long now, they're here,' the icy voice said.

Lisa climbed slowly up the creaking stairs; Samantha was searching the rooms downstairs, while Lisa would search upstairs. Lisa stood on the landing and listened for any strange sounds. The only sound she could hear was Samantha moving about below her.

'There's nothing of interest down here,' Samantha said.

Lisa looked down at Samantha, who stood at the bottom of the stairs.

'It's strange, I'd thought I'd be wetting myself by now,' Lisa said.

'They do say, it's good to face your fear,' Samantha said.

Lisa shook her head.

'I don't mind facing this old broken-down house, but I don't want to face him,' Lisa said.

Samantha climbed the stairs and stood beside Lisa, who looked up at her bright green eyes.

'If you do have the misfortune of bumping into this human monster, I know you are very strong, and you'd probably give him a good fight.'

Lisa ran a hand over Samantha's right cheek.

'But he gets inside your head, you have to be careful, Sam, very careful,' warned Lisa.

Samantha was already aware of that, unlike Lisa when she first came against him, Samantha had an idea of what sort of foe she was fighting against.

'I shall be watching myself as I have your safety to think of, I'm not going to do something rash and put you in danger,' Samantha assured her.

Lisa gave the tall girl a hug, she had a strong respect for Samantha, and it had given her the strength to accompany her to this place.

Evelyn had her ankles untied and he pulled her off the bed and onto her feet, she was roughly pulled out of the room and onto the landing.

'You are going to be the bait.'

Samantha left the house and entered the house next door by the open front door. Lisa stayed in her old home. Samantha told her to shout out if she got in trouble and Lisa assured her, she would scream the house down, which would not be hard considering the state it was in after so many years of neglect.

Evelyn gazed down the stairs as she tugged at the rope that held her wrists to the wooden banisters. Evelyn found she was securely tied and there was no escape. Her overactive mind conjured up an evil monstrosity slithering up the stairs to consume her for a tasty snack. Evelyn shook her head to clear her mind of such scary thoughts. Her situation was frightening enough, without her mind adding to it.

There suddenly came a sound from down below and Evelyn gazed over the banister and down to the hallway below. A tall figure stepped into view wearing a long brown coat, the head came up and Evelyn saw a familiar thin face – it was the girl she had met in the apartment building, Evelyn guessed she was looking for the man who was holding her captive. Samantha walked to the stairs and looked up, she saw the white face of Evelyn, she saw the fear in the expression and wide grey eyes of the young girl.

Lisa wanted to leave the house to get some air, as the atmosphere in the old bedroom was stuffy and stale. She walked towards the door. She wondered how Samantha was getting on; she hoped the demon was not at home, Lisa did not want any harm to come to the tall, likeable girl. As she got to the door, which was ajar, it was thrust open and he stood on the threshold; his dark eyes stared at her hungrily. Lisa stepped back, she wanted to scream but she could not find her voice.

'Don't go, we have some unfinished business to attend to,' the icy voice said.

Lisa managed to let out a sharp piercing scream, but he moved sharply and grabbed her arm and placed a hand over her mouth. He pushed her further into the room and pushed her onto the bed; she stared at him in terror, and it was going to happen again. He was strong and had a strong mind; he was going to get inside her head again. He lashed out with his right fist and hit her full in the face, there was an explosion of pain then blackness came over her mind as she slipped into unconsciousness.

He pulled the coat off the girl; she wore a short dark green dress underneath.

'You've grown into a lovely young woman.'

Samantha slowly made her way up the stairs, the young girl was shaking her head, she could see Evelyn was tied to the banisters, she was staked out like a lamb to slaughter.

'Stay calm, Evelyn.'

Evelyn thought that was easy to say, when you had something nasty behind you. A sharp object was jabbed in her back. More pressure was applied, and she felt the sharp point cut through her clothes and touch the skin of her back; it brought cold shivers that ran down her spine. She watched Samantha get ever nearer to her. Evelyn wished she could call out and say it was a trap, but she would die the instant she spoke out and she would not be able to help Samantha. All the light had been blocked out in the house and the landing was gloomy and full of dark shadows. Evelyn thought the killer must have excellent eyesight as he enjoyed working in the dark. That did not worry Samantha as she could see just as well in the dark as she could in daylight. He was there somewhere lurking in the dark of the landing. Samantha would need all her predatory skills if she was going to survive this and bring Evelyn out of this unharmed.

If you want my advice...

Right on cue her conscience wanted to air its opinion.

'No, I don't.' Her voice sounded strange in the silence.

Evelyn made up her mind, it was up to her to make the first move, and Samantha had stopped just over halfway up the stairway. Evelyn hoped the tall girl was fast on her feet as Evelyn had no thoughts of sacrificing herself. She gazed up at the ceiling and saw a fluorescent bulb above her. After ten years of neglect perhaps the fittings were unsafe. Evelyn stared hard at it and concentrated her brain on the fluorescent light, she hoped something would give, she had moved little things when experimenting alone in her bedroom, this was the largest test she had ever attempted, and she just had to hope it would work. She felt the sharp point stab her back, as if he was aware she was up to something. Evelyn kept her concentration on one thing: the fluorescent light above her.

Samantha wondered what the girl was looking at and stared up at the ceiling. She thought the young girl was up to something, perhaps the killer was just behind the staked-out girl. As soon as Samantha was close enough, he would kill the girl and then go for her.

He kept the long thin blade pressed against the back of his captive; it was very sharp and would slide easily into the young girl's body. He saw his prey had stopped moving up the stairs, he wondered what she was waiting for. She must be aware he was up here somewhere. She had to decide about the girl he had staked out, she was going to be the first to die whatever happened, was his prey going to try to save her? He silently urged her to take a few more steps upward. The girl was nothing, it was him she wanted. He pushed the blade, so it cut into the flesh of the captive's back. Evelyn ignored the pain and concentrated hard on the overhead light. She gritted her teeth; Come on, come on, her mind screamed silently.

Samantha moved up another step, Evelyn's life would be left to fate, she had to concentrate on the killer, it would be suicide not to. She could see part of him behind Evelyn. She took two more steps then fate took a hand.

Evelyn's ears picked up the sound of the fluorescent light shifting, she kept her mind focused as her brain kept pushing, and her body was covered in a cold sweat. Then everything seemed to happen at once, as the fluorescent light came away from the ceiling. Evelyn let herself fall and she started to slide down the stairs until the rope tying her wrists to the banister stopped her descent. There was an explosion of sound as the fluorescent tube hit the banister and shattered, showering Evelyn as she lay on the stairs. She closed her eyes tight and held her breath. Samantha was nearly caught out, but she had the sense to keep her mind on one thing, the creature that was lurking in the shadows of the landing. The creature of nightmares but this creature was real and had a human shape.

Samantha saw her chance and took it; she flew up the remaining stairs avoiding the fallen girl as she did so. The tall figure at the top of the stairs moved back into the shadows of the landing. He held the long thin blade in his right hand. He did not want to kill his prey yet, he just wanted to subdue her, she had to be aware of her surroundings when he worked on her. At the top of the landing she faltered in her forward rush, he got a clear view of her face and it was not the face he was expecting, but the brightness of the shining green eyes told him this was the one.

Keeping her eyes on the long silvery blade she lunged at him and as they came together his right hand shot forward and Samantha turned sideways, and the blade narrowly missed her body. She lashed out with her left hand and hit him under the chin with the heel of her hand, his head was knocked back, he swiftly swung his right-hand round and the blade was headed towards her body. She tried to move out of the way, but the blade cut into the material of her coat and slid harmlessly passed her left hip. Samantha brought her right fist down on his wrist. He grunted and kept a tight grip on his weapon and swung out with his left fist and struck her on the left side of the head. Samantha moved backwards and shook her head.

'You're good, I'll give you that, but I will win in the end.'

His voice was cold and arrogant, and it reminded her of the tall slim aliens that she had discovered on the huge spaceship further out in the solar system. The nasty feeling she had about this serial killer was coming true. He moved towards her again and she took two steps back, then she rushed at full speed at him; as she crashed into him, she felt the blade slide into her body, they crashed into the banisters and the old wood splintered loudly in the silence. Part of the banister broke up and Evelyn found herself sliding all the way down the stairs as the rail she was tied to broke away. When she landed painfully at the bottom of the stairs, she got shakily to her feet and made her way out of the front door.

Leaning against the handrail he lashed out with his left fist and struck Samantha full in the face. She jumped away from him; she felt a pain in her side where the thin blade had slid into her body. He kicked at her and struck her in the stomach, and it knocked the wind out of her. The killer had a quick look at the stairway and saw his captive had got away. He did not care as her job was done. Now he had injured the tall female predator, it would soon be over. He stared at the prey as she stood against the wall trying to get her breath back. He went for her again and she dived away towards the bedroom nearest the stairs.

'There's no escape, you just aren't strong enough to take me.'

Samantha was well aware of that, she hoped to delay his victory until Evelyn could get to Lisa or Steven. The pain in her side was aching slightly and her flesh seemed to be getting numb where the blade had entered. As she dived into the bedroom, she tried to kick the door shut, but he kicked it before it closed, and it swung at her. The door hit Samantha as she tried to move away from it and he lunged at her with the blade and it struck her in the back. He kicked her again with a force that knocked her backwards and she landed on her back. The killer dived on top of her.

He dropped the blade and grabbed her head in both hands and lifted it and then brought it down hard on the floor. She wriggled madly under him as he lifted her head again and it was once again slammed down on the hard floor; she groaned as the back of her head was full of pain. He picked up the long thin blade and the point cut into her coat and the blouse she wore underneath. He smiled with triumph as he eased the blade into her body.

Lisa came to and found herself lying on the bed, her arms were up over her head and her wrists were tied together; she suddenly remembered where she was and who was with her. Lisa blinked her watery eyes and focused them on the man who was sat on the bed staring at her; he wore a pair of black overalls. As he had not killed her yet, Lisa was sure he wanted to torment her first. He had removed her coat but not her dress. She turned her head and gazed towards the window and wondered how Samantha was getting on.

'If you are hoping for your tall friend to come and save you, it's not going to happen as she has her hands full and you won't be seeing her again.'

He stared at her with his yellowy eyes and she turned her head away, he grabbed her jaw and turned her head so he could look into her eyes, he saw the fear on her pretty face.

'Why don't you just kill me and be done with it?' Lisa cried.

She closed her watery eyes and then she felt the sharp sting of a slap on her right cheek. Lisa opened her eyes and tears ran down her cheek.

'I'm not going to kill you, Lisa, you are too important to me.'

He ran his hand softly over her right cheek which still hurt. His eyes bored into her own, Lisa knew he was trying to get inside her head, and she felt unable to stop him.

Samantha lay on the dusty floor stunned and weak. She was aware this could be the end for her. There was now the only hope that Evelyn had been able to contact her friends. Her executioner stood over her, the gleam in his bright purple eyes showed that he saw she was finally at his mercy. He kicked her twice in the side to see if she had any fight left. She groaned and showed no sign of retaliation. He pulled her up to a sitting position and removed her coat. He then removed her blouse and bra. He laid her out on the floor again and then pulled off her skirt and panties. He gazed at her face and her dull green eyes stared back, as she tried to focus on the hawkish face. A smile spread over his thin lips.

'You will notice your flesh will be getting numb, you will feel no pain and you won't be able to move a muscle.'

Samantha tried to find her voice, when she spoke it was shaky and just understandable.

'You are alien; I have met your kind.'

He held the long thin silvery blade in front of her eyes for a moment then it was moved away out of sight.

'Yes, I know, I've been told about you.'

He placed her clothes under her head, so she was able to look down at her body. Samantha saw the wound at the base of the ribcage where the blade had slid into her. He knelt down at her side and stretched out his hand and slid the blade into the wound and slid the blade across her body leaving a red line in its wake.

'Can you feel any pain? Your flesh should be numb enough, the blade is hollow and injects a fluid into your body, which will quickly spread throughout your body,' he explained.

Samantha tried to move her arms and legs; she seemed to be paralysed all over. That showed the alien spoke the truth about the weapon he used. She watched the blade reach the side of her body and then move downwards, until he got to her groin, then he pulled the blade out of her.

'You will be conscious throughout so you will be able to watch me work, I don't want you to miss a thing.'

Samantha could see the alien was going to have a good gloat, as she was powerless to stop him from working on her body with the long thin blade. She stared mesmerized as it slid into the first wound and moved across to the left side of her body then it moved downwards. There was no pain just the sensation of it moved through her flesh.

'You can talk if you want; I want to know what's in your mind.'

'What's there to say?' she asked, weakly.

'You can tell me what you think about my work, nobody is going to disturb us.'

'You are very expert in what you do,' she said.

'I'm glad you think so, I want to appreciate the skill I show, as I work on your body.'

He had the skill of a surgeon and he made sure he did not cut any vital organ. She was the product of two worlds, and he had to find out how much of his world she consisted of.

CHAPTER XLVIII:

DESPERATION

Evelyn ran to the exit of the housing estate and ran into Xanthe; she quickly told her about Samantha, while Xanthe untied her wrists. Steven came up to them. Evelyn told them where their friend was. Xanthe asked about Lisa but Evelyn had not seen her. Steven ran down the road with a gun in his hand, Xanthe told the young girl to get in their car, and then she raced after Steven with her automatic in her right hand. When they got to the house, they cautiously approached the open door. Steven entered the house and listened; there was no sound, and he slowly went up the stairs; Xanthe followed behind him. They reached the landing and they stood still for a moment.

Lisa lay on the dusty bed and gazed at the man as he stood by the window. He had seen the man and the girl enter the other house. He turned away from the window and went to the bed and stared down at Lisa.

'Your friends have arrived; you're not going to make a sound, are you?'

Lisa stared at him blankly, her head ached.

'You don't want them to find you, do you?'

His voice was soft and hypnotic, she shook her head.

'Good girl.'

He sat on the bed and ran a hand over her cheek, Lisa could feel him inside her head; she groaned.

Steven eased himself through the half open bedroom door. He tried to prepare himself for whatever horrific scenario he might walk into. But what met Steven's eyes was a blow even for his strong constitution. Some daylight was filtering through the cracks between the boards that covered the window. Steven aimed his gun at the dark dressed figure that bent over Samantha's still body. He had his back to Steven, and he was too intent in his work to hear Steven silently enter the room. He aimed for the back of the bulbous head and fired twice, and the head exploded showering the nearby floor with blood and brains. The body fell forward. Steven pocketed the gun and took out his cellular phone and contacted headquarters and told them to get a helicopter and paramedics to the housing estate full speed.

Xanthe dragged the body across the room then knelt down beside Samantha; she stared at the dull green eyes, and they looked as if all life had drained from them, then they blinked and Xanthe saw the poor girl was still alive. She stared up at Steven who stood over her.

'I don't know how, but she still has a spark of life inside her.'

Xanthe felt for a pulse and found it was very weak.

'It's going to be touch and go, if your colleagues get here fast enough,' Xanthe said.

Xanthe left the house and went next door to see if her friend Lisa was there. Up in one of the bedrooms she found Lisa's coat and nothing else. She walked slowly down the stairs; tears ran down her cheeks, she was sure she would never see Lisa again. There came the sound of a helicopter flying over the house.

Evelyn watched a car draw up to her as she sat in the back of Steven's car. She saw a familiar face in the car, and she got out. A tall man in his late forties approached Evelyn and gave her a warm smile.

'Hullo Professor, what are you doing here?' she asked.

He put a friendly hand on her shoulder.

'I need your help with something; I have contacted your mother.'

The man guided her to his car, and she got in the back and the car drove off.

Samantha was placed in the helicopter, Steven and Janice stood close by, and they were both depressed about the state of their friend.

'I hope she can be saved,' Steven said, softly.

'We'll do the best we can, time will tell,' Janice observed.

They watched the body of the killer being loaded onto the helicopter and then they got in and the helicopter lifted up into the sky and flew off at maximum speed.

CHAPTER XLIX:

GOING UNDERGROUND

Red, everything was red, she was drowning in a river of red. Blood, it was blood, lots and lots of it, the acrid smell of it clogged her nostrils and she could taste it in her mouth, she was drowning, she tried to find something to cling onto, so she would not slip further in, so she would never get out. She screamed out.

She sat upright and struck her head on something above her, she swore loudly. She blinked her watery eyes and tried to focus on her surroundings. A dream, just a dream, she was awake because the pain in her head told her so. She looked down at her body, she wore a long nightgown. There was no red and no blood; she gave a sigh of relief. She was not dreaming of herself. A dark lurid thought drifted up from the depths of her mind. Samantha, it was her, she was dead or dying, and all that blood in her dream belonged to Samantha. She had been in the girl's mind for an instant, part dream, part reality.

The memories started flooding back, she had been in an explosion and a house had fallen in on top of her. Someone had taken an instant dislike to her and wanted her dead. She was sitting in a life support capsule, the cover lifted up and she sat up and looked round the room, there were two capsules one either side of her. The room was misty, and a strange odour assailed her nostrils. She clambered out of the capsule and stood beside it and tested out her legs to get them used to her body weight again.

She began to cough, and she realised the oxygen content of the room was diminishing. She moved away from the capsule, she noticed the lift doors at the far wall, and she made for them. The gaseous mist that was slowly filling the room thickening and making her eyes smart, everything in the room was becoming an opaque blur. Here we go again, she thought. As she reached the lift at last, she collapsed to her knees. She stretched her left arm upwards in an effort to get to the lift controls. She had fits of coughing as the gas was replacing the oxygen in the room and getting into her lungs. When the lift doors opened, she collapsed and once again fell into the dark pit of unconsciousness.

General Heywood and Dr Sally Hamilton stared down at the body on the slab; the back of the head had been opened up like a splattered melon. Now they had evidence there was one hostile alien on Earth, they had to find out if there were others, the General thought it unlikely there would be just the solitary alien. Sally told the General, he would be the scout to find out about the strength of the natives. There would be many, but they would have a scout ship somewhere near.

They left the room and entered the operating room, where Dr Blake and Hilary were exercising all their medical skills in trying to save Samantha's life. Dr Hamilton went to the head of the operating table and looked down at her daughter's pale face; she noticed Samantha had had some work down on it to hide her identity. It was still touch and go if her daughter would survive her ordeal. Sally Hamilton never questioned her decision to put Samantha in the firing line. She had to be dispassionate where her daughter was concerned, she came from a world where her daughter would have to go and do what she had to do despite the extreme dangers there might be about. The trouble was the human part of Samantha's brain, which sent her off the track she was following, just to track down a predator that was seeking out her newfound friends.

'If she survives this, we'll have to give her mind some retraining, so she avoids running after homicidal maniacs,' Dr Hamilton said.

'It's because she cares about the people around her,' Dr Blake said.

They stared at each other over the operating table; she had tried to educate Dr Blake about her civilization, not letting compassion get in the way of getting the job done. He saw her as a hard and uncompromising as far as her daughter was concerned, that was her way, but it did not mean she had no love for her daughter. Dr Hamilton had a burning desire to rid herself of menace that had kept them under foot for a millennium and Samantha was her weapon against them.

'The city has a very competent police force; the catching of serial killers can be left to them. Samantha should keep her mind on the job at hand,' Dr Hamilton argued.

The pathologist looked up from the body on the slab as he heard someone enter the room by the double doors behind him. He spun round and watched two people approach him. The man was a high-ranking army officer, beside him was a tall striking blonde woman, who walked past him and stopped at the mortuary slab; she gazed down at the body of the dead girl that was on it.

'Can I help you?' the pathologist inquired.

The tall blonde woman answered him.

'We have come to view the body, we know her.'

'And you are?' the pathologist asked.

Dr Sally Hamilton gave him a smile and introduced herself and told him who her companion was. The pathologist wondered what a general had to do with a murdered girl. Dr Hamilton gazed down at the body impassively. The girl had been opened up with skilful precision, the ribcage had been cut away and the lungs and heart were revealed to the eye. Nothing was missing, the killer was examining what lay under the flesh, he was finding out what made her tick. She could tell the killer had been the one that had attacked her daughter.

'Have there been any other murders like this one?' she asked.

The pathologist nodded his head and told her to follow him and they went into the next room, where the bodies were kept, he pulled out two drawers that contained the two girls. Dr Hamilton gazed at the two bodies for a while, and then she looked up at the pathologist.

'The killer that murdered these two girls is not the same one that killed the girl in the other room,' she said.

'You think so?'

'Yes, the weapon used is different in both cases. The girl in the other room, our PR officer, we have got the right person who did that crime, he was killed while attacking another of our colleagues. The killer of these poor girls was of a different character,' Dr Hamilton said.

She could not give him more information because she could imagine what the pathologist would say, if she told him one of the killers was alien, she knew the weapon and it was not a product of this world. She turned away from the bodies and walked out of the room and joined General Heywood in the next room. They left the City Mortuary and got into their car and Steven drove away.

JANUARY 2134

Her eyes fluttered open, she took a deep breath drawing in the rich oxygen atmosphere into her lungs, and she held her breath for a moment then exhaled. She lay in an oxygen tent, just like the time she first woke up at the age of twelve.

'Jenny!'

A hand reached into the oxygen tent and touched her forehead.

'How are you feeling, Jenny?'

She found her voice.

'Sick.'

She closed her eyes and dozed off. Valerie Peterson left the room and went to report Jennifer had come to again.

The next time Jennifer opened her eyes the oxygen tent had gone. She pulled the sheets back and swung her long legs over the side of the bed. She sat with her head in her hands. Someone was out to get her; miraculously she had survived another attack. She wondered how many lives she had been blessed with. She must get out of here, Jennifer thought. She stood up and looked round the small white walled room and saw the door and made for it. The door slid open and she found a tall blonde woman barring her way out. She wore a white lab coat,

'Going somewhere?'

Damn right!

Jennifer glared at the woman, as anger raged inside her.

'After being electrocuted, blown-up and then gassed, do you really think I want to stay here?'

Dr Sally Hamilton smiled at the girl; she had a point. Dr Hamilton had just returned from Exeter, her daughter was still hanging onto life, she was unconscious, and her pulse was very weak. She left Dr Blake and Hilary in charge of keeping Samantha alive, while she had to get back to see to Jennifer. If her daughter did not survive then Jennifer would have to take her place, though physics was not her field.

'Yes, I'm sorry about that, the security seems unable to stop the attacks on you.'

Jennifer told her exactly what she thought of her security.

'Who am I? What do you want of me?' Jennifer wanted to know.

'Your name is Jennifer,' Dr Sally Hamilton said.

The ice-blue eyes blazed at her; Sally could almost feel the anger burning inside the girl.

'Jennifer! Jennifer who? And why was I cloned?'

Sally walked over to the bed and sat on it; Jennifer came and stood over her.

'You know about that?'

Jennifer told the woman she had discovered the first clone dead in the overgrown copse, she was a mess.

'That's one mystery solved; we never did find the body.'

Jennifer sat on the edge of the bed beside her.

'You had a difficult birth and you were in a coma until you were twelve. We had no idea if you would ever come out of it. So, I took some of your cells and cloned you.'

'You did?'

'I'm Dr Sally Hamilton.'

'I've never heard of you.'

Jennifer thought for a moment, her mind began to churn away at her memory files. Then it came to her.

'You are Samantha's mother.'

Dr Hamilton gave her a wry smile. The girl did not miss much.

'Your time on the computers was not wasted, I see.'

She stood up and told Jennifer to follow her. They left the room and stepped into a long corridor.

'Has something happened to Samantha? I had a dream, there was lots of blood, and I thought it was me, but when I awoke, I was unharmed. So, it must have been Samantha, who was hurt,' Jennifer said.

Sally stood and stared at the girl in astonishment,

Jennifer was trying to tell her there was a mind link between her and Samantha. That was an exciting thought.

'Samantha was attacked by a serial killer, who commenced to cut her up, it is still touch and go if she survives it.'

'I hope she does, I like her, we can work together, much better than your clones, and Samantha can't stand them.'

They went a little way up the corridor, and they entered a room on their left. Sally told Jennifer this was her living quarters and told the girl to get dressed, as she was still wearing a long white nightgown. Jennifer pulled off the nightgown and tossed it onto a chair. Jennifer went through another door that led to a small bedroom. She went through the cupboards to see what sort of clothing she was provided with. After a few moments she picked out a short turquoise dress and put it on. She put a pair of white socks on her bare feet then a pair of black shoes.

They left the living quarters and walked along the corridor until they got to the end and the panel slid up and they stepped into a large room. Jennifer gazed around it in wonder. The hum of the computer systems was music to her ears, her brain throbbed with excitement, and she went around the room and ran a loving hand over the high-tech machinery.

'This is all yours, we are underground,' Dr Sally Hamilton said.

'Am I going to be down here on my own?' Jennifer asked.

Dr Hamilton shook her head.

'Of course not, you can have whoever you want to accompany you down here.'

Jennifer was ushered into another large room full of communication equipment. A secret underground scientific facility, Jennifer was intrigued.

'Are there many people who know about this place?'

'No not many, it's for an undefined future,' Dr Hamilton said.

Jennifer sat in a swivel chair and gazed up at the doctor, there was something about the woman she found disturbing, but Jennifer could not fix her mind on what.

'Is Michelle Gowning still on the team? Samantha thinks highly of her.'

Dr Hamilton nodded her head and Jennifer told her to send the girl down to her.

Dr Hamilton turned away from the glaring ice-blue eyes. The alien mind was right, but it was not the universe that Jennifer was going to bring chaos to.

'You don't think you're an outcast, do you, Jennifer?'

The ice-blue eyes that stared at her back darkened.

'No, but I think you are,' Jennifer said, slowly.

Dr Hamilton spun round. The smile on Jennifer's face was challenging, she saw Jennifer was sure of her and was not scared to attack when the chance presented itself.

'You have a low opinion of me.' The smile turned to a look of anger.

'I just don't like being cloned without being asked first,' Jennifer complained icily.

'You were in no position to be asked. You were in a deep coma and I did not know if you were going to come out of it.'

'Well, you won't need any clones, I'm here to stay,' Jennifer said, confidently.

Let's hope you're right

Dr Hamilton left the room and made her way to the surface. Jennifer went in search of a storeroom, when she found it, she checked the racks and opened cupboards in the hope they had plenty of spares she could use when she went to work on the computer control desk. Jennifer found what she was looking for and carried a full box back to the computer control room. She got on her hands and knees and crawled under the control desk and got down to work. Jennifer was so engrossed in her work, she did not hear Michelle arrive until she spoke.'

'Jenny.'

Jennifer lifted up her head and struck it against the underside of the control desk; she swore loudly and rubbed the top of her head.

'That's not very ladylike, Jenny.'

Jennifer crawled out from under the computer control desk and stood up. She looked the newcomer up and down; Michelle Gowning wore a short pale blue dress that hugged her full voluptuous body. Michelle adjusted her steel rimmed glasses. Samantha had told her about this Jennifer and being caught in an explosion in Samantha's house. Michelle was glad the girl had survived it.

'Michelle, you look delicious,' Jennifer said.

Michelle blushed.

'I've been assigned to work down here, so I asked if I could have you here to work with me. I hope you don't mind.'

Michelle shook her head and went to Jennifer and hugged her.

'I'm just glad you are in one piece, Samantha told me about your misfortune.'

Jennifer went back under the control desk to finish her work, Michelle offered to help her, and Jennifer got her to hand her the tools she needed. Then she crawled out again and Michelle helped her to work on the top of the control desk. Michelle wondered what Jennifer was up to; Michelle was told she would find out when the work was done. Jennifer pulled the top of the control desk apart and added new parts and then reassembled the control desk; when she was done Jennifer turned the power back on. Jennifer placed her right hand on a lighted panel.

'Identification Jennifer, record my handprint.'

Jennifer told Michelle to place her hand on the lighted panel and repeat the same words. As she laid her hand on it, her flesh started to tingle, and Michelle found she could not move her hand.

'Identification Michelle, record my handprint.'

The computer released her hand and Michelle took it away from the control desk.

'It's nice to be back at work and I'm here to stay,' Jennifer said.

PART SIX:

TEARS FOR AMY THORNTON

CHAPTER L:

A QUESTION OF LOYALTIES

FEBRUARY 2134

Sarah Mullen marched into the Administration Building and made for the twenty-ninth floor where Gerald Pollard had his office, she knocked on his door and marched straight in before he had time to say 'come in'. General Heywood had given her some time off to see her colleagues – she had been informed about the beauty parlour being burnt down and she had been furious when the General did not allow her some leave then. Her father was also keeping a tight lead on her, more for safety reasons than she might be causing trouble for him, as an opposition to his leadership. David Calvert was given the job of sticking close to her, in case the people who attacked Lisa and Xanthe decided to have a go at her. Sarah told them in a loud voice, she could look after herself.

Gerald got out of his seat and met her on the other side of his desk; he put his arms round her and gave her a warm-hearted hug.

'You'd better sit down, Sarah, I've got something to tell you and you're not going to like it.'

Sarah walked across the office and sat on a couch that stood on one side of the office. She smoothed the hem of her skirt down over her thighs. Gerald sat beside her. He told Sarah her friend Samantha had turned up and gone in search of a serial killer, taking Lisa with her and they were now both missing.

'Also, Lisa and I have had an agent checking up on us.'

Sarah stared at him with a shocked expression.

'What!'

Gerald told her about the two murdered girls that had been attached to them and how Samantha had learned they were Government agents.

'Xanthe tells me, Zenobia thinks they are linked with the people who attacked Xanthe at her place and the destruction of Lisa's beauty parlour.'

'This must be Daddy's idea, no wonder he had me spirited away, it left him an easy path to shut my organisation down,' Sarah stormed angrily.

Gerald laid a hand on her shoulder.

'I don't think your father has any designs on harming you or your friends. I'm afraid the people who are guilty of doing this, don't only want the organisation shut down, they want us dead too,' Gerald said, gravely.

Sarah sat in stunned silence.

'Your friend Samantha broke into an apartment above Lisa's. She found a chart inside with several small photographs on it. We think the serial killer has been assigned to kill the people on the chart; we're on there, Lisa and Xanthe. Zenobia and some of her friends are for the chop as well,' Gerald said.

'What has that woman got to do with us?' Sarah wanted to know.

'Zenobia has an idea about that, and she wants to see you as soon as possible.'

'She would; I don't trust women with money,' Sarah said.

Gerald laughed and kissed her on the cheek.

'I'm working closely with the police,' he said.

The door of the office opened and to their surprise the Premier Graham Mullen walked into the office. Sarah stormed over to him and accused him of setting spies on her colleagues. He stared at her blankly as he had no idea what his daughter was talking about.

'I've always been honest with you, if I want to know what you are up to, Sarah, I shall come straight to you,' he assured her.

Graham told her he would look into it and Sarah left the office and made her way to the next floor, where Sarah hoped to find the other man who was in a position to send people to spy on her interests. If Sarah was to realise her ambition to be her father's successor, he was the one man she would have to beware of. Henry Jackson was the head of local government in Exeter and he would be her main rival. He was very ambitious and had thoughts of climbing up the next rung of the ladder to power. Sarah was going to make sure he fell off before he reached the top.

Henry Jackson was shuffling through some files on his desk when Sarah entered the office unannounced. He stood up and bowed to her respectfully.

'Miss Mullen, what a delight to see you,' he said, smoothly.

Sarah stared across the desk at him and informed him it had come to her notice that two government agents had been assigned to look into her affairs and keep watch on Gerald and Lisa. Sarah made him aware she blamed him for the fire on Lisa's property and the attack on Xanthe, as she was sure all cases were connected. Henry Jackson knew all about the incidents as Gerald Pollard had already informed him. He assured Sarah if her friends were being investigated by the City Security Agency, he knew nothing about it. He apologized to her for any distress caused by somebody's thoughtless actions. Henry Jackson assured her he would look into it.

'I've got great respect for your father so I would do nothing to harm his daughter,' Henry said.

Sarah walked out of the office and bumped into a tall young man with sandy coloured hair. He gave her a warm smile.

'I'm glad I bumped into you.'

Keith Stockley was an assistant to Stephen Jenkins who was head of the City Security Agency. Henry Jackson asked him to look into the cases of the two girls who were murdered, as his boss was away. He told Sarah the two girls had been working for a private contractor, whom he did not have a name for at the moment.

'When I find out more, I shall tell Gerald about it,' Keith assured her.

'Thank you, I thought it might be Henry.'

Keith shook his head and told Sarah, Henry Jackson was not involved, and he wanted to keep in the Premier's good books, so he wants to keep on the right side of his daughter.

'What about Zenobia Madison, has she got any skeletons in her closet?'

'We haven't found any, she's a very influential and shrewd businesswoman,' he said.

'I don't think she's so squeaky clean as she seems,' Sarah said.

'Time will tell,' Keith said.

Zenobia Madison sat on the low wall front of the house where one of her old school friends used to live; the house was now a burnt-out shell. Zenobia had not lived on the estate; she had been free of mishap. Zenobia looked towards the burnt-out house where her friend Amy Thornton used to live; Christopher, Amy's brother stood closer to the house, he had not been home at the time of the tragedy. At the time Zenobia and her other school friend Jacqui had seen no sign of depression in Amy or insanity. On the night Amy set her house ablaze with her parents still in it, Zenobia and Jacqui were out of town, so they were unaware of Amy's state of mind on that night. Zenobia felt guilty over that as did Jacqui. Zenobia learnt from Xanthe that she felt the same guilt over her parents and her sister. Lisa had felt guilty over her own wickedness of letting something get inside her head and make her do things she regretted.

When Zenobia returned to the country after ten years abroad, she had one aim in mind and that was find the truth about Amy and her parents. Something had come to the housing estate and turned everybody's life upside down and left them scarred and guilty. The evil entity was still around and had Lisa with him. Zenobia was going to find him and destroy him; it would be for Amy and the others that had their lives ruined. She had one problem: whoever was responsible was aware she was after them, because they had sent someone to get her first and anyone else who might want to get to the truth; they also had Lisa for a hostage, anybody moving against them and Lisa would be sacrificed.

Christopher Thornton turned away from the house and went to Zenobia.

'Let's do it,' he said.

Zenobia had just told him what she planned, it had not taken long to make up his mind, and it was his duty to clear his sister's name.

'Yes, let's,' Zenobia echoed,

Xanthe knocked on Gerald Pollard's door and it was opened by Sarah Mullen. She entered the house and Sarah shut the door. Xanthe took off her coat and hung it up. Sarah went to her and hugged her tight and kissed her on the lips. They parted and went through to the kitchen and Sarah made some coffee.

'Are you still working for that woman?'

Xanthe shook her head and sighed deeply.

'If you mean Zenobia, yes I am.'

Xanthe sat on a chair and Sarah handed her a mug of strong coffee.

'I'm sorry about Lisa, I hope they find her soon,' Sarah said.

Xanthe sipped the coffee, she was sure when they found Lisa, she would probably be dead.

'I shall probably be next,' Xanthe said.

Sarah put a hand on her shoulder.

'What do you mean?'

'Has Gerald told you about the chart, Samantha found?'

Sarah nodded her head.

'Then you'll know we're all in danger, including that woman as you call her,' Xanthe said.

Sarah finished her coffee and placed the empty mug in the sink. She wondered what Zenobia had done to be marked down for execution.

'This Zenobia, could she be involved with the fire at Lisa's beauty parlour?'

Xanthe shook her head and took hold of Sarah's hand.

'You are barking up the wrong tree; it was Zenobia who pulled Lisa out of the burning building,' Xanthe said.

Sarah walked out of the kitchen and went into the lounge, Xanthe followed her and they sat on the couch.

'A lot of hard work on our part had gone up in smoke with that building,' Sarah said.

Xanthe placed her hand on Sarah's left knee.

'It's not all lost.'

Xanthe placed a finger to her head.

'The most important files I keep up here. When you've got a memory like mine, you use it to its full capacity. Someone setting fire to our offices was a possibility,' Xanthe said.

They heard Gerald Pollard entering the house and Xanthe stood up.

'Zenobia wants to see you first thing in the morning, if you can't trust her, then trust me, our long friendship must count for something,' Xanthe said.

Xanthe walked across the room and met Gerald at the door.

'Are you going soon, Xanthe?'

'Yes, I've got things to do.'

Xanthe let herself out of the house and Gerald sat beside Sarah on the couch.

'I've had the summons, the great lady wants to see me,' Sarah said.

'You'd better go, and then we'll all know what she's up to,' Gerald observed.

Sarah frowned as Gerald gazed at her sparkling grey eyes.

'If she was up to no good, I can't see her letting me out of the building alive.'

Gerald put his arm round her waist and kissed her on the cheek.

'If that was the case, Xanthe would have found out by now and told us,' Gerald argued.

'Can we trust her to be loyal to us, now Xanthe is working in big business?'

'Knowing Xanthe as I do, she would not let us down,' Gerald assured her.

Sarah lay back on the couch and gazed at his handsome face. Sarah suddenly felt she was being hard on the girl – after all, her main problem was Zenobia and what sort of threat she may represent. If the woman was going to give her an offer to finance Sarah's political ambitions, all well and good, but you don't get something for nothing, Sarah was well aware. The big pay-out would be something to do with her father, Sarah was sure. Well the Premier can look after himself; Sarah just wanted to make sure Zenobia was not going to cause her any problems.

'No, I don't think she would, Zenobia is the one we have to watch,' Sarah said.

Gerald kissed her on the lips and started to unbutton her blouse.

Zenobia Madison sat in her office staring down at the photograph on her desk. It showed the close up of her dead friend's face, Amy Thornton. She put the blame of her death solely on the shoulders of the people that worked in the Research Laboratories. They owned the land the housing estate was built on and most of the residents worked at the complex.

Christopher Thornton had not been able to get a reasonable account of Amy's strange behaviour before it ended in tragedy. His sister had been spirited away and nobody knew what had happened to her, and two months after the fire, her body had been found floating on the River Exe. Zenobia and Christopher were ready to turn up stones and find what lay beneath. Why Amy had not confided in her friends if she was having problems, Zenobia would never know; it was a failing to see anything wrong in Amy's character that Zenobia felt guilty about. Now Zenobia had the money and the power, she was going to do something about it.

Xanthe walked into the office and placed a mug of coffee on the desk in front of Zenobia.

'When do you want me to go?'

Zenobia looked up at her. They had both talked about sending someone into the Research Laboratories, but they had not mentioned any names, and she did not want Xanthe to be the one as she was an asset to her company that she did not want to lose.

'You are too valuable to me here, to risk your life in this venture,' Zenobia said.

Xanthe stood behind the chair and started to massage Zenobia's shoulders.

'It has to be me, I have my own ghosts I must exorcize, and perhaps they are keeping Lisa there.'

Zenobia had to give in to Xanthe's argument, but she was not going to let Xanthe go until all the safety angles were explored. Zenobia had lost too many friends in her life; she did not want to lose any more.

'They can't do any worse to me that haven't already been done, I'm a big girl now, I want to stand and face my fears,' Xanthe said.

'Reluctantly I'll have to give in to your argument, but I'm going to make sure we have everything covered to stop anything nasty happening to you,' Zenobia said.

Xanthe bent down and kissed her on the cheek.

'Don't worry, I won't do anything silly; I shall keep my eyes open and ears sharp to any sound and make sure I'm one step ahead of them,' Xanthe assured her.

Zenobia drank her coffee and stood up.

Sarah Mullen awoke with the morning sun shining on her face; she stretched her limbs and sat up in bed. Gerald Pollard entered the bedroom and handed her a mug of strong tea and kissed her on the mouth.

'I've got in touch with Zenobia and told her we'll be with her in an hour,' he said.

Gerald left the room and Sarah drank the tea and then got out of bed and had a shower and then got dressed, she joined Gerald in the kitchen where he was fixing breakfast for them both. Sarah had her mind fully on her impending meeting with the mysterious Miss Madison. Her father briefed her on the woman's childhood and her rich father, but of Madison the woman he had no idea, except that after her father's death she had inherited his mass fortune and was making a fortune of her own. Sarah also had a wealthy father, but she had gone her own way to make money, which irritated her father, as he thought she was mixing with the wrong sort, but all her colleagues and friends were honest. Sarah did not trust people like Zenobia who were handed a fortune on a plate, as Zenobia could afford to make a mistake as she had plenty of money to pay for any failures. Sarah had to make sure there were no slip ups financially. She had friends that made sure there were none.

Gerald drove his car down to the underground car park of the Zen Industries building. He slipped into a vacant space and got out and Sarah followed him to the lift. Xanthe leapt out of her seat when they entered the outer office.

'I'm glad you've decided to come, Sarah.'

'I hope you haven't given Zenobia too many of our secrets.'

Xanthe shook her head disappointedly – after all the years they had known each other Sarah would be sure of her loyalty.

'I'll only tell Zenobia what you want her to know, I've never betrayed your trust in me and I'm not going to start now. Zenobia is not after your secrets, she just wants to be of help to you, just hear her out, that's all I ask of you,' Xanthe said.

Sarah walked to the main office door and knocked on it and a female voice told her to enter. Sarah opened the door and walked into the luxurious office and closed the door behind her. Sarah strolled majestically over to the desk. She stood behind the desk and gazed at the woman sitting on the other side of it. Sarah had conjured up in her mind several visions of what Zenobia Madison might look like. All were wrong, the strong facial features were fixed in a pleasant smile, the soft silky voice that thanked her for coming in to see her, was well trained and articulate. The woman was too smooth by far, the main reason Sarah did not like people like Zenobia was the fact they were in a position she desired for herself, though she would not admit to herself. On entering the office Sarah had half expected Zenobia to turn out to be the missing girl Naomi in disguise, as the girl was bound to turn up like the proverbial bad penny, but Zenobia having the same hazel eyes was the only match with Naomi as she was a much heavier person – Zenobia was older and tall, slim and elegant, something Sarah was sure Naomi would never be.

Zenobia waited patiently for her visitor to finish her assessment of the woman she was facing; she could see the dislike and suspicion in Sarah's expression. It was only natural; Zenobia was the one that had to present herself to Sarah and show she was a woman that could be trusted and could help Sarah in many ways.

'Xanthe told me to listen to what you have to say, so here I am.'

Zenobia motioned her to sit down and Sarah pulled up a chair. They stared at each other across the desk. Sarah gazed at the angular face surrounded by long fair hair; the manicured hands were clasped together on the desktop. Sarah admired the precious stones set in the many rings that adorned the fingers. Zenobia was no beauty, but she was not ugly either, outwardly the woman was not bad, and Sarah was impressed – but what was going on inside her head, Sarah wanted to know, Zenobia had a hidden agenda, Sarah was sure of it. The woman was clever and intelligent, the fact she had got Xanthe working for her had shown that. She had wealth and power, what did Sarah have? A father who happened to be running the country; if Zenobia hoped to get to him through his daughter, she was in for a disappointment – though Sarah disagreed with a lot of her father's opinions, she was loyal to him.

'I'm glad you could come, I'm sure this meeting can be beneficial to us both.'

Zenobia gave her a warm smile.

'That remains to be seen,' Sarah observed.

The smile stayed as Zenobia sat back in her seat.

'Indeed, it does.'

'How much has Xanthe told you about me?' Sarah wanted to know.

Zenobia shook her head; Sarah really had no need to question Xanthe's loyalty.

'Nothing you wouldn't want her to; if I want to learn about you, I'll do it face to face, that's why you're here,' Zenobia explained.

Zenobia stood up and crossed over to the wall covered with the worldwide chart. Sarah got up and joined her.

'I'm in a position to assist you, if you'll let me.'

Sarah stared at the chart; Zenobia's communications set up was impressive.

'I don't trust your motives.'

Zenobia turned and stared hard into the bright grey eyes; she knew it was not going to be easy to convince the intelligence behind them that she was no danger to Sarah.

'My motives are clear and precise,' Zenobia assured her.

Zenobia told her about the chance meeting with Naomi Evans in the Capital. After doing a business deal with her, Naomi told her about Sarah and her ambitions for the future. As Zenobia showed interest in Sarah, Naomi proposed Zenobia should put some of her resources into Sarah's ventures.

'That's why you are here, Sarah, so I can learn more about you.'

Sarah hoped that would mean she could learn more about Zenobia. She was mystified about the fact Naomi had told Zenobia about her, as their first meeting in college did not go well and their relationship got steadily worse, Naomi had ideas of her own and like her father, Naomi did not like the people she associated with.

'My worldwide business enterprises can help your political campaigns with the finances and resources you need, and I can offer you a power base for your organisation.'

Sarah was well aware of the benefits of having the backing of a woman like Zenobia.

'Where's the catch?' Sarah asked, cynically.

Zenobia smiled broadly, Sarah was a challenge and she liked that.

'Never accept anything at face value, quite right, Sarah. Let's get down to business.'

Zenobia motioned Sarah to follow her out of the main office and up to the next floor, which was all one room filled with work desks and computers. This was the operations room, the heart and brain of Zenobia's business empire. Sarah gazed round the room in wonder; it showed that Zenobia indeed had a lot to offer her. But she was still going to be careful. Sarah did not want to be sucked in by Zenobia's smooth tongue and sophisticated business technology.

'This is the nerve centre of my business enterprises. I have employment here for you, if you want it.'

Zenobia gave Sarah a tour round the room, the people working in the room ignored them as they walked past them, as they were concentrating hard on their work.

'I need a director with vision and high intelligence, and you are the ideal person for the job.'

'I'm honoured,' Sarah said.

Zenobia sat on a vacant desk and smoothed her skirt down over her slim thighs. Sarah sat on the swivel chair and gazed at the woman's pretty face.

'I'm not offering you any loans that your father and his Government would frown on. Our association will be ethical, and you will be beyond reproach.'

Sarah was glad at that as there were several things she had to be careful of when she was associated with a mega-rich person like Zenobia.

'I have all the power I need, so I'm not using you to get a hold on the Government of this country.'

Zenobia offered Sarah a salary that was beyond her wildest dreams; like the offer Xanthe had accepted, it was one Sarah could not refuse either.

'You really can trust me, Sarah. We just have to get to know each other, that is all,' assured Zenobia.

CHAPTER LI:

A QUEST FOR THE TRUTH

Zenobia left Sarah with her thoughts and let her ponder over the offer of a directorship in Zenobia's business empire. A few seconds later Xanthe entered the operations room, she grabbed Sarah by the arm and pulled her up onto her feet. They crossed the operations room and made for another door on the other side of the room from the door they had entered from. Xanthe drew an electronic key from her blazer pocket and slid it into the lock, the door slid open and Xanthe pulled Sarah across the threshold and the door slid shut behind them. It was a small room with filing cabinets and desks with computers.

'Most of the information on our organization is here, I have the only key, so I'm the only person who can get in here.'

'Do you think we can trust her?'

'Without question,' Xanthe assured her.

Xanthe could see by Sarah's expression the older girl was still doubtful. She ran a caressing hand over Sarah's cheek.

'I have a high regard and respect for you and most of all you are a very close friend, I swear if you put your faith in Zenobia's ability to help us, you won't regret it.'

'I have faith in you, Xanthe, so if you can put your trust in Zenobia, then I can too, I shall tell Zenobia – I shall take her appointment here,' Sarah said.

Xanthe hugged her and assured Sarah she would not regret it. They left the room and Xanthe locked the door securely with her electronic key. They left the operations room and entered a large conference room, where Zenobia, Gerald and Christopher Thornton were sitting round the conference table waiting for them. Sarah sat beside Gerald. Xanthe sat beside Zenobia and whispered in her ear, and then the woman looked across the table at Sarah.

'Glad to have you on board, Sarah,' Zenobia said.

Gerald and Sarah exchanged glances; Sarah told him she had had an offer she could not refuse. Inside she hoped she did not live to regret it. Zenobia was speaking and she concentrated on the woman as she spoke of her investigation on the experiments going on behind the high fences of the Exeter Research Laboratories. For Sarah's benefit, she started at the beginning, as the others round the table had already discussed it, while Sarah was in the other room deciding to take up Zenobia's offer of a directorship of Zen Industries Incorporated. She informed Sarah of their suspicions that the security staff at the research laboratories were involved in the burning down of Lisa's beauty parlour and Lisa's abduction. They had, Zenobia was sure, been experimenting with the residents of the housing estate that had been built on land owned by the Research Laboratories, she wanted to find out the truth about the strange things that happened there and who killed her friend Amy Thornton.

When it was announced Xanthe was going to infiltrate the secret establishment, Sarah gazed across the table at her. It was understandable as Xanthe was another victim, and she was obviously looking for information that could clear her sister's name. She was the only person in the room who had ever been there, she would have an idea of what to expect.

'I hope you have thought seriously about the danger you may be walking into,' Sarah said.

Zenobia assured Sarah they were not going to let Xanthe go until her position was secure. Christopher Thornton would be there to keep an eye on her.

'I've always been in danger, they know where they can get me and they haven't acted so far, so I will be in no more danger there than outside,' Xanthe said.

When the meeting broke up Sarah and Xanthe stayed behind.

'I have two companions working there, I shall tell them to keep an eye out for you,' Sarah said

'Why didn't you tell Zenobia about them, they might be able to give her valuable information about what exactly is going on behind the high fences?'

Sarah shook her head.

'Their anonymity must be preserved at all costs; if they contact you, you must honour that, so I want you to say nothing to Zenobia,' Sarah warned.

'I will do as you ask, but their secret would be safe with Zenobia.'

They walked towards the door.

'I'm sure it would, it's just the fewer that know about them the better,' Sarah said.

Xanthe stood by the river gazing across at the far bank, where the Research Laboratories was situated, she tried to access the memories of an eleven-year-old, and who had been deposited on the other side of the high fence, where she was questioned and prodded and probed. Would there be anyone there now who would remember her as a child, frightened and alone. She turned around and a car drove up to her and stopped. Steven Calvert got out and stood beside her.

'What can you tell me about that place?' Xanthe asked.

'It's a civilian establishment, if it had been under military control, I would have been able to tell you more; and the director is a woman scientist, Victoria Beresford.'

'When I was taken there at the age of eleven, I was put under the guidance of Frederick Fairclough; he was monitoring the E S P in children.'

Steven nodded his head, he knew about the Professor, Janice and Juliet had been working with him.

'You think there's something suspicious about his work?' Steven inquired.

Xanthe giggled, she mistrusted scientists, especially those that worked at the Research Laboratories across the river.

'That girl we found at the housing estate is missing, I believe he has her over there,' Xanthe said, pointing to the complex on the other side of the river.

'I think Lisa might be held there too. '

'You want me to look out for you?'

Xanthe nodded her head; she knew Steven could give her added security so she could get out of this alive.

CHAPTER LII:

GIRL ON A MISSION

NOVEMBER 2134

Xanthe drove up to the main gate of the Research Laboratories. The gate slid open and she drove slowly into the compound and made for the security building; the guard came out and she showed her pass to him. He surveyed her with a critical eye; she greeted him with a stony stare. He returned her pass and she drove away towards the main building. It was a large, sprawling flat-roofed building made up of two levels, one above ground and the other below ground. Xanthe parked her car close to the entrance of the building and picked up the small case on the passenger seat beside her and vacated the car.

Xanthe entered the building and found herself in a small room. She approached the security desk and showed the guard her pass, and she lay her case on the desk and opened it for inspection. He handed back the pass and went through her case. When he had finished his search, she closed the case and took it off the desk. Xanthe walked round the desk and headed for the lift doors behind it. She entered the lift and it took her down to the underground level. When it stopped, she got out and walked across the tiled floor.

Marcus Bradley watched the girl leave the lift and make for the reception desk, where he sat with his companion, a tall slim blonde-haired girl. His searching eyes gave her the full examination, as she made her way towards him. She was very smart in her dark brown blazer and matching skirt; her black hair was cut short. As she presented her credentials to Marcus, he studied her full round face and was drawn to her dark intelligent eyes. Xanthe was fully aware the man was putting her under a microscope; she hoped he liked what he saw.

'Xanthe, what an unusual name,' Marcus said.

The smile she gave him was alluring.

'I'm an unusual girl.'

Marcus handed her identity computer disc to his female companion, who had looked up from her work and made her own visual examination. Carol took the disc and placed it into the slot in her desktop computer. Her sharp blue eyes flitted from the screen to Xanthe's face.

'I was told to report to Dr Hilary Calvert,' Xanthe told her.

'You carry a firearm?' Carol inquired.

Xanthe nodded and put her hand inside her blazer and drew out her automatic slowly. Carol held out her right hand and Xanthe placed the gun into it. Carol turned to Marcus and nodded; she handed the ID disc back to him.

'Everything seems to be in order, thank you,' Richard said, as he handed the disc back to the owner.

'I'm licensed to carry it, a girl needs all the protection she can get,' Xanthe said.

Carol jotted down the identity number of the automatic and checked the calibre of the bullets; after a while she handed the gun back to Xanthe. Marcus Bradley gave her an identity tag and told her to wear it at all times. He gave her directions to where she had to go next. She turned and walked away and turned left and went through an open doorway.

'What do you think of her?' Carol asked her companion.

Marcus smiled at her.

'She's very nice to look at.'

Carol scowled and stood up.

'That's not what I meant,' she said in a cold voice.

Carol walked away. He watched her retreating back and sighed; Carol was so beautiful when she was angry.

Xanthe entered a locker room and walked along the rows of lockers. The man had given her a key with a number tag and she soon found the locker with the corresponding number on it. She opened it and removed her jacket; she removed the automatic from the inside pocket and slipped it into the pocket of her skirt. She hung the jacket up on a hook in the locker and placed her small case in it also. She closed the door and locked it and placed the key into her skirt pocket. Xanthe made for the other side of the room and opened the doors of a large cupboard and took out a folded white lab coat and put it on; she clipped the identity tag onto the lapel.

'Miss Moss,' a female voice spoke behind her.

Xanthe was using her mother's maiden name. She spun round and faced a tall, slim woman in her early forties; Xanthe had not heard her enter the room.

'I'm Hilary Calvert, it's nice to have you on the team, and my stepson Steven has told me about you.'

Xanthe shook the offered hand.

'It's an honour to be working here,' Xanthe said.

Xanthe followed Hilary out of the locker room and into the reception area, they turned left and walked down a long corridor, at half way Hilary stopped and turned to a door on the right hand side of the corridor, it slid open and Xanthe followed the woman into a small office. Hilary sat behind a desk and told Xanthe to give her some details about herself for the files.

After half an hour Hilary stood up; she was most satisfied with Xanthe's response to her questions, she had gone through her credentials. Xanthe sighed deeply inside; the first phase of her mission was progressing well. She was in the Research Laboratories and over the last few months she had been working hard to gain the qualifications needed to get work there. Xanthe chose the medical department which was based underground, because if Lisa and Evelyn were kept on the compound, which would be the likely place, they would be kept away from the general flow of Scientists on the upper level. It was also the place she would gain information on Samantha and her well-being.

They left the office and crossed the corridor and went through a doorway opposite. Xanthe gazed round the large white-walled room, it was filled with rows of hospital beds mostly empty.

'We have many care and nursing rooms like this, for 130 patients,' Hilary said.

They walked out of the room and Xanthe walked back up the corridor to a door she had noticed on the way down. It had a small round window in it, and she looked through it and saw a narrow passage on the other side of the door. Xanthe pushed against it and it did not budge. She heard Hilary come up to her.

'That's the quarantine area; we make quite sure nothing harmful can reach the surface.'

As Hilary guided Xanthe down the corridor away from the locked door, she wondered who was being kept on the other side of it. That was something she was determined to investigate. At the end of the corridor they entered a large storeroom; Xanthe spied a tall curly haired girl looking through several racks of supplies. She stopped her work when they approached her and turned to face them. Xanthe thought her friend Lisa was the most beautiful girl in the country; now Lisa had a competition for that title.

'Janice, this is our new recruit, Xanthe Moss.'

Xanthe looked the girl over as they shook hands, this was Steven's girlfriend, and he had told her about Janice, his description of her was not exaggerated. Janice wore a short yellow dress that hugged her well-built curvaceous figure, she was well aware of the effect she had on people, the dark eyes of the new girl staring at her made Janice feel she was standing in the room with no clothes on. Xanthe apologized for staring at her and hoped she did not take offence.

'That's all right, I'm used to it.'

Janice picked up some boxes from the racks and seeing Janice had got her arms full, Xanthe offered to lighten her load.

'Thanks, I hope you enjoy working with us.'

Xanthe took some of the heavy boxes from Janice; Hilary left them and made for some lift doors on the other side of the storeroom. Xanthe followed Janice out of the storeroom and back down the corridor. When they reached the locked door Janice stopped and placed her boxes onto the floor. She took out an electronic key and slid it into the lock on the door and it slid open. Xanthe followed Janice down the short passage and through a doorway at the end of it. They entered a small room and Janice placed the boxes she was carrying onto a metal table – Xanthe placed the boxes she was carrying beside them. Janice turned and left the room and walked back up the passage; Xanthe followed behind her.

'Have you anyone in quarantine at the moment?' Xanthe inquired.

'Not at the moment.'

They walked out to the outside corridor and Janice locked up the quarantine door. They entered the office and Janice told Xanthe to wait for her there and she went through another door opposite the one they had come through. Janice entered the operating room, lying on an operating table was the clone Jennifer Russell, the ice blue eyes watched Janice approach her and remove a tube from a bandage round the clone's arm.

'How much more blood are you going to take out of me?'

Janice picked up the blood sample bottle and turned her back on the girl.

'Oh, we'll be sure to leave enough to survive on,' Janice said.

'You're all heart, Jan.'

Hilary entered the operating room and Janice handed her the blood sample.

'I wish we did not have to use her blood for the serum, there's something just not right about her,' Janice said.

'She has the closest blood type for our purposes, we'll keep a close eye on her to see she does not get up to any good,' Hilary assured her.

Janice entered the office and Xanthe leapt out of her seat and waited for orders, Janice told the girl to follow her and they left the office and walked down the corridor. When they were out of sight Hilary crossed the corridor and made for the quarantine area with the bottle of serum in her right hand. She took the electronic key from her white lab coat with her left hand and unlocked the door. She walked down the passage as the door slid shut and locked behind her. She went through the doorway at the end of the passage, she crossed the small room and made for a locked door opposite and opened it with her electronic key and walked into a small ward and went to the occupied hospital bed. Machines surrounded the bed monitoring the faint life signs of the girl in the bed. Hilary gazed at the pale face on the pillow; for months she had been lying as in death, inside her the body was working furiously to mend the damage done to it. If she ever woke from the coma time alone would tell, the only thing Hilary and Janice could do was do what they could for her. Hilary prepared a hypodermic needle and drew the serum into it, and then she injected the serum in a bare arm of the girl lying on the bed.

Xanthe was kept busy and had little time to ponder how she would start her mission. Hilary hoped they had not worked her too hard on her first day. Xanthe shook her head.

'I like being kept busy, I'm enjoying the work here, I've been waiting for interesting employment like this for ages,' Xanthe said, enthusiastically.

Down past the offices were the shower rooms and toilets, separated compartments for men and women, further down the corridor on the same side were the lounge and kitchens. Xanthe went to the shower room and found all the cubicles vacant so she had a choice of all of them. She went to one of the changing compartments and undressed and then went to the shower cubicle and got under the hot running water; she gave a deep sigh of relief. Xanthe relaxed and let the shower drive the tiredness from her body. When Xanthe left the shower, she dried her body and went to the changing compartment. As she pushed the door open, someone came up behind her and pushed her into the room. Something hard was pressed into her back and Xanthe was sure it was a firearm.

'Get on your knees on the floor.'

It was a female voice, hard and demanding. Xanthe did as she was told.

'You have a nice figure, if you want to keep it, you will have to do as I say.'

Xanthe tried to move her head but got a bang on the head for her pains.

'Don't turn around; if you see my face, I will have to kill you, Prue. Be under no misconceptions, I will do what I say, my safety comes higher than yours.'

Xanthe was surprised the person had used her former Christian name. She supposed Sarah must have told her.

'They don't like spies here, so you'll have to be very careful.'

The person moved away and Xanthe heard a chair behind dragged up behind her. She could not recognise the voice, but it could have been any one of the women she had met in the course of her work. Except Janice and Hilary, as Steven would have told her about any connection with Sarah, but Xanthe thought this female was an old friend of Sarah, that was how she knew her name had once been Prue.

'Why don't you tell me, why you are here, then I can see what kind of help I can give you.'

The barrel of the gun ran gently down her spine and it made her bare skin tingle.

'Before I tell you anything, you must convince me that I can trust you, if not, then you'll just have to kill me.'

'You are a tough cookie; Sarah always chose her friends well. I assure you what you tell me won't go past these four walls.'

Xanthe took a deep breath and gave an explanation of why she was in the Research Laboratory, the female told Xanthe she knew something of her and Lisa's horrific past. Xanthe did not mention her involvement with Zenobia, she just mentioned Amy Thornton's name as just another victim like herself and Lisa, though it had been fatal for Amy.

'I can check to see if anyone fitting the description of your friend Lisa is about the place, I'll let you know, though if she is here, she may well have been brought in secretly.'

The person behind her stood up.

'Don't move until I close the door, if I find out anything, I shall contact you.'

'When you do, make sure I have some clothes on, I'm self-conscious about my naked body.'

The female laughed and left the room. After a moment, Xanthe stood up and inhaled deeply and let the air out of her lungs through her mouth. She got dressed and went to the kitchens and made herself a strong cup of coffee and sat in the lounge and drank it. Hilary joined her a moment later and told Xanthe, she would show her where she could bed down for the night.

Janice drove out of the main gate and turned left and drove alongside the river. After a short distance she turned right and parked her car up a driveway of a large house, she got out of the car and knocked on the door of the house. The door opened and Steven Calvert gave her a welcoming smile. Then he stood aside to let her in, and then closed the door behind her. It had been some months since the last time they had been together, as she had been tied to Samantha's bedside working hard to make the girl well again. Now it was down to the waiting game Janice decided to see what her companion had been up to.

'How is she?' Steven asked in deep concern.

Janice shook her head; her expression was full of sadness.

'Samantha still hangs onto life, but she is still in a deep coma.'

Steven put his arms round her and kissed her on the lips; she rubbed her body against him.

'She'll pull through, Samantha's not going to desert us just yet,' Steven said.

'I hope you're right.'

They had a meal together then they went to the lounge and sat comfortably on the couch.

'I suppose you've had loads of women flocking round you, while we've been apart,' Janice said.

Steven gave her an expression of complete innocence.

'I've been the proper gentleman; I've been true to you, my love.'

'Yeah, like you expect me to believe that,' Janice scoffed.

Steven put his arm round her waist and Janice pulled away from him.

'We had a new girl start with us today, she says she knows you,' Janice said in a hurt voice.

'You are barking up the wrong tree, Xanthe would be more interested in you,' Steven assured her.

Janice remembered the way Xanthe stared at her with those dark depthless eyes.

'She's not my type.'

Steven pushed her against the back of the couch and began to unbutton her blouse.

'Glad to hear it,' he said.

As Xanthe slept troubled dreams plagued her sleeping mind, memories of when she was last here as a little girl of 11, tall dark figures in the dark that came to torment her and find out what she knew and what she might have seen. They had not been very nice when they interrogated her. It was a reminder if the same people were still here, now she was a woman they would treat her worse, all the tortures her mind could think up, they would use to hurt her. Her sanity would be threatened as they tried to preserve their secrets. Xanthe moved about restlessly in the bed, her body was covered in a cold sweat as her mind ran over more old memories.

Steven woke and gazed at Janice's sleeping face, the morning sun shone through the window and settled onto the bed. He kissed her on the lips, and she woke and gazed up at him.

'You look lovely when you're asleep,' Steven told her.

Janice poked her tongue out at him and slid out of bed and walked out of the bedroom; he gazed at her bare bottom as she went. Janice went into the bathroom and showered, she then returned to the bedroom with a towel wrapped round her body, Steven was getting dressed.

'Are you going to stay for breakfast?'

Janice nodded her head and he left her to get dressed.

After breakfast, they left the house and Janice got in her car and opened the window; he kissed her hard on the mouth.

'Don't take too long to come and see me next time,' Steven said.

Janice promised to see him the next night; their night of love had shown her how much she had missed him.

'I'm your girl, Steven, as long as you want me.'

'I want you forever, Jan.'

They kissed for a few minutes more and he ran his hand over the front of her blouse. Then he moved away and watched her back the car onto the road and drive away.

Xanthe woke and pulled the sheet off her sweaty body, she felt awful and she could still remember the bad dreams of the night. She swung her legs over the side of the bed and sat with her head in her hands. After a while she stood up and left the sleeping cubicle and made for the showers. She removed her bra and panties and got under the stream of hot water; she closed her eyes and let her mind go blank. The cold sweat was washed from her body; the dreams had disturbed her, and she had to forget them. Fifteen minutes later she turned off the water and stepped out of the shower. She dried her body and put on her bra and panties and went back to her room. She got dressed and put on the white lab coat and she went in search of breakfast.

She met up with Hilary and they went to the storeroom and made for the lift doors; they slid open and they entered the lift and it took them up to the ground level of the main building. The doors opened and Xanthe looked out at a large lounge area.

'You find a vacant table and I'll get the coffees,' Hilary said.

As Xanthe made her way through the lounge eyes were suddenly turned her way. She found an empty table and sat down, a few minutes later Hilary joined her and placed a mug of strong coffee in front of her.

'Thanks.'

Xanthe stared across the large room and spied a girl of about 15; the dark hair and pretty face were familiar. Xanthe excused herself and strode quickly across the room and grabbed the girl by the arm. Evelyn stared wide-eyed at her. Xanthe dragged the girl to the table and sat her down; Hilary gazed at the young girl.

'What are you doing here?' Xanthe asked.

Evelyn explained how Professor Fairclough turned up that night and told her to get out of Xanthe's car and she got in his and he drove her here so she could undergo more tests on her brain power.

'I was 11 when I was brought here, Evelyn, what can you do?'

Evelyn lowered her head and fixed her eyes on Xanthe's coffee mug. Xanthe watched the mug as it slowly slid across the table away from her. In the middle of the table it stopped, and Evelyn looked up and Xanthe gave the girl a warm smile.

'I'm impressed.'

Evelyn had her hands on the table, and she played nervously with her long slender fingers, Xanthe stretched out a hand and took hold of Evelyn's fidgeting fingers.

'You look like a girl that needs someone to trust, I'm not going to hurt you,' Xanthe said, comfortingly.

Evelyn gazed at the friendly face opposite her and made up her mind.

'The man who had held me captive in the old house is here.'

Xanthe shook her head and told the girl he had been killed.

'There were two of them, he had got hold of me, so the other one could use me as bait to catch Samantha, I can feel his presence somewhere near the testing room.'

Hilary gazed at the young girl then turned to Xanthe.

'What is going on here?'

'There is a professor here by the name of Frederick Fairclough, who is testing children for ESP. I was here when I was eleven and tested until I reached the age of sixteen, then they let me go; they are testing Evelyn here, there is something sinister about it, I'm sure.'

Xanthe was sure the man who had grabbed Evelyn had Lisa under his control, her friend might be her with him, and Xanthe had to hunt him down.

'Why don't you show me the testing room?' she said to Evelyn.

Xanthe excused herself and said she would not be long; the young girl stood up and walked across the room beside Xanthe. She suddenly found courage while she was close to the older girl. They left the lounge room and they entered a long corridor; Evelyn took the lead. There were doors on each side of the corridor at intervals.

'Where are we now?' Xanthe wanted to know.

'Those doors lead to the living quarters.'

Evelyn stopped at a door and opened it.

'This one is mine,' Evelyn said.

Xanthe entered the room; it had all the comforts of home. Xanthe had had one when she had been tested.

'A nice home from home, let's gets to the testing room.'

Evelyn closed the door and guided Xanthe down the corridor. Halfway down she stopped in front of a large door and she gazed through the glass panel and into the large room beyond the doors. She turned to Xanthe.

'There's only two in there, a boy and a girl,' Evelyn said.

Pamela Sisson stood with a fixed stare at the large rectangular mirror on the wall. She was fourteen and she had been under the tests for a year; behind her stood her boyfriend Francis Powell, who was a year older than her. She did not know about two-way mirrors, but she had a sense that told her, someone was watching them from the other side of the mirror.

'What do you see, Pam?'

Pamela only saw the mirror, but she knew what Francis meant, she could not see him visually, but she could sense him.

Xanthe walked into the room, while Evelyn stayed by the door as if there was something in the room she did not like. In the centre of the large room were two conference tables surrounded by chairs. Xanthe turned to Evelyn; she could see the young girl was ill at ease. It made Xanthe wonder what the tests entailed.

'You can come further into the room, Evelyn, there's nothing in here, as far as I can see, that can cause you harm.'

Evelyn walked slowly towards Xanthe.

'Whereabouts do you feel the presence the strongest?'

Evelyn pointed to the wall opposite where the rectangular mirror was; a boy and a girl stared at them with interest. Evelyn followed Xanthe across the room, Pamela moved away to let the older girl approach the mirror. Xanthe ran a hand over the surface, Pamela watched her with eager interest. Xanthe gazed at her reflection, the dark eyes stared back at her accusing, the timid, afraid eleven-year-old was gone, the face in the mirror showed a hard and determined expression now she was in the lion's den, but the dark eyes showed her a guilt she felt deep inside – how far into danger would she step, before she ran away scared with her tail between her legs? Xanthe shook her head, it was not going to happen, she was going to be strong, just like her sister, she wanted Phoebe to be proud of her, that mattered more than anything to Xanthe. She was going to hold her head high and meet the devil face to face.

'What are you looking for?' Pamela asked.

Xanthe ran her fingers over the edge of the mirror starting at the top and moving round it in a clockwise direction

'It's probably a two-way mirror, there's someone on the other side watching the ESP tests,' Xanthe said.

'He's not there now, as soon as you came up to the mirror, he left,' Pamela informed her.

Xanthe stared at the pretty chubby face, the sapphire coloured eyes stared back at her.

'You are a remarkable young girl,' Xanthe said.

Her searching fingers touched a small lever and the mirror slid back, Xanthe gave a cry of triumph, the boy came up beside her.

'I wonder what secrets are hidden in the darkness before us,' Xanthe muttered.

'I wonder,' Francis echoed.

Evelyn gazed at her; she had an idea of what Xanthe was going to do next, and the young girl shook her head.

'You're not going in there, are you?' Evelyn inquired, nervously.

Xanthe grinned at the worried girl.

'Why not, nothing ventured, nothing gained.'

'I will go with you,' Francis said.

Xanthe looked the tall teenage boy up and down, he looked strong and capable. 'You will?'

'Yes, I will protect you,' he said.

Xanthe smiled, the boy's expression told her, and he was honest in what he had said.

'OK, it'll be nice to have someone watching my back,' Xanthe said.

Xanthe told the two girls to go back to their rooms and say nothing about her and Francis's whereabouts. They promised to keep silent. Xanthe watched the two girls leave the testing room, and then she turned and moved through the opening made by the mirror shifting its position. Francis followed; when they were on the other side of the wall, the mirror slid back.

Xanthe and Francis stood in darkness, suddenly a beam of light stabbed the darkness and she stared at Francis, who held a small torch.

'Do you always carry a torch in your pocket?' she asked him.

'I always come prepared,' was his answer.

They walked along the passage. Xanthe had a feeling the path they were following was going slightly downhill. The passage came to an end at a locked door. Francis shone the torch on a keypad at the right-hand side of the door.

'Simple enough,' he said.

Francis ran the fingers of his left hand over the keypad; when he found the right sequence the door slid open.

'Amazing,' Xanthe said.

'It was nothing,' Francis assured her.

'And modest with it,' Xanthe said.

They passed through the doorway and the lights came on and they found themselves in a small room furnished as an office. Xanthe decided to try the filing cabinets first and searched through the drawers; Francis sat on the desk and watched her with interest. Xanthe found a file on her friend Lisa Booth; it contained her whole life history. Lisa had not told her all the horrors she had gone through, when the dark stranger had come to live next door to her, but it was all here in the file. Xanthe could see why poor Lisa wanted to keep it a secret, now the fiend had his hands on her again. She quickly went to the files under 'c' and found a file for herself and her sister. She went through them all and the files were on all the residents that lived in the same housing estate. She found Amy Thornton's file. It had deceased on the bottom; it gave her no idea who had murdered the girl. All the files had a case number and they had been under a Dr Stonehouse; the name was vaguely familiar. It was obvious he had been experimenting on his subjects to see what they feared the most. Xanthe shivered: she had been one of them.

'Did you find what you were looking for?' Francis asked.

Xanthe approached the desk and Francis slid off it. The doors of the desk were locked; she could shoot off the locks with her automatic, but she did not want to damage anything, she did not want anyone to know she had been here. She crossed the room to a second door. Xanthe decided to vacate the office by that way.

'Are you going to do the honours?' Xanthe asked.

Francis used the same combination on the keypad that he had used on the first door, it slid open and Xanthe stepped into the darkness beyond. The door slid shut and Francis switched on his torch and shone it on the floor of the passage they found themselves in. They walked a short distance and Francis grabbed her arm and pulled her back, he pointed to the floor where he was shining the torch beam; there was a gaping chasm. Xanthe got onto her hands and knees and felt down the edge and found a rung of a metal ladder. She told Francis of her discovery and told him she would go first. Xanthe clambered over the edge and by the light of the torch she got on the metal ladder and started down; Francis followed her down. At last she reached the bottom. Xanthe figured out they were now in the underground level. After feeling about in the dark for a while she found the way forward; it was a shaft she had to go along on her hands and knees. Francis followed behind her keeping the torch beam shining forward.

After they had gone a few yards Xanthe told Francis to turn off his torch, as he did so she saw a speck of light up ahead. She came to the end of the shaft; a mesh panel barred their way, to the room beyond.

'What do you see?' Francis asked.

Xanthe gazed through the mess and at the medical room beyond. She studied the hospital bed with the machinery surrounding it, she then turned her attention to the occupant of the bed, and Xanthe recognised the thin pale face. It was Samantha. Xanthe gave a sigh of relief as she saw the tall girl was still clinging to life.

'Let's get back before we're missed,' Xanthe said.

Francis led the way back to the small office room. Xanthe went to the desk; Xanthe wished she had something to break open the locked drawer. As if reading her thoughts, Francis handed her a pocket knife; she took it and slid the blade in and forced the drawer open. She riffled through the papers, most of them were scientific and beyond her. At the back of the drawer she found a sheet of paper folded up, she unfolded it and read what was on it, then she refolded it and placed it in her skirt pocket.

CHAPTER LIII:

THE MIND OF EVELYN STEVENS

Evelyn Stevens sat curled up in an armchair, she was thinking of Xanthe and was hoping nothing serious had happened to her, Evelyn liked her. There came a knock on the door, and she got out of the chair and opened the door. She stood aside and let her visitor walk into the room. Evelyn closed the door and looked up at Professor Frederick Fairclough; he was a tall, slim man in his late thirties. He was head of the department that was testing Evelyn and others like her. He had a pleasant nature and Evelyn felt at ease when he was around.

'Is anything bothering you?' the Professor asked in a soothing voice.

Fairclough gazed down at the upturned, impish and slightly freckled face. Her wide dark eyes studied his face. He could see she was a pretty girl with striking facial features, he was sure the intelligence behind the dark eyes was a lot more intense than the girl was outwardly projecting.

'Why don't you tell me what is on your mind, Evelyn. I can help you get over your worries.'

Evelyn dropped her head and gazed down at the floor.

'I know there is something inside my head that makes me different from other people. I just want to be like other normal fifteen-year-old girls.'

Fairclough put a comforting arm round her shoulders.

'I don't know what you want of me. When you have found out my strange abilities, what are you going to do with them?'

'I'm not going to make you do anything you don't want to,' he assured her.

Evelyn sat down in the armchair and looked up at the Professor as he stood in front of her.

'We are heading for an uncertain future and it will be with the help of people like you, Evelyn, that will help us get through it,' he explained.

The wide dark eyes stared hard at him, as if trying to see into his mind.

'Sometimes I feel I have been cursed. I don't want to be used,' Evelyn said.

'I just want to help you learn about yourself, you are a very intelligent girl, Evelyn, I would never use you for anything that went against your wishes.'

Evelyn held out her right hand and he took it and squeezed it gently. She gave him a smile that showed she was putting her trust in him. Fairclough was not going to betray Evelyn or her trust in him.

'Everything will work out fine, you'll see, Evelyn,' Fairclough told her.

Professor Fairclough left the living quarters and Evelyn went to the sleeping compartment; she walked towards the bed, she felt tired and drained. She heard a sound behind her. Evelyn was grabbed from behind and something wet and clammy was clamped over her nose and mouth. Fumes entered her lungs and it stung; after a few moments she lost consciousness.

Hilary opened the door that led to the quarantine area. As she stepped into the passage beyond someone grabbed her arm. She turned and faced Xanthe as she closed and locked the door.

'You shouldn't be here,' Hilary said.

'Your friend is in great danger, we have to talk,' Xanthe said, urgently.

Hilary walked up the passage, Xanthe kept close behind her.

'There's something about yourself that you haven't been honest about, Xanthe?'

Xanthe explained to Hilary the reason she was here in the Research Laboratories. She was making a private investigation and she was not spying, or trying to steal any national secrets.

'Whoever was responsible for Amy Thornton's death is here at this moment and I'm sure he will harm your friend Samantha, if he learns she still lives,' warned Xanthe.

They entered the medical room where Samantha lay still in a metal bed, Xanthe pointed up at the mesh grill high up the wall where she had looked into the room some time before. Hilary gazed up at it then went to see about her patient.

'Have you any idea when Samantha will become conscious?' Xanthe asked in a voice full of concern.

Hilary checked the machines that were monitoring her patient's life signs. They showed Samantha was much stronger, but she would not come to life until her body was fully recovered, so it could be anytime.

'Hopefully it won't be too long,' Hilary said.

As Hilary finished speaking Samantha's eyes flashed open, Hilary rushed to the wall and turned down the lighting. Xanthe stood by the bed under the gaze of two bright green eyes.

'Where am I?'

Hilary told Samantha she was safe underground in a research facility just outside the city. Her last memory floated into her mind, there was so much blood, Samantha was sure she would not survive, her body was better at repairing itself than her mind had thought. She was regenerated and ready for action. Hilary detached the wires from Samantha's body and turned off the monitoring machines.

'What about the foetus?' Samantha wanted to know.

Hilary gave her a reassuring smile.

'It's unharmed and growing naturally and healthily. I have not told anyone that you're pregnant. I'm sure you'd like to drop that bombshell on the General yourself.'

Samantha struggled to sit up and Xanthe gave her a helping hand and pulled the pillows up behind Samantha's back.

Samantha could feel the new life moving around inside her. There it would have to stay for the time being, Samantha could not afford to give birth just yet. She had much to do and little time to do it in.

Evelyn Stevens came to in darkness and fear seized her waking mind. Then she realised something was covering her eyes. She moved slightly and found she was lying on a hard surface and her hands were tied behind her back and her ankles were tied together. Evelyn decided she was in for another bad day.

'Your guest has just woken up.'

It was a female voice some way off from her position which she guessed was on the floor as the voice was some way above her.

'Good, Evelyn is going to be our next experiment,' said a man's voice close by.

Evelyn recognised this voice only too well; it was the man who had abducted her and held her at the old housing estate. Evelyn heard footsteps approach her and a hand touched her bare arm; the touch made her skin crawl. He felt her flinch away from him. Evelyn was aware of him, which was good.

'Keep calm, Evelyn, I'm not going to harm you. I'm just going to test your unique talent. You may have fooled Professor Fairclough, but you don't fool me.'

Evelyn felt his hand stroke her cheek, she tried to control her fear, as her body trembled uncontrollably.

'We shall work together, Evelyn. I have a use for a brain like yours.'

Evelyn did not like the sound of that; he only wanted her for evil means. Her mind and body were in mortal danger from this man.

Xanthe made her way to Evelyn's room and found Pamela Sisson standing outside. She had knocked on the door, but Evelyn had not shown herself. Xanthe opened the door and walked into the room and called Evelyn's name. When she got no answer to her call, Xanthe went into the sleeping compartment in case Evelyn had dozed off on her bed. She was not there. Xanthe sniffed and detected a faint obnoxious odour, she left the living quarters and told Pamela to return to her own room and the young girl did as she was told. Xanthe was anxious for Evelyn's safety. She went in search of Christopher Thornton, and she found him on the ground level in the lounge area. She sat opposite him and told him she had found what she had been searching for, she gave him the note she had found written by his dead sister, and she sat silent while he read it. He read it twice and they looked up at Xanthe.

'What did they do to her?'

Xanthe stood up and laid a hand on his shoulder.

'We must go and see Zenobia and I will tell you all I have found out, I'll meet you in the car park,' Xanthe said.

Xanthe returned to her own room and as she walked into the room her senses were immediately alert; she heard a sound behind her, and a gun was pressed against her back.

'After our first meeting, I decided to catch you with your clothes on,' a female voice said behind her.

'How very gracious, I don't suppose you'd let me see your face,' Xanthe said.

'Why not, just don't turn around too fast.'

Xanthe heard her visitor move back; she was relieved not to have the weapon pressed against her back. Xanthe turned slowly round and found her staring down a barrel of a gun. The girl holding it was of average height and had a slim figure; she recognised the pretty round face. It was the blonde girl behind the reception desk when Xanthe first arrived.

'Have you found what you're looking for?' Carol Moreland inquired.

'Part of it, I don't think my friend is here, but I know Amy Thornton was here before she was murdered, so is the murderer.'

Carol placed the automatic back in the inside pocket of her blazer. She had a girlfriend who had been brutally murdered a few months ago. Finding out the killer might be roaming around the laboratories unnerved her.

'Can you identify the killer?' Carol asked.

Xanthe shook her head, her memories of a girl of twelve were a nightmare best forgotten and she kept it blocked out.

'I don't know who or what he is, only that he kills and enjoys it,' Xanthe said.

Xanthe sank into a chair and Carol stood over her.

'What are you going to do now?'

Xanthe looked up at her. 'I've done what I came here for; I have other work to do.'

Carol put a hand on her shoulder.

'If you let me know how I contact you, I can give you any news that may be helpful to you.'

Steven Calvert walked into the private ward room Samantha had been moved into, she was sat up in bed and received him with a warm smile. He sat on the bed and kissed her on the lips. She pushed him away and shook her head.

'You mustn't, what if Janice comes in and catches you kissing a strange girl,' she warned.

Steven ran a hand over her cheek.

'She knows I care for you, we're both glad you have survived that horrible attack.'

He kissed her on the cheek.

'Anyway, you're not strange, just a little weird, that's all.'

Samantha pushed him off the bed as Hilary walked into the room; she scolded her stepson for tiring her patient. She gave Samantha an injection in the right arm. Samantha looked up at Steven.

'Ever since I came back to life, your stepmother has been sticking needles into me,' she complained.

'She's supposed to, she's your doctor,' Steven said.

'That's it, son, you tell her. She is very lucky to be alive.'

Samantha held onto Hilary's right arm.

'I know I owe my life to you, believe me, I am very grateful,' Samantha said, sincerely.

'Now that you are up and fit, I suppose you are eager to get away,' Hilary said.

'Not until you give me the go ahead, I shall not leave until you think I'm fit enough to do so,' Samantha assured her.

'I'm glad to hear it, now lie down and get some rest, I don't want you overdoing it,' Hilary ordered.

Samantha slid down under the sheets and watched Steven and Hilary leave the room. Then she closed her eyes and thought about her next plan of action.

As I'm loathe to say it. I'm glad you have survived. It's been boring in here without you to irritate.

Samantha sighed deeply; being near to death had not rid her of the voice in her head.

'So, my being so close to death has not relieved my head of you,' Samantha said out loud.

So, it seems, so we'll have to find another way for me to return to my rightful place.

Evelyn Stevens felt herself being picked up and carried across the room, she felt nauseous as if she was in the clutches of something utterly loathsome. She wondered what sort of torture she was going to be put through. Evelyn was sure it was going to be something really nasty. He carried her out of the secret office and down the dark passage that led to the control room he was using for his own private use. He sat her in a metal chair; he untied her wrist and clamped them to the arms of the chair. He placed a domed headset which was attached to a computer over her head. The hum of electronics filled her ears.

Sight had been taken away from Evelyn, only her ears could tell her what was happening to her and the thing on her head told Evelyn she was being connected to a machine, something was going to be done to her mind.

He ran his fingers over the computer control desk, a few more adjustments and the computer would link with the girl's brain. He felt someone come up beside him. He looked up from his work and gazed at Lavonia's smiling face.

'What will happen to her when you've fed her brain to the machine?' she asked.

'Evelyn won't come to any serious harm; I don't want to kill her.'

'What do you want to do to her?'

'I want to put her through a few tests just to see if she has a mind we can use for our own purposes.'

Samantha stood in front of a full-length mirror on the door of the wardrobe, and gazed at herself. She had on a long light blue dress that came down to her ankles. She was satisfied with her appearance. She heard the door open and someone made their way towards her. Samantha turned and Steven grabbed her and kissed her on the mouth, then she pushed him away with ease.

'You're impossible; I don't know how Janice puts up with you.'

Steven gave her a wicked smile.

'It's just that you look ravishing in that dress.'

Samantha turned away from him shaking her head. She picked up a dark blue blazer that was hung over the back of a chair and she put it on.

'What are you planning?' Steven inquired.

Samantha gave him a sad face.

'Have you been able to find out what has happened to Naomi?'

'John has been to London to investigate the car crash she was involved in, the car was a burnt out shell, the evidence is inconclusive that Naomi may have died in the crash. If your friend is alive, she must have gone to ground,' Steven explained.

Samantha left the room followed closely by Steven.

They entered the lounge and Samantha sat at an empty table; Steven went to get some coffee for them both. Xanthe entered the room and spied Samantha sitting alone and sat next to her. Xanthe told Samantha how pleased she was to see her back up on her feet again.

'So am I, what have you been up to?'

Xanthe told Samantha about her mission and told her of the depressing files she had found dating back more than ten years. She gave her the news that Evelyn had been abducted again and there were no clues to where the girl was.

'The person who attacked you was not the one who had kidnapped Evelyn as bait to get you,' Xanthe said.

'Who ever this mystery person is, he hasn't finished with Evelyn yet,' Samantha said.

Steven arrived at the table with three cups of coffee and he placed one in front of Xanthe. He sat opposite them.

'What are you going to do now, Xanthe?' Steven inquired.

'Go back to my day job, I'm tempting fate to overstay my welcome here,' Xanthe said.

'If you have any trouble with the authorities, let me know and I'll sort them out for you,' Steven told her.

When they got outside Xanthe saw two men in grey suits standing by her car. They saw her and the larger of the two men made his way towards her; Samantha moved closer to her for protection.

'Miss Cross, can you come with us, we want to ask you some questions about your sister,' the man in the grey suit said.

Steven stood in front of him and showed the man his I D. The man stared at it.

'Military intelligence,' the man said, for the benefit of his partner behind him.

'That's right and Miss Cross is working for us at the moment. If you want to question her, you'll have to contact General Heywood. I'm sure your boss knows his number,' Steven said.

'We just want to know if she has had contact with Phoebe Cross,' the man said.

'I've not seen my sister for years,' Xanthe said.

The second man drew alongside his partner.

'I hope you'll let us know if Phoebe contacts you. We are not going to harm her in any way, we just want to talk to her,' the man said.

Xanthe just nodded her head that she understood and walked past them and made for the car. As Xanthe drove away Steven and Samantha waved her away. Then Steven guided Samantha to his car that was parked nearby. He drove up to the main gate, where Xanthe had stopped to pick up Christopher Thornton. They went in different directions. Steven drove to the house he was staying at with Janice. They entered the house and discovered Janice was not at home. Samantha asked him where the shower was, as she wanted to have a shower.

'Can I scrub your back?'

Samantha stared at his innocent expression.

'No.'

Samantha walked up the stairs and Steven followed her.

'Spoilsport,' Steven said.

They went into the spare bedroom and Samantha undressed. Steven gazed at her body, her skin was pale and unblemished as ever, there was no sign of the horrible injuries she had suffered.

'It's amazing how your body has mended itself after your ordeal.'

Samantha placed her hands on her bulging belly, she felt a sharp kick. Telling her the baby she was carrying had big feet.

Keep still, Darling. You are a lot safer where you are.

The baby gave a final kick and then became still. Samantha sighed, the baby was in a hurry to be born, but her mind and body still had control over the new life inside her and that was the way it had to stay, Samantha had work to do and a doomsday machine to construct. She had dangerous people to avoid, so she did not have time to bring up a baby.

Sometime later Samantha made her way down the stairs, her skin tingled after the shower and she felt much better. She went into the kitchen and Steven came up to her and put his arms round her.

'You look and smell nice,' he said.

Samantha allowed him one kiss and then pushed him away, showing him, she had not lost any of her unusual strength.

'You are sex mad, Steven,' she scolded.

'I know and I don't want to be cured.'

Samantha moved away from him and sat at the table and dug into the meal he had prepared for her. When she had finished Samantha got up and went to the back door and opened it and gazed across the garden and to the river beyond. She looked up at the darkening sky and saw it was starting to snow.

'Are you expecting trouble?' Steven asked.

'I'm always expecting trouble,' Samantha said, seriously.

He put a hand on her shoulder.

'It's a pity you can't try harder to avoid it.'

She turned and gazed at his face.

'You've looked death in the face and survived, next time you might not.'

Samantha closed the door – the cold air made her shiver.

'I made a stupid mistake, I was not ready to face them, I shall be more careful next time,' Samantha declared.

A female voice spoke from the other side of the kitchen.

'Let's hope so, we may not be able to glue you back together next time.'

Samantha moved away from Steven and moved towards Janice who had entered the kitchen quietly.

'I'm aware I owe my life to you and Hilary; I do appreciate it.'

They hugged each other; Janice hoped the tall girl had learnt a vital lesson.

'Let's hope you don't go off on your own again.'

They parted and Samantha gazed at Janice's serious expression, Samantha felt she was going to get her wrist slapped.

'We are supposed to be friends and we are supposed to be working as a team. It's too dangerous for you to keep running off on your own,' Janice said.

'The dangers are only just becoming clear,' Samantha said.

Steven put a hand on her shoulder.

'What do you mean?'

Samantha turned and faced him.

'That alien that almost finished me off, has been on Earth for some time, so I guess they have a scout ship somewhere near here. This mystery man, who has Lisa and Evelyn, is obviously involved with them.'

'What about Dr Stonehouse?' Janice asked.

'They were helping him with the experiments on the young people of the housing estate Xanthe came from. Her sister Phoebe could verify that if we can find her. '

'What are we going to do first?' Janice asked, putting emphasis on; we.

Samantha smiled at Janice.

'Naomi had something of mine, I'm going to visit her father, to see if she left it with him,' Samantha said.

They left the house Steven got into his car and drove down the driveway to the road; Samantha and Janice walked together down the path. Samantha was being watched through the telescopic sights of a high velocity rifle, in a car parked five houses up the road. It was centred on her swollen belly pushing against her dress, as she had her blazer open. The finger tightened on the trigger; her life was in his hands. A hand settled onto the shoulder of Barnaby Morgue and the finger on the trigger relaxed and he lowered the rifle. He gazed at his female partner who sat beside him.

'Not yet, we must find out where she is hiding the power crystal,' Lavonia said.

Lavonia picked up the rifle and sighted it on the back of Samantha's head, as she reached Steven's car.

'Oh Sam, what would I give to blast your brains all over that car,' Lavonia sighed.

Barnaby watched the car drive away and he drove onto the road and followed the other car at a safe distance. Steven Calvert made for the Governmental Administrative building; George Evans lived close by. He parked outside and Janice got out and entered the building, Steven turned down Cathedral Close and parked outside the large house owned by George Evans.

'I'll try the front door, Steven, you go around the back just in case,' Samantha said.

Samantha rang the doorbell and a few moments later the door opened. George Evans looked over at his caller; his daughter had told him about Samantha, so he decided this was the girl. He stood aside and watched the tall girl duck her head and enter the house.

'I'm Samantha. Has your daughter, Naomi, told you about me?'

George nodded his head and guided her down the hallway, they turned into the lounge and he told her to sit down. He walked out of the room and returned a few moments later holding a metal and plastic case. He handed it to Samantha.

'Naomi told me to give you that and there's a letter inside explaining everything,' George said.

Samantha laid the case on the floor and opened it up and inside lay the lead box, on top was a large envelope. She picked it up and ripped it open and found some documents and a letter, which she unfolded and started to read.

Dear Sam, as you may have heard about my death, I thought I'd let you know it is greatly exaggerated. The unfortunate person in the car got it instead of me. There's a lot of nasty people about, who, if they have targeted me, will also be after you, so take care.

While I was in London I met up with a very rich lady by the name of Zenobia Madison. It was a chance encounter you pray for. Zenobia had just what we needed: money and plenty of it. So, I struck up a working partnership with her. While I'm doing this thing for you, I need someone to look after my interests and Zenobia turned out to be the very businesswoman I needed. I also told her about Sarah Mullen and her big ambitions, which interested Zenobia and I told her about Sarah's loyal friends so she can work her magic on them.

The documents with this letter tell you details of my new I. D. and how you can contact me on e-mail. My father is giving me support and helping me a lot and he even thinks we shall succeed, which should please Sarah, so she won't kill us both.

So, until we meet again in person, keep yourself safe and don't take too many crazy chances.

N.

Samantha placed the letter back in the case and closed it up; she held onto it as she stood up.

'When you see her next, thank her for me,' Samantha said.

'I will. There's a car parked on the opposite side of the road, it might be waiting for you,' George said.

Samantha went to the window and looked out and saw the car was occupied. She decided to play safe and leave the house by the back door. She found Steven waiting outside and Samantha told him to take the car and meet her outside the Government building. Steven made his way to the front of the house as Samantha made her way down the back garden; he looked across at the car opposite as he opened the car door. He drove off and noticed the other car did not follow; he was sure it was Samantha they wanted. He drove quickly to the next street to head off Samantha just in case they had someone watching the back of the house. Steven did not want anything to happen to her, he was very interested in what secret she held in the case she took out of George Evans' house.

On the thirtieth floor of the Government building Janice sat in front of one of the many computers in the room, she stared at the data on the screen about Naomi Evans. It was about time they ran a thorough investigation into the girl. She knew about the information on her in the Research Facility, she decided to check the database for information about Naomi, they did not know. She had to use her military security number to get past the access denied data that Janice found very interesting. Naomi Evans was a dedicated scientist and qualified medical doctor;

she was also a Government Agent. Samantha had told her Sarah thought Naomi was a spy, now Janice could tell her, she had been right.

Janice fed the name Phoebe Cross into the database and not to her surprise the ACCESS DENIED came up, alarm bells rang round the room and across the City at police headquarters a buzzer sounded in Chief Inspector Roberts' office. Charles Roberts gazed at his computer screen and saw someone was trying to activate the Phoebe Cross file. He went to the next office and a tall brown-haired woman turned away from the window.

'Come on, Kerry, someone is looking for Phoebe.'

Detective Inspector Kerry Hunter followed Charles out of the office, and they left the building. They got in his car and drove swiftly towards Government Building.

Gerald Pollard was sitting in his office when the computer came to life and warned him someone was trying to get into some sensitive data. Gerald stood up and left his office and got into the lift. He entered the database room and made for monitor 62, down the centre aisle, he stopped at the desk and gazed at the beautiful blonde girl seated at the computer.

'Can I help you, Miss?'

Janice looked up at the man.

'And you are?'

'Gerald Pollard, the Home Secretary assistant.'

Janice stood up and handed him her ID card.

'Military Intelligence; why are you interested in Phoebe Cross?'

'We have come across her in our investigations and we want to find out more about her,' Janice said

'What have we here, Gerald?'

Janice ran an eye over the newcomers, the man was tall and well built in his middle thirties, the tall pretty woman was about the same age, and her bright brown eyes gazed at Janice inquisitively.

'Hullo Charles, how's Kelly?'

Chief Inspector Roberts hoped his thirteen old daughters was safe at home, his wife had been dead for three years.

'Safe at home while Phoebe and the serial killer are loose in the neighbourhood.'

Janice moved closer to him; Charles stared at the bright blue eyes.

'Do you think there's a link between the two?'

'Are you a reporter?' he asked. Janice shook her head and handed him her ID card.

'Are all the females in Military Intelligence as young and pretty as you?'

Janice ignored the question.

'The sooner someone gives me data on Phoebe Cross, the sooner we can track her down,' Janice said.

'We haven't had much luck so far, she seems to have gone to ground,' Charles said.

'We know where she was May last year,' Janice informed them.

'Will you accompany us to police headquarters?' Charles inquired.

'I'd love to,' Janice said.

Back at police headquarters Janice sat at Charles Roberts's desk, she told him about Dr Stonehouse's clinic and finding Phoebe Cross there. Phoebe had gone by the time Janice got there so she did not know what the girl looked like. Charles took a file out of his filing cabinet and gave it to Janice, who opened the file and began to read it; when she had read it all, Janice wondered what was fact and what was fiction.

CHAPTER LIV:

VISIONS OF HELL

Phoebe Cross clung to the steering wheel as she sped along the road towards the Government building, she was back home, after keeping her head down and avoiding people who wanted to lock her up and throw away the key and people that just wanted her dead. She was a survivor; she had been through all kinds of madness and come through it with her sanity intact, though slightly scarred. Phoebe was not staying alive for herself, but for her sister, whose vision in her mind had stopped Phoebe from slipping into the dark pit, where there was no return. Phoebe wanted to be where the action was, danger drew her to it like a moth to flame. Which was why she was in big danger now, ever since her fourteenth birthday? Her hardness and bitter temper made her careless in the face of danger. Phoebe had been an angry young girl; she had been angry with her parents and angry with herself for putting up with them. She only stayed at home for her younger sister. Prue Cross had been a little angel at the age of eleven, she did not understand her big sister's anger, but she loved Phoebe all the same.

Phoebe swerved round a right-hand corner and spied a tall girl walking leisurely along the pavement; she deliberately headed the car for the pedestrian. Phoebe recognised Samantha in an instant; she had seen the oncoming danger but even Samantha could not avoid the speeding car, it hit her hard and she was knocked sprawling onto the road surface. The car screeched to a halt and Phoebe got out and picked up the heavy case that lay on the pavement and tossed it onto the back seat of the car.

'Sorry, Sam, but you could be just what I need to gain my freedom.'

Phoebe dragged the unconscious girl to the car and put her in the back. Phoebe got in and drove the car speedily to her next destination.

Steven Calvert sat in his car close by, not close enough to prevent the mad girl driver catching Samantha and bundling her into the car.

Janice gazed at the photograph DI Kerry Hunter had given her of Phoebe Cross as she sipped a mug of coffee. The mobile phone in her blazer pocket buzzed and she took it out and listened calmly to Steven's report of him losing Samantha to a crazy female driver dressed in black. Janice asked him to describe her face.

Then she put the mobile phone back in her blazer pocket. She gazed at the face on the photograph; the young round face was crowned by a thick shaggy black hair. Janice was drawn to the dark eyes; it was like staring into two dark pools that hid the horror of Phoebe's incident-filled life. Janice could see Phoebe was a stronger individual than her younger sister. She slipped the photograph into her blazer pocket. She stood up and faced Chief Inspector Roberts and told him about the driver running down her friend and that the culprit was probably Phoebe. Steven had not got the licence number as it did not have one, but Janice gave Charles the colour and make of the car.

'If I get any other information about her, I'll let you know, Inspector.'

CI Charles Roberts and DI Kerry Hunter watched Janice walk majestically out of the office.

'I wonder if we offered her more money, she might work for us,' Charles said.

'We couldn't afford her on our budget,' Kerry informed him.

Barnaby Morgue held the rifle steady as he peered through the telescopic sight. George Evans left the house, closing the door behind him. The finger tightened on the rifle's trigger. The high velocity bullet hit the politician in the chest and his heart exploded. As George Evans hit the ground Lavonia drove the car at high speed, and Barnaby tossed the rifle onto the back seat.

'That's one of your father's opposition out of the way,' Barnaby said.

'Yes, it's a pity we couldn't get Sara as well, the slippery girl must have escaped out the back way,' Lavonia said.

Janice met up with Steven outside the government building; she showed him the photograph of Phoebe and asked him if she fitted the description of the girl who drove away with Samantha. He nodded his head.

'Yes, it could have been her, so that's Xanthe's infamous sister. Not much alike are they, except for the dark eyes.'

They went back to their car and drove back to the house, where they found another car parked in their driveway.

'We have visitors,' Steven said.

Janice got out of the car.

'Dr Bishop has arrived at last.'

They found Dr Anthony Bishop in the kitchen making tea, sitting on a stool was a pretty girl of seventeen. She wore a light green dress and a dark green blazer that was unbuttoned.

Janice gazed at the pretty face and the dark glasses, as she placed a hand on the girl's shoulder.

'You brought Charlotte with you?'

Dr Bishop handed Janice a mug of tea.

'I couldn't leave her there, it seems I'm the only person she feels safe with.'

Janice sat at the table and placed the mug of tea on it; Charlotte slid off the stool and sat beside Janice.

'Do you mind me being here?'

'Of course not, I'm glad you are out of that horrible place,' Janice assured her.

'How is Samantha?' Dr Bishop asked.

'We've lost her again,' Steven told him.

'What!'

Steven told Dr Bishop of Samantha's abduction. Janice showed him the photograph of Phoebe Cross. Bishop went to the briefcase he'd left on a chair and pulled out a file and laid it on the table in front of Janice.

'You should read that, Samantha could be in grave danger,' he said.

Charlotte had been listening to them and she was aware of the girl they spoke of. She had been at the clinic when Phoebe had been brought in. They had ignored Charlotte because of her blindness, but there was nothing wrong with her hearing. It had made Charlotte wonder what Phoebe had done for Dr Stonehouse to lock the girl up on the top floor of the clinic.

'There's no reason to believe she will harm your friend,' Charlotte said.

'And there's no reason to think she won't,' Steven said.

He was sitting at the table opposite her and Charlotte turned her attention on him.

'If Phoebe had wanted to kill Samantha, she would have run her down and drove away. Phoebe has taken your friend because she wants something,' Charlotte observed.

Janice had been reading the file Bishop had given her; Janice looked up and placed a hand on Charlotte's shoulder.

'And what is that?'

'Freedom from persecution,' Charlotte said.

'She can always give herself up,' Steven said.

Charlotte shook her head.

'And they'll just lock her away again, she doesn't want that.'

'The violent killing of her parents doesn't warrant Phoebe being locked up?' Janice inquired.

'You must go through what you know of the girl with a fine-toothed comb and try to discover what is missing.'

Charlotte turned on her chair and placed a hand on Janice's shoulder.

'You must read that file and try to determine what it does not tell you,' Charlotte explained.

Bishop moved closer to Charlotte and ran a comforting hand through her long hair. She knew the contents of the file and he wondered what Charlotte had picked up that they were unable to see.

'What is it you are trying to tell us, Charlotte?'

'The tests and experimentation Phoebe went through at the hands of Dr Stonehouse – who was in charge, him or someone else?'

Bishop and Steven stared at her but kept their thoughts to themselves. Janice kept reading. As she did Janice read between the lines and did as Charlotte told her and worked out what this file was not telling her.

JUNE 2123

Phoebe Cross could never remember when her troubles first started because she was always in trouble. When her sister was born Phoebe got the impression her parents had lost interest in her. As Prue (Xanthe) got older and was walking and talking, they still had no time for Phoebe. When Prue tried to get close to her wilder older sister, their parents showed their irritation, which pleased Phoebe. Phoebe loved her little sister and she had no intention of harming her. From the age of thirteen Phoebe spent more time away from home and sometimes did not return until the early hours of the morning. It made her little sister think she was driving Phoebe away, but she assured Prue that she was in no way to blame.

On a warm June night at the age of fifteen, Phoebe was walking through the wood at the north side of the housing estate where she lived. She was heading for her worst nightmare, as she made her way homeward. When she got to her house, her father was waiting outside the door and Phoebe knew she was in trouble again. She stood defiantly in front of him and Albert Cross glared at his oldest daughter.

'You didn't have to wait up for me,' Phoebe said, insolently.

Albert Cross moved back into the open doorway and picked up a suitcase and stood it at his daughter's feet.

'What's this?' she asked in a trembling voice.

He told Phoebe she was uncontrollable, and they had had enough of her and they were going to find another home for her. Albert told her to pick up the suitcase, which she did at once as the sound of his voice was unnerving her. He marched her to the large mansion at the rear end of the estate. It was owned by a certain psychologist named Brian Stonehouse. The large grand house and the owner had an air of mystery over them. As Phoebe was forced down the path by her father towards the front entrance of the large house, she got the feeling once she entered the formidable house, she would not be coming out.

They entered the house and walked down a large spacious hallway. Albert came to the second door on the right and knocked on it and a gruff voice from inside the room told them to enter. Albert opened the door and pushed his daughter into the room and closed the door behind her, he turned away and left the house, hoping he would not see Phoebe again.

Phoebe stood in the middle of a large room furnished as an office and consulting room; it had pink walls and a grey ceiling. She stared across the room in apprehension at a large built man in a grey suit sitting behind a large mahogany desk. He gave her a warm smile and motioned her to move closer to the desk. She left the suitcase on the floor and stood in stony silence behind the desk. Dr Stonehouse assured Phoebe there was nothing to be frightened of; he just wanted to have a talk with her and find out what the problem was.

The problem as Phoebe saw it was, she and her father had grown apart as he found out Phoebe was not going to be the daughter he wanted. She did not care he was a scientist and did not want to know about his work at the Research Laboratories. Phoebe was suspicious of him and his work, when she learned the housing estate was part of the laboratory complex and she felt her life was going to be worked out by them. Phoebe had a mind and a will of her own and she wanted the right to make her own mind up at what course she was going to take in life.

As Stonehouse started to ask her questions the door behind him opened and a tall slim man in a charcoal coloured suit stepped into the room and stood beside the seated psychologist. He stared at Phoebe with yellowy hypnotic eyes. He had a hawkish thin face with long nose and thin lips. Phoebe found the man cold and evil; he was a person she would have to be wary of. Phoebe looked down at the floor; she did not see the change in the man's expression. His false smile turned into a look of frustration.

Phoebe treated the interview with Stonehouse, with boredom and disinterest. She wanted to get away, she wanted to run away and leave her troubles behind her, but for Phoebe, her troubles were just beginning. She stared at the tall man as he tried to outstare her. She imagined he was trying to see inside her head.

He stared into her wide coal black eyes and he tried to visualize the mind behind them. The round pretty face showed no fear; Phoebe was not going to be intimidated by the tall evil looking man. After the interview was over, Stonehouse stood up and walked round the desk and laid a comforting hand on her shoulder. He told Phoebe she would be staying, and he was going to take Phoebe to her room. Phoebe picked up her suitcase and followed Stonehouse out of the room into the hallway. She followed up a large staircase that curved up towards a long passage. Phoebe gazed around the mansion in amazement; she was impressed with the grandeur and splendour of Dr Stonehouse's home. Phoebe followed him up to the halfway point up the passage and he stopped and opened a door and motioned her to enter the room. Phoebe opened the door and walked into a large spacious bedroom luxuriously carpeted. She laid her suitcase on a large bed and looked around her; Stonehouse stood beside her.

'What is going to happen to me?' Phoebe wanted to know.

'There's no need to be distressed, you are perfectly safe. We'll soon find someone more suited to your needs to take you in,' he said.

He left the room to let her get settled in. Phoebe crossed the bedroom to another door and opened it and went in and the light came on automatically and she found herself in the bathroom. Phoebe peeled off her clothes and went to the shower and let the hot water run over her body.

'She's the one.'

Stonehouse had entered his consulting room and found his dark companion sitting at his desk.

'Good, her father doesn't seem to care what happens to her,' Stonehouse said.

'She's a wild child, Albert doesn't understand her.'

'But you do.'

Dr Stonehouse stared at his companion as he grinned at him and nodded his head.

'Of course, she has a strong mind and she will be a challenge, just what my associates want.'

Phoebe returned to the bedroom with a large bath towel wrapped round her body. She went to the bed and opened the suitcase her father had packed. She took out her clothes and carried them to a large teak wardrobe; she placed the empty suitcase under the bed. She heard a slight sound by the door, and she spun round and glared at the tall threatening figure of Stonehouse's strange companion. The bright yellowy eyes regarded her with interest.

'Do you have to creep up on people,' Phoebe complained angrily.

A ghost of a smile flitted over the thin lips.

'Did I frighten you?'

The sharp piercing voice was making fun of her.

'Of course not,' she said.

Then why are your knees knocking together

'Good – because I'm not here to harm you,' he said.

Phoebe was not so sure, the voice lacked sincerity.

'You intrigue me; I find your dark eyes fascinating.'

As they stared at each other Phoebe felt a sensation inside her head, like the time when she first set eyes on this mysterious stranger. Phoebe had a strange feeling he was somehow trying to get inside her head. Phoebe was sure she was strong enough to keep him at bay.

'You are strong willed and can stand up for yourself.'

He placed a hand on her shoulder, and it made her body shiver.

'I'm sure you are ready for the challenge ahead of you.'

He moved away from her and silently left the room, closing the door behind him. Phoebe shivered and goose pimples covered her skin. Phoebe locked the door and turned off the light and made her way to the bed and pulled the towel from her body and slid under the sheets; she tried to get some sleep, but he invaded her dreams like a dark phantom, warning her of bad things to come.

Phoebe woke late morning and bright sunshine came through the window. She sat up and gazed round the room; nothing had changed, and nobody was standing in a corner watching her. Phoebe thought about her sister and if she had been told she would never see her older sister again. Their father would make sure they never came together again. Phoebe knew she was in danger, but from who or what she could only guess.

Phoebe got out of bed and got dressed. She left the bedroom and went down the stairs and met Stonehouse in the hallway. He asked her if she was ready for breakfast; she nodded her head. He gazed at the short olive-green dress she wore and told Phoebe she looked very pretty in it. After breakfast he took her to his study a large room with walls full of racks of books.

'Will I be allowed out of the house?'

Stonehouse stared at her and tried to imagine what was going on in her mind.

'Of course, are you thinking of running away?'

Phoebe shook her head; she wanted to see her sister before she disappeared.

'I wouldn't get very far; I have no money and I want to say goodbye to Prue before I leave here.'

'I can help you there, I shall put you to work and I'll pay a good wage,' he offered.

Phoebe was surprised, she was not expecting that; it was not going to put Phoebe off her guard.

'Thank you, I appreciate that, I hope I won't let you down.'

After three days of working as Dr Stonehouse's secretary, Phoebe had still not managed to get outside; she was kept so busy she was unable to leave the great house. Both Dr Stonehouse and his freaky companion were trying to work out what was going on in her head. But she wanted to keep her secrets to herself. While they were keeping in the house Phoebe decided to find out if they had any secrets, they wanted hidden, she wanted to find out if there were any skeletons in Dr Stonehouse's cupboards.

The fourth night she crept out of bed and put on a black sweater and jeans. She opened the door of her room and stepped out into the passage and stood and listened for any sound and the darkness was all quiet. She closed the door quietly and turned left and that took her to a junction, and she took the left fork and made her way slowly to what she knew would be the stairway up to the top floor of the house. She went slowly and quietly up the stairway and as she reached the top the door before her slid upwards and a tall dark figure was silhouetted against a bright light.

'What are you doing here?'

The piercing voice was cold and menacing.

'I couldn't sleep so I went for a walk, I must have lost my way in the dark,' Phoebe said.

He grabbed her by the left arm above the elbow.

'You've lost your way all right, in more ways than one.'

He pulled her over the threshold into the bright light and the door slid down. She looked him in the yellowy eye.

'What are you going to do with me?' Phoebe tried to hide her fear.

'You'll soon find out.'

He kept a tight grip on her arm and almost pulled her along a short passage. At the end the panel slid up and they entered a large lighted room filled with machinery. He took her to one side of the room and sat her in a metal chair; he clasped her wrists to the arms of the chair. Her dark eyes glared up at him, her face was reddening, and he could see her fear was being replaced by anger. He grinned at her and placed a domed headset on her, which covered her eyes. She could hear him moving about.

'Keep calm, Phoebe, you're not going to be harmed.'

Phoebe did not believe him; she was not here for her health. The headset started to hum and vibrate softly, Phoebe felt a throbbing inside her head. She heard footsteps approaching and a vibrant female voice spoke out.

'Who is this female?'

'Phoebe, she's a very favourable subject.'

'I hope she's better than your other subjects,' the female said.

'Absolutely, Phoebe is just what we are looking for,' the man said.

The throbbing in her head was getting worse, she felt as if something was pulling at her brain, and then she passed out.

When Phoebe came to, she found herself lying on a hard floor, she was surrounded by darkness. She heard a slight sound nearby.

'Who's there?'

Phoebe sat up and stared into the darkness; a hand settled on her shoulder and she almost screamed.

'Don't be scared, we are in the same boat,' a female voice said.

The hand moved from her shoulder and caressed her cheek.

'Who are you?' Phoebe wanted to know.

'Amy Thornton.'

Phoebe knew Amy by sight but had never talked to the older girl.

'You are Phoebe Cross, you have a bad reputation, I can understand why Dr Stonehouse has you here,' Amy said.

Phoebe stood up, she wished there was light so she could see. Amy was four years older than her and Phoebe would have liked to keep an eye on the girl.

'You shouldn't believe all the stories you hear about me.'

'I don't,' Amy assured her.

Amy told her they were in a small room with no windows and one door which is locked.

'How long have you been here?' Phoebe asked.

'Five days.'

'Your parents must be worried about you; do they know Dr Stonehouse has got you in his house?'

'My parents want me out of the way,' Amy said, dramatically.

Phoebe knew what she meant, and Phoebe told Amy she was here for the same reason.

'I wonder when they are going to do it.'

'Do what?' Phoebe inquired.

'Kill us, of course.'

That was what Phoebe thought Amy would say. But Phoebe was sure she would not be killed yet, she was sure Dr Stonehouse's companion had other ideas about her fate.

'Perhaps they have something else in store for us – before I ended up in here, I was sat in a chair and wired to a machine,' Phoebe said.

'They must have done something to your mind, and they put you here to kill me,' Amy said, nervously.

'I don't think so, I have no intention of harming you, my anger is directed at Dr Stonehouse and his freaky associate,' Phoebe said.

'You've met the evil one?'

'Yes, do you know if he has a name?'

'No, I know nothing about him, only that he is cold and evil, he can get inside your head,' Amy said with fear in her voice.

Phoebe assured Amy he had not got in her head yet.

'You are lucky, perhaps he wired you to the computer to see why he had failed to get a hold of your mind,' Amy said.

'It wasn't a very pleasant experience,' Phoebe said.

'You can be sure things will get more unpleasant when he comes back for you,' Amy assured her.

Phoebe was well aware of that, there was only one thing in her mind and that was escape. If they failed to take over her mind, they would kill her, and they would take her sister and experiment on her. Phoebe had to make sure that did not happen.

'I'm not going to let him take me without a fight,' Phoebe said, defiantly.

A large shaft of light cut through the darkness and Phoebe saw the girl she had been talking to, Amy Thornton, was sitting on the side of a metal bed; she wore a white tennis dress, and Phoebe was standing within touching distance of the girl. Amy looked as if she had been through hell and Phoebe guessed the girl probably had and she was about to go through the same hell herself. She turned her head to face the source of the shaft of light. He stood tall and lean in the open doorway. He called her name and Phoebe faced Amy again.

'It looks as if I'm wanted, if I get the impossible chance of freedom for us both, I shall take it, and I shall not forget you are here, Amy,' Phoebe promised.

Phoebe was about to move away from Amy, when the girl shot out a hand and grabbed her arm.

'He's not human, Phoebe.'

'I've worked that out already,' Phoebe said.

Amy shook her head and her long fair hair cascaded over her thin shoulders.

'Things are not as they seem, he is not like us,' Amy said.

The wide eyes stared intently at her; the gaunt features of Amy's thin face brought a chill to Phoebe's mind and body. Phoebe walked away from Amy and approached her captor. He grabbed her by the arm and pulled her into the passage, the door slid shut, at the other end of the passage the door slid open and Phoebe was pulled into the large machinery filled room where she had been clamped to a metal chair and wired to the computer. There were two tall menacing figures in the room and she finally understood the meaning of Amy's last words to her. The two beings her captor dragged her towards were not human; they were not even of this planet.

Well, Phoebe, my girl, you are really in it this time.

One of them was obviously female and almost seven-foot-tall, her slim body was hidden by a long flowing blue gown that came down to her ankles. Phoebe gazed at the head, which was domed, and the short cut glossy hair was red, the face was thin, and the wide ruby red eyes were deep set, they bored into her skull like lasers.

'This is Zindra, she has an assignment here on Earth and you are going to help her.'

Phoebe looked away from the piercing red eyes.

'And if I don't you will kill me,' Phoebe observed.

The man tightened his grip on her arm.

'You have no choice; you will do what we tell you.'

She always had a choice, Phoebe was sure of that, she knew her own mind. The tall alien female moved closer to her. Phoebe felt small under the gaze of the bright ruby red eyes.

'You don't agree.'

The voice was sharp and vibrating.

'Your friend here has been trying to get a hold of my mind ever since we met. He hasn't succeeded yet,' Phoebe said, clearly and coolly.

'You have a strong mind, but we only have to find a weakness and your mind will be ours,' Zindra said

'Not if I have anything to do with it,' Phoebe said, defiantly.

Phoebe was dragged over to the computer and sat in the metal chair, her arms and legs were clamped to it. The domed headset was placed on her and all went dark. Her body could not help her now; Phoebe had to rely on her mind to get her out of this one. The headset started to hum, and her head started to throb. Phoebe had no memory of what had happened to her, when she was first wired to their computer. The only thing she could rely on that was a help to her, was the fact they were trying again, which meant their first attempt to get inside her head had failed.

She had a headache and had a sudden feeling of something tugging at her brain. Phoebe suddenly thought of her sister, why Prue should come into her mind Phoebe was not sure. She hoped the girl was safe. Phoebe wished they were together and far away from here and these people that were trying to destroy her. Phoebe felt a hot anger towards her father, who had sent her here to be tortured and experimented on. Her hands balled into tight fists. Her anger turned to blind rage, she wanted to lash out at her enemies, but she could not, she was tied down.

All feeling and sense were suddenly gone. When Phoebe came back to consciousness her head was still covered, but there was no sound and no bad feelings inside her head. She wrestled with the clamps that held her wrists and they suddenly became free. She put her hands up to her head and pulled off the headset. She was alone in the room and she let the headset fall to the floor. Phoebe unclamped her legs from the metal chair and stood up. She looked round the room and spied the doorway she had entered the room by; she strode over to it and hoped it would open for her. The door slid away, and she entered the passage beyond. She walked to the end of it and the other door slid away to allow her to enter Amy's prison. The girl leapt off the bunk and ran to Phoebe. She could not believe what she was seeing.

'I told you if I get the chance of freeing us both I would grab it.'

'That was hours ago, I thought they had killed you,' Amy said in an excited voice.

'How long?' Phoebe inquired.

Amy pointed to her luminous watch, and told Phoebe she had been taken away five hours ago. She could not believe what she was hearing, it seemed as if she had only left the room moments ago. She told Amy what had happened to her and Phoebe suddenly realised she must have passed out while she had been wired to the computer and had been out for five hours. They must have thought she was not coming to and left her sitting there alone.

'What are you going to do now?' Amy asked.

Phoebe grabbed her hand and guided Amy out of her prison and into the passage.

'We've been locked up in this place for long enough; we are going to find a way out,' Phoebe said, confidently.

They entered the computer room and thankfully found it unoccupied. Phoebe still holding Amy's hand made her way to the door that would give them access to the house and possible freedom. The door slid open and they made their way down the steps to the landing. Nobody challenged them and Phoebe took Amy to the room she had been staying in and showed her to the bathroom. While Amy had a shower Phoebe went down the stairs and checked all the downstairs rooms and found them all unoccupied. Dr Stonehouse and his creepy associate did not seem to be about. When Phoebe returned to her room, she found Amy sitting on the bed with a bath towel wrapped round her body.

'There doesn't seem to be anyone about, so hopefully we can just walk out of here,' Phoebe said.

Amy stood up and put her arms round Phoebe and hugged her.

'You've saved my life; I'm indebted to you.'

Phoebe kissed her on the cheek.

'That's all right, I'm just glad to help,' Phoebe assured her.

Amy removed the towel and put her underwear and dress back on.

'Will you go back home?'

Amy shook her head violently.

'No, my parents want me dead, they have changed.'

'Have you got any friends you can go to?' Phoebe asked.

'Zenobia has an apartment in the city, I can stay with her,' Amy replied.

They walked to the door and Phoebe opened it and stepped out and told Amy all was clear. They went downstairs and went into the large kitchen and left the house by the back door. They hugged each other and wished each other luck and went their separate ways.

Phoebe still had her key and she opened the door, then she became aware of him lying in wait for her in the darkness. He pushed her into the hallway and threw her against a wall and knocked the wind out of her; then he dragged her up the stairs. Phoebe saw her young sister come out of her bedroom to see what the noise was. Phoebe was thrown against her sister and Prue was knocked backwards into her bedroom, Phoebe was kicked viciously several times before being pulled into the bedroom and the door was slammed and locked. Phoebe sat up on the floor; her body hurt all over; her little sister clung to her, asking her to explain what was happening. Phoebe listened to the noises and screams that came from the next room. Then there was silence then she heard footsteps outside the door telling her he was coming back to cause her more pain.

The door opened and she saw her sister dive under the bed, he grabbed Phoebe and threw her round the room as if she was lightweight, she cried out in pain. He dragged her into the next room, and she gazed on the carnage in horror, he stood over her like a carnivore getting ready to tear her apart. Phoebe was sure she was going to end up like her parents. He moved down on her and set about her, Phoebe closed her eyes and gritted her teeth; she tried to blank her mind of the things he was doing to her.

Sometime later he was gone. Phoebe struggled to get to the next room, and she called out to her little sister. Prue wriggled from under the bed and went to her older sister; Phoebe took Prue's small face in her hands.

'Listen to me, Prue darling,' Phoebe's voice was weak and shaky.

'You must forget what you've seen. If you know nothing, no one can hurt you. You must do as I say; we are both in danger, only you by wiping this from your mind can save us both.'

Tears ran down Prue's cheeks; Phoebe kissed her on the forehead.

'You know how much I love you, little sis. You must do this for me; nod your head so I know you understand. You must keep silent about this, if they ask you about it, you must tell them you don't remember.'

Her little sister nodded her head and Phoebe kissed her on the cheek.

'Good girl, sweetie. I will be all right as long as you keep silent. We are going to be apart for some time, but don't worry about me; we shall be reunited one day.'

The police came and dragged her away. The police van she was in was involved in an accident and Phoebe took her chance to escape. Phoebe made sure she put some distance between her sister and herself; the further apart they were the safer her little sister was. Phoebe hoped he would come looking for her and leave Prue alone. The killer of her parents caught her a few times and tormented her and beat her, but Phoebe managed to escape him. He did not want to kill her, just cause her pain and humiliation. He was having fun with her. Phoebe longed for the time when she could turn the tables and rent her rage on him, but for the moment he was the stronger, he was the experienced predator; she had to wait for her chance and Phoebe was good at waiting.

DECEMBER 2134

Phoebe stood and stared out of the window and watched the snow drift across the city. Somewhere out there was her sister, wondering if her older sister was still alive and sane. Phoebe had kept hold of her sanity as she needed it to get revenge on those who hurt her and her little sister. Phoebe had almost been tipped over the edge a few times, but she was well aware madness was not going to help her get what she wanted. Phoebe focused her mind on plan at hand. She turned away from the window and gazed across the room at Samantha, who was sat on a couch with her hands tied together behind her back and her ankles were also tied together. Carrie Scott was in the process of untying them. She had just come into the room.

'What are you doing?' Phoebe asked.

Carrie untied Samantha's ankles and reached behind the tall girl's back and untied her wrists. She turned to Phoebe who was walking steadily towards her.

'I'm not having a girl in her condition tied up like that,' Carrie said, coldly.

'Yes, I forgot you were the caring nurse,' Phoebe said, in a sarcastic voice she really did not mean.

Samantha gazed at Phoebe. She wore a black dress that came down to her knees, she had grown her jet-black hair, it was now thick and bushy, and the dark eyes were wide and menacing. She was just less than six foot in height, and she was big and strongly built. Her round pretty face and expression spoke volumes, Samantha could see she had been through hell and survived. Samantha felt a deep respect for the girl, as she been through all sorts of hell herself.

'If there is something you want me to help you with, you only have to ask,' Samantha said.

Phoebe gave her a wry smile.

'You are going to help all right, Sam.'

Phoebe turned to Carrie and told her to make some tea for their guest.

'I'm glad your enemies have failed to kill you, it's good to see you again.'

'They don't just want me dead, which would be too easy; they want to drive me out of my mind. I want more freedom so I can fight back. I want the authorities off my back; that's where you can help me.'

Phoebe sat on the couch next to Samantha.

'Your friends are in military intelligence; I have information their boss would be very interested in. I want you to set up a trade, amnesty for me and I will give them the information.'

Samantha saw nothing difficult in that and asked Phoebe to give her a phone. Carrie had come in with three mugs of tea and Phoebe asked her to give Samantha her mobile phone.

Janice was explaining to Steven what she had read in the file Bishop had given her to read, when his mobile phone bleeped. He took it out of his pocket and put it to his ear, then looked across the table at Janice.

'It's Sam.'

Samantha told him to contact General Heywood; she wanted to speak to him urgently. Steven told Janice to use her mobile to contact the General, while he kept Samantha on the line.

'Is Phoebe there with you?' he asked her.

Samantha gazed at Phoebe, who was walking aimlessly round the room sipping her tea; Carrie was sat in an armchair gazing at her friend.

'Yes.'

Steven warned her to watch Phoebe closely, he told her about a file on Phoebe written by Dr Stonehouse. Steven told Samantha that Phoebe had been experimented on, using electronics to study her mind. Steven warned Samantha Phoebe could be dangerous; she was a manic-depressive with a touch of paranoia.

'I'm not surprised after what she has been through, she's not mad, she's speaking clearly and acting sanely.'

Phoebe had stopped moving and was staring at her.

'They've been reading a file written by Dr Stonehouse, it is not very complimentary,' Samantha told her.

'I can imagine,' Phoebe said.

Samantha assured Steven Phoebe was not going to harm her and he had no need to worry. She looked across at Phoebe.

'Do you want your sister to know you are here, Phoebe?'

Phoebe moved closer to the couch.

'What has Prue been up to?'

Samantha told her about Xanthe entering the Research Laboratories to get information on Amy Thornton, a friend of a friend of hers.

'The little fool, I could have told her about Amy. The friend wouldn't be Zenobia Madison by any chance?'

Samantha nodded her head. Phoebe had not known the woman was back in the country.

'I wonder why Prue picked a strange name like Xanthe, to call herself.'

Samantha shook her head and told Phoebe she would have to ask her sister about that.

An hour later General Heywood drove up to the house; the Premier was with him. Carrie opened the door for them and said Phoebe and Samantha were in the lounge waiting for them. The General walked into the room and stopped dead in his tracks when he saw Samantha was heavily pregnant.

'You've been busy, who's the father?' Heywood inquired.

Samantha gave him a wide smile and told him to mind his own business.

'What is it, a boy or girl?' asked Graham Mullen who was standing behind the General.

'It's a girl and her name will be Sally.'

General Heywood turned to Phoebe who was sitting in an armchair.

'You have some information for me?' he asked.

'When I get my amnesty, I have things to do and I can't do it with the authorities chasing after me.'

Graham Mullen stepped forward and gave Phoebe some documents.

'The information about you on the database has been wiped and replaced with more favourable facts. You are a free girl again, Phoebe,' Graham informed her.

'Thank you, sir, I appreciate this, I really did not kill my parents, but I know who did, I don't know his name, but I will get him or die trying, it's me or him,' Phoebe said.

'If you need any help in your quest, let me know,' Graham said.

Phoebe told the two men about Dr Stonehouse and his mystery associate and how they had been experimenting with the young boys and girls that had lived on the estate, like they had with Phoebe herself with the help of an alien female being called Zindra. They also had been experimenting on Samantha when they had her at Stonehouse clinic; they had got Phoebe to help them fit the implants to Samantha's head, which was why she knew how to remove them without damaging Samantha's head or brain.

'You didn't tell me that,' Samantha said.

'I thought you might think I'd helped them willingly,' Phoebe told her.

CHAPTER LV:

THE POWER OF ZINDRA

Phoebe entered the foyer of the Zen Industries Building, Jacqui Taylor was sitting at the reception desk, and she was talking to Christopher Thornton, who stood beside her. Jacqui turned her head and saw a well-built girl approaching the desk. She pointed the visitor out to Christopher. He greeted her with a smile and asked her if he could help her.

'I was told my sister works here, I'm Phoebe Cross.'

Christopher and Jacqui gazed at each other in surprise.

'She's out at the moment, but I would like to speak to you, Phoebe,' Christopher said.

Christopher guided Phoebe into a small office behind the reception desk, he pulled up a chair for her and he sat behind the desk. Christopher told her he was Zenobia's security officer.

'Your sister discovered a letter written by my sister, Amy and she mentions your name,' he said.

Phoebe told him how she had met Amy in Dr Stonehouse's old mansion.

'I had hoped when we escaped that house that Amy might have been able to get some help from one of her friends, but I discovered later she had been found drowned in the river close to the Experimental Laboratories. I'm very sorry for you, I liked her,' Phoebe said.

'Amy told me to look you up and thank you for rescuing her from the house.'

'It was a case of out of the frying pan into the fire for the both of us; whoever is to blame I shall make sure they pay for her death,' Phoebe assured him.

'If you need any help let me know,' he said.

'I will, thank you,' Phoebe said.

Xanthe drove her car out of the compound which housed Zenobia's castle home. She would be glad to get back to her normal work; she was not cut out to play the spy, she would leave that sort of thing to her older sister, if she was still alive. She drove at a leisurely speed, she came alongside a right hand turning on the road and a large white van shot out at her and she tried to swerve out of the way, but the van struck her car and knocked her off the road. She switched off the motor, a tall slim man got out of the van and ran to her car and opened the car door and dragged her out and struck her hard over the head and knocked her senseless.

Xanthe came to; She was sitting at a conference table, she was in a large compartment, she was not alone – standing on the other side of the table was the tallest female she had ever seen. She gazed at the long thin face and domed head, the deep set ruby red eyes glazed back at her with contempt. Xanthe could feel the power of the seven-foot female like something tangible. Xanthe returned her malevolent stare with a defiant stare of her own.

Zindra had an arrogant single-mindedness that was a trademark of her species. She had a very malignant character that made her own kind tread softly around her. The evil mind inside her head was amazed the captive was not trembling with fear.

'What are you going to do to me?'

'Nothing yet, I'm sure we'll find a use for you later,' Zindra said in a cold vibrating voice.

A door slid open behind her and a huge bulky alien came in and pulled Xanthe out of her chair. She stared at the reptilian monster with shock, she felt it was going to tear her to pieces. It dragged her out of the compartment and along a dimly lit passage. At the end of the passage the alien opened a hatch and pushed her through the opening and closed the hatch. She was sat on a cold metal floor; the compartment was dimly lit, and it was full of shadows. She heard a sound of movement in front of her.

'You've come to join the party, Xanthe; the accommodation is basic to say the least.'

A dishevelled figure moved out of the shadows. Xanthe stared at the small grubby round face, her eyes filled with tears; it was her friend Lisa Booth.

Phoebe drove alongside the river as she headed for the Experimental Laboratories. Samantha relaxed on the back seat. She had persuaded Phoebe to help her, as Naomi was not around, and Phoebe had met the alien menace they were fighting. Phoebe gave her a description of Zindra and told Samantha the alien female was a powerful being. Steven and Janice would be leading a search to find Dr Stonehouse and his mystery associate, who was also a serial killer. Phoebe was sure if they found them, it would lead them to Zindra's power base.

Phoebe drove through the main gate and made for the security hut, where Phoebe and Samantha showed their passes to the guard. Phoebe parked the car and the two girls made for the main entrance. Samantha carried the metal case containing the lead box that contained the alien power cell. They entered the main building and they approached the reception desk; Carol Moreland noticed the buxom girl in the black dress had similar facial features to Xanthe, she also knew the tall ginger haired girl was called Samantha, Sarah had mentioned her. Carol took their ID discs and placed them in the desktop computer.

'I'm not sure I will be any use to you, Sam, I'm not very scientific,' Phoebe said, as they passed through some double doors that led to a long white-walled corridor.

'You'll be fine; it will give us a chance to get to know each other. You've seen similarities between me and this character Zindra.'

'I did not know you were a mind reader,' Phoebe said.

'I'm not, I saw it in your expression and voice when you described Zindra to me. I'm only half alien, my father was human, my mother is a different race to Zindra, she is here to find my mother and kill her and me as well,' Samantha explained.

As they walked along the corridor Samantha checked the door numbers until she got the one that matched the number on the electronic key that Carol had given her. She found the right door and slid the key into the electronic lock and tapped out the security number on the door keypad. The door slid open and they walked into the laboratory. Henry Jones was working at the computer; he turned and greeted them with a boyish smile.

'I see you got the short straw, Henry,' Samantha said.

'A straw I was happy to receive, Melanie is here with me,' he said.

Samantha knew the girl – she was working with Dr Hilary Calvert. She had heard Melanie McAllister did not get on with the General.

'I thought she was the general dogsbody,' Samantha said.

Henry shook his head.

'You do Melanie a disservice. She is a very bright girl and if you had witnessed the fights she had with the General, you would see her in a different light,' Henry assured her.

While they were talking Henry gazed past Samantha and ran a critical eye over her companion in the black dress.

'Who's your friend?'

Samantha introduced him to Phoebe. As they shook hands Henry felt himself being drawn in by the dark pools of her captivating eyes.

Samantha placed the case on the work bench in one corner of the room and opened it up. She took out the lead box and placed it on the bench. She flitted through the documents at the bottom of the case and pulled out a computer disc. She strode over to the computer and called Phoebe over to her.

Samantha slid the disc in the slot and the screen lit up. Phoebe stayed a little distance away. Samantha grabbed her arm and pulled her closer.

'It's all right, Phoebe, I'm not going to wire you into the computer, I just want to give you an idea of the work we will be doing,' Samantha explained.

Samantha sat her firmly down on the chair; Phoebe stared at the computer screen, which was showing Samantha and Naomi working on the prototype machine built by Dr Sally Hamilton. Phoebe concentrated on the visual report of their work, while Samantha went back to the work bench. She put on a pair of protective gloves and then opened up the lead box. She was bathed in a cold green light. She moved back slightly from the work bench. Henry came and stood beside her.

'What's that?' he asked.

'It's an alien power cell and Angie Russell found it and that's what killed her.'

The door slid open and a tall slim figure walked into the laboratory. Samantha did not have to turn around to see who it was. The hairs on the back of her neck stood up and a cold chill ran through her body. The baby inside her detected it and started to kick.

'I've been ordered to help you,' a voice said behind her.

Samantha took control of her and spun round. The tall thin girl with the pale face and long silvery blonde stood silent and expressionless, waiting for Samantha to give her the first instructions. The clone Jennifer Russell gazed at Samantha's expression of distaste with interest.

'It's nice to see you again, also, Samantha.'

She gave Samantha a wry smile.

'I promise, I won't cause you any grief and I will do as you tell me.'

Samantha did not believe a word of it. She was going to keep a sharp eye on her and if she caused any trouble, Samantha would have her thrown out and thrown in the nearby river.

Jennifer Russell moved round Samantha and gazed at the lead box and the glowing green crystal it contained.

'What do you think of it?' Samantha asked.

The clone could feel the alienness of the power cell. The cold energy caressed her pale skin.

'It's not of this world,' was her only comment.

'Go to the top of the class,' Samantha said.

Henry giggled and the clone stared at him. Her brain functioned on logic and Samantha's sarcastic remark was lost on her.

'It would help if you told me, what you were going to use it for,' the clone said.

Fair enough, Samantha thought. Samantha told the clone to follow her and they went to the computer and Phoebe turned and gave her a smile. She stood up and the clone sat in the chair she had vacated; Samantha reran the computer disc to give Jennifer Russell information on the work they were going to do.

'I've got to redesign that machine and condense it into a more workable machine,' Samantha told Phoebe.

Samantha guided her to a door on the left side of the computer and they entered a small room with lockers and cupboards. She opened one, found it full of clean white lab coats, and took one that would fit Phoebe and gave it to her, and Samantha selected one for her and put it on.

'That tall girl's not a relation of yours, is she? You two being so tall and you did not seem too pleased to see her.'

Samantha gave Phoebe a horrified expression.

'She's not a real person, that girl is a clone,' Samantha informed her.

It was Phoebe's turn to be horrified.

'You mean they clone humans here, is nothing sacred?'

'Jennifer Russell was not cloned here, the girl she was cloned from, lay in a coma since birth and they weren't sure if she would come out of it, so they cloned her, not successfully, I might add.'

They returned to the laboratory, Jennifer Russell was standing by the work bench gazing at the lead box and the contents. She was enthralled with what she had seen on the computer disc, it was a problem her brain could get its logical teeth into. She was also glad Samantha was not going to punish her for the things she had done to her.

'You are hoping to power the modification with this alien power cell.'

Samantha nodded her head. The girl was keen to get started, Samantha could see that, but it was going to be hard working with someone she could not stand.

'It's very hypnotic, the power cell draws your mind into it,' the clone observed.

Samantha gazed at the ice-blue eyes as they fell on her, she could almost hear the brain behind them ticking over as it ran over the information it had gained from the computer disc.

'To find the final stage your machine with evolve into, we'll have to use the computer, feed in the information of the original design and start from there.'

Samantha stared at her. The clone might be arrogant and overbearing, but she knew her stuff. Computers were her forte, so Samantha told her to get started. The thin pale face beamed, and she turned and strode over to the computer.

'Can you trust her?' Henry asked. Samantha shook her head.

'No, not an inch, but she's willing to help us.'

Samantha decided to buy her two friends a coffee and they left the laboratory and made their way to the lounge area. While they were sat down at a table, Steven joined them and gave Phoebe some bad news about her sister. Phoebe jumped out of her seat and asked Steven to take her to the place where her sister's car was found. Samantha told Henry to keep an eye on Jennifer Russell and then joined Phoebe and Steven.

The land was covered in a blanket of shining white snow. Phoebe stood by the crashed car, they had found out the vehicle that had hit it had been heavy and painted white. Phoebe told him it had been a large white van. She looked across at Samantha,

'I would rather have killed Prue myself, than let her fall into his hands,' Phoebe confessed.

Phoebe walked off road and made for the nearby wood. Samantha and Steven followed her. They walked through the wood in silence; Steven knew the place Phoebe was making for. On the other side of the wood was an abandoned farm. Zenobia Madison had inherited it from her father, though she did not know it, she had other things on her mind to occupy her. Phoebe stepped out of the wood her hands deep in the pockets of her fur lined coat. She stood still and surveyed the scene before her. Amongst the scatter of farm building were three police cars and two police vans. She watched the dark figures standing out in the whiteness of the thick carpet of snow. Phoebe moved forward; her boots trudged through the crisp snow. Steven and Samantha followed her, as she seemed to know where she was going.

'She's been here before,' Steven observed.

'I expect Phoebe was held here at some time or other. Tortured and tormented by her mystery man,' Samantha said.

'Pity we haven't got a name for him,' Steven said.

'Just call him Mr X, when we find Dr Stonehouse, he can tell us his name,' Samantha said,

Phoebe had moved forward past a parked police van; she stopped at a large two storey building. Phoebe stared at it as if something nasty was about to leap out of it and attack her. The door was open, and she walked into the building. The large room was devoid of furniture, the floor was covered with a thick layer of dust which had newly made footprints over it, and she could hear the sound of movement up on the second floor. Memories of the last time she entered the building. He had dragged her across the very same floor she stood on; he was going to give her the last painful punishment for not giving him what he wanted. Phoebe remembered she had felt no fear; she was past feeling fear, there was not much he could do to her that he had not done already. Up till then he had somehow been reluctant to kill her as it was not part of his agenda.

'Phoebe! Are you all right?' Samantha asked softly.

Phoebe remained rooted to the spot as she stared at something ahead of her. Phoebe stood silent in the present, but her mind was in the past. Samantha placed a hand on her shoulder and after a moment Phoebe turned her head and gazed at the tall girl with dark eyes full of pain and misery.

'This is it, Sam. This is the place.'

Phoebe moved forward followed by Samantha and Steven.

'What's wrong with her?'

Samantha silenced him with a wave of her hand.

Detective Sergeant Pearson came down the staircase at that moment. He could not believe his eyes when he saw Phoebe walking across the lower floor as large as life, almost larger than life. He looked up at Janice who was coming down behind him. He raced down the stairs and headed for Phoebe in a way that gave Janice the impression the detective did not know Phoebe was now free. As Phoebe got to the far wall Pearson grabbed her arm and she spun round, and he got the full glare of her bottomless dark eyes. It made him release her arm. She gave him a wry smile and took a document out of her coat pocket and gave it to him.

'Haven't they told you, Sergeant, I'm free of all charges against me, signed by the Premier himself,' she said.

The detective sergeant stared at the document of amnesty in disbelief; he knew his boss would be as shocked as he was.

'How did you get this, kidnap his daughter?'

Phoebe giggled and that made him madder. Steven stepped in between them.

'It's quite genuine, I assure you Phoebe is on our side now,' Steven told him.

Pearson shook his head.

'The governor's not going to like this.'

'He'll just have to get used to it,' Phoebe said, sternly

Pearson was sure Chief Inspector Roberts would not, as he had been chasing her for years and he wanted to lock her up and throw away the key.

'If he sees you, I suggest you speak very quickly, he'll most likely shoot first and ask questions afterwards.'

'That's why we're here, to make sure he doesn't,' Samantha said.

Pearson looked up at the tall girl as if wondering how she came to be so tall. Samantha was used to it now and kept her expression placid, so he would feel at ease in her presence. It was hard for Pearson to look up to a face that was over a foot above his head. He looked down and turned to Janice, who was of similar height as himself.

'Don't you find your friend's height intimidating?'

Janice laughed and shook her head.

'Of course not, Sam's quite harmless,' Janice assured him.

'I'll take your word for it,' the detective sergeant said.

Samantha smiled at him then joined Phoebe, who was standing by the wall and running her hands over it.

'What is it, Phoebe?'

Phoebe clawed at the wall as her mind went back into the past. Samantha could see by the girl's expression that Phoebe was now unaware of them standing round her. After a while her exploring fingers found a small panel and it lifted up to reveal a keypad. Phoebe ran her fingers over it. Suddenly the floor under Samantha's feet started to lift up and she jumped backwards and watched parts of the floor lift up to reveal a flight of steps. Phoebe moved to the gaping hole in the floor and started to descend the stone steps; Samantha decided to follow her at a slight distance.

Phoebe might know what she was stepping down to, but Samantha did not. Down below was a dull green light.

Phoebe moved off the bottom step. The damp cellar was lit up by an eerie green light; she stared across at the far wall in a trance-like state. She was looking into the past, she saw herself manacled to the wall, he stood over her, he was mad at her because he had failed to get inside her head, there was a barrier and he could not probe her mind. His alien associates had tried everything their technology possessed, but Phoebe remained impervious to their efforts to take over her body and soul. It was all coming back to Phoebe as she started to remember the memories that had been hidden to her. While they had her imprisoned in Dr Stonehouse's home, she had been brought here to this cellar to work on her. Zindra had gone away and he had brought her here for the last time to kill her and bury her somewhere about the abandoned farm, but he wanted to punish her for one last time. Phoebe had tried to blank out the pain and humiliation. Phoebe kept her eyes tight shut, she felt immense pain all over her and she felt tired and weak as he beat the strength out of her. A vision of her sister came to her mind, the person she was taking this pain for; she had to protect Prue at all costs even if it meant her death.

'What's happening, Phoebe, what do you see?' Samantha asked softly, as she placed a hand on her shoulder.

Phoebe stayed still as she watched a vision that she only could see.

'This is the place, I was brought here to see if I was the sort of person they wanted for their plans,' Phoebe said in a monotone voice.

'What was that, Phoebe?' Samantha asked, softly.

'That creature Zindra, some of her people had no bodies; just a mind; an essence. They wanted one of them to enter my head, but my brain somehow formed a barrier against them.'

Steven and Janice joined Samantha and she turned to them and put a finger to her lips.

'Of course, one person would be ideal for them, but I must protect her.'

'Xanthe,' Samantha called out.

'While they experimented on me, Prue would be safe, as long as they had me, they would not bother with my sister. That's why I had to defy Father and not be the daughter he wanted, I had to stay near to Prue, so save her from evil.'

The vision she watched came to an end, he had not killed her, and he just left her hanging limp in the manacles that kept her fixed to the wall. He left her to die, but months later someone had made their way down to the cellar and found her near death, but a spark remained, a part of her mind wanted revenge and more important she had a sister to protect, nothing mattered in the world but Prue. She had been taken to a hospital where the spark grew bright and she came out of the coma and when she was strong enough, she managed to make her escape from the hospital.

Phoebe turned and faced Samantha.

'I've failed Prue, now they have her at their mercy,' Phoebe said.

'If she loves you as much as you love her, your sister won't blame you. We will help you find her,' Samantha said.

They searched the cellar, but it had been stripped of machinery and only the eerie light remained. They climbed up the steps and left the building. Detective Sergeant Pearson stayed with them. Phoebe marched ahead through the snow past the two-storey building and she made for a long low building a hundred yards away. When she got to it Phoebe pulled open the huge door and stepped inside the building, Samantha was close behind her. She gazed across the large expanse of metal floor; the inside of the building was still and quiet. Janice ran a Geiger counter over the floor and got a high reading. Phoebe gazed at her and smiled.

'They had to have somewhere to hide their spacecraft,' Phoebe advised.

'Where is it now?' Steven asked.

They all looked around at each other hoping someone had the answer. Phoebe was aware that when they found it her sister would be there too.

They made their way back to the farmhouse, they met up with Detective Chief Inspector Charles Roberts, and he stared at Phoebe in surprise as his sergeant told him the girl was not wanted by the authorities anymore. He looked at Janice.

'What other startling news have you failed to inform me of?'

Janice assured him she was being honest with him; she just imagined his superiors would have informed the Chief Inspector about Phoebe.

'What did you find in the farmhouse?' Janice inquired.

They had found the farmhouse had been lived in recently and they found a coat belonging to Lisa Booth, but they found no clue as to what might have happened to her. Phoebe guessed her sister had a friend accompanying her wherever she was being held.

CHAPTER LVI:

VISIONS IN A GREEN EGG

Two hours later Samantha and Phoebe returned to the laboratory. The two police detectives and Steven went to visit Zenobia Madison to see if she had visited the abandoned farm since her return to England. Zenobia assured them she had not been near it, as she had other business that she was tied up with. Her father owned several properties in the area, and she had not had time to visit them all.

When Samantha and Phoebe walked into the laboratory, they found Jennifer Russell hard at work, assisted by Henry. Phoebe walked over to the computer and stared at the alien power cell that sat on the control desk inside a force field.

'It's a very powerful thing,' she said to Samantha.

'You were standing over the power cell when it was on the bench,' Samantha said.

'Do you think it was the cause of the visions I had at the old farm?'

Samantha nodded her head; she remembered the experiences she had when working with her mother's machine. Samantha gazed down at a small table beside the computer; on it was a smaller version of the prototype she had wrecked. Jennifer Russell turned off the force field and wearing protective gloves she picked up the power cell and placed it in an opening in the machine she had constructed.

'I had bombarded it with several isotopes, and I found its appetite insatiable,' the clone said.

'So is mine,' Phoebe said.

The four of them went to the canteen for lunch. After they had eaten, Henry went to the medical room to find Melanie, and Phoebe retired to her quarters to rest. Samantha and Jennifer Russell returned to the laboratory. They wired the new machine to the computer then Jennifer Russell activated it and a low vibrating hum filled the room and it bathed them in an eerie glow. Samantha sat in front of the machine and ran her fingers over the control box. The clone stood at the computer as it monitored the workings of the machine. Samantha closed her eyes and relaxed. A vision came to her mind.

The little girl woke suddenly in the middle of the night; she stared at the surrounding darkness. A voice had woken her, and she could not tell in what direction it had come. The girl sat.

Sammy. Sammy.

A soft whisper floated about her head; she could see no one else in the room. The disembodied voice spoke softly.

Sammy, can you hear me.

'Who are you? I don't see you,' the little girl said, in a fearful voice. The voice got colder.

Of course, you can't. I am inside your head.

That did not sound right to the little girl.

'How did you get there? I can't have anybody in my head, except me,' the girl observed logically.

That's what you think, I'm not overjoyed to be here, I can tell you. In fact, it I don't get out of here. I shall drive you mad.

The strange voice sounded cross – the little girl did not want to be driven mad.

'That would not be good for you, being in the head of a mad girl'.

Just get me out of here.

The voice sounded very angry, the little girl wished her mother was with her, would know what to do.

Silence, the voice had gone, the girl lay down and buried her head in her pillow and cried with fear.

In the morning the little girl woke and got dressed, she went to find her mother. The little girl told her of the strange dream she had had, the girl was sure it had been a dream. Her mother was disturbed at what her daughter had told her. The girl asked her mother if she had ever wanted another little girl to like her. The woman decided to tell her little daughter about her tiny twin sister that had been born dead. The little girl stared at her mother.

The next night she woke again, and she felt something stirring inside her head and the voice came to her again.

Sammy.

'I would have had a twin sister, but she died during birth,' the girl said to the surrounding darkness.

Died! How do you know if I am dead or alive? Can't give birth to twins, without mucking it up. She calls herself a mother. I shall give her a piece of my mind, when I am out of here.

'How are you going to do that?'

That machine your parents are working on, they must put you through an experiment with it.

'What if they won't do that?'

Force them, have a tantrum or something.

The voice went silent and the girl snuggled under the warm sheets and was soon asleep.

The girl did not have to have a tantrum, because the following afternoon, her father took her by the hand and led her to the machine and sat her in front of it. He told the girl there was nothing to be worried about. She was sure of that as she trusted her parents. She gave him one of her sweetest smiles to assure him of the fact.

'Concentrate on the green glow, Princess,' her father said.

The girl stared at the black and silver machine as her father activated it. The machine was long and bulky with switches and coils. It started to hum and vibrate; she gazed at the green glow filtering out of the front of the machine. The voice floated about her head.

Concentrate, Sammy, concentrate.

'I am,' the little girl said.

Her father looked across at her when he heard her speak.

'What is it, Princess?'

'Nothing, Daddy,' the girl said.

Keep your eyes on the green egg.

The girl stared intently at the oval green light in front of the machine. The man kept his eyes on his daughter's thin face; the bright green eyes stared ahead of her.

'Are you all right, Princess?'

The little girl did not answer her father; her mind was no longer inside her head. She wanted to scream but she had no voice and she had no body.

Oh damn! She has gone instead, what a mix up.

The girl's mother came into the room and went to her daughter; the man turned off the machine. The woman slapped her daughter on the cheek gently; the green eyes flickered and stared at the woman. The girl was glad to be in her body once again. She did not like the experience she had just gone through. She put her arms round her mother, and she was lifted off the chair and carried out of the room.

In the night she stayed awake as she lay in bed, the voice was soon with her again.

That machine is all wrong. No wonder it does not work properly.

'Something strange happened, I was in the dark and had no body,' the girl said.

You and me, both. The machine is too big, it needs condensing down and there is something missing.

'What's missing?' the girl wanted to know.

Ah, there is the rub.

Samantha shook her head and turned off the machine. She looked up at Jennifer Russell, who was stood by the control desk of the computer. She was fascinated by the machine and she wondered what was going through Samantha's mind as she sat in front of it. Samantha stood up and walked out of the laboratory and went to her quarters and lay on the bed. That was a shock to the system; she knew the little girl in the dream was herself. She was in two minds about continuing with the machine. She wanted to leave it and run and hide somewhere, but something was nagging at the back of her mind; the only way she was going to learn more about her was to continue and she wanted to rid herself of that annoying voice in her head.

Samantha got off the bed and undressed and slid between the sheets and into a troubled sleep.

The girl sat at a small round table; she was surrounded by darkness. On the table in front of her was a green glowing globe. The eerie green light obscured the girl's thin white face, the long blonde hair cascaded over her thin shoulders. The long thin fingers curved round the globe as it sat on a matt black plinth. The thin lips were fixed in a wry smile.

At first light Phoebe slid out of bed and showered, then got dressed. She made her way to the laboratory and found Jennifer Russell working at the computer. Henry Jones stood nearby watching her. Phoebe approached him.

'Sam not up yet?' she inquired.

Henry shook his head and Phoebe left the laboratory and made for Samantha's quarters. She knocked on the door several times and got no answer. She tried the door and found it unlocked, she opened it and walked into the room. Phoebe found Samantha still asleep in bed. She left the room and bought two cups of coffee and returned to Samantha's quarters. She sat on the edge of the bed and shook the sleeping girl. The green eyes flickered open and Samantha groaned.

'And Good Morning to you, too,' Phoebe said, amusingly.

Samantha sat up and Phoebe handed her a cup of strong coffee and she sipped it.

'You look as if you've had a rough night,' Phoebe commented.

Samantha gave her a weak smile; the vision and the dream had given her a headache.

'Not as rough as the ones you have to put up with.'

Phoebe drank her coffee, she wanted to put pain and misery and sleepless nights behind her. Phoebe wanted to keep her mind clear and alert; she had a sister to find.

'I have nothing to whinge about, Xanthe and Lisa are in a worse position than me.'

Jennifer Russell stood at the computer control desk and gazed at the screen. Henry stood by the machine and activated it. He stood away from the energy field created at the front of it. He did not have Samantha's lack of regard to personal safety, as she dived headfirst into every task she was given. He looked across at Jennifer Russell, who nodded to him to show she was getting results, as the computer monitored the experiment with the machine closely as it went through the data it received on how the machine worked. She was enthralled in her work with the strange machine; she found it fascinating. She gazed at the data on the computer screen and tried to analyse what she was seeing.

Henry suddenly looked towards the far wall that the front of the machine was facing; there was a circle of green light on it that was produced by the energy field that was being created by the machine. Inside the confines of the circle of light something was appearing.

Evelyn Stevens sat strapped firmly to the control seat; the headset probed her brain as the computer was linked to her mind. She yearned to be free, so through the computer she hoped to find a way out. The computer she was linked to start to draw data from the other computers in the facility, her mind sifted through the incoming data searching for something to use to free herself from the torment she felt. Then she saw it. Someone was running an experiment with a new mind machine.

Evelyn concentrated hard and she managed to make contact with the experiment.

Jennifer Russell was suddenly alert as she became aware of someone locking onto the experiment. Henry gazed in amazement at the vision in the green circle of light, it was of a girl strapped to a metal chair, the head was covered by a domed headset, but he could tell the sex of the person because she was wearing a black dress. He looked across at the Russell girl, who had her attention on the computer; he called her and pointed to the far wall. She gazed at the apparition in the circle of light.

'Fascinating.'

Henry turned off the machine and the light and girl disappeared. The girl turned back to the computer and continued with her task to modify the machine. She put her own theories to the computer; she stared at the screen as diagram after diagram was constructed and then being discounted as unreliable. Henry sat in the chair and watched the tall girl work at the computer. She was certainly dedicated to the experiment. After some time, she was rewarded from her hard endeavours, as she came up with the logical design approved by the computer.

'Eureka!'

Henry came and stood beside her and gazed at the computer screen.

'You're a genius,' Henry said.

The tall girl gazed at him and gave him a smile of satisfaction.

'I know.'

'Modest as ever,' Henry observed.

'Someone was locking onto our experiment – wherever that person is, that's where the vision in the machine's energy field originated from,' she informed him.

'Can you fix the position where the interference is coming from?' he inquired.

Jennifer Russell nodded, all the computers were connected to a central brain in the complex, she was sure she could plot the precise place the person was working from. Henry told her to get on with it and the tall girl ran her long thin fingers over the control desk and a map of the facility came onto the screen. After a while a tiny red light came on in the map and the girl pointed to it.

'There,' she said, triumphantly.

CHAPTER LVII:

THE DREAM MACHINE

Samantha walked into the laboratory mid-morning; Phoebe followed behind her. Henry and Jennifer Russell had started to construct the smaller modification to Samantha's machine. Henry walked away from the work bench and went to Samantha and guided her to the computer, she would see he was excited about something. She stood silently by the computer and listened to Henry as he explained how Jennifer Russell and the computer came up with the final blueprint. Samantha knew what the modification was going to look like before it came up on the screen. As she had already seen it in a dream. Henry also told her about the apparition created by the machine, and someone was trying to disrupt their experimenting through the computer system of the facility. Samantha was sure who this someone was. Henry was mystified by the wide smile on her face.

'Do I read from your expression that you know who it is?' Henry asked.

'Yes, it's a remarkable young girl called Evelyn, I was afraid she may have been murdered, but it seems the girl still lives.'

They went to the work bench and Jennifer Russell walked away and went to the computer. Henry grinned at Samantha as she gave a deep sigh of relief. All the rest of the day the four of them worked feverishly to bring the modification into reality. At the end of the day Samantha was being painfully pressurised by her body. Her mind raced as she felt the world crushing in on her. Her heart pounded in her chest and the new life in her belly kicked mercilessly. Samantha did not want to go into labour now. The baby wanted to be born, she was in a hurry to get out into the world and see what it was like. Samantha mind-linked with her baby in a hope of calming her down.

Samantha gazed at the pulsating green glow before her, sat on the table was the vision of her dream, the green globe sat on the matt black plinth, inside the globe was the alien power cell. The baby settled down and was still, Samantha gave a deep sigh of relief. She was being punished, she was angry, and she wanted Samantha to know it.

Hands settled onto her shoulders and started to massage them, she looked up at Phoebe who gave her a warm smile of sympathy.

'You look shattered.'

Samantha gave her a weary smile; Phoebe planted a firm kiss on her thin lips.

'Why don't you go and rest, I'll take care of here and I'll look in on you later,' Phoebe advised.

Samantha stood up on shaky legs. Phoebe stood by her to make sure she did not fall, after a few moments they made for the door, and outside in the passage Samantha turned to Phoebe.

'I want you to do something for me.'

'I'm here to give you all the help I can,' Phoebe assured her sincerely.

'There's a professor by the name of Frederick Fairclough here working with young people with special gifts.'

Phoebe nodded her head, she knew all about Professor Fairclough and his work, as she had been one of his subjects when she had been thirteen. Just like her father the good professor could not get rid of her fast enough. Samantha told her about Evelyn Stevens and the fact the young girl was being held captive somewhere in the facility. Samantha wanted to know if Fairclough had any idea where the girl was being held and if his work was a private venture or if it was being run by someone with a more sinister objective.

'See if he ever had Amy Thornton in his charge.'

'Do you think Fairclough may be responsible for her death?' Phoebe inquired.

'We're sure she was not responsible for her parents' death, but she would know who was and she had to be silenced.'

Phoebe saw Samantha to her quarters then went in search of Professor Frederick Fairclough. She went to the testing room first which was at the other end of the passage.

Francis Powell sat at the table and stared across it at the Professor who was testing him to see what special talent he was gifted with. His mind was only half on the interview, the other half was on Pamela Sisson who stood close to the two-way mirror, as if she was trying to look into it to see what was on the other side. Francis turned his head and gazed across the room where Pamela stood still and silent gazing into the two-way mirror. As if aware of his eyes on her, Pamela spun round and grinned at him.

'Are you all right, Pam?' Francis asked.

Pamela nodded her head and walked towards the conference table. Professor Fairclough could see Francis was not giving his full concentration to the interview. He obviously had his mind on the girl, he had wanted to test them separately, but they wanted to be together as if they had forged a bond between them.

'I think we should end it for the day,' the Professor said.

Francis and Pamela walked towards the door, until it opened, and they stopped dead in their tracks. They studied Phoebe intently as she walked towards them.

'Did that girl ever mention she had a sister?' Pamela inquired.

'No, there is a similarity,' Francis told her.

'I thought so too, it's the dark eyes,' Pamela said.

Phoebe walked past the two teenagers and approached the tall man in a navy-blue suit. She was glad to be out of the stare of the boy and the girl – for some reason they seemed to unnerve her. Francis walked out of the door; Pamela hung back and waited for the visitor to announce herself to the Professor.

Frederick Fairclough stared at the newcomer with a mixture of shock and surprise, he recognised Phoebe Cross in an instant, though the last time he had seen Phoebe, she was just thirteen. He had heard she had been cleared of her parents' death and was glad, as he did not believe she had done it. Phoebe had been a girl with a lot of anger inside her, but he was sure Phoebe was not capable of murder. She stood in front of him and he studied the face of the twenty-seven-year-old girl; the hardships she had gone through were etched on her face.

'Hullo Phoebe, I'd heard you are now a free girl.'

Phoebe smiled; she was glad he remembered her.

'Bad news travels fast.'

Fairclough offered her a seat and Phoebe sat down, he seated himself, so he faced her.

'It's not bad news to me, I was sure you did not kill your parents or anyone else. Now how can I help you?'

'A friend sent me to see you about Evelyn Stevens, we think the girl may be in danger.'

Fairclough had not stopped thinking of the young girl ever since she disappeared. He was still waiting in hope the girl would be found safe and well. He assured Phoebe he had no idea where the girl was, he mentioned the fact that her sister was around at the time of Evelyn's disappearance. He noticed a grave expression on Phoebe's face.

'Anything wrong, Phoebe?'

'My sister has gone missing also, her car was crashed, and she was taken by somebody.'

'Any ideas who it was?'

'The same person who has Evelyn, she is being held somewhere in this facility,' Phoebe said and waited for that information to sink in.

That piece of news brought mixed emotions: he was relieved to hear Phoebe was sure Evelyn was still alive, but he was anxious about her being held by someone intent on causing her distress.

'Have you any idea where exactly she is being held?'

'We are in the process of working that out now,' Phoebe assured him.

Fairclough stood up and paced the room, she watched him with interest.

'Did you ever come in contact with a girl named Amy Thornton? She was being tested here ten years ago, she was murdered and thrown into the river near here,' Phoebe said.

Fairclough stopped his pacing and spun round and faced her, the dark staring eyes were accusing as they studied his expression intently. He remembered the girl of thirteen with dark eyes and a power behind them, now fourteen years on the power awesome and he felt himself being drawn into the dark depths of Phoebe's staring eyes. He had no reason to lie to the girl and he was sure Phoebe would be able to detect every lie if he ever gave her any.

'Yes, I met her for an instant, but she never became part of my work and I did not kill her.'

Phoebe smiled and the dark eyes let him go and he relaxed.

'I was not accusing you of her killing.'

'No, but your eyes were,' he observed.

Fairclough sat down.

'I just wanted to be certain, Amy's brother and friends want justice for her murder.'

'If I knew anything about her murder, I would have told the police at the time,' he assured her.

'After the murder of my parents, Prue was brought here; I was hoping you could tell me about her, Prue is very special to me.'

The Professor gazed at the softening of Phoebe's expression, he saw the love she had for her younger sister on the sad expression, and he took her hand and squeezed it gently and told her of the timid and frightened twelve year old that was brought to his attention. Prue had had the same dark eyes, but they looked away from Fairclough when he faced her, as if she had a secret, she wanted to keep to herself. He had worked with Phoebe's young sister for four years as he took charge of her education up to her sixteenth birthday, when she left the facility. He assured Phoebe he had treated Prue with a lot of care and consideration.

'Was she questioned about that night?' Phoebe wanted to know.

'Not by me, I did not mention it as I did not want to distress her any more than she was already. She came to trust me, and I did not betray that trust. Prue was a very pretty and intelligent young girl and you could not help but like her. I pray that eventually she will be back with you alive and well.'

The dark eyes were watery as they gazed upon him.

'Thank you for that.' The Professor took her to the lounge area and bought her a hot strong coffee, they sat at a table and he told her more of the time he had spent with her little sister.

Samantha had all the lights turned out and most of the laboratory was in darkness, except close to the computer where it was illuminated by an eerie green glow that come from the pulsating globe sat on a table close to the computer control desk. Samantha sat at the table and ran her fingers over the control box on the plinth. Henry and Phoebe stood beside the computer waiting patiently for something to happen. The low hum started to get louder, and data started coming up on the computer screen.

'They're back,' Henry said.

Samantha knew who he meant – just as Samantha had hoped, someone was hacking into their experiment. Samantha looked across at Phoebe and gave her a smile of encouragement, as she knew Phoebe had been in the same position as Evelyn. Wired to a machine that was trying to take over her mind, Phoebe knew exactly what Evelyn was going through and she wanted to free the young girl as much as Samantha did. An energy beam was suddenly emitted from the globe; at the end of the beam something started to happen. A green haze grew up in the surrounding darkness, it moved up to a six-foot column and a shapeless mass started to evolve inside the green haze and then started to form into a figure they could recognise.

'Come on, Evie, you can do it,' Samantha said.

Henry worked with the computer and Phoebe kept her eyes on the figure materializing in the green haze. She saw it was a young girl.

'That's it, girl, use your insight,' Samantha urged.

They gazed at the small impish face inside the column of green haze. The lips moved and Samantha was sure the apparition was calling her name. She moved to the end of the energy beam and stood close to the figure of Evelyn. She watched the lips move: 'Sam.'

'I'm here, Evie and we are coming for you, hold on, we will save you,' Samantha said, softly.

Evelyn was tiring, the mental energy she was using was sapping the strength in her young body. She slipped into unconsciousness.

The figure of the young girl faded, and the green haze faded away. Samantha turned off the machine, Phoebe turned on the lights, and she stared across at Samantha.

'When do we start?' Phoebe asked. Samantha went to the computer and Henry pointed to the plan of the facility on the computer screen; it showed the two levels side by side. A tiny pulsating red light told them where Evelyn was being held prisoner. There were many passages like the ones Xanthe had discovered on the other side of the two way mirror. There were several entry points they could take so she decided to call on Steven and Janice to help her. Also they did not know who or what had hold of Evelyn, and Samantha wanted to be ready for any eventuality.

Steven Calvert stood between two huge turbines as he stood inside the engine room. Janice was just making her way up a metal stairway that rose up between them. After a while she stopped and gazed down at her partner.

'Come on, Steve, aren't you coming, or are you afraid of heights?' There was a slight mocking in her voice.

Steven started making his way up the metal stairs; Janice turned and made her way upwards whistling cheerfully. Janice eventually reached a metal walkway high above the two turbines; she waited a moment for Steven to join her then she moved along the walkway. Steven kept his eyes on her back as he followed her; he avoided looking down over the side of the metal walkway. Janice suddenly stopped and looked down at the engine room way below them.

'It's a great view from up here, Steven,' she said in a taunting voice.

Steven moved past her and made his way towards the end of the walkway, Janice followed close behind him. She was glad he was hurrying as they had a deadline to meet. They had to enter the passages between the two levels at the same time as Samantha and Phoebe. At the end of the walkway Steven opened the door and walked into a metal lined passage. They gazed at each other quietly asking if the other was ready to carry on. They walked side by side down the passage. There was a line of lights down the centre of the ceiling that lit their way; it was dimly lit, and the long metal passage was full of shadows. They came to a T-junction. They looked both ways and then stared at each other.

'Which way now, left or right?' Steven offered.

'According to the diagram of these passages, we should keep on the left,' Janice said.

Steven came to a decision.

'I'll check the right passage for a little way; we don't want someone coming up from behind us.'

They went their separate ways.

CHAPTER LVIII:

THE ALIEN WARRIORS

They reached the small secret office between the two levels without mishap; Phoebe had a quick survey of the files in the several cabinets round the small room. She had known some of the people on file. Phoebe had suffered the same hardships they had suffered. There was nothing in the files to give them an idea of what the aliens were after. Samantha hoped Evelyn would be able to tell them more when they rescued her. Samantha stood by the desk and stared at the wall behind it. Phoebe stepped over to join her.

'According to the diagram, there's a passage behind that wall.'

Phoebe helped Samantha pull the desk away from the wall. Phoebe ran her hands over the wall. Samantha stood back and waited; she was sure Phoebe knew what she was doing. After a few moments there came an audible click and the wall in front of them slid away revealing a dark passage. Phoebe walked forward into the darkness as if she was in a hurry to get to grips with her enemy. Phoebe was ready to do battle with whatever she was about to face. Samantha followed her and the partition slid back behind her. Samantha followed the sound of Phoebe's hurried footsteps until her eyes changed a different shade of green and her night vision could see the dark shape of Phoebe a hundred yards ahead of her. Samantha moved faster and caught up with Phoebe as she came to a T-junction.

'Do we split up, or keep together?' Phoebe inquired.

'We have to keep to the right,' Samantha said.

Phoebe took the right-hand passage and kept up the brisk pace.

'I hope you're keeping alert; I don't want you to rush into danger,' Samantha warned.

'The sooner we get to Evelyn, the sooner we can free her from suffering,' Phoebe said.

'Just take it easy, we want to get to her in one piece,' Samantha said.

Phoebe was aware of what Samantha meant, if they rushed into something nasty on the way, it would not help Evelyn. But Phoebe had faith in Samantha and the tall girl would be able to do well whatever crisis she ran into. Phoebe was in a hurry to get the action started.

Evelyn opened her eyes and found she was free of the domed headset; the room was lit up by an eerie green light, which was joined by the flashing lights of the surrounding machinery. The tall thin man was staring down at her.

'I'm glad to see you're back with us again. You have done well, Evelyn.'

Evelyn was weak and weary in mind and body. She was sure Samantha was on her way to rescue her. Evelyn knew she had to hold on to that thought.

Rhan stood in the middle of the room waiting patiently for orders from his masters. His red scaly skin glistened in the green eerie light that illuminated the control room. The Ixxion had not always been under the domination of the Monox. They had been rulers of their part of space for a millennium before they were invaded by the more technical powerful Monox. The Ixxion were soon overcome and became part of the Monox Empire and they used the Ixxion warriors to keep their empire strong. They did not have to fight any opponent that seriously threatened the Monox superiority. Their biggest problem was nearer home, on their home world to be exact. The planet had two large continents: one in the Northern hemisphere and the other was in the Southern hemisphere.

The Monox were made up of two races not unidentical to each other but had a different philosophy. The other thing the Ixxion noticed was the people in the Southern hemisphere were mostly female with a few males about. The Monox that had conquered the Ixxion lived in the Northern hemisphere and they were mostly male. When the Ixxion warriors entered the crystallized cities of the Northern Monox they were placed under the leadership of a tall awe-inspiring female, who went under the name of Zindra. The warlike Ixxion found them bowing down before her penetrating ruby red eyes. She was waging a personal war on the people of the Southern hemisphere and she sent the Ixxion to raid their continent on a regular basis. They found it too easy as the people did not seem to own any offensive weaponry. Their orders were clear: if they found any twins they were to be put to death, the Ixxion did not ask the reason for this, they followed their orders whatever they were. The Ixxion were also commanded to catch a tall red-haired female, who was their leader. They found that easier said than done, as Imera was as slippery as an eel and unlike most of her people, had a venomous nature as the Ixxion warriors that faced her found out. Like the warriors she took no prisoners.

Imera led her people up to the high snow-capped mountains to the far south of their continent. The Ixxion warriors followed them part of the way, but were forced back down by a shower of rocks that their prey rained down on them. The warrior force was left guarding the lowlands just in case Imera brought her people down from their mountain stronghold, but she was too intelligent for that and Imera stayed up in the mountains planning her revenge on the Monox. Zindra sent her forces up into the mountains scouring for signs of where her enemies were hiding. Some of them came back to her with tales of strange sounds and terrors that plagued them in their search. Some of the Monox returned out of their minds. The Ixxion were determined to keep up their facade of being afraid of nothing, but looking at some of them, Zindra could see some of the warriors were worse for wear. So Zindra decided if she wanted to capture Imera, she would have to do it herself. Zindra led an elite force up into the mountains. She reached a high gully that ran through the mountain range and it was near where they were that the strange things started to happen. Zindra guessed correctly that they were near Imera's stronghold. They moved forward along the gully slowly and cautiously, then all hell broke loose. The attack on them was swift and powerful, all manner of hellish creatures was among them, a sound of thunder roared above them echoing around the mountain range. Monsters of their myths and dark past tormented the force and broke them up and they ran for their lives, except Zindra, who stood quite still and stared at the melee around her. Zindra was highly intelligent and she grasped the fact they were not under attack by anything tangible. It was their minds that were being battered by an invisible force; it told her Imera had developed a weapon that was potent as well as successful. Zindra returned to the Northern hemisphere. The Monox bombarded the mountains continually hoping they could destroy Imera's stronghold.

Two months after the bombardment had stopped, Imera showed Zindra she was still alive and kicking by the audacity of leading an attack on the Monox Northern stronghold and getting away with it. Security was stepped up and when Imera attacked again her force was killed in the battle and only Imera and her daughter survived; they stole a spacecraft and escaped into space. Zindra followed in one of their star ships and the hunt was on. Zindra wanted Imera and details of her mind weapon.

Zindra strode majestically over to Rhan commanded him to take some of his warriors into the passageways and search for their enemies. She was sure someone would come and rescue the girl and Zindra hoped it would be Imera's grandchild, the one known as Samantha.

CHAPTER LIX:

THE POWERFUL ENEMY

P hoebe made her way slowly along the dimly lit metal passage, she had lost sight of Samantha and she supposed the tall girl had taken another route. After a while she spied a tall bulky figure lumbering towards her. She stood still and gazed at the first sight of an alien being and Phoebe suddenly knew she had a fight on her hands. The Ixxion warrior was glad he had come upon the enemy at last. As he moved closer, he saw it was female – he would have preferred a male, but he was sure the female would put up a good fight.

Phoebe waited for him to come closer. She did not like the look of this ferocious looking creature, Samantha had told her, and freeing Evelyn would not be easy. She could see her opponent was armed to the teeth, but he did not go for his weapons, so Phoebe thought perhaps the alien on seeing she was only a female had decided to tackle her with his bare hands.

'OK, buster, gives us your best shot,' Phoebe said in her best fearless voice.

Phoebe prepared herself for battle as the alien warrior moved in for the kill. Phoebe set her mind on one thing: survival. This was just one more horror she had to face in her trouble filled life. The Ixxion warrior gazed at the face of his prey; there was no fear, only deep concentration on the matter at hand, to avoid being his next victim. His right hand flashed out and gripped Phoebe by the throat; she lashed out with her right fist and struck him on the side of the head. The warrior gave an angry grunt, the grip on her throat relaxed and she grabbed the offending arm and pushed him away, showing her opponent she was no weakling. The Ixxion drew his long sharp blade from his weapon belt. Phoebe was aware of his move and was ready for his attack. She saw the slim silvery blade that was aimed for her right side as he held it in his left scaly hand. She moved fast and leapt sideways away from the deadly incoming blade; Phoebe thrust out with her right leg and hit the alien on the right knee with the solid tip of her shoe. The Ixxion howled angrily. He swung his left arm round and Phoebe ducked under it and the blade passed over her head. Phoebe dived forward head butting the alien in the chest forcing him back against the metal wall.

Janice came around the corner and stopped dead as she saw the two dark figures grappling with each other. She was glad of the gun she held in her right hand; she moved cautiously forward. As she suddenly recognised Phoebe, Janice wondered where Samantha was, as they were supposed to stay together. Janice kept a sharp eye on the monster Phoebe was wrestling; she could not fire while they were close together. Janice was amazed at the strength of Phoebe as she fought to keep on equal terms with the tall bulky alien.

The Ixxion had dropped his killing blade on the metal floor as he found he needed both hands for this slippery female. He had to admit she was a worthy opponent – if he threw her to the floor, she was up in an instant and throwing herself at him before he had a chance to draw a weapon to dispatch her with. Phoebe was enjoying the workout and knew she was not getting all the pain and was glad she was strong and fit enough to stop the alien from overpowering her. Once again Phoebe found herself being thrown off him and landing on her back. Before she could leap to her feet there were too loud reports and two bright flashes, and she was showered with green blood. She watched the alien warrior collapse to the metal floor. She sat up and turned to face the person who had brought their fight to a bloody end.

'Spoilsport, I was just about to deliver the final blow,' she complained.

Janice grinned at her.

'Not from where I'm standing,' Janice observed.

Janice held out her left hand and Phoebe took it and she pulled Phoebe to her feet.

'Where's Samantha, has she gone off on her own again?'

Phoebe shook her head.

'We got separated and I lost sight of her,' Phoebe explained.

'I'm not surprised, it's like a maze down here,' Janice said.

Rhan stood outside the control room; he had heard the discharge of a weapon not far away and knew one of his warriors had come into contact with the enemy. He was unaware of the light of two green eyes behind him, watching and waiting for the right moment to attack. Rhan moved slowly along the dim metal walled passage; his right hand went down to his weapon belt. The tall silent figure behind him moved closer to him; she had seen the red sheen of the warrior's scaly skin. He was a commander and the kill would be more honourable. She was not going to make any mistake this time. Rhan suddenly stopped and sniffed the air, he caught her odour at the exact time she attacked, a well-aimed bony knee hit him in the hollow behind his right knee and the leg folded, a hand grabbed his right wrist and broke the bones and he dropped the thin blade and growled in pain and anger.

He was thrown hard against the metal wall and a slim bony fist hit him full in the face, breaking more bones. The attack was fast and furious and soon over, Rhan fell to the floor and a foot stamped on his head and crushed the skull like an eggshell. She knelt down and removed the weapons from the belt round the thick waist. She detected a slight sound behind her, and she swung round in a flash of speed and aimed the blaster at the figure moving towards her. She relaxed and let the tension fade from her body and the finger slipped off the firing button and she stood up.

'You really shouldn't creep up on me like that, it could be the death of you,' Samantha said in a husky voice.

Steven Calvert gave a sigh of relief as he realised he had been close to death.

'I'll remember that next time,' he assured her.

'Where's Janice?'

'I took another passage to see where it would take me, Janice can't be far behind,' Steven said.

'Well, it seems to be up to me and you,' Samantha decided.

Steven stared at her as he wondered what she had in mind.

'You're just going to rush in there, all guns blazing.'

Samantha ignored his sarcasm.

'I don't suppose there are many of them guarding Evelyn, they won't be expecting us to rush in there and we're armed.'

Samantha stepped towards the control room door with the dead Ixxion's blaster in her right hand. Steven took out his gun from the inside pocket of his jacket and readied himself to follow Samantha into hell. The door slid open and Samantha rushed into the room. A green Ixxion standing close to the door just had time to spin round before Samantha blasted him out of existence with a burst from her alien weapon. She saw Evelyn slumped in a metal chair wired to the computer systems running along the far wall. She pointed the blaster at the tall figure standing close to her. Samantha could not make out the face in the dim gloomy green light, so she could not determine if it was human or alien. He started to move away from the girl clamped to the chair.

Zindra moved back into the shadows as she realised it was time to go. In front of her was Anris Bruton, who had his weapon out and was ready to kill the tall female that had rushed into the control room, when Steven ran in behind her shifting the alien's concentration as he fired and the energy beam missed Samantha as she went to help Evelyn. Samantha spun round to face her enemy and saw him fall to the floor after Steven fired at the alien several times in quick succession. She faced the tall female alien behind the fallen Monox male. Zindra touched the bracelet on her left arm as she studied the one they called the hybrid; Zindra could see why: the bright green eyes glowed in the dim lit room. Samantha stared at the hostile expression on the tall female alien's face, the ruby red eyes burned with a furious hatred for her. Zindra started to fade and was soon gone from the room.

'They must have a spacecraft nearby,' Samantha said.

Samantha went to Evelyn and released her from the chair and helped her up onto her feet; the young girl clung to Samantha.

'I knew you would come and free me, Sam.'

'If you hadn't interfered with my experiments with the computer, I would never have found you. You have an exceptional mind,' Samantha said.

Janice and Phoebe came into the room.

'Nice of you to join us, though you have missed all the action,' Steven said.

'I got into an argument with an alien monster and Janice helped me sort him out,' Phoebe explained.

They made their way out of the maze of passages. Phoebe returned Evelyn to Professor Fairclough so he could take the girl back to her mother. Steven and Janice left the research laboratories and got in touch with General Heywood telling him to set up a search for a hidden alien spacecraft. Samantha made her way to her laboratory.

Barnaby Morgue strode over to the table close to the computer system; he stood over the glowing sphere that sat majestically on the black control box. The pulsating green light bathed him with a cold energy, which brought goosebumps to his skin.

'You have come to kill Samantha?'

Barnaby spun round and faced the owner of the voice. The tall thin girl with long silvery blonde hair looked like a ghost; the pale blue eyes stared at him with interest. She had just met her controller and he had told her someone was coming to kill Samantha and she had to grab the machine and take it to her controller.

'It will be nice to see an end to that obnoxious ginger haired bitch; I hope you will make her death very painful.'

Barnaby moved closer to the girl and ran a hand over her cheek and grinned at her.

'Your wish is my command,' Barnaby assured her.

The clone gave him her best evil smile and made her way to the computer. Barnaby made for the door just as it slid open and Samantha entered the laboratory. She sensed the danger immediately and readied herself for action. Barnaby stared at the bright green eyes, as he put his hand in the inside pocket of his jacket and pulled out his automatic and aimed it at the tall ginger haired girl, the expression on the thin white face never changed.

'Have you got authority to be here?'

Her voice was sharp and commanding as if the gun in his hand did not mean a thing to her.

'This is all the authority I need,' Barnaby assured her, as he waved the gun at her.

Samantha walked past him and went to the glowing sphere, Barnaby tightened his grip on the gun and was ready to fire the moment she made an aggressive move.

Samantha gave the clone that stood by the computer control desk a stony stare. She worked on the control panel on the black plinth that held the green glowing sphere.

'What are you doing?' he asked, sharply.

The sphere glowed brighter and a low hum echoed round the room. Barnaby ordered her to turn it off and Samantha ignored him. She heard the report of the gun and then felt a bullet hit the back of her right thigh. She fell forward against the table and another shot rang out and she felt an immense pain in her left shoulder. Samantha gritted her teeth against the agony and moved away from the glowing sphere. A third shot rang out and a blazing fire burned in her back and Samantha fell to the floor and another bullet slammed into her body and she blacked out.

The clone knelt down beside the body; a happy smile crossed her thin lips.

'Is she dead?' Barnaby inquired.

'Not yet.' The clone stood up and went to the computer control desk and touched a switch and part of the wall next to the computer slid away.

'Follow the passage and it will lead you to the outside,' she said.

Barnaby put his gun away and picked up Samantha and carried her still body over his shoulder and he stepped through the opening in the wall and the partition slid back behind him.

He made his way along the dimly lit passage and he eventually found the way out; it was freezing, and it was snowing. He saw his car parked nearby and made for it. He tossed the lifeless body unceremoniously onto the back seat. He covered it with a large rug and then got in the driving seat and drove towards the main gate.

Inside the laboratory the clone stared down at the humming, pulsating sphere. She had felt the pain of the ginger haired girl, now she felt nothing; perhaps the girl was truly dead, she thought happily to herself. She drew a chair up to the table and sat before the glowing sphere, the bright green light shone in her long silvery hair bringing a green aura flared about her head. She felt the device tugging at her mind; the cold energy entered her head and ran through her body. Her mind was falling into a dark pit, a dark well of darkness and emptiness. Then she was gone forever.

CHAPTER LX:

WINTER KILLS

Barnaby Morgue drove steadily along the road because of the treacherous conditions. The windscreen wipers fought against the driving snow which was almost a blizzard. He made his way to the place where his employer would be waiting to relieve him of his dying passenger on the back seat. He had been paid very handsomely for this hit.

Barnaby kept his concentration on the road ahead; he heard a slight sound behind him and before he could react; talons of steel gripped his head pulling it violently back. He lost control of the car and it skidded over the icy road. The vice like grip wrenched his head round and the bones in his neck splintered and broke noisily and all went black. The car veered off the road and smashed into the roadside hedges. The back door opened, and Samantha slid out of the car and fell into the thick snow. Agonizing pain tore at her nerves; blood seeped from the bullet holes in her body. The worse news was the pain in her abdomen, she was going into labour, the baby wanted out and there was nothing she could do about it.

A car approached the crash and stopped; a tall heavy figure stepped out of the car and went swiftly to the stricken girl lying in the snow. The fur lined hood was pulled down revealing the grim-faced Phoebe Cross. She knelt down and surveyed the damage done to Samantha. She saw the blood in the snow and knew the girl was in a very bad way. The back of the white lab coat was saturated in blood; she turned Samantha over onto her back and stared at the deathly white face. Phoebe lifted the girl up onto her feet and supported her as they made for the car. Samantha groaned painfully at every step; she was fighting to stay conscious. The baby inside her was making its way to the outside world. Phoebe laid her out on the back seat and slammed the door. Phoebe got in the car and drove carefully away from the crashed car. The snowstorm was slowly abating.

Samantha struggled to sit up and lay her back against the car door, she unbuttoned her white lab coat and pulled up the hem of her skirt, she groaned painfully as she removed her panties. The baby's head was just starting to emerge; she pushed and cried out in pain.

'What is it, Sam?' Phoebe asked, with her voice full of concern for her friend. 'Baby,' she muttered softly.

Phoebe slowed the car and turned her head and saw what Samantha meant.

'You don't do things by halves do you, Sam.'

'I held up the birth for as long as I could, but she is determined to be born.'

Phoebe turned back to keep her eyes on the road, she was nearly at her destination. When she reached the small cottage she was making for and parked the car round the back, Phoebe leapt out of the car and opened the back door; she stared open mouthed as she heard the baby cry.

'Well, Sam, I've never heard of anyone giving birth in the back of a car before.'

Phoebe rushed into the cottage and picked up the medicate and a large thick bath towel. She came back to the car and cut the umbilical cord and wrapped the baby in the thick bath towel and took her to the cottage and turned on the heating. When she returned to the car, she found Samantha had slipped into unconsciousness. Phoebe heaved the girl out of the car and carried the limp body over her shoulder and carried her into the cottage.

Phoebe laid Samantha on the bed and removed her clothing and rolled the girl onto her front so she could tend to her wounds.

Jennifer stood in the underground medical room, she gazed down at the frozen face of the clone, and it was strange looking down at herself. Jennifer was glad she was not lying on the slab, there was no brain activity and the body was completely lifeless. The trap she had set for the clone with the device she had built had been blowing to say the least. Jennifer's esteem for Samantha had reached new heights.

'Brilliant, Sam, your genius is almost comparable with mine.'

Melanie McAllister stood beside her.

'You're so modest, Jenny.'

Jennifer turned to Melanie and stared hard at her, Jennifer was not too sure of the girl yet; she was bright enough and sure of herself. Jennifer decided the girl warranted further study.

FEBRUARY 2135

Phoebe stared out of the bedroom window at the night sky. A few moments later a light appeared in the sky; her body tensed as the light grew bright as the object in the sky came closer to the cottage. Something large hovered over the back garden; she sucked in her breath, as a vibrating hum shook the cottage. It stayed hovering for a few minutes then shot up higher into the night sky. She waited for the light to disappear then she turned and went to the bed and gazed down at the sleeping face on the pillow.

'Well, Sam, even UFOs are searching for you now.'

Phoebe turned out the light and left the room and went to her own bedroom. Phoebe woke at first light and got dressed and had her breakfast. Samantha spent most of her time in a deep sleep as her body desperately mended itself. Baby Sally lay comfortably in a cot by the bed.

PART SEVEN:

THE WAY OF THE PREDATOR

CHAPTER LXI:

THE THING IN THE NIGHT

JUNE 2136

Jennifer made one of her regular nocturnal escapades from her underground world- They did not want her up on the surface, because they felt it was too dangerous as she had several attempts on her life in the past, so she had to make her way up to the surface in secret. The plans of the underground complex were in the computer and she had found several points where she could make it up to the surface. She always went up at night so there was least chance of discovery. It was cool and a slight breeze ruffled her long silver-blonde hair. The sky was clear of cloud and the moon shone brightly. She made her way to the hill in the hope of finding some of Samantha's old friends. She moved round the base, there seemed nobody about. She moved towards the overgrown copse, she suddenly heard voices and she dived into the bushes. A boy and a girl walking hand-in-hand come into view. They came close to where Jennifer was hiding in the cover of the bushes in the overgrown copse.

Juliet Prentice, now twenty-one, walked happily with the boy she had attached herself to, he made her laugh and he was good company. They stopped walking and Juliet gazed up at the night sky.

'Something up there is coming to get us,' Juliet said.

Malcolm put his arm round her waist and kissed her on the cheek.

'Don't worry, I'm here to protect you,' Malcolm assured her.

Juliet stared at him. Malcolm took nothing seriously, which was why she liked him so much.

'That's what I'm worried about,' Juliet said, light heartedly.

'I shall be the perfect gentleman, I would not cause you harm.'

They started walking towards the hill.

'I wonder why you like me, I'm the original bad penny, and I get the blame for everything that goes wrong round here. People are disappearing and it's got them frightened of their own shadows, I'm just as frightened of the unknown as they are,' Juliet explained.

Malcolm stopped and put his arms round Juliet and kissed her lightly on the lips.

'You have nothing to fear, while I'm with you, I shall never let anything happen to you,' he said.

Malcolm tried to drive away her fears but some of them were deep rooted and of a time before he came to the research facility. Juliet managed to conjure up a smile and he held her tighter and kissed her lips more firmly; she did not struggle and kept still as he kissed her several times.

'I don't blame you for anything and I never listen to other people talking about you. I like you, Juliet, I like you a lot,' Malcolm said, sincerely.

Jennifer kept still and quiet, she suddenly felt guilty; she did not want to make a sound in case they thought she was spying on them. Jennifer moved her head down so she could not see them, as they hugged and kissed each other.

'I like you too, Malcolm, you are so nice to me,' Juliet said.

Suddenly something crashed through the copse close to where Jennifer was hiding and startled her. Malcolm released Juliet and turned towards the sound, Juliet moved away from the overgrown copse and made for the hill; her pretty face was a mask of fear. Something huge and bulky ran out of the overgrown copse and attacked Malcolm as he was about to follow Juliet. He was gripped tightly and dragged into the overgrown copse, he could not make out any features, but he knew whatever had got him was big and strong. A strong force tore his body apart and crushed his head like an eggshell.

Jennifer ran out of the overgrown copse, with the sound of growls and breaking bones, as something nasty tore Malcolm to pieces. The arrogance and aloofness faded, and fear took over. Not wanting to be next on the menu, Jennifer followed Juliet's example and ran for her life.

Juliet did not stop running until she reached her cottage; she searched the darkness to make sure she had not been followed. She opened the door of the cottage with her electronic key, she shut the door and ran up the stairs. As she reached the landing, Wendy Goodman – who was now twenty – came out of her bedroom and switched on the light. Juliet blinked as the bright light stung her eyes. Wendy stared at the look of fear on her friend's face.

'Juliet, what's happened?'

Juliet ran into her own room and Wendy hurried after her. Juliet dived onto the bed and tried to regulate her rapidly beating heart; she took deep breaths. Wendy sat on the bed and ran a soothing hand over Juliet's face. Wendy had been living with Juliet for six years – as a new arrival they had put her with Juliet as she lived alone. This was the first time she had seen fear on Juliet's face.

Slowly Juliet told her what she had seen and the horrible death of Malcolm, who had arrived at the same time as Wendy; she was shocked to hear of his death.

'You're safe now, Juliet, I shall protect you,' Wendy said.

Juliet just stared at her and Wendy kissed her lightly on the lips, she helped Juliet out of the grubby dress and Juliet got into bed and Wendy got in bed with her and held Juliet tight; the girl was still trembling with fright.

'Thank you, Wendy, promise you won't leave me.'

Wendy kissed her on the cheek and hugged her tighter.

'I promise, we've been friends too long not to care for each other,' Wendy said, softly.

Michelle Gowning awoke sharply and sat up in her bed. She gazed around the sleeping compartment to see what had woken her. She could see nothing in the darkness; she slid out of the bed and activated the lights. She went to the door and it slid open; the corridor lights were on and she saw Jennifer standing by her door shivering and a look of fear on her thin pale face.

'What is it, Jenny?'

Jennifer pushed past Michelle and entered the room and sat on her bed. Michelle stood over her.

'He's dead,' Jennifer mumbled.

Michelle left the sleeping compartment for a moment and returned with two mugs of strong coffee; she had put a drop of brandy in the mug she gave to Jennifer. Michelle sat beside her and sipped her coffee, she waited patiently for Jennifer to compose herself, then Jennifer blurted out her tale; when she had finished, she continued to sip her coffee.

'We'll have to tell the General, he won't be very pleased to know you went to the surface without permission.'

'They must never know I was out there; they will probably accuse me of the murder. I have the strength to do that to a person,' Jennifer said.

Michelle knew how strong Jennifer was, but she had worked long enough with the tall girl to know she would not kill Malcolm.

'They'll have to know what happened, if there is something dangerous on the loose, they must be told.'

'Juliet was with him, she will probably tell them,' Jennifer said.

Michelle told Jennifer to go to bed and they would sort it out in the morning. Jennifer stood up and put the empty mug on the bedside table and pulled off her T-shirt and dropped it onto the floor.

'What are you doing?' Michelle asked.

Jennifer removed her shorts and stood beside the bed in her bra and panties.

'I hope you don't mind, Michelle, but I'd like to sleep with you tonight, I don't want to be alone just now,' Jennifer appealed.

Michelle nodded and turned off the lights. Michelle got into bed and Jennifer snuggled up to the older girl.

'You are such a good friend, Michelle,' Jennifer said.

Jennifer had a disturbed sleep full of monsters trying to devour her. Jennifer woke in the morning covered in a cold sweat. She found herself alone, so she got out of bed and left the sleeping compartment and went to the shower room. She found Michelle in the showers; Jennifer removed her underwear and got in the shower with Michelle.

'You look as if you had a bad sleep, when I woke you were tossing and turning,' Michelle said.

Jennifer gave her a weak smile and told Michelle about her dreams.

Michelle gave her a hug. She was concerned about Jennifer. Working with her for so long, Michelle thought the girl was afraid of nothing, but the fear Michelle had seen on the face of her friend told her otherwise.

'I really do value our friendship,' Jennifer told her sincerely.

Michelle moved further in the shower so Jennifer could get under the flow of warm water.

'Some people say you are arrogant and overbearing, but I've never found you that way, when I've worked with you,' Michelle explained.

Jennifer gazed at Michelle as the warm water flowed over her naked body.

'I have liked you, Michelle, from the first day we met, and you have been a good friend to me.'

They changed places and Michelle rinsed her body under the shower, Jennifer stood and ran her eyes over Michelle's fuller figure.

'You have a lovely body, Michelle; you make me look skinny.'

Michelle turned the shower off and gave Jennifer a warm smile.

'You are not skinny, Jennifer.'

They walked out of the shower and Jennifer put her arms round Michelle and kissed her on the lips.

'Thank you, it's nice of you to say that.'

Jennifer went to her own sleeping compartment and got dressed; she went to the computer room, and waiting for her was the tall commanding figure of Dr Sally Hamilton.

'You've been up on the surface,' accused the tall woman.

Jennifer shook her head.

'No, I haven't,' she lied.

'You were out last night; the girl Juliet saw you.'

Jennifer silently cursed the girl, even though she was scared stiff, she was observant.

'Someone was killed last night; it could have been you.'

Jennifer walked away from her and went to the computer banks.

'You'll stay here, whether you like it or not.'

Major Harrington stood and stared down at the grisly sight in the overgrown copse; he had never seen a body pulled apart. Wendy Fraser had informed General Heywood about what Juliet had seen. The major walked away, and he saw Colonel Collins approaching him. Juliet followed behind him; her expression showed she wished she was somewhere else.

'It's not a pretty sight, whatever did it, must have had immense strength,' Harrington said.

'Juliet was with the boy when he was killed,' Collins said.

An ambulance drove up and Hilary jumped out of the back with two male paramedics.

'It's not a pretty sight,' Harrington told her.

'Death never is,' assured Hilary.

Juliet watched the two paramedics carrying the stretcher that contained the remains of her dead friend. Some soldiers were going through the copse for signs of the assailant. Hilary stopped and gazed at Juliet.

'You've had a bad shock, how are you feeling, Juliet?'

'I'll feel a lot better when they catch the thing,' Juliet said.

Hilary gave her a warm smile and made her way to the ambulance. Juliet followed Major Harrington into the overgrown copse. The day before Dr Anthony Bishop had returned and Juliet had learned what had been happening to her friends while they had been away. Juliet had thought they were having all the fun, as nothing out of the ordinary had happened at the Research facility; until now. Something had come amongst them, now it was their turn to face danger.

Dr Sally Hamilton walked into General Heywood's office deep in thought. Jennifer was becoming hard to handle, she knew the cause of the friction between them, and Jennifer disliked and distrusted her because she kept Samantha in the dark about her being very much alive and kicking. The two girls coming together had been a mistake that could not have been avoided because of Jennifer. She was proving to be a slippery customer, being able to escape from any confinements they put her in. So, their meeting would have been inevitable, they did not know what was going on in Jennifer's mind when she had come out of the coma. Dr Hamilton knew she should have some idea of the character of Jennifer, but the girl was still a bit of an enigma, as well as being defiant and disrespectful.

'Having trouble with Jennifer again?' the General asked, echoing her thoughts.

General Heywood gave her a sheet of paper and told her; Juliet had made a sketch of the thing she saw last night. She stared hard at it.

'Do you recognise it?' he asked.

Dr Sally Hamilton recognised it only too well; her people had been fighting the Ixxion for a millennium. She had been there when Dr Bishop gave his report about Samantha and her friends' battle with the aliens. Samantha was lost; Steven and Janice were out looking for her.

'They are somewhere near keeping an eye on this place. Somehow, we have to keep Jennifer in the underground base; it was lucky for her the boy Malcolm was seen instead of her, the next time she may not be so lucky.'

General Heywood stood up and walked round his desk.

'I'll go and have a word with her,' he said.

When they walked into the underground computer room, Jennifer was sat at the device Samantha had designed, she had it working, and she had been able to get to the surface. She had it connected to the computer, so it could activate the machine when she wanted to get back to the underground facility. Jennifer looked up when they approached her.

'Is there something missing from your life, Jennifer,' he asked.

Jennifer stood up and faced the General.

'Now you come to mention it, yes.'

Standing behind the General Sally Hamilton stared at the girl's eyes, which at the moment were ice blue.

'You are aware of the death of Malcolm; it is now vital you stay down here for the time being. We can't protect you, if we don't know where you are,' Heywood said.

'I can look after myself,' Jennifer said, in defiance.

Dr Sally Hamilton moved forward and the blue in Jennifer's eyes darkened. She had only to be in the same room as Jennifer, to ignite the girl's anger.

'You are to stay down here; if we have to lock you up, we will,' she said.

She got the full force of Jennifer's anger, her eyes were a deep blue which showed Dr Sally Hamilton had put herself in a dangerous position. They did not know what the girl was capable of if her anger was in full throttle. Jennifer pushed past the woman and went towards the computer desk. The General followed her. When they got to the computer she spun round and faced him. Michelle stood close by and could see the anger boiling up in Jennifer.

'I get bored sitting here twiddling my thumbs, I want to get out into the fresh air,' Jennifer stormed.

Michelle laid a hand on her shoulder.

'Easy, Jenny, don't blow a gasket,' warned Michelle.

Jennifer closed her eyes and regulated her breathing and calmed the storm in her head.

'We'll have to get you some more mind-numbing work to do, you'll still have to stay down here where it is safe,' General Heywood said.

The relationship between Jennifer and the General was a lot different. Jennifer looked up to him and respected his rank. Jennifer had first seen him after she had come out of the coma and at the age of twelve, she could see he was a man she could respect and admire as a role model. Jennifer was aware he was not a man who would let her get away with anything or wrap round her little finger, which was a reason she admired him.

'All right, but someday I have to get out of here,' she said.

The General moved away and went towards the doors; Sally Hamilton could not resist another taunt at the girl.

'We will lock you up if you go out again without permission.'

Jennifer stared at the woman red faced, the blue eyes darkened, and Sally Hamilton turned away and followed the General.

'That woman is insufferable,' Jennifer said, turning to Michelle.

Jennifer stared back at the retreating back of her antagonist and poked her tongue out at her.

'If she thinks I'm going to be locked up, she has another thing coming,' Jennifer said, coldly.

Michelle put her arm round Jennifer and kissed her on the cheek.

'You shouldn't let her get to you, Jenny; you are more intelligent than that.'

Jennifer faced Michelle.

'You are right, of course, another reason why I like you so much.'

Michelle put her arm round her and guided Jennifer out of the -room.

'I'll have to find something to combat your boredom,' Michelle said.

They made their way to the canteen.

CHAPTER LXII:

JENNIFER GETS HER WISH

Late next morning Jennifer found herself in front of General Heywood's desk. She wondered what she had done now; Jennifer was sure she was going to get another telling off. He gazed at the thin face and ice blue eyes as Jennifer stood at her full height and stared back at him. He remembered the countless times he found himself at odds with Samantha. He did not want the same thing happening to Jennifer, at the moment the girl had respect for him and his orders. Dr Hamilton wanted her caged up, but Heywood knew that would be no good. He would have to let her go; he had a job for her.

'As you and Dr Hamilton have a volatile relationship, I've decided to find a way to keep you two apart.'

'You let Samantha go, there seems no idea what I'm wanted for, until you make up your mind I want to be allowed to see more of the country I'm living in,' Jennifer said

He stood up and walked around his desk. He stood in front of her.

'I can't let you run off anywhere, I need to know where you are at all times, in case we need you,' he said.

Jennifer nodded her head.

'I will follow every restriction you want to place on me, just let have a look round the country, see it with my own eyes,' Jennifer said.

General Heywood sat on the edge of the desk; there was something in her voice that told him he could trust her word.

'OK, I'm going to trust you; I have a job for you.'

'I shall do anything you ask of me.'

The search for Samantha was at a dead end; he was sure the girl was still alive. They had found her blood in the crashed car and on the snow. She had had the strength to kill the driver, who was a well-known contract killer. Steven and Janice had been unable to find her. He was sure Jennifer could do no worse. They were still not sure of Jennifer's capabilities; this would be a good exercise to find out more about Jennifer and how she would cope in the wide world. He would not let her go alone; he had the right person who could accompany her. He told her Samantha was missing and he wanted her to try and make contact with the missing girl. Jennifer was thrilled at the prospect of getting close to Samantha, her face lit up and a broad smile crossed her thin lips.

'I have not felt anything strong regarding Sam, so you are right, she is still alive and kicking, I will find her for you, there is a bond between us,' Jennifer said.

'I don't want you running away and losing yourself,' he warned.

'I have given you my word, you can trust me, I shall not let you down,' Jennifer assured him.

He studied her face carefully and saw he could trust her; she wanted to prove to him she was a person he could depend on and she could take any assignment he gave her. He was more than willing to let Jennifer prove herself.

'I believe you, Jennifer. You won't be travelling alone; I have picked someone to go with you.'

Inside Jennifer jumped for joy; she hoped Michelle was going to be the one to join her in what she decided was a new adventure. The door opened and Jennifer spun round, but her face fell as Melanie McAllister walked into the room and slammed the door behind her. Jennifer noted the expression on Melanie's face, and it matched her own. Melanie was wondering why Jennifer was here. She stood at the side of the desk that was the furthest away from Jennifer.

'What have I done now?' Melanie wanted to know.

'Nothing that I know about, I have a job for you,' Heywood told her.

General Heywood explained to her why Jennifer was in the room and why she had been ordered to his office. Melanie stared at him as her anger once against boiled up and made her face red, seeing Jennifer once and a while was enough for her, driving around the countryside with the girl was too much.

'You're joking,' she stormed.

'Not at all, you are always bleating that you want to get away from here, now's your chance,' he offered.

Melanie stared at Jennifer, she did not like the tall girl and Melanie was determined to get out of it.

'I'd rather stay here, than drive around with her,' Melanie said, coldly.

'I have a name, you know,' Jennifer said, calmly.

Heywood stood between the two girls.

'This assignment will do you both good, being close to each other for some time, you'll have to get on with each other. You, Melanie, might find out Jennifer is not as bad as you think.'

'I doubt it,' Melanie shot out.

'Well you'll just have to deal with it, because you're going with her, whether you like it or not,' he told her firmly.

'Is that an order?' Melanie asked, insolently.

'If you want it that way, I'm ordering you to take this undertaking with Jennifer.'

General Heywood dismissed them and told them to leave as soon as they were ready; there was a car ready and waiting for them. They left the office building together and then Melanie shot off away from Jennifer as if she was contagious.

Jennifer watched her with a smile on her face. The journey they were about to take together was going to be more of a pain for Melanie than Jennifer.

Melanie left the compound and went to her cottage at the far end of the estate. She found Henry Jones there waiting for her; he grabbed her and kissed her firmly on the mouth.

'You look very annoyed – who's rubbed you up the wrong way, this time, Mel?'

Melanie rubbed her body against him as Henry kissed her again.

'That man, now I have to play nursemaid to that freak Jennifer.'

'I hear she speaks highly of you.'

Melanie was not amused and gave him a slap.

Melanie waited in the car outside the Research Facility for her passenger; she was not looking forward to driving around the country with the girl Jennifer. She heard the boot opening and she turned around and saw the tall girl placing a suitcase in the boot and she slammed it shut, she walked round the car and opened the passenger door and sat in the seat beside Melanie and closed the door.

'I'm glad I'm getting away from there, Mel,' Jennifer said, cheerfully.

'How nice for you and the name's Melanie to you.'

Melanie started the engine and before she could drive away, Jennifer gripped her wrist.

'Before we go, let's get one thing straight. We have to work together, so it would help if you could change your hostile attitude towards me. I have nothing against you, and I find you not unpleasing. Perhaps you could offer me the decency of waiting to know me more before you treat me like a monster – if you let me – I can prove to you – I'm not as nasty as you seem to think I am.'

Melanie stared at the pale face and ice blue eyes; she suddenly felt guilty about the things she had conjured up in her mind about Jennifer. Her wrist was firmly gripped showing her the strength of Jennifer's hands.

'OK, I suppose it's only fair.'

Jennifer released her wrist and Melanie drove the car away from the Research Facility. Jennifer sat back in her seat and enjoyed the scenery.

DULVERTON, DEVON.

Janice stood by her car parked in the public house car park. The sky was cloudless and blue, the bright sunshine was warm and pleasant, and she wore a short yellow dress. She kept an eye on the cars entering the car park as she waited for Melanie and Jennifer to arrive at the appointed time and place. She had mixed feelings about seeing Jennifer again. She was sure the girl would have changed from the last time they were together, before she was injured in the explosion at Samantha's house. Jennifer had been pleasant enough then, but after the trouble with clones, Janice was apprehensive about the character of the older Jennifer.

A light blue car entered the car park and moved slowly towards her and parked alongside her car. A tall girl wearing a white T-shirt and white shorts slid out of the car and approached Janice with a pleasant smile on her thin pale face.

'Hullo Jan, how's your head?'

'Fine, it's nice to see you again, Jenny.'

Jennifer hugged her and stepped away; she was glad to see Janice again as she was sure the girl liked her.

'Why don't you bring me up to date with what's happened so far, leave nothing out, Jan, I need to know everything,' Jennifer said.

Janice nodded and started to tell her all that had happened so far, Jennifer listened intently and concentrated deeply on what Janice was telling her. Her brain sifted through the information it received. Somewhere amongst the strange happenings Janice was relating was something that would be her idea of what Samantha had been planning and where she might be hiding out. When Janice at last got to the point where the crashed car had been found with the killer who had taken Samantha and her body was nowhere to be found, she stopped talking and gazed at Jennifer waiting for her to comment on what she had heard. Her face was a mask of concentration; Janice could almost hear the girl's brain churning over the information it had just received.

Melanie got out of the car and went to the public house to quench her thirst; she met Steven Calvert on his way out. They greeted each other and Steven went to the car, Jennifer nodded her head to him as he stood beside Janice and put his arm round her waist.

'Your friend Juliet had a boyfriend who has been killed by something close to the description of the aliens you spoke of. The girl Phoebe you spoke of, I would love to speak to her, what she knows about them, would be invaluable to us.'

'If we can find her,' Janice said.

Jennifer leaned her bottom against the bonnet of Janice's car. She kept her eyes on Janice.

'Do you think that if we do find Phoebe, Samantha would be with her?'

'Samantha had lost a lot of blood so she was in a bad way and she was about to give birth; someone had to assist her in getting away from the crash and Phoebe would be the ideal person as she had left the research laboratories just after the killer had driven off,' Janice explained.

Jennifer moved up away from the car, her mind still going over the data Janice had given her.

'The Professor Fairclough you speak of, interests me and his work, I suppose you haven't found out what he is looking for in these young people he is examining?'

Steven answered her.

'It's some Government project, something to do with the alien ship approaching Earth. Perhaps the Professor thinks his experiments will give us something to fight the aliens with.'

'That girl Evelyn and her telekinesis certainly would,' Jennifer observed.

Melanie came back sipping a glass of lager; she gave Jennifer a glass of orange juice. She thanked her and was glad of it as her mouth was dry.

'Though the aliens are not our only problem, we have enemies within,' Jennifer said.

'You mean that snake, Lavonia?' Janice inquired.

Jennifer nodded her head.

'Though she is not the only one, I have a score to settle with Lavonia,' Jennifer said.

'I expect we'll bump into her somewhere along the way, she always manages to turn up like a bad smell,' Janice said.

Jennifer turned to Melanie and grinned at her.

'Melanie thinks the same about me, don't you, Mel?'

Melanie took her empty glass and went back to the public house.

'I don't suppose you found out who the father of Samantha's baby?' Jennifer inquired.

'We asked her, but Sam told us to mind our own business,' Steven told her.

Jennifer went to the car she had been travelling in and took out a map they had been following and laid it out on the bonnet. Janice and Steven stood at each side of her.

'Have you any ideas of where Sam might be at the moment?' Jennifer asked the both of them.

'There have been several sightings of a girl fitting Phoebe's description, so we've been following these. I believe Samantha has been lying low and getting Phoebe go out for supplies,' Steven said.

'We'll have to section up the map and we can split up. Melanie's got a mobile phone, she can give you the number. Then we can let each other know if we find anything,' Jennifer said.

Jennifer scrawled some lines over the map and handed it to Steven; she had another map in the car that Melanie could follow. Steven went to his car.

'Are you armed, Jenny?' Janice asked.

Jennifer nodded, General Heywood had allowed her to have a weapon and warned her not to shoot herself with it, but Melanie declined being armed because if she had a weapon, she would not know what to do with it.

'Take care, Jenny,' Janice told her.

'I will and make sure you do the same.'

Janice went back to her own car and Jennifer walked round the car and got in and sat beside Melanie, who started the car and drove out of the car park.

DUNSTER, SOMERSET.

Jennifer sat on the low wall of the eight-sided Yarn Market, she gazed up at Dunster Castle on the hill, and trees hid the lower part of it. Melanie stood close by. She was bored but she was not going to tell Jennifer that.

'Nice castle, Mel. How would you like to live in a place like that?'

'We're not on a sightseeing tour,' Melanie pointed out.

Jennifer stared at her companion.

'You're such a bore, Mel. You really are,' Jennifer complained.

Melanie poked her tongue out at Jennifer, who slid off the wall and walked towards the castle; Melanie fell in step beside her.

'Your friend Sam doesn't seem to be here,' Melanie said.

Jennifer stopped walking as she noticed a tall auburn-haired girl walking towards them; she stopped in front of Melanie and gave her a malicious grin.

'Well what have we here?' Lavonia inquired coldly.

Lavonia stood over Melanie, who glared at her in defiance, Jennifer moved away from them and controlled her temper as she had an uncontrollable urge to place her hands round Lavonia's throat.

'Nice to see you again,' Melanie lied.

Lavonia looked away from Melanie and stared in distaste at Jennifer. Then she turned back to Melanie.

'I see they've got you running around with that thing,' Lavonia said, nastily.

Jennifer moved in front of Lavonia.

'I'm not a thing, the name's Jennifer.'

Lavonia stepped back from the icy stare of the pale blue eyes. Melanie watched the confrontation with interest. She wondered if Lavonia had realised, she was facing the original Jennifer and not one of her clones.

'We have things to sort out between us, you and me. The failed plan of yours to kill me with a power surge from the computer, you have not suffered the consequences yet, but you will, I guarantee it,' Jennifer said in a soft steady voice full of venom.

For the first time Lavonia realised who she was facing. Melanie was getting to like Jennifer – anyone who could put the wind up the malicious bully that Lavonia had become. She saw something in Lavonia's expression she had not seen before. Fear. Lavonia spun round and walked hurriedly away. Jennifer turned to Melanie.

'There's something not quite right about that girl,' Jennifer said.

Melanie smiled at her.

'You noticed that, did you?'

Jennifer walked up to the castle determined to have a closer look at it; Melanie kept with her. Melanie had now decided that if Jennifer wanted to do some sightseeing while they were doing the General's bidding, it was all right with her. When Jennifer had had a good look over Dunster Castle they returned to the car and drove towards Minehead. Jennifer saw the sea for the first time as they drove onto the coast road.

'So that's what the sea looks like.'

Melanie giggled and Jennifer stared at her.

'Yes, I forgot you've led a sheltered life.'

Melanie drove into Minehead and found a car park. She told Jennifer she was going to buy her some fish and chips. It was sometime since they had last eaten. Melanie found a restaurant and she ordered for the both of them.

After they had eaten, Melanie was true to her word and took Jennifer shopping. Jennifer did not really trust Melanie, yet and was sure the girl was up to something and it was probably something to annoy her. Later they went down to the beach and Jennifer removed her T-shirt and shorts revealing the light blue bikini Melanie had bought her. Melanie removed her yellow blouse and green skirt and accompanied Jennifer down to the sea. Melanie ran a critical eye over Jennifer and decided her figure was shapely enough; she caught Jennifer catching her quick glance and Melanie assured Jennifer, her body was just fine, and nobody was going to make fun of it.

'I can understand why Samantha wanted to get away, it's so good to be free,' Jennifer said, as they stepped into the salt water.

'Don't get any ideas about disappearing too, the General will go ballistic, if you got yourself lost,' Melanie warned.

'It's nice to be wanted,' Jennifer said with a sigh.

Melanie giggled as she kept close to Jennifer as they moved forward and the water came up to their waists. Jennifer had not learnt to swim so Melanie had to make sure she did not get into trouble.

'Mind how you go, I shall be in hot water if I allow you to drown yourself,' Melanie warned.

CHAPTER LXIII:

FIRST CONTACT

JULY 2136

Melanie drove casually along the road; Jennifer had the road map laid across her thighs, as she acted as navigator. After a while she looked across at her companion. Melanie wore a short dark green dress and the hem had ridden up her tanned buxom thighs. Jennifer knew Melanie had a better figure than her. Melanie turned her head slightly and noticed Jennifer watching her.

'Anything wrong, Jennifer?' Jennifer shook her head.

'No, I was just admiring your shapely legs.'

Melanie gazed at the road ahead as they approached Allerford. She found a place to park the car and Jennifer got out and went for a walk. She came to an ancient packhorse bridge and walked past it as the road bent round to the right; she saw a car coming towards her. Jennifer stopped walking and the car went slowly past her. There were two girls sitting in the front of the car, the driver had long blonde hair and her companion had short jet-black hair and she wore dark glasses. Jennifer suddenly felt a headache starting. She watched the car drive away, towards where Melanie had parked her car.

The driver of the car took several deep breaths and let the tension drain from her body. She was surprised to find she had had an urge to run down the tall girl standing at the side of the road. She had resisted the temptation and drove past her without giving her a second look.

Jennifer made her way back to the car and she found Melanie laid out on the grass behind the car.

'Are you comfortable?' Jennifer inquired, as she sat beside Melanie.

Melanie lay on her back and she gazed up at the clear blue sky. The day was warm, and a slight breeze was blowing.

'Very, I suppose you want to get on the road again.'

'There's no hurry, you've been driving around for some time, so you deserve a rest.'

Melanie turned her head and stared at Jennifer; she could not believe what she had just heard.

'That's decent of you, Jennifer.' Jennifer sat on the grass beside Melanie.

'I like you, Melanie and I can't drive, so we don't want you to overdo it,' Jennifer said.

Jennifer lay on her side and gazed at her companion. She had noticed that Melanie had changed her attitude to her for some time now; Jennifer hoped it would continue, because Jennifer felt they could work better together if they had equal respect for each other.

'I admired the way you stood up to Lavonia; I even saw fear in her face. You were right what you said before we started out, I was condemning you, before getting to know you properly and I apologise.'

Jennifer smiled at her.

'That's all right, I just want us to get on as we will be working together for some time, Mel, and I hope you don't mind me calling you that?'

'On one condition,' Melanie said.

'What's that?'

'I call you Jenny.'

Jennifer sat up and held out her hand to Melanie.

'It's a deal.'

Two hours later they drove out of Allerford and headed for Luccombe. Jennifer was silent and gazed out of the side window. She was deep in thought about the car with the two girls in it, she had felt strange when it had passed by her and it had brought a throbbing inside her head.

'You're quiet, Jenny, anything wrong?' Melanie inquired.

'No, I'm just thinking.'

'Don't do too much of that, it hurts the brain,' Melanie said, light-heartedly.

'It certainly does,' Jennifer agreed.

Melanie drove into Luccombe and stopped the car alongside a high hedge; on the other side of it stood the church. Jennifer got out and asked Melanie to stay with the car. She watched the tall girl walk away and wondered if Jennifer was following a scent she could not detect. Jennifer walked steadily down the street gazing at the assortment of houses, some had thatched roofs and others had dark ochrous tiled roofs. She moved between a cottage and a large house, she stopped dead when she came up to a blue car, she gazed at the registration number and it was the same car she had seen in Allerford.

She went to the back door of the cottage; something was tugging harder at her brain, and something had drawn her here. Jennifer had been in no doubt she would be successful in her quest to find Samantha, as soon as the blue car had passed her,

Jennifer knew she had to find out about the two girls in it. She tried the door and found it unlocked. She walked into the kitchen; she passed through the room and stepped into the hallway. All was silent, nobody seemed at home. Jennifer made her way up the stairs. When she got to the landing, she passed by the first room which was the bathroom, she turned left and walked along the short passage.

A tall figure emerged from behind the door of the bathroom and rapidly moved forward and got close to Jennifer and stabbed the weapon into the small of Jennifer's back.

'You must know, I have no option but to kill you,' a female voice said.

Jennifer was pushed into the doorway ahead of her.

'Killing me will be disastrous for the both of us,' Jennifer said.

Jennifer was pushed onto the bed and she sat and stared up at a tall thin girl with long blonde hair, Jennifer recognised her as the driver of the blue car. She held a strange weapon in her right hand, and it was pointed at Jennifer's head.

'I have a friend with me, if I don't turn up, she will come and look for me.'

'When you've killed once, it becomes easy; I will kill your friend too.'

The girl walked away from the bed and went to the window and looked out. A car was drawing up to her own, and two men got out of it. Jennifer watched her turn and call to her to join her at the window. Jennifer got up and went to her and looked out of the window.

'Are they friends of yours?'

Jennifer assured the girl they were no friends of hers.

'Perhaps I should give you to them.'

Jennifer turned away from the window; she did not like the sound of that.

They heard the two men enter the cottage. Jennifer was grabbed by the arm and pushed across the room and out of the door.

'What are our chances?' Jennifer wanted to know.

'Yours are nil.'

Jennifer was pushed towards the stairway, she was going to be used as a shield if the two men were armed. Jennifer had to do some quick thinking, and she was in no hurry to die yet. One of the men appeared at the bottom of the stairs. Jennifer dived to one side and the discharge of the weapon in the girl's hand was thunder in her ears. Jennifer gazed at the man at the bottom of the stairs, as his head exploded. The girl let go of her arm and kicked her viciously down the stairs. She rolled down the stairs and tried to protect her head the best she could. She fell on the headless body at the foot of the stairs; the other man came in view and glared down at Jennifer. He kicked out and his shoe came in contact with her nose and blood dripped down her lower lip. She lay against the wall stunned. He did not get the chance to damage Jennifer even more, as the weapon was discharged a second time and the man joined his companion on the floor in a headless condition, Jennifer was showered with blood and brains.

The girl slipped the weapon in her skirt pocket and came down the stairs and pulled the dazed Jennifer to her feet.

She dragged Jennifer across the hallway and into an open doorway and entered the room and threw Jennifer onto the couch.

The girl left the room for a moment then returned with some rope and tied Jennifer's hands together behind her back and tied her ankles together. Jennifer stared at her captor's face; the eyes were blue.

'I can understand why someone would want to preserve their freedom,' Jennifer said.

'You do, do you?'

Jennifer nodded; she was enjoying her own kind of freedom. Jennifer stared hard at the girl's eyes; Jennifer was sure they were not the original eye colour. Jennifer tried to make contact with the mind behind them; the girl was not going to tell her what she wanted to know, so Jennifer had to get the information some other way. The girl grinned broadly at her then struck her viciously across the right cheek. Jennifer's eyes watered, there was a vivid red mark on her pale cheek, and it burned with a sharp pain.

'Don't do that.'

'I'm sorry, who were those men?'

The girl shrugged her shoulders.

'I suppose there's no harm in telling you. On the outside they are human, but the mind in their heads is alien.'

Jennifer stiffened.

'What do you know about aliens?'

The girl walked to the door and then turned to Jennifer.

'I'm not going to tell you everything; you have a brain, use it.'

The girl left the room and went into the next room, where a nineteen-month girl sat on a chair, her wide deep blue eyes stared at her mother accusingly.

'Come on, kiddo and don't stare at me like that.'

Sally got off the chair and followed her mother out of the cottage. When they got to the blue car, the girl put her daughter in the back and put the seat belt tightly on her. She got in the driving seat and backed out though the gap between the red brick house and her white walled cottage. Melanie stood behind a large tree in the back garden and watched the blue car drive away. Melanie made for the cottage and entered it by the back door. Melanie put her hand to her mouth when she saw the two headless bodies. She turned away from the gruesome sight and stumbled into the room opposite. She gave a sigh of relief when she saw Jennifer was still alive. She moved to the couch and gave Jennifer a humorous smile.

'I was getting worried about you, Jenny. I can see you're tied up at the moment,' Melanie giggled.

Jennifer glared at Melanie as she untied her.

'Your jokes are terrible, Mel.'

Melanie noticed the red hand mark on Jennifer's pale cheek.

'I see she slapped you around a bit – how are you feeling?'

'She's got a lot of power in her right hand; it felt as if she nearly knocked my head off.'

Melanie sat beside her and kissed Jennifer lightly on the lips.

'What was that for?' Jennifer asked, in amazement.

'You looked as if you needed it,' Melanie replied, softly.

They stood up and left the cottage and walked up the road towards their car.

'Was it her?' Melanie asked.

'Yes, she's obviously wearing a wig and she has changed the colour of her eyes, but it was Sam all right,' Jennifer said.

'She has a little girl aged about twenty months,' Melanie told her.

'Janice told me Sam had conceived; I'm intrigued to know who the father is.'

When they got to the car, Jennifer looked around and saw nobody about; she swiftly removed her soiled dress and threw it onto the floor below the back seat. She opened the boot of the car and pulled out her suitcase and opened it and took out a white T-shirt and white shorts and put them on, then placed the suitcase back in the boot and slammed the lid and got in the car beside Melanie, who had the med kit open on her lap. Jennifer let her smooth some white cream on her battered cheek. Her nose had stopped bleeding, but it was still sore. Melanie cleaned the blood off Jennifer's lower face.

CHAPTER LXIV:

PREDATORY INSTINCTS

Melanie and Jennifer walked to the access to Horner Wood. Melanie gazed at Jennifer's long shapely legs; she thought the tall girl looked good in shorts, and Melanie knew she could never have the courage to wear shorts, as she had the fuller figure.

'It's a nice evening for a walk in the woods,' Melanie said.

'And a nice evening to be ravished by a wild animal,' Jennifer said, casually.

Melanie stopped walking and stared at Jennifer, trying to decide if she was joking or being serious.

'Did you have to say that?' Melanie complained.

Jennifer turned and smiled.

'I'm sorry, Mel. We won't bump into anything nasty,' Jennifer assured her.

They walked through the depths of the shady ancient woodland.

'I don't know about that, Lavonia is roaming about the countryside somewhere,' Melanie said.

Jennifer laughed.

'You won't have to worry about that, she's not that brave, to go running about in the woods,' Jennifer said.

Jennifer moved off and Melanie watched her creep quietly through the thick leaf mould. The tall girl seemed to be in her element as she moved gracefully amongst the trees. Jennifer stopped occasionally and sniffed the air. She moved slowly forward, and she espied a deer ahead of her and Jennifer stood still and wondered how near she could get to it before it sensed her. Jennifer knew she was downwind of the creature and it would not hear her above the usual sounds of the dense wood.

Melanie moved quickly to keep Jennifer in sight, which was not difficult because of the colour of her clothes: Jennifer was a ghostly white figure moving through the undergrowth. Melanie in her short dark green dress was more suitably attired for moving about the many shades of green of the wood. Melanie suddenly stepped on a twig and it snapped, and the deer bounded away and so did Jennifer.

Melanie lost sight of her and called out her name. She had a sudden feeling Jennifer was stalking her. Melanie retraced her steps back to where they had entered the wood. When she got there, she stood still and waited for Jennifer to show herself.

'Come on, Jenny, stop fooling around,' Melanie called out.

Melanie was suddenly grabbed from behind and she screamed, she was released, and she spun round and glared at Jennifer, her face flushed with anger.

'What are you trying to do, scare me to death,' Melanie raged.

Jennifer stared at Melanie and could see she was not very happy with her.

'I'm sorry. I could not resist it; it was so easy to creep up on you.'

Melanie shook her head and sighed deeply and let the anger fade from her mind and body.

'You'd make a good predator, if you wore something other than white.'

Jennifer's face beamed with pleasure at Melanie's compliment. She moved closer to Melanie and kissed her on the lips.

'You looked as if you needed that, I'm truly sorry for frightening you, I see now that it was very stupid of me. Please don't stay angry with me, I do so want us to be friends,' Jennifer said, sincerely.

Melanie turned away and Jennifer followed her to where they had parked the car.

MALMSMEAD, DEVON.

AUGUST 2136

Steven Calvert drove into the car park in the farm and parked alongside a sleek green sports car. Janice got out and stared down at the registration and saw it was the car they were trailing. Steven stood beside her.

'Our Phoebe loves fast cars,' he pointed out.

'She is standing on a knife edge. She is not all she seems, I'd love to find out who's running her,' Janice said.

When Melanie had informed them, they had made contact with a girl they were sure was the runaway Samantha, Janice had decided to target Phoebe. Ever since reading the file on the girl, Janice was intrigued, and she wanted to know more about the girl and more about what the file was not telling her. Janice was sure if the authorities really wanted Phoebe locked away for life they would have done it long ago. Janice had an inquiring mind and the information she had about Phoebe just did not add up.

'You're not just being overly suspicious?'

'If you had read the file on her, you would be suspicious, too.'

Janice walked out of the parking area. Steven made off towards the gift shop, where he had a vantage point to watch the green sports car and lie in wait for the owner. Janice walked casually along the side of the road, her eyes peeled for any sight of her quarry. It was a pleasant afternoon with a clear blue sky; her body felt the warmth of the sun through the material of her sky-blue dress. The road curved round to the right and at the apex of the curve was a large grey roofed house. The surrounding area was bordered on both sides and at the back of the house and outbuildings. Janice made a quick scan of the grounds around the house and near the rear she saw Phoebe standing by a tree talking to a tall, solid-looking man. Janice recognised him at once. What did the head of Central Intelligence want with a supposed female homicidal psychopath? Now Janice knew who was controlling Phoebe, she was determined to find out more about the strange alliance. She would be able to tell Steven she had had a right to be suspicious of Phoebe Cross. She had been unstable as a child – what was she really like now that she was an adult? She would be having to be treated with care, something Janice was very aware of.

Director Henry Jackson had first met Phoebe when he had been the head of the City Security Agency; he had been in the interrogation room when she was questioned about the murder of her parents. After the interrogation he was left alone with her and he asked Phoebe if she would do some work for him. The police did not believe her story, but Henry had, knowing something of the unidentified serial killer and how he worked. Phoebe consented and he organised her escape. She kept in touch with him by several means he had set up for her. The more she learnt about the killer, the more Jackson thought the man was in authority, Phoebe could not put a face to the man as it was always masked.

Phoebe moved away from the tree and turned and saw Janice staring towards her. She told Jackson she had to go. He told her to take his car. Janice had dived into the cover of the trees and hoped Phoebe had not seen her. She heard the sound of a car starting.

Phoebe headed the silver-grey car along the driveway and out of the open gates; she shot past Janice, who was skulking amongst the trees at the side of the road. She swung the car round to the right and drove fast down the road. She heard a sound behind her, and something was pressed against the back of her head.

'Why don't you stop the car, there's a good girl,' a female voice said behind her.

Phoebe kept going and she passed a car parked at the side of the road; it started up and followed her.

'Who are you?' Phoebe asked.

'The name's Jennifer, now stop the car.' The voice was sharp and menacing.

Phoebe gazed up at the mirror and at the reflection of the pale silver haired girl behind her. Phoebe also noticed the car following close behind.

'If I don't, you are going to shoot me?'

'I want to talk to you, not kill you,' Jennifer said, calmly.

The car behind her shot forward and drew alongside Phoebe then it passed and swung into her path forcing Phoebe off the road. Luckily there were no trees or hedges along the side of the road, and she stopped the car in the field she found herself in.

Melanie McAllister got out of her car and opened the front door of the silver-grey car and asked the dark-haired girl to get out. Phoebe stared at her with wide dark eyes.

'Why don't you do what the nice girl says,' Jennifer told her.

Phoebe turned around and gazed at the slim girl sitting on the back seat, who still had the weapon aimed at her head. Phoebe gave a deep sigh and eased herself out of the car and stood over Melanie, who was slightly shorter than her. Jennifer vacated the car and kept Phoebe covered with the weapon in her right hand. Phoebe looked the tall girl over from head to foot.

'You're very tall; you wouldn't be Samantha's sister, would you?'

Jennifer shook her head and assured Phoebe she was not related to Samantha. Jennifer gazed down the road at the direction they had just come, and she saw Janice running towards them.

'Talking of Samantha, can you tell me where she is?' Jennifer asked.

'I don't know; we parted company ages ago.'

'Yes – you drove past me some time ago – when I was crossing a bridge,' Jennifer said.

Phoebe thought for a moment. 'Yes, I remember – Samantha was about to run you down – then thought better of it.'

Janice joined them and stared at Jennifer in surprise.

'What are you doing here?'

'Just after you contacted us and told us about Phoebe having a green sports car, we came across it on our travels, so we followed it here,' Jennifer explained.

'What do you want me for?' Phoebe wanted to know.

Jennifer moved swiftly and stood in from of Phoebe.

'You have valuable information that would be very useful to us.'

'Such as?' Phoebe wanted to know.

Janice stood beside Jennifer.

'You have had contact with the aliens, Jennifer thinks you can help us to understand their motives for being here,' Janice said.

'What's in it for me?'

'The chance of having your sister back with you safe and alive,' Jennifer said.

'Do I have a choice?'

'Not really,' Jennifer observed, dryly.

Jennifer and Melanie went back to their car and drove away. Phoebe decided to go with Janice – if she could help her find her sister, Phoebe was willing to give Janice and her employers all the information she could about the aliens.

CHAPTER LXV:

THE KILLER INSTINCT

MAY 2137

THE NORTH DEVON COAST.

The sun broke out of the thick cloud cover at last and the bright light and warmth settled on Jennifer's sleeping face. She woke and turned away from the window and the glare of the sun. Jennifer slid out of bed and left her sleeping space and crossed the passage and entered Melanie's sleeping cabin. Jennifer was glad the rain had gone at last. For the last two months there had been torrential rain. She had ventured out into the rain a few times and returned looking like a drowned rat. It did not bother Jennifer as she had found it an exhilarating experience. Melanie had stopped trying to influence Jennifer into behaving properly, she was a wild thing and being confined in the camper for weeks on end was getting the tall girl down. The experience in Horner Wood had shown Melanie Jennifer's real aptitude, the ancient wood had woken up something of Jennifer's ancestral genes. She wanted to be out and in the woods with the other wildlife.

They had returned to the Research Complex in the winter months. Jennifer got Phoebe to tell her all she could about her experiences with the aliens and the mystery serial killer, as Jennifer was very interested in him also, he was a predator and she wanted to battle her wits against him. Melanie was in the room as well and she stared at the mask of concentration on Jennifer's face. Melanie could almost hear her brain working furiously over the information Phoebe was giving her and locking it away into the memory for future use. After that Jennifer had gone to General Heywood's office and had a long conference with him. Melanie had not been invited and she had a strong urge to know what they were hatching up between them. To Jennifer's surprise he gave her leave to depart again from the Research Complex and he granted all her wishes and approved her ideas of what to do next. Jennifer wanted Melanie to accompany her again to act as driver,

General Heywood declined at first, because he wanted Melanie where he could keep an eye on her, but Jennifer argued non-stop about letting Melanie go, so he decided to let Jennifer have her way.

They were given a large camper vehicle which was loaded with the instruments needed for their mission. They set off in sunny weather, which lasted two days; the sky was then covered with thick cloud and down came the unending rain. Melanie asked Jennifer if she wanted to return because of the bad weather, but Jennifer adamantly declined and told Melanie they were not going to let a little rain spoil their freedom. Melanie was glad to follow Jennifer's lead, as she had no wish to go back either.

Jennifer pulled the sheets off Melanie and shook her awake. She rubbed her eyes and glared at Jennifer because of the rude awakening. Jennifer beamed at her and Melanie could see the girl was happy about something. Their friendship had grown, and they enjoyed each other's company.

'You can't stay in bed all day, the sun is out, and it's stopped raining,' Jennifer informed her.

'I don't believe you,' Melanie said and gazed out of the small window to see if Jennifer was telling her the truth.

Melanie swung her legs over the side of the bunk bed.

'Do you have to run about in the nude?'

Jennifer looked' down at herself as if realising for the first time she was naked. She went to her own sleeping cabin to get dressed. Melanie stood up and went to the wardrobe and took out a dark brown dress and put it on; she put on her white ankle socks and shoes and went up to the top of the camper, where the small kitchenette was and started on the breakfast. Jennifer came in and Melanie handed her a mug of hot strong tea; she gazed at Melanie with a critical eye.

'The dress is too long,' Jennifer complained.

Melanie poked her tongue out at Jennifer and gazed down at the hem of her dress which came down to her knees. She looked up at her partner. Jennifer wore a white T-shirt and blue shorts, her long legs and feet were bare – she did not believe in being overdressed.

'After two months of inactivity, the hunt is back on,' Jennifer said. Melanie shook her head.

'You're enjoying this, aren't you, Jenny?'

They had breakfast and then got back on the road. Jennifer gazed up at the sky, the thick cloud cover was breaking up and revealing clear blue sky and it was getting warmer. Jennifer looked across at Melanie, who was concentrating on her driving. Jennifer placed her hand on the hem of Melanie's dress and started to ease it up her buxom thighs. Melanie took her left hand off the steering wheel and slapped the offending hand off her leg and then pulled the hem back down to her knees.

Melanie drove into Hunter's Inn car park. They got out and Melanie went to the toilets, Jennifer noticed a large white van and she went to have a look at it. There was nobody in the cab. She went around the back and saw the windows in the back doors were covered, so she could not see into the back of the van. She turned away and one of the covers on the windows was moved aside and two grey eyes watched Jennifer walking away.

'Enjoy your freedom, Jenny, I'm coming for you.'

Jennifer walked towards the camper unaware of the eyes watching her. When she got to the camper, she found Melanie had returned and she went off to the toilets. When she got back, she got in the cab and sat next to Melanie, who handed her a mug of coffee.

'Thanks, Mel, you're an angel.'

Melanie sighed and shook her head. She finished her coffee and then drove out of the car park. She headed down the Heddon valley. Jennifer gazed in wonder at the thick expanse of woodland; she had an inner urge to get out of the vehicle and dive into the wood. The call of the wild, she could hear it as if it was shouting in her ear. Melanie took a swift glance at Jennifer then turned back to the road ahead.

'What are you daydreaming about, Jenny?'

Melanie's voice brought Jennifer back to reality.

'Some strange intangible force is pulling me towards the dense woodland,' Jennifer said.

Melanie, not for the first time, wondered what was happening inside Jennifer's head. It seemed after spending so much time cooped up in the underground complex, her mind was having some problems coping with the wide world. Her mind was spreading out as was her knowledge and experiences.

'You are a strange girl, Jenny; I'd love to meet your parents.'

'So would I,' Jennifer assured her.

Jennifer yearned to know who had brought her into the world, her questions about the subject had been ignored, they told her all would be revealed to her in time. Dr Hamilton told her to be patient, but Jennifer's patience was growing thin.

'At least you have friends who care for you,' Melanie assured her.

Jennifer looked away from the view out the window and gazed at Melanie.

'I also need a special friend I can trust, that's why I persuaded the General to let you come with me again on this mission.'

'You can count on me, Jenny. You only have to tell me what you want me to do,' Melanie said, sincerely.

Jennifer placed a hand on Melanie's left thigh and squeezed it gently.

'I appreciate that, Mel.'

Melanie drove off the road and parked in a field. Jennifer got out of her seat and opened the door at the back of the cab and walked into the camper. Melanie followed behind her.

Melanie went into the kitchenette section of the camper and Jennifer went into the section opposite; she sat down in front of the instrumentation and activated it and a screen lit up before her and showed a map of the surrounding area, a light flashed which showed the place where the camper was parked. If the alien scout ship was nearby the instruments would find it. They were connected to Samantha in a way and they were after her. If they found one the other would not be far away, Jennifer supposed.

The huge helicopter was cruising southwards; below it was the Heddon valley. Joanna Lumsden was piloting the huge craft; John Stephenson sat beside her acting as navigator. Behind them sat Henry Jones staring at a computer screen in front of him and taking swift glances at the green globe sitting on the black plinth on his left.

'Got anything yet, Henry?' John asked.

'No, I haven't even picked up Jenny and Mel.'

'Missing your loved one, Henry?' Joanna inquired.

'You could say that.' John gazed out of the window at the different patches of green below them. They passed over three farms and as they flew over the huge camper the globe started flashing.

'We have something,' Henry said. Down below John spied the huge white camper.

'It's Jenny and your girlfriend, they are just below us,' John informed him.

As they flew away from the camper the globe flashed slowly and then it stopped. When Jennifer had started working with the green sphere made by Samantha, she had tuned it to her brain, so it worked the same for her as it did for Samantha. If Jennifer and Melanie ran into trouble and seemingly disappeared without trace, the device could be used to seek her out. The helicopter headed for the village of Parracombe.

The door opened and Jennifer looked away from the screen as Melanie sat on the edge of the couch on her right.

'The complex's helicopter has just flown over us, I expect Jo is flying it,' Melanie informed her.

'They couldn't have found anything yet, because they did not call in,' Jennifer said.

Melanie told her lunch was ready and Jennifer placed a hand on Melanie's right knee.

'Are you all right about being the driver and cook?'

'Of course, you can't do any of those things and I've also got to look after your health.'

'What I meant was, I don't want you to think that's all you're here for, I want your input as well. If you have any ideas, I want to hear them.'

Melanie gazed at the pale face and the ice blue eyes; she could not believe this highly intelligent girl was going to ask her opinion on anything. Jennifer could almost see what Melanie was thinking.

'I have never thought of you as anything but a bright and intelligent girl. I have never thought anything bad you, I assure you,' Jennifer said, sincerely.

Melanie placed a hand on Jennifer's hand that still lay on her knee.

'I'm sorry I can't say the same. Though those clones they made from your cells must take most of the blame, they were just like Lavonia, trouble with a capital T.'

'Like I told Sam, they are not me, I'm a different person,' Jennifer said.

Melanie gave her a warm smile and squeezed her hand gently.

'I just thought as the clone was made from your cells it must be the same, but I could see the differences, you are not cold and hard like the clone is.'

'Samantha once told me, the clone made her physically sick whenever they were close, it gave her severe headaches. But when I met up with her, Samantha was surprised that I did not affect her that way and we got on well.'

Melanie touched Jennifer's cheek with her hand.

'It's the same with me; you are a much better person.'

Jennifer stood up and Melanie slid off the table and they left and went into the kitchen area and had lunch.

Late in the evening Jennifer went out for a walk and Melanie lay on her bunk and read a book. Jennifer wore a grey sweatshirt and grey shorts. The night was closing in and a stiff breeze blew over the land. She crossed the field and walked into a wooded area. She stepped into the cover of the trees. She moved slowly and silently; she took a deep breath taking in the wild odours of the wood. Jennifer was in her element as she listened for the slightest sounds.

He watched her flit about the trees, he admired her tall slim figure, and she was very shapely, he thought. He moved closer to her; he could see the way she moved the girl was something special. He crept forward, the long thin blade in his right hand.

Jennifer suddenly stopped moving and gazed about her. The wood was full of dark shadows. She suddenly saw a glint of silver and she backed away from it, her sharp hearing picked up the sounds of something coming towards her. The ice blue eyes went to a deep blue then they lit up, and she saw a tall dark shape coming towards her on her right-hand side. Jennifer waited for the figure to get near to her. Jennifer was sure it was a man; she wanted him to know she had the nerve to face him; she was not going to turn and run. As he came up to her, Jennifer moved swiftly and the blade meant for her chest slid harmlessly away from her body; she was a foot taller than her assailant. She lashed out with her right fist and hit him on the side of the head. He lashed out with his right foot and hit her in the abdomen. She moved quickly backwards as she ignored the pain.

He thrust forward with the blade, she moved rapidly sideways and her fist came down on his right hand, knocking the blade out of it. He saw the girl turn and run; she disappeared into the darkness of the wood. He heard a sound behind him.

'Jennifer is a very slippery customer, you'll have to do much better than that, if you want to carve her up,' Lavonia said.

He turned and faced her.

'Jennifer is a predator, I know it would not be easy, you could learn something from her,' he said.

'She's got more lives than a cat, I want her dead and I don't care how we do it as long as we put her life at an end,' Lavonia said, wildly.

'We'll have to bring some more people in; just make sure they know that Jennifer and Melanie must never return to the Research Complex,' he said.

Jennifer returned to the camper and dived into Melanie's sleeping area and asked her to move the camper. Melanie slid off the bunk and ran through the camper and went through the door that led to the cab. Jennifer sat beside her and told her of the attack in the woods. Melanie drove at a leisurely pace along the road towards the village of Parracombe.

Melanie parked the car just outside the city and the two girls left the cab; they went into the kitchenette area and Melanie made some coffee for them both. Jennifer sat on a stool.

'That'll teach you to go off on your own, Jenny.'

'I didn't think there was a homicidal maniac running amok round here.'

'So did his victims. I wonder if he is the one killing those poor girls in Exeter.'

Melanie sat on a stool beside Jennifer.

'Phoebe told me about him, he devised a plan to trap Samantha and it almost brought about her death; perhaps he is still after her blood,' Jennifer said.

Melanie turned to her and they faced each other. Jennifer knew what she was going to say before she opened her mouth.

'Now he had seen you, he will be after your blood too.'

'Well he won't find me a pushover.'

Melanie stared at the girl; she seemed to have no problem over the idea that someone wanted to murder her.

'You're a cool one, Jenny. Don't you feel any fear?'

'You have no time for fear, when your life is under threat. I'm still finding out about myself. The first time I went into the wood, I felt a change come over me, that's why I was stalking that deer and why I silently crept up on you.'

'Yes, I remember that, you really shook me up that time,' Melanie said.

Jennifer placed the flat of her right hand on Melanie's left thigh below the hem of her skirt.

'And I'm still sorry I did it to you.'

Melanie laid the empty mug on the table and lifted Jennifer's hand off her leg. Melanie stood up.

'I'm off to bed, I advise you to do the same.'

Jennifer followed Melanie down to the rear of the camper. Melanie entered her sleeping area and Jennifer watched the door close behind her. Jennifer went to her own compartment and sat on the bunk bed in the dark and gazed out of the small window. Jennifer hoped that everyone like her were safely inside while the predators hunted in the night. Jennifer had enjoyed her night out and she had felt no fear when the killer descended on her. Instead she had felt a thrill run through her body, it was what she wanted, to face the ultimate danger. She could have ended up like Samantha, at the mercy of a predator skilled with a sharp dissecting blade. Jennifer was overjoyed she had faced him and got away with her body and life intact. She was invincible and indestructible. Jennifer was ready to face any danger the aliens could throw at her. She had some tremendous power inside her head, a part of her mind told her so, but how she could learn how to tap into it. That was what she had to discover.

She lay on the ground, her arms and legs outstretched; she could not move. Deep golden eyes gazed at her as he worked on her slim body, the light glinted on the silvery blade, and her blood ran along channels dug into the ground.

Jennifer woke with a start; her body was covered in a cold sweat. It was daylight; someone was bending over her calling her name, her eyes focused on Melanie's face.

'Jenny, it's just a dream.'

Jennifer sat up; her body was shaking. Melanie handed her a mug of hot strong tea, then she left the sleeping compartment and returned a moment later and injected an amber liquid into Jennifer's upper right arm. Melanie ran a soothing hand over Jennifer's cheek.

'That was a rough dream you were having.'

'It certainly was, in more ways than one,' Jennifer agreed.

Jennifer drank the tea then slipped off the bed; she put on a white blouse and black skirt. Melanie wanted to know what was going on inside her head.

'Do you think the dream was a warning?'

Jennifer sat beside her on the bunk bed and put on her shoes.

'It's telling me how much danger there is surrounding this mission; if you want to go back, I shall not think less of you.'

'I'm not going back without you, I won't get paid if I do,' Melanie decided.

Jennifer put her arm round Melanie and kissed her on the cheek.

'I appreciate that; we make a good team, you and I.'

Outside something hit the side of the camper and Melanie leapt to her feet, she went around to the other side of the bunk bed and opened the window and put her head out. Steven Calvert stared up at her.

'You're awake then?'

'We heard the helicopter flying over us – did they find anything?'

Steven told her they were sure Samantha was staying at a public house in Parracombe. They had the place watched and they would grab her when she came out. Melanie told him Jennifer and she were ready when needed.

Jennifer and Melanie wandered leisurely down a narrow street with houses on each side of them. They approached the Inn. Melanie stood on the bridge and gazed down at the river that ran under it. Jennifer looked across at the car park and noticed a large white van parked in it. She entered the inn and Steven came up to her. Jennifer told him she would go up and speak to the girl, she would soon know if it was Samantha or not. She made her way up the stairs to the top floor and walked along the passage to the end door and knocked on it. Jennifer waited a moment and then opened the door and stepped into the room and closed the door behind her.

'You are becoming a real nuisance, Jenny.'

Jennifer stared across the room at a tall girl standing by the window opposite the door; she had long dark brown hair. She wore a navy-blue dress that came down to her knees.

Melanie sat and sipped her beer and gazed across the table at Steven and Janice. She had told them about the attack on Jennifer, when she went for a walk in the wood during the night. Janice turned to her partner and shook her head; she was sure Jennifer was trying to look for trouble. Janice did not want Jennifer ending up like Samantha had, Jennifer might end up unlucky and not survive as Samantha had done. They hoped Jennifer would be able to persuade the runaway girl to come back with them – If the girl staying at the inn was Samantha.

Jennifer sat on the bed and watched the girl as she stood by the window, she stared at the new face and could not see through the disguise and the colour of the eyes had changed from the first time she had caught up with her.

'Why did they send you to find me?'

Jennifer told her about the underground complex she now worked in and about how she was getting bored with not much to do, she escaped at night for a change of scenery.

'The General found out and sent me out to try my talents on trying to find you.'

Samantha moved away from the window and sat beside Jennifer on the side of the bed.

'Wasn't he worried that you might run away like me?'

'The longer I stayed away the more I was tempted to do a runner, but I gave my word to the General, I would not disappear,' Jennifer explained.

Jennifer stared hard at the girl's face their eyes met and Samantha laid a hand on Jennifer's cheek.

'The last time we met, you tried to get inside my mind, that's why I slapped you.'

'Yes, I regretted doing that, you intrigue me, Sam. I want to find out all there is to know about you, I'm drawn to you like a magnet.'

Jennifer moved closer to Samantha, who suddenly felt her breath on her face. She remembered when she had Jennifer in her home and how the strange girl had got close to her.

'I'm still not sure of you, Jenny.'

'You have nothing to fear from me, I am still the same girl you had in your home, we worked well together, I like you Sam, I really do,' Jennifer assured her. Jennifer put her hand on the girl's knee.

'We are to fight this alien menace together, why should I harm you, there's enough enemies after your blood, its allies you want. Tell me what I have to do to convince you of my loyalty to you.'

Samantha gazed at the ice-blue eyes; she had a sudden vision of her swinging an axe and splitting Jennifer's skull and having a look at what was behind those hypnotic pale blue eyes.

You should have killed her the first time you two met

Samantha felt slightly dizzy and she knew Jennifer was trying to get inside her head again. It would do her no good, Samantha could block her out. If Jennifer wanted something from her, she would have to give something in return.

'What are you after, Jenny?'

'The story I heard was your mother was from outer space. I don't hold that against you, but if you let me read through your memories, I might find something helpful to fight these aliens with,' Jennifer said.

Samantha laughed. Jennifer was almost a split personality; her outward character was not as forceful, as the cold intelligence that hid behind the ice-blue eyes. Samantha would love to know how strong her mind was; the only way Samantha could discover that was to let Jennifer have her way. It might be a two-way thing and Samantha hoped to feed off Jennifer's mind while she was probing her brain.

'OK. How are we going to do this?'

Jennifer put her arm round Samantha's slim waist and stared into her eyes.

'Just relax, Sam and let me do the work. I'm not going to hurt you, I promise.'

Samantha watched the ice-blue eyes slowly change to a deep blue; detecting no opposition from Samantha, Jennifer forged on. The nearness of Jennifer made Samantha's body tremble. Jennifer placed a hand on her face, the touch was electric, and it made her skin tingle. She was getting a slight headache, she took a few deep breaths as she let Jennifer keep control, the excitement of the moment ran through her body, adrenalin built up in her veins. Jennifer felt ecstatic, it gave her extreme pleasure probing into another person's feelings and emotions. She closed her eyes and surveyed the images she was getting in her mind's eye.

'That's it, Sam, concentrate, let your memories flow, I'm getting it, don't leave anything out,' Jennifer said, softly and seductively.

Samantha felt the heat being generated by Jennifer's body, as her mind fed on the data she was getting from Samantha's brain. Jennifer had been developing her mental powers ever since the first experience with Samantha when they had first come together. She did not know why but Samantha was the best person she had worked on. It was all part of the way she was drawn to Samantha, she needed the girl's full co-operation in the joining of their two minds, as Jennifer had just found out Samantha could lock her out if she wanted to, so she had a mind as strong as her own.

'You're doing fine, Sam, what you are giving me is very interesting.'

Samantha was reacting to the intimate moment with Jennifer. She felt the zip at the back of her dress being pulled down and Jennifer's hand went inside her dress and ran caressingly down her bare back. Samantha shivered as the touch brought a tingling to her skin.

'I like you, Sam. I have certain feelings towards you.'

'You have a lovely soft touch, Jenny.'

Samantha closed her eyes and concentrated on the mental power probing her brain. She finally made contact with Jennifer's brain and she started to access her memories. Jennifer was too engrossed in probing Samantha's brain to realise her own mind was being invaded. She came across darkness in the depths of Samantha's memory she could not penetrate. As she tried to probe deeper the contact with Samantha's mind was disconnected. Jennifer moved away from Samantha and rubbed her eyes. Samantha blinked and gazed at Jennifer.

You should be careful when letting people rummage around inside your head, they might find out about us, that would never do.

The voice inside Samantha's head had no idea it was close to the body it searched for.

'Are you all right, Jenny?'

Jennifer was not sure, it was not Samantha who broke the link, and she had felt another presence.

'You've been through some rough times, Sam and I thought I had problems.'

Samantha pulled the zip on the back of her dress up and moved close to Jennifer and kissed her on the cheek.

'I've survived it all, that's what matters.'

Samantha stood up, she picked up a shoulder bag from a chair and took out a gun and held it in her right hand.

'We must go,' Samantha said.

That girl is dangerous, you must kill her.

Samantha did not know why, but she thought that would not be the thing to do. She was also unaware, the body the voice was seeking was in front of her.

Jennifer opened the door and stepped out into the passage. After a few moments Samantha joined her. They slipped out of the inn by the back way, they crossed the gardens at one side of the building; they vaulted over a stone wall and landed at the roadside on the other side of the wall. They crossed the road to where Samantha had parked her car. Samantha opened the passenger door and told Jennifer to get in and slammed the door shut after her. Samantha got in beside her and tossed the shoulder bag onto the back seat; she started the car and drove away.

'You have a very powerful mind, Jenny.'

'I've been going through a few changes lately, I don't like being cooped up, there are several things happening inside me, that I have no explanation for yet.'

'We could experiment further some time; there is a blank in my memory for the time when I was under 6. You might be just what I need to unlock the door to them.'

'That would be nice, I would certainly help you in any way I can,' Jennifer said.

Samantha took the left-hand corner without slowing, Jennifer saw Melanie crossing the road and she shouted at the girl. Jennifer gave a sigh of relief when she saw Melanie dive safely out of the car's path. The car flew up the main street. Suddenly the window beside Jennifer shattered and a high velocity bullet buried itself in the floor of the car between her feet.

'You lead a charmed life, Jenny.'

Samantha drove faster to get out of the village, and then she stopped the car.

'It's time to part company.'

Jennifer moved close to her and kissed her on the cheek.

'Take care, Sam.' Jennifer got out of the car and watched Samantha drive off at high speed. Jennifer carried on walking up the road until she reached the camper and stood and waited for Melanie. Ten minutes later a car drew up to the camper and Melanie got out. Jennifer waved at Steven and Janice.

'Did you have your little talk with Samantha?' Melanie inquired.

'Yes, I found it very enlightening.'

'Why don't you tell me about it, I could do with some enlightenment,' Melanie said.

Steven asked Jennifer if Samantha had told her where she was heading for. Jennifer shook her head and told him Samantha had things to do before she returned to captivity. Steven drove off and Jennifer and Melanie entered the camper. Melanie made some tea. Jennifer went to her sleeping compartment and removed her T-shirt and shorts and lay on her bunk bed and gazed up at the ceiling. A little while later Melanie came in and handed her a mug of strong tea. Melanie sat on the bed and sipped her tea and gazed at Jennifer.

'Did Samantha have that little girl with her?'

'I didn't see her; she wasn't in the car with us.'

Jennifer sat up and patted the bed with her hand and Melanie moved beside her; Melanie wore an emerald green bikini bra and pants. Jennifer ran her hand over the top of Melanie's left thigh.

'Samantha wants to bring up her child on her own, she could not trust them not to experiment on her child,' Jennifer said.

'I can understand that.'

Jennifer did not have to worry; she would never have that problem as she was unable to have children.

'She goes to ground now, and we won't hear from her until she re-emerges,' Jennifer said.

'Do you want to go back?' Jennifer turned her head and smiled at her companion.

'Not yet – what about you?' Melanie asked.

Melanie stared down at Jennifer's right hand that lay still on her thigh.

'You're not tired of my company already, are you?'

Jennifer shook her head and squeezed Melanie's thigh gently.

'Definitely not.'

Melanie put her empty mug on the floor. She moved down and lay out on the bunk bed.

'I'm glad to hear it.'

Jennifer looked down at Melanie and was glad to see she was at last wearing minimal clothing. Jennifer looked down at her face and studied the bright brown eyes. She wondered what Melanie was thinking about. Jennifer would not do to her, what she had done with Samantha, not without Melanie's permission.

'Are you trying to read my mind?' Melanie asked.

Jennifer shook her head.

'I don't read minds, but I was wondering what you were thinking, that was a very inspirational question.'

Melanie swung her legs over the side of the bunk, Jennifer moved behind her and started to massage her shoulders. Melanie gave a sigh.

'That's nice, Jenny, keep it up, that's just what I want.'

CHAPTER LXVI:

A PAINFUL EPISODE

JUNE 2137

Melanie drove through Lynton on the North Devon coast. The days were getting hotter. She gazed up at the clear blue sky and it made her want to drive down to the blue-green sea and jump in. She followed the directions Jennifer gave her; the tall girl was sitting at her instruments and Melanie would need a crowbar to prise her away from them. Jennifer was following a faint signal picked up by her equipment. If it was the alien scout craft, she could not tell yet. Time would tell; if they were close, they would know about them as Lavonia and her creepy friend were shadowing them in a large white van. Jennifer was sure in failing to get hold of Samantha, they would try for her and she was ready for them.

Melanie came in and Jennifer ran her eyes over her companion, she wore a light green top and a short dark green dress, her midriff was bare. She looked hot and bothered. Jennifer turned away from the electronic equipment and faced her companion.

'Have you passed any large white vans on the road?'

'Several, but none of them were following us,' Melanie replied.

Jennifer stood up and ran a hand over Melanie's cheek.

'You look as if you need cooling off,' Jennifer observed.

Melanie took hold of the hand on her face.

'And I'm going to do just that, I'm going for a dip in the sea, are you coming with me?'

'Why not.'

Melanie turned and Jennifer slapped her bottom gently as she stepped out of the control compartment.

'Jenny, you're impossible.'

They left the camper and Melanie locked it up. They walked down towards Lynmouth and the sea. They turned eastward and walked along the water's edge.

After a while Melanie walked across the sand to the trees that covered the lower part of the hills that led down to the strip of sandy beach. Melanie placed her shoulder bag on the ground and then took off her top and skirt; she wore a blue bikini under them. She turned to Jennifer.

'Are you coming?'

'Nor I'll stay here and admire the view.'

Jennifer grinned at her and Melanie shook her head and made for the water's edge. Jennifer gazed at the girl's shapely bottom. She watched Melanie slip into the sea, Melanie was an expert swimmer and Jennifer saw the girl was as at home in the water as she was on land. Jennifer watched her for a few minutes then she started to walk back to Lynmouth. While Melanie enjoyed herself, she had enemies to look out for. As she wandered aimlessly through the harbourside village, she gazed at the people she passed and gazed at their expressions of surprise of seeing a girl so tall. Jennifer had got used to looking down at people and the strange looks they gave her. She walked up the steep road that led back up to Lynton. She made it to the car park where they had left the camper. When it came in sight Jennifer stopped dead; parked next to it was a large white van. She ducked down behind a car. Lavonia was standing by the cab of the camper as if waiting for someone. Jennifer moved round to another car so she could get a better look at what Lavonia was up to. She noticed a pair of legs sticking out from under the cab. After a moment a tall, well-built man crawled out from under the cab and stood up, Lavonia spoke to him and he nodded his head. They got in the van parked next to the camper and drove off. Jennifer made her way to the camper and got on the ground and slithered under the cab. Her suspicions were confirmed – they had planted a bomb under the cab.

Jennifer crawled out from under the cab and stood up, she took the key out of the back pocket of her shorts and let herself into the camper, she pulled the large tool box out from behind the driver's seat and carried it outside and dragged it under the cab with her and set about removing the bomb from their camper. When she had done that, she put the tool box back in the camper and locked it up. She went back to where she had left Melanie. When she got there Melanie was just coming out of the sea, she rushed over to her and showed her the bomb. Melanie stared at her in horror. Jennifer threw the bomb as far as she could out to sea.

'I'd really like to get hold of that girl and throttle the life out of her,' Jennifer said.

They walked up the beach to where Melanie had left her bag.

'Let me know when you do and I'll give you a hand,' Melanie said.

Melanie took a towel out of the bag and dried the front of her body.

'Do you want me to dry your back, Mel?'

Melanie shook her head and was about to say no, as Jennifer could not be trusted to keep her hands from wandering.

'OK, but behave yourself.'

'I don't know what you mean,' Jennifer said, innocently.

Jennifer slowly and meticulously dried Melanie's back. When Jennifer got down to her waist, for one horrible moment she thought Jennifer was going to pull her bikini pants down, so she could dry her bottom, but Jennifer did as she was told and behaved herself.

'You know you can trust me, Mel.'

Melanie put on her top and skirt and picked up her shoulder bag and the two girls went back to the camper. Melanie went into her sleeping compartment; Jennifer was about to go into her own when Melanie called her in. She sat on the bed and watched Melanie undress and put on a change of clothes. She moved to the bed and gazed down at Jennifer; the pale blue eyes stared back at her.

'That bomb has got to you, hasn't it?'

Melanie nodded her head; Jennifer ran a caressing hand over her left thigh.

'I'm taking no chances, that's why I'm on the lookout for them and it paid dividends: I caught her at it,' Jennifer said.

'I'm glad I brought you along,' Melanie said, trying to be light-heartedly.

Melanie kept staring at the ice blue eyes, now they were heading into danger, she would be relying more on Jennifer now as she seemed unperturbed about what was going on around them. Melanie thought Jennifer was unemotional as a machine when she first met her, but her feelings towards the girl had changed.

'I like you, Jenny, I'm really sorry for the bad things I've said about you,' Melanie said, sincerely

Jennifer kept stroking the soft skin of Melanie's left thigh, the touch was almost electric, and she did not want to knock the hand off.

'I'm not going to hold that against you. I like you too and I'm going to make sure you come to no harm.'

Melanie sat on the bunk bed beside Jennifer, who put her arm round her waist and pulled Melanie closer to her.

'You are the strong one of the two of us.'

Jennifer stared into the bright brown eyes.

'If trouble comes, I am certain I shall not find you wanting,' Jennifer assured her.

'I wish I could share your optimism.'

Jennifer kissed her lightly on the lips.

'I have faith in you, Mel, that's why I kept on at the General to let you come with me,' Jennifer told her.

'I'll try not to let you down.'

Jennifer kissed her again and Melanie gave her a warm smile.

'You are certainly not the unemotional girl I accused you of, Jenny.'

'I was once, but Michelle taught me to be more responsive to people and she put up with my overbearing ways, I decided to change, and you obviously noticed the change.'

Melanie decided it was lunch time and she stood up and Jennifer followed her to the kitchenette compartment. Two hours later they were on the road again. Melanie sat in the cab by herself as Jennifer went back to her electronic equipment. Melanie followed the coast road; a sea breeze blew in the open window. Melanie headed towards Porlock Weir. When she reached the destination, she parked the camper. She left the cab and made some coffee and took a mug in to Jennifer.

'Where are we?' Jennifer inquired.

'Porlock Weir, it's a delightful place,' Melanie said.

Jennifer sipped her coffee and gazed up at Melanie.

'What are you thinking?' Jennifer wanted to know.

'Don't you know?'

Jennifer shook her head. Melanie had always had a strange feeling when she looked at the ice blue eyes, she was always sure Jennifer was looking into her mind. She told Jennifer about it.

'Very perceptive of you, Mel. But I told you I don't read minds. I don't look into their eyes and immediately see what they are thinking written on their forehead.'

Melanie giggled, it told her Jennifer had some way of telling what was in a person's mind and she told the girl so.

'And you want to know what it is?'

Melanie nodded her head vigorously; she wanted to learn as much about Jennifer as she could.

'I can't do it without your permission,' Jennifer assured her.

Melanie bent down and kissed her on the cheek.

'You have it, Jenny; you did say we had to learn more about each other.'

Jennifer put the empty mug down and took Melanie's hand and pulled her down onto her lap. Melanie put her arm round Jennifer's shoulders and gazed into the ice blue eyes.

'What do I do now?' Melanie asked.

'Just keep looking into my eyes and concentrate, open your mind,' Jennifer said, soothingly.

Jennifer ran her hand gently over Melanie's cheek; her skin tingled at her touch.

'The best way I can explain it is, I get your brain to act like a computer, I access your memories and download them to my memory, I read the data as it flows from one memory to the other. It works better when there are certain emotional feelings between us.'

'I had noticed, but I don't mind now.'

Jennifer stared hard at the bright brown eyes; Melanie felt the warmth of Jennifer's body as they sat close together. She concentrated on the pale blue eyes, as

Jennifer probed Melanie's brain. She made contact and filtered through Melanie's memory.

'Keep calm, Mel, concentrate, I will not harm you.'

Melanie had a slight headache and Jennifer broke the contact; Melanie blinked her eyes.

'Are you all right, Mel?'

Melanie stood up; the throbbing in her head had faded away.

'That was a strange experience.'

'Just as long as you haven't suffered for it,' Jennifer said.

'I'm fine, you needn't worry.'

Jennifer stood up and caressed Melanie's cheek with a soothing hand.

'You've got a lot of anger inside you; I can see now why the General was reluctant to let you go.'

'Keep it to yourself.'

'Of course, Mel. Your secrets are safe with me.'

Melanie was glad of that; she knew she could trust Jennifer. There was one secret she wanted kept deep inside her memory. They left the camper; Melanie had a quick look round but saw no large white vans in the vicinity. They were in a small inlet below wooded hills, which Melanie pointed out to Jennifer, who assured Melanie she was finished making her way through some dark wood for a while, as her last experience was still vivid in her memory. They walked along the quay and Jennifer gazed at the many brightly coloured yachts moored along the quay wall. Melanie noticed her interest in the boats, and she asked Jennifer if she would like to go out on one. Melanie had been out sailing several times and she assured Jennifer, she would be in safe hands. Jennifer was enthusiastic about the idea, so Melanie went to see about hiring a yacht for a couple of hours.

The sea was flat and placid, a stiff breeze blew ruffling their hair, and Melanie guided the yacht out to sea, while Jennifer leant on the rail and gazed down at the blue green water. Melanie warned her to be careful and not fall overboard. She turned the yacht towards the east and Jennifer gazed at the coastline with interest. She gazed across at the flat coastal plain that was Porlock Bay. Jennifer wondered if there was anyone there watching their yacht. Lavonia and her friends were still close by, she wondered if they had found out their bomb had not been a success. Jennifer turned and saw Melanie standing at the stern; she was removing her blouse which revealed a blue bikini bra she wore underneath. Jennifer was envious of the girl's fuller figure. She watched Melanie remove her skirt. Jennifer strode over to her.

'How are you enjoying being out at sea?' Melanie asked.

'It's a great experience.'

Jennifer detected a faraway sound and her sharp hearing told her it was getting closer, she told Melanie something was coming. Jennifer looked up at the blue sky; she looked around then saw a black shape coming from the west. She nudged Melanie and pointed to the thing in the sky. They watched it get bigger and take shape of the alien scout craft, it shot past them and flew off eastwards and towards the land. The two girls stared at each other.

'A UFO and they didn't stop to say hello,' Melanie said.

'Have you got your mobile on you?'

Melanie picked up her shoulder bag and rummaged in it and then pulled out her mobile phone.

'Contact your friend the General and tell him about the spacecraft.'

'He's no friend of mine as you well know,' Melanie said, coldly.

They turned the yacht round and headed back to Porlock Weir. Once back inside the camper Melanie started it up and headed for Porlock to the east. Jennifer sat in front of her instrumentation and tried to track the spacecraft. Melanie drove through Porlock without stopping; she kept on the coast road as she had always enjoyed the beauty of the scenery the road ran through. She drove into Bossington and parked the camper.

They walked out of the village of Bossington and followed a footpath up to Hurlstone Point. It was bordered on one side by a wooded area; sometimes the footpath entered into the wood and then veered out again. Melanie made sure Jennifer did not wander off and try to creep up on her when they entered the tree line. Melanie had dressed to fit the surroundings; she wore a lime green blouse and dark green pleated skirt. Jennifer complimented her on how she looked.

'I hope we don't run into that UFO,' Melanie said.

Jennifer hoped they did so they knew exactly where it was. She had worked out and plotted its course and it had come to ground not far from where they were now. She kept Melanie in the dark about her search for the alien spacecraft and gave her other things to occupy her mind.

'You were whingeing earlier because they did not stop to give you a wave,' Jennifer said.

Melanie turned to her and growled, Jennifer giggled, and if she got the chance to wind-up Melanie occasionally, she took the chance.

'You wouldn't be so glib, if they did and you found they were bigger than you.'

Jennifer stared hard at Melanie; she hoped the girl did not still find her tallness intimidating. Melanie was just over six foot so she should not find her height too much of a problem.

'The bigger they are, the harder they'll fall. I hope you aren't holding it against me, because I'm so tall; it's not a threat to you, Mel, I assure you.'

They left the wooded area behind them and Melanie started to climb up the hill that would lead her to Hurlstone Point, Jennifer moved up behind her. She looked up at the sky and saw it was clouding over. It was a cool evening and a breeze was blowing in from the sea. They reached the highest part of the point and Jennifer took a gadget out of her shorts pocket and pressed a button on it. Melanie gazed at her in interest. Jennifer pointed the gadget towards the east, on a small screen on the front of it a red light blinked. Melanie moved close to her.

'What are you up to now, Jenny?'

'I'm trying to get a fix on our alien friends.'

'So we can go in the opposite direction?' Melanie hoped.

Jennifer looked at her and grinned slyly.

'Well I'm not going to do battle with them,' Jennifer assured her.

Jennifer started walking eastwards along a footpath that followed the coastline. Melanie followed behind her, as she wondered where the girl was going to now. She had discovered long ago, Jennifer liked to keep things to herself on occasions. They followed the path round the base of the high spread-out hill, Melanie was glad she was fit, because she had to walk fast to keep up with Jennifer's long striding walk. The footpath ran parallel with the road on their right. Just up ahead of them a car was parked at the side of the road and two men got out and up the hilly moorland towards them. Jennifer suddenly sensed danger. Melanie drew level with her.

'Do you think they're looking for us?' Melanie asked, nervously.

'We'll soon find out.'

They kept walking side by side, the footpath curved towards the road as they came level to the parked car, the two men hurried towards them. One of them shouted out and Melanie stopped walking, but Jennifer kept going. Melanie saw one of them men take a gun out of the pocket of his jeans and aim at Jennifer, Melanie shouted at her and the man fired. Jennifer moved swiftly but she was not fast enough: the bullet burned a furrow across the side of her right thigh, and she fell to the ground. Melanie was about to run to her aid but one of the men grabbed her and held tightly onto her. The man with the gun went to Jennifer and pulled her roughly up onto her feet.

'You are coming with us.'

Jennifer glared at him.

'Have we a choice?' she inquired, coolly.

'No!'

The two men marched the two girls to the road, Lavonia got out of the car and waited for them to reach her.

'What have we here?'

Jennifer gave her a stony stare, Melanie looked away from her.

'Nice to see you again, Lavonia,' Jennifer lied.

The two men pushed the two girls into the back of the car and one of the men got in beside Melanie. Lavonia got in beside the other man who drove away from the side of the road. Melanie took the med kit out of her shoulder bag and tended to the wound on Jennifer's thigh. She gave Melanie a smile to assure her she was not too badly hurt. Jennifer turned her head and gazed out of the window to see where they are going. They drove into a village and Jennifer recognised it as Allerford, as she had been there before. When the car drove out of the village it was manoeuvred off the road and along a gap between two large buildings, one a two-storey house and the other a long single storey structure. The car turned left and drove past the house and headed for another long single storey building. Gazing out of the window Jennifer spied the scout craft parked at the side of the house; she nudged Melanie and pointed to it.

'There you are, Mel, you'll be able to say hello, after all,' Jennifer said, lightly.

'Doesn't anything scare you, Jenny?'

Melanie was exasperated by the flippant attitude Jennifer showed in the face of danger.

'Not that I know of,' Jennifer said.

The two girls were pulled roughly out of the car in a way that made Jennifer seriously think of hitting one of them, but the tine was not right yet and they were outnumbered. They were dragged into the single storey building; it consisted of one large room, and the floor was covered in dust and straw. The two men knocked Jennifer to the floor and tied her ankles together, then her wrists. They walked out and locked the door; Lavonia kept a tight hold on Melanie as they approached the house.

'What do you want of me?' Melanie cried, irritably.

Lavonia swung her left fist and hit Melanie brutally in the face, her eyes watered and she forced herself not to cry. Blood trickled from her sore nose.

'I want to cause you pain, I have a strong dislike for you.'

'I'm not mad about you, either,' Melanie declared, defiantly.

Lavonia punched her in the stomach, and she doubled up and fought for breath.

'That's it, Mel, keep giving me causes to hit you, I'm really enjoying this,' Lavonia assured her happily.

The wind and fight were knocked out of Melanie and she kept quiet, as she was dragged into the house. She was sure it was going to be a painful session with Lavonia.

Jennifer lay on the dirty straw-covered floor, the atmosphere of the building was stale and musty, and there was also a strong animal smell. She wondered what sort of torture Melanie was going through. She felt a strong feeling of failure as she had let her friend down, as she had been unable to stop Melanie from getting hurt. Jennifer wondered what her own fate was going to be. Some time later the door was opened, and Melanie was thrown into the room and the door was closed and locked. Melanie crawled over to Jennifer and sat up and lay her back against the wall, her face and body hurt all over, her assessment of the situation had been right, Lavonia just did not like her.

'Have you upset Lavonia again, Mel?'

Melanie looked down at Jennifer through watery eyes; tears ran down her bruised cheeks.

'It was my fault; I kept banging my face against Lavonia's fist.'

Jennifer stared at the girl; she could see Melanie was putting up a brave face for her.

'I'm sorry, Mel, I have failed you. The last thing I wanted was for you to get hurt.'

'There's no need to blame you for this, Lavonia is a beast,' Melanie said.

'I did not want you harmed; I'd hoped they took their hatred out on me.'

Melanie moved across the floor and untied Jennifer's ankles; she turned onto her front so Melanie could untie her wrists.

'You can't predict what is going to happen, you aren't superhuman, Jenny.'

They heard the door being unlocked and it opened, and two men walked in and lifted Jennifer to her feet and they dragged her out of the building; the door was closed and locked again, and Jennifer was taken to the house. She was taken into the front room and was sat down on a wooden chair. Lavonia stood over her.

'We are going to have a little talk.'

One of the men stood behind Jennifer and gripped her shoulders. Lavonia tied Jennifer's ankles to the legs of the chair; she did not want the tall girl kicking out at her. The second man held onto her right arm and Lavonia grabbed her left hand and gripped her little finger, Jennifer gritted her teeth as Lavonia pulled the finger back until there was a loud snap. Lavonia stared at her face waiting for Jennifer to cry out, but she kept silent and kept the pain to herself.

'It's nothing personal, Jennifer, it's just that I'm cruel,' Lavonia said, giggling.

'Yes, I had noticed.'

'I want you to tell me where I can find Samantha.'

Jennifer shook her head.

'I don't know where she is, I'm looking for her myself.'

'That's unfortunate for you,' Lavonia said.

The man behind the chair held Jennifer tightly against the back of the chair. Lavonia started to pummel her fists into Jennifer's body; she fixed Lavonia with an ice-cold stare, like a venomous snake about to strike. Lavonia hit out at the tall girl in a fit of blind rage, pain ran through Jennifer's body. Lavonia eventually stopped and stood back.

'I'd really love to know what you are, before you die.'

'So would I,' assured Jennifer.

Two figures entered the room and stood beside Lavonia.

Jennifer knew she was looking at the owners of the spacecraft. Zindra moved forward and stared down at Jennifer, who stared back in amazement. She felt no shock seeing the domed head and thin face of this alien creature, the deep-set ruby eyes blazed down at her with a blazing fury. Jennifer could see how much cosmetic surgery Dr Hamilton had had to make her resemble a human. Jennifer gazed at the long thin nose and thin wide lips that gave the creature a cruel countenance. The alien female wore a glittering gold gown that came down to her feet. Jennifer was not going to be intimidated by the overbearing alien.

'Are you afraid?' The voice was high and resonant.

'Should I be?'

Zindra brought a hand up and Jennifer stared at the long thin hand with long sharp talons on the end of the fingers.

'I am Zindra, you intrigue me.'

Zindra studied Jennifer with a critical eye, the thin face and ice-blue eyes disturbed Zindra. She gripped Jennifer's jaw and her mouth opened slightly and Zindra gazed at the sharp teeth – as Jennifer did not have molars, Zindra knew she had to beware of this one, she could sense the intelligence behind the pale eyes.

'What are you going to do with her?' Zindra asked Lavonia.

'I'm going to have her killed, also her companion.'

Zindra turned away from Jennifer and joined her companion, who was like her but male.

'Good idea, there's something about this one I don't like,' Zindra declared.

The two men untied her ankles from the chair and lifted her up onto her feet and dragged her out of the house. Lavonia followed the two aliens to the scout ship by the side of the house. Jennifer was taken across the yard to the single storey building; one of the men took her in while the second man went to the car. Once inside the building Jennifer went into action, she clung to him and forced him down to the floor. He found out how strong the girl was, as she moved on top of him and gripped his head and with all her strength she twisted the head round, the sound of breaking bones was loud in the quiet room. Jennifer went through the pockets of his trousers and pulled out his gun. Melanie stood up painfully and moved towards Jennifer.

'You certainly took a beating.'

'Lavonia has a serious attitude problem,' Jennifer said.

Jennifer tried to put the aches and pains in her body to the back of her mind and concentrate on getting Melanie out of this dangerous situation. She looked out of the dirty window and saw the man standing by the car, waiting for his companion to kill them and return to the car. Melanie stood at her side.

The vision of Jennifer trying to screw the man's head off was still vivid in her mind, Melanie was glad she had not made Jennifer angry enough for her to do that to her. Jennifer looked towards the house and she saw the scout ship lift off.

'Lavonia's alien friends are leaving,' Jennifer told Melanie.

Jennifer moved away from the window and went to the door, she told Melanie to keep her head down. Jennifer held the gun tightly in her right hand and pulled the door open with her left.

'Good luck,' Melanie whispered.

Jennifer moved slowly and silently out of the door. The man was at the rear of the car, the boot was open ready to take their dead bodies. He was bending down looking into the boot. Jennifer, keeping the gun gripped in her right hand, held out her arms in front of her, aiming the gun over the top of the car. The man suddenly looked up and Jennifer fired several shots in quick succession and all the bullets buried themselves in the man's skull. The man fell to the ground. Jennifer called Melanie, telling her it was all right to leave the building. Jennifer went to the back of the car and closed the lid. She searched the man's pockets and found another gun.

'You are getting used to this killing lark,' Melanie said.

'It's them or us.' Jennifer gave Melanie the other gun she had found.

'Place that in your knickers, you'll need it.'

Melanie lifted her skirt and placed the gun down the waistband of her panties. Jennifer suddenly felt groggy and fell against the car, Melanie was immediately at her side.

'What's the matter?' Melanie asked in a voice full of concern for her friend.

Jennifer moved away from the boot of the car and went to the front and collapsed into the passenger seat. Melanie rushed to the house to see if her shoulder bag was still there. She returned to the car with it and got in the driving seat, she took the med kit out of the bag, and she opened it and took out a hypodermic needle and injected the drug into Jennifer's upper arm.

'You need to get to a hospital, we don't know what damage Lavonia has done to your insides, with that beating she gave you,' Melanie said, anxiously.

'Don't worry about me, just concentrate on your driving and get us away from this place.'

'I do worry about you, I don't want you dying on me, I shall get the blame for it,' Melanie said.

CHAPTER LXVII:

THE KILLING GROUND

Jennifer came to and groaned at the aches and pains that gnawed at her nerves. A hand settled on her forehead and she turned and faced Melanie.

'How are you feeling?'

'Bloody awful, where are we?'

They were parked at Horner, close to Horner Wood. Melanie was anxious about Jennifer and the state of her health. While Jennifer had been unconscious, her breathing had been shallow, almost non-existent. Melanie was very worried and was glad Jennifer was conscious. Jennifer undid the safety belt and moved forward and folded her arms on the dashboard and laid her head on her arms. Melanie ran a hand gently up and down her back. Jennifer groaned and sighed.

'I've contacted the General, and Steven and Janice will be picking up the camper, I told him about Lavonia and the spacecraft.'

Jennifer sat up.

'We'll have to get rid of this car, they'll know we've escaped their execution and they'll be after us.'

Melanie gave her two white pills.

'What's that?'

'Never mind that, take them,' Melanie commanded.

Jennifer popped them in her mouth and swallowed them. She opened the car door and swung her long legs out of the car and got out. She stood by the car, leaning against it. Melanie was quickly at her side. Jennifer gazed at the dark sky; the night was warm, and a slight breeze blew over the moor. Jennifer went to the boot of the car and opened it up. There were several boxes inside. Jennifer rummaged through them and her face lit up. She found two heavy handguns and a rifle; there was plenty of ammunition for each. She asked Melanie if she had the gun she had given her. Melanie lifted her green pleated skirt and showed the gun butt sticking out of the waistband of her panties. Jennifer gazed at her buxom tanned thighs; Melanie let go of the hem of her skirt.

'You'll need that before long,' Jennifer said.

'I don't know if I've got the nerve to use it, I haven't the killer instinct like you, Jenny.'

Jennifer put her arm round Melanie's waist. She gazed at Jennifer's face; the ice blue eyes stared back at her, the marks of the beating she had got still showed on her pale features, Melanie knew her face was no better and her body still ached from what Lavonia had done to her.

'When it comes to the crunch, you'll find the courage, I have faith in you,' Jennifer said.

Jennifer picked up the rifle and weighed it up in her hands, it was light, and she checked it and found it loaded. She put it in the boot and continued to look through the boxes, she found a sheath about six inches long, she took hold of the ornamental hilt and pulled the blade out of the sheath, it was long and thin and very sharp, it glittered silvery in the moonlight. Staring at it she remembered what had happened to Samantha with a similar blade. She replaced it in the sheath and slid it down the front of her shorts.

'That'll come in handy,' Jennifer said.

'You'll be armed to the teeth with all that fire power,' Melanie observed.

Melanie took out a rucksack from the back of the car and Jennifer put the two handguns and the boxes of ammunition into it. She held onto the rifle and Melanie slammed the boot shut. They got back in the car. Jennifer lay back in the seat and closed her eyes.

'We'll stay here until daylight, so get some sleep, Mel.'

Melanie settled down in her seat. She did not feel like sleeping, the realization that other murderous people were coming after them with the same type of weapons that lay in the boot. It did not seem to bother Jennifer, she was all set to do battle with them, and Melanie had seen her kill without a moment's thought. There was a dark side to Jennifer which came out now and again. Melanie kept assuring herself the tall girl would be no danger to her. Melanie prayed they got back to the Research Facility before their enemies caught up with them.

Jennifer woke with the sun shining in on her face. She sat up and stretched out her body and groaned at the aches and pains she still suffered from. She nudged Melanie in the ribs, and she opened her eyes and growled at Jennifer, for giving her a fright. Jennifer kissed her on the cheek.

'Let's go and get some breakfast, then we can be on our way,' Jennifer said.

They returned to the car after they'd had breakfast, unaware they were being watched by two men in shirt sleeves in a car parked a fair distance behind them. They watched the car drive away; the driver started his car and followed the car at a safe distance away. The man in the passenger seat contacted control and told them they had made contact with the target. On the other side of the line Lavonia smiled with glee, the two girls would not escape them this time; Lavonia was setting a trap for them, which Jennifer would not wriggle out of. Lavonia was going to make sure she would be in for the kill. Melanie drove at a leisurely pace along the road. Jennifer gazed at huge expanse of Horner Wood on their right; she was thinking of leaving the car and making their way to the Research Facility through the wood. Jennifer was sure she had a better chance of fighting their enemies in the depths of the shady wood.

'Where do you think they'll attack us?' Melanie inquired.

Jennifer turned her head and kept her eyes on Melanie.

'Any minute now, they will want to stop us from getting home,' Jennifer said.

Melanie slowed the car and stared at her companion.

'I don't like the sound of that.'

Jennifer laid a hand on Melanie's thigh and squeezed it gently.

'You've got me to protect you, just do as I say and you will be safe,' Jennifer assured her.

Jennifer ran her hand caressingly up and down Melanie's thigh.

'I will make sure they have their attention on me.'

Melanie put her foot down on the accelerator and the car picked up speed, she kept her eyes on the road, while Jennifer kept caressing the soft skin on the inside of her left thigh.

'I failed you once; I shall not give them another chance to hurt you, Mel.'

'I trust you, Jenny.'

Jennifer moved close to her and kissed her on the cheek.

'We're going to get through this,' Jennifer said, confidently.

Melanie kept her eyes on the road; she hoped Jennifer was right; you could not fault her optimism. Melanie looked up at the mirror and noticed there was a car behind them; she told Jennifer and she turned her head and looked out of the back window. There was no way to know if the car behind them was a danger to them, but to be on the safe side, Jennifer decided to take it that the people in the car were after them.

Up ahead Lavonia was making the final preparations to their trap, the car following the two girls was keeping in constant contact with her and they were almost upon them. She had three men with her, and they were in position. The road Melanie was driving on came close to the edge of Horner Wood; the two men following them were a car's length away. The road turned into the wood. Jennifer reached over to the back seat and picked up the rucksack.

'I take it you think they are going to hit us now,' Melanie said.

Before Jennifer could remark there was a flash up ahead of them in the cover of the trees. Jennifer grabbed the steering wheel, Melanie let go of it and Jennifer swerved the car off the road. The rear of the car exploded as Melanie dived out of the car. Bullets hit the trees as she dived for cover.

The car crashed into the trees at the side of the road and Jennifer rolled onto the road, still clinging to the rucksack.

A bullet grazed her side. She slid the rifle out of the rucksack, and she saw a man running towards her from the other side of the road. Jennifer brought him down with a hail of bullets from the rifle; she then fired into the trees on the opposite side of the road. She then turned her attention on the car that had been following them as it came into view, she fired at it and the car headed for her position at the side of the road and she decided it was time to go.

Melanie moved deeper into the wood. She held the gun Jennifer had given her in her right hand, she knew Jennifer would soon catch her up, if they did not fill her full of holes before she could get away. Jennifer was making sure they did not have the chance. The first man who rushed into the wood was dropped with a torrent of bullets in quick succession. Lavonia was some way away, but she had Jennifer in sight, she was in no hurry as she was skulking amongst the trees, she had a rifle with a telescopic sight, she was not going to kill Jennifer quickly, she was going to watch her die very slowly and painfully. Lavonia brought the rifle up and looked through the telescopic sight; it was centred on Jennifer's head.

'It's too easy,' Lavonia muttered.

She brought the rifle down and the sight centred on Jennifer's left shoulder. Her finger tightened on the trigger.

'You are not going to die just yet.'

Jennifer heard another man rushing towards her. She aimed the rifle at the direction of the sound. There was suddenly an agonizing pain in her left shoulder, and she looked down and saw blood spurting from a bullet wound; a sniper had her in their sights. A man came into view in front of her and Jennifer shot him down and ran a zigzag course away from the danger area. Lavonia rushed forward to keep her in view. She had a radio and she contacted her men, telling them the position Jennifer was at. She also radioed ahead where more of her people were lying in wait for the two girls.

Jennifer stopped to take a breather; she listened to the sounds of the wood and gazed about her. Lavonia sighted the rifle on Jennifer's left thigh; she was going to play her for a while, to let Jennifer know she could be killed at any time. She fired the rifle. Jennifer grunted as a bullet imbedded itself in the top of her left thigh just below the leg of her shorts. She was knocked to the ground by the force of the bullet. She raised the rifle and fired along an arc around her, bullets thudded into the trees, Lavonia dived to the ground. Jennifer got up and limped away. Lavonia waited for her companions to reach her. There were two of them left; she told them she had hit the prey twice.

Melanie crouched down behind a tree and waited to see if Jennifer was anywhere near. She heard someone moving through the trees on her left; she held her breath and kept still and silent. Jennifer came into view limping towards her, blood was running down her left leg and her white T-shirt was soaked in blood. Melanie stood up and went to her and Jennifer collapsed to the ground. Melanie took the rucksack off Jennifer's back and took out the med kit. Jennifer lay on her back and groaned. Melanie surveyed the damage to the shoulder; she decided to remove the bullet. Jennifer watched her remove the bullet and dress the wound, then Melanie worked on the bullet hole in Jennifer's thigh.

'Thanks, Mel, you're a life saver.'

Jennifer sat up and leant against Melanie, who put her arms round the injured girl and kissed her on the cheek.

'It looks like I'll be earning my wages today,' Melanie said.

'You'll have more work to do yet, the person who shot me could have killed me anytime, they're playing a game with me,' Jennifer said.

Melanie put the med kit in the rucksack and Jennifer gave her the rifle. Jennifer took the sheath out of the pocket of her shorts and slid the silvery blade out.

'What are you going to do with that?' Melanie wanted to know.

'I'm going hunting, stay here and keep your head down.'

Jennifer moved away from Melanie, she could see by the girl's expression, Melanie did not want her to go. She put her hand on her chin and kissed Melanie lightly on the lips.

'Don't worry, I'll be careful, I won't be long,' Jennifer said.

Jennifer rubbed the leaf mould and dirt into her clothes, so they were no longer white. They stood up and Jennifer gazed at Melanie's bright brown eyes.

'Please be careful,' Melanie said.

Jennifer promised Melanie she would do just that. Melanie stared at her wondering if she could believe her. Jennifer ran a hand over her cheek and kissed her again.

'That should convince you I won't be leaving you,' Jennifer said.

Melanie watched her go and disappear amongst the trees.

Jennifer held the blade in her right hand. She moved quietly amongst the trees in search of her prey. When she heard someone approaching, she kept still and quiet. A man came into view and she waited until he passed close to her, then she rose up behind him and wrapped a leg round the front of his legs and her left hand gripped his face and pulled his head back, her right hand came up and slid the sharp blade over his throat cutting deep, he made a gargling noise and Jennifer let his body fall to the ground. She got on the man's back and buried the blade into the back of his neck. Jennifer stood up; she felt ecstatic; she had enjoyed that – the thrill of the hunt and the kill.

She heard a sound behind her, and she froze. Something moved closer to her, Jennifer turned around slowly and saw a tall figure emerging from the shadows. She was ready to spring onto this new prey.

Melanie stopped as she surveyed Jennifer's face, it was almost unrecognizable. The deep-set eyes glowed a deep blue; it was like viewing Jennifer's face in a distorted mirror. She could see Jennifer was about to leap at her.

'Jenny, it's me, Mel,' she shouted quickly.

Melanie waited with bated breath, a change came over Jennifer and the hard-predatory lines of her face faded, and her facial features softened, the deep blue faded from her eyes and they were back to their normal ice-blue. Melanie gave a sigh of relief.

'Did I frighten you, Mel?'

Melanie nodded her head and Jennifer apologized and assured Melanie she would never hurt her. Melanie put her arms round Jennifer and hugged her. Then she looked up at Jennifer's face and gave her a smile.

'I know you will never injure me, Jenny.'

Melanie kissed Jennifer softly on the lips.

Jennifer kept her ears listening out for signs of danger.

The camper drew up to the crashed cars and stopped. Steven Calvert got out and surveyed the scene, Janice got out and pulled out her rucksack from behind her seat and put her arms through the straps and secured it to her back. The door slid open and Henry came out of the main compartment and sat in the driving seat.

'We'll keep in touch, try not to worry too much, Jennifer will make sure nothing happens to Mel,' Janice said.

'Take care, Jan,' Henry said.

Janice went to Steven who was standing over the body lying in the middle of the road.

'Jenny and Mel are not making it easy for them,' Steven said.

'I'm not surprised, knowing Jennifer's got the strength to twist somebody's head completely round, it wasn't a pretty sight,' Janice observed.

Janice turned away and walked towards the crashed cars, Steven watched her retreating back, and he gazed at her perfect bottom encased in a pair of tight shorts. She walked into the wood and found the second body. Steven caught up with her near the third body.

'It looks as if Jennifer's been busy,' Janice said.

'I'm glad she's on our side,' Steven commented.

Janice stared at him; Steven gave her a smile.

'I hope Jennifer sees it that way too,' Janice said.

Janice walked away from him before explaining what she meant. Jennifer was still partly a mystery to the both of them. Janice had tried to get information on the girl's parentage from Dr Hamilton, without success. They made their way through the wood, quickly and carefully, they were some way away from the several footpaths that ran through Horner Wood and they hoped to get onto one soon. Janice hoped the two girls would keep to the footpaths, so they could catch up with them sooner. They came across the fourth body; Steven grimaced at the sight of a man's head separated from his body. Janice wondered why he had been killed in a different way to his companions.

'It looks as if Jennifer is carrying a sword about with her,' Steven said.

Janice got on her haunches and studied the corpse; she could see the head had been removed cleanly; the instrument Jennifer had used had been very sharp and had cut through bone as easily as it had through flesh. She was sure it had been the same sort of weapon that had been used on Samantha. If it was how Jennifer got hold of it, she certainly knew how to use it. Janice stood up and gazed across at Steven.

'Our Jennifer is getting to be a very expert killer, I just hope, as you say, she's on our side.'

'So, do I, for Mel's sake,' Steven said.

Steven radioed back to Henry and informed him what they had found and told him to report back to base. Steven assured him they had found no clue that Melanie or Jennifer had been harmed. They moved on, Steven kept close to his partner and ran his hand over the back of her shorts and patted her bottom affectionately. Janice nudged him in the ribs and moved away from him.

'Don't touch what you can't afford.'

Steven laughed and watched her walk away from him.

John Stephenson expertly settled the helicopter onto the road; he saw the two crashed cars were being taken away by pick-up trucks. Dr Hamilton, who was seated beside him, got up and joined her paramedic team as they left the helicopter and went to remove the dead bodies from the road and the wood. When she got to the corpse with his head severed, she lingered over it for a while staring down at it. She silently congratulated Jennifer on a job well done; she had bitterly resented the General for letting Jennifer out into danger. Now she was glad the girl was taking her survival seriously. It seemed a good idea now for Jennifer to be out in the wild world, she had been coping all right up till now, and any enemies had been swiftly dealt with. She had had no fears that Jennifer might have disappeared like Samantha; Dr Hamilton understood why Samantha wanted to be free to bring up her child. Jennifer would not have that problem, so she had no reason to run away.

Jennifer and Melanie came upon a footpath and Melanie inquired if she was going to follow it. Jennifer nodded, she saw it as a way to get back to base easier and quicker, but she warned Melanie, their enemies would realize that too, so they had to tread very carefully. Melanie nodded her head and showed Jennifer she understood.

CHAPTER LXVIII:

HUNTER AND THE HUNTED

The footpath the two girls were following ran parallel to the west bank of the river. Consulting the map they had, Jennifer was aware if they kept in touch with the footpaths and river, they would not get lost, as she did not want roam the great ancient wood forever. As they had not been shot at lately, she supposed the sniper had lost sight of them. Which was the case. Lavonia was some way in front of them as she was still in the wood roaming about a few yards away from the footpath. She had the one remaining member of her team with her. After seeing the corpse of the last man Jennifer had killed, made her sure the girl was not human, she was a monster and Lavonia was going to treat Jennifer as such. She had similar ideas about Melanie. Lavonia had already contacted the alien scout ship, which was concealed close to the Research Facility, and they had to make sure Jennifer did not make it back there. The two girls would be hunted down, and their death would not be a quick one, Lavonia would see to that.

Jennifer stopped walking and Melanie collided with her. It was now dark, and Jennifer was getting tired and her damaged shoulder and the bullet wound in her thigh were giving her grief. She told Melanie it was time to rest up for the night and wait for morning. Melanie did not fancy the idea of sleeping out in a wild wood, with homicidal maniacs hunting them. Jennifer took the girl by the arm and pulled her off the footpath and into the cover of the trees and the darkness. Melanie had to put her faith in Jennifer's night vision, as she could not see a thing. Jennifer told her what the ground was like, so she would know where she was putting her feet. Jennifer pulled her down to the ground and sat with her back against a tree, she took the rucksack off Melanie's back and she moved between Jennifer's thighs and snuggled up to her and rested her head against Jennifer's chest. She had hold of the rucksack.

'The only thing you have to worry about, Mel, is having creepy crawlies creeping up your skirt,' Jennifer said, giggling.

'Thank you for that wonderful thought.'

Jennifer closed her eyes and waited for sleep.

'I thought you would like it.'

Steven and Janice came along the footpath. Steven had a small torch in his hand to light their way, they passed the point where the two girls left the path and their two friends were now behind them.

Jennifer woke and gazed up at the tops of the trees; the sunshine filtered through the tops of the trees. She looked down at Melanie's head that still lay on her chest. She was still asleep; Jennifer listened for any sound that meant danger. It was humid and she felt the sweat running over her body. Melanie woke and kissed her.

'We're still alive, then?' Melanie observed.

Jennifer ran a hand through Melanie's long brown hair.

'They're not going to kill us in our sleep.'

Melanie could feel Jennifer's heart beating as her head lay on Jennifer's left breast.

'That's very considerate of them,' Melanie said, sarcastically.

'They're nowhere near us, at the moment,' informed Jennifer.

Melanie stared at her. 'What do you mean?'

Jennifer gave her a sly smile.

'I made a slight detour and moved towards the South East, while they went in the opposite direction,' Jennifer said.

'You're brilliant, Jenny, you think of everything,' Melanie said in admiration.

Jennifer gazed at the bright brown eyes as she ran a hand over Melanie's cheek.

'How's your shoulder?'

Jennifer assured her it hurt like hell and it was stiff.

'I've got plenty of pain killers.'

Melanie took the med kit out of the rucksack and took out two white pills and gave them to Jennifer. She swallowed them and Melanie gave her a bottle of water, she drank some and washed the pills down.

'How are you feeling, Mel?' Melanie grinned at her and moved close to her again.

'I should still be frightened out of my wits, because there are people out for our blood, but every time I think the game's up for us, you get us out of a sticky situation time after time. You are an amazing person, Jenny. You give me the belief that we'll beat them and get back home.'

Jennifer stared at Melanie; they had become very close in their long journey together.

'I said, I'll get you back in one piece and I will, Mel. I care for you very much,' Jennifer said, sincerely.

'What are your feelings about what we did yesterday?' Jennifer then asked.

'It's the first time I've been intimate with another girl. Ever since the first day's journey, you couldn't keep your hands to yourself. Yesterday, as you have saved my life a few times, I thought it was time to let you have your way. I thought it was the right thing to do, as I care for you so much, now, Jenny,' Melanie explained.

Melanie stood up and picked up the rucksack, she held out her hand and pulled Jennifer up onto her feet. Jennifer made for the footpath and Melanie followed behind her. After a while Jennifer moved off the footpath and Melanie followed her into the thick of the wood.

'Where are we going?' Melanie asked.

'We've got to get back on track and move towards the west of the wood.'

Melanie took hold of Jennifer's good arm and they faced each other.

'Where do you think they'll be waiting for us?'

Jennifer had a good idea what their stratagem would be. Lavonia knew what part of the wood they would exit to get to the Research Facility. If the alien scout ship was about then Lavonia would have help. They would spread out and wait for them to walk into their net. Jennifer knew she had a much higher intelligence than Lavonia, but the alien mind inside her head – she still did not have enough information on them. If anything came to stalk them, Jennifer was confident she would sense them first.

'I expect they'll wait for us near home, they know where we're headed, they can afford to wait for us to go to them,' Jennifer said.

That did not sound good to Melanie; she hoped Steven and Janice would be close by, when they were closer to danger.

'Stay here, Mel; I'll do some scouting ahead. Keep your courage up; I've got a lot of respect for you, Mel. I haven't brought us to this point by myself, you have helped, your medical training has worked wonders in keeping me on my feet,' Jennifer said.

'I'll have no trouble with my courage, Jenny, with your support.'

Jennifer put her arms round Melanie and looked down at her upturned face.

'Whatever your feelings towards the General, he chose well when he picked you for this mission,' Jennifer observed.

'Well I suppose a person does one good thing in their lives,' Melanie decided.

Jennifer laughed and then moved away into the shadows of the wood. Melanie sat down on the ground to wait for Jennifer's return.

Jennifer kept off the footpaths, as she moved towards the west of the wood. Suddenly a sound was picked up by her sharp hearing. She stopped and listened; something was moving towards her. One of their enemies was scouting around like Jennifer. She crouched down and waited. A moment later a red deer moved into view, Jennifer stood up and the animal stood for a moment and then bounced away, it was wild and free, something Jennifer yearned for. Jennifer moved forward. Some time later she halted her progress through the wood again; she detected some movement ahead of her. Jennifer got down and merged into the undergrowth. Two men came into view moving cautiously towards her. Silently Jennifer moved position so they would not trip over her. They both held handguns. In her new position Jennifer kept still and quiet. They stopped close to her and one man turned and moved back the way he had come. Jennifer made a move and crept silently up behind the man that was standing still. When she was close enough, Jennifer dived forward and leapt onto his back; using her immense strength, she brought him down and swiftly brought the killing blade out from the back of her shorts. The handgun had fallen from his grasp and he called for his companion. She drove the blade into the back of his neck cutting into the brain stem. The thrill of the kill ran through her mind and body: the predator was back. She heard the second man coming back to help his companion.

Jennifer stood up, her heart thumping faster in her ribcage; she was exhilarated by the kill, and it was almost the ultimate pleasure. As she heard the second man getting near to her position a feeling of ecstasy ran through her slim body. She got ready to tackle the second man when he came into view. They caught sight of each other at the same time, but Jennifer was too quick for him; she knocked the gun out of his hand and drove the blade into the man's chest and he fell like a stone, she got onto his back and slid the blade into the back of the neck of her prey. She severed the head from the body. She wiped the blood off the blade and slid it into the sheath that lay down the back of her shorts. Jennifer retraced her steps and ran into a very surprised Melanie, her finger tightened on the trigger of the handgun she held.

'Careful, Jenny, I nearly shot you.'

'That's why I told you to stay where you were,' Jennifer said, breathlessly.

Melanie slid the gun into the pocket of her skirt. Jennifer slid down to the ground and Melanie got down beside her and put her arms round Jennifer.

'You look as if you've run into some trouble,' Melanie said.

Jennifer waited for her rapidly beating heart to slow down and she regulated her breathing.

'There are two less for us to worry about,' Jennifer said, at last.

'You'd better rest for a while, before we start off again,' Melanie advised.

Jennifer made no complaint and laid her head on Melanie's shoulder.

'You smell nice, Mel.'

'I'd smell better, if I had shower – my underwear is soaked with sweat,' Melanie complained.

'Yes, it's very humid in this wood.'

Jennifer started to unbutton Melanie's blouse. When the girl did not stop her, Jennifer undid all the buttons and pulled the blouse out of the skirt.

'That should be better, get some air moving round your body,' Jennifer said.

Jennifer put a hand on Melanie's chin and moved her face close to her own.

'You are very beautiful, Mel.' Melanie gazed at the thin pale face before her: Jennifer was not a beauty.

Melanie did not find it unpleasing, though.

'I think you are quite striking too.'

Jennifer planted a kiss on Melanie's cheek.

'For a person who can twist someone's head off, Jenny, you are very passionate,' Melanie said.

Jennifer ran a hand up and down Melanie's back.

'There's something I've been meaning to ask you,' Melanie said.

'What's that?' Jennifer nuzzled the side of her neck.

'Why are Lavonia and her new friends helping these aliens?'

'Do you remember those spheres that fell to Earth?'

Melanie nodded her head.

'I found a complete sphere in the marsh and I had it opened up.'

Jennifer laid her back against a tree and Melanie lay against her.

'What did you find?'

'It was an alien mind; all the broken spheres must have contained one. Lavonia was infected – she is no longer human.'

Melanie laughed and could not help voicing her next thought.

'I don't think that girl was ever human.'

It was Jennifer's turn to laugh and she hugged her friend.

'You are a naughty girl, Mel.'

'That tall alien with the burning red eyes, what did you think of it?' Melanie inquired.

Jennifer thought back to her first impression of the tall female alien.

'She took an instant distaste for me. I could tell by the way the alien moved and stared at me with those piercing ruby eyes. She was a predator, probably as good as me,' Jennifer said.

'That's what I like about you Jen, you are so modest.'

Jennifer pushed her away and stood up.

'With that gem, Mel, it's time to go.'

They made for the footpath that ran along the west back of the river; Melanie took off the rucksack and told Jennifer to keep a sharp look out. To Jennifer's amazement Melanie quickly removed her clothes and slid into the cold water of the river. Jennifer stood and stared at Melanie as she cooled off her hot sweaty body. After a few minutes Jennifer took her hand and pulled her out of the river.

'Having fun?'

Melanie grinned and gave her a quick kiss and got dressed.

'Why don't you cool off, Jen. I'll keep an eye out for danger.'

Jennifer did not bother to remove her clothes she just stepped in the river and splashed water over her hot sweating body. She got out and they followed the footpath.

'I feel a lot better now, it's very handy to have running water, when it's so humid,' Melanie said.

'When we first went on this mission, the last thing you would have done is take off all your clothes.'

Jennifer marched along the footpath, all her senses alert for danger. Melanie tried to keep up with her, as Jennifer had a longer stride because of her long legs.

'I know you better now, Jen, I have no qualms about you seeing me naked,' Melanie said.

They came to a footbridge and Melanie grabbed Jennifer to stop her steady march forward.

'What is the best way here, cross the bridge or stay on the path we're on?' Melanie inquired.

'The path on the other side of the river doesn't take us anywhere we want to go,' assured Jennifer.

They followed the footpath for a mile and Jennifer was getting more apprehensive, her major senses could not detect danger, but her sixth did – the fact they had not come across anyone with murder in their minds, made Jennifer nervous. If you could not see it or hear it or even feel it, it did not mean danger was not there. Jennifer obeyed her sixth sense without question. Jennifer told Melanie to move out of sight and stay down. She took the handgun out of the pocket of her shorts. Jennifer moved cautiously forward and came to a point where the footpath split into two. One path ran towards the west, which was no good to them; the other was no good because they would be in the open. It was time to move into the wood, she had a compass so that would keep them on a course towards the south.

Melanie was keeping low in the dense undergrowth; she held the gun tight in her right hand. She suddenly heard movement close by, it might be Jennifer and it might not.; Melanie wanted to make sure before she made a move. A man came into view and moved past her and headed for the footpath. Making sure he was alone, Melanie moved cautiously behind him.

Jennifer made her way slowly towards the place she had left Melanie. Lavonia was watching her through the telescopic sight of her sniper rifle. She could not make up her mind which part of Jennifer's body she should hit first. The rifle was fully loaded, and every bullet had Jennifer's name on it. Not that Lavonia was ever a good person; she had crossed the line that made her positively evil. There were several of her team in the woods to make sure Jennifer did not escape her. They had orders not to kill her. Lavonia wanted that pleasure all to herself.

Melanie had a decision to make as she kept the man in sight. She had a weapon and she was aware it was no use having one if she did not mean to use it. The man moved towards the footpath. Melanie stopped moving.

Jennifer had her eyes fixed on the man. She wondered how many more of them were skulking in the shadows of the wood. Suddenly the man turned and faced her direction, Jennifer could see he had detected something; it was not her as Jennifer knew she was too good at moving around the wood silently. Jennifer smiled to herself, Melanie was close by and the man had sensed her. Jennifer got ready and aimed her weapon at the man's head. When he was close enough Jennifer fired twice at the man's head and he fell to the ground, Jennifer moved swiftly and just in time, as a bullet thudded into a tree close to her.

Jennifer put the handgun in her shorts pocket and pulled out the pulse rifle out of her rucksack. She fired a torrent of shots at the area she supposed the sniper was hiding. Lavonia and her team scattered away from danger. Jennifer heard something rush towards her. Jennifer put the pulse rifle back in her rucksack. A moment later Melanie bumped into her and Jennifer brought her down to the ground.

'Keep your head down, Mel, if you want to keep it.'

Melanie lay on her back and Jennifer sat astride her stomach.

'That was good shooting, Jen.'

'A sniper took a pot shot at me, our friend Lavonia, I suppose.'

'If we had her as a friend, we wouldn't need all these enemies that are after us,' Melanie said.

Jennifer gazed at the front of Melanie's green blouse as the girl calmed her rapidly beating heart and breathing.

'Are you going to sit on me all day?' Melanie inquired.

'I'm just enjoying the view.'

Jennifer rolled off her and moved forward. Melanie followed her, and she did not need Jennifer to tell her to keep her head down.

Lavonia in her new position kept her eye fixed on the sight of her sniper rifle. She scanned the area where she last saw Jennifer. Suddenly she spotted movement and she caught a glimpse of Melanie. Lavonia fired.

Melanie screamed as a bullet hit her in the left thigh. She lay on the ground groaning in pain, Jennifer fired the pulse rifle and fired at the area ahead of them for a few moments, then got down and studied Melanie's injured thigh.

'It's all right, Mel, you'll live.'

Jennifer got out the med kit and took out an instrument she could get the bullet out with.

'Grit your teeth, Mel, this may hurt,' Jennifer said.

Melanie sat with her back against a tree and watched Jennifer probe for the bullet in her thigh.

'Why did I get hit?' Melanie complained.

Jennifer looked up at her.

'You are a big girl, Mel; you are easier to hit.'

'You're enjoying this.'

Jennifer grinned at her and then got on with getting the ballet out of Melanie's thigh. When she had done that, she dressed the wound. Jennifer held out her hand and Melanie took it and she pulled the girl to her feet. Jennifer held onto her to give support.

'Sorry about the pain Mel. I can't do anything about that.'

Jennifer moved off in a different direction they went before, Melanie limped behind her. Jennifer did not want Melanie getting shot again, so Jennifer had to seek Lavonia out, while making sure Melanie was at a safe distance behind her. Jennifer moved to the west for a while then returned to her original direction. Behind her Melanie kept a sharp look out for anyone that might creep up on Jennifer.

Jennifer came across the westward footpath. She wondered if Lavonia was anywhere near. Unfortunately, Lavonia was making her own search pattern and she suddenly spied Jennifer. She steadily sighted the rifle and fired.

Jennifer moved forward again, and something slammed into her back, fire burned her nerves, she dived to the ground. Lavonia fired again and watched Jennifer's body jerk as another bullet slammed into her. Jennifer lay still so Lavonia fired again. Jennifer cried out at the agony in her body, her eyes watered. Another bullet slammed into her body.

Melanie came upon the sniper and was not too surprised to find it was Lavonia. Without a moment's hesitation, she fired at the horrible girl and hit her in the shoulder, the gun dropped to the ground and Lavonia ran off. Melanie kept after her. Jennifer struggled painfully to her feet, she fought to stay conscious, she had to keep going for Melanie's sake, and she had an obligation to get her friend to safety. She got onto the path that would lead her home and just up ahead of her Lavonia broke cover and as soon as Jennifer recognised her, Jennifer fired at her with the handgun. Melanie came out of the trees and stopped dead, as she did not want Jennifer to shoot her by accident.

Lavonia lay groaning on the path. Jennifer limped up towards her, Melanie stared down at her, Jennifer stopped and aimed her handgun at Lavonia's head, who stared up at Jennifer with an expression of pure hatred, and Jennifer pulled the trigger and shot her in the middle of the forehead. Jennifer looked at Melanie.

'That's one monster out of the way,' Melanie observed.

A shot was fired, and a bullet hit Jennifer in the left side. She shoved Melanie away from her and dived in the opposite direction, she felt another bullet hit her in the left thigh. The man moved forward to finish off his prey. Melanie got her handgun out and kept low and looked about for the shooter. She saw him and fired three shots at his head. Melanie waited to see if he had any friends nearby, then she got up and made her way to where she last saw Jennifer. She found her standing by a tree surveying her wounds.

'Good shooting, Mel, I'm proud of you,' Jennifer said.

Melanie grimaced when she saw the side of Jennifer's T-shirt covered in blood and blood running down her left thigh.

'I don't know how you can stand it; you must be in a lot of pain and you don't complain.'

Jennifer had no intention of complaining, she wanted to keep the pain to herself. Melanie was relying on her to get them home in one piece. She was determined not to let Melanie down.

'I'm made of stronger stuff.'

Melanie got the med kit out and tended to the bullet wound on the left thigh. Jennifer kept a sharp eye out for trouble. Melanie bandaged up the thigh wound, and then she stood up. Jennifer removed her T-shirt and Melanie fixed the bullet wound in her side.

'Thanks, Mel, you are a life saver.'

Melanie got up on tip toe and kissed Jennifer on the lips.

'I don't want to lose a special friend,' Melanie said, sincerely.

Jennifer ran a hand over Melanie's cheek.

'You are special to me also, Mel.' Jennifer hugged Melanie and gave her a long firm kiss.

CHAPTER LXIX:

AN ALIEN PERSPECTIVE

Jennifer and Melanie made their way round a tree covered dome shaped hill, Jennifer suddenly stopped, and Melanie bumped into her. Jennifer pointed to a clearing ahead of them. Melanie gasped in horror at the alien scout ship lying beside the tree line.

'What do we do now?' Melanie asked.

Jennifer stepped out of the dense wood; Melanie followed her. They approached the alien scout ship. The hatch slid open and Melanie saw a thing from her worst nightmare exit the scout ship.

'We'll have to find another route to take.' Melanie said.

'I'll distract him, while you run for it.'

Melanie stared at her open mouthed.

'You're joking; it'll make mincemeat of you.'

'Oh, you of little faith,' Jennifer said.

Melanie tried to argue with Jennifer to stop her from tackling the large alien warrior. Jennifer ignored her worries and told her to run for it when the time was right. Melanie tried all she could to change Jennifer's mind, but she would not be dissuaded. Melanie gave up reluctantly and watched Jennifer move towards the scout ship, thinking she would never see Jennifer alive again.

The Ixxion Rhan turned towards the tall scruffy female that was slowly approaching him. She was taller than him; she had many signs of battle on her body. Her life force was leaking from several wounds. Rhan gazed at the weapon in her hand; her intent was plain to see. Rhan moved to accept the challenge. The tall female being stopped moving and stood still; the ice blue eyes glared at him.

Avin Perox sitting on the flight deck gazed at the view screen and stared at the strange confrontation. Avin could not be sure if the inhabitant of this planet was being brave or being downright foolish. Avin was sure Rhan would have no trouble defeating the tall female. Avin watched them, sizing each other up; he waited with anticipation for Rhan to tear the alien female to pieces.

Rhan rushed at the tall female as she aimed the weapon at him.

Jennifer pulled the trigger, and nothing happened, she swore and threw the gun away – it had run out of ammunition. Rhan gripped her shoulders and thrust forward knocking her over backwards, she brought her legs up and as she hit the ground, she thrust her feet into his body and kicked upwards and the alien flew over the top of her. Rhan quickly got to his feet and saw the female was up and ready for him. She was fast on her feet, this one, he thought to himself. Jennifer had the blade in her right hand. She watched him slide out a machete shaped weapon out of a scabbard on the left side of his weapons belt; the large flat blade was eighteen inches long.

As Avin Perox gazed at the view screen someone moved up and stood beside him. Zindra stared at the screen; she could not believe the tall silver-haired girl was still alive. Zindra hoped the Ixxion would do better than the converted humans they had sent after her.

Rhan lunged forward, his sharp-edged weapon sliced through the air towards Jennifer's head. She ducked her head at the last moment and it sailed harmlessly over the top of her head. Jennifer thrust forward with the long thin blade out in front of her; she drove it into the creature's chest. She dived away from the falling alien taking the blade with her. She picked up her opponent's weapon and hacked off his head with it.

Zindra turned away from the view screen. Aplon Whan, the second in command, moved towards her.

'Who shall we send out to get her this time?' he said.

'There's something about that female, I don't like,' Zindra said.

A tall elegant shape moved close to Zindra, Aplon Whan did not have to look at the newcomer to know who it was. He kept his eyes on the view screen.

'She's strong and fast, she's an expert killer,' he said.

Zindra turned to her companion, who had just come onto the flight deck. The tall sleek and shapely female was a product of Monox genetic engineering on her species, that lived on a jungle planet not far from their own. The Monox females were dying out and they needed to make Zelphas and her kind into a replacement for their diminishing females. They could not take the predator out of Zelphas, so she was beautiful as well as being repulsive, she wore a shimmering translucent green gown that hugged her body. Her head was similar to Zindra, the same domed skull and tapering slender lower face and jaw. Her skin had a light greenish tinge. Her hands were long and slender and elongated and ended in sharp claws. When Zelphas opened her mouth it gave her expression the final proof of her murderous intent, the upper jaw would show off two long sharp fangs, which showed she was a carnivore. The mind and brain lurking behind her bright yellowy eyes was highly intelligent and powerful.

Zelphas was aware Aplon Whan had a complete dislike for her. It did not matter, it was his right as a member of the elite, Zindra had patience, and her time would come.

Zelphas stared at the view screen with relish.

'Delicious, do you want me to go out and kill her?' Zelphas asked.

Zindra shook her head; she did not want to jeopardize Zelphas, as Zindra needed her at her side for the moment.

'I see a lot of Axerus in her, they have the same fearless aggression,' Zindra observed.

Aplon Whan moved closer to the view screen and stared hard at the pale thin face of the alien female.

'Do you think Imera's daughter would dare to evoke the myth?'

Zindra stared at Aplon Whan and then gazed at the view screen. The warrior female stood with her legs apart, as if waiting for the next opponent. She looked battle weary and she was wounded in several places; it showed Zindra, the fighting female was made of strong stuff.

'Axerus is erratic and psychopathic, nothing like Imera, and Axerus is capable of using the myth against us. I wonder what she has spawned, we must find that hybrid of yours and destroy her and that thing out there,' Zindra said, icily.

Zelphas placed a clawed hand on Zindra's shoulder.

'Send out Ruin to kill her and bring the body here, so we can dissect her and see what she's made of.'

'Good idea,' Zindra agreed.

The Ixxion warrior named Ruin stepped out of the hatchway and gazed at his female opponent. She was tall and lean just like his masters; he approached the adversary slowly. Jennifer kept a sharp eye on the alien warrior and kept the hilt of the long thin blade held firmly in her right hand. Ruin suddenly rushed at her and Jennifer side stepped and thrust out with the long thin blade; Ruin dodged the blade and rammed a fist against the side of her head. Jennifer yelped painfully and Ruin grabbed her and lifted her up into the air, then threw Jennifer painfully to the ground, knocking the wind out of her. Ruin bent down and picked up the blade the fighting female had dropped and then moved towards her.

Jennifer lay panting on the ground; she was in agony and she did not know if she had the strength to defend herself from this new threat on her life. She stared at the long thin blade as it moved towards her lower body and watched it slide in under her ribcage. Jennifer gazed at the Ixxion and stared at the yellow eyes. Ruin silently honoured the brave adversary for the fearlessness in her face and deep blue eyes; it seemed she was getting ready for death.

Ruin bent down to pick up the prey and carry her back to the scout ship. Jennifer heard the report of a weapon and a torrent of bullets ripped into the Ixxion and he dropped her and fell backwards with the force of the bullets slamming into him. Jennifer lay where she had been dropped, too tired and weak to move.

Steven Calvert and Janice ran to where Jennifer was lying. They heard a roaring sound as the scout ship lifted off the ground, they dived down flat and it flew over the top of them and disappeared over the tops of the trees. Janice got up and ran to where Jennifer was lying, she carried a med kit and she got on her knees on the ground beside her stricken friend, she opened the med kit and injected a drug into her arm.

'Do you think Jenny will live?' Steven inquired.

Janice looked up at him and shook her head, only time would tell. Steven looked up at the sky as a helicopter flew over their heads and landed in the clearing. Two paramedics left the helicopter carrying a stretcher. They went to where Janice was tending to Jennifer, who had slipped into unconsciousness. They laid Jennifer on the stretcher and carried her to the helicopter. Melanie sat in her seat and Janice told her Jennifer was still alive; she gave a deep sigh of relief.

CHAPTER LXX:

JENNIFER THREE

When Dr Hamilton came out of the operating room, General Heywood was outside waiting for her. She washed her hands and then walked down the corridor with the General. He asked how Jennifer was and she told him the girl would survive.

'You must be glad Melanie was not in the same state?'

'She's not speaking to me, so I've not had her report yet.'

'When are you two going to bury the hatchet, you're as bad as each other. I'll see if Melanie will feel like giving her report to me,' Dr Hamilton said.

'Thank you, I'd appreciate that.'

Melanie and Janice wheeled the trolley carrying Jennifer's unconscious body into the lift. Janice left the lift and the doors slid shut. Melanie stared at Jennifer as the lift went down to the underground complex. When the lift stopped, and the doors slid open Melanie wheeled the trolley out of the lift and into the large underground medical room. She pushed the trolley to the centre of the room, where Dr Hamilton waited beside one of the life support capsules. She gave the girl a friendly smile.

'The General tells me you haven't given him your report about what had happened to the both of you. Melanie shook her head and told her; she could not face the General while Jennifer's life was still in danger.

'Why don't you tell me, in your own words and in your own time?'

Melanie helped Dr Hamilton lift Jennifer off the trolley and into the life support capsule. Jennifer lay serene and unmoving, just a slight raising of the chest showed the girl was still hanging onto life. A probe attached to the capsule ran up and down Jennifer's body. There was a monitor on the top of the capsule that showed what was happening inside Jennifer's body. Melanie fixed her eyes on the screen. Dr Hamilton noticed how intently the girl gazed at the monitor.

'What are you looking for?' Melanie did not take her eyes off the screen.

'I need something to tell me how her body can take so much punishment and she did not moan or cry.'

'Jennifer is made of flesh and bone, just like you.'

Melanie looked away from the monitor and fixed the woman with a stony stare.

'What's the secret of her unusual strength? Jennifer said once, she was indestructible, and she certainly proved that true.'

Melanie looked down at Jennifer and gazed at the pale thin face and started to tell the doctor of their adventures. Dr Hamilton listened without interruption. When Melanie had reached the end of her narrative, she gazed up at the monitor. Dr Hamilton thought over what she had just heard. Jennifer had triumphed over insurmountable odds; she realized what Melanie had meant. She had been interested in what Melanie had told of the change in Jennifer's facial features when she killed. She asked Melanie to go over that part of her story again. Melanie was still not sure of what she had seen, the wood was shady and full of shadows and Jennifer's face seemed to be blurred.

'I had to shout out her name and tell her who I was; I really thought I was going to be her next victim.'

Dr Hamilton closed the lid of the life support capsule and moved onto the one next to it and the lid hissed sideways. After a while the occupant sat up and stared at the tall woman. Melanie watched the doctor help the tall thin girl out of the capsule. Her gaze fell on Melanie.

'You are Melanie, I remember you,' the monotone voice said.

The doctor strode over to Melanie, who had turned her back on the third clone.

'I would have thought when the last one had fallen into Samantha's mind trap, that would have been the end of the clones,' Melanie said.

'It'll be a long time before Jennifer is back on her feet. This clone can take her place in the meantime,' Dr Hamilton said.

The clone stood watching the both of them, knowing they were discussing her.

'Samantha found them a pain, in the real sense of the word,' Melanie said, with a smile.

'There were problems with the other two; I hope the third will be more responsive to our needs.'

'As long as she hasn't got the same attitude problem as the other two,' Melanie warned.

Melanie was told she would be keeping a watch on Jennifer and monitoring her slow recovery. Dr Hamilton was very pleased with Melanie and how she had applied herself to the work she gave the girl. Melanie had gone through the medical training with the ability that told Hamilton that Melanie was going to make a good doctor. She trusted the girl and had no worries regarding giving Melanie a more responsible position. Melanie was glad to stay in the underground complex; she wanted to be near Jennifer and be involved in the girl's recovery. Melanie had faith that Jennifer would eventually pull through. She had already proved her body was very strong and could take a lot of punishment.

Dr Hamilton went over to the clone, which was looking through the transparent window on the lid of the life support capsule that contained the girl who owned the cells that had made her. She guided the clone to the lift, and they entered it and went up to the ground level. Melanie walked across the room to the office, where she would work.

SEPTEMBER 2137

Inside the observatory Paul James walked down the aisle between the desks and computer terminals. He carried two mugs of steaming coffee. Paul stopped when he got to his co-worker and handed her one. Hazel Johnson looked up at him and Paul kissed her on the lips. At twenty-one Hazel had not changed her outlook on life and kept her happy and joyous character, which made her very popular and people saw that Hazel kept her head while others were losing theirs. Paul gazed at her small round freckled face, as she beamed up at him; he ran a hand through her thick curly auburn hair.

'Look what the cat's brought in,' Hazel said.

Paul James placed his coffee mug on the table and spun round. Erika Strausberg entered the room; the tall lean woman did not give them a glance as she walked past.

'Never mind, her bite is worse than her bark,' Paul misquoted.

Hazel giggled and was pleased the evil woman ignored them. Hazel was sure there was something nasty about Erika, she had a cold hard voice and she enjoyed bossing people about. Erika targeted Hazel for her easy-going manner and happy smile, which seemed to irritate the tall slim woman. Hazel watched the woman pass through the double doors that led to the computer room. Paul sat down next to Hazel; they heard someone else enter the observatory and turned to see the clone approaching them. Hazel greeted her cheerfully and just got a grunt in reply.

'She's really the life and soul of the party, that one,' Hazel observed, humorously.

'I think she's rather cute,' Paul said.

Hazel stared at him open mouthed, she could not believe he had said that.

'You're joking, of course.'

Paul moved closer to Hazel and kissed her.

'Of course, I am, I'd rather have the real Jennifer any day: she's weird, but she's a lot more fun.'

Hazel nodded in agreement, she had tried to find out how Jennifer was, but nobody would tell her anything and she had not seen Melanie to ask her about the stricken girl.

In the computer room Erika stood by the control desk, she gazed at the large matt black sphere that stood on a turntable beside the desk; it was enclosed in a force field. Erika ran her fingers over the controls and hoped it would not take long to deactivate the force field. Erika worked quickly and after a few minutes the force field was down. Erika picked up the black sphere and carried it to an open window. A man in a security uniform stood outside and took the sphere from her. She closed the window as the clone entered the computer room.

'Oh, I'm sorry, I did not know you were working here, shall I return later?' Jennifer Russell inquired.

Erika shook her head.

'You can carry on, I'm just going.'

Erika once again walked past Paul and Hazel without comment; they were too engrossed in their work to notice her.

Erika returned to her living quarters and the security guard was waiting for her, the black sphere lay on a table. She walked up to him and he put his arms round her.

'We'll get revenge for Lavonia's death, I assure you,' the man said.

Erika stared at his yellowy eyes. They had tried to get their hands on the injured girl and Melanie, but the security was too tight round them. They had to wait until a chance availed itself to them; Erika had been responsible for several death attempts on Jennifer and was very irritated when the girl survived them all.

'Don't worry, we'll get them in the end, it's only a question of time, our newfound friends will help us.'

There came a knock on the door and Erika went to open the door. Professor Andrew Atwood walked into the room. She guided him to the table where the black sphere sat, she ran her fingers over it, and she broke the sphere apart. Atwood stood beside her and stared down at the green glowing mass inside the sphere. He felt the alien mind probe inside his head.

'We need your help, Professor Atwood, this alien mind can give us a great jump forward in technology,' Erika said, in a soft vibrating voice.

'What do you want me to do?'

Professor Atwood had worked a long time with Erika Strausberg, and he trusted her high intelligence. Her singlemindedness in getting what she wanted almost frightened him, he was sure she would stop at nothing to prove her theories about extra-terrestrial life. Now she had found it and he was staring down at something alien. The glowing mass lifted out of the split sphere and rose up and enveloped Professor Atwood's head. Then it disappeared. Erika stared at his eyes and noticed the green tint in the whites.

Bauros was glad to be once more in a warm-blooded body.

He was free from his prison and it was the end of his exile. He was free to move about the universe once again. He scoffed at the entities throughout the universe that played at being god, he would not have to imitate a god, and he was a god. But there was something here that was a danger to the universe; he remembered when he had touched a female mind, which had opened the sphere for the first time. She would bring chaos and darkness to the universe; she had to be utterly destroyed.

As if she was aware someone was thinking about her, Jennifer's eyes flashed open. The lid of the life support capsule was up, and Melanie was standing close by staring at the monitor of the medical probe. Jennifer's hand shot up and gripped Melanie's arm – making her jump and scream.

'Did you have to grab me like that, you nearly gave me a heart attack,' Melanie complained.

The sense of extreme danger had brought her out of the coma. There was another alien presence about and a lot more evil and menacing than the Monox and the Ixxion. Jennifer remembered the time she had opened up one of the black spheres that had fallen from space. An inner sense told her, the mind had escaped its confines and it had found a host. Her body was still weak and in pain. Jennifer felt herself slipping back into the darkness of unconsciousness. Melanie held her wrist feeling her weak pulse. She gazed at the pale face; Melanie was deeply concerned about her injured friend.

'You look like death warmed up.'

'Thanks, Mel, but as you can see, I'm not at my best,' Jennifer said, in a weak voice.

Melanie let go of her wrist and gave Jennifer an injection. Jennifer raised her right hand and touched Melanie's right cheek.

'You must warn the General to be vigilant, there is an extreme danger close by and it's gathering its forces; when the time is right, they will attack. You must be watchful, Mel.'

Jennifer closed her eyes and slipped back into the dark pit. Melanie stared at her friend, she did not understand what Jennifer had meant, but she knew the girl enough to get her message to General Heywood and she was also going to be vigilant – if someone was coming to get Jennifer, she was going to be ready for them.

CHAPTER LXXI:

PAUL STEVENS

EXETER EXPERIMENTAL LABORATORIES

APRIL 2139

Paul Stevens and Jocelyn Wotton were on the ESP programme. She was doing experiments on his telepathic abilities. Paul was able to keep track of his sister's journey through life – he was amazed at her talents – he knew about her telekinesis abilities – but connecting her mind to a computer was something new to him – Paul wanted to know more about that.

One night he was walking down the corridor where the living quarters were housed, and he spied a young girl standing by an open door. She had gushy auburn hair; she wore a green dress with a small linked gold chain round the waist. Paul moved quickly to her and grabbed her arm. She turned and green eyes flashed.

You are hurting me.

Her lips never moved.

'I'm sorry I grabbed you so hard, I did not mean to harm you. I just wanted to talk to you,' Paul said.

Paul let her arm go and the hostility faded from her pretty face.

'It's late – we'll have to talk in the morning.'

Paul nodded. 'I've never met a girl like you before.'

The girl smiled: 'No you haven't,' she assured him.

The girl went into the room and closed the door. Paul shook his head and made his way to his own rooms. In the morning Paul told Jocelyn Wotton about the meeting with the mystery girl.

'You've met my daughter at last, her name is Pauline.'

'Do you test her in programme?'

Jocelyn shook her head and told him – her daughter had no interest in the tests.

'That's what she wants you to think. Pauline is telepathic,' Paul said.

Jocelyn stared at him wide eyed. 'Are you sure?'

Paul told her what had happened when he accidently grabbed the girl's arm.

'Do you mind if I talk to her and find out more about her abilities?'

Jocelyn thought for a while and smiled. 'Not at all – I hope you get somewhere with her.'

They went to the testing room and after the long session Paul went in search of Jocelyn's daughter. Paul found her in the offices sitting at a computer work desk. He went to the drinks machine and took out two coffees and placed one on the desk beside her. He pulled up a chair and Pauline looked up from her work and sipped the coffee Paul had handed her - she stared at him.

'You are the secretary? Paul asked.

Pauline looked up from her work and took a sip of the coffee he had brought her.

'Amongst other things,' Pauline said.

Paul smiled. 'Of course,' he said.

'I'm working with your mother – I hope we can be friends.'

'You look a nice person – I don't see why not,' Pauline agreed.

Paul smiled and drank his coffee while Pauline continued her work with the computer. He put the empty cup down and watched the girl's face and concentrated hard to try and sense what the girl was thinking – after a while Pauline turned her head – the green eyes stared hard at him.

'What are you doing?'

'Nothing, I was just watching you work,' Paul said.

'Are you a mind reader?'

Paul smiled. 'What makes you say that?'

Pauline sat back and swivelled the chair round to she faced him. 'That's what they are looking for round here.'

'A telepath?' Paul asked.

Pauline nodded.

'You are one,' Paul said.

Pauline shook head.

'I'll prove it to you,' Paul said. Paul got up and walked out of the office. In the evening he stood outside his living quarters and he saw the girl walking down the corridor – she wore a pink blouse and maroon skirt. When she was near; he asked her in for coffee. Pauline nodded and followed him into the room.

'Mother warned me about talking to strangers – but you are no stranger to my mother.'

'You are perfectly safe – I only want to talk to you – your mother does not mind,' assured Paul.

Pauline sat at the table and she watched Paul as he stood at the coffee machine. 'That's all right – then,' Pauline said.

Suddenly she said, 'White please.'

Paul spun round. 'Gotcha,' he said.

Paul placed a mug of coffee in front of her.

'That's unfair,' she said.

Paul sat opposite her and sipped his coffee. 'I'll keep your secret – but why don't you let your mother know?'

'I don't want to be a guinea pig in their tests,' she said.

'You are definitely a girl who knows what she wants – I like that.'

Paul told her about his experiences in the tests and he was enjoying finding out what he could do. He told Pauline about his sister and her talents. Pauline was impressed. They talked for a while and then Pauline left. When Pauline got to her room, she went to bed and stared up at the dark ceiling. She did not want to know what talents she may have. She was not sure she could read minds. Pauline was glad her mother was not pushing her into anything.

Paul managed to have several talks with Pauline – but he was not able to get her to join him with the tests. Paul stayed at the EEL until May 2141 – then he left for the USA and settled in New York.

CHAPTER LXXII:

GO AND FACE THE DRAGON

DECEMBER 2141

Samantha stared out of the window and gazed at the snow-covered landscape. The sky was darkening, and it was still snowing. She noticed a large white van parked across the road. She moved away from the window and ran out of the lounge and rushed upstairs to her bedroom. Samantha packed a large suitcase. She left it on the landing and went into her daughter's bedroom and packed the girl's belongings in a smaller case. Seven-year-old Sally sat on the edge of the bed staring at her mother flitting round the room.

'Where are we going, Mummy?'

Samantha did not answer and placed the case on the bed beside the little girl, she laid a fur-lined coat on top of it. She went to the window and looked out and saw the white van was still on the other side of the road. A little voice behind her repeated the earlier question.

'Where are we going?' Samantha mimicked.

She regretted saying it as soon as it was out. She crossed the room and got on her knees in front of her daughter. Tears were running down her cheeks. Samantha kissed the girl's right knee and then placed her chin on her daughter's knees and gazed up at her small round face.

'I'm sorry, baby; I should not be taking the mickey out of you. Forgive me?'

Sally nodded her head.

'I love you, Mummy.' Sally wiped her watery eyes with the back of her hand.

'I love you too, and all I do is make you cry.'

Sally ran hands through her mother's long hair.

'It's not your fault, Mummy, I see the pain you suffer, and I haven't got enough love in me to drive away the demon that plagues you.'

Samantha stared at her daughter; the deep blue eyes stared back at her. At seven her little girl was very bright and observant. Samantha had long ago given up hiding things from Sally.

'I should have had you put into foster care, while I sorted myself out.'

Sally stared in horror at her mother.

'I don't want anyone else; I want only you, Mummy. What kind of a daughter would I be if I left you in your hour of need?' Sally said, loyally.

Samantha lay her head on her daughter's knees to hide her tears from her daughter – it was the longest speech her daughter had ever made; it had touched her. It had been rough for the little girl, when her mother was irritable and bad tempered. Samantha had to live with the pains and voice in her head. She would shout at her daughter, but she never hit her – if there was any danger of that she would walk out of the room. When things were bad Sally made sure she walked round the house softly. When her mother's head was clear and without pain, Sally saw the love her mother had for her, so she did not blame her mother for anything. It was the demon inside her head that was to blame.

'I know you will never hit me, the love in you would not let you. It's my job to stand by you, when things get rough,' Sally observed.

Sally laid her arms on top of her mother's head – Samantha felt the throbbing – she tried to raise her head – but her daughter kept her arms on her head. Sally looked across at the window.

'Leave my mummy alone.'

The throbbing started to ease – Sally lifted up her arms and Samantha raised her head; she kissed her daughter on the cheek and stood up. She wished one day she could give her daughter the love and tenderness she deserved. The little girl would not say a bad word against her. Samantha did not think she deserved such loyalty. Sally stood up and put on the thick warm coat, she picked up her small suitcase. She followed her mother out of the room and down the stairs. Samantha told her daughter to leave the house by the back door and she would meet her by the road.

Samantha went into the lounge and gazed out of the window; she saw three men walking away from the white van towards the house. Once again, she had to fight her way to a getaway. She took the handgun out of her coat pocket and smashed the window with it and shot the lead man, who was just approaching the front door. Samantha ducked down and dived away from the window, as it shattered further by a hail of bullets. She ran into the hallway, the lock was blasted off the front door, she stepped into the doorway of the back room, and she put the gun in her coat and pulled out the long thin blade. She waited for the first man to move near to her, she was relaxed and ready for action. Her strike had to be swift and final. When the first man came level with the doorway, her right hand flashed out and she embedded the blade in the man's temple; he fell to the floor. She was aware of the other man in the lounge looking to see if she was in it. Samantha slipped into the darkened room as the dead man's companion left the lounge and went to his fallen partner. Seeing he was dead he turned his attention on the prey they hunted. She had killed twice, he had to make sure he would not be the third.

The man moved into the room and switched on the light; Samantha stood behind the door holding her breath. She had placed the blade in her coat pocket, and she had a strange shaped gun in her right hand; she aimed for his head. He stood and gazed round the room, she fired her weapon and the bolt entered his head and exploded. His head blew apart.

Little Sally Hamilton sat on her case by the side of the road; she stared up at the night sky and watched the snowflakes floating down to earth. The cold froze the tears on her cheeks; she wondered how long her mother would keep her waiting. A hand settled on her shoulder and she leapt to her feet and swung round and stared at the smiling face of her mother; the shock turned to relief.

'I'm sorry I made you jump.'

Sally moved to her mother and Samantha opened her coat and Sally laid her head against her mother's breast; she was comforted by the warmth of her mother's body. Samantha closed her coat over her daughter. Sally felt the rapid heartbeat inside her mother's chest. The heart gradually slowed its beating, as Samantha relaxed, and the tensions faded from her body. A decision had been made, the constant running away from the evil that was feeling out for her had to stop, it was time to go back and face her destiny.

'Where are we going?' Sally asked.

Samantha felt her daughter snuggled tightly against her body. She was old enough now, for Samantha to face her demons.

'We're going to face the dragon.'

PART EIGHT:

GHOSTS

CHAPTER LXXIII:

THE CONSPIRACY THEORY

JANUARY 2142

Shirley Gallagher drove into Westminster and drove her car down into a basement car park underneath a tall apartment building. She slid the sports car into an empty space and turned off the motor; she sat back in her seat. She waited patiently for the subject of her inquiries to make her appearance. As a freelance journalist Shirley had dedicated her life in searching out conspiracies. Anyone faking their death and turning up with a different ID was up to something and she felt there was a conspiracy in the air. James Radford, the deputy Premier who had informed her about the supposed death of Naomi Evans in a car crash close to Westminster ten years ago. The car had been so burned out the charred remains inside were beyond identification. Shirley had been on the case for two years; she had gathered up all the information about Naomi Evans she could acquire. She could get nothing on her work at the Research Installation on Exmoor. Shirley wondered if her murder or disappearance had anything to with that part of Naomi's life. Naomi was a qualified scientist working on improving medical technology. Shirley hoped Radford could get her into the secret complex because she smelt a very good story in it.

Shirley was forty-one and very experienced in her work, she practised her craft all over the world and had crossed swords with Zenobia Madison many times and her interest was aroused when she learned that Naomi had formed a partnership with the woman just before the car crash. Shirley did not trust Zenobia mostly because she was beautiful and rich, she was a shrewd businesswoman, and Shirley had to give her that. What she had learnt about Naomi the girl was intelligent enough to know what she wanted in life and how to get what she wanted out of people who were slightly dubious. Shirley had enthusiastically taken the deputy Premier's assignment. She took the premise that Naomi was not the body in the car, and she was alive and well and still living in the Capital. She would need a new

ID and a new life. Shirley went through all the data involving females of Naomi's age new to the Capital from the day after the car crash. Naomi would change her appearance to enable her to hide from her enemies and carry out any covert operation the girl might have in mind. Shirley jotted down the likely names and looked into their biographies and crossed them out as she discounted them as they were obviously not the person Shirley was looking for. She eventually whittled her suspects down to one. James Radford and the Premier were in for a surprise, as she was part of the Home Office.

Footsteps echoed around the underground car park and Shirley sat up instantly and was alert. A tall sturdy female walked into view wearing a navy-blue blazer and pleated skirt that came down to her knees. Her dark hair was cut short and the face was strong and beautiful. She carried a large briefcase in her right hand. Shirley watched her walk past and get in a car three spaces down from her own. Shirley waited for the girl to drive out of her parking space and head for the exit, and then she started her car and drove off in pursuit.

Eve Hatton was aware she was being followed and knew all about Shirley Gallagher; Eve had been well prepared for the eventuality of someone looking into her past. Shirley was a dangerous woman and Eve knew she had to treat the woman with respect, when the time came to deal with her. Eve had almost done what she set out to do and she hoped Sarah Mullen would appreciate the work she was doing on her behalf. Sarah and her followers should be aware that their ideals were being put into practice. Eve had sent for Gerald Pollard who was Sarah's chief supporter and confidant. Eve had tried to get in touch with Xanthe and Lisa, but they were unavailable, and she had no idea they had been abducted.

Eve drove her car into a car park at the rear of a tall office block. She entered the building and made her way up to the offices of Capital Intelligence. In the outer office a beautiful blonde sitting at her desk gave Eve a warm smile of welcome. Eve recognised the face and Eve was immediately on her guard. She had met Carol Moreland at a nearby nightclub and she had a different story to tell about herself, which was a long way from being in the employment of Capital Intelligence.

It looked like she was under scrutiny from two sides, but it was nothing Eve could not handle. She strode over to the desk calm and unperturbed.

'Hullo Eve, you're looking lovely this afternoon.'

Eve stood upright and gazed down at Carol's bright blue eyes.

'So, your job's not so boring after all.'

'Well I couldn't really tell you the truth about my employment; you might have got the wrong idea about me.'

Carol Moreland was quite sure Eve did not believe her; she was too intelligent for that. Carol had been pulled out of the Research Laboratories and enlisted into Central Intelligence for her exceptional security work. Her confidante Sarah Mullen was pleased with Carol's promotion and it gave her the chance to keep tabs on anyone who was sent to spy on Sarah and her companions. Three years ago, her boss Henry Jackson was moved to the Capital and she went with him. Being good at her job Carol soon latched on to the realisation someone was implementing Sarah's ideals into the outer Government. Her search for the culprit came up with the same person as Shirley and Carol went to investigate Eve. She had no idea a freelance journalist was after her too for another reason entirely.

'Is Mr Jackson in?' Eve asked. Carol stood up.

'Yes, I'll tell him you're here, what is it you want to talk to him about?'

'I'll tell him myself,' Eve said.

Carol moved away from her desk and went into the inner office. Eve waited patiently as she tried to decide what she was going to do about Carol and Shirley, and she did not want her plans going wrong at this late stage. Carol came back and told Eve that Henry Jackson would see her now. Eve strode past Carol's desk and entered the inner office, closing the door behind her. Carol sat at her desk and turned on the communicator so she could hear the discussion between Eve and Henry Jackson.

Eve walked slowly and majestically towards the large mahogany desk. Eve wanted someone strong willed and ambitious for the last part of her plan and Henry Jackson fitted the bill perfectly. She was aware of his political ambitions and she was sure he would go for her offer – he could not refuse. She sat on a chair at the side of his desk and delicately crossed her legs; she was aware of his eyes studying her face and body.

'Well, Miss Hatton, what can I do for you?'

Eve gave him a warm smile and unbuttoned her blazer and opened it out, she wore a crisp white blouse underneath that fitted snugly against her ample bosom.

'It's what I can do for you, that matters,' Eve said, smoothly.

Henry Jackson ran a critical eye over the woman, he guessed rightly that Eve was in her late thirties, pretty and had a nice full figure. It was the first time he had met her face to face, though his agents had been keeping an eye on her since she first appeared in the Capital. Now she was here in his office, he could find out who she was working for.

'I'm well aware of your ambitions, Mr Jackson and I have a proposal for you that can realise those ambitions.'

Henry Jackson sat back in his chair and smiled at the woman; he was all in favour of listening to proposals that would increase his lot in life.

'I'm all ears.'

Carol Moreland listened to Eve's silky voice coming from the communicator speaker. She had to admit the woman was a good talker and she was putting her case well. Carol knew Sarah could not have done better, but Carol was surprised Eve had picked the same person Sarah had her sights on, the final cog of her political machine. Carol was sure Jackson would go for her proposition as it was what he yearned for. Carol had worked long enough with Henry Jackson to know where his aspirations lie. It was also handy for Carol, she could take over as head of Capital Intelligence, which was something she had yearned for ever since the agency first started. Everything was falling into place nicely; Eve Hatton was definitely her kind of woman.

Two hours later Eve walked out of Henry Jackson's office a happy woman, the final phase of the plan had been set in motion. Carol Moreland quickly switched off the intercom but not quick enough as Eve noticed what she was doing.

'Tut-tut, listening to other people's private conferences, you are a very naughty girl.'

Carol gave Eve her best expression of innocence.

'It's purely for security reasons; you wouldn't tell me why you wanted to see him.'

Eve stared hard at the bright blue eyes; they had been running rings round each other for some time.

'Well, now you can report to Sarah, everything is in place.'

Carol did not try to hide her surprise.

'My dear Miss Moreland you're not as solid as you think you are. I know all about you from Xanthe. As soon as you turned up in the Capital, you'd be a danger to me. As a secret agent myself, I know all about you and Central Intelligence, my uncle happens to be one of its agents.'

Carol stood up.

'Why don't you come to my apartment tonight and we can talk about this there?'

Eve thought for a moment and nodded her head; Carol gave her the address of her apartment.

'OK, I'll meet you there at seven this evening,' Eve said.

Eve left the offices and made her way down to the next floor, she had to see one more person before Eve disappeared for good. Eve made for the offices of the Home Secretary Gordon Hammond. As she walked along the long corridor, Sarah Mullen and Gerald Pollard turned a corner and made their way towards her. As Gerald stopped to talk to her, Sarah stared at her in suspicion; Eve hoped Sarah could not see through the disguise. When Eve walked away, Sarah smiled at Gerald.

'Who's your friend?'

'Eve Hatton, I met her a few years back, she's a very remarkable woman and she's been helping you a lot,' Gerald informed her.

Sarah turned around and saw Eve had disappeared.

'I seem to have helpers I don't know about,' Sarah said.

'Your friend Carol has been keeping an eye on her,' Gerald said.

Eve walked into the offices of the Home Secretary; he was absent, which pleased Eve, as it was his wife she wanted to see. Eve sat on the side of Hammond's private secretary's desk. Barbara Hammond stood up and offered her coffee and Eve nodded.

'Your nemesis was here just now,' Barbara told her.

'I've just bumped into her, I thought I might bump into her sometime,' Eve said.

Barbara handed her a cup of coffee, Eve sat on a seat by the desk and sipped her coffee.

'How did you get on with Mr Jackson?' Barbara asked.

Eve gave her a tired smile.

'Everything is in place; it's been a long ten years.'

Barbara pouted her lips at her.

'And you haven't aged a second in all that time,' Barbara said.

Eve finished her coffee and stood up.

'It's time for Eve Hatton to disappear.'

'I hope you'll say goodbye properly, before you go,' Barbara said.

They stood up and put their arms round each other and kissed passionately, after a while they parted – they had been friends since their school days.

'Of course, it'll have to be tomorrow night; I've got a date with Carol Moreland tonight.'

'And you've got Miss Gallagher to sort out too, you are between the devil and the deep blue sea,' Barbara said.

'I have a plan for that nosy reporter,' assured Eve.

Barbara kissed her lightly on the lips.

'Watch yourself, those two women can be dangerous,' warned Barbara.

'So can I,' Eve assured her.

Sarah and Gerald walked into Norman Jameson's office; he was the Premier's adviser. To Sarah's dismay, he was talking to Shirley Gallagher. The woman got up and held out her hand to Sarah, who chose to ignore it.

'You won't find any conspiracies here,' Sarah told her coldly.

Shirley smiled demurely; the frosty reception from Sarah was the usual response Shirley expected from the people she met.

'Are you sure of that, what can you tell me about Eve Hatton?'

The expression on Sarah's face told Shirley she had hit a nerve.

'You should ask Gerald here; I've only just heard of the woman.'

Sarah sat in the seat the reporter had vacated, Shirley stood over her.

'Doesn't your office tell you about the people you employ to run your affairs while you are away?'

Sarah stared up at the infuriating woman, the grey eyes flashed a warning to Shirley.

'Obviously not,' Sarah said.

Sarah turned her attention on Norman Jameson; she had no time for reporters and even less time for people like Shirley Gallagher.

'Perhaps your father employed the woman to check up on your political regime.'

Shirley was exasperatingly persistent in her inquiries.

'The Premier doesn't have to spy on his daughter,' Jameson said quickly before Sarah got up and hit Shirley.

'Goodbye Mrs Gall…'

Shirley interrupted Sarah. 'Miss, but you can call me Shirley.'

'I know what I'd like to call you,' Sarah said, icily.

Shirley swept out of the room.

'Why hasn't anyone shot that woman yet,' Sarah wanted to know.

'She has been many times, but they fail to hit a fatal spot,' Gerald said.

Sarah swept the irritating woman from her mind; she had more important things on her mind. She turned to Gerald Pollard.

'What do you know of this woman, Eve Hatton?'

Gerald Pollard had first met Eve at the Government Building in Exeter with Sarah's political adviser, Adam Gorman. Eve had turned up in his office with a letter from Sarah and expert qualifications that were ideal for putting Sarah's political ideas into action. Gerald had been impressed with her as Adam had been. Sarah had never heard of the woman so someone who knew Sarah well had put Eve on the scene. She suddenly remembered telling Samantha about her ambitions, the girl had disappeared, and nobody had heard from her for years. Sarah had to get in touch with her colleague Carol Moreland; she was in a good position to find information about Eve.

Shirley Gallagher made her way down to the underground parking lot, where she had left her car. To her surprise Eve Hatton was waiting for her. That warned her trouble was brewing. Eve greeted her with a stony silence full of menace, she brought out a gun from the inside pocket of her blazer.

'You drive; I'll give you instructions to get to my apartment.'

They got in the car and Shirley drove carefully out of the car park, Eve kept the gun trained on Shirley.

'This is not the first time someone has pulled a gun on me.'

'It might be the last, I shall kill you if I have to,' Eve assured her, coldly.

Shirley followed the directions Eve gave her, as her mind worked on a way to make sure she did not wind up dead. She could see Eve was a dangerous female. She had kept quiet and let Shirley concentrate on her driving. When they had reached the apartment building, Eve told her to drive down to the underground car park. Shirley slid the car into an empty space and switched off the motor. Eve held out her hand.

'Car keys, please.'

Shirley sighed deeply and tossed the keys to Eve, who caught them easily. They got out of the car and Eve locked it up and, keeping the gun trained on Shirley, they made for the lift doors nearby. When they got to Eve's apartment, they entered the main living room and Eve ordered Shirley to sit in a chair. Eve got some rope and tied Shirley's hands together at the back of the chair and tied her ankles to the front legs of the chair.

'What are you going to do to me?'

Eve gagged her and left the room and entered the bedroom. She undressed and went into the bathroom and had a refreshing shower. She dried herself and went back to the bedroom. She stood in front of a full-length mirror and gazed at her body. It had taken a lot of effort and hard work to get her weight down and give herself a slimmer figure so she could slip into another persona. She gazed at her face, now devoid of the disguise. It showed all the thirty-eight years of her life, she had removed the wig and her black hair was cropped short, she was now going to let it grow thick and bushy, just the way Naomi Evans liked it.

She went to the wardrobe and took out a khaki blouse and olive-green skirt; she put them on. She put on a pair of short white socks and grey trainers; she went to the mirror and gazed at her reflection.

Naomi was back in circulation and looking great. She went to the lounge and told Shirley she was borrowing her car. Naomi resisted the temptation to tell the reporter not to go away, when she tested the bonds that tied Shirley's hands and legs to the chair. She left the apartment and went down to the underground car park and drove Shirley's car to Carol Moreland's house. When she got there, Sarah and Gerald were just leaving. She drove up the driveway and parked next to Carol's car. Naomi got out of the car and watched Sarah get into a car parked close by; Gerald glanced her way and then got into the car and drove away. Naomi went to the front door and rang the doorbell. The door opened and Carol stood and stared for a moment as if trying to decide who her visitor was, as Naomi was no longer made up as Eve.

'Hullo Carol, I thought I'd dress the part and let you see who I really was.'

Carol stepped aside and let her visitor step into the hallway. Carol closed the door.

'Naomi Evans, I presume, Sarah was sure it was you and has just told me about you.'

Carol escorted her to the dining room.

'I hope Sarah was not too mad at me, I did not really want to do it, as we did not hit it off at our first meeting at university. But Samantha was adamant that I was the right person for the job.'

'Sarah had an idea Samantha was behind it,' Carol said.

Naomi sat at the dining table and ran an admiring eye over her host. Carol was average height that made her a head shorter than Naomi; she wore a short figure-hugging cream coloured dress that showed off her perfect long shapely legs, she was a girl who knew what she had and how to flaunt it.

'We'll eat first, and then we can talk,' Carol said.

Carol turned and went into the kitchen. Naomi was left to wonder how much she could tell the girl, it all depended on how much Sarah confided in her, would she tell Carol, would Sarah tell her there might be an invasion from an alien race. It was something she had to know, it was part of her job to see if Carol knew anything about the spaceship heading for Earth and if she did, Naomi had to make sure Carol did not spread it around.

All through the meal Carol engaged Naomi in small talk to find out the differences between her and Eve in the hope their friendship would be the same. Naomi did not want to talk about her other persona as that part of her life no longer existed; she did not mind talking about her real self. After the meal, Naomi went into the lounge and went to the wall where a large painting of a spaceship hung; she had been fascinated with it because of her experience on a real spaceship with Samantha. Carol came in a few moments later and handed her a mug of coffee.

'Do you think we'll ever find extra-terrestrial life, when we eventually leave the Solar System?' Carol asked.

'As a scientist, I'd like to think so; I don't think we're alone in the Universe.'

Carol moved towards the sofa and settled herself on it folding her legs under her bottom. Naomi turned and faced her.

'We're not,' Carol assured her.

Naomi stood still and stared hard at her; Carol knew something – that was obvious. She studied the beautiful round face; the sparkling blue eyes glittered at her and a smile played on her full red lips. After a few moments Carol asked her when the last time was she had contact with Samantha; when Naomi told her, Carol decided to inform Naomi about the happenings at the Experimental Laboratories, her former workplace. Being part of security there, she was involved in clearing away the alien bodies and making sure the story did not get out. Naomi listened without interruption, even when Carol informed her Samantha had killed the man who had assassinated her father. A tear ran down her cheek and she went to a nearby armchair and settled down onto it.

'I'm sorry, Naomi, if there's anything I can do, just ask,' Carol said.

When the lights went out at the back of the house two dark figures detached themselves from the bushes and made for the French windows; the lead man worked on the lock and got the French windows open without too much noise, then they entered the dining room. The man had a tiny torch in his hand, and he manoeuvred his way round the furniture as he made for the door; his partner followed silently behind him. When he got to the door, he eased it open and stepped into the dark hallway.

Carol finished her coffee and stood up; she took Naomi's empty cup.

'Thanks for giving me that information; it was something I needed to know, it also tells me how much you know about our problem from space.'

'I want us to be honest with each other, I want us to put our cards on the table,' Carol said.

Carol left the room. The light from the room moved into the darkness, she moved along the hallway. Just before she reached the kitchen, she sensed danger, and someone grabbed her from behind and a hand covered her mouth. Carol struggled as he got a tighter hold on her; another man moved towards her and hit her viciously in the stomach, knocking the wind out of her.

Naomi walked to the door and called out for Carol but got no answer. She turned off the light and stepped into the hallway. The house was in darkness. What was Carol playing at? Naomi did not fancy playing hide and seek with the girl. She moved slowly down the hall towards the dining room on her right. Naomi took her gun out of her skirt pocket and gripped it tightly and readied herself for action. Counting her steps, Naomi stopped walking as she drew level with the dining room doorway. There was danger nearby, she could sense it, all she had to do was reach out and touch it.

Brogus clung onto the girl, while Bacus stood on the girl's feet to keep her legs from kicking out, he had a heavy handgun aimed at the open doorway. They had been told the other girl was dangerous and had to be killed, what they did to the girl they held was up to them. His finger tightened on the trigger as the sound of the other girl approaching the door.

Naomi suddenly darted forward, and a shot broke the silence like an explosion, she spun round and fired into the dining room, she could not have done better if the lights had been on, the bullet buried itself in the centre of Bacus' forehead.

As soon as Carol felt the body fall at her feet, she wrenched herself sideways in an attempt to free herself from the second man. The light suddenly came on and Brogus kept a tighter hold on his captive using her as a shield as he faced the tall girl standing in the doorway; the gun in her hand was aimed at him.

'I wouldn't fire if I were you, you might hit your girlfriend,' Brogus said, defiantly.

The gun in Naomi's outstretched hand did not waver.

'Let's see, shall we.'

Naomi fired as she spoke the last word, Brogus tried to move down behind the girl he held, but he was not quick enough and the bullet entered his mouth and blew the back of his head off. His body fell to the floor and Carol found herself lying on top of his body, as his dead arms still gripped her. Naomi pocketed the gun and went to Carol's aid and freed her from the dead body and helped her up onto her feet.

'You are pretty lethal with a gun in your hand, Naomi.'

Naomi checked the pockets of the two dead men and found no IDs.

'You'd better get on to your boss, so he can clear the mess up in here.'

Carol left the room still shaky from the men grabbing her and Naomi shooting them without hitting her. Carol was amazed at the deadly accuracy of Naomi's shooting.

Naomi left the house by the open French windows; she had suddenly remembered she had a reporter tied up in her apartment. Shirley would be in danger if someone was sent round to attack her there. Naomi rushed round to the front of the house and got into the car she had borrowed from Shirley. She drove down the driveway onto the road and shot off in the direction of her apartment building. When she got back to her apartment Naomi found nothing had changed and Shirley was still gagged and tied to her chair. Naomi pulled the gag out of her mouth.

'I thought you'd forgotten about me,' Shirley said.

Naomi untied her and Shirley rubbed her wrists. It was not the first time she had been tied up and Naomi had no reason to trust her.

'I did for a while, but something had happened to cause me concern about your safety.'

'You're not going to kill me then.'

Naomi shook her head.

'I'm no murderer and I have a better use for you,' Naomi declared.

James Radford opened his door and smiled when he saw who was on his doorstep. Shirley stood still while his eyes ran over her slim figure; she wore a short red dress. He stood aside and she stepped into the hallway; he closed the door behind her.

Radford guided her into the lounge and Shirley perched herself comfortably on the couch folding her long glorious legs under her bottom, she removed her shoes; her feet were long, slim and elegant.

'What have you got for me?'

Shirley stared hard at his face as he sat in an armchair in front of her. Shirley informed him Naomi was very much alive and living in the Capital under the alter ego of Eve Hatton. She was working at the political office of Sarah Mullen. Radford had seen both of the young women in question and found it hard to see they were the same person. Naomi wore loose fitting garments and her long thick black bushy hair had an untidy style about her head. Eve Bradley was the direct opposite; her movement was refined as were her clothes.

'I can't picture Naomi changing into Eve,' Radford said.

Shirley smiled and stood up and moved towards his chair.

'I wasn't always like you see me now. When I was young, I was a tomboy, scruffy and reckless. It's a wonder what a little cosmetic surgery can do these days,' Shirley explained.

Shirley sat on the arm of his chair and bent over and kissed him on the lips.

'So, Naomi is working undercover for the Premier's daughter.'

Shirley shook her head.

'No, not Sarah, she still thinks Naomi's dead, she's just helping Sarah realise her political ambitions; if Sarah knew Naomi was involved, she would go ballistic.'

'I don't think Graham will be too pleased either, that's why he sent her packing to the Research Facility in Exmoor, to keep her away from the people she was getting involved with.'

'Not really, it was for her own protection, Naomi and one of Sarah's companions were attacked tonight, from the same people that would harm Sarah, if they got hold of her.'

James looked up at her and Shirley studied his face, the deep concern of his expression was real enough. He was another person Naomi could cross off her list.

'I'd better get hold of Graham, were they hurt?'

Shirley assured him the two girls were all right and Naomi had killed the two men, who had carried no ID.

'I wonder what Naomi is up to, if she's not careful, she could end up like her father.'

'She's not going to let her father's death go unvented,' Shirley assured him.

'She should leave that kind of thing to the professionals.'

Shirley returned to the couch and settled down on it, she sat back and stretched her long legs out.

'Naomi is a professional, there's more to Naomi than what's on the database.'

James Radford stared hard at her. He could see by her expression; Shirley had a story to tell. He stood up and made his way to the couch and sat beside her.

'What are you trying to tell me?'

Shirley moved close to him and kissed him on the cheek.

'I shall be forever grateful to you for giving me this job. Naomi has confirmed my life's work is not for nothing. She is, for want of a better word, a spy.'

Shirley commenced to tell Radford everything Naomi had told her to tell him. Radford did not interrupt her even though most of it was a surprise. There was a conspiracy, but it was still in its birth stages. Naomi had blundered into it while doing her normal work, which was why she was almost killed, and her father being murdered.

When Dr Richard Blake got his post at Research Complex at Exmoor, Naomi Evans who was part of his staff wasted no time in getting him to take her with him. Naomi had a cousin working there and she had not heard from her for some time. Having a father who was in the government was useful in authorisation to work in the secret establishment. As soon as she got there, she went through their database to find out about her cousin. She found the name Patricia Evans, she had supposedly left, and no reason was given, she made a nuisance of herself with security and they would not give her any other information about her cousin.

Naomi questioned everyone who was at the Complex at the time of her cousin's disappearance. They did not give her much information; it was a case of one day she was there and the next she was gone.

One day she was called to the main administrative building and she was ushered into the main office and found herself standing before the Premier, Graham Mullen; the director of the Research Complex was with him. The two men told Naomi they were concerned about her cousin's disappearance. That was not the only strange occurrence that happened in the history of the complex. A lot of accidents had happened, and a lot of people had been injured and a few unsolved murders had been committed on some of the staff. As Naomi had started asking questions, Graham had a job for her. When he told her what it was, she was flabbergasted. Naomi never thought of herself as secret agent material and told Graham so. He assured Naomi, when he had heard about her inquiring after her cousin and after a discussion with her father, she was the right girl for the job.

Professor Harris, the director, would be there to receive any information she gathered that would be important. Working in the complex's hospital she got to know the scientific staff by being in charge of their periodic medical examinations. She discovered nothing unusual until she came in contact with Samantha. As soon as she put the unconscious girl in the brain scan machine, she went in search of Dr Blake. Naomi found him in his office, and he told her to sit down. He told her about Samantha and her uniqueness. Naomi stared at him opened mouthed, this was science fiction to her, but Richard assured her it was fact and the girl was lying in a hospital bed testifying to the situation. He wanted her to get close to Samantha and be a friend to her. As she was taller and stronger than normal, Samantha was being alienated by nearly everyone she came in contact with. Naomi assured Dr Blake she would do her best and when the girl regained consciousness Naomi was there to administer a thorough medical examination on the tall girl. Naomi made sure Samantha realised she was there to care for her.

When Naomi got to the Capital to carry out the plan Samantha had formed with her help, their conspiracy almost ended before it began. One morning she went down to the underground car park and made for her car and found a tall bulky woman waiting beside it and immediately sensed danger. Naomi placed her right hand in her blazer pocket where she had her gun. She faced the woman and asked what she could do for her. The woman took her hand out of her coat pocket and aimed a gun at her; Naomi heard someone behind her. An icy male voice told Naomi she was going to take a drive out of the Capital as she was not welcome here. The woman told her to open the car door and get in. Naomi got in and started the car and the woman got in beside her, the car door was slammed shut by the woman's male companion – Naomi only saw him as a fleeting dark figure. Naomi drove out of the car park and up the ramp to the ground level. The woman kept the barrel of the gun pressed against her midriff. Her mind was racing to work out a plan how to get out of this predicament without losing her life. The woman did not seem to care what route she took out of the Capital, she had her mind on killing Naomi when they left the city. Naomi drove up onto a flyover and increased speed; she gazed down at the gun in the woman's hand. Naomi took her left hand off the wheel and brought the edge of her hand down swiftly onto the woman's wrist, she heard the sound of bone snapping and the woman cried out in pain, Naomi's left arm flashed out and her fist smashed into the woman's nose and blood splattered her face. Naomi opened her door and swung the steering wheel round and swerved the speeding car towards the edge of the flyover, Naomi vacated the car and rolled over and over across the roadway. Luckily for her there were no other vehicles nearby, the car crashed through the barrier and over the edge of the flyover. Naomi ran to the barrier and looked down and watched the car hit the road below, where it exploded and disintegrated. It was working out well for Naomi, she was not officially dead, and she could slip into another persona.

Three years later Eve Hatton walked into a wine bar in the centre of the Capital. She spied a tall, elegant black-haired beauty standing by the bar; a long black dress hugged her slim body. Eve walked up to the woman and tapped her on the shoulder; she turned, and her dark eyes widened, and her mouth fell open.

'My God; it's a ghost from the past.'

'Babs, I thought it was you,' Eve said.

Barbara Hammond was out enjoying herself as her husband was away in Exeter. Naomi and Barbara had been close school friends, they both would dress up in outlandish clothes and disguises, they would invent identities, and one name Naomi thought up was Eve Hatton. Barbara was only too pleased to be her partner in crime, so to speak. Barbara took her home.

Barbara Hammond sat on the couch and Eve lay on it; her head lay in Barbara's lap.

'You've done well for yourself, Babs and you've kept your gorgeous body in fine condition.'

'I always thought you would end up as a spy.'

'That comes from having an uncle in Capital Intelligence,' Eve said.

'I like Sarah, I've met her a few times and I like her political ideas and it will be great working with you, after all these years,' Barbara said.

Eve sat up and kissed Barbara on the lips, Barbara stood up and took Eve by the hand and guided her upstairs to her bedroom.

Naomi sat in her car and gazed across at the Hammond house; a car in the driveway told her Gordon was at home. She wanted to say goodbye to Barbara and warn her of the dangers she may be in. Naomi got out of the car and crossed the road; there were no lights on at the front of the house. Naomi decided to go around the back.

The large spacious back garden was surrounded by a high wooden fence, Naomi opened the back gate quietly, and she turned back and gazed suspiciously at a large white van parked across the road. She closed the gate and walked down the paved path towards the back of the house; a frosty wind tugged at her blouse and skirt. She did not mind the cold, or the night filled with dark shadows. Naomi had no time for fear in her line of work. She kept her mind clear and alert. As she reached the back of the house, she noticed a dim light in the kitchen windows. She moved towards the conservatory and found the doors open; Naomi took the automatic out of her skirt pocket, and she felt the lock and discovered the door had been forced. Naomi hoped she was in time to save Barbara from any serious harm.

Naomi made her way through the conservatory and made for the kitchen and stopped dead at the open door. In the dimly lit kitchen, she saw a man standing with his back to her facing Barbara, who had an expression full of fear. Her eyes fell on Naomi who she put a finger to her lips warning Barbara to be quiet. The man started to turn, and Barbara grabbed him so he would not discover Naomi moving silently towards him.

'You are a very beautiful woman,' he said.

'It would be a shame to kill me then,' Barbara assured him.

He moved closer to Barbara and she put her arms round him and let him kiss her on the lips, she kept her eyes on Naomi as she approached them, Barbara felt his hand slip down the bodice of her dress, she wore no bra. Naomi slammed the gun viciously across the back of his head and Barbara moved away to let his unconscious body fall to the floor.

'Are you hurt, Babs?'

Barbara shook her head, tears ran down her cheeks, and she moved close to Naomi, who put her arms round her. Barbara began to feel better, feeling her friend's strength as she comforted her. After a while Barbara kissed Naomi on the lips.

'I'm so glad you came, two men are holding my husband by gunpoint,' Barbara said.

Naomi assured her she would get her husband out alive; she gave Barbara her mobile phone and a number to call. She told Barbara to leave the house by the conservatory as the doors were open.

'Take care of yourself, Naomi; I want you both to come out of this alive.'

Barbara gave her a long lingering kiss on the lips and rubbed her body against her.

'I don't aim to get myself killed just yet,' Naomi assured her.

Naomi stepped rapidly into the room, pushing the door wider. The man sitting next to Hammond turned towards the sound of the female voice, and he stared open mouthed as he saw the flash of her gun; the bullet hit him in the head and exploded in his brain. Naomi knew she had the edge because the man that had the door between him and her would be surprised to see she was still alive and kicking. She heard a roar of anger as he came for her, Naomi quickly fired at the two small lights and the room was in darkness. Naomi hoped Hammond had the instinct to keep his head down. He collided with her and they crashed into a chair, it went over and Naomi rolled over it, the gun was knocked out of her hand. She got up and rushed to where she knew the doorway to be, he was after her and caught her in the hallway and pulled her down at the foot of the stairs. Something stuck in her right side that told her the man had a knife.

'Where have you been hiding yourself all this time, Naomi?'

'I've been around.'

He was heavy on her as Naomi tried to wriggle away from the knife point he had jabbed in her side.

'Don't struggle; it will be more painful for you if you do.'

His voice was cold and menacing, she was not going to lie there and let him carve her up like a chicken. Her right arm was trapped under her body, she brought up her left elbow, but he was ready for her as if he could see well in the dark hallway and he quickly avoided her strike. He grabbed the back of her head with his free hand and struck her forehead against the bottom step; she saw stars.

He stood up, pulling the stunned girl with him.

'There's nothing you can do to stop me, Naomi.'

He shoved her against the far wall, and she bounced off it and he grabbed her. He held her arms round her back. He moved towards the kitchen; Naomi hoped Barbara had managed to get hold of the authorities. Naomi was convinced she was in the hands of a demon; he certainly had the strength of one. He suddenly threw her forward and she hit the floor hard face down. The man she had knocked out walked out of the dimly lit kitchen.

'Have you let that woman escape?'

The man complained he had been attacked from behind. He ordered his companion to leave the house and start the van so they could make a quick getaway, as Barbara would soon be back with some armed men. He lifted Naomi up onto her feet; she hurt all over, and he threw her with immense force through the open doorway of the conservatory. Naomi crashed into a chair and landed on the floor on her back. He stood over her. Naomi stared up at the luminous yellow eyes.

'Your infernal meddling into my affairs has not changed a thing.'

He bent down over her and gripped her throat, strong fingers dug into her flesh.

'I'm planning for the future, it has all been carefully mapped out, people like you, Naomi, have been prepared for, so you are an irritation and no more than that.'

He stood up straight.

'I shall not kill you, Naomi, I would not want to do that, as I would like you to discover what has happened to your cousin.'

He walked out of the conservatory. Naomi got painfully to her feet and switched on the lights, and she then went to the lounge and switched on the main light. She found Gordon Hammond sitting on the floor with his back against the couch, his hands and feet were tied, and Naomi got down and released him. She assured him Barbara was safe and going for help. Once untied, she helped him onto the couch; he had been viciously beaten and was in much pain. She went to the door just as Carol Moreland and two armed men rushed into the room. Naomi told Carol to contact her people to look for a large white van that had been parked at the back road behind the back garden. Carol noticed the blood on the side of Naomi's blouse.

'You're injured.'

'I'll live,' Naomi assured her.

Naomi went into the hallway then into the kitchen and found Barbara there. She saw the blood and ordered Naomi to sit down so she could tend to her wound. Barbara unbuttoned her blouse and Naomi winced as the material of her blouse was pulled off her wound.

'Thank you for getting yourself and my husband out of this alive,' Barbara said.

'You have both done so much for me, I would do no less for you. I would never have got started without your help; I appreciate what you have done for me.'

Barbara kissed her on the lips, Naomi had been a good friend to her, and Barbara enjoyed working with her.

'I'd like to see Sarah reach her full potential the same as you. We are friends, you and me, and we don't hesitate to help one another, I've enjoyed working with you and I hope you will keep in touch.'

Barbara got the med kit and fixed up the wound in Naomi's side.

'What are you going to do now?' Barbara asked.

'I have a meeting with Graham, to let him know about this man, who invaded your home; I still don't know his identity.'

Sarah Mullen walked the floor like a caged tiger watched by her father who sat at the long conference table. General Heywood sat beside him. The door opened and James Radford walked into the conference room followed by Shirley Gallagher. Sarah stopped her pacing and stared at the tall slim woman.

'What's she doing here?' Sarah asked in a hostile voice.

Shirley turned and smiled at the young woman.

'It's nice to see you, Sarah.' They sat at the table and Sarah faced her father.

'Just what are we waiting for?' she demanded.

Her father faced her with a cool expression. His thoughts were on Naomi and the hope she was on her way here.

'You'll know soon enough,' he assured her.

Their relationship was at an all-time low. His plan to keep his daughter hidden away so she would not have contact with her associates had failed and they were stronger than ever. He had questioned her about Eve Bradley who was working on her behalf, he would not believe Sarah, that she had nothing to do with this mystery woman. She had not informed him that Eve was really Naomi in disguise. She had not made up her mind whether to kill Naomi when they next met. Sarah turned away from him and faced the door as it opened, and Naomi Evans stepped into the room. She had changed into a short olive-green dress; she carried a thick folder under her arm. She sat opposite Graham and handed him the file. General Heywood had just been informed by the Premier that Naomi was alive and working for him.

'Nice to see you in one piece, Naomi,' the General said.

'General, has Samantha made an appearance yet?'

Heywood shook his head.

'I guess she'll turn up when she's ready,' he said.

Graham Mullen flipped through the file Naomi had given him. She assured the Premier the close associates that made up his Government were clean, and he had no worries about being attacked from within. Sarah stared at Naomi; she could not believe what she was hearing, and as her father told her of Naomi's work that she was doing for him. Graham told her the conspiracy they were trying to seek out was after her as well. Naomi smiled at her. Naomi hoped Sarah would realise her possible rise to fame would not be an easy road and Naomi did have her safety at heart.

CHAPTER LXXIV:

OUT OF THE DARK – INTO THE LIGHT

When Sarah left the conference room Naomi raced after her and held her arm as she caught up with Sarah in the corridor.

'I hope you don't hate me too much, Sarah, I know we did not hit it off when we first met.'

Sarah faced Naomi; she had decided not to kill her.

'Whatever you think of me, I really do hope you get everything you want. My work on your behalf was sincere, I'm a scientist and I gladly leave the politics to you.'

The frosty expression disappeared from Sarah's face.

'I don't hate you, Naomi, I did when I first found out this Eve person was really you. I should have realised, because some of your trademarks were involved and reminded me of our conversation at university, when I told you about my ideas.'

'I told Sam, that's why she got me to set up this organisation. I told her you would not like it if I was involved. These uninvited guests we have on this planet must be kept in the area they are in at this moment and implementing your plans at this moment in time will help us do that.'

Sarah nodded and told Naomi she understood everything.

'I had an e-mail from Sam, yesterday, telling me to put all the blame on her. The biggest shock was finding my father using you to be his spy.'

'I have told him nothing about you as I have no wish to spy on you. You may not feel it, but you can trust me, Sarah.'

'What about Zenobia? I take it it was your idea for her to contact me and offer me some financial help.'

Naomi nodded her head; Zenobia Madison was a shrewd businesswoman and assured Sarah the woman was very trustworthy.

'I'll take your word for it.'

'Did Samantha give you any idea when she was going to surface?' Naomi wanted to know.

Sarah gave her a nod and told her Samantha was on her back. Sarah walked away and Naomi stood in the corridor; a moment later Shirley came out of the room and joined her.

'I'm going to your Research Facility; Radford was true to his word and gave me a pass and authorization to get in there.'

'Good, perhaps you'll let me accompany you on the drive down to Exmoor.'

'Of course, it'll be my pleasure,' Shirley said.

The car sped out of the Capital. Shirley was driving and Naomi lay back in the seat beside her. She had spent the rest of the long night in her bed and she had made up a bed in the spare room for Shirley. As soon as it was light, they had breakfast and then they hit the road.

FEBRUARY 2142

THE FORTRESS, EXMOOR.

A car drove up to the high main gates of the Fortress. It stopped and a tall ginger haired girl got out and walked up to the gates and shouted to the security guards to let her in. The gates slid open and a guard approached her; Samantha promptly handed him her pass. She advised the guide to let General Heywood know she was here right away, but the guard informed her the General was away in the Capital. Samantha walked back to her car and got in; she looked across at the seven-year-old girl who sat beside her.

'We're here, kiddo, this is a special army unit, they might want you to enlist, and how would you like that?'

Sally stared at her mother and was sure she was making one of her strange jests.

'If it would help to protect you, Mummy, I would,' the little girl said in all seriousness.

Samantha laughed. Even at her tender age Sally was sure of her station in life. Samantha drove into the compound and parked the car beside the administrative building. She made her way up to the operations room where she found Colonel Hopkins, who was in charge while General Heywood was away. He told her it was nice to see her again and she would have to attend a War Council when the General came back later in the afternoon. Samantha was given the same living quarters she had had the first time she had been here. She got a small bunk bed brought in for her daughter to sleep on.

Four hours later Naomi arrived at the main gate, Shirley dropped her off and then drove away. She showed her pass and she went to see Colonel Hopkins to let him know she had arrived; he told her of the arrival of Samantha and Naomi rushed out of the office and made for the buildings that housed the living quarters. She banged on the appropriate door, it opened, and Naomi flung herself at Samantha and gripped her friend in a bear-hug.

'It's good to see you again, Sam.'

'You survived Sarah's wrath, I see.'

Samantha made coffee for them both and Naomi told her all about her life after she left her. When she had finished, Samantha told her story. Naomi scolded her for almost getting herself killed twice. They compared notes about the mystery man that they were both sure was not quite human. Samantha told Naomi about Phoebe and her run in with this serial killer and how he had been working with the aliens as they experimented on the inhabitants of a housing estate where Phoebe and her younger sister lived.

'He tried to mess with her mind, he killed her parents and Phoebe got the blame for it,' Samantha explained.

'Where is she now?' Naomi asked.

Samantha stood up.

'She's next door, I'll introduce you to her, and then you can see if you can help her.'

Naomi followed her out of the building and knocked on the door of Phoebe's living quarters. After a few moments the door was opened and Samantha walked into the living quarters followed by Naomi; the door was shut behind her. The windows had been covered up and the room was dark.

'Doesn't your friend like the light?'

Naomi retraced her steps back to the door and moved to the right and pulled the shade away from the window. Naomi looked round the room as the afternoon light flooded in.

'That's better,' Naomi said.

Naomi turned to Samantha, who was standing over a well-built girl in a black dress, who was sat at a table with her head in her hands. This must be Phoebe, Naomi thought. She strode over to them. The girl Phoebe stared at her with wide dark eyes, she was also having a bad hair day as Naomi stared at the thick bushy thatch covering her head.

'Phoebe, this is Naomi, she's a doctor, I want her to look you over, you can trust her,' Samantha said.

Upon her arrival at the Fortress, she had locked herself in the living quarters and would not open the door to anyone; the horror visions kept playing inside her head. When Samantha arrived and was told about Phoebe, she knocked on her door repeatedly until the girl opened the door to let her in. Phoebe told Samantha of the torment she was going through with the visions inside her head; she was being punished because she was unable to protect her sister. Samantha told Phoebe that was not true. Now Naomi was here they could get Phoebe up off her knees and bring her back to the tough girl she used to be.

'I'm beyond medical help.'

'Why don't you let me decide whether you're a helpless case or not,' Naomi said.

Phoebe stared at the woman. If she was a friend of Samantha, Phoebe was sure she could trust her, but she felt no one had the power to exorcize the demons that plagued her nights and days.

'Let Naomi help you, Phoebe,' Samantha said.

Phoebe turned her head and stared up at Samantha, she gazed at the expression of concern on her face.

'It takes courage to come out of the dark, have you got the nerve to fight the demon that keeps you from the light?'

Phoebe stared hard at Naomi as she spoke. The woman was challenging her; Phoebe knew she was a girl who never turned down a challenge.

'I used to think so,' Phoebe said.

'Go for it, Phoebe, what can you lose?' Samantha urged.

Phoebe stood up and stood in front of Naomi.

'OK, what do you want me to do?'

RESEARCH FACILITY, EXMOOR.

Shirley Gallagher walked into the director's office and strode up to his desk; Robert Houston stood up and welcomed her to the research complex. He told Shirley he was glad to see her again, as she had met him before on one of her assignments. Robert told her he had been following her career with interest and hoped she would enjoy her work here.

'You are a very intelligent woman, just the sort of person we want for our P.R.O.'

'I'm flattered you think so highly of me; I hope I can justify the faith you have in me.'

They left the compound and Robert took her to the village that had grown up beside the complex. Shirley surveyed the scenery as they walked along the winding road that ran through the scattering of thatched cottages, which housed the people that worked at the Research Facility. There were several people going about their daily business; they gave Shirley a quick glance and she greeted them with a smile. Robert stopped and guided her down a path that led to a small cottage, he unlocked the door and ushered Shirley into it and handed her the key.

'I'll leave you to look over your new home; the cupboards have been well stocked up with provisions.'

Shirley went around the cottage checking every room in turn and ended up in the bedroom; she took off her shoes and lay on the bed. She closed her eyes and relaxed, she was glad of the rest after the long drive down. She soon dozed off.

Two hours later, Shirley woke and got up and went downstairs. She left the cottage and looked around her. Standing by the door of the cottage on her left a girl stood watching her. She was just below average height with a well-built figure, the wind ruffled her short black hair, the pretty round face was slightly freckled. She wore a short black dress; Shirley greeted her with a friendly smile.

'Who are you?'

Shirley walked over to the girl and held out her hand.

'I'm Shirley Gallagher, I arrived a couple of hours ago, and I'm the new P.R.O.'

'I did not know we had an old one.'

The girl took the offered hand; the girl had a strong grip, as they shook hands.

'Juliet Harris is the name, I'm the black sheep of the family.'

'It's a pleasure to know you, I hope we can work amiably together,' Shirley said.

'So do I,' Juliet agreed.

At twenty-six Juliet discovered she still had the same problems she had had when she was a child. She still felt like an outcast, the person she could mostly confide in was gone and it did not seem Janice would be coming back. She now knew her real name – when Samantha found the name Melissa Harris, she contacted Professor Harris and asked him about the woman, and he confessed to Samantha – the woman was his wife and Juliet was his daughter. He decided to tell Juliet the truth. He could not tell her what had happened to her mother – he hoped she would turn up sometime – safe and well. As she walked towards the Research Facility with Shirley, Juliet hoped she could make friends with the woman; she seemed a nice enough person. They entered the compound and Juliet made for the building that housed the laboratories 2 and 3. Shirley made her way to the offices' building. Juliet saw John Stephenson by the doors carrying some heavy boxes.

'Give us a hand, Juliet.'

Juliet took some of the boxes from him and they walked towards the helipad. She helped him load the boxes into the helicopter.

'If you've got nothing to do, Juliet, you can come with me,' he said.

Juliet's round face lit up. She got in the seat beside him and strapped herself in. The helicopter rose up into the sky and she looked down and waved a happy farewell to the complex far down below them.

Dr Richard Blake gazed across the office to the far desk, where Melanie McAllister was writing up another report on the condition of Jennifer, who was still in a coma though the machines monitoring her life signs were showing her body was slowly mending itself. Melanie looked up from her report and saw Dr

Blake watching her. A lazy smile flittered over her pretty strained face. She got up and walked to the window near her desk and opened it and let the cold wind blow in her face.

'Are you all right?' Dr Blake inquired.

Melanie nodded her head; Melanie knew he was looking out for her, searching for the real Melanie lurking inside her. He had witnessed some of the arguments Melanie had had with General Heywood; there was a hidden secret there if he could find the reason for the hostility between the two of them. She was not afraid to speak her mind to even the highest authority, he admired and respected Melanie, and she was a very efficient paramedic and a hard worker.

'I'm just once again wondering what the future holds for us,' Melanie said.

As she finished speaking there came the loud roar of an explosion on the other side of the compound and it made Melanie jump.

'What now?' she muttered.

Dr Blake joined her at the open window. A thick column of black smoke rose up into the evening sky.

'I'd better go and give my services to the victims,' Melanie said.

Melanie left the hospital building with a med kit and rushed across the compound. The explosion had demolished a side wall of the laboratory 3 building. Three technicians had been killed and several people injured. Hilary Calvert and her staff were already there when Melanie got there, and she helped with the wounded. Colonel Collins was with the bomb disposal squad as they sifted through the wreckage as they searched for the reason for the explosion. They soon found what they were looking for: an explosive device had been fitted against the outside section of the wall. Inside the building the room was a mess, racks that had stood against the demolished wall had been blown across the floor, littering it with trays of cultures and other genetic material that had filled the shelves of the racks. Hilary was glad there had been nothing virulent in the containers of solutions that were strewn across the room.

From a window of the next door building that housed labs 1 and 2, eyes surveyed the damage from the explosion with a confidence of a job well done. Erika Strausberg turned to her companion, who was a heavy man in his early fifties; his plump face showed an expression of aggression.

'That's certainly started off our plan with a bang,' he said.

Erika turned away from the window and strolled across the room, laughing, as she left the building on her way to survey the damage at close hand. She spied a stranger coming from the direction of the office building; she made her way to the tall elegantly dressed woman.

'Hello, I'm Erika; you're new here, aren't you?'

The woman took Erika's offered hand.

'I've just arrived, Shirley Gallagher's the name, and I'm the new P.R.O.'

'This is not a very good beginning to your position here.'

'I'm not a newcomer to death and destruction,' Shirley said.

Shirley walked away as Erika's stare bored into her back; she was a good judge of character as it was a must for her work, and she knew this woman Erika would be her enemy number one. Shirley was going to find out as much as she could about the woman. She made her way to the scene of the explosion to see if she could provide assistance. She spied a young woman administering to the injured; Shirley went to her and offered her help, which Melanie gratefully accepted.

The Fortress: Military Research Establishment.

Naomi and Sally watched the helicopter settle down on the helipad. John Stephenson switched off the motors and Juliet got out of her seat and waited for the rotors to stop turning and she got out and started to unload the cargo. As she placed the boxes on the tarmac, a seven-year-old girl came over and bent down to lift one of the boxes. Juliet warned her they were too heavy for her to lift. Sally gave her a smile and lifted up the heavy box with little effort. Naomi joined them and Juliet looked at Naomi as the young girl marched off with her prize.

'She's quite strong for her age.'

Naomi grinned at her. 'She should be, Sally is Samantha's daughter,' Naomi informed her.

'Who's the father? Samantha did not bite his head off – like the praying mantis?'

Naomi shook her head.

'You haven't changed much, Juliet; your jokes are as bad as ever.'

Naomi moved away from Juliet and greeted John with a smile.

'I've got some important news for the General. Is he in a good mood?'

'He's busy giving Sam a roasting at the moment,' Naomi said.

'Has she been a naughty girl again?' John inquired with a smile.

Naomi nodded and told him the story as they walked towards the office building.

Juliet carried one of the boxes and followed the young girl, who seemed to know where they were to be taken. She was amazed at the pace the little girl was going with the heavy box she was carrying; Juliet had to run to catch her up.

'Are you always in a hurry, girl? My name's Juliet by the way.'

Sally giggled and continued her march across the compound towards the medical buildings. Juliet managed to keep in step with Sally.

As John and Naomi reached the offices, they encountered Samantha coming out of the building. John gave her a wide grin.

'I hear you've been a bad girl again, Sam.'

'They just can't understand I have to go away and be on my own for a while,' Samantha complained.

'Eight years is a long while,' John observed.

John and Naomi made their way up to the operations room, General Heywood followed behind them. He hoped Samantha was going to keep her mind on the mission and she was here to stay this time, he understood she had a daughter to bring up and she wanted to do it away from the confines of the Research Facility and she did not want them to treat Sally as a test subject. Samantha had assured him she had kept abreast of what was happening and if anything serious had happened that needed her talents, she would have made an instant reappearance. Samantha had told the General she had enemies and for her daughter's sake, she had to hide from them.

They walked into the operations room and Graham Mullen moved away from the minister of science, Trevor Duxbury, and greeted Samantha with a welcome home smile and a strong handshake. He was glad to see her again.

They all sat at the conference table; John Stephenson told the assembled about the explosion in the genetics lab. Samantha felt this was the start of a major attack on the Research Facility. With Jennifer lying in a coma it was now up to her to take the fight to the enemy; Samantha knew she just had to show up for the monsters to come out of the woodwork.

'I think they're ready for an all-out strike, we should get ready for that, especially me.'

General Heywood stared hard at Samantha across the table.

'You're ready for that?'

'Ready as I'll ever be, Jennifer risked her life, now it's my turn,' Samantha assured him.

'We'll put you through a vigorous training programme; we'll soon get you into shape.'

Samantha smiled at him; she could imagine the rough ride he was going to put her through, as punishment for being away so long. They would all be waiting for her to fall flat on her face.

'I can't wait,' Samantha said.

Phoebe sat up in a hospital bed as Naomi placed a headset on her. Phoebe fought back the sensation to get up and run screaming from the room. Seeing the anxiety, Naomi gave her a reassuring smile.

'Just relax, Phoebe, you've come this far,' Naomi said.

The wires from the headset led to a machine on the opposite side of the bed to Naomi, and Juliet stood beside it as it monitored what was going on inside Phoebe's head. Dr Anthony Bishop stood at the end of the bed. He had just arrived, and Naomi was glad of his help in giving Phoebe her mind back on track. Naomi adjusted the settings on the headset, Phoebe closed her eyes and the flashbacks started and her head started to throb. Naomi saw the pained expression on her face.

'You will feel pain in the areas of your brain the aliens had been working on. As soon as we have identified them, I can start to repair the damage they've done,' Naomi explained.

'What's going through your mind, Phoebe?' Dr Bishop asked.

Phoebe kept her eyes closed and recited the horrors that were replaying inside her head.

'Why don't you try to think of the pleasures in your life,' Naomi said.

Phoebe tried to call up a memory she could say was the best thing that had happened in her life. But her mind seemed to be locked on the fascination she had for a tall dark man who just wanted to cause her pain and misery.

Phoebe kept her eyes tight shut and the visions of horror were suddenly gone and were replaced by her sister's face at the age of 12.

'Do it for me, Phoebe, you are stronger than they are.'

Tears leaked from her tightly shut eyelids and ran down her cheeks.

'I love you, Phoebe.'

The vision of her young sister's face faded away and there was only darkness.

'I love you, too,' Phoebe murmured.

'Are you all right, Phoebe?' Dr Bishop asked.

Phoebe nodded her head and opened her eyes; she dried them on the sleeve of her white nightgown. The pain in her head was abating and the headset vibrated softly as it continued to read what was happening in her brain.

'Never felt better,' Phoebe replied with a wide grin.

Naomi gave her a glass filled with a light green liquid. Phoebe sipped it and grimaced at the sour taste; Naomi told her to drink it all.

'That'll put you out for a few hours and when you wake everything will be all right,' Naomi said.

Phoebe stared at her face to see the sincerity of her words.

'Promise?'

Naomi nodded her head.

'Trust me.'

Phoebe sank down into the sheets and the strong sedative worked quickly and she was soon in a deep sleep. Naomi went around the bed to where Juliet stood studying the machinery monitoring Phoebe's brainwaves. Dr Anthony Bishop was impressed with Naomi as she was sure of what she was doing, and it was obvious the woman knew she was going to succeed.

'What happens now?' he asked.

'There's no serious damage to her brain – sleep and the substance I gave her to drink will help Phoebe cure herself,' Naomi said.

Samantha came into the hospital ward room and stopped dead in the middle of the room when she saw the black-haired girl standing next to Naomi.

'Juliet?'

Juliet moved towards her old friend; she had thought long ago Samantha was no more as she could never get any information about the tall girl.

'I thought you were dead, Sam, I am glad to see I was wrong,' Juliet said.

Samantha gazed at the twenty-six year old young lady in a short black dress that clung to her full figure.

'You are very beautiful, Juliet, I hardly recognised you.'

Juliet hugged her. 'Thank you for finding out about my mother – Professor Harris owned up about being my father.'

They parted and Samantha told her it was a pleasure.

'Are you coming back with us? There is something close by that is killing people in a horrible way,' Juliet said.

Samantha saw the fear in Juliet's expression, she guided Juliet to an empty bed, and they sat on the edge of it and Samantha asked her to explain. In a shaky small voice, she told Samantha about the death of her friend Malcolm, she described the dark creature she had caught a glimpse of in the moonlight.

Samantha realised she was talking about an Ixxion warrior; she said nothing and let Juliet continue her story. A few years after Malcolm's death, Juliet had woken with a start in the middle of the night, the moonlight filtering in through the window. A tall dark demon with bright yellowy eyes stared down at her. Dark thoughts had run through her agonized mind, she had thought it was going to be her last moment on Earth as it stood over her. Death loomed over her, it was as ugly as it was terrifying.

Talons of steel gripped her and lifted her bodily out of the bed as if she weighed nothing. It lifted her above its head and her head hit the ceiling. Juliet had expected to be torn apart at any moment. She did not scream out as there was nobody near to save her. The creature hurled her at the window, and she crashed through it with a shattering roar, thin fingers of glass raked her skin and nightdress. She landed painfully in the bushes below the window. She sat up on the ground and waited to get her breath back, then she got shakily to her feet just as the demon came rushing out of the back door. Juliet shot away as if the devil himself was after her. Juliet managed to escape it and sometime later she returned to her home.

Juliet had made friends with David Murray, she got on well with him and he believed in her. One morning she went to his house and found the back door forced open. Something inside her grabbed her heart as she entered the house. The kitchen was full of red; she stared at the carnage in the room. David's body had been torn apart, she screamed out as she stared at David's crushed head. After a while she ran out of the house and made for her own home and found a dark place to hide from her fears.

Samantha put a comforting arm round her waist and Juliet laid her head on Samantha's shoulder.

'I'm scared and not ashamed to say it, they are after me and everyone keeps away from me as if I'm possessed.'

Samantha gazed at the girl's deathly white face; her body shivered uncontrollably as she leaned against Samantha.

'We'll have to do something about that, we shall need each other in the coming fight, I'll have a word with John, and so he can bring you all together. You are a nice girl, Juliet, I can't believe your old friends would completely ignore you,' Samantha said.

'I hope you're right; I don't really want to be alone,' Juliet assured her.

'You won't be alone for long when I get back, I shall need you at my side, I know that tough teenage Juliet is still somewhere inside you,' Samantha said.

CHAPTER LXXV:

MISTY HAPPENINGS

J uliet was quiet on the flight back and John concentrated on piloting the helicopter and left the girl to her thoughts. When they arrived back at the Research Facility, Juliet thanked John for taking her and then returned to her home. John went to Colonel Collins' office to report on his meeting with General Heywood. He found Steven and Janice there; they had just arrived from their return from Exeter. They were glad to hear from John that Samantha had turned up again and was almost ready to return, just in time as they were told about the explosion in the laboratory. As soon as the dawn of the next day came up, Steven and Janice were going to search the surrounding area for signs of their enemy.

Shirley was gazing out of the living room window and she saw Juliet approach her home next door. She walked out of the room and went to open the front door; she wanted to have a talk with Juliet and get to know the girl. She stepped onto the path and greeted Juliet with a warm smile.

'Have you eaten?' Shirley inquired. Juliet walked up to the woman and shook her head.

'I've just prepared my evening meal; will you join me?' Shirley offered.

'Yes, thank you, that'd be very nice, I'm too tired to cook myself.' Juliet gratefully accepted the offer of a meal.

Just as the dawn light was spreading across the moorland, Steven Calvert was walking at a leisurely pace along the track that passed beside the hill and the copse behind it. A spreading mist was moving across the land as he made his way to the old Hamilton house. The sound of voices drifted towards him on the wind, he stopped walking and tried to determine the direction the voices were coming from. He was at the edge of the overgrown copse and facing the old orchard of dead apple and pear trees. Just inside the edge of the old weathered trees stood Paul James and next to him was a tall slim woman in a long dark blue dress; he could not see her face, but Steven heard her cold hard voice. She held a weapon and it was aimed at Paul.

'Your usefulness to us is at an end,' she said.

Paul dived towards the cover of the cops, but he never reached it. An energy beam emanated from the weapon the woman held and Paul was bathed in a red energy glow and he fell face down on the earth and lay still. The tall figure of the woman slid like a spectre into the orchard as the mist moved into it.

Juliet opened the window and gazed at the mist as it moved across the grounds at the back of the house. She saw it as an omen, today was not going to be a good day. Her enemies would find it easy to creep up on her in the mist covered land. Juliet was glad she did not have to report for work early.

Steven Calvert approached the dead body of his fallen friend. He turned him over onto his back. Steven wondered if Hazel knew anything about what Paul had been up to.

Hazel left her house and saw Janice walking along the road towards her gate. Hazel ran to her and hugged her.

'When did you arrive back, Jan?'

Janice told Hazel she had come back last evening with Steven. Hazel stared at the mist slowly enveloping the small village; she accused Janice of bringing it with her.

'I can't do anything about the weather. How is Paul?'

A dark cloud came over Hazel's small bright face; tears came to her hazel coloured eyes.

'Paul has been quiet and distant of late. I don't know what's ailing him. I just can't get through to him, I leave him alone and hope it wears off in time,' Hazel explained.

Janice put her arm round Hazel's slim waist and they made their way to the Research Facility.

'I'll have a word with him, Hazel.'

Steven made his way through the overgrown ancient orchard until he came to the clearing where the old Hamilton house stood. He ran to the right side of the house and bent under a window. He got into a comfortable position and with his eyes level with the bottom of the window; he looked into the room beyond. The tall woman that had killed Paul was there, and standing close to her was one of the alien warriors he had come across at Exeter. Standing before them erect and upright was the tall elegant figure of Zindra; he stared at the ghoulish thin face with deep set ruby eyes.

As they got to the main gate Janice and Hazel met Colonel Collins coming out in his jeep. He told them to get in the back. When they sat on the back seat the jeep headed for the hill, Collins told Hazel he had some bad news for her. She immediately knew something terrible had happened to Paul. Janice comforted Hazel when she was told of Paul's murder. The driver drove carefully through the mist as he headed for the old orchard. He stopped the jeep and Hazel jumped out of the vehicle and ran to where Paul's body lay. Janice ran after her. They knelt down and stared at the horror of death etched on Paul James's face. After a preliminary examination of the body Colonel Collins helped Janice place the body in the back of the jeep. Steven joined them and told the Colonel what he had seen in the old Hamilton house.

Janice moved away from them and stepped cautiously into the broken-down trees of the old orchard. She gazed at the weird shapes of the dead trees in the gathering mist. She made her way carefully through the overgrown orchard. Up ahead she heard voices and Janice stopped still. The sound of voices came nearer, and she ducked down into the undergrowth amongst the old fruit trees. The dark shapes of a tall stout man and tall slim woman came into sight.

'What is your plan of action for tonight? Something equally nasty, I hope,' the man said.

'You can be sure I shall keep the pressure up,' the woman said.

The man laughed.

'I shall keep striking out at them until they are sufficiently worn down and we can take over,' the woman continued.

Janice waited for them to move off then she got up and moved back the way she had come. Just before the edge of the orchard she stopped and gazed through the mist surrounding her. Janice had a feeling something was stalking her.

'Who's there?' she said in a shaky voice.

Janice moved forward, unknowingly she was walking towards the watcher. When Janice was close the watcher moved silently behind the girl. Janice suddenly sensed the nearness of another person; she listened for the slightest sound that would betray the stalker. She listened to the phantoms riding the wind that whistled through the trees. She heard her name being called softly behind her, a female voice taunted her, Janice felt she could reach out and touch her tormentor. A claw like hand gripped the back of her neck; an icy coldness ran down her spine, her body shivered uncontrollably.

'You are about to die,' an icy female voice said.

The hand let go of her neck.

'Why don't you run, see how far you get before I send your life forever.'

The cold hard voice vibrated on the wind. Janice dashed forward and she heard a blast of energy behind her, then a searing pain ran over her back. Janice fell to the ground and blacked out. The huntress moved back into the heart of the orchard, satisfied over a job well done.

Down in the underground medical unit Jennifer lay in the life support capsule, the monitoring machinery put her body strength up to 88%, her heart began to beat faster, and the brainwaves got stronger and wakened her sleeping mind. The eyelids flashed open and the ice blue eyes stared up at the lime green ceiling. The room outside the capsule was dimly lit. Her left hand felt for the lid release button, her long delicate fingers found it and activated the lid release and the lid rose up and Jennifer sat up and pulled the sensor pads away from her head and body. Jennifer clambered out of the life support capsule, she was wearing a long white nightdress, her feet were bare, and the floor was cool to her skin. She went to the office where she could see Melanie inside with her back to the room. She quietly pushed the door open and silently approached the back of Melanie and grabbed her arm. Melanie shrieked and spun round and stared angrily at Jennifer.

'Give me a heart attack, why don't you.'

'Sorry, Mel, I did not mean to frighten you,' Jennifer said, sincerely.

'How long have you been back with the living?'

Jennifer told her friend she had awakened just this moment. Jennifer sensed something was up, she asked Melanie if anything strange was happening. Melanie told her about the explosion and the death of Paul James, she told Jennifer that Janice had been shot with an energy weapon, she was out cold but alive.

'Things are hotting up,' Jennifer observed, logically.

'And it's misty up top, nice weather for an attack,' Melanie said.

'It looks as if I woke up just in time,' Jennifer realised.

Melanie took hold of Jennifer's thin left wrist and felt for the pulse.

'Are you strong enough to be up and about?'

'We'll soon find out, I can't spend any more time on my back, if this is an all-out attack, I must be up and alert,' Jennifer observed.

The crisis was at hand as the occurrences of the morning were speeding up. The girl opened her eyes and felt the throbbing at the back of her head. Someone had come up behind her and struck her down. She blinked her watery eyes. She had a splitting headache. She found herself strapped to a metal chair which was wired to a machine beside it; her body ached all over, as if every nerve in her body was under attack. She was dressed in a white blouse and black skirt; she had been working as usual on the computer, when someone knocked her out. The third clone of Jennifer knew she was in trouble.

CHAPTER LXXVI:

COUNTDOWN

The clone stared up at the wall clock, she had been out for some time, and she moved her head so she could see the lighted computer panel. An icy dread joined the pain in her body, when she saw the flashing red words.

THE COUNTDOWN FOR SELF-DESTRUCT SEQUENCE IS IMMINENT. THE AUTHORISED HANDPRINT IS NEEDED TO STOP THE COUNTDOWN.

She realised she was not the only person in trouble. She wondered if the girl she had been cloned from had recovered from her injuries, she was the only person who could halt the countdown. She heard the door opening and she watched Erika Strausberg enter the room and stood in front of her captive, the watery ice blue eyes stared appealing up to her.

'You must release me at once, before it's too late. '

Erika ignored the warning.

'Sorry, I can't do that.'

The clone stared transfixed at the computer panel and the flashing digits on it, the countdown had started.

5:00

Down in the underground computer room Michelle Gowning stared at the flashing digits. She was mesmerized by them, the vibrating electronic voice echoed round the room.

'What am I supposed to do now?' she appealed to no one in particular.

'Pray,' Henry Jones offered, as he stood beside her.

'That's not very helpful, Jennifer can't be out of the coma yet, or Melanie would have told us.'

4:30

Jennifer and Melanie strode along a white corridor, unaware of the imminent crisis. They headed for the living quarters so Jennifer could get some clothes on.

4:20

Pamela Sisson woke with a buzzing inside her head. She sat up in bed and realised it was buzzing outside her head also. She slid out of bed, she was enjoying her new life at the Research Facility, she was glad all the tests and brain probing was at an end and they had some real work for her to do. She was now twenty-two with the excitement of at last being let loose into the wide world. She put on a long olive-green dress and shoes and slid out of the quarters into the brightly lit white corridor and made her way to the operations room to see what the buzzing was for.

4:00

Erika Strausberg stared down at the clone as she appealed to her for her release. She saw the agony on the girl's expression as the machine wired to the metal chair continued to cause the girl pain.

'If you don't release me soon, we are all doomed.'

Erika grinned at her captive.

'I shall be fine; it will serve our purposes if this place is destroyed.'

With the realisation that her life was going to be counted out in minutes, the clone bowed her head and prayed the girl Jennifer was a long way from the imminent explosion.

3:00

Pamela ran into the operations room.

'What's going on?' she wanted to know.

'The computer thinks it's the end of the world,' Henry told her.

'That's the trouble with machines, no imagination,' Pamela declared.

Michelle worked frantically at the computer, but all her ideas were dashed as the warning buzzes and the countdown went on. She hoped someone was working on the computer above them; there was nothing Michelle could do to influence that.

2:20

As they entered the corridor where the quarters were situated, Jennifer and Melanie gazed up at the flashing red lights along the ceiling.

'Something's up,' Melanie theorized.

Jennifer dashed into her quarters and was met by a loud buzzing sound.

'You're very astute, Mel.'

Jennifer threw off her nightgown and put on a long cream coloured dress. She brushed her long silvery hair.

She sat head bowed, she only had to endure the pain in her body for less than two minutes more and her troubles would be over. Erika had left the room and locked the doors so nobody would be able to save her.

1:00

Jennifer and Melanie ran along the corridors towards the operations room.

Inside the operations room Michelle and Henry were scratching their heads trying to decide what to do next.

'If I have any trouble with a machine, I usually kick it,' Pamela said.

They stared across at her, Michelle wanted to slap her.

0:40

Francis Powell sat in the communications room and was trying to get in touch with the surface without luck. Pamela stood behind him as she had been evicted from the operations room by Michelle. She was glad she had not been parted from her friend, she liked Francis a lot and Pamela knew he liked her. Francis told her the moment they were on their own.

0:20

Erika Strausberg sat in her hut and waited for the big bang, as she mentally counted down the seconds in her head. Everything was going to plan. The door opened and the tall figure of Dr Sally Hamilton walked in. Erika stared up at her.

'You wanted to see me,' Hamilton said in a commanding voice.

'Yes, I have a surprise for you,' Erika said.

There was a tone in the woman's voice that warned the doctor of danger.

0:10

The door opened again.

'Look behind you, there's someone here who wants to meet you,' Erika said.

0:09

Dr Hamilton turned and faced the tall figure that stood by the door.

0:08

The face had had surgery to make her look human, but the eyes told Zindra everything. This was Imera's daughter.

0:07

'You didn't think you could avoid me forever,' Zindra said.

'No, I'm ready for all eventualities, this is a fight I'm going to win.'

0:06

Juliet stood beside the hospital bed and gazed down at the pale and serene face of Janice. Steven sat on the other side of the bed.

'I have this feeling something dreadful is about to happen,' Juliet said.

0:05

'I have that feeling, all the time,' Steven assured her.

0:04

Francis and Pamela entered the operations room in the hope Michelle had come up with something, but the buzzing siren and the vibrating electronic voice told them she had not.

0:03

Jennifer rushed into the room behind them.

0:02

'What's up?' she wanted to know.

0:01

Pamela stared at the tall silver haired stranger, and Michelle pointed a finger at the computer control panel.

0:00

'Bloody hell,' was all that Jennifer could think of saying.

CHAPTER LXXVII:

UNDER A CLOUD

The dawn mist still lingered when Samantha started her rigorous training exercise. Major Moore and Dr Bishop watched Samantha make her way through the tough assault course. Major Moore was following the General's orders to be as tough on her as he could. Bishop was there to remind the Major though Samantha was at the moment part of the army, she was still technically a civilian. Along the course the soldiers were about keeping an eye on her progress waiting her to land on her backside. Samantha was up for the challenge and she showed them she had the strength and fitness to compete with any of the watchers. When she eventually got to the end of the course, she was hot and out of breath. Anthony Bishop was immediately at her side.

'Are you all right?' he asked, in a voice of deep concern.

Samantha gave him a wide grin.

'Of course, I'm a tough old girl.'

Major Moore came up to her and slapped her on the back and commented on her ability to get through the tough course without showing herself up.

'I think I'll go around a second time before breakfast, I don't want you reporting to the General that I've been slacking,' Samantha said.

'There's no chance of that, I'm very impressed.'

Samantha completed the course a second time without mishap and she made her way to her quarters. When she entered the building, she saw Naomi and her daughter already having breakfast.

'We started without you,' Naomi said. Sally gazed up at her mother.

'Was it tough, Mummy?'

Samantha kissed her daughter on the cheek and assured her it was going to be even tougher later on. Samantha went into the shower room and got under the spray of cool water and let it run down her body. When she came out of the shower Naomi was waiting and handed her a large bath towel; she commenced to dry herself.

'How is Phoebe?' Samantha asked.

'She's still asleep, untroubled I'm sure.'

In the hospital ward Phoebe was having a dream, she was fifteen and her twelve-year sister was by her side as they walked through the wood at the end of the housing estate. Phoebe was trying to assure Prue all the things that her father was saying about her were untrue, Phoebe assured her little sister she would never hurt her. Phoebe told her there was danger here for the both of them. As Phoebe was the bigger sister, it was her job to protect her younger sister.

Prue took her older sister's hand and stared up at her.

'If I had any doubts about your love for me, which I don't, your eyes, voice and expression tells me all I want to know about your true feelings towards me, I'm so lucky.'

'You are the best little sister a girl could ever have, I'm the lucky one,' Phoebe said.

Phoebe gazed down at Prue with watery eyes. She had to protect her little sister with her life.

'I love you, Prue.'

The dream ended and Phoebe woke, with eyes full of tears. Phoebe sat up. Tears ran freely down her plump cheeks; she had failed Prue and they had her little sister. Phoebe had to believe Prue was still alive and she could fight the odds and rescue Prue.

I know you will save me, Phoebe.

Phoebe stared at the far wall and for the first time for a very long time, it was just a wall, a plain light green painted wall, no visions of horror imprinted on it, showing her past life.

'Naomi walked into the room and stood by the bed.

'How's the head?'

'Fine, my head is clear and I'm getting no flashbacks. I'm in your debt.'

Naomi disconnected Phoebe from the machines and went to get her some breakfast. Phoebe got out of bed and went to the shower room. As the hot water ran over her naked body she sighed deeply. After a few minutes she dried herself and went back to bed. Naomi came in and handed her a tray and she tucked into her breakfast.

'I had forgotten how good it was to feel normal.'

'I wouldn't know, I left normal years ago,' Naomi said.

Samantha walked out of her quarters to continue her training; Dr Bishop was outside waiting for her.

'You are becoming a regular soldier.'

Samantha giggled; she was dressed in a military uniform and she was ready for action. They made their way to the assault course. Dr Bishop was shocked to see the strain on her thin pale face, he knew she would never admit to fatigue. He had tried to get the General to release her in his care, so he could be sure of the fitness of her mind, but it seemed she was Government property.

'Don't worry about me, I'll survive.'

Samantha trotted over to the soldiers who were going to put her through more pain. Dr Bishop stood beside Major Moore.

'Do you care what happens to Samantha?' Dr Bishop asked.

Major Moore turned to him and nodded his head.

'Of course, she's a hell of a character and she's very fit and tough. Like you, Doctor, I have a soft spot for her, but don't tell the General or he'll have me shot,' the Major said.

After a long hard training session Samantha walked proudly up to the Major and Dr Bishop.

'What did you think of my efforts at getting through this hard assault course?'

'Very good, you are stronger and fitter than most of the troops I've got here,' the Major informed her.

Samantha was glad to hear it and she made her way to her quarters, followed by Bishop.

'Do you really want to go through with this?' Bishop wanted to know.

'A girl has to do, what a girl has to do. I have done with running away from my destiny; I must face the menace that threatens us.'

Dr Bishop could tell from her tone that she was determined to fulfil her obligations to the General and the project. He was worried she might end up being shot up like Jennifer. Samantha had already miraculously survived one attack, she might not be so fortuitous next time, and he told her about his misgivings about her position in this campaign.

'I'm fighting for my sanity and my very existence, I have to go through with it,' she said in a very determined voice.

They stopped at the door of her hut.

'You were the first person to make me feel like a real person and not a freak.'

He put a comforting arm round her waist and kissed her on the cheek.

'There's nothing freakish about you, Samantha, whatever you may think of yourself,' he assured her.

'Thank you for that, I look on you as a good friend, as well as a doctor.'

'I'll leave you to get changed, I'm off to see your warlord,' Bishop said.

Dr Bishop walked away with Samantha's laughter in his ears. He found General Heywood still in the operations room with the Premier and Naomi was there giving her report on the condition of Phoebe Cross. She could not tell them why the aliens wanted to unite her brain with their computers, which was something they had yet to discover.

'Could you theorize something?' Graham Mullen asked.

Naomi nodded her head and smiled.

'I could think of quite a few, they may be just trying to gauge her intelligence and mental powers.'

The General stood by a hologram wall chart that showed the solar system. A red pulsating red light showed the position of the alien star ship; it was in an orbit round Mars. Naomi looked away from the General and stared at the map. The General turned his attention on the psychiatrist.

'Has Samantha still got the mind for the job?'

'Yes, she's as stubborn as you, in that respect,' Dr Bishop replied.

'Don't blame her for that, she's headstrong and she knows what she wants, and her physical strength and fitness will get her through this.'

They stared at each other for a moment.

'She won't be on her own and she'll get all the protection she needs. Whatever you think of me, Doctor, I really do care for Samantha.'

Dr Bishop stared hard at the army officer and saw he meant every word, he really did care for her.

'In that case you can help me, to help her. I'd like to stay, so I can let her know I'm here for her. '

'I hoped you would, as you are one of the few people Samantha really trusts, you would be an asset to me in that respect,' the General explained.

Before they knew it, Samantha had slipped silently between them.

'Talking about me, again?' Samantha said, fluttering her long eyelashes at them.

Samantha stared at the hologram wall map and the winking red light that circled the red blob that represented Mars.

'They're getting close, an attack on the Research Facility must be imminent,' she observed.

'It's already started,' the General told her.

General Heywood gave her the report he had got from Colonel Collins of what Steven had seen in the old Hamilton house and the attack on Janice. They had lost communication from the Research Facility after Colonel Collins had made his report. Samantha would have to find out what was going on at the Research Facility when she eventually got back there.

A thunderous roar broke the oppressive silence, the observatory building shook as the explosion ripped into the computer room. The wall was blown into the control room, Hazel Johnson and Wendy Goodman were closest to the partition wall and they were blown off their seats, while everything was crashing down around them, Wendy had ended up under her desk, Hazel lay on the floor and the desk she had been working at now lay on top of her. Wendy waited for the roar of the explosion to die down and things to settle down before moving from under the desk.

'Are you hurt, Hazel?'

Hazel gazed towards Wendy; her body hurt where the desk had hit her, but she did not think any bones were broken. Wendy got up and pulled the desk off Hazel and pulled the girl up onto her feet.

'Thanks, Wendy, that was close.'

'Someone doesn't like us.'

'Don't take it personally, Wendy.'

The two girls made their way to the exit doors, as the building was being evacuated. Hilary and her medical staff were tending to the injured.

Dr Sally Hamilton stared at the tall creature before her. The ruby red eyes bored into her own. She listened to the sound of the explosion outside and wondered where it had come from, she was sure Erika was involved in it and the other explosion as well.

'Are you going to blow up the whole Facility, Erika?'

Erika grinned at the tall doctor.

'It's just a softening up process before me and my associates take over.'

Dr Hamilton shook her head.

'You won't get any thanks from this monster, Zindra has a dislike for all things, and even her friends don't trust her. '

Dr Hamilton turned her attention back to Zindra and saw she now held an energy weapon. She had a sudden apprehension that she was about to be killed; she had hoped Zindra would keep her alive to get her help in catching Samantha. Zindra had the weapon on a low setting and she fired it at her enemy and smiled when she watched the woman fall to the floor senseless.

'Have you killed her?' Erika asked.

'No, I shall need her later, when we get hold of her daughter.'

Ian Henderson looked away from the window when he saw Dr Hamilton being shot by the alien weapon. He had seen the strange looking female enter Erika's quarters and he immediately approached the hut and looked through the window. He watched as Dr Hamilton's body was bathed in a blue glow and she collapsed to the floor. He moved away from the building and ran across the compound towards the blockhouse in the centre of it. He ran into Hazel, who had left the observatory and was on her way to see if Janice was conscious. A strong wind was blowing a black choking cloud across the complex. He took her hand and told her to come with him. Ian went to the door of the blockhouse and tapped out the secret combination on the door lock keypad. The door slid open and Ian pulled Hazel into the building and the door slid shut.

'Where are you taking me?' Hazel wanted to know.

A dim light on the ceiling lit up the inside of the blockhouse; Ian went to one side wall and pulled a bench away from it. He knelt down and pulled up a small metal tile from the floor, which revealed a small control box. Hazel watched him press a button on it and a trapdoor lifted up.

'We are going underground; I must know if they're all right down there.'

Hazel knew about the underground complex and one day hoped she would go down and have a look round, so she was happy to go with Ian.

'You go first, Hazel.'

Hazel gazed down the dark hole, as he told her it was a shaft which they would descend by means of a metal ladder. She clambered over the edge and moved slowly down the metal ladder, Ian followed her down the shaft, the trapdoor shut, and the electronic lock was engaged. Ian heard Hazel gasp as they were in darkness. He reassured her, he was close by and there was nothing in the dark to harm her, he told her to keep a tight hold of the ladder. Sometime later she came to the floor of the shaft and Hazel told Ian. She moved away from the ladder so Ian could move off the ladder. Ian saw a path of small lights on the floor of a horizontal shaft and they showed the way forward; Hazel followed behind him.

The troops in the military encampment beside the hill were thrown into action after the explosion. A fully loaded truck swung out of the main gate and headed for the Research Facility. Steven Calvert and Shirley Gallagher stood outside the gate and watched the truck speed past them.

'It looks as if I've arrived here just in time. I love being in the thick of it.'

Steven stared at the woman; Shirley had told him she was a journalist. Steven hoped she had not bitten off more than she could chew.

'You might regret saying that,' he said.

Before Shirley could respond to his statement, there came a loud wailing sound in the sky above their heads. They both looked up and saw the alien scout ship descend from the thick cloud and settle down in the middle of the military encampment.

'Wow, my first UFO,' Shirley shouted, triumphantly.

Steven laughed at her.

'It's a flying object, but it isn't unidentified,' assured Steven.

Shirley gazed at him with a puzzled expression.

'You were expecting it?'

'Something like that,' he said.

Shirley slipped her arm round his.

'What do we do now, panic?' Shirley asked.

The sound of the spaceship's motors faded into silence. Shirley stared at it and watched a hatch open. The soldiers were arming themselves and got ready to do battle with the occupants of the spaceship. The Ixxion warriors filed out of the open hatch. They were ready to fight, and they were glad their opponents were too. Steven grabbed Shirley by the arm and told her it was time to move and they ran towards the Research Facility.

CHAPTER LXXVIII:

UNDER ATTACK

Jennifer stood rigid as she stared at the computer screen, as the ceiling and walls shook. The lights flickered, as she wondered why she was still alive. Michelle stood by the control desk and gazed at the tall girl.

What now, Jenny?

Michelle called out to Jennifer, who stared up at the ceiling as if expecting it to fall on her. Michelle rushed to her and shook Jennifer roughly.

'Snap out of it, Jenny, we have to find out what is happening up there.'

Jennifer shook her head and tried to clear her confused mind; she turned and walked out of the operations room and walked along the corridor to the next door and strode into the communications room. Simon Beresford was sat in front of the transmitting equipment; he had been trying without success to get in contact with those up above. When Jennifer and Michelle approached, Simon stood up and anticipated their first question and told them he had not yet been able to make contact with anyone.

'At the moment, we seem to be on our own,' Jennifer reasoned.

'You'll be taking charge then?' Simon inquired.

Jennifer shook her head and turned to Michelle. Jennifer knew they would only follow someone they could trust, and Jennifer knew she was not the most popular person amongst them. Michelle was the most likeable person and there was another factor in the girl's favour.

'Michelle is the senior here, she will be in charge,' Jennifer decided.

Michelle started to protest as she was not sure she was up for the job as leader.

'You are the ideal choice for leader, Simon here can be your second in command,' Jennifer said

Melanie approached them and told them she was going up to the surface to help with the injured, she also would be able to find out what had happened to the computer up above them. Jennifer crossed the room and made for the lift doors.

'Take care, Mel, I owe you a lot,' Jennifer said.

'Not as much as I owe you,' Melanie assured her.

Jennifer stood by the closed lift doors for a moment then turned away and joined Michelle and Simon.

In the military encampment the soldiers were fighting it out with the alien warriors. Aplon Whan watched the battle on the viewer, Zelphas stood beside him. They could see the Ixxions were not having it all their own way, as the soldiers stood up to the alien onslaught.

Erika Strausberg stood beside the hospital bed that Janice lay still in. She was slowly recovering from the energy bolt Erika had fired at her. She had not killed the girl because she had a use for Janice. Things were happening inside Janice's head, the excruciating pain in her body had woken the thing in her brain that had entered her head when she went into the marsh to investigate the object that had fallen from space and landed in the marshland. It had remained dormant for years until the time was right for it to take action. The energy filaments of the alien mind hiding in the depths of her brain gathered information from Janice's memory cells. It had no wish to harm the host it had inhabited and when the body had been seriously hurt, it went into action to revive the mind and body of the host.

Janice came to her senses and her eyes opened and gazed at Erika, who stood staring down at her. Janice was sure she was in trouble.

The lift door slid open and Melanie stepped out and walked across the operation room of the observatory. She walked to the destruction of the side wall, where the rubble was being cleared away. She was told fortunately nobody had been injured in the observatory, when the side wall had been blown in. She made for the exit doors and left the building; she gazed up at the cloudy sky and saw the thick black smoke that was spreading over the compound like a shroud. A strange sound met her ears and she saw the alien scout ship descend out of the thick cloud bank. It landed beside the blockhouse. She stood still and watched the hatch open and a horde of alien warriors came striding out. The attack had started.

Janice got out of the hospital bed and found her clothes and got dressed. Erika waited patiently for her.

'You are going to work for us, Janice.'

Janice gave her a wry smile.

'What do you want me to do?'

Erika grabbed her arm and almost pulled her out of the room. They entered the operating room; they approached a life support capsule and Janice gazed at the lid to see who was in it. She stared down at the still face of Dr Hamilton.

'What have you done to her?'

Erika stood close to Janice, she had never liked the woman, and her manner was too icy for Janice.

'She's still alive; we shall need her, when her daughter eventually arrives.'

Footsteps approached them; Janice turned and stared open mouthed. Two Ixxion warriors approached them, their reptilian plated skin glistened in the light, one was coloured green and the other was red. Their sloping foreheads ran down to a broad bridged nose, there was a small slit for a mouth underneath. They wore a black leather uniform with a large belt round their waists which held many formidable weapons. They were tall and muscular.

'Are they friends of yours?' Janice asked.

Erika just nodded and kept her eyes on the door and Zindra made her entrance. Janice stared hard at the tall alien female. This was the big boss, Janice thought, the expression on the thin alien face and the deep ruby red eyes told her that.

'Who is this?' Zindra demanded.

'This is Janice, she is going to help us, she is a geneticist,' Erika answered, immediately.

Zindra turned her burning red eyes on Janice, she felt them burning into her brain.

'You are going to betray your own kind?'

Janice shrugged her shoulders.

'I want to be on the winning side.'

Zindra grinned; she silently complimented Janice on her excellent reading of the situation. Janice wanted to stay close to them, so she could discover what they were planning to do.

'Good, you will act as mediator, if your people do as they are told, they won't be harmed,' Zindra told her.

'I'm yours to command,' Janice said.

Janice hoped the tall alien would be true to her word, it would make her job easier, she just hoped everyone would trust her.

Melanie made for the long single storey building that held Lab 1. It was close to the explosion that had destroyed the observatory computer room. She saw the side wall of the laboratory building had been blown in by the explosion. She entered the building and found Hilary and her medical team removing the dead bodies and tending to the wounded; she was glad of Melanie's help. She told Hilary they were about to be invaded by alien warriors. She thought Melanie was joking until she saw the serious expression on her face.

'It looks as if we're in trouble,' Hilary observed.

Jennifer silently agreed with Hilary, as she listened to the transmission sent by the electronic bug Melanie carried on her person. Jennifer soon came to a decision; she turned to Michelle, who stood behind her.

'We must disable the lifts, when they are in charge up there, they won't waste time getting down here.'

Michelle nodded in agreement.

'There are at least two people up there working against us, it is me they're after. They know I am a threat to them,' Jennifer said.

She advised Michelle to get everyone in pairs to fix every lift that led to the surface. Michelle rushed off to the armoury which was down another corridor not far from the communication room. Jennifer contacted the others and told them to join her. When they were all assembled Michelle came back, with a box of explosives and weapons in case the aliens managed to get down amongst them before they were able to disable all the lifts. Jennifer went to the lift doors in the room they were in and opened them, she got in the lift and reached up her longs arms and lifted off the inspection hatch and pulled herself up through the hatch and onto the top of the lift. She set the explosive in place and eased herself through the hatch and onto the floor of the lift. Simon stood there waiting for her.

'Michelle has told the others, I'm with you.'

'When the lift goes back up the explosive will go off when it hits the top. I'll contact Melanie and get her to make sure none of our people try to use them,' Jennifer said.

To get around the underground complex quickly there were rail cars which ran along an electric rail in the middle of the floors of the many corridors that made up the base. Just outside the communication room was rail car 4; Pamela and Francis got in it and headed across to the other side of the complex where they would find Terminal 3. Michelle and Henry had the longest trip as Terminal 1 was at the other end of the underground complex. They got in one of the rail cars at Terminal 2 which was a short walk away.

Melanie was impeded in her efforts to treat the injured by the tall bulky Ixxions that strolled about the medical lab as if they owned it. Melanie shouted at them, but they ignored her. One of the tall slender Monox came into view and she flew at him, shouting and waving her arms about and brandishing the heavy med kit she carried.

'If you are going to kill us all, then get on with it, if not, then get these goons away and let me get on with my job.'

Aplon Whan gazed at the furious alien female in bewilderment. He saw one of the warriors make a move towards the shouting creature and got the heavy med kit in the face for his troubles; as he fell back Melanie made a grab for his weapon and held it on him to make sure he did go for her again. Aplon waved him away and Melanie handed him the Ixxion's blaster. Melanie went back to helping the injured. Aplon Whan cleared the warriors from the laboratory.

'You certainly told him, Mel,' Hilary said.

Melanie became aware of a bleeping sound coming from her blouse pocket. She looked about to see if any of the aliens were about, then took the communicator out of her blouse pocket and she heard Jennifer's voice.

'How's it going, Mel?'

Melanie tried to keep the tremor out of her voice as she explained about the carnage made by the explosion in the medial laboratory. Melanie told her they were still digging the dead and injured out of the rubble.

'We've booby trapped the lifts in case the aliens try to get down here, so make sure our people don't use them. They'll have to use the emergency shafts.'

'OK, Jen, take care.'

'And you, Mel.'

Just hearing Jennifer's voice was a boost to her confidence, Melanie moved towards the other paramedics that were carrying the injured to the operating rooms in the undamaged part of the building. Hilary came up to her.

'Are you coping all right Mel?' Melanie nodded her head.

'I just got a call from Jenny; she's fixed the lifts in case they have unwelcome guests.'

'That's a relief to know she's up and about,' Hilary said.

Jennifer and Simon entered the large room that was Terminal 2; she brought down the bulkhead that blocked the corridor they had just come out of. Simon opened the doors of the lift and stepped into it; Jennifer joined him. She reached up and opened the inspection hatch.

'It's certainly a help being so tall, Jenny.'

Jennifer pulled herself up through the hatch and fixed the explosives to the mechanism of the lift. Jennifer went back through the hatch and jumped down to the floor of the lift.

'That's two done and two to go, let's see how Michelle and Henry are getting on.'

When they reached the Terminal 1, Henry jumped out of the rail car and ran to the lift doors; Michelle stopped the car. She went to the lift doors and Henry informed her someone was coming down.

'We're going to have visitors,' Henry said.

'How are we going to know if they are friend or foe?' Michelle wanted to know.

Henry took a handgun out of the inside pocket of his jacket. Michelle put a hand into her white lab coat and brought out an automatic pistol.

'Shoot first and ask questions afterwards,' she said.

They stood on either side of the lift doors ready for action. The doors slid open and something was thrown out of the lift. A cloud of obnoxious gas filled the terminal room, Henry fired at a huge bulk that emerged from the lift, and Michelle held her breath and moved away from the lift. Her eyes tried to penetrate the thick foul mist. She suddenly lost all senses and dropped to the floor.

Jennifer and Simon reached Terminal 1 and saw the gas cloud moving towards them. She told Simon to hold his breath and run as fast as he could towards the other end of the terminal. Simon nodded and Jennifer closed down the bulkhead. While Simon made his way to the other side of the terminal room, Jennifer moved cautiously towards the lift doors, her feet made contact with something lying on the floor; she reached down and found it was Michelle lying unconscious on the floor. A large shape came out of the mist. As the alien warrior grabbed her, Jennifer was knocked backwards and she landed on her back. Jennifer kicked up with her long powerful legs and the monster flew over her head. Jennifer jumped up and took the automatic pistol out of her skirt pocket and fired several times at the alien warrior as it made a move towards her. As it hit the floor and lay still, Jennifer lifted up Michelle and carried her swiftly towards the other side of the terminal room. Her immaculate vision tried to see a way through the foul mist.

Simon and Henry stared into the thick mist, they had heard the shots and they hoped Jennifer and Michelle managed to make their way towards them. Jennifer came into view carrying her burden and Henry helped her place Michelle carefully into the rail car.

'I'll fix the lift; you two take Michelle to the medical room. Get ready to drop the security bulkhead when I get there,' Jennifer ordered.

Jennifer took a deep breath and made her way back to the lift; the alien gas was thinning so it was getting easier to see. She fixed the explosives she had been carrying to the lift walls. When that was done, she raced towards the end of the terminal room and out into the corridor; behind her came a deafening roar of a loud explosion. Jennifer turned and saw a ball of flame in the terminal room, the alien gas had ignited, and the fire was heading for her. Jennifer ran at full speed down the corridor.

Simon stood and gazed down the corridor, hoping Jennifer was going win her race for survival. He silently willed her on. When Jennifer was close enough, she shouted to Simon to drop the security bulkhead, as it came down Jennifer dived under it and reached the other side safely. Simon stopped her slide across the floor and helped her up.

'I think you've broken some kind of record, Jenny,' Simon informed her.

'Thank you, Simon, I was just making sure I didn't get singed,' Jennifer said, grinning.

They entered the medical room and Jennifer found Michelle sitting up in one of the hospital beds.

'How are you feeling?'

'You saved my life, Jenny,'

'You are the one person I can't do without, Michelle.'

When rail car 4 entered Terminal 3, Pamela had the explosives in her lap. She was exhilarated now the action was in full flow. She was sure this was what all the tests were for; Pamela was determined not to fail. Francis stopped the rail car and they got out and went to the lift doors.

'I never thought I'd be trying to fight of a lot of annoying aliens, when I got here,' Francis said.

'That's why we went through all those weird tests,' reminded Pamela.

When they got to the lift doors, they noticed the lift was on the way down.

'Looks as if we got here just in time,' Francis said.

'We have to make sure whoever is using the lift, is friend or alien,' warned Pamela.

'How? We're not armed,' Francis said.

Pamela grinned at him and produced a handgun from her dress pocket.

'I never go into action unprepared,' Pamela assured him. She stood at one side of the lift doors waiting for them to open, the handgun aimed at them ready in case it was the aliens who came out of the lift. Francis gazed at her and thought Pamela was a cool one, he had to admit. The doors slid open and Pamela tightened her finger on the trigger. A tall army officer stepped out of the lift and Pamela relaxed. Professor Albert Harris followed him and a dark-haired girl in a red dress brought up the rear. Wendy Goodman smiled at Pamela and nodded to Francis.

'You are just in time, we were going to fix the lifts in case we get invaded down here,' Francis said.

Pamela pocketed the handgun and went into the lift. Francis followed her.

'Lift me up Francis, so I get open the inspection hatch.'

Francis grabbed her by the waist and lifted Pamela up so she could reach the hatch.

'It's a good job you aren't too heavy, Pam.'

Pamela crawled up onto the roof of the lift and fixed the explosive to the lift mechanism. She slid down into the lift and Francis grabbed her hips and helped her down to the floor of the lift. Francis put his arms round her and kissed her on the lips, and then she pushed him away.

'Control you, Francis,' Pamela said, firmly.

Jennifer and Simon took the rail car and headed for the communications room; Henry stayed with Michelle in the medical room until she felt better. When they got there Jennifer tried to contact the Fortress, to tell them of their predicament. After getting no response Jennifer had to give up.

'It's no use, we need a genius,' Simon observed.

'What we need is Hazel,' Jennifer said.

A small voice spoke behind them.

'Did I hear my name mentioned?'

Jennifer spun round and stared at Hazel and Ian standing by the doorway.

'How did you two get down here?' Jennifer inquired.

Ian Henderson told her about their journey down the emergency shaft under the blockhouse. Jennifer informed him they had had some unwelcome visitors, while they were making sure the aliens did not use the lift. Jennifer asked them if they had seen Juliet. They both shook their heads. Jennifer hoped the girl had not been caught in the explosion in the medical laboratory.

'Janice is being held by the aliens, they shot Dr Hamilton,' Ian said.

'That'd be unfortunate if she died twice,' Jennifer thought out loud.

They did not know what she meant, and Jennifer did not explain herself. Hazel went to the communication desk and got down to work; Ian sat beside her.

Janice stood studying Erika and her alien companion as they listened to the sound of firearms being discharged at the bottom of the lift shaft.

'Your friends are having trouble, that's not their weapons firing,' Janice said.

Janice had been sure Jennifer would not be caught napping.

'A minor setback, we'll get down there eventually,' Erika said.

'You won't find Jennifer a pushover,' assured Janice.

Aplon Whan and Zelphas marched into the room. Janice stared at the female monstrosity as she approached her. Aplon Whan went to Zindra and told her they had the Research Facility under their control. Janice had thought Zindra had been a bad dream, but this new female alien was a nightmare. The domed head and deep-set amber eyes, the slightly elongated muzzle was open, and it revealed to long white fangs amongst the smaller needle-sharp teeth. Janice could see the alien female was a carnivore; the burning eyes stared down at Janice, as if she was going to be the next meal.

'Do you want me to get information from this one?'

Erika shook her head and informed Zelphas, Janice was already working for them. Janice had eye to eye contact with the creature and Zelphas ran a long blue tongue over her long fangs.

'You are very wise to work with us, your safety will be guaranteed,' Zelphas assured Janice in her low growling voice.

'I'm glad to hear it.'

Erika gripped Janice by the arm and guided her out of the building, Zelphas followed behind them. Janice stared up at the sky, the great smoky cloud hung over the Facility like a dark shroud. They moved towards the long low building that housed Labs 1 and 2. Janice gazed across to the other side of the building which was in ruins destroyed by the vast explosion in the computer room of the observatory building that stood close by; it was still burning furiously sending more acrid smoke into the atmosphere. Fire appliances were working hard to put the fires out in both buildings. Two Ixxion warriors stood by the main doors, they walked past them and entered the building. Several Ixxion warriors were striding along the corridor making sure the inhabitants of the Facility did as they were ordered. Erika pulled Janice towards the lift that would take them down to Terminal 2 in the underground complex. Zelphas ordered three Ixxion warriors to accompany her into the lift. Janice hoped they were ready for them down there. She wondered if Jennifer was up and about yet, they would need her strength and intelligence.

As the lift came up from the underground base, Janice pulled free of Erika and moved away from the lift doors, she was sure Jennifer had made sure the aliens could not use the other lifts. When the lift hit the top of the shaft; there came an ear-splitting explosion, the doors were blown out and the three Ixxion warriors were killed. Hot dust and debris hit Janice and Erika, as they moved further away from the destruction of the lift.

'I told you, Jennifer is no fool.'

Zelphas rushed out of the building and made her way to the scout ship. She met Zindra and Aplon Whan standing by it, Zelphas told them about the second failed attempt to gain access to the underground base.

'We should use the teleporter, that's our only option,' Zelphas advised.

Zindra agreed and they went into the scout ship, Zindra and four Ixxion warriors stood in the teleport pad and Zindra worked the controls.

Jennifer stood by the computer desk and looked up at the screen that showed a map of the underground complex. Michelle came up to her. After two failures they were sure the aliens would try something else. They were all putting their minds together to try to figure out what it would likely to be. Wendy was at the other end of the computer system, gazing at a large glass sphere standing on a matt black plinth; it intrigued her. Then it started flashing. She moved away from it; Wendy was sure she had not touched it.

'Hey Jenny, your crystal ball is flashing,' Wendy called out.

Jennifer and Michelle rushed over to her.

'I didn't touch anything, honest,' Wendy assured them.

Jennifer stared at the flashing globe for a moment then rushed back to the computer desk. Michelle followed behind her.

'They are using a teleport machine, we'll have to find out where they are going to materialize,' Jennifer said.

Jennifer spanned the map of the base on the computer screen and suddenly there were two glowing pinpoints of light appeared at Terminal 2. Jennifer called Simon and Henry over and made sure they were armed. She told Michelle to keep an eye on the map and contact her if there was any more transportation. The three of them left the operations room and made their way to the entrance to the terminal. Jennifer told Simon and Henry to stay back so they could handle any alien that materialized behind her. Jennifer lifted the bulkhead and they saw two Ixxion warriors approaching them.

'Are you sure you don't need any help with them, they look pretty mean to me,' Simon said.

'I'll be all right; they are probably more scared of me, than I am of them.'

'I can believe that, Jenny,' Simon assured her.

Jennifer moved into the terminal room. She stopped and stood with her legs apart and hands on hips; it was a challenge to the two bulky alien warriors. They had to get through her to proceed any further. The leading Ixxion had seen this silver haired female before; he had been in the spacecraft when Jennifer had come out of the wood to combat with one of his fellows. It was time for him to get revenge. She stood firm as they pointed their energy weapons at her.

Jennifer took her hands from her hips and held them up in front of her. Jennifer hoped they were more honourable than shoot an unarmed female. She enjoyed a good fight and she wanted to get to grips with them. She was happy to show them who was boss.

One of them stepped forward and the tall female, she was in a better condition than when he last saw her. His adversary, she was taller than him and even taller than Zelphas their commander. The Ixxion had been warned about the fact she was strong and fast on her feet. She was the perfect predator. The Ixxion put the blaster away and pulled out the broad fighting sword. The challenge had been made, he moved towards her.

In her mind Jennifer was going over the first fight she had had with them; it was going to be different this time. Jennifer felt stronger than she had ever before; a new forceful power was surging through her athletic body. The adrenalin was building up in her blood as it raced through her veins. The tension building up inside her was electric.

The Ixxion suddenly rushed at her. Jennifer took a step back. As he raised the machete like sword up as he was about to bring it down on her head. Jennifer reached up and grabbed the arm and then brought her right knee up into his stomach, the Ixxion let out a roar of rage and pain. Jennifer keeping a grip on his arm with one hand, she swiftly spun round and leapt onto the warrior's back and wrapped her long legs round his broad body, with her free hand she said the long thin blade out of the sheath attached to the belt on her skirt. Jennifer slid the blade into the back of its neck, she kept thrusting it in until the alien lay still.

Jennifer jumped up and got ready for the second Ixxion, who was bearing down on her, a clawed fist flashed by her head, she ducked out of the way. His other fist hit her in the stomach; her strong muscles took the blow, so she did not have the wind knocked out of her. Jennifer swung her right fist and hit the Ixxion in the throat with all her strength, crushing his larynx. In her left hand was the long thin blade and she drove it into the side of the warrior's head.

Jennifer returned to Simon and Henry.

'Remind me not to get in an argument with you, Jenny, we're sure glad you are on our side,' Simon said.

Henry closed down the security bulkhead. Michelle came running up to them and told them there were three more visitors along the living quarters' corridor.

CHAPTER LXXIX:

THE FEMALE PREDATOR

Jennifer moved down the corridor slowly towards the living quarters; she was alone. She came to the point where another corridor veered off to her left. She held the alien broad sword in her right hand; Jennifer thought it would come in useful, when she encountered the other three unwelcome visitors.

As soon as she came level with the left-hand corridor another warrior rushed out at her and crashed into her, the heavy bulk knocked her to the floor, and she landed on her back. The Ixxion aimed his blaster at her head and Jennifer rolled away and it fired at the floor where her head had been. Still holding the alien broad sword, she swiftly lopped off the clawed hand that had held the energy weapon; the creature gave a loud growl of pain and shock. Jennifer stood at her full height with her legs apart, swung the wide bladed weapon and it sliced through the warrior's neck and the head and body parted company.

Jennifer moved forward towards the living quarters. On the other end of the corridor out of sight was Zelphas and the other Ixxion; she had seen the fight between the silvered haired girl and Rohn. She was intrigued by this tall athletic native of this planet they had landed on. The tall creature was a good fighter, cunning and deadly as herself; Zelphas could not wait to match her predatory skills with it. Zelphas had been disappointed she had not been sent out to dispatch the alien creature, when they had encountered it by the wood. Now Zelphas had a chance to learn the secrets of this remarkable alien female.

Jennifer kept her eyes focused on the empty corridor ahead of her. All the doors of the living quarters were shut except one, her own. Jennifer reached it and stood still, she sensed danger; she moved over the threshold and stared into the room. Jennifer heard her name being called and then something slammed into her back and pushed her further into the room; the door was slammed shut. Jennifer managed to keep on her feet and spun round. She stared transfixed at the monstrosity that stood by the door. Jennifer remembered the female alien she had met at the old farmhouse. This alien who stood watching her with amber eyes was similar, but different. It was slightly shorter than the other, same domed skull but slight elongated jaws. The body was slim and wiry; the skin was white and had a sort of luminosity about it. It wore a long transparent gown that went down to the bare feet which were long and slender. Jennifer stared at the long white fangs that protruded from the upper jaw. This female alien was a hunter and killer. Jennifer felt a new thrill run through her mind and body, she was ready to tangle with this new threat, and it was a challenge to her ego.

'You intrigue me.'

The creature spoke in its own language, but Jennifer was able to understand it, as she had had the reports from Samantha about the alien language.

'I hope you're a better fighter than your warrior friends,' Jennifer said.

Zelphas moved forward and gave Jennifer her impression of a grin. Jennifer stared at the sharp teeth and thought once the creature had killed her, it would eat her as well, and Jennifer wanted to make sure both things did not happen.

'We have come to take back what's ours.'

Jennifer shook her head.

'There's nothing of yours down here,' assured Jennifer.

'We have the mother, now we want the daughter, the hybrid, the one you call Samantha.'

Jennifer smiled; Zelphas took another step towards her.

'We want her.'

Don't we all?

'I have the power down here and I'm not going to relinquish it,' Jennifer said, icily.

Zelphas leapt at her, Jennifer swung her right fist, but Zelphas ducked under it. The clawed hands gripped her by the waist and the domed head butted her hard in the chest. Jennifer moved backwards to keep herself on her feet. Clasping her hands together Jennifer brought them down hard on Zelphas' back. She growled angrily and the grip on Jennifer was released. Jennifer bounded away from the creature. Zelphas stood up and glared at Jennifer.

'You are a very fast and slippery prey.'

Jennifer laughed; the alien monster had got that wrong.

'You're underestimating me, not a wise thing to do,' warned Jennifer.

Zelphas shot forward and Jennifer got ready for her attack. Zelphas lashed out with her right hand, Jennifer shifted her position and the sharp talons flashed past her face, Jennifer rammed her right fist against the side of the alien's head. Zelphas lashed out with her right foot and hit Jennifer under her rib cage. She moved back from the alien and it was quickly onto her again, Jennifer grabbed Zelphas and swung round and threw the alien female against the wall. Jennifer stepped back as Zelphas slid to the floor, the deep-set amber eyes burned full of hatred.

'Had enough?' Jennifer asked. Zelphas got to her feet; she was fighting something a lot quicker and stronger than she had ever done before. Zelphas felt no fatigue so she could still continue the fight with the tall alien; Zelphas hoped it would get complacent.

'You're good, but not that good.'

Jennifer smiled at the alien's idea of a compliment; she would show the creature that she was that good.

'We'll see.'

As they grappled with each other, each trying to get the upper hand, Jennifer had to concentrate harder than she had ever done before, she had to avoid the flashing hands that had four fingers and an opposable thumb, each ending in sharp claws, and Jennifer knew that could easily rip the flesh off her bones. Zelphas was not just a ferocious predator, in the animal senses, she was also highly intelligent, in climbing up the evolutionary ladder, and she had brought her ancestral savagery with her. Zelphas was now aware their speed and agility was well matched, she had to avoid Jennifer's hard bony fists – they hurt when they struck her body. Jennifer used her height to good advantage, keeping her head away from the sharp claws better than Zelphas could keep her head away from Jennifer's well aimed fists.

When Zelphas managed to grab a hold on her, Jennifer had to watch out for the long gleaming white fangs, which were waiting to tear into her flesh. Every time Zelphas opened her jaws wide, Jennifer got a blast of her hot foul breath and she would throw the creature off her. Her skin glistened with sweat and her heart thumped inside her chest at her exertions. Jennifer realised it was coming down to stamina. Jennifer was sure the creature was feeling the pressure as she was.

The battle suddenly stopped with Zelphas standing by the door, Jennifer sat on the edge of a chair on the other side of the bed. Zelphas opened the door and an Ixxion warrior entered the room.

'Bringing in reinforcements?' Jennifer inquired.

'We must do something about this stalemate,' Zelphas observed.

Jennifer stood up, now it was two against one. Zelphas took the energy weapon off the warrior and adjusted the setting. Zelphas aimed at Jennifer and fired, she dived out of the way and Zelphas swiftly fired again and Jennifer was hit. A searing pain ran through her body. Zelphas handed back the energy weapon to the Ixxion and went for the wounded prey. Jennifer fought to clear her mind of the pain, she watched Zelphas approach her. When the creature was near enough Jennifer dived forward and gripped Zelphas round the waist, the force of Jennifer's body hitting her made Zelphas lose her footing and they crashed to the floor.

Jennifer wrapped her long slender hands round Zelphas scrawny neck, claws ripped into the back of her blouse and digging into her flesh. Jennifer heard the sound of the energy weapon being discharged and once again her body felt excruciating pain. Feeling the grip on her neck loosen, Zelphas shoved Jennifer off her and leapt on top of her. The long blue tongue ran across the two long gleaming fangs, a clawed hand was clamped over Jennifer's chin. Fatigue from the battle with the alien monster and being shot twice by an energy weapon, had left Jennifer weak and in pain; she stared at the amber eyes that glared down at her.

Zelphas gazed at the slender white neck, as the prey wriggled madly under her, trying to throw her off. Zelphas snarled as she opened her jaws wide, saliva and hot foul air sprayed Jennifer's face. She stared at the long white canines as they hovered near her face. Zelphas lifted Jennifer's head and then brought it down hard on the floor; she saw stars.

'Bitch,' Jennifer shouted. Over and over again Zelphas slammed the back of her head against the tiled floor. Zelphas stared at the changing shades of blue in the prey's eyes, as she waited for the sign to tell her the prey was stunned enough to start the second phase of getting her prey under her control. Jennifer groaned in pain and discomfort. Her head felt as if it had been split open. The long white fangs moved down closer to her neck. The hot breath caressed her face and neck. The tips of the fangs scrapped the skin of her neck and brought cold shivers to her flesh. Zelphas noticed the struggles underneath her were lessening; she struck the prey's head against the floor a few times more. Then she stared at the pale blue watery eyes; it was stunned enough for her to feed. Jennifer cried out as the long fangs slid into the flesh of her neck.

For ten minutes Zelphas drank hungrily on Jennifer's blood as the fangs drew it from the veins in her neck. Then Zelphas got up and went to the Ixxion warrior by the door and told him to go back to the ship and report. Then she went back to her prey; behind her the Ixxion dematerialized. Jennifer did not have the strength to move from her prone position on the floor, she watched the alien creature move down on top of her, and Zelphas clamped her jaws on the white neck and fed on the prey's warm blood. Zelphas was the victor and she was collecting her reward.

Sometime later Zelphas lifted her head and gazed at the thin white face of her prey.

'You are good, but you have been beaten by a superior being.'

The ice blue eyes looked glassy and wet, the gentle rise and fall of the chest showed the victim was still alive. Zelphas would keep her weak and manageable, so she could work on the victim's mind. Zelphas stood up; Jennifer lay still in a heap on the floor.

'You are mine; I have your life force inside me, and I'm going to discover your secrets.'

Zelphas sat on the bed and ran her clawed fingers over the communication bracelet on her left wrist. She contacted Zindra.

'I have her, she is weak and sedate, and she will stay that way so I can get into her mind.'

'Good work,' congratulated Zindra.

'She is in my power, I have fed on her life fluids,' Zelphas said.

Zelphas stared across at her prey that still lay in a heap on the floor.

Pamela Sisson walked along the corridor and made for her room. When she got there, she looked across the corridor at Jennifer's door, which was opposite her private quarters. Pamela tapped her intercom against the door and called out Jennifer's name; she got no answer, and they were getting worried as they had not heard from Jennifer for some time.

'Are you all right, Jenny?'

Pamela put her ear to the door and listened for any sound coming from inside Jennifer's private quarters. All seemed quiet so she went to her own room to get some rest. Zelphas waited for the footsteps outside to disappear, and then she got off the bed and went to where Jennifer lay still on the floor. Zelphas kicked the prey several times to see if there was any fight left in it. Jennifer groaned at the rough treatment, Zelphas grinned as she kept kicking her prey. After a while Zelphas got down and gazed at the ice blue eyes, she ran a clawed hand gently over one cheek. Then her head went down and Zelphas slid the long fangs into Jennifer's neck, she groaned weakly as the alien fed on her blood.

Ian Henderson sat beside Hazel as she worked on the radio transmitter. Captain Goodwin stood behind them, keeping an eye on their work. Because of the alien interference Hazel was finding it hard to contact the Fortress. Suddenly an old memory came back to her mind. When they were younger Hazel and Samantha had worked together on the shifts at the observatory. To pass away the many hours of inactivity they had thought up a scenario, like the one they were in at the moment, a hostile force was jamming the frequencies so they could not get a message out. Hazel started to put the transmitter back together with help from Ian.

'Let's hope that Samantha is on her way here,' Hazel said.

In the operations room Francis Powell stood at one side of the computer system and stared down at the green globe. He had seen Jennifer working on it when he first arrived at the underground facility. It was still wired to the computer. It started to glow in a pulsating rhythm. He called out to Michelle and she came and stood beside him.

'Is it supposed to glow on its own, like that?' he asked.

Michelle shook her head and went to make another attempt to get hold of Jennifer. She went to the intercom and buzzed Jennifer's private quarters.

'If you are there, Jenny, please answer me.'

Zelphas lifted up Jennifer and carried her to the bed and laid her onto it. A loud voice came out from the intercom on the bedside table. Zelphas slapped Jennifer's face to make her conscious, Zelphas slapped her a second time and Jennifer groaned, she kept moving in and out of consciousness. Jennifer stared up at the amber eyes. She heard a voice shouting her name.

'Aren't you going to answer it?' Zelphas asked.

Jennifer had a sore throat and one side of her neck was numb, she tried to find her voice.

'And tell them what? There's an alien monster in my room?'

Zelphas shook her head, being called a monster, hurt her feelings.

'That's not very nice, after all we are going to be close companions, you and I,' Zelphas said.

Jennifer moved her aching right arm up to her head and ran the hand down the part of her neck that hurt the most, and then she looked at her hand – it was covered in blood. Her body weak and aching, she wondered what fate was going to befall her. She was aware the creature had complete dominance over her, as she was too weak to fight because the creature kept feeding on her blood.

'See what she wants, her voice is getting on my nerves,' Zelphas said.

Jennifer reached across slowly to the intercom on the bedside table and pressed the button.

'What is it, Michelle?'

'At last, Jenny. Your green sphere is pulsating, what does it mean?' inquired Michelle.

Jennifer moved closer to the intercom.

'It means Samantha is close by,' Jennifer said in a weak voice.

Jennifer switched off the intercom; she rolled back on the bed and gazed up at the ceiling. Zelphas ran claw over her cheek, she turned her head, Zelphas gave her a contented smile as far as the long canines would allow. There was a gleam in the amber eyes.

'That is welcoming news. You will help me trap your friend, Samantha,' Zelphas said.

'What if I won't co-operate?' Jennifer inquired, coldly.

Zelphas raked her clawed hand gently over her face.

'You will, you have no choice,' Zelphas said in a confident voice.

'Is blood the only thing you consume?' Jennifer asked, after a few minutes silence.

Zelphas moved closer to her until their bodies touched.

'Does that disturb you?'

'Only because it's my blood you are feeding on.'

The clawed hand caressed her throat.

'It won't disturb you for long, you'll get used to providing meal fuel for my metabolism,' assured Zelphas.

Zelphas slid over her body and she closed her eyes as the long fangs bit into her flesh. Jennifer closed her eyes as she felt the fangs embedded in her neck, the sounds of Zelphas feeding assailed her acute hearing. The fact there was no struggling from her prey told Zelphas, she had the prey exactly the way she wanted it.

CHAPTER LXXX:

FIRST STRIKE

The large helicopter flew over the large group of cottages close to the Research Facility. John Stephenson was piloting it and Samantha sat beside him. Naomi was seated behind them. They stared at the huge black cloud hanging over the complex. Samantha was backing home with the ghosts and demons ready to reclaim her. Something disastrous had happened and she was going to be dropped in the middle of it, there was no going back.

Samantha had been quiet for some time and John had left her to mull over her thoughts. He suddenly became conscious of a nearby voice. It seemed to emanate from the kitbag that rested on Samantha's lean thighs.

'Your bag seems to be talking to you.'

Samantha rummaged through her kitbag and pulled out a radio communicator of her own design, she heard a girl's voice coming from it loud and clear. She knew who it was without trying to recognise the voice: it could only be Hazel.

'OK Hazel, I have you loud and clear,' Samantha said.

'At last, Sam, have you come to join the party?'

'Yes, though things look pretty grim from up here.'

Hazel explained to Samantha what had happened, and they were now overrun by a band of marauding aliens. Hazel told Samantha she was speaking from the underground complex.

'Is Jennifer down there with you?'

'Yes, but she's locked herself in her room and won't communicate with us,' Hazel informed her.

'How very tiresome of her,' Samantha said.

Hazel broke into a fit of giggles and Captain Goodwin took her place at the communications desk. He asked Samantha if she had any orders for him from the General.

'I've got some sealed orders for the Colonel, is he not with you?'

John swung the helicopter away from the black smoke that hung over the complex, he flew over the hill and turned back towards the small village. Michelle's voice came over the communicator.

'That machine of yours is flashing madly; it's not going to blow up, is it?'

'It's perfectly safe, I want someone to work it from there, and I hope Jennifer explained it to somebody.'

'Jennifer went through a few experiments with it, I was helping,' Michelle told her.

'Good, it's up to you then, Michelle, connect it to the computer, I will call back next, when I'm ready to join you.'

'I'll be ready, 'Michelle assured her.

John Stephenson expertly guided the helicopter down on the road in front of the village, Samantha opened her door and dived under the moving rotor blades. He shouted to her to keep her head down and be careful. She waved a hand to him and slung the kitbag over her right shoulder. John lifted the helicopter into the sky and turned north and headed back to the Fortress.

Pamela stood staring down at the green sphere as it was pulsating rapidly. It lit up her pretty round face, Francis stood close by.

'I wonder what it does,' Pamela said

Michelle moved between them both and got Francis to help her carry the table to the computer control desk. Michelle wired it to the computer.

'It is going to help us transport a friend here, from outside the Facility,' Michelle said for Pamela's benefit.

'A matter transmitter; why didn't you say so? It's all clear now,' Pamela said, in an air of superiority.

'It is, is it?' Michelle said.

Pamela nodded her head enthusiastically.

'We'll have to get a map of topside on the screen and plot where your friend will call back from.'

Michelle worked at the computer control desk, Pamela gazed at the screen and a map of the Facility came up and she studied for a while.

'I expect your friend will enter the Facility,' Pamela theorized.

'Dicey,' Michelle observed.

Samantha made her way to the main gate; she moved slowly with extreme caution. There was nobody on guard at the gate, so she entered the compound.

'She will want to be in the best possible position for a perfect teleportation,' Pamela observed.

Michelle shook her head, she was not sure if Pamela knew what she was talking about, or the girl was having her on.

'Which would be just above us close to the administration building,' Pamela said.

Michelle went to the computer control desk.

'I hope you're right, let's go.'

Hazel dashed into the room and told Michelle, Samantha was ready and waiting. Michelle nodded to Pamela; she ran her hand over the control box on the black plinth the pulsating green globe sat on.

Samantha stood by the administration building. She held the transport transmitter in her hand, she had tapped in the coordinates Hazel had given her to transport herself down to the underground base. Samantha hoped she would arrive in one piece, after she had been put together after the transition.

JUST HOPE AND PRAY, SAM

Samantha closed her eyes and pressed the activation button.

Down below her feet, Michelle was saying the same prayer – if it went wrong and Samantha materialized inside the computer, the girl would never speak to her again. Professor Harris stood beside Pamela; he had seen Jennifer experimenting with the glowing globe. He was sceptical about the idea of Samantha transporting herself down into the operations room with them.

'I hope Samantha knows what she's doing,' he said.

'Of course, she does,' Pamela said.

'I wish I could share your optimism, young girl.'

Pamela looked up at the Professor and gave him a wink.

'When will we know, when it is starting?' he inquired.

Michelle took off her metal rimmed glasses and polished the lenses with a clean cloth she took out of her white lab coat pocket. She put her glasses back on as a beam of green energy emanated from the globe and fixed itself to a point on the floor in the centre of the room.

'It's started,' Pamela said.

'Let's hope Samantha survives the experiment,' Michelle said.

'Amen to that,' the Professor said.

Samantha stood still as the air around her became charged with energy. Samantha felt it pulling at her body. She felt dizzy and she blacked out.

Inside the operations room a column of green light rose up from the floor to a height of seven foot. Hazel and Ian entered the room and stared spellbound at the tall column of energy in the centre of the room. Something was forming inside it. A low hum echoed round the room, the dark form inside the energy field slowly took the shape of a tall slim female. The globe stopped glowing and retracted the energy beam. All in the room stood and held their breath and stared at the tall figure in the centre of the room dressed in army uniform. Samantha opened her eyes and took a deep breath and sighed, as she saw her body was all there in one piece. It had been a strange experience.

One day you are going to take one chance too many, Sam.

'But not today,' Samantha said softly to herself.

Samantha stepped over to the computer; Michelle smiled at her, showing Samantha she was relieved the experiment had worked out all right.

'You did well, Michelle,' Samantha said.

Pamela joined them and Michelle told Samantha, Pamela had taken charge of her invention and Michelle could not have done it without her help. Samantha turned and gazed down at Pamela, she thanked her and felt she had met the girl before and she asked Pamela where she had come from and she informed Samantha she had been working with Professor Fairclough in Exeter. Samantha remembered his tests on children for ESP, at the Experimental Laboratories. She could see Pamela had a certain talent about her, as she had worked the matter transmitter successfully.

'I was only a kid when you first saw me, but I'm all grown up now, so you can rely on me, Samantha.'

'I'm sure I can.'

Samantha turned to Michelle.

'Who's in charge down here?'

Captain Goodwin moved forward and told her he had taken charge on his arrival recently. He informed her Colonel Collins was being held captive in the administrative building.

'We had put the lift terminals out of action so the attackers can't get down here,' Michelle told her.

Michelle stared hard at Samantha's face, she was shocked at the strain etched on her expression, she remembered the last time she saw the tall girl at eighteen. Michelle wondered what Samantha had been doing all this time since then.

'How is the security down here?' Samantha inquired.

Michelle smiled as Samantha was showing off her authority over them – the tall girl had not changed in that respect, she was taking charge and Michelle was one who was not going to complain about it.

'We were organising that before Jennifer locked herself away in her room.'

Samantha allowed herself a weak smile.

'Yes, Jennifer, we'll have to do something to get her out,' Samantha decided.

'We've blown the lift terminals down here, so they won't get to us that way,' Henry told her, as he moved close to Michelle to give her support.

'What about the vertical shafts?'

Ian Henderson, who had used one of them to get down to the underground base, informed her they were electronically locked from those up on the surface and the people who knew about the shafts were down here.

Samantha told Michelle to override the security lock on Jennifer's private quarters. Samantha turned to Henry and asked him to show her the way to the private quarters. They walked out of the operations room and Michelle went to the computer to unlock Jennifer's door. As Samantha strode along the corridor Henry found himself almost running to catch up with her.

'If you don't slow down, you'll get there before I do,' Henry complained.

Samantha slowed down and Henry fell in step beside her.

Zelphas slid off the bed and contacted Zindra on the wrist communicator; the she lifted the unconscious girl off the bed and slung her over her shoulder.

'OK, Zindra, we're ready to come back.'

They started to fade and when Samantha burst into the room, they had completely dematerialized. They had a quick look round the room; they found blood stains on the floor and on the bed.

'It looks as if they've got her, I hope they find her as irritating as we do,' Samantha said.

They walked out of the room and returned to the operations room; Michelle was not very happy about the news of Jennifer being captured by the aliens.

'Are you going to try and get her back?' Michelle asked.

'No, she's big enough to look after herself,' Samantha said.

Samantha and Henry made for escape shaft 8H, which was close to Terminal 3. When they got there, Henry opened the hatch to the escape shaft.

'Ladies first.'

Samantha stared at his grinning face.

'I'm going to have to have a word to Mel, about you.'

Samantha hoisted herself up the metal ladder. Henry followed behind her. They made a steady progress up the shaft; when they reached the top, Henry gave her the security number and she tapped it out on the keypad by the hatch door. It slid away and Samantha moved out of the shaft. Henry shut the hatch. They were behind one of the walls in the office building storeroom, there was another lit keypad and Henry tapped out the security number that would shift the panel so they could enter the room.

The panel slid shut behind them. The storeroom was full of filing cabinets and racks full of supplies of one thing and another.

Samantha crossed the room and opened the door; she peered out, but there was nobody in sight. She stepped out into the corridor and Henry followed her. Samantha made her way to the main offices.

She stood by the door leading to the inner office and listened for any sound coming from beyond it. Hearing nothing, she opened the door and pushed open, she got down and moved into the room; Henry crouched down and followed her. Samantha made it to the partition, which separated them from the main office. She slowly raised her head until her eyes came up to the glass partition and stared into the main office. On the other side of the glass, Justine Mason was sat at her desk, a bulky Ixxion warrior stood by keeping a guard on her. Justine had nothing to do but stare at the monstrosity that stood over her, now her secretarial duties were over for the time being.

On the other side of the office Colonel Collins sat at his desk and had his own bulky reptilian alien guarding over him. Collins was giving the creature an icy stare to show he had no fear of the alien. Rwan was a good reader of faces of his adversaries; he was a warrior like himself. The uniform told Rwan, he was part of the fighting forces of this planet. Rwan guessed he was hoping to get a chance to reverse their positions. Colonel Collins wanted desperately to get out of the offices and see what was happening outside the building. He knew he would not be able to fight the alien with his bare hands. The creature was too big and furious for him to handle alone.

'There's two, one each,' Henry said.

Samantha moved towards the door; Henry took the handgun out of the inside pocket of his jacket. Samantha stood up and slowly opened the door.

Rwan sensed danger as the door slid open, the sound averting his eyes away from the captive. He drew out his blaster as a tall female launched herself at him from the widening doorway. The short cropped red hair and blazing green eyes touched a chord in his memory. This was no docile captive female, this one was out for blood: his. Rwan fired his blaster and Samantha dived under the destructive beam. She struck him like a battering ram and Rwan was forced backwards. Samantha dug her bony elbow into his throat; Rwan gave a grunt of pain as the blow damaged his vocal chords. Henry, moving into the room behind her, fired at the second warrior with his handgun. Justine dived to the floor, where it was safe.

Samantha was now well experienced in doing battle with these armoured heavyweights and being over a foot taller she used the advantage of height with full effect. At this moment she was in a hurry and as she grappled with him, Rwan found her immense strength comparable to his own, she forced him back towards the window, then her hands gripped him in a vice-like grip and she threw the alien warrior against the window and it exploded in a loud sound of breaking glass and wood, as the alien went through it and fell to the ground below. Samantha did not bother to see what had happened to it. She turned and walked calmly to the Colonel, who was standing staring at her in disbelief.

'Sam. Remind me not to get in an argument with you.'

Samantha smiled and saluted respectfully.

'I don't like the way they roam about as if they owned the place.'

'I'm afraid at the moment they do,' Colonel Collins informed her.

'I'm going to do something about that,' Samantha assured him.

Justine Mason approached her and gave her a welcoming hug.

'I've heard about you, Samantha, I arrived here after you left, it's good to have you back.'

'It's nice to be back.'

They left the offices and returned to the storeroom; Samantha gave Colonel Collins a sealed envelope the General had told her to give him. He asked Samantha what she was going to do now.

'I'm going to find out more about them, I'm expendable.'

'I don't think you're expendable, Sam, I don't think I've ever seen anyone explode into a room like you.'

Colonel Collins followed Henry and Justine into the shaft, which would take them down to the underground facility.

'I'm in communication with Hazel, so I shall contact her when I have some news for you.'

'Good luck, Sam.'

She saluted and the panel slid across the shaft head. She tapped out a different set of numbers on the keypad of the electronic lock and pulled some of the filing cabinets against the shaft panel. She took the communicator out of her bag and contacted Hazel,

Hazel Johnson ran into the operations room and told Michelle that Samantha wanted someone to activate her teleport machine. Michelle sent Francis to call Pamela to operations; she was resting in her quarters. He knocked on her door.

'Wake up, Pam, you're wanted.'

After a few minutes the door slid open and Pamela Sissons walked out into his arms. Francis kissed her full on the mouth.

'We haven't got time for that, I've got work to do,' Pamela scolded.

Pamela strode quickly along the corridor and Francis fell in step with her. He was amazed at how Pamela was coping with the tension in the complex now they were under threat. They had grown up together and he had an idea how her mind worked. When they were younger Pamela was happy to let him take charge of their relationship. Now she was twenty and a young adult, she had a more independent mind. Her ability to understand the teleporting machine had surprised him, there was a lot more to find out about Pamela yet and Francis was going to enjoy finding out the secrets she was hiding about herself.

Pamela entered the operations room and Michelle told her everything was fixed up and ready to go. Michelle gave her the coordinates to tap into the machine. Pamela sat at the desk and stared at the glowing green globe, she tapped in the first set of coordinates.

In the storeroom of the administrative building Samantha gave a sigh of relief as the transporter beam lit up the control box she was holding. She heard noises coming from another part of the building, she wondered if she would get away in time.

A beam of green light moved across the room then stopped and made a circle of green light on the floor, a shape started to form. Pamela stared at it and saw it was someone in a crouching position. She tapped in the second coordinates. Francis stood close, watching the proceedings.

'That's a long way from here,' he said.

'It is the old house she was born in,' Michelle said.

'I wonder why she is going there,' Francis said.

Pamela watched the figure in the green light fade away.

'Perhaps she's going to exorcize some old ghosts from her past,' Pamela philosophized.

Zelphas stepped off the teleport pad carrying her unconscious prey. Zindra walked beside her as they walked down the corridor towards the rest rooms. Zelphas told Zindra about the battle with the tall female creature, Zindra could hear the respect for a fellow predator in Zelphas' voice. Zindra had a lot of suspicions about the tall silver haired creature, something was just not right.

'You've done a good job, Zelphas, I want you to discover everything you can about this creature,' Zindra said.

'It is malleable now. When I have got all the information out that you want, may I have the prey afterwards?'

'Of course, Zelphas, all the work you have done for me, you deserve it.'

They walked into a small compartment and Zelphas dropped her prey onto the bed. Zindra stared down at the pale thin face, the confidence Zindra had seen on the face the first time they met had gone. Zelphas had done her work on it. Zindra left the room and Zelphas tied Jennifer's wrists together, and then tied her ankles together. It was getting dark now; at first light, she would get into the prey's head, and then it would only be too pleased to tell them all they wanted to know.

CHAPTER LXXXI:

GHOSTS

The wind blew through the broken panes of the attic window, blowing up clouds of dust. In the middle of the attic a green glow appeared and started to glow brighter, a dark figure materialized inside it. The green light faded, and Samantha was sitting on the wooden floor, she stared up at the roof beams, she was back home, older if not wiser. The phantoms of her past would be coming out of the woodwork to torment her once more. Samantha had to confront them before she could go any further, she just had a few images of life before she was six, and the answers to her existence lay in her first six years of life. She stood up and gazed round the large attic room. This was where her parents conceived and tested their machine and put their daughter up as guinea pig ending up with two Samanthas. It was not like staring into a mirror, the image she saw was solid and three dimensional and it was the past Samantha looking into the future. Samantha wondered if the ghost of that past Samantha was still about; unfortunately she could not tell Samantha anything that would help her, as the past Samantha did not know any more about her existence than the future Samantha did.

The old house is full of echoes of the past.

Samantha left the attic and went down to the landing. She made for the small room at the end of the landing, her old bedroom. The air was stale and dusty; she stared down at the small broken-down bed, where little Samantha had been introduced to the voice in her head. The one ghost she could never exorcize.

You'll miss me, when I'm gone.

'Yeah, like a hole in the head.'

Samantha laid her backpack on the bed and walked round the small bedroom. There were lots of fluffy toys and little girl books. Things to make little Samantha think she was normal, but she was not.

What is normal?

'What indeed?'

Samantha sat on the bed after making sure it would not break up under her weight. She put her head in her hands and closed her eyes. She tried again to access her hidden memories – whatever had happened to her in the first five years of life should be there somewhere. But she could not recover them; the time she got forgotten memories was when she was bathed in a mild radiation, like when she was testing her parents' invention.

Dr Sally Hamilton gazed down at her five-year-old daughter lying on a hospital bed; Dr Richard Blake was working to modify the skull so the girl would look more human, so they could keep her alienness well hidden. He had to flatten the high dome that was the top of the skull and reshape the back of the skull; luckily all these improvements would not cause any damage to the brain or brains, because the girl was part alien, she had two separate brain parts connected by several filaments that carried the neural messages to and fro from both brain segments. After he had finished the operation, Dr Blake bandaged the head of the little girl and she was wheeled out of the operation room.

'As soon as the bones knit together, we shall see if we are successful,' Richard Blake said. Sally Hamilton nodded her head.

'I'm sure that was the easy part of the procedure, operating on her brain will be a more difficult part of making her into a more normal human child.'

The next morning the little girl's eyes opened and gazed up at her mother's worried expression.

'Is everything all right, Mummy?'

Sally Hamilton kissed her daughter on the cheek.

'Of course, darling, just lie still and rest.'

Samantha opened her eyes and found herself lying across the old bed, her head throbbed, and she felt tired and listless. She gazed up at the ceiling.

'What's happening to me?'

The little girl wondered why she visited the hospital so much; she decided to tackle her mother about it.

'Is there something badly wrong with me, Mummy?'

'No, darling, whatever gave you that idea?'

'I seem to be in the hospital a lot.'

Sally Hamilton hugged her daughter and kissed her on the cheek.

'It's just for a regular check-up, we have to be careful as you are at a young age; when you get bigger and stronger, you'll be fit and healthy.'

Just after her sixth birthday the little girl woke up in a hospital room. She pulled the sheet down and slid off the bed. She went to a neighbouring bed and saw another little girl lying on it. She was in a deep sleep; her thin face was deathly white, and she had long flowing blonde hair.

'I hope you will wake soon and be my friend.'

Dr Sally Hamilton came into the room and picked up her daughter and carried her out of the room.

'Who was that girl, Mummy?'

'Just another little girl like you; who is very ill,' her Mother said.

'When she gets better, will she be my friend?' her daughter asked.

'She'll be more than that.'

Samantha's eyes fluttered open; she struggled to get to her feet. She went to the window and opened it and took some deep breaths. The small bedroom was becoming warm and oppressive. She went to the bed and heard a bleeping sound coming from her backpack.

Samantha rummaged through it and took out the radiation monitor and ran her eye over the readings. Radiation was filtering into the room from somewhere, it was not fatal, but it was doing her head in and not doing much good to her body either. She walked round the room holding the monitor, the strongest reading she got was at the head of the bed. She pulled the headboard away and found a metal panel in the wall. She removed the panel and gazed at the flashing lights and coils inside the wall.

'What have we here?'

Samantha studied the machine and found the control box; she hoped there was an off switch. After a long careful examination, Samantha was able to shut down the machine and activate a dampening field around it. She left the room and made her way down the stairs. She mulled over in her mind what the machine had been doing to the brain of the young Samantha, as she lay unexpecting in the bed and what it meant to her mind now. She left the house; darkness was falling and a slight wind blew around her. The search for her destiny was about to begin and Samantha was glad to see her mind was as clear as it had ever been. No voices inside her head for which she was grateful,l her own conscience gave her enough grief as it was, she did not need a disembodied spirit nagging her about making dangerous decisions. She moved slowly through the old orchard; the gnarled shape of the ancient fruit trees made frightening monster shapes in the gathering darkness; she knew all about monsters, real and imaginary. Samantha breathed a sigh of relief when she exited the orchard unscathed. She walked round the copse as the memories came flooding back of her first meeting with Jennifer inside it as the mysterious girl stood over her clone. The image came into her mind's eye, the pale blue eyes and mischievous smile on her thin lips.

'Hullo, I'm Jennifer,' the girl had said as she reached out a thin cold hand to her.

It had been a rollercoaster meeting that had turned her life upside down. The girl had forced emotions out of Samantha, she never knew she had. When she had dealt with the invading aliens, Samantha had to deal with Jennifer, when it came to the crunch Samantha was going to make sure she was the one who walked away from the head on collision.

At that moment Juliet Harris was dealing with her own ghosts, she tossed and turned in the bed, the demons outside were after her, they invaded her dreams, which were vivid images of what the demons would do to her if they caught her.

Juliet had evaded them ever since they had arrived. She could trust no one; she had to survive on her own. The demons constantly patrolled the area of the scattered houses and she had managed to dodge them so far. She was hiding in Samantha's old house, she felt safer there and she was waiting for Samantha's return. Now they were in trouble Juliet was sure the tall girl would come back and save them from the trouble they had brought upon themselves. Juliet could trust Samantha and she knew the tall girl would not let her down.

Juliet woke with a start and drew the sheet off her body, she stared into the darkness of the bedroom, nothing moved. She slid off the bed and stood up. She could hear some sound outside the house, she left the bedroom and made her way down the stairs and kept an eye out for any movement in the lower part of the house. At the bottom of the stairs Juliet stood still and listened and all was silent. Juliet was not taken in by the silence, something had woken her, and Juliet sensed danger. Her nerves and senses were strained to the limit. Her mind was constantly on survival mode and tried to keep her fears from bringing her down.

Juliet turned and walked down the hallway towards the kitchen. As she reached the door it was suddenly opened and a dark shape stood over her, red eyes glared at her.

Shirley Gallagher sat by the window and stared out at the darkness, searching for any movement coming their way; Steven Calvert was asleep on the sofa. Like Juliet they had been dodging the alien patrols. She was not a newcomer to avoiding hostile factions at home and abroad. Being an investigating journalist Shirley made sure she got to most of the trouble spots round the world. Shirley had her own ghosts to deal with, mainly friends and colleagues she had lost in her line of work, most of them were killed though some had disappeared mysteriously. Shirley had lost her best friend in mysterious circumstances – Helen Bright would really have enjoyed being in the position Shirley had found herself in. Helen would have no trouble with alien encounters, she had had an open and inquiring mind, and she would have treated this mission like any other of her investigations. Shirley missed her and hoped one day she would find out what had happened to Helen.

Shirley suddenly caught the sight of a huge dark shape moving towards the house, it was not a patrol but just a single alien. When it got close to the house it stopped and looked around then moved away. Shirley got up from her crouched position and left the room. She took the handgun out of her skirt pocket. She made her way to the kitchen and gazed out of the glass in the back door, she watched the dark shape move away from the house and merge with the darkness of night. Some of the tension drained from her mind and body but not all.

She went to the work surface and switched on the kettle and started to make herself a coffee; she had everything at hand, so she did not need the light. She heard Steven enter the kitchen.

'One of our alien friends just passed by,' Shirley told him.

Steven walked over to the back door and looked out, a few moments later there came the distant report of two shots. Shirley moved towards him and handed him a mug of coffee.

'I hope that's not the sound of him catching up with Juliet,' he said.

'No, it wasn't an alien weapon, it was a pulse rifle,' Shirley said.

'You know your weapons, I'm impressed,' Steven said.

Shirley sipped her coffee; she had used all sorts of weapons to keep herself alive in her dangerous work.

'Perhaps it's a sign,' Steven said.

Shirley looked up towards the ceiling. 'What, from him upstairs?'

Steven shook his head and smiled in the darkness.

'Divine intervention, no I don't mean that. A friend of mine once told me, she would leave a sign to say she was back with us.'

'You mean Naomi's associate, Samantha?' Shirley inquired.

'That's right, perhaps she's here at last,' Steven hoped.

Juliet spun round and started to dash down the dark hallway, the alien warrior rushed forward and kicked at her and he caught her sharp blow with his foot and fell forward onto the floor. The huge alien rushed forward and grabbed the girl and lifted her up and with no effort tossed her against the wall, knocking the wind out of her. He went for Juliet as she lay hurt and gasping for breath; as the alien reached out for her the front door opened and the alien looked towards the intruder. There was a pulsating sound and the alien's chest was ripped apart, another shot took his head off.

Janice Clarke sat on her bunk bed in her hut; an alien warrior stood outside the door making sure she stayed put. She wondered if Steven was somewhere safe, she missed him very much, but she was compelled to stay behind and act as if she was to help the aliens in their schemes. She had to work out their strengths and weaknesses. So they could fight back. This was what she had been educated and trained for. Information gathering, that was her mission. The authorities outside the complex were relying on her to be their eyes and ears, Janice had to discover all she could about them, and then she had to discover a way of getting the information to the people outside the complex.

Janice got up and went to the window and looked out. It was dark, some of the complex main lights were on and she saw several alien warriors moving about, but none of her own kind – they were probably locked up like her. Janice turned away from the window and her thoughts suddenly turned to Samantha. Janice had faith the tall girl would be back among them sometime in the near future. Then it would begin.

CHAPTER LXXXII:

CRUEL TO BE KIND

Juliet came to and she found the bedroom full of bright sunshine, her body was full of aches and pains. When she had seen the demon, Juliet was sure her number was up. She turned her head and saw someone sitting on a chair beside the bed.

'Don't you ever learn to pick on someone your own size?'

Juliet stared in disbelief and open mouthed at the slim lean girl sitting in the chair, the face was thin and strained, and she could see Samantha had gone through a lot while she had been away.

'You look as if you've seen a ghost,' Samantha said.

'Perhaps I have, it looks as if you've had a bad time of it,' observed Juliet.

Samantha came and sat on the side of the bed, the door opened, and Naomi came in carrying a tray with three mugs of hot strong tea.

'The patient's awake at last.'

Naomi put the tray on the bedside table and handed Juliet a mug of tea. Samantha gave Juliet a short version of what had happened to her over the years. Naomi went to the window and looked out. It was snowing heavily.

Jennifer woke and found herself in a well-lit room, her body was still weak and full of aches and pains, her neck hurt the most. She remembered the blood sucking alien and that made her more depressed. She found her hands were tied to something behind her head; she moved her legs and found her ankles were tied together. She was helpless and under the power of her assailant. The bunk bed she lay on was along one wall. She turned her head and saw a computer console, close to the bed and a small cubicle beyond that. The door slid opened and Zelphas glided into the room at the other end of the bed. Jennifer was grabbed by the shoulders and pulled up, so her head lay against the wall. Zelphas sat on the bed and stared at Jennifer, studying her pale face.

'Do you think your red-haired friend will try to rescue you?'

If they were hoping for that, Jennifer knew they were wasting their time, even if Samantha knew where she was, which she did not.

'She has other problems, she won't worry about me,' assured Jennifer.

'Doesn't that make you mad, you all tied up and nobody is coming to set you free?'

Jennifer could almost see a smile on the muzzle full of long sharp teeth.

'I expect you will have drained my body of blood, by the time anyone got here,' Jennifer said.

'That depends on how quickly you give us the information we want.'

'You are going to kill me, so why should I betray my world?'

Zelphas ran a clawed hand over her neck.

'You'll give me the information we need; it is inevitable.'

Zelphas moved closer to her and Jennifer tried to move away, but there was nowhere to go. Jennifer cried out as Zelphas clamped her jaws on her neck, Zelphas was in no hurry, she would get what she wanted eventually, Zelphas knew she had the stronger mind.

Juliet gazed at Samantha and Naomi, they both wore military dress, olive drab blouse and matching skirt, she could see they were ready for a fight. Juliet hopped out of bed and looked down at her naked body; she looked at Samantha who was sitting on the bed.

'You've cleaned me up.'

Samantha shook her head and pointed to Naomi, who stood by the door.

'I'm a trained physician, I had to clean up the damage to your body,' Naomi explained.

Juliet found some clean clothes on the chair by the bed; Samantha had been to Juliet's home to get them. Juliet got dressed and followed her two friends out of the room, then stopped still as she realised where she was.

'The old school, what are we doing here?'

'It's a good place to work out our stratagem,' Samantha said.

Samantha took the lead down the styled wood staircase down to the bottom floor and she made for the gymnasium, Juliet wondered what Samantha had in mind. When they stepped into the gymnasium, Samantha slapped her gently on the back.

'That's what happens; if you are going to continue to pick on something bigger than yourself. We're going to toughen you up a bit" Samantha said.

Juliet glared up at her tall friend.

'I don't like the sound of that, Sam.'

'We've got to get you fighting fit and ready for action,' explained Samantha.

It had been a long time since Juliet had visited the gymnasium. Juliet thought she was fit enough. Naomi took her by the arm and assured her they would be gentle with her. It was lucky she did not see the expression on Samantha's face – she was going to be anything but gentle to Juliet, time was of the essence, and they had to work fast.

Samantha stood staring out of the window, she was keeping a sharp eye on what was going on outside. She did not want anything nasty creeping up on them, when they were not looking. She heard Juliet going through the vigorous exercise routine Naomi had devised for her. Naomi was monitoring her progress throughout. When Naomi called a halt, Juliet sank to the floor, puffing and panting after her exertions. Naomi handed her a plastic bottle and Juliet drank the liquid inside slowly.

Samantha came over and sat on a nearby vaulting horse and gazed down at Juliet. The girl had done well, her next test would be to assess her fighting skills, which Samantha would be supervising, because of the coming battle, and she was going to be hard on Juliet, because she wanted the girl to survive.

'We'll soon knock you into shape,' Samantha said.

Juliet looked up at her, as she wondered what she had in store for her; whatever it was, it would not be good. Naomi walked out of the gymnasium and left the building to have a scout around the area. When they arrived, they had to avoid a few alien warrior patrols. Naomi was going to keep an eye out for them, while Samantha gave Juliet some training on fighting something that was a lot bigger than her.

Samantha got off the vaulting horse and sat on the floor beside Juliet, who turned and stared hard at the weathered thin face, she had travelled a long hard road, from a tall lanky fifteen-year-old, to a trained killing machine. Juliet thought back to the time before Samantha went away, she had felt she had got close to the real Samantha hiding behind the deep-set emerald eyes. Even more Juliet felt guilty over the grief she had given Samantha when they first met.

'What is our part in the manner of things?' Juliet asked.

Samantha thought for a moment about the meaning of the question asked.

'The propaganda is we are special people with a very high IQ and various unique talents. We are the future. This is an elaborate experiment to see if we can survive an alien invasion from space.'

Juliet suddenly felt she was a lab rat in a maze.

'That's what all those ESP tests you and Janice had were for.'

'Professor Fairclough did not give us any idea what the tests were for,' informed Juliet.

'That's the Conspiracy Theory.'

Juliet giggled.

'Shirley Gallagher, yes I've met her. I would say she's been dropped right in it.'

This time it was Samantha's turn to laugh.

'Haven't we all.' Juliet stood up and gazed down at her friend.

'I had the usual military training when you went away. They thought I was too short to be a soldier, which was fine with me, I enjoy being a scientist,' Juliet explained.

Samantha stood up and put an arm round Juliet's shoulder.

'Well you're going to be a soldier now,' informed Samantha.

Samantha guided her across the gymnasium to one corner where there was a large mat on the floor; it gave Juliet an idea of what was going to happen next.

'You're going to get revenge on me for the entire bad things I said about you, when we were young.'

Samantha shook her head.

'You should know me better than that, Juliet.'

Samantha took off her shoes and stepped on the mat, she waited patiently for Juliet to join her. After a few minutes Juliet took off her shoes and stepped on the mat; she stared up at Samantha, who towered over her.

'I suppose you are going to tell me, this will hurt you more than me,' Juliet said.

'No, I just want to teach you how you can make it hurt less,' Samantha said, sincerely.

Juliet readied herself to do battle with someone a lot taller and stronger than herself. Samantha was going to coach Juliet, to use her short stature as an advantage when the odds were unequal.

Naomi crossed the track between the school building and the infirmary; she made her way round to the rear of the medical building and made her way to the rear of the boundary fence around the Research Facility. Keeping low she rushed to the other side of the boundary fence. When she got there, she stopped and knelt down and surveyed the inside of the compound. Before they could come up with the right attack plan, they had to know what was going on. Naomi searched for a place where they could enter the complex and come across less opposition. She had just passed the rear of the accommodation huts and that was clear, now she could see the front of the huts; they were heavily guarded, so was the spacecraft parked close by.

Keeping close to the base of a tree-covered hill, Naomi moved cautiously parallel to the north side of the boundary fence. When she had reached the far end of the fence, Naomi noticed the side gate was open. Making sure nothing was looking her way, Naomi moved through the open gateway and rushed behind the concrete pylon of the radio telescope. She stared across at the observatory building. She surveyed the damage done by the destruction of the computer room. It had demolished half the building. Naomi ran across the few yards between the pylon and the building, she passed by the huge mound of rubble and made for the part of the observatory that was still standing. When she got to the other side of the building, she heard voices and stood still. Naomi slowly took a peek round the side of the building.

The alien mind that had occupied the sphere Jennifer had picked out of the marsh now inhabited the head of Professor Atwood, the director of the observatory. He stood beside his companion, the alien Zindra, who was animated now she had been informed by Zelphas that their quarry was close. Erika was standing around the corner of the building so Naomi could not see her, but could hear her voice.

'Your patrols should catch Samantha if she is in fact hiding somewhere near.'

Zindra stared at Erika, who could almost feel a heat coming from the blazing red eyes. Zindra did not have to speak; Erika knew the capture of Samantha was up to her.

'I failed killing Samantha the first time, I won't fail this time.'

The confidence was thick in her voice.

'The sooner we get rid of this creature of yours, Zindra, the sooner we can get away from this backwater planet,' Bauros (Atwood) said.

Zindra bowed her head; she was grateful that her Lord had granted her this one thing, as Bauros had schedules of his own.

They walked away from the building and made their way across the compound. Naomi had been studying the tall alien, as she had learnt a lot about Zindra from Phoebe, as it was in charge of the experiments on the girl. If she eventually came up against Zindra, Naomi wanted to know the stature of the creature and how she moved. Erika came out from behind the observatory building and made her way to the main gate. Naomi kept a sharp eye on her. As Erika came up to the second radio telescope pylon, Naomi took the automatic out of her skirt pocket and rushed forward and grabbed Erika with her free hand and placed the barrel of the automatic against her temple. Naomi pulled her behind the concrete pylon.

'We knew there was someone working against us, I should have thought of you, which was very lax of me.'

'What are you going to do, Naomi, shoot me in the head?'

The voice was irritatingly cool under the circumstances.

'That's a good idea, Erika, why didn't I think of that,' Naomi said, sarcastically.

'You won't get away from here alive,' Erika assured her.

'Neither will you.'

They were close to the main gate; there were no guards near it or in the security hut. Erika was trying to think of ways to turn the tables on Naomi. Erika had not known Naomi was a Government Agent, until she had been told about what Naomi had been doing in the Capital. Erika was aware Naomi knew what she was doing and that made her dangerous. Naomi pushed the woman in the direction of the main gate, keeping a tight grip on her arm and the handgun pressed into the small of her back. A freezing wind blew against them. Naomi was glad there was no snow in it. Naomi reached the open main gate without being challenged. Unfortunately, outside the main gate a patrol was returning from a scouting trip around the area outside the compound. Naomi had to move fast as they were far enough away for her to make a run for it.

'Now what are you going to do, Naomi?'

Erika believed she could now get the upper hand. Naomi did her best to keep Erika between her and the advancing alien patrol. She was well aware Erika was a treacherous female and Naomi had to be on her guard. They passed through the main gate; Naomi kept a tight grip on Erika's right arm.

'Your friends don't seem to be too bothered about you.' Naomi said.

Erika slid her left hand into the pocket of her white lab coat; she gripped the energy weapon and got ready to do something about Naomi. The patrol, now a hundred yards away, did not quicken their pace, as they were used to seeing Erika moving freely about the Research Facility; they saw nothing wrong. Directly opposite the main gates were the first two cottages of the small housing estate for the scientists and workers. Erika slid her left hand out of her coat pocket keeping a tight grip on the energy weapon. Sensing danger from the change in Erika's hardened expression, Naomi released Erika's arm and swung her left fist and hit Erika on the point of the jaw; she crashed to the ground and the weapon was knocked out of her hand. Naomi dashed across the track and leapt over a low hedge and keeping low moved between the two cottages.

Naomi did not take long to get back to the schoolhouse. When she got to the gymnasium, she found Juliet was still trying unsuccessfully to put Samantha down on her back. Naomi decided to give Juliet a little advice.

'Use your head, Juliet, use your head.'

Samantha stared across at Naomi, turning her attention off Juliet, who ducked her head and rammed into Samantha, knocking the surprised girl down onto her back. Juliet sat on her chest keeping her knees pressed down on Samantha's shoulders.

'You're beautiful when you're mad, Juliet.'

After a while Juliet stood up and walked off the mat. Naomi raised her right hand and Juliet hit it with her own. Naomi stepped onto the mat and held out her hand to Samantha, who took it and Naomi pulled her up onto her feet. They went to the shower rooms; while Juliet and Samantha refreshed themselves in separate showers, Naomi told them what she had been up to.

CHAPTER LXXXIII:

INTO THE LION'S DEN

Melanie McAllister strode out of the Lab 3 building. The freezing afternoon air penetrated her white lab coat and her clothes underneath. As she strode across the compound, she hoped the alien invaders disliked the weather more than she did. Melanie made her way to the accommodation huts. She passed alien warriors who stood on guard all over the Research facility without being challenged, though she was aware their eyes were on her constantly as she went about her business, seeing to the medical needs of other technicians. They did not bother her, as Melanie had already made her point and they moved away so the angry female could get on with her work.

Melanie came to the hut where Janice Clarke was being kept captive. A green Ixxion stood outside the door, making sure Janice stayed inside the hut. The alien looked down at Melanie with respect as she had shown no fear of them, even though she was alarmed, except for her loud voice. Melanie noticed the creature looked unhappy standing in the ice-cold wind; she was very pleased about the alien's discomfort. Melanie indicated she wanted to enter the hut. The alien moved away and that moment when it turned away from Melanie, Naomi and Samantha came from the side of the hut. When Melanie opened the door, Samantha rushed forward and pushed Melanie into the hut.

'Hey!'

Melanie spun round to face her assailant and she could not believe her eyes.

'Samantha.'

Samantha grinned at her shocked expression; behind her Naomi quickly shut the door.

'Sorry I had to be rough, Mel; I wanted to get in before your friend saw us.'

Melanie stared at the strain on the older girl's face.

'You look rough, Sam. I've seen corpses in better health,' Melanie observed.

Naomi giggled and got a sharp look from Samantha.

'Thanks, Mel, I knew I could count on you to give it to me straight.'

The sound of voices brought Janice out of the sleeping area. She gazed at her visitors; her body ached from the punishment the invaders had exerted on it. When she saw Samantha, her face lit up. She had never been gladder to see someone in her life before; she hugged Samantha.

'You've made it at last, Sam.'

'Yes, Jan, I'm ready to do battle with our enemy,' assured Samantha.

Melanie gazing at Samantha; she was not so sure.

'I hope you aren't thinking of rushing in blindly,' cautioned Melanie.

'No, we aren't,' Naomi said, sharply.

Janice sat on the bed and Naomi sat beside her. Samantha stared down at Janice with a critical eye. She could see the pain and tiredness in her face.

'You look as if you've had a rough time of it, Jan.'

Janice gazed up at the bright green eyes – they did not miss much, and Janice was tired physically and mentally.

'I decided to let them feel that I was on their side, they were not very gentle in their ways to see if that was so.'

'You are a brave girl, Jan,' Naomi said, sincerely.

Naomi ran a caressing hand over her cheek and moved the curly hair away from the side of her head. Naomi stared at the sore red marks on her skin. Naomi saw they had put Janice through the same experiment they had put Phoebe and Evelyn through. These aliens were searching for something, Naomi decided, but what was it?

'It looks as if they've been probing inside your head, Jan.'

Janice turned and gave Naomi a tired smile.

'They wired me to their machines to see how I tick.'

Naomi shook her head.

'It's more than that,' Naomi assured her.

Melanie placed a mug of strong coffee in Janice's hands; she sipped it and found it had been laced with brandy.

'Thanks, Mel.' Samantha sat on the other side of Janice.

'Did they seem pleased with the results they got from you?'

Janice shook her head, they seemed very disappointed.

'Do you remember the time, when you were a child and one night you found yourself down by the marshes?' Samantha asked, softly.

Janice never forgot the experience; it had haunted her dreams – the cold slimy water creeping up to her waist and the green glow rising up from the dark waters. It moved up her body to her head, a whispering female voice telling her there was nothing to fear.

'I have not remembered anything new.'

'We can alter that,' Naomi said.

Janice was about to turn her head, when Naomi put a hand on her cheek and told her to keep her head still as Naomi ran a medical device over her head.

'What are you doing?' Janice asked.

'I think something got inside your head when you were at the marsh. It's about time we found out what,' Samantha said.

Samantha gazed at Janice's bright blue eyes.

'Do you trust us, Jan?' Samantha asked.

Janice nodded her head.

'With my life; Sam.'

Naomi gazed at the tiny screen on the device she ran over Janice's head; it showed her what was going on inside Janice's head. Suddenly the device picked up something. Naomi called Samantha over and she got off the bed and stood beside Naomi; she gazed at the small screen on the device in Naomi's hand.

'Good work, Naomi.'

Naomi turned up the power of the probing device.

'Your head will start to ache, Janice, tell me if it gets too much,' Naomi said.

Janice nodded as her head began to throb. Naomi stared at the screen in deep concentration as the device probed deeper into Janice's brain. Samantha sat beside Janice again and held her hand. If the thing inside her head wanted to take over Janice, it would have done it by now. If it was lying dormant all this time waiting for something certain to happen, it would be useful to Samantha to know what it was.

Suddenly a green aura appeared above Janice's head, Naomi deactivated her device. The four girls stared in amazement as something materialized just in front of them. Samantha stood up and watched the shimmering luminous green aura as it slowly took shape and turned a glowing blue column of energy. Samantha moved close to it.

'Well, what have we here?' Samantha muttered.

Samantha found herself gazing at a six-foot, shimmering, glowing female. The apparition was not solid, it was translucent, and veins of different colours ran through it. Samantha was fascinated – this was a life form made of living energy.

'What are you?' Samantha was not sure if she would get an answer, as the creature probably would not understand her. Samantha repeated the question in the Monox language.

'That was not very nice.'

Samantha got a soft rhythmic female in her head; the creature was telepathic. What the creature had said told Samantha it was not very pleased in having Naomi's brain probing device pull it out of Janice's head.

'It wasn't meant to be,' Samantha said.

Naomi got up and stood beside Samantha.

'You are made up from two different life forms, you are a hybrid.'

That word again, Samantha wished they would stop calling her that, she found it very insulting.

'Nobody's perfect, I can see right through you,' Samantha said.

Naomi stared at Samantha and wondered why she was holding this one-sided conversation.

'Is this a private conversation, or can anyone join in?' Naomi inquired.

Samantha informed her the translucent creature was telepathic.

'Is that what I had in my head, Sam?' Janice inquired.

Samantha turned to her and nodded.

'It's just another life form.'

'That's a relief; I thought it might be a god.'

'That's exactly what I am.'

The four girls got the telepathic voice in their head, the alien was not being arrogant, and it was just stating a matter of fact.

'And modest with it,' Janice said.

Samantha moved closer to the entity.

'Why don't you tell us who and what you are,' Samantha said.

PART NINE:

THE MYTH OF JENAGUE

CHAPTER LXXXIV:

THE MYTH

'I am Auria, there are two of us, and Aurus is here somewhere.'

Auria probed the brain of the tall female standing in front of her. She was intrigued by the life form made up from two different worlds. Samantha moved away as her head started to throb, telepathically Auria assured Samantha she meant her no harm.

'You have a presence inside your head; I can fix it for you.'

Samantha smiled and nodded.

You will miss me, when I am gone.

There was a sharp pain in her head and then she felt better; she could concentrate better now her conscience, as Samantha called the ever-present voice in her head, was silent at last. Auria communicated to the four girls telepathically and told them of the Galactic Empire she was deity to, along with her companion Aurus.

As deities they were expected to keep the Empire wealthy and strong, which is what Aurus and Auria did for several millennium – until an evil presence materialized amongst them. Bauros and Zindra were of the Zelphines, an obnoxious race of parasitic minds, through time and space they moved in other life forms' brains. They became High Priests of the Empire's powerful religious sect, which gave Bauros the chance of dealing with Auria and Aurus and putting them out of harm's way. Soon after the Empire was attacked by a mysterious marauding alien race, thought to be extinct several millenniums ago. When Auria's race was numerous in the Galaxy, a great war ensued between them and the marauding aliens they knew little about and did not know what they looked like. At the end of the conflict Auria and Aurus were all there was of their race and the marauding aliens were pushed out of the Galaxy and they were no more, or that was what they thought.

The second invasion by the marauding aliens was as brutal as the first. What was left of the Empire was torn apart. Auria and Aurus used all the power they could muster against the attacking aliens, but there were only two of them and they were fighting a losing battle. Then something amazing happened to turn the tide. The marauding aliens had run into a powerful being of unrelenting ferocity.

'What was this being?' Samantha asked

'Her name was Jenague; Bauros called her a pariah because Jenague unleashed a destructive force the Universe had not seen before.'

Samantha smiled; Jenague seemed a girl she could get on with.

'I'm intrigued, tell me all about her,' Samantha said.

The twins were relaxing on a beach on the largest moon of their home world. It had an atmosphere and a pleasant climate. Jenague sat on a rock and gazed down at her twin, Sanamera, who lay naked on the warm golden sand. They had just finished a long hard-working term at the Great Hall of Learning. The moon was bathed in the warm heat of an orange sun. Jenague wore a shimmering ice blue gown that covered her tall slim body; she was envious of the fuller figure of her twin and she was regularly told Sanamera was the more beautiful twin. That did not hurt Jenague as she agreed with them. Sanamera noticed her twin gazing down at her.

'I love being here alone with you, Jen.'

'Your friends think you're mad spending your free time with me.'

Sanamera sat up and smiled warmly at Jenague. Sanamera knew what she meant, twins were rare and the twin like Jenague surviving was even rarer, in fact Jenague was the only one, to become a strong female with a powerful mind. The society they lived in thought the survival of Jenague would bring them bad luck. Sanamera thought they were talking rubbish and she told them so in no uncertain manner.

'You are my twin, Jen and I love you,' Sanamera said, sincerely.

Sanamera stood up and stood close to Jenague and started massaging her shoulders.

'Everyone's jealous of your high intelligence and your entry into the Hall of Sciences next season,' Sanamera said.

Jenague shook her head and her ice blue eyes stared up at her twin.

'It's more than that, the differences between us are clear to see, San. They are afraid of me. Even though I assure them, they have nothing to fear from me,' Jenague explained.

Sanamera kissed her on the cheek.

'We are two sides of the same coin, there is a bond between us nothing can break,' Sanamera said.

Jenague stood up and hugged her.

'The Society won't stop trying, my sweet twin,' Jenague observed.

Sanamera picked up her golden gown that lay on a rock and put it on. Jenague ran a hand through Sanamera's long flowing ginger hair; Jenague had her blonde hair cut short.

'If they hurt you, Jen, they will have me to answer to.'

They walked up the beach towards the headland; they ran up the slope and walked along the flat scrubland towards their spacecraft. Suddenly they heard a roaring sound up in the sky above them, they turned their eyes up to the sky and saw a huge spaceship descending and cutting them off from their spacecraft. Jenague stopped and Sanamera ran into her. Jenague eyed the newcomer with distaste. Their home world was outside the Empire, but Jenague had heard about the marauding aliens that were attacking it; now they had reached her home world.

'Who are they?' Sanamera inquired.

'The Empire is under attack by an unknown race of beings, now it is our turn,' Jenague said.

Sanamera shivered at the tone of her twin's voice.

'You are frightening me, Jen.'

Jenague hugged her. 'The Universe is in turmoil, we must be strong, San.'

They kept walking away as the huge spaceship landed. A horde of tall dark figures rushed out of the spaceship and pursued them. Jenague grabbed Sanamera's hand and ran across the flat land swiftly away from the invaders from space. They could not get to their spacecraft so Jenague decided to make for the distant mountains. There were too many and Jenague could not fight them all. She had to get Sanamera away from them. Jenague knew several places in the mountains where they could hide out and hope the invaders would get fed up and leave them on the moon.

The twins kept running as fast as their long legs could take them, the sound of pursuit got closer; they made it to the rocky ground just before the mountains. Sanamera stumbled on the loose rocks and as Jenague lifted her up onto her feet the horde was upon them. They grabbed and subdued Sanamera easily, but they found Jenague a different prospect – using her fists and feet, she let their attackers know she was no pushover. Her long muscular legs could deliver a blow that would cripple a foe, the horde found out they were tackling a furious fighting machine. But force of numbers soon wore her down and the horde carried the twins to their spaceship.

They were taken to a large compartment and thrown to the metal floor. They were struck with energy sticks that brought a severe pain throughout their bodies. Jenague kicked out at them, other aliens tore the shimmer gown off Sanamera and savagely beat her naked body, her screams echoed inside Jenague's head. She was held securely by several of the marauding aliens with their sharp talons gripping her body. They had their heads covered so Jenague had no idea what they looked like. They were heavily built and were very strong, but they had found Jenague was the stronger.

The rage built up in Jenague's head as she was forced to watch them abuse her twin; the rage inside Jenague reached boiling point. She saw Sanamera's face appealing to her do something to stop the pain. Her heart beat faster in her chest and the blood raced through her body. The horde found themselves holding onto a force that was about to explode. Jenague let out a blood curdling roar as she based her long sharp fangs. She tore herself violently away from her captives and pulled a blaster away from one of her captors and fired it at her twin.

'Forgive me, Sanamera.'

Jenague moved swiftly and fired the blaster at every alien around her. After a while she was the only living thing still standing. Jenague stared at the scorched body of her twin.

'They will pay for this, San. They will die, every last one of them. I swear it, San, you will be avenged,' Jenague said, icily.

Jenague bent over one of the hordes and lifted off the helmet that covered the head. She stared at the face of her aggressor, Jenague got the shock of her life, and the marauding aliens were no longer a mystery to her. Jenague saw why she was feared by her own people. She was the reminder of an ancient evil.

Jenague raced out of the compartment and made her way to the flight deck, dealing out death to every marauding alien she came across. When she got to the flight deck Jenague had a blaster in both hands. Amongst the aliens was a tall female with burning ruby eyes. Zindra watched her companions blasted out of existence. Zindra made good her escape. When there were no aliens to kill, she took charge of the spaceship and headed out into space towards the dying Empire. Jenague set her voyage of destruction into motion. Because of her dead twin she was going to bring chaos to the Universe. She purged the Empire of the marauding alien. With a powerful mind and a powerful spaceship Jenague was going to have her revenge for her dead twin. Jenague raced through the Galaxy dealing out death and destruction to every planet overrun by the horde. Jenague moved relentlessly towards their home world and disappeared into the realms of myth.

Samantha turned away and sat on the bed beside Janice.

'Sanamera and Jenague, I see a connection,' Janice said.

'I'm trying not to,' Samantha admitted.

Naomi stayed close to the shimmering alien female.

'Can you give me a mental vision of this Jenague?'

Auria placed a mental image of Jenague into Naomi's mind, the strange alien was a formidable figure, but it did not show to Naomi how she conjured up so much power to run amok in the Galaxy. She turned and gazed at Janice and thought of Phoebe's experiences. The answer was there somewhere, if she could think of it. Samantha looked at Naomi and saw the concentration on her expression; Samantha could almost hear her brain working over a certain problem.

'Do you see something in this myth?' Samantha asked.

'To do as much destruction like that, you need a lot of power, more than one spaceship and one powerful mind.'

'An awesome force if we could find out what it was,' Samantha said.

Naomi grinned and stared at Samantha.

'Physics is your subject.'

Janice rubbed the side of her head and looked at Naomi.

'You asked for an image of Jenague, what was she like?'

Naomi moved away from the shimmering form of Auria.

'It tells me there's more to Jennifer than we think.'

Melanie stood quietly and took everything in, running it through her mind.

'There's a creature here with red eyes, could it be the same one Jenague saw?'

'Zindra can exist for thousands of years, there are plenty of bodies around for her mind to take over,' Auria said telepathically to all of them.

'This Zindra had a special interest in Jennifer,' informed Melanie.

'I can understand why,' Naomi said.

'Perhaps they wanted to know what made her tick, just like they did with me,' Samantha said.

'We must rescue her,' Melanie said.

Samantha gazed at Melanie and could see she cared a lot for Jennifer.

'Easier said than done,' observed Naomi.

Samantha strode over to the window and gazed out across the compound. The alien spacecraft stood close by; she speculated Jennifer would be held inside it. She turned to Melanie.

'I've got a job for you, Mel.'

The Ixxion guard that had been guarding Janice outside the hut was now by the spacecraft talking to its glorious leader, Aplon Whan, the Monox Samantha had met on the mother ship.

'Here's our chance, their No. 2 is talking to Janice's guard by the spacecraft. I want you, Mel, to tell him you believe they had one of us captive on the ship. Don't tell him how you know, just say you want to check on their health,' Samantha explained.

Naomi took her med-kit and opened it and took out two phials and a hypodermic syringe. She gave them to Melanie.

'Use both phials – that should get Jennifer up on her feet,' Naomi said.

'What is it?' Melanie wanted to know.

'It's similar to the drug usually used on Jennifer; I've made an improvement, whatever they have done to her, that should fire her up,' Naomi said.

Samantha gave Melanie a quick instruction in the alien's language.

'You'll be able to swear at them in their own language now, Mel,' Samantha said.

'That's very handy, Sam.' Melanie left the hut. Samantha and Naomi stood by the door, waiting for Melanie to make contact with Aplon Whan, so they could get away while his attention was on Melanie.

Melanie strode purposely towards the spacecraft. when Aplon Whan caught sight of her, Melanie could almost see a frown on the alien's face. Melanie stood defiantly close to him; she noticed with pleasure the alien guard had moved away from her.

'You have a captive in your spacecraft, I demand to see them.'

Melanie spoke in half English and half in the alien language in her best voice of authority.

'You do.'

Melanie stood firm under the gaze of the amber eyes. While Aplon Whan had his attention on Melanie, Samantha and Naomi hurried round the side of the hut towards the rear boundary fence.

'I want to be satisfied you are not harming them in any way,' Melanie said.

Aplon had seen Zelphas carry her prize onto the spacecraft; she was not under his command so he had no idea what Zelphas was going to do with her captive, but he was sure she would be doing as much harm as she could to the captive.

'I haven't seen your companion since they were brought here.'

Aplon Whan turned and entered the hatch at the front of the spacecraft, Melanie followed him. Melanie McAllister was on a journey of discovery, as much about herself as the aliens suddenly invading her world. Jennifer had taught her to face the things she feared the most. That fight through the deep dark wood had taught Melanie a lot about herself, the anger she felt inside her, it had taught her to channel it against the things that wanted to take her over. Following the tall alien through the spacecraft, Melanie had decided what she had to do. Jennifer had saved her through that long trek through danger; now it was her turn to do something for Jennifer. Melanie would take anything the aliens threw at her.

Melanie made a mental note of the corridors and compartments they traversed; she was sure Samantha would find the layout of the spacecraft useful.

Aplon Whan arrived at the holding cell that contained Zelphas's captive, the door slid open and they walked in. Aplon gave a sigh of relief when he saw Zelphas was not there. Melanie went to the bunk bed and sat on the edge and gazed in horror at Jennifer's condition. Jennifer lay on her back, still as a corpse. Melanie was afraid she had come too late. She picked up a thin wrist and felt for a pulse and found a very weak one. Melanie gazed at the blood on her neck and saw the two puncture marks.

'First aliens, now vampires.' Melanie took the two phials and the hypodermic syringe out of the pocket of her white lab coat. She injected both contents of the phials into Jennifer's arm. Then she grabbed Jennifer by the shoulders and shook her gently. The eyes suddenly opened and seemed to look right through her.

'Jenny, speak to me,' Melanie pleaded. Melanie shook her again and a hand ran over her cheek.

'Mel.'

Melanie helped Jennifer up into a sitting position and dressed the wounds on her neck.

'I've just seen Samantha and Naomi.'

'I remember Naomi; she treated me when I was hit by the computer power surge.'

'Naomi gave me a drug to inject in your bloodstream, I've done that, and she said it will get you on your feet.'

Jennifer gave her a weak smile.

'If Naomi said that, then that's what will happen, I trust her medical knowledge, as I do yours, Mel,' Jennifer said, sincerely.

Melanie took a notebook and pen out of the inside of her white lab coat and drew a diagram of the journey she had taken through the spacecraft and gave it to Jennifer.

'I'll try and get some food out to you. You have done a lot to build my confidence, now it is my turn to do something for you, Jenny.'

Melanie stood up and made for the door carrying her med kit.

'Take care, Mel.'

Melanie met Aplon Whan outside the door; he locked it and escorted Melanie off the spacecraft. She made her way to Janice's hut. As she was about to open the door, something grabbed her arm and pulled her hard round to the side of the hut. She found herself staring at the smiling face of Henry Jones. He kissed her hard on the mouth and she clung to him; after a while she pushed him away and. slapped his face.

'That's for giving me a fright,' she said.

Henry ran a hand over her cheek.

'You've got a great right hand, Melanie, but keep it for the enemy.'

Melanie grinned at him, she was very glad to see Henry, but she was not going to tell him that.

'It'll teach you to creep up on me like that,' Melanie complained.

They walked across the compound towards the medical laboratory building.

'What are you doing here anyway?'

'I wanted to keep an eye on you, Mel. You are my girlfriend,' Henry replied.

Melanie coughed and stared at him. 'I am?'

Henry nodded his head and opened the door of the lab building; she stepped into the building and Henry followed her.

'I'm glad you didn't slap me for kissing you.'

'I still might,' Melanie said.

CHAPTER LXXXV:

LURKER IN THE DARK

In the late evening Samantha slid out of the back door of her old foster home. Naomi and Juliet were inside resting, as Samantha had told them they were going to be busy in the coming night. She had given them no idea what they would be doing. Samantha was not going to say anything until she had Plan A fixed in her mind. She made her way down the track between the infirmary and the school building. The hard-packed snow under her feet crunched too loudly for her liking. Samantha was ready to tackle the enemy if she ran into them. She looked towards the research facility gates and saw nothing coming her way. Samantha turned and stepped onto the grass and made her way between the first two houses and stepped onto a courtyard; nothing moved to alert her senses. Samantha was sure something would be lying in wait for her. Naomi had told her what she had learnt when she had bumped into Erika and her friends. They would be out searching for her day and night. She strode between the next two thatched roofed houses. There were no lights on, Samantha was sure there would be nobody at home, and Erika would make sure of that.

Samantha crossed a dusty track and came to a curving privet hedge, which she could see over the top. She stared across at the house Steven Calvert lived in, she remembered nobody knew of his whereabouts. She followed the hedge until she came to the opening and made for the house. The front door was open, and she stepped into the hallway, she stood still and listened for a sound in the dark house. If a predator was lying in wait, it would see the green light of her bright green eyes. If something leapt out of the darkness at her, she would have to make sure she would move the fastest. The door to the lounge was open and she peered into the room. All the dark shadows in the room were organic. No monsters in there then.

Samantha walked down the hall to the next room; she noticed the door was open. As she got to the entrance to the room, a broad dark shape came out at her. Samantha swung her left fist with all her strength at the place where the head was; the silence was broken by the sound of cracking bones and a loud roar of pain. She kicked out with her right foot and buried the steel toecap of her boot into the creature's belly. The bulky alien fell to the floor. Samantha knelt down and felt for the alien's weapon belt and pulled out the machete-like weapon out of the sheath and with one swift action she beheaded the Ixxion. She cleaned the blood off the weapon and slid it into the weapon belt round her own waist. Samantha stood up and heard another alien enter the house by the open door, probably looking for his fallen comrade.

Samantha turned to face her enemy. The tall heavy alien flew at her with revenge in the deep purple eyes. Hand to hand fighting with a heavy bulky alien was something Samantha was enjoying with the fullest of pleasure. The first assault of the alien was to grip her in a bear hug and crush the life out of her, but Samantha showed she was no pushover as she easily threw him off and the alien hit the banister of the staircase with a loud sound of splintering wood. Clasping her hands together she struck the side of the thick neck, then she gripped his head in her hands and violently twisted it round, the breaking of bones and ripping sinew was loud in her ears.

'I wish you wouldn't do that.'

Samantha looked up and saw Steven Calvert staring down at her from halfway up the stairs; her expression did not betray the feelings going on inside her. Shirley Gallagher stood behind him; she was glad to see another friendly face, after having to avoid the patrols of alien monsters roaming about. Shirley stared at the bright luminous green eyes; they looked eerie in the darkness. Steven met Samantha at the bottom of the stairs, she grabbed him and pressed him against the wall and kissed him hard on the mouth. Shirley stared at them in amazement. After a while Samantha stepped back and slapped Steven on the left cheek with her right hand.

'And that's for making us think something bad had happened to you.'

Samantha turned away and moved into the kitchen towards the back door. Shirley met Steven at the bottom of the stairs.

'I think she likes you,' she said.

They joined Samantha outside the rear of the cottage. Her eyes and ears could not detect any danger. She was glad Steven had turned up uninjured; she needed all the help she could get, and Shirley was a bonus. Samantha did not necessarily want the woman for her fighting skills; she had another idea for the journalist. Steven wanted to know what her plans were for freeing their world from the alien menace. Samantha told him he would find out later, she had other things on her mind at that moment. She moved slowly and cautiously amongst the cottages and outbuildings.

Steven had his gun ready in his hand for trouble as he and Shirley followed close behind her.

'Not very talkative is she?' Shirley observed.

Steven explained to Shirley about Samantha and her aloofness. When Samantha was younger she was given only the barest of information by those she worked for, Dr Sally Hamilton had wanted her daughter to use her brain to its fullest capacity and Steven and the others were there to give Samantha their input to make Samantha aware of what was going on around her. Now she was older Samantha wanted to proceed on her own so she would not have to put other people in danger. She did not want to risk the people she cared for.

'It's time for you to convince her to break out of that hard shell she has encased herself in,' Shirley said.

'We'll have to see what her plan is, and then I'm sure she'll open up more,' Steven said.

When Samantha had passed the last building she moved through a line of trees, she heard Steven and Shirley keeping close behind her. Samantha stopped walking and took the rucksack off her back and laid it on the ground.

'What are you going to do now?' Steven asked.

Samantha knelt down and rummaged in the rucksack and pulled out her radio transmitter; she looked up at Steven.

'I'm going to contact the General; I want the helicopter to bring some things I will need.'

Samantha took out a signal beacon and activated it and gave it to Steven. She told him where to place it. Samantha got in touch with the Fortress and informed the General of her needs; she told him it was time to enter the lair of the enemy and face her destiny. General Heywood cautioned her to be careful; getting herself killed was not an option. Samantha laughed; she did not know he cared. She put the radio transmitter back in the rucksack and fixed on her back again. There was nothing to do now, but wait for the helicopter.

'Have you two been having fun, while you were hiding away?' Samantha asked.

Shirley stared at her bright green eyes. The girl did not seem too serious in her inquiry.

'I wouldn't go as far as saying we were having fun, but I'm very glad you turned up when you did.'

Steven was walking round the moorland as he waited for the helicopter keeping his eyes and ears open for any sight and sound. Samantha kept an eye on him as she talked with the alert journalist.

'I don't want to get in the way, when the fighting starts,' Shirley said.

'You won't be getting in the way; I have a job for you.'

Samantha had a use for her journalistic powers in this struggle against the alien menace.

'I shall make sure you are well protected, Shirley; you are part of the biggest story of your life.'

Shirley nodded and grinned, she had an idea of what Samantha wanted of her.

'After all this is over, I have a daughter to bring up, you are going to be my insurance for getting what I want.'

'You can count on me, Sam.'

Steven approached the two conspirators and informed them the helicopter could be heard approaching them.

'What plan are you hatching up between the pair of you?' Steven inquired.

Samantha handed him a torch.

'None of your business, just shine the beam up to the sky, so John knows where to land,' Samantha said.

They could see the navigation lights of the helicopter as it approached their position; they stood far apart so the helicopter could land safely inside the area where they waited. When the helicopter had landed, Samantha waited for the rotor blades to stop turning then she approached the cabin of the helicopter. The door opened and John Stephenson leapt out and gave Samantha a strong hug.

'It's great to see you in one piece, Sam.'

'I hope I'm in the same state when this is all over.'

Steven approached them.

'If you let us help you out, I don't see any reason why you can't come out of this in good health,' observed Steven.

'There goes the voice of my conscience,' Samantha said.

Joanna Lumsden leapt out of the helicopter; as she was a major Samantha saluted her respectfully. She told Samantha she was glad to be working with her again. While they were talking a slim silent figure left the helicopter by the opposite door of the cabin. The supplies and weapons Samantha wanted were packed into three knapsacks, Shirley and Steven carried one on their backs and Samantha carried the spare in her arms. John and Joanna were going to stay with the helicopter until Samantha contacted them again. Samantha and her two companions made their way slowly back to the cottage where Juliet and Naomi were waiting for Samantha.

They got to the cottage without mishap; they had no idea they were being followed. Samantha did not disturb Naomi or Juliet as they were still asleep. Shirley made coffee and they sat round the table drinking and nibbling a biscuit or two. Sometime later there came the sound of someone trying to get in by the back door, Samantha shot up out of her chair and picked up the assault rifle that lay across the back of chair. Steven and Shirley stood up and moved back. Samantha approached the back door as it slowly opened. Her finger tightened on the trigger as the door swung open; when Samantha saw who was trying to get in, she dropped the weapon and moved forward, she gripped Sally under the arms and lifted her high up and stared at the small round face.

'Foolish girl, you nearly got your head blown off,' Samantha said, angrily.

Sally stared down at her mother; she had made her mad again.

'Why are you here anyway, we aren't playing a game here?'

Sally could not find her voice; she did not think how angry her mother would be, when she found out she had stowed away on the helicopter. Sally was sure her mother would need her help and Sally missed her; she would rather have an angry mother, than no mother at all. Samantha was angrier with herself; she was within a hair's breadth away from ending her daughter's life, and she had not gone through the pain of childbirth, just to blow her daughter's life away in an instant. Inside Samantha was shaking like a leaf, as she brought her daughter down. Sally wrapped her long legs round Samantha' s waist and put her thin arms round her neck.

'I'm sorry, Mummy; I just miss you too much.'

'I missed you too, Kiddo.'

Samantha placed Sally back on her feet, she turned to Shirley.

'Can you do me a favour, Shirley? Keep little madam out of trouble.'

'I'd be pleased to.'

'I appreciate it very much,' Samantha said.

Samantha told her daughter to do everything Shirley told her. Shirley took the young girl by the hand and took her to the lounge.

'Mummy's mad at me again,' Sally said, in a trembling voice.

'You noticed that,' Shirley said, lightly.

Steven stood close to Samantha.

'Silly question, are you all right?'

Samantha turned and stared at him and shook her head, now she had Sally to worry about her problems had doubled.

'My daughter's rash action has complicated things,' she said, sternly.

Steven put a hand on her shoulder.

'Keep your mind focused on what you have to do, we will see nothing happens to Sally.'

'I'm glad you turned up when you did, I can't do this without you, Steven.'

Steven kissed her and Samantha walked through the hallway to the front door. Steven looked in the lounge to see how Shirley and Sally were getting on. Samantha slipped out the front door and stood and listened for any sound in the darkness. They were lurking out there somewhere, waiting for her to walk into their trap. Samantha had settled herself down after her daughter's turning up and unsettling her nerves. As Steven had said, she had to keep her mind on her mission. She had to be the hunter not the hunted. Samantha moved slowly away from the small cottage. A freezing cold wind blew across her path; her body raised the heat to combat the frosty air. She stopped at a line of trees close to the infirmary building; she heard something moving towards her.

Samantha held the assault rifle ready. She could hear the heavy movements of an alien warrior patrol making their way on the other side of the trees, moving across her path. Someone with a lighter step moved towards her. Samantha stood still and waited.

Erika Strausberg moved to the treeline not knowing someone lay in wait for her. She was going to stay out all night if need be, until she caught her quarry; she was well aware of Samantha's abilities, but she had injured the girl before, now she would injure the menace fatally. Her alien companions were close by, she passed between two trees and a voice spoke out close to her.

'Erika!'

Erika spun round and found herself looking down the barrel of an assault rifle.

'Looking for me?'

Erika grinned at her enemy, she showed no fear, but Samantha was unimpressed.

'Unlike you, I like to face the enemy while I end their life,' Samantha said.

'I'm not alone,' Erika said, confidently.

'I can hear them; my hearing and night sight is better than yours and theirs.'

'I should have killed you, when I caught you in that spacecraft,' Erika snarled. Samantha agreed with her.

'Yes, you should. You also killed my mother, punishment for that is death.'

Erika smiled at the fact that Samantha did not know her mother was not dead. They were still keeping her in the dark.

'It's my job to rid the world of tiresome people, you included,' Erika said, defiantly.

Samantha smiled; she was not the one staring down the barrel of a weapon. She should blow her head off and be done with it.

'It's my job to rid the world of you,' Samantha assured her.

Samantha heard Erika's companions coming their way, Erika moved away from her. Samantha watched the dangerous woman.

'Your job is redundant.'

Samantha was hoping that Erika would go for a concealed weapon, she was obviously armed. It would make it easier for Samantha to shoot her. One of the alien warriors was moving her way; Samantha knew Erika was aware of it. It was time for Erika to underestimate her, Samantha had noticed Erika move slowly away from her and move her right hand down to the pocket of her jeans. Samantha was happy for her to go for a concealed weapon; Samantha was a lot faster and stronger than Erika and her alien companions. Samantha faced Erika and the alien was approaching her left side, Samantha slowly rotated on her left foot and then everything seemed to happen at once. Erika swiftly moved sideways and brought the gun out of her jeans pocket and she found out Samantha was well in command of the proceedings; she fired a volley of shots at Erika and spun round and blasted the alien warrior as he came upon her. The battle had started, the other alien warriors were moving towards her after the sound of weapon fire.

Samantha dashed towards the cottage; she saw Steven standing by the door as he had been alerted by the weapon fire, and she waved him back out of sight.

Samantha stopped and listened, there would be more than one patrol, they were determined to get their hands on her, and they could be all round her. Samantha glanced towards the boundary fence of the Research Facility and saw nothing coming towards her from that direction. She moved to the left side of the cottage. At the rear of the building was part of the large ancient wood. Samantha went back to the front of the cottage, the enemy would not attack her in a pack, they would spread out and hunt her down, and Samantha was well equipped to show them who was the best predator.

Steven left the cottage by the back door and searched the darkness for danger and saw none, so he walked round to the other side of the cottage fully alert for any sight and sound of danger. Steven kept his eyes on the scattered trees on his left, beyond them was the school. As he reached the front of the cottage, he sighted movement and a darker shadow moved out of the darkness. The gun already in his hand, he moved swiftly and fired as the Ixxion was almost upon him.

Samantha moved towards the gun shot as it echoed through the still night. An alien warrior leapt out at her roaring loudly as if it might impress the tall female predator. Samantha dropped the assault rifle and kicked out with her right foot and struck him hard in the stomach. Samantha swung her bony right fist and struck the alien in the side of the head, cracking the skull; the warrior fell to the ground and Samantha finished the job by stamping on the alien's head and crushing it. Samantha picked up her assault rifle as another Ixxion decided to try her out, she swung the heavy weapon and struck the alien in the face, she swiftly rammed the barrel into the alien's right eye and pulled the trigger, the alien's head exploded and she was showered with blood and brains.

Naomi leapt off the bed as if fired from a cannon, she grabbed the weapon she had left on the bedside table and rushed out of the bedroom and dashed down the stairs to the front door. She slowly slipped out into the night. Samantha had one of the alien warriors by the throat and held it up against the wall of the cottage; Samantha lifted the alien up off its feet.

'When are you going to learn, you just aren't good enough to take me on,' Samantha yelled.

Samantha strengthened the grip on the alien's throat, her long fingers slid into the flesh; when she had throttled the life out of the alien, she let it fall to the ground. She saw a dark shape move close to her.

'Was it something he said?'

Samantha turned and relaxed as she saw Naomi and grinned at her.

Steven joined them and they went back into the cottage. Juliet was coming down the stairs, she saw Steven and wrapped her arms round him.

'Where've you been hiding?' Steven inquired.

'I was going to ask the same question,' Juliet said.

Juliet walked into the lounge and Sally leapt off the couch and went to Juliet and hugged her.

'I bet your mother is glad you're here.'

Sally shook her head. 'No, she isn't.'

Juliet laughed softly as Sally told her how she had got here.

Naomi went into the kitchen and made some coffee to wake herself up, she had to be very alert when the fun started. Samantha stood by the front door that was partly open so she could see the coming danger. The battle with the alien and the killing had the adrenalin running through her body, which was fighting another battle as her alien metabolism melded with her human genes. Her mind was tuned on one thing only: Survival.

Suddenly the door splintered by a blast outside, Samantha spun round and dived down to protect her face and head.

Samantha swore.

Samantha recovered and held the assault rifle steady and fired a volley out into the darkness. Naomi dropped her coffee cup and ran out of the kitchen, Steven told her to get back and watch the rear of the cottage. He went to Samantha.

'If the coast is clear at the back, get Naomi to take the others out towards the school building; you are with me,' Samantha ordered.

Samantha moved outside and gazed out into the darkness; nothing moved as she counted a few more dead bodies. Their attack on her was getting very costly. She waited for Steven to join her, then they ran away from the cottage to the cover of trees, beyond which stood the school building.

'What's the plan?' Steven asked.

'We've got to get to the military camp for reinforcements and we have to let the Major know what's going on,' Samantha explained.

'Do we take the direct route, or take the picturesque route?'

Samantha shook her head; his since of humour was lost on her, even more now danger was all around them.

'If you mean we keep clear of the Research Facility, I would have thought that was obvious.'

'I was just testing.'

Steven stared at the bright green eyes as she tried to determine what he was thinking.

'I'm not alone and I have others to think about; as you said, I must focus on the job at hand. You can relax, I'm not going to rush blindly into this,' Samantha said, honestly.

'I'm glad to hear it.' They went in search of the others.

'We were brought up as a team of special human beings to fight a battle like the one we have here, because I was different and I was given the smallest of information to guide me to a solution, I went off on my own,' Samantha explained.

Steven was well aware of how the authorities ran Samantha, he had never liked it, so he tried to keep close to her, so she could see she had a friend.

'And now?'

Samantha turned and stared at him; Samantha knew she could trust Steven with her innermost thoughts.

'I need all of you if I am to succeed in what I have to do. You know I trust you more than anyone, I even see you as my conscience,' she said, sincerely.

Steven was seeing another side of Samantha; the tall girl still had secrets he had to discover.

'I have only one objective and that is to make sure you come out of this alive and in one piece.'

They moved out of the trees and made for the front of the school building.

'Your objective is harder than mine, Steven.'

Steven laughed and slapped her on the back.

'Isn't that the truth?'

Samantha was aware the final solution to their problem might end in her death, though she kept it hidden in the depths of her unconscious mind; her only vulnerability was to go off blindly on her own – she had fixed that as she needed the others of the team working with her.

'If anyone can save me from myself, it is you, Steven.'

'I hope I don't let you down, Sam.'

They found Naomi and Juliet waiting for them at the school building entrance, Shirley and Sally were inside the building.

'What now, oh, mighty one?' Naomi asked, saluting her.

Samantha ignored her attempt at humour and told the two girls what had to be done. Hearing the voice of her mother, Sally came out followed by Shirley. Samantha gave them the positions they would be in, they were not going to be bunched up, though they would be close enough so they could watch each other's back.

Samantha and Naomi would take the lead, making sure they kept away from the enemy. Samantha had no idea how many alien warriors Zindra had at her disposal, there would not be an inexhaustible supply of them, a lot of them had already been disposed of. Ruin their leader was still about, Samantha was eager to her hands on him. The other problem was Zelphas, Samantha had not bumped into her yet, though Samantha knew about her, from her mother's computer disc she had found at the sight of her car accident that killed both of Samantha's parents, or so she thought.

Samantha knelt down in front of her daughter and put her hands-on Sally's shoulders.

'You must stay close to Shirley, your hearing and night sight is as good as mine, so stay alert, if you hear anything let Shirley know, I'm counting on you, Kiddo.'

'I love you, Mummy.'

Samantha hugged her and kissed Sally on the cheek.

'I love you, too.'

Samantha stood up and nodded to Naomi, they crossed the track and moved slowly towards the scattering of two storey and single storey dwellings, the owners Samantha hoped were all alive, though trapped in the Research Facility by the aliens. She was glad there was no moon to light their way. Naomi did not have her night sight so she had to keep close to Samantha, who would make sure she did not collide with anything hard or fall flat on her face. Steven followed a few steps behind; he could not hear Samantha moving ahead of him, but he heard Naomi stumbling about in the dark, trying to keep close to her friend. Juliet kept her ears on the sounds of Shirley and Sally behind her; if Sally detected anyone coming up behind them, she would have to give Juliet a sign.

Shirley was no stranger to wandering about in the dark, with Steven she had been moving about the dwellings in the dark ever since the aliens arrived, making sure they were never caught by their patrols that had regularly searched the area. The young girl kept close to her. When Sally looked up at her, Shirley stared at the strange bright luminous sapphire eyes, two bright stars in the dark. Knowing how old the young girl was, Shirley was surprised at how tall she was. Sally peered into the darkness taking stock of her surroundings. She was glad her mother had given her something to do; it was her job to protect her mother from the things in the world that were there to hurt her. Sally knew her mother was the most important person in her life. They needed each other. Sally knew her mother would not agree, but it was her duty to keep an eye on her parent.

Suddenly Sally stopped and listened, Shirley put a hand on her shoulder.

'What is it, darling?' Shirley whispered.

'Something is moving behind us to the right, in an erratic manner,' Sally said.

They moved quickly forward until they got to Juliet and Sally told the older girl what she had heard in the darkness behind them.

'What did those special eyes of yours see?' Juliet inquired.

Sally stared at her and smiled; Sally liked the older girl, and she was fun.

'Tall, slim and shadowy, moved like Mummy, when she is searching for things that might come and hurt me,' Sally said.

'I can see why Samantha wants to keep her daughter away from the people she works for,' Shirley said.

'Samantha doesn't want Sally to be poked and prodded, experimented on like she was,' Juliet said.

They kept moving forward and Sally kept her senses alert.

'Putting you in charge of Sally shows the trust Samantha has in you, Shirley.'

'I won't let her down,' assured Shirley.

Samantha and Naomi stood between the last two buildings waiting for the others to catch up. When they were all together, Sally told her mother something was creeping about behind them.

Samantha knelt down in front of her daughter.

'They are moving slowly and light-footed, just like you do, Mummy.'

'Female?'

Sally nodded her head; on occasions Sally had sniffed the air and she could smell her.

'She is strange, doesn't smell nice like you, Mummy.'

Samantha stood up and stared at Naomi who was trying to stifle a giggle.

'Have you any idea who it can be?' Steven asked.

'It's not Erika, I've disposed of her,' Samantha said.

Beyond them they had cover of Ash and Beech trees – Samantha wanted to make her way through them before they crossed the track and made for the overgrown copse and the military camp beyond. Samantha gave orders to the others and moved forward to scout ahead; Naomi was about to follow, and Steven grabbed her arm.

'Guard Samantha with your life, her safety is your responsibility.'

'You don't have to worry, Steven; I wouldn't have it any other way.'

Naomi moved off to catch up with her leader. Sally moved close to Steven and stared up at him.

'You care deeply for my mother?'

Steven ran a hand through her thick curly blonde hair. 'You'd better believe it, Kiddo,' Steven said, smiling down at her.

Sally smiled back at him; she was glad her mother had so many loyal friends.

When Naomi had caught up with Samantha, she told Samantha what Steven had said to her.

'Don't mind Steven, he's just being overprotective,' Samantha said.

They moved slowly through the trees; Samantha tuned her senses on detecting danger ahead of them. When she detected movement some way in front of them, she told Naomi to go back to the others and tell them to stay where they were, then return swiftly. When she met them, Sally told her the shadowy female was still tracking them.

'Whoever it is, is probably waiting to pick us off one at a time, we are too good at protecting each other, it finds that a problem,' Naomi said.

'Plus, the fact we have our own danger detector,' Steven said, gazing down at Sally, who gave him a wink.

Juliet knelt down in front of the young girl and ran a hand over her cheek.

'That makes you the first target, will you keep very close to me. Your mother will be mad at me, if anything bad happens to you.'

Sally kissed her friend on the cheek.

'I know what it's like when Mummy gets mad, I won't let you down,' promised Sally.

Naomi went in search of Samantha moving quickly but silently, keeping alert for movement ahead of her.

Samantha stood silent by a tree. She could hear two Ixxion moving about in front of her, Samantha was sure who one of them was. She had an old score to settle with Ruin, he was the Ixxion leader, taller, heavier and more treacherous than his fellows, just the odds Samantha liked, and the bigger they were the harder they fall. She heard Naomi coming up behind her and Samantha turned and stopped her before she ran into the enemy.

'There's two of them, the red one is the leader, I'll take him, I'll leave the green Ixxion to you,' Samantha said.

'Our female shadow is still about, Sally is doing a good job tracking her,' Naomi said.

'Sally is my child, what you expected.'

One good thing had come out of Sally disobeying her orders; she could warn the others when the alien female was ready to attack. Samantha knew Steven and Juliet would protect her daughter from harm. She had to keep her mind focused on the threat in front of them and keep the problem of her daughter in the back of her mind, until the main priority had been solved. Samantha told Naomi what she wanted her to do, she gave Naomi the assault rifle, Samantha knew the Ixxion leader would be hoping to tackle her with his bare hands, which was all right for Samantha, as she had Naomi to keep the second Ixxion from sneaking up behind her. Samantha moved forward and when she moved out of sight, Naomi moved to the left of Samantha's position where her target lurked in the dark.

Ruin waited patiently for Imera's granddaughter to come to him. Ruin knew she was aware of him, her night vision was better than his. Ruin had to forget about the first fight he had had with her, the alien predator had evolved since then; amazingly the creature had survived everything his superiors had thrown at her. She was a credit to the memory of Imera. Ruin had never defeated Imera and neither had his superiors.

Samantha moved out of the trees; she saw the huge red Ixxion waiting for her by the dwelling she had once lived in with Jennifer. She could hear the second Ixxion behind her amongst the trees and Naomi who was keeping close to him.

'I hope you fight better than your underlings,' Samantha said, in the Ixxion language.

Ruin ignored her words; he was going to avenge his fallen companions. As she stepped closer to him, Ruin stared at the thin, battle-worn face, the green eyes were a dark emerald green, and his adversary was in battle mode. Ruin had to keep in mind she was a product of two worlds, she possessed something Imera did not have. He must not take this hybrid too lightly; he had seen what she had done to his dead companions.

Samantha was prepared for Ruin to make the first move after they had eyed each other up.

'I'm not worried what happened at our first meeting, I learn from my mistakes, I hope you do,' Samantha said, calmly.

'I don't intend to make any.'

Ruin lunged at his enemy and grabbed her with his thick muscular arms, Samantha spun round and shook him off, showing him the immense strength her tall, slim body contained, and his adversary was not as fragile as she looked. Samantha was not going to ignore the brutish strength of the Ixxion. Samantha had the advantage of being light on her feet and she could move faster. Ruin was stung by the pain her thin bony fists inflicted on his body and she used her feet as she gave him many painful kicks. Ruin was finding this tall female a slippery customer; Ruin felt his adversary had come a long way since their first meeting. He hoped Roth was still close by.

Roth moved slowly out of the trees and moved to the front of the building, keeping an eye on the fighter at the side of the dwelling. Naomi moved slowly behind him, she was sure the alien warrior was hoping to help his master. She could see Samantha was on top and waiting for the right moment to penetrate the alien's defences. Naomi hoped Samantha had the stamina to keep up with her heavier opponent.

There came a halt in the fighting as Ruin swiftly moved away from the tall female. Samantha stood still and kept her eyes on him, her heart was thumping in her chest, and the hot blood rushed through veins. Samantha was sure this would be the time Ruin's companion would step in; she hoped Naomi had her eye on him.

Roth took his energy weapon out of the belt round his waist and aimed it at the ginger haired female. Naomi moved closer to him, now she saw what the alien warrior was up to. She raised the assault rifle and fired a volley at the enemy.

Ruin moved forward to initiate the final round with the female predator, he was sure Roth was in position and ready. There came the echoing sound of weapon fire. Ruin turned his head as he saw it was not his enemy who was being fired at. Samantha saw her chance and took it. She leapt forward and struck Ruin hard in the gut with her left foot and moved swiftly and wrapped her right arm round his neck and strengthened her grip as she pulled Ruin down to the ground. Samantha rammed her left knee into his back as her strong muscular arm tightened against his throat. Ruin gasped for air as his adversary continued to throttle him. Samantha placed her left hand over the top of Ruin's head and gripped it tight with her long powerful hand and fingers, Samantha twisted his head round, the snapping of tendons and cracking of bones was loud in the still night.

Samantha slowly stood up and the sound of something approaching made her instantly alert and she turned sharply, but she relaxed when she saw Naomi moving towards her.

'You are one hell of a strong person, Sam.'

Samantha ran a hand over Naomi's cheek.

'You have nothing to be worried about, I won't lose control and hurt my friends,' Samantha assured her.

Samantha stared at the house she had lived in with Jennifer, partly destroyed by an explosion that nearly ended her life.

'We never did find the culprit,' Naomi said.

'I'm sure he's still about, at least he won't have Erika helping him out.'

The others joined them, and Sally told her mother, they were still being followed. Samantha told her to keep close to her friends. Samantha and Naomi stood by the damaged house; they watched Steven guide the others across the track to the overgrown copse. Samantha waited for the female monster to move out of the cover of the trees. Naomi sped across the track and stood between the hill and the overgrown copse. Whatever was tracking them might not go straight to Samantha. Naomi hoped to keep between their enemy and their friends. Samantha had advised Naomi, if she heard anything, she should shoot first and ask questions afterwards. Naomi told Samantha to make sure it was not her she heard. Samantha assured Naomi she had nothing to worry about.

Samantha moved away from the house and went to the trees to see if she could sense the lurker in the dark. Samantha had a sense this was going to be a new test for her abilities and predatory skills. This was a new kind of monster that was hunting her. There was no sight or sound of her nemesis. Samantha left the cover of the trees and sped across the track and made for the overgrown copse. When she got there, she stood and listened. She heard movement way ahead of her; Samantha smiled to herself, because Naomi was a heavier built girl than her, Naomi was unable to be completely silent as she moved through the trees and bushes. Samantha moved slowly forward silently moving through the undergrowth. Naomi was changing the direction she moved every now and again, as Samantha had advised her to do. Samantha moved closer to her, then Naomi was silent; the hunter was close to her.

'Come out, wherever you are.'

Naomi was standing still, she had heard something at her left, and she heard the voice of her friend behind her. Naomi dived down and moved slowly through the undergrowth.

Zelphas was disappointed when her first target disappeared out of sight, she could not detect the prey by sound. Zelphas heard the voice of her main target. Zelphas had kept her eye on the prey when she was in combat with the Ixxions – they were good fighters, but Zelphas had seen the ginger haired prey was too good for them. Zelphas could see Imera's style of fighting in the prey as they were related. Zelphas had never bettered Imera, when they had fought together. Zelphas had seen the ancestral link between her and the tall pale creature she held captive in the spacecraft. They inherited a certain gene, that gave the idea they evolved from the same ancestor, Zelphas was aware Imera was higher up the evolutionary ladder than her. The Moran had been captured and experimented on by the Monox to eradicate the gene that produced Moran like Imera, who had slipped out of their net by her resourceful mother.

Zelphas was not just a ferocious predatory animal that struck an enemy fast and silently. She was an intelligent being.

There were not many of her race left and Zelphas was the only one that had gone into space. She had been a companion to Zindra ever since she had brought chaos to their Empire and Zelphas had gained a wealth of knowledge from her. Zelphas would need some of that knowledge to overcome Imera's grandchild. Zelphas was not going to underestimate the enemy; the hybrid had shown it had immense strength and agility. It knew how to kill with ease. They both had the same stealth and cunning to bring down a prey before they were aware of the fact they had been hunted. But this female predator had genes from another world. She was also more evolved.

Samantha kept staring into the darkness waiting for any sign of movement; Samantha had hoped she would have caught sight of her elusive opponent. She could detect Naomi, so she hoped Naomi was keeping low and out of sight and sound of the female predator's radar. She moved forward keeping her senses alert for danger.

Naomi kept low and still; she suddenly heard movement coming towards her. Naomi held her breath, something came close to her, and Naomi peered hard at the dark undergrowth to catch a sight of what was moving close to her position. She suddenly saw movement, a tall slender figure glided perilously close to her. Naomi stared at the shadowy nightmare – even in the dark the skin of the creature showed the luminescence of the orange skin and underlying flesh, two small yellowy orbs of light glared out of the two deep set eye sockets. The creature moved away, and Naomi exhaled slowly and fought hard to steady her frayed nerves. She heard another sound and she kept down amongst the bushes and waited. When Samantha moved into her sight, Naomi stood up and Samantha put a finger to her lips. Naomi took the hint and kept silent, she pointed a finger in the direction the alien creature had gone, Samantha moved off and a moment later Naomi got up and slowly moved through the copse in a different direction from Samantha and her alien opponent.

CHAPTER LXXXVI:

THE ANCESTRAL PARADOX

Jennifer woke from a nightmare that made her body sweat and her head throb, her eyes were a deep sapphire, her brain was in turmoil, her blood ran hot through her veins, and the adrenalin was running through her body. She had a strange sensation to find something to kill. Melanie had been able to keep giving her the drug Naomi had given her, it was now firing up her metabolism. The hold Zelphas had on her mind was being relinquished. She had been dreaming of Samantha and she was walking into danger. Jennifer sat up, her hands were free, but her feet were tied together. Her long delicate fingers worked furiously to free the bonds that tied her, eventually freed her feet and she swung her long legs over the side of the bunk bed, she ran her hands over her slim thighs massaging them, then she rubbed her calf muscles. When she had finished, she stood up.

Jennifer slowly made her way to the computer and sat in front of it. She ran through the data Zelphas was working on, it was all to do with genetics, it was not her subject, but Jennifer thought she was a quick learner. When Samantha had gone to the Monox mother ship, they had taken a sample of her DNA while they had her tied down, Jennifer studied the gene sequences then she looked over the data of her DNA Zelphas had got out of her, while she had been captive. They were similar, but there was something different about Samantha's DNA, they were related somehow. It had occurred to her when they first met, their eyes shone in the dark and they had the same perfect night vision. Their bodies had the same immense strength. Jennifer got a surprise when she found data on the DNA of Zelphas – it looked they had come out of the same gene pool. She found data on DNA sequences of the Monox and the Moran, something very significant: the Monox were all male and the Moran were female. Their ancestors had a lot to answer for.

Jennifer stood up. She had to escape and get hold of Samantha. She went to the bunk bed and sat down; she closed her eyes and concentrated. She had been able to get inside Samantha's head when they were close together; Jennifer hoped she could get some kind of link with Samantha, though they were far apart.

Zelphas picked up her first target again, she had sensed the hybrid moving slowly through the vegetation. Zelphas was studying the hunting skill of the hybrid female, and she wanted to learn more about her adversary before she went in for the kill.

Naomi was getting close to the edge of the overgrown copse.

Suddenly the alien nightmare appeared in front of her. She held the assault rifle up, her finger tightened on the trigger.

They stared at each other. Samantha had taught Naomi well, and she kept her attention on the bright amber eyes. Zelphas stared at the weapon that was aimed at her head. She looked up at the grey eyes, there was no fear in them, this prey was a fighter and was due respect. Naomi decided she had the advantage, as however fast the creature was, she would fire the weapon before the alien moved across the distance between them. Naomi had been well trained in keeping cool under pressure and she had no intention of getting herself killed just yet, Naomi had another mission to complete.

Zelphas stared at the weapon aimed at her then at the distance between her and the enemy, calculating the exact path she should take to get a victory over the enemy. It happened in the flicker of an eye; Naomi had never seen something move so fast, she fired her weapon. Zelphas had moved in the exact right way to avoid being hit by the volley of bullets, but not avoiding the hand that gripped her by the throat. Zelphas hissed at the bright green eyes that shone out of the darkness. Naomi was also surprised at the arm that shot out and grabbed the alien creature.

Samantha threw the loathsome creature against a tree, an arm flew out and long pointed talons missed her face by inches. Samantha kicked the creature hard in the midriff; as Zelphas doubled up, Samantha struck her on the back of the neck with the edge of her right hand. Naomi came close to her and shone the beam of the light on her left sleeve on Zelphas.

'People thought I was ugly,' Samantha said.

Naomi stared at her and grinned.

'I didn't,' Naomi assured her.

Samantha picked up the unconscious alien and carried Zelphas over her shoulder as they moved out of the overgrown copse. They found the others at the side of the military camp. Samantha laid Zelphas on the ground, and Juliet came close to her and stared down at the female alien.

'Go on, Juliet, say it, I know you are dying to,' Samantha said.

Juliet stared at her innocently.

'I wouldn't dream of it and I don't want your daughter to thump me.'

Samantha laughed as Sally came up to her and Samantha gave the young girl a motherly hug. Naomi took some rope out of her knapsack and tied up the unconscious alien. Steven and Samantha made their way to the main gate of the military camp.

'Sally is quite a girl, just like her mother,' Steven said.

Samantha kept focused on the ground before her, there were no alien guards at the gate, and they were probably roaming about inside the compound. Steven kept close to her, he had to wait, and they had other things on their minds. Steven was very interested in who the father of Sally was – he was an obvious candidate.

The main gate was open, and Samantha moved slowly into the compound. She made for the building on her left, which was Major Harrington's office. Steven Calvert kept a sharp eye out for the enemy. As she neared the building an alien warrior appeared from the side of the building, the speed in which Samantha did battle with the tall stout alien still surprised Steven, even though he was aware of her capabilities. It made him slightly nervous around her in case he annoyed her, although Steven was sure she would not harm him. Steven went to the right-hand building, which was the canteen; he was ready for a fight.

Samantha tried the door and found it locked. She aimed a heavy right boot at the door and the lock splintered and the door flew opened. Samantha took the heavy torch out of her knapsack and shone the beam into the office.

'Does anybody here want to be rescued?' Samantha asked.

Major Harrington got up and approached the tall figure in the doorway.

'If I'd had a bet about the first person coming through that door, you would be the last person, Samantha.'

Samantha grinned at him.

'You know me, Major, I'm the bad penny round here,' she said.

Samantha took the sealed orders out of the inside pocket of her combat jacket and gave it to the Major.

'Colonel Collins and Captain Goodwin are safe down in the underground base,' informed Samantha,

Harrington was glad to hear that and glad that Samantha was alive and kicking – he had a soft spot for the girl, as he knew she was a tough customer. As they marched towards the barracks building, Steven joined them.

'Nice to see you are still with us, Steven, I was never sure what happened to you and Miss Gallagher.'

Steven told the Major he had been keeping his head down, until Samantha turned up.

'You just can't get the staff, Major,' Samantha said.

For the first time in ages Major Harrington managed a smile as he gazed at Steven's expression.

Naomi and her small band entered the military camp by the small gate at the rear of the compound. With the help of Juliet they managed to rid themselves of two alien warriors, Naomi shot the lock off the door of the barracks, the soldiers there knew Naomi and were glad to see her. The NCO saluted her and asked about the Major. Naomi assured him Major Harrington would be with them. Naomi was not in the army, but she worked for the Government and she had authority over the soldiers. Sally sat on one of the beds, Shirley sat beside her. Naomi approached them and took off her knapsack and combat jacket and draped it over the young girl's shoulders and smiled down at her.

When Samantha entered the barracks, Sally got up and ran to her, Samantha saw fear in her bright blue eyes.

'What is it, Sweetie?'

'She is here, very close, your dragon,' Sally said.

Samantha hugged her. Samantha knew what she meant. Jennifer was trying to contact her, but Samantha knew she would not be able to get inside her head, so she had made contact with her daughter.

'Did you get voices in the head?'

'No, just a headache and a sense of something evil, there is something out there Mummy, that wants to harm you.'

Samantha stared at Naomi.

'It looks like that concoction you made for Jennifer is working, she is getting stronger,' Samantha said.

Naomi looked down at the troubled expression on Sally's face.

'I thought Jennifer was on our side.'

'She is, but I don't know if I can fully trust her, she is still an unknown factor. She is Sally's dragon,' Samantha explained.

'I'll keep a sharp eye out for her,' Naomi assured her.

Juliet was listening close by and she approached them.

'So will I, she's not a very likeable person.'

Samantha laughed and patted Juliet on the back.

'You just don't like the girl.'

'There's that too,' Juliet said.

CHAPTER LXXXVII:

A PLAN OF ATTACK

Jennifer stood up, she was disappointed she had been unable to contact Samantha, she had touched another mind, it had been young and inexperienced, but the mind had put the shutters down and forced her out. The experience had set her thinking. There was a child about with a strong and strange mind. Jennifer knew Samantha had a child.

'I must get out of here.' Jennifer went to the door and it slid open. Framed in the doorway was one of the Ixxion warriors; Jennifer hoped she had the strength to overcome it. Jennifer stepped back as the heavy alien moved into the compartment. The left claw shot out and gripped her by the neck, Jennifer brought her right leg up hard between the creature's thick thighs, it gave out a loud roar, the grip of her throat slackened, she gripped the arm and brought her right knee up and Jennifer listened to the gratifying snap of breaking bones. The other clawed hand came up and hit her in the face; luckily for her the sharp claws did not rake her face. Jennifer kicked the alien hard in the belly; as it doubled over, Jennifer brought her right fist hard down on the thick broad neck. Her eyes were a dark blue, the blood raced through her veins, her face gave away the exertion her body was putting out to combat a heavier opponent. She hoped the injections Melanie had been giving her was providing her metabolism the boost it needed after Zelphas had been trying to suck the life out of her.

Jennifer screamed out as she lifted the alien warrior high above her head, then she brought the heavy alien down on the computer system; it brought a loud hiss and sparks of energy from the machine, an odour of burning flesh reached her nostrils.

Jennifer left the compartment. She strode down a long corridor. It was a pity there were not notices on the wall to inform her of the layout of the alien spacecraft. Jennifer wanted the quickest way out of it and that was the teleport compartment. She came to a junction in the corridor; Jennifer decided to keep straight on forward. She came to a door and it slid open as she came up to it, she entered the compartment: she had found the teleport room.

Jennifer stood on the pad and surveyed the control panel. Jennifer wanted to teleport herself into her sleeping quarters down in the underground facility. She wanted to get some clothes on before she faced her companions, Jennifer had no qualms about her nudity, and it had not been an issue when she grappled with the alien warrior. The atmosphere in the spacecraft was pleasantly warm on her body. Jennifer punched in the co-ordinates then she stood still and waited. Strange feelings ran through her body as she began to fade, her brain was trying to interpret the messages received by her nerves.

A crescendo of alarm bells and flashing red lights made every person in the underground facility jump. Michelle stared at the large plan of the underground base on the wall and saw a red light marking Jennifer's quarters, and she contacted Ian Henderson and told him to get there as fast as he could. When he got there, Ian had to override the security lock on the door, it slid open and he entered the room, and he stared in shock at the naked figure of Jennifer standing in the centre of the room.

'Stop gawking at me, Ian, haven't you seen a naked girl before?'

Ian turned his back on Jennifer as she got dressed. Then she tapped him on the shoulder, and they made their way to the control room. Michelle grabbed Jennifer and hugged her.

'I thought we had seen the last of you.'

Jennifer told Michelle to turn off the alarm system, she told Jennifer it had been Samantha's idea to have alarms sound out when someone teleports into the facility.

'Good idea, I suppose she also told you to keep a guard on me, if I teleported back here,' Jennifer said.

Michelle nodded her head guiltily.

'You don't have to worry; I would have done the same.'

****

Dr Sally Hamilton slowly came out of unconsciousness, her body ached, and she remembered the pain of being shot by an energy weapon. She had thought in an instant that would have been the end of her. Keeping her alive was a mistake by her enemy, it was obvious Zindra did not want to give her a quick death and it would be the same for her daughters. She was very confident she would win out against her enemies. As long as she was still alive, she was still able to fight back. Like her mother Imera, she was of the view it was a danger to keep an enemy in your power, the chance to fight back. Zindra was keeping her alive for bait to reel in Samantha, but Zindra did not know Samantha had no idea her mother was still alive. Sally made sure that fact was kept from Samantha by her companions.

She sat up and looked round the room, there was no guard standing in the room. She gazed out of the window at the morning light. When she turned her head there was a tall shimmering figure beside her bed.

'Who are you?'

A thought came inside her head. She did not like telepathic entities.

'I am Auria, it is my job to destroy Bauros and Zindra, you and your cub will help me.'

When she had been Axerus, she had heard of Imera speak of Zindra having a companion, a male of her species. She knew nothing of Auria.

'I do not know this being you call Bauros.'

'They are Zelphines, an old race like mine. When they destroyed the Galactic Empire, Aurus and I were sent out to destroy them. '

'Then your mission is the same as mine. Zindra has been helping the Monox to keep my people in slavery.'

'You may have to sacrifice your cub, to get what you want.'

If that was indeed the fact, she still had another daughter to throw into the fight. Auria caught the thought.

'She is not complete, part of her essence is in the other twin, it is tearing her apart, I have nullified it at the moment; what happens when it wakes is in the hand of fate.'

Dr Hamilton was shocked at the revelations, it gave her a clue to the headaches and blackouts the young Samantha had and the failure of the clones that Samantha had a revulsion to.

She was sure Jennifer had no idea what she was doing to Samantha.

The helicopter settled down by the barracks of the military camp. John Stephenson and Phoebe Cross exited the helicopter; Steven and Samantha were waiting for them. Samantha explained to Phoebe she would be joining Naomi and some of the soldiers in a raid on the spacecraft, Samantha was sure Phoebe's sister was being kept in it. When Phoebe had entered the barracks, John followed Steven and Samantha out of the military camp. They crossed the track and went to the side gate in the research facility. They kept a look out for the enemy, as they made their way to the Lab 3 building. Zindra would have her depleted force hidden in the hope Samantha would eventually come to her.

Janice Clarke was marched out of her quarters by two of the alien warriors. She did not know why but she had the feeling the end was near. The final outcome was not within her radar. She blanked out her fears and anxieties, she kept as calm as she could. A cold wind blew across her path, she stared up at the dark grey sky, and the clouds of doom were still hanging over them. As they approached the Lab 3 building, Janice gazed towards the building that housed Labs 1 and 2 and beyond in the hope she could see the cavalry coming to her rescue. She hoped Samantha was close by.

Samantha was watching her being led across the compound; she found it significant that the enemy had decided to put their prime captive to work. She turned and gazed at Steven and he gave her a nervous smile – Janice would solely be his concern. Samantha, Steven and John entered the Lab 3 building by the hole that had been breached in the side of the building. Samantha was glad to see the floor had been cleared of debris. She swiftly crossed the room and made for the half open door.

Samantha put her head round the door and gazed down the long corridor, she saw Janice and her captors moving down to the other end of the building. She rushed across the corridor to the door opposite. She opened it and walked into the locker room, Steven followed her, and John Stephenson stood outside and kept a look out for the enemy. There were two technicians wearing white coats inside the locker room. It made Samantha instantly suspicious, none of them would be left to roam about on their own without a guard. She put a hand in the pocket of her combat jacket and gripped the weapon inside firmly. One of the men approached her while the other kept close to the locker he was looking in. Samantha kept a sharp eye on the man as he approached her. There was another enemy lurking around them, hidden from sight even though they could be a few feet away.

Behind Samantha, Steven was settling down on a bench; he had suddenly felt dizzy, he felt his head throb.

KILL

The technician in front of Samantha started to lift a hand out of his white lab coat. With one swift movement Samantha pulled her hand out of her jacket and fired the weapon she held point blank range at the head of the technician, the head exploded; Samantha dived away from the shower of blood and brains.

The other technician moved towards her then stopped, the body started to tremble, and the face was a mask of terror, a moment later the technician fell to the floor and lay still. Samantha turned and saw Steven slumped onto his bench, in front of him was a tall shimmering luminous figure.

'Auras, I presume,' Samantha said.

'Auria is nearby; as you know me, she must have made contact with you.'

Samantha went to Steven and he looked up at the shimmering alien then stared up at Samantha, hoping she had an answer to what had just happened to him.

'It's all right, Steven, you'll live,' Samantha assured him. Samantha turned to the shimmering alien.

'Auria is helping me rid this planet of these invading creatures,' Samantha said.

'I will help you.'

John Stephenson came in and stood and stared at the shimmering apparition.

'He's a friend, John, we haven't time for explanations,' Samantha said.

Samantha went to the laundry cupboard and took out two white lab coats and gave one to John and put one on herself; she told Steven to stay where he was.

Samantha gazed through the glass in the door that led to the medical ward. After a moment she pushed the door open and strode into the room, she turned left and strode into the offices, giving Dr Hilary Calvert a fright as she sat at the desk computer; she shot up and faced Samantha.

'Sam!'

Hilary gave her a hug.

'It's nice to see you are still in one piece,' Hilary said.

'Let's hope at the end of this, I'm in the same state.'

Hilary sat back down in her chair; Samantha sat next to her.

'Can you contact the underground facility with that computer?'

Hilary nodded.

'Contact Jennifer and tell her I have a job for her,' Samantha said.

Jennifer was sat at the computer control desk when the message from Samantha came over the screen before her. It did not tell her what Samantha had in mind; she would find that out when they met in the Lab 3 building. When the message was complete Jennifer stood up and crossed the room. Evelyn Stevens was sat at the glowing sphere of the device she had been working on with Jennifer. Since her arrival in the underground scientific facility, a year ago when she was grabbed from University, she had been getting to know the world her friend Samantha had been born into. The most fascinating person she had come across was Jennifer, she was a person full of contradictions, the girl reminded her of Samantha as they were both tall and slim. Evelyn could see the predatorial instincts in the both of them; Jennifer showed a deep fascination of Evelyn's telekinesis capabilities and gave her all sorts of strange tests.

Jennifer disconnected the device from the computer; Evelyn took the headset off and stood up.

'What's up, Jenny?'

Jennifer stared at the pretty 22-year-old girl; the grey eyes stared back at her. Jennifer wondered why Samantha wanted Evelyn to accompany her.

'Samantha needs us; we are taking this with us.'

Jennifer picked up the device and put it in a large box, Evelyn put the headset in and other assortment of fittings.

They left the control room and got in a railcar and made their way to the Exit Shaft 2B. That would take them up to the main laboratory. Evelyn kept questioning Jennifer about what they were about to do, but Jennifer kept silent, so Evelyn gave it up.

Samantha had to deal with three Ixxion warriors that were keeping guard on the medical staff and patients in the long wardroom. The alien Aura helped her to find anyone infected by the followers of Bauros and Zindra; fortunately they found none. Melanie McAllister took it all in her stride as she had seen enough aliens not to be spaced out by the materialisation of another. Her only comment was to

Samantha about her strange companions. Henry Jones was glad they were going to fight back at the alien invaders. She had told them the military had been freed from their camp and when she gave the word they would be coming in, it was up to Henry and John to get everything ready for them.

Samantha and Steven entered the main laboratory room. There was nobody about, all the experiments left and probably forgotten, as the scientists had other things to worry about. They went to the computer room and Samantha went to an alcove. The panel at the rear slid up and Jennifer strode out of the shaft carrying a large box, Evelyn followed behind her. Seeing Samantha, Evelyn hugged her and stood on tip toe and kissed Samantha lightly on the lips.

'It's nice to see you again, Sam.'

'How's it going, Evie?'

'I'm having a great time, Jenny's very intrigued by my talents,' Evelyn said, enthusiastically.

Jennifer grunted as she connected the device to the computer. Evelyn sat on a chair and smoothed the hem of her black dress down over her slim thighs. Samantha gazed at her round freckled face as she put the headset on.

'How is everything inside your head, Evie?'

Evelyn gave her a warm smile and assured Samantha her mental state was as healthy as it ever was.

'Working here will change that,' Jennifer said.

Evelyn giggled as she switched on the device and her face was bathed in a green glow. The headset hummed, she let her mind drift, and she concentrated hard

'Are you going to give me an idea of what you are up to?' Jennifer asked.

When Samantha told her what the plan was, Jennifer thought she was mad, but what Samantha had been through already, she had a reason to be.

'Are you sure about this, it might not work,' Jennifer said.

'That's not like you, Jenny, I thought you were always sure of your talents,' Samantha said. Jennifer shook her head; she felt Samantha was sacrificing herself.

'We have to be well synchronized, Sam, a miss either way will be the end for you.'

'Then we'll make sure we get it right,' Samantha said.

Samantha stared at the ice blue eyes.

'I won't let you down, Sam, I hope you know that,' Jennifer said, sincerely.

Samantha ran a hand over Jennifer's cheek.

'We were born to work together; I do have faith in you, Jenny.'

Samantha turned to Evelyn who stared up at her.

'I have contacted a mind calling out a name continuously,' Evelyn said.

'What is it?' Samantha inquired.

'Phoebe Cross,' Evelyn said.

Samantha took her cell phone out of her jacket pocket and contacted Naomi and told her the target was on the alien spacecraft.

Naomi and her group were resting in the hut Janice had vacated. Phoebe stood by the window and looked out at the alien spacecraft; Naomi moved alongside of her.

'Sam has made contact, she did not say how, but she can now certify your sister is being held on the spacecraft.'

Phoebe turned her head and Naomi stared at her large dark eyes.

'When do we start?' Phoebe asked.

'When Sam calls back. How are you feeling?' Naomi inquired.

'I'll answer that when I have Prue back with me.'

Naomi was keeping a close eye on Phoebe, she had her mind concentrated on just one thing, and Naomi was surprised how well Phoebe kept her emotions in check. Naomi had given up trying to determine what the girl was thinking.

Jennifer sat in front of the glowing sphere, her mind was furiously active, her blood raced through her veins. She stared at the green glow in the centre of the pulsating globe. Evelyn sat opposite to Jennifer; Evelyn kept her eyes closed as her mind concentrated on the data coming through the headset. She was one with the computer, everything throughout the building was powered by the computer and Evelyn was aware of what was going on in the laboratory building as her brain sorted out the data coming in through the headset.

Samantha removed the white lab coat and left the laboratory; Steven kept his on and followed her down the corridor. Samantha was clear headed and calm about what she had to do. Steven had no idea what she had in mind or what Jennifer and Evelyn were hoping to achieve; his one purpose was to make sure Samantha came out of this alive and well.

Dr Hamilton sat on the edge of the bed. Janice stood on her left and Zindra stood in front of her glaring down at the person who had dared fight against her power. Sally Hamilton was calmer than she thought possible at this moment in time, she had been moving towards in an unavoidable collision with fate. She stared up at the blazing ruby eyes that tried to burn two holes in her skull.

'You make too many mistakes, Zindra, you never beat Imera and you won't beat me or my twins.'

Being arrogant and self-opinionated, Zindra was unaware she was capable of making mistakes.

'You should never leave an enemy alive, as soon as you captured me and Imera, you should have killed on the spot.'

'I could easily destroy you now, but I want you to see the death of your twins,' Zindra said.

Dr Hamilton grinned and shook her head.

'You have tried to destroy them on many occasions, but they still live. You know how dangerous Jenague was, you were there.'

The visions of the myth flowed through her mind, it showed her why they had tried to eradicate the Jenague gene from the Moran. Imera had slipped through the net and now they had another pariah around to bring more chaos to the Universe.

'On that ship Jenague saw something go on a voyage of destruction, what did she see, Zindra?'

Zindra spun round and saw the simmering figure of Auria by the door.

'I thought we had destroyed you.'

'We are still on your tail, Zindra, you can't get rid of us that easy.'

The shimmering luminous shape of Auria dematerialized, Zindra turned back to Dr Hamilton.

'Nothing is going to save you or your blasphemous twins,' Zindra spat out.

'You are the blasphemy, Zindra and that thing that follows you,' Dr Hamilton said.

Zindra stormed out of the room. Outside the door were two figures dressed in a brown habit with a cowl drawn over their heads.

'Keep an eye on them, I'll let you know when it is time to kill them,' Zindra said.

Zindra's followers moved into the room, Janice had moved to the window and looked out. Dr Sally Hamilton still felt weak and she lay out on the bed.

'Don't worry, Janice, Samantha won't allow any of her friends to be killed.'

Janice turned away from the window.

'Talking of mistakes, not telling Samantha you are alive is a mistake.'

'Perhaps,' was all Dr Hamilton could think of to say?

Jennifer felt a burning pain in her head; she opened her eyes and stood up. Evelyn stared at her.

'I felt it, Jenny, what is it?'

Jennifer remembered the sphere she had fished out of the marsh and the mind it had contained. A cold, malignant corrupt mind that had left her cold and shivery in mind and body, Jennifer had just felt it again, it had called her a pariah and a chaos to the Universe and it was a lot stronger than her.

'I don't like this, I don't like it at all,' Jennifer murmured.

Auria materialised in front of Samantha and she stopped still. Steven stared at the shimmering energy that was in a female shape.

'Your male companion is out and helping us weed out Zindra's followers from our people,' Samantha said.

'Good, are you ready?'

Samantha grinned and thought she was as ready as she ever was. Samantha took out her cell phone and contacted Naomi.

"The time has come, see you in hell, Naomi.'

'They won't let us in, Sam.'

Samantha contacted Major Harrington and told him to start the proceedings as she was about to give herself to the devil.

'If I don't make it, Major, make sure the General gives Sally a good home.'

Steven placed an arm round her shoulders.

'You've got to make it, Sam, the General will give us hell if you don't,' he said.

Samantha kept silent; she had her mind on other things beside her untimely demise. She moved on to the end of the corridor and walked into the office room; she sat at the computer and tapped out a message for Evelyn.

Naomi came around the front of the spacecraft with Phoebe behind her, Corporal Morris and the other four soldiers came around the rear of the spacecraft. Two Ixxion warriors were guarding the entry hatch. Naomi aimed her assault rifle and fired a volley of shots at the alien warrior close to her, while Corporal Morris dealt with the second alien. Naomi stepped through the open hatch. She found three passages to follow. Naomi decided to split up the group, Phoebe and one of the soldiers took the central passage, Corporal Morris and two of his men took the right passage and Naomi took the remaining soldier with her and went down the left passage.

Phoebe marched down the well-lit passage; thankfully she found no bulky bad-tempered alien to bar her way. She opened every door she came to and she found the small rooms empty, until she got to the last two doors; one was the room Jennifer had been kept in, the last room off the corridor. Phoebe found a woman lying on a bunk bed, her back was turned to Phoebe and the soldier. Phoebe turned the woman onto her back and two dark brown eyes stared up at her, with a pain that Phoebe knew so well.

'Who are you?' Phoebe asked.

The woman tried to get off the bed and Phoebe helped her to stand.

'Melissa Harris. Does this mean I'm free at last?'

The soldier moved out of the room to check the corridor. When he told them it was clear, Phoebe and the woman left the room. They went back up the corridor to the entry hatch and Phoebe told the soldier to take Melissa away to safety. Phoebe went in search of Naomi.

Samantha moved out of the office room; she saw three figures in habits with cowls over their heads. She turned to Steven.

'Zindra has sent the advance guard, I see,' she said.

It is time for you to show these vermin, what you are made of, Sam.

Samantha moved towards them and Steven stayed back. The three hooded figures surround Samantha as she marched down the corridor.

'Take me to your leader,' she said.

CHAPTER LXXXVIII:

THE FINAL TEST

Phoebe made her way to the flight deck of the spacecraft. Naomi was standing menacingly over Aplon Whan as he sat in the operations seat. He turned his head as Phoebe emerged from the open hatch, he recognised the female as one of the subjects Zindra had experimented on. He stared back at the female that had a weapon trained on him. He was under orders of the Supreme Leader on the mother ship and his mission was slightly different to the one Zindra was on; over the years he was of the opinion it would be best to take the spacecraft and his men and leave Zindra and her followers stranded on the planet, they wanted to be rid of her as much as the Moran were. Because Zindra was taking so long to get hold of the hybrid, he did not think Zindra was as all powerful as she thought herself to be – over the years the natives of the planet had run rings round her and it seemed Zindra was still no nearer catching her prey. Aplon Whan was beginning to have respect for Axerus and her hybrid cub, but they were rebels and they had to be brought to justice.

'What's the hold up?' Phoebe wanted to know.

Aplon Whan stared at the dark stout female; he could see Phoebe was in a hurry.

'I'm having a chat with our alien friend here,' Naomi said.

'Why not just kill it; we have more pressing things to sort out.'

'Sam doesn't want that,' Naomi assured her.

Auria – the female energy being – materialised beside Naomi.

Aplon Whan stared at her. 'It is time for Monox to leave this planet – when we have secured Zindra, Zelphas and Bauros and any other of your kind who are still on this planet – we will be leaving,' the shimmering female said.

Phoebe left the flight deck and turned left and then took a right turning. She heard the sound of weapons firing.

Jennifer opened her eyes and got off the chair, she could hear weapon fire in other parts of the building. The battle had started. She gazed at Evelyn who was watching her while she concentrated on her work. She winked at Jennifer. She turned away and found they had been joined by Michelle and Ian Henderson.

'We've come to join the action,' Ian said.

Jennifer told him the fighting seemed to have started, she told them to make sure none of the enemy appeared in the room they were now in.

'I hope you brought some weapons with you,' Jennifer said.

They both nodded, Michelle wore her military outfit olive drab shirt and skirt. Ian had on fashionable casual wear, as he was a civilian. Michelle Gowning held the rank of major. She opened the door and moved into the next laboratory room; Ian followed close behind her. The door at the far end of the laboratory room, the main door, slid open and alien warriors entered the room. Michelle dived to her right and slid across the floor behind a work bench, Ian weapon in hand and firing as he dived after Michelle.

'You all right, Michelle?'

Michelle nodded her head as she moved to the end of the bench, Ian stayed where he was.

'Keep your head down, Ian.'

Michelle moved out of sight as she made her way across the floor towards the next workbench, she could not hear the enemy; they were probably waiting for a clear sight of them. Michelle slowly lifted her head up until her eyes were up to the top of the bench, she saw the two aliens moving down the other side of the laboratory room. Michelle lifted the military handgun out of the pocket of her skirt. She drew her head down and moved to the side of the bench. She peered across the room and the leading Ixxion came into view. Michelle aimed the weapon and fired off a volley of shots and the alien warrior fell to the floor. The other Ixxion swiftly fired his energy weapon in the direction of the shots. Michelle moved swiftly across the floor to the next workbench, just in time as the bench she had moved from disintegrated with the full force of the energy weapon.

Major Harrington stood in the medical office staring down at Juliet as she sat at the computer; she suddenly looked up at him.

'There's energy fire in the main laboratory,' she informed him.

Juliet had got data from the computer that Evelyn was in charge of it, the whole idea of wiring someone to the computer system freaked her out. Juliet enjoyed working with them, but she did not want to be part of a machine. She stood up.

'Evelyn Stevens has control of the computer system, Jennifer is with her, and they are doing something for Sam. Michelle and Ian are in the laboratory,' Juliet said.

'It's time, are you joining us?'

Juliet gazed at him then walked out of the office, Major Harrington raced after her.

'Ask a silly question,' he said. They moved out of the locker room. They moved into the main corridor, where his military force waited for him.

Phoebe kept a firm grip on the assault rifle as she moved cautiously through the various compartments of the spacecraft. The sound of weapon fire was still going on somewhere to her left, at first it had been in front of her, now she had moved beyond it. Phoebe decided to come up behind whatever had the soldiers bogged down.

Phoebe came to the rear of the spacecraft; she stood by the bulkhead beyond which was the engine room. She gazed across at the doorway beyond that was the gun battle, she moved towards the open doorway and an alien warrior came into view and she fired the assault rifle until the creature fell to the floor.

'Another one bites the dust,' Phoebe said, without a hint of humour.

Phoebe was not a trained soldier and had not been trained to kill. It had not been the first alien monstrosity she had dealt with, there were a few others behind her. Nothing was going to stand in her way, she was on a mission, and her mind was coldly concentrated on the job at hand. She moved slowly out of the doorway, her weapon firmly held ready; she spied the group of Ixxions holding the soldiers at bay. She pressed hard on the trigger, the sound of the assault rifle was deafening in the passageway, a hail of bullets struck down the enemy and she stopped firing. The two soldiers moved towards her.

'That's sorted that little problem out,' Phoebe said.

'You don't believe in taking prisoners,' Corporal Morris said.

Phoebe turned away and went back through the doorway and stood in front of the hatch that led to the engine room.

'Are you behind there, Prue, give me a sign?'

Janice Clarke stood by the bed and stared across at the two hooded figures standing by the door. Dr Hamilton was sitting on the side of the bed; they could hear the battle going on outside. Janice wished she had a weapon, her friends needed her. Suddenly the door opened distracting their captors, and she dived across the room and tackled the nearest of the hooded figures; Steven Calvert who had entered the room, tackled the other one. Steven shot them in the head with the weapon Samantha had given him.

'What's going on out there?' Janice asked.

Steven did not know much as he had been sent to rescue Janice and Dr Hamilton; he told them Samantha had gone to meet Zindra.

'Have you any idea what she is going to do?' Dr Hamilton asked.

'I only know she has Jennifer doing something for her that Sam hopes will help.'

Dr Hamilton smiled, she was sure her twins would take down Zindra and her followers. Janice put on one of the habits their captors had been wearing and pulled the cowl over her head; she asked Steven if he had any other weapons. He nodded his head and took out a handgun out of his jacket; Janice took the weapon Samantha had given him. She opened the window and got Dr Hamilton to climb out of it and get quickly to safety.

Steven and Janice left the room and parted company. Janice went down the passage Samantha was taken. She hoped to mingle with the other hooded followers of the alien Zindra. Steven gazed up the other passage and noticed a group of alien warriors waiting outside the main laboratory doors; he moved out of sight and kept an eye on them. Luckily, they were not looking his way.

He gazed at the double doors at the other end of the corridor; the military would be coming through them at any time. Steven stared at his watch, it was all a matter of timing, as they moved irresistibly along the path where there was no detour, they were heading for an explosive climax and Samantha would be in the centre of it.

The door slid open and Samantha stepped into the room; her companions stayed outside. The door slid shut behind her.

YOU ARE WELL AND TRULY IN THE SPIDER'S WEB NOW, SAMMY

Samantha sighed deeply; it was not the time to have a voice in her head insulting her. Hopefully in a few moments she would be free of it.

OR THE UNIVERSE WILL BE FREE OF YOU

'That too,' she observed.

Samantha moved to one side of the room and spied a computer console. She moved between it and a worktop, she switched the computer on and typed in Evelyn's name, informing her it was nearly time for her to act. She turned away and looked up past the worktop. Zindra stood staring back at her with the burning ruby red eyes.

'You are here at last; you are an elusive creature.'

Samantha stared at Zindra – this was the creature that could destroy empires and keep other cultures down into slavery.

Outwardly there was nothing impressive about Zindra; the power was locked inside the domed head.

'It was not the time to take you on: now it is.'

Samantha moved round the worktop, keeping her eyes on Zindra.

'You think your mind is capable to match a mind as powerful as mine.'

Samantha smiled.

'Of course, I would not be here otherwise.'

Zindra stared at the bright green eyes, she saw no fear and the thin face was calm and assured. If this was Axerus's cub, it was everything Zindra thought it would be; that was why she must be destroyed and the silver haired one.

'Where is your twin?'

Samantha shook her head; she did not know what Zindra was talking about.

I DO

'I haven't got one, there's just me, I don't fear you, every overbearing being has a weak spot.'

Zindra laughed, the sound was cold and resonant with no humour in it.

'The one who spawned you was of the same mind, thought we made too many mistakes.'

Zindra watched the green eyes darken; the cub was getting angry, that was good.

'That's another reason I'm here, to avenge my mother's death and I'm more dangerous when I'm angry, I know how to use that emotion to aid me in your destruction.'

Samantha gazed at the ruby red eyes, they flashed brighter, and the great Zindra did not like that. Samantha smiled broadly. Zindra flashed out with her left arm the talon gripped Samantha by the throat.

'You are just a hybrid, not one thing or the other. Axerus breeding with a native of this world has weakened the Moran gene pool,' Zindra observed.

Samantha had an answer to that.

'I have killed a lot of your Ixxion warriors, I have also beaten Zelphas, I am stronger than you give me credit for,' Samantha said.

Janice still wearing the brown habit and the cowl over her head, entered the room and saw the two antagonists squaring up to each other. It did not look good for Samantha as Zindra had her by the throat.

Samantha grabbed Zindra's lower arm with both hands, the tips of her long slender fingers dug into the flesh, she twisted her hands in different directions around the circumference of the long bony arm of the alien. The grip on her throat weakened as Zindra became aware of the strength of her nemesis. Samantha pulled the arm away from her as the clawed hand was detached from her throat. She swiftly brought her left leg up and kicked the loathsome creature away from her.

Samantha moved away from the worktop she had been leaning against; she became aware of the hooded figure standing close by. Samantha moved towards Zindra, a clawed hand lashed out and Samantha moved her head just in time; the razor-sharp talons missed raking her face by inches. Zindra swiftly changed direction and got behind Samantha and a thin arm wrapped round her throat, Zindra swiftly got a bony elbow in the face for her pains. Samantha spun round, Zindra fought hard not to wilt under the gaze of the dark menacing green eyes. The predator was ready, armed and dangerous, the eyes of Imera were staring back at her, an adversary Zindra was unable to defeat, in death she reached out from the burning green eyes before her.

'I fear nothing, your time has come, Zindra, death is at hand.'

That's fighting talk, Sam.

Janice moved between the worktop and the computer, she kept an eye on Samantha. The tall girl had her left hand behind her back as she faced Zindra, she was pointing at something,

Janice gazed at the computer then at the screen.

PRESS ENTER AND ALL HELL WILL BREAK LOOSE

Good luck, Sam.

Janice sighed deeply.

'She's going to need it, Evie.'

Janice placed her hands on the keyboard, ready to bring the whole building down on their heads.

Juliet gazed through the glass panel in the double doors, down the corridor beyond alien warriors stood outside the doors of the main medical research laboratory; she turned around and smiled at Harrington.

'Do we rush them?'

Juliet held a heavy military pistol in her right hand, her left pulled open one of the doors; she turned her head and gazed at the group of soldiers behind her. Sergeant Anderson moved beside her.

'I don't fancy yours,' he said to Juliet, smiling at her.

'As Sam said once, I'm going to kill them, not make love to them,' Juliet said in all seriousness.

Juliet pulled the other door; it was time to get at them. At the other end of the corridor, Steven watched the doors open and the alien warriors turned to face Juliet and the soldiers coming behind her. Steven fired at the alien that first raised a weapon at the force starting to come at them. Steven kept firing the automatic as the alien fell to the floor. A gas canister exploded amongst the aliens and Juliet rushed forward. Half way down the corridor a huge shape moved out of the gas cloud, Juliet dived to the floor firing her pistol as she went, the alien discharged his energy weapon just before it fell to the ground. Juliet felt a burning pain in her left side as she hit the floor. The soldiers fired into the gas cloud for a few seconds until a voice called out to cease fire, somewhere in front of them.

Steven Calvert strode out of the gas cloud and saw Juliet on the floor with her back against the wall; he held a hand out to her.

'Come on, Juliet, this isn't the time to have a rest.'

Juliet gave a grimace of pain as Steven pulled her up onto her feet.

'You're hurt?' Steven asked in deep concern.

'I'll live, Sam is our main concern,' Juliet said.

Jennifer sat eyes closed and breathing deeply, the green glow of the transparent sphere lit up her pale face. She could sense the cold alien mind of Zindra, she was in confrontation with Samantha, Jennifer was having trouble reading her thoughts, and something was blocking her out, another mind, with similarities to her own. Jennifer remembered the time she had tried to get into Samantha's head in the hotel room, something had thrown her out of Samantha' s mind, it was now blocking her from probing Samantha, but that would be disastrous to their plan.

'Anything wrong, Jenny?'

Jennifer opened her eyes and stared at Evelyn's round pretty face; the grey eyes stared back at her.

'Everything,' Jennifer said.

'We can't have that, not now, Jenny,' Evelyn said, sternly.

Jennifer closed her eyes and took a deep breath.

'Tell me something I don't know.'

Michelle Gowning stayed crouched down behind the workbench, as she could hear the alien warrior moving close by and she did not want her head blown off, she had no idea of Ian Henderson's position in the room. She had heard the firing outside the laboratory and decided the war had started.

Ian Henderson had moved to the other side of the laboratory, hoping he and Michelle could attack the enemy in different positions. He moved silently round the computers. He heard the main doors open and the Ixxion turned towards the new sound. Ian moved between two computers and stood up and aimed his automatic. At the same time Michelle moved along the workbench she was crouched behind and raised her head. She saw the alien with his back to her and she noticed Ian standing between the computers, about to fire at the enemy. Michelle aimed her heavy military pistol and fired just after Ian and the alien was caught in their crossfire; it collapsed to the floor.

Michelle made her way to the main door. Major Harrington stood surveying the scene. Michelle stood in front of him and saluted.

'It seems you have everything under control here, Michelle.'

Michelle smiled and Ian came up alongside her.

'Yes, sir. Jennifer and Evelyn are in the computer room as part of Samantha's strategy, we are keeping the enemy away from them,' Michelle explained.

Steven and Juliet raced down to the end of the corridor; the soldiers followed behind them. Steven stopped at the end and turned right. At the end of that corridor the followers of Zindra were waiting for them.

'It's strange we are going to fight people we used to work with,' Juliet said.

'They are something different now,' informed Steven.

Steven and Juliet marched slowly towards the hooded figures that stretched across the corridor ahead of them, they held their guns firmly and ready, as were the soldiers behind them.

Samantha stood waiting to hear the plan Zindra had for her; Samantha slid her hand into the left pocket of her combat jacket. She gripped the butt of her weapon which was designed to kill creatures like Zindra – she could kill Zindra by hitting her body, and she had to go straight to the head and the alien mind inside it.

Samantha sensed something behind her, a slight sound then a feeling of cold dread touched her mind, and something nasty was creeping up on her. Samantha was reminded of what Jennifer had felt when she had opened up the sphere she had found in the marsh. If Jennifer was the pariah, then what kind of evil was bearing down on her?

Samantha lifted the hand out of her combat jacket, it still held the weapon firmly, and she kept her attention on the piercing red eyes that blazed at her as Zindra moved closer to her.

Kill me and your troubles will be over.

Her mind and body did not waver from the course Samantha had set out for herself: this was it.

In reality – they've only just begun.

With one swift action Samantha lifted the weapon and fired twice at Zindra hitting the blazing red eyes, the domed head exploded, and Samantha was showered with blood, bone and brains, the energy bolts of Samantha's weapon would have blasted the evil mind into oblivion. Samantha's grandmother had got her revenge.

One down – One to go.

Samantha spun round to face the danger behind her.

It was a tall thin man wearing a security uniform, it was someone she had never met before; the amber eyes were full of anger and hatred.

'Bauros.'

'You know me?' The cold echoing thought ran through her brain, telepathies put her teeth on edge, and she had enough voices in her head as it was. To free herself of them she was taking the only option open to her. Fight fire with fire, energy with energy.

The tensions building up in the bodies of Jennifer and Samantha were almost explosive. Jennifer was covered in a cold sweat as her body was bathed in a green glow, her emotions and passions were running riot as she tried to force her mind to break down the barriers inside Samantha's head. She was also aware of the alien thing called Bauros, knowing she had already touched the mind once before. Jennifer kept her eyes closed and concentrated hard; perspiration covered her forehead and ran over her long eyelashes.

Evelyn stared across at Jennifer; it was a strange sight, the tall girl inside a green glowing mass emanating from the green glowing sphere in front of her. Jennifer's thin pale face was a mask of concentration. Evelyn herself was calm before the storm, as she waited for a sign.

Janice stood still by the computer and her hands lay on the keyboard ready. She gazed at Samantha and the man who faced her, Janice could almost sense the mental exchange between the pair of them. Outside the room she heard a gun battle, she wondered who was winning.

Bauros was not a creature to be taken lightly,

Samantha could feel the cold alienness of the mind behind the amber eyes that stared back at her. Though she was ready to sacrifice herself in ridding the Universe of this alien evil, she still ready to find a way to survive as she was an organism of the Universe, it was her duty to find a way to survive.

Two clawed hands flashed out and grabbed her by the throat; she was pushed hard against a computer console behind her.

You are one of the Universe's big mistakes.

Samantha brought her right knee up and struck her adversary in the stomach, she brought her right arm up and struck him in the chin with the heel of her hand. The grip on her throat relaxed.

'Not if I can help it.'

That's it, you tell him, Sam.

Samantha dived at him and using the weight of her body, she pushed the enemy backward knocking him off balance. He landed on his back and Samantha landed on top of him. She shouted at the top of her voice.

'Now!'

Janice still having her hands on the computer keyboard, hit the enter key and stood back. There was a flash of sparks of escaping energy and the power surge exploded in the machinery around her and Janice sped for the door; she did not bother looking back at Samantha. Out in the corridor she bumped into Steven – Juliet and the soldiers were behind him, they had dealt with the habit wearing followers of Bauros.

'We've got to get out of here, now,' yelled Janice.

Hearing the urgency in her voice they rushed after Janice, behind them there came a loud roar; Steven turned and saw a fireball run across the corridor.

Sam, save yourself.

Steven turned and followed the military and his friends to the end of the corridor and left the building by a side door.

Evelyn pulled the headset off her head, she pulled the wires from her chair and leapt out of it. She went to Jennifer, who was unresponsive when Evelyn told her the building would be falling down around their ears. She went to the emergency shaft and started to descend down the metal ladder towards the underground facility.

Bauros threw Samantha off him and she crashed against the machinery, the computers and machines were exploding around them.

'It is the end for both of us, Bauros; you won't bother the Universe anymore.'

Samantha stood up and moved across the room towards the windows, hot air assailed her body. He grabbed her, and Samantha spun round and pushed her assailant violently away from her, he hit the machinery as it exploded, and his body flared up in a walking fireball. Samantha rushed to the windows; behind her the mind of Bauros rose out of the burning body's skull. She charged at the window and as she hit it coldness entered her head, the glass splintered at her body hit and went through the window.

Sally had wandered away from Shirley who was supposed to keep an eye on her. Sally had made her way to the research facility and she walked along the inside of the boundary fence. Sally eventually came up to the rear wall of the Lab 3 building, just in time to see her mother exit the building via the window.

Samantha collided with the hard-frosty ground giving her battered body more pain to grieve over. Her head throbbed and it was full of voices, the alien mind of Bauros had entered her head.

Let me in, Sam. Or this is not going to work.

Jenny?

Samantha stared through watery eyes; something was moving towards her. Her eyes cleared for a moment and she saw her daughter coming towards her. Samantha thrust out a hand.

'Stay away, Sally, don't come any closer.'

Sally stopped dead in her tracks, she saw the pain on her mother's face, Sally wanted to go to her aid, but she had to obey her mother's command.

Jennifer was aware of the invasion of Samantha's brain. Using the mind probe she pushed her thoughts into Samantha's mind.

Listen to me, Sam. Ignore everything else, concentrate on my thoughts alone.

Samantha tried to concentrate on Jennifer as she thrust her thoughts into Samantha's fuzzy brain. Bauros was making it hard for her, but Samantha had to force herself, she had the stronger mind.

PART TEN:

THE GEMINI PROJECT

CHAPTER LXXXIX:

SLIPPING BACK IN TIME

o back, Sam.

G Samantha let her mind drift back through her memories up to the age of six, then she came up to a barrier, the lost memories, a dark place she must not venture into.

Force it, Sam. Remember, go back.

'I can't,' Samantha mumbled.

You must, what is it you are forgetting?

Jennifer's thoughts in her head were very urgent. The other voice in Samantha's head was very interested in what was going on.

Yes what?

Jennifer felt a shock run through her senses, the thought was not part of Samantha, as Bauros was not, she was suddenly afraid for the pair of them, but she had to concentrate.

Break through, Sam.

Samantha forced her mind into the dark of her lost memories; a nightmare dream came back to her thoughts.

Let me out.

Someone was locked in an opaque glass prison, bony fist beat against the glass, and two pinpoints of blue light stared out at her.

Let me out.

Samantha remembered as her age counted down, six – five – four – three – two – one. Back in the womb, she was not alone, another consciousness was close by.

What kind of mother does not know she is giving birth to twins?

That was what Jennifer wanted to know, as she became aware of the other thoughts inside Samantha's head.

'Mother, what have you done?'

That was something Jennifer wanted to know, as she felt the first signs of anger fuelling her mixed emotions running through her mind and body, as she was about to learn something bad, very bad.

Let me out.

The opaque glass prison shattered, two burning deep blue eyes searched for someone to hurt for her imprisonment.

'Jennifer!'

Jennifer, now it is all clear, you are my twin, Sam.

Little Sally's dragon was free.

I'm free. Free at last, Sam.

The mind probe sphere changed from blue to a glowing green as it captured Bauros's mind, a spark of energy floated up from the sphere and floated around Jennifer's head and disappeared, and it was home again. A roaring explosion and a burning wind took hold of Jennifer's body and threw her across the room, her head hit the wall and she saw stars. Her anger was at boiling point.

I am going to kill you, Mother.

Contortions ran through her face and body, all the pain she and the clones had brought on Samantha, Jennifer was getting back with interest. Jennifer laid her long hands and fingers over her face, her mind full of guilt and anger.

How do you feel, Jenny?

You and the clones are not all that different after all.

The sphere was destroyed along with the alien mind inside it. Jennifer lay in a heap by the far wall contemplating her guilt. Everything she had passed onto Samantha, because of the part of her that was inside her brain, came back to Jennifer two-fold. Her mind and body were in chaos.

Samantha lay on the icy ground and a few feet away Sally stood, her mind in turmoil, a fight between her impulse to go and comfort her mother and the last command from her mother. Tears ran down her cheeks.

'Please, Mummy.'

Samantha opened her eyes, her sight was a misty bluer, her head ached, and her body was full of aches and pains. At least Samantha had the inside of her head to herself, no voices to irritate her. Her vision cleared and she saw Sally standing a few feet away, Samantha stared at the sad face and tear stained cheeks. Samantha held out her right hand. Sally saw it was a sign to free her from the command that was stopping her from saving her mother. She ran to her mother and knelt down on the cold hard ground; Samantha raised her head and stared at the watery blue eyes.

'I always make you cry.' Sally held her mother's head to her chest.

CHAPTER XC:

FREEDOM OF SOULS

S ally stared down at her mother's pale green eyes, she was in pain and worn out, Sally knew all too well the meaning of the different shades of green that her mother's eyes went through, this paleness of green in her eyes was bad. Mother was dying.

'Forgive me.'

The voice was a faint whisper.

'What is it, Mummy?'

Samantha tried to raise her voice.

'Forgive me, Sally, please say you forgive me.'

Sally gazed at her mother's pleading expression.

'I forgive you, Mummy.'

Major Harrington and some of his men came around to the rear of the burning building and saw Samantha and her daughter. He told the NCO to get the paramedics. Sally watched the military office approach, when he was standing over her, Sally looked up at him.

'Please help, Mummy's dying.'

Dr Hilary Calvert and her medical team were outside the front of the Lab 3 building. When Michelle and Ian came out, Melanie grabbed her by the arm and asked her about Jennifer, they had heard Evelyn had got down to the underground base safely, but no Jennifer. Michelle shook her head; there was no way they could get to her from where they were. Melanie made for the doors; Hilary grabbed her arm.

'You'll never make it through there, Mel,' Hilary warned her.

'I have to find her, I can't let Jenny die alone, I just can't,' Melanie said.

Melanie rushed through the entrance door, there were no fires to stop her from getting to the next doors along the corridor, and she passed through the doors and made for the doors that led to the main laboratory room. Distant explosions came to her ears, the burning heat in the room made it hard for her to breathe. Melanie kicked the doors inward and rushed into the room, she kept away from the burning and exploding machinery. She made it to the door that led to the main computer room where Jennifer was laid out on the floor. A rush of hot air hit Melanie as she passed through the doorway, an explosion pushed her forward and her left leg got caught and her body turned as she fell to the floor; there was a loud snap as her left femur snapped, an agonizing pain ran through the nerves of her left leg, her eyes filled with tears. She crawled along the floor, she stared through the smoke and spied Jennifer on the floor by the far wall, she crawled towards Jennifer, pain burned in her left thigh. Tears ran down her cheeks.

Melanie got to where Jennifer lay with her back and head against the wall, her face was covered with her hands. Melanie grabbed her thin wrists and pulled the hands away from Jennifer's face; the thin pale face was contorted and vague.

'Jenny!' The blue eyes darkened.

'It's me, Jenny. Mel.'

Jennifer focused her sight on Melanie's face, the tremors in her face and body subsided.

'Mel.'

'We have to get out of here,' Melanie said.

Jennifer saw the pain in Melanie's expression.

'You are hurt, Mel.'

Melanie gave her a weak smile in spite of the pain in her left leg.

'I forgot you were a mind reader.'

Jennifer struggled to her feet.

'I don't need to read your mind, the pain is written all over your face,' Jennifer said.

Jennifer lifted Melanie up, she screamed out as she put her weight onto her right leg.

'I'm sorry, Mel.'

'We've got to get out of here; you have to help me to save you, Jenny.'

Jennifer laughed. She lifted Melanie off her feet and carried her towards the exit shaft that led down to the underground facility. She eased Melanie onto her right leg, Jennifer turned, and Melanie put her arms round Jennifer's neck and wrapped her right leg around the tall girl's waist. Jennifer got on the metal ladder.

'Hang on tight, Mel.'

Phoebe Cross stood gazing at the hatch at the rear of the spacecraft – if she stared at it long enough it might open on its own. Naomi entered the compartment and stood beside Phoebe.

'Did you bring a key with you?'

Naomi shook her head, Phoebe sighed deeply.

So near, yet so far away.

An apparition appeared beside Naomi, the shimmering form of Auria stood close to Naomi.

'Having problems?'

Naomi thought of the hatch opening for them, Auria moved close to it. A few minutes later the hatch opened.

'Who's your friend?' Phoebe asked. Naomi gazed at Phoebe and winked.

Phoebe.

The thought was faint.

Phoebe stared at Naomi thinking she had spoken. Phoebe turned back to the black darkness beyond the hatchway.

HERE YOU GO, PHOEBE, BACK INTO THE DARKNESS

'Are you all right?' Naomi asked. Wide dark eyes stared back at her.

'The dark and I are old friends.' Phoebe said.

Phoebe stepped into the dark, from within the darkness two eyes peered at the shaft of light coming from the open hatch; a large dark shape was coming in from the light.

Phoebe.

Phoebe moved slowly into the blackness, the voice in her head continued to call out her name.

'Prue!'

Phoebe stood still; something moved to her left.

I knew you would come.

Naomi moved into the dark and switched on her torch, the light beam settled on a dark form moving towards Phoebe, the eyes blinked not used to bright lights.

'Prue?'

Xanthe stopped in front of her sister, tears flooded her dark eyes.

'I knew you'd save me, Phoebe.'

Phoebe caught her before she fell senseless to the floor. Phoebe carried her sister out of the darkness and moved through the hatch. Naomi had shown the torch along the catwalk between the spacecraft's silent motors. She shined the torch in any crevasses; suddenly she stopped when she heard a noise. Something moved ahead of her. Lisa Booth stared at the tall large figure moving towards her. The torch shone in her face and she blinked as it hurt her eyes.

'It's all right, I'm going to get you out of here,' Naomi said.

'You aren't a hallucination; I'd given up hope.'

Naomi put the torch in her combat jacket pocket and picked up the girl in her arms and carried her out of the spaceship's engine room.

Evelyn and Wendy Goodman were waiting at the bottom of shaft 2b as Jennifer got to the bottom with her burden, Wendy went to get a stretcher and Jennifer carefully laid Melanie on it and got her to one of the hospital beds in the medical room, Dr Richard Blake saw to her broken leg.

'Your father will be proud of you,' Blake said.

Melanie did not know whether to laugh or cry, the anger she had against her father was fading.

Phoebe sat at her sister's bedside; a drip feed was fixed to her right arm. Lisa lay in the next bed, Phoebe could feel the girl's blue eyes boring into her skull, and Phoebe gazed at her.

'I owe you an apology, Phoebe, Xanthe was forever saying you would save us, but I did not have her faith in you, I kept telling her you had forgotten her.'

'Nothing could be further from the truth.'

Phoebe stood up and walked round the bed and moved to the bed Lisa lay in.

'I did what I had to do, to protect my sister, I want through all sorts of terrors and experiments, as long as they had me, Prue was safe.'

Lisa held out her hand and Phoebe took it gently in her own.

'You know the thing that killed my parents; he has touched you, got inside your head.'

'You are innocent, Phoebe.'

'Perhaps, perhaps not,' Phoebe said.

Phoebe returned to her sister's bed and sat down, Naomi came in wearing a white coat, and she gave Phoebe a mug of hot strong coffee.

'How is Sam?'

'She is alive, and in a coma, her body is very weak, it's down to if she wants to live or not,' Naomi said.

'Sam does not seem the type of girl to give up her life easily.'

'Let's hope you're right, Phoebe.'

The military engineers worked hard to fix the lifts that were sabotaged by Jennifer and her team, except the one in the destroyed Lab 3 building. When the lift to the Lab 1 and 2 building was fixed, General Heywood was able to get down to the underground complex, and he made his way to the medical room. Melanie was lying comfortable in bed, she watched him approach her.

'Jennifer has told me you went to find her, while the building was falling down around your head.'

'Well you know me, Daddy, big mouth and small brains,' Melanie said.

General Heywood smiled; it was a long time since his daughter had called him that.

'You are not the same girl who arrived here. When your leg gets better, you can leave here and go where you want with my blessing.'

Melanie grinned at him.

'You can't get rid of me that easily. Besides, I have a lot of humble pie to eat, after the way I treated you and the anger inside me.'

He took her hand and squeezed it gently.

'Your mother would be very proud of you, as I am.'

Melanie watched him walk away; Henry Jones appeared at her bedside a moment later.

'Would you be mad at me, if I kissed you?'

Melanie smiled at him.

'I'll be mad at you, if you don't.'

Henry bent over the bed and kissed her full on the mouth.

'The General told me you were staying with us,' Henry said.

'Of course, who's going to make an honest man of you, if I go?' observed Melanie.

Henry sat on a chair by the bedside and took hold of her hand.

'Nobody I can think of, but it's going to take you a long time, Mel'

Melanie laughed and he kissed her fingertips of the hand he held.

Sally sat at her mother's bedside, machines were wired to her head and monitoring her life signs. Hilary had warned Sally it might be sometime before her mother regained consciousness. Behind Sally the door opened, and she spun round. A tall slim girl entered the room, Sally stood up and stared at the thin face and ice-blue eyes.

'You are the one,' Sally said.

Jennifer stopped and stared at the young girl, her fists were clenched and down at her sides.

'If you have come to hurt, Mummy, I won't let you,' Sally said, firmly.

Jennifer stared down at Samantha's child, the little girl showed no fear; she had one thing on her mind, to protect her mother. Jennifer turned and walked out of the room. Sally sat back down and stared at her mother's face.

Jennifer made her way to the hospital offices, where she found the person she looked for. Dr Sally Hamilton turned in her seat as Jennifer entered the room, she could see Jennifer was angry, the girl pulled a gun out of her skirt pocket and held it to Dr Hamilton's head.

'Give me one good reason why I shouldn't blow your head off,' Jennifer said, coldly.

'I'm your mother.'

'You'll have to do better than that. I've caused Samantha a lot of pain because of you. When we were in your womb, something happened and a part of my consciousness was trapped inside Samantha's head, it was me, not the clones that were causing her headaches and blackouts.'

Dr Sally Hamilton stared at Jennifer; she could see why her daughter wanted to kill her.

'I'm sorry, Jenny, but Samantha has a right to decide what happens to me.'

Jennifer placed the weapon back in her skirt pocket.

'Stay away from me, if our paths cross, make sure you walk softly and slowly,' Jennifer said, icily.

Jennifer walked out of the office. She had to find something to vent her anger on.

Xanthe Cross woke and found she was lying in a hospital bed; she saw her sister sitting at her bedside dozing, and she lifted her hand and ran it over Phoebe's cheek. She sat up and stared at her younger sister.

Phoebe held onto her sister's hand.

'We are together again, Phoebe, I won't let them take you away from me again.'

Phoebe ran a soothing hand over her sister's forehead.

'I was waiting for you to recover before informing the authorities, when they get here, you can work your magic.'

'I love you, Phoebe.' Phoebe kissed her on the cheek.

'I love you too, Prue.'

Xanthe sat on the bed and at the window, the sun was shining into the room, the door opened, and Phoebe came in and Xanthe stood up.

'Are you ready, little sis?' Xanthe hugged her.

'Let's get the show on the road,' Xanthe said

They left the bedroom and went down the stairs and entered the kitchen. Two men sat at the table: the Home Secretary Gerald Pollard and next to him was Superintendent Charles Roberts. Naomi Evans stood by the back door. The two girls sat opposite the two men. Xanthe closed her eyes and the memories flooded into her mind, she started the narrative calmly and kept her voice steady, Roberts wrote it all down, it came in his mind that these were memories of an 11-year-old girl; he wondered how Xanthe kept such horrors locked in her head for so long. Phoebe held onto her sister's hand. Pollard watched the two sisters and could see the love they had for each other; he could see the strain on Xanthe's face as she kept her emotions in check as she recited the horrors of her childhood.

When she had finished telling them about the murder of her parents, Xanthe bowed her head and tears dropped onto the table, Phoebe put her arm round her waist.

'It's all over now, Prue, you have done well.'

Xanthe raised her head and stared across the table at Chief Inspector Charles Roberts.

'Have you got what you want, can I have my sister back?'

The two men stood up.

'Lisa is here, Gerald, I hope you'll see her before you leave,' Xanthe said.

Gerald nodded and held his hand out to Phoebe.

'You're free to get on with your life, Phoebe, I'm sorry it took so long.'

Phoebe shook his hand.

'As long as everybody was after me, they would forget about Prue, her safety was paramount,' Phoebe said.

The two men left, and Naomi sat next to Xanthe.

'I don't know how you coped all those years with those horrors inside you head.'

Xanthe smiled at her.

'The memory of that day was not forever floating about in my mind; it was moved to a dark corner of my memory, until it was needed, until my brain sent the right signal to recall it. When I was part of the ESP program. Professor Fairclough thought I was uninteresting – of course that was what I wanted him to think.'

Phoebe stared at her sister.

'Being unimportant kept her safe,' Phoebe said.

'What are you going to do now?'

Xanthe had a job to go back to at Madison Industries Limited; she had contacted Zenobia and told the woman she would be back at work in a few days. Phoebe had been offered a post at the Research Facility, which she was happy to take, so she could be there when Samantha woke from her long sleep.

Jennifer stood at the rear of the compound close to where they were reconstructing the Lab 3 building. She still had not come to terms with the return of the missing part of her mind. How much was it going to change her character, what would Samantha think of her when she woke from the coma she was in? Little Sally was her relation, yet Jennifer could not get close to her, the young girl still thought she meant Samantha harm. Juliet Harris now reunited with her mother, was having an enjoyable time baiting Jennifer, as she had done to Samantha, when they first met. Jennifer had to ignore the insufferable girl.

The sky was grey and overcast; a strong wind blew rain into her face and ruffled her long silver blonde hair. She stared across at the boundary fence. Her senses were suddenly alert.

Printed in Great
Britain
by Amazon